Abigail's Curio Life

(The Curio Chronicles)

Robin John Morgan

First published (Paperback) in the UK in 2025 by Violet Circle Publishing.

Manchester, England, UK.

Print ISBN: 978-1-910299-50-0
Digital ISBN: 978-1-910299-51-7

British Library Cataloguing in Publication Data.
A catalogue record for this book is available from the British Library.
All paper used in the production of this book are sourced only from wood grown in sustainable forests.

Human Authored. No A.I. Content contained within this book

www.violetcirclepublishing.co.uk

Also, by Robin John Morgan.

Heirs to the Kingdom.

Book One, The Bowman of Loxley.
Book Two, The Lost Sword of Carnac.
Book Three, The Darkness of Dunnottar.
Book Four, Queen of the Violet Isle.
Book Five, Crystals of the Mirrored Waters.
Book Six, Last Arrow of the Woodland Realm.
Book Seven, Bridge Of Sequana.
Book Eight, The Circle of Darkness.

The Curio Chronicles.

Part One, Abigail's Summer.
Part Two, Curio's Summer.
Part Three, Curio's Christmas
Part Four, Abigail's Wedding
Part Five, Curio's Carnival
Part Six, Abigail's Curio Life

Of The Ravens of Berengar Trilogy

Rise of the Raven.
The Countess of Darkness
Violet Stone

Sword for the Sky

Oaken of the Winds

Other works.

Han's Cottage

Life is a curious thing. There is always going to be wind and rain, and at times there will be snow, and the river may freeze. But at some point, the ice will melt, the rain will dry, and the water will warm up as the sun shines.

Be You... Appreciate Each Other.

Chapter 1

Life is not what you think.

It is strange how through our lives we change, and yet we are all still caught in the circles of life, doomed to keep repeating certain patterns, until hopefully at some point, we see the error of our ways and alter our course. Bradley Wheeler once told me "Stay your course Abigail," but what is that? Birch tells us, we are born naked, will die naked, and everything else in between is up to us, but is it really, can we really force the changes we need to live a happy life? For months, my mind has been filled with these kinds of thoughts, as I have fulfilled my dreams and lived the life I once thought would be the right one for me. As I stand here, a famous Author, talking into the microphone, as I deliver my speech under the spotlight, I am wondering, if life will ever be the way I once wished.

I cannot help but ask, is this who I really am, or have I fallen into the same trap as my mother, and allowed the Parish Council to take me away from the truth of who I really should be? All I know is something is missing, some part of me that should be here, is absent, and there is a yearning that is growing inside me, and I have no idea at all of what that is. All I really know, is I cannot continue until I get to the bottom of all of this, I want the time and space to work it all out, and find what is lacking so maybe, I will have some joy back in my life, because the truth is, here in this room filled with thousands of adoring fans, I feel like I am utterly isolated, and the loneliest person here today.

I took a deep breath as I glanced down at my notes on the podium, I was almost through it, and I felt like this one conference lecture, had really cemented what had been the largest part of my life, and my love of gothic stories. I took that last final deep breath.

"And so, as we walk into the darkness, and we feel the chill of the night surround us, and stir our inner souls, always remember, that no matter what the dawn may bring, it is the warmth of our love, and the strength of our hearts that will sustain us always... Ladies and Gentlemen, I offer my hearty thanks, for giving me the opportunity to present this key note address for this convention... Thank you."

I took another deep breath, as I stepped back with a smile, and the audience rose from their seats, and gave a thunderous applause, as cameras flashed all over the hall. I stepped out from behind the podium and stood centre stage, gave a bow, as the applause continued, and I simply stood and smiled, and gave them just a little bit longer.

I glanced to the side, and saw Anita waiting at the side of the stage, I smiled to the audience as they continued to cheer, gave another bow, turned, and walked towards the edge of the stage where Anita smiled at me, and handed me a bucket, but actually, I was fine, how weird is that?

"Wow Abby, that was an amazing speech, did you see them, they lapped it up?"

My throat was dry, and I really needed a drink, my stomach was jittery, but it was excitement, not nerves. We turned, and walked towards the dressing room, Anita filled me in as we walked down the steps, and into the long corridor, and I started to feel happy.

"Right, your schedule is clear for a whole two weeks, then we have a few days with River Studios doing cast selection. After that, you will have nothing until July and the American Curio event, so go on, get to your hiding place and give Jemi a huge hug for me, and I will see you when you get back." She stopped and turned to me; she looked a little concerned.

"Abby, really rest up, you know you are looking exhausted, it has been a grueling six months for both of you, just keep her in bed, and both of you relax." She smiled as I nodded.

"Anita, I am fine, all I want is some space, some sanity, and I really need some time with her, I have hardly seen her for months." She gave a nod, and lifted her hand to my shoulder.

"I know, but Richard can be a real stickler for events, the man is a machine, he has no idea of family, he is all promotion and no awareness of life."

"Yeah... He is Katie's puppet." Anita shrugged.

"Well, there is that, but come on Abby, that was ten years ago, all that is in the past, even Katie does not hold a grudge for that long, she gets too bored. Just go to Birch, and take some time for both of you. Everything is in your car, I got Gary to load it up an hour ago, just jump in, and drive, here are your keys."

She slid her hand in her pocket, pulled them out, and handed them to me, I gave her a smile, and pulled her into a hug.

"Thanks... You know, for getting us this time off." She gave a chuckle.

"Abby, I work for you, honestly, if you don't want to do something, you can just say no. I could use the rest to, and some Tabby time." I gave a smile as I broke apart.

"I wanted to do this one, key note at a convention is the best gig in town. Have fun with Tabby, you know, you could use the break too. I will see you when I get back."

Once changed into plainer clothing, and having removed some of my heavy makeup, I left Anita outside the dressing room, and made my way down to the lower car park, and over to my A6 Tourer. Yep, I actually own a car these days. I bought it two years ago, as I found it was faster and a lot more luxurious a drive than Petal. I love to be able to jump in, whiz off, and get to an event quickly, and with Birch also taking bookings for events, as her books have sold really well, she gives a lot of talks at conventions, so she takes Petal. I had started hiring cars, or booking limo's, which appeared to be a waste of good money.

The simple truth is, I love driving alone, so when I bumped into Andrew Mc Anderson the car dealer who supported us at Curio Live during a charity auction, we talked, and I asked his advice for a good sound saloon vehicle. Nothing too sporty, just a good all round quality ride, and he put me onto a dealer friend of his. As soon as I saw the dark grey car and slid inside, I bought it.

I got the private plate of DEADLY 01, and I thought it was brilliant, and to be honest, I have driven all over in it, riding in comfort. I love it, although, it does need a clean, motorways can be really dirty, and it shows.

I jumped in, and made my way out of London, avoiding the press, and connected my phone with the blue tooth, and hit music, and Avril played softly in the background as I made my way onto the M4, heading south, for two weeks at Sunny Bank alone with Birch, and boy did I need it.

I relaxed at the wheel and watched the road, it was so nice being away from London, and knowing by tonight, I would be alone, curled up with Birch and looking forward to two weeks alone together, in her favourite place, and I hoped the weather would improve.

It has been hard this year, and to be honest, Anita is right, I really am feeling the strain, I try to hide it, but I am really exhausted. The final book of the Cursed Books of Krisandra series came out in late January, and my life has been a whirlwind, because I have had to promote it, which has meant bouncing all over the country for the last few months, and I have hardly been home.

Birch has done well, and just like her mother, she has been a massive success, selling her books the Sham of Shame, Your Inner Self, and Marriage Wise. She has been in huge demand and has been on TV, Radio, and the guest speaker circuit for almost two years on and off. To be honest, because Anita was exclusive to me, and Katie promotes the Dixon Group, she has ended up being managed by Richard Babcock, Katie's number one ass kisser. Remember him, he was the young trainee she stuck me with to run off to Birch's graduation?

Yeah, some things never change, she behaves herself these days, and I hardly see her at events, but you cannot tell me, she does not enjoy knowing she can find ways to keep us working apart. Three years ago, we both stepped down from the Parish Council, having spent seven years at the helm, and took two weeks alone at Sunny Bank, but apart from two weeks in Crete a year and a half ago, we have been working none stop. To be honest, it is becoming really hard to try and keep our relationship going, we hardly seem to be home at the same time.

On the few occasions we are actually home at the same time, we are either too exhausted to do anything together, and just sleep, or we are working on other projects. It has felt recently, like I am either on the road, or living at my desk alone in my room.

This year has been really tough, apart from the week between Christmas and New Year, we have been crossing paths since. As she comes home, I have an event, and as I get back, she is off to another talk or lecture, and I am reaching a point where dare I say it... To me, she has lost her sparkle, and honestly, I am lonely, and I miss her, thank God for Anita and Chloe, without them, I would be lost.

I miss the Curio's too, life at home has changed so much, and at times I wonder why we live there, well apart from my arch, I mean, I am never selling that house, not unless I take my arch with me. Chloe is my sanity, I know, weird right, she has hardly changed as we have all grown up, she still paints, fucks, and swears like a sailor, but she is adorable, and I love her to bits.

Chloe still lives for her art, and through D&D we have organised some really high profile shows for her paintings. She has done really well, and has sold so many paintings, I have lost count. She is really well known in the art community, and even gives her time to the art college in Oxendale, where she joins with Hatty and gives talks on painting and after hours workshops. Hatty is retired; can you believe it? I never thought she would give up teaching, but when the time came, she had no hesitation grabbing her pension, and buggering off with Clive to tour the Mediterranean.

They both live together now on Manor Road, he sold everything and moved in with her, I mean, it is unheard of, she now shares her studio, but insists marriage is out of the question. I love her to bits, she is my second mum, and she is still as wild as always. I left the Parish Council after seven long years as Chair, and left it in good hands, because Hatty is still there at the grand old age of sixty eight, swearing like a trooper, and keeping a watchful eye on the accounts, with mum at her side.

Mum is great, her and Patrick have had a wild time seeing the world and living life to the full. After all those years of suffering, she finally found a man to make her happy, and they have been everywhere. She paints a lot, the guest house is now an art studio again, although, she left the bedroom exactly as it was. It is funny how that room is so important to both of us.

Patrick moved in four years ago, sold his share of his legal practice and retired. He spends his time working in the garden, cleaning the pool, and taking care of mum. I have really grown very fond of him, and his humour is wonderful. Mum paints and smiles when she is not in the gallery, which has been a huge success for her and Ellen, and even though mum is now sixty nine, and Ellen fifty eight, the pair of them have no intentions of throwing the towel in yet. Bradley still runs his business, but to be honest, Margret or as I lovingly refer to her, 'The Shredder,' has sold her practice and now works at his side. She does most of the work, and yes, she still scares the shit out of me, she has not softened with age.

Deb's and Jimmy are still going strong, although they now have three children, just as she always wanted, Jennifer, Helen, and Gem. Battered Taco split up, their album 'Tell it as it is' went massive, and made them a global hit, which they followed up with 'Rock till death.' Family life changed Jimmy, and had a strange effect on Floyd, who asked Gail to marry him, as he saw what Jimmy had and felt he wanted something similar. They married a good few years back, and Floyd has a son called Dylan. He is working on a solo album at the moment with Jimmy, and it is very laid back stuff from what I have heard, how life has changed us all, are we all becoming normal?

The thing was, the band lived a pretty wild life, and to be honest, it got a little too wild. Floyd liked a drink, but he loved music more, he did get out of it, but when threatened by losing his place in the band, he cleaned up his act. I think Gail played a part in that, as she became his long term girlfriend, then his wife.

Once married, Jimmy calmed down. Zac had a long term girlfriend, and was pretty happy, but Doug and Emerson, they got pretty wild and lost control, and things went downhill from there, and the band broke up. Doug and Emerson ended up in rehab, and got the cure, Emerson lives on a farm in Wales, and raises sheep and bees, I know right, it is a strange combination. Doug built his own studio, and does movie scores, and he has done really well out of it.

With Jimmy out of the band and at home a lot, he has become more involved with Deb's business, and Cogs and Wheelers is now a chain of book shops, and they are looking at more. He invested heavily, and they now have five shops, which they take it in turns to visit and manage. Denise is pretty much the full time manager of the village shop. I don't see as much of Deb's as I would like; it feels at times like the Curio's are drifting apart again, there is only Anthony and Chloe left at home now.

Edwina got married, and her and Luke lived with us for a year, but then she got pregnant, and had a little boy called Samuel Anthony, they moved to Millington, where Luke bought a warehouse for G5, and expanded the security business. Deli dated Eric for two years and he popped the question, and she now lives on Garden Street, with Eric, and their two children. With the help of Birch and me, we helped her set up a children's nursery on the wasteland between the train station and Norman and Daisy's Plant nursery, right next to the big play park, we built when on the council.

To make things even quieter, two years ago Izzy moved in with Malcolm Forbes Benedict at number seven... See, we knew that was where the dungeon was built and the club was established, you never know what goes on behind closed doors in Wotton.

Nothing really changes on the outside in Wotton, it is still the picture perfect village, which is immaculate at all times, and has many tourists flowing through it. All the shops and buildings have had a massive upgrade, as I raised the funds to take on a sand blasting and renovation program, and over a hundred years' worth of grime was removed. Then as promised, we painted the whole village, and it looks as good today as it did two hundred years ago.

Dursley Woodland now has park status, and Birch and myself set up a friends of Dursley Woodlands Group, to manage it. Today, it is the most beautiful it has ever been, with a cleaner stream, and lots of benches, and areas where the villagers and tourists can have picnics, we have had quite a few there over the last few years. I have such fond memories sat on the grass, under the trees, sipping wine, as Birch laughs and chuckles on our old travel rug from the guest house.

Molly and Nigel joined the council, and today Nigel is Vice Chair, Deb's is Chair and has continued the work started by Birch and myself. Anthony refused to run, but is still a heavily involved officer, and Edwina stepped down when she moved to Millington, which is a shame, but she still maintains a lot of the local websites as a sub contractor for the council.

Nigel has actually changed a lot, he is still with Sophia, and to be honest, they really make a beautiful couple. She works with Deli at the nursery, and Rupert is now 12 and in high school at Oxendale. Just like his dad, he really is clever, although, I have to say, he is much cooler and not quite so nerdy. We put that down to the influence of Sophia, after all, she has an eye for fashion and trends, and she gives him some great advice. She is now an influencer on Insta, she has well over a million followers, as she gives out advice to help parents make their kids cool.

We all grew up, who would have believed it, but I will not deny, I miss them all. There are days when the house is so quiet, I find I slip back into the hermit like creature that lived alone in the guest house. I have become quite solitary, but I do have days where I miss all the banter, and the endless sexual innuendo, and crazy happenings.

We are supposed to all head over the water to the States in July, but as yet, apart from Chloe, Birch and myself, the others have not decided. I had hoped for a Curio Live reunion, it would be nice, but sadly, life is getting in the way of everything. It is just not that easy to move forward with so many commitments. I must admit, I have not really had time to write, I have been so busy, and I miss it.

I cannot deny, deep down inside, I just want to cut all the ties and break free, and I have often wondered if this is what happened to my mum, did life get so involved it took over and killed her free spirit? That is how I feel, and my mind has been fixed on whether or not to just quit everything and stop. I really want to spend my time with Birch over the next couple of weeks, and talk it over with her. God, I really want to just be alone with her for more than a day, I feel trapped and like I am suffocating. That crazy teenager inside me wants to be free and let out again, and honestly at the moment, I really want to just let go, and let her out to go wild.

I will be, by Avril came on the player and played through my speakers, up ahead, I could see the signs for the services. I needed coffee, my travel mug was empty, so I pulled into the inside lane and indicated. The next junction would be the M5, and I would be heading south to Dartmoor, and not long after, she would be in my arms, and mine for two whole weeks.

Edwina walked in through the side door with Samantha talking.

"Just get him to sign the contract and then we should be fine. I have to shoot up to Manchester, they are having problems with the system, and I think we need to replace or repair the server. I tried remotely, but it cannot be done from here and Aden is tied up all week." Chloe leaned around the door.

"If you are making coffee, I could use one." Edwina flicked on the kettle.

"I thought you were going to get your hair done yesterday?" Chloe got up, and walked out of the studio.

"Anthony needs more dye, his new trainee screwed up, and he used it to do a cover up." Edwina smirked.

"That is what happens when you open the top floor to more staff. You cannot keep your eyes on them all the time, where was Delphine?" Chloe smirked.

"At the doctors, Janis was supposed to be supervising her, but was rushed off her feet, and Anthony was busy downstairs with deliveries." Chloe looked around.

"Where is little Sammy?" Edwina frowned.

"School, where else would he be? Which reminds me, I have to get a move on, the roads will be crazy soon, and I have to pick him up." Chloe looked disappointed as she sat down at the island.

"I was hoping to see him, it feels like ages."

"Chloe it was last week at my place, and don't forget, you have to take mum shopping today at four." She nodded.

"I know." Edwina stared at her.

"I hope you will be wearing clothes, and behave, no pissing about like you do with Abby... Where is she anyhow?" Chloe smiled.

"She is giving the key note at the Gothic Revival Festival, then heading to the farm house to meet Birch, they have some time off... Finally!" Edwina put her cup down in front of her.

"Good, those two need it, both of them have been too busy recently, and Abby is looking really burned out, some time alone with Birch will do her good." Chloe nodded and gave a soft smile.

"Yeah, she has been really quiet recently, I was telling Baz the other night, I am worried about her. Her and Birch are spending too much time apart; it's that red haired bitches' fault. She keeps

Birch too busy, and she is always booking more and more stage events, the old hag needs dropping off a bridge, that is the only way those two will get a break." Edwina rolled her eyes.

"Not again... Chloe, I know you love them both, but honestly, don't you think it is time you got over it, Christ, it was bloody years ago, all that is done with? I mean, Jesus, Katie is what, fifty now, and she is fatter and uglier, look at Abby, she is almost the same as she has always been, and still good looking. To be honest, I think she is more beautiful than she has ever been. I am telling you, that fat slapper has not got a prayer, Birch will only ever love Abby." Chloe scoffed at her.

"Oh yeah, then why is she never here, and why is Abby always alone and sad, tell me that smart arse?" Edwina gave a sigh.

"Chloe, look at them, both of them have been chasing their dreams since they first met, and now they have finally got there. Abby is huge you know? She has sold millions of books, and Birch is not that far behind her. Dixon have loads of new writers, and a lot of them write gothic stuff, Abby is a legend now and a massive influence on all of them, her fan base is huge. I hate to say it, but fame has its price, and having to be high profile is a part of that. Look, it will soon calm down, they have both had to promote, it won't last forever, and then they will be back here together and acting like idiots again." Chloe lifted her cup, and looked over it as she took a sip.

"I wish I was as sure as you, I am telling you Weena, I think they both need to take a break, and honestly, I am scared that they won't. I am really worried about Abby, if you ask me, Birch needs to remember who she is, all this fame and glamour is clouding her mind, and she is forgetting the most important thing in her life, and that will not be good for us." Edwina smiled as she finished her coffee.

"You worry too much, look, life gets busy and complicated, there will always be bumps in the road, it is called growing up. Not all of us have the luxury of spending all day naked with purple paint on our tits, some of us have a complicated life... Shit, is that the time?" Edwina stood up, and grabbed her bag.

"I have to go, or I will get stuck in traffic. Chloe relax, they will be home smiling and happy soon, you will see." She leaned down and kissed her on the cheek.

"I will bring Sammy on Saturday." She smirked.

"Funny isn't it, you say you don't want kids, and yet you cannot wait to see them. It is never too late sis, but the clock is ticking?" Chloe frowned and looked up her.

"Fuck that, I don't need any, I got Sammy, and Jenny, Helen and Gem, and Deli's two, why the fuck do I want all that shit and mess? No, I am fine as I am." Edwina laughed as she walked down the hall.

"See you Saturday." Chloe sat back with her cup, and looked up at Samantha.

"I am not wrong you know, Abby is my best friend, I know her, and although she is hiding it, she is lonely. Birch needs to wake up, because if she does not, she will lose Abby, everyone laughs at me, but I am not wrong on this."

I felt tired, it is a long drive, but as Sunny Bank came into view, I felt my spirit's lift. I pulled off the road onto the drive filled with trees and shrubs. They had overgrown a little, Birch had still not found a gardener since the loss of Seth two years back. I turned at the end of the roadway, and the house came into view. I smiled as I saw it, I have so many happy memories of this place, it really has been my saving grace at times. Our hidden get away, where time stops and Birch is who she was always meant to be, and honestly, I need this time with her.

It was good to just get out of the car and stretch, I grabbed my bags, and headed up for the green door, there was no Petal, so I was earlier than her. I walked up the path and pulled out my key, wow, this old green door has seen some visitors, I wonder what it would say if it could talk. I smiled as I remembered her lifting me screaming, and carrying me inside.

I turned the key and stepped in, and it felt nice, I pushed the door back, and closed it with my bum, and leaned on it dropping my bags, and just for a moment, I closed my eyes, and gave a long sigh.

"Finally, some peace and time for us to be alone."

The routine never changes at Sunny Bank, in a way, it is our idea of normal, whatever that may be. You arrive, open all the windows, open the back door, click on the kettle, and then unload the supplies and put them away, and then comes my favourite moment. I step out of the back door sweating, slip off my shoes, and just stare at the trees, as I dangle my hot feet from driving in the stream, and just remember all the joy this place has been.

I leaned back and gave a long gasp of air, Christ, this water is cold, but oh my God, it feels so great. I lifted my cup and smiled, I could almost see her with that bright happy face, and those dancing green eyes, filled with such life, and her bright happy smile, all framed by that amazingly white hair filled with black patches, as she turned and lifted her arms in the air.

"See Sweetie, I told you I made the swing." I have missed her so much. I lifted my phone, and hit speed dial; it rang... Then went to voice mail.

"Hey Baby, just letting you know I made it to the house, call me when you get this, and let me know when you will be here... I love you." I ended the call, and put the phone down, time for another coffee.

My feet felt numb as I got up, and walked back into the house, and headed for the kettle, my phone came alive and I looked at the screen and smiled.

"Hi Baby, how far away are you?"

"Deads, I just landed in Paris."

"What... Why the frig are you in Paris, you are supposed to be here?" I heard her sigh.

"Give me a moment Deads... Richard, just give me a second, I am talking to Abby... Sorry about that, he is being a real pain in the ass. Deads, I am booked in at the Relationship Conference, I did tell you."

"When!? Birch, I am at Sunny Bank, we were supposed to be spending two weeks together." The phone was silent for a moment; I heard her sigh.

"Deads, I forgot, I have been rushed off my feet, and Richard has booked me solid. Honestly, I completely forgot, I am sorry... Look, I will make it up to you."

I felt my heart completely break, and I felt angry, we had planned this a month ago, and I had cancelled everything for this. I really wanted it so badly. I could not help but feel so utterly let down.

"Deads are you still there?" I gave a sigh.

"I am always here, what a shame you never fucking are... Forget it." I ended the call.

Birch looked at Richard as he signalled looking pissed off. "Deads... Deads, are you still there?"

"Jemi, we need to go, the limo is waiting, for God's sake, just ring her later, we have a deadline you know?" Birch took her phone away from her ear, and grabbed the handle of her case.

"Keep your shirt on, I am coming, you know Richard, you work for me, and maybe you should remember that."

I threw my phone on the table, I could feel the surge of emotions swirling up inside me, and I turned with my coffee, closed the door, and headed for the stairs, and our room. I knew what was coming, it had been building inside me for weeks, and I needed to be alone and out of sight.

I saw the bed, and it hit me, as I flopped into her pillow, pulled it close, and up came the tears, how could she have forgot? I buried my face into it, and bawled my brains out.

Chapter 2

Moment of Clarity.

I opened my eyes and blinked, it was dark, I sat up and slipped to the edge of the bed, and gave a long sigh. I looked back for my phone, it was not there, but my cold coffee was. I rubbed my face, I needed a drink, but not coffee.

The good thing about this house, is it has a good wine store. I headed down to the kitchen and grabbed a bottle out of the fridge, I unscrewed the cap, my dad would faint if he saw me drinking this stuff. With a glass and a full bottle, I wandered out into the garden and over the bridge, the grass was longer than normal, but felt good on my bare feet, it was a little chilly, and I shivered a little.

I sat at the old picnic table, and poured the wine, and looked out at the old trees, with their slender white trunks and black patched lines around them, illuminated by the lights of the house. They seemed to glow in the late evening darkness, just as her hair did in the darkness of our room at home. God, is there no escaping her image? I sat there feeling alone, depressed, exhausted, and heart broken, simply staring into the darkness, as I drank my wine.

It was quiet, and still, and I felt more isolated and remote than I ever had. For the first time in a long time, I felt all those feelings I had a long time ago, sat alone in the guest house, knowing Birch was thousands of miles away from me, and my love for her was eating me away. I gave a sniffle as the tears once again filled my eyes. How could she have forgotten, had I really become so unimportant in her life now?

Is this what life comes to, the love you felt fizzles away, and you end up lost and alone, out of reach and out of mind? It certainly felt that way, I have this huge pain inside me and I really do not know what to do about it. I have spent weeks smiling for people, signing books and pictures and appearing as promised, but the truth is, all I want was to just be left alone in my room, snuggled up to Birch. Now it feels like she has also forgotten me, and suddenly, I am alone in a boat, cast adrift and sailing away from everyone. Was this the life of my mother repeating on me?

I looked at the bottle, it was empty, hell, how long had I been here? It was pretty dark, I snatched it up with my glass, and stood up, my head swirled and my legs wobbled. Oh God, I feel pissed, I have not been drunk in ages, and actually it felt good, scratch that, it feels bloody wonderful. I staggered to the left, and giggled, the trees were swaying, or was that me? I laughed at myself.

"Hell girl, you have not been this pissed in ages. Almost a year I think?"

Yeah, I talk to myself a lot these days, I guess it helps to have someone who understands what it is like being me around. I grabbed the table as I swayed.

"Okay, I have done this a thousand times... I think?"

I giggled, I could see the bridge, lit by the light from the kitchen window, the problem was it kept moving, or I did, I was not sure. I staggered over to it, and missed with a loud giggle, I took another unstable step, and everything blurred, and then, splosh! I felt the ice cold water running down my back, and gasped with shock.

"Oh hell, that is cold!"

Talk about a shock to the system, I caught my breath in surprise, and looked up at the bridge, and lay back feeling the water as it ran over me, and stared up at the sky as I shivered, it was dark and the moon was obscured. I felt the drop hit my face, then another, and another, it was starting to rain. I have no idea why, I just started to laugh. I lay there soaking wet staring up into the darkness, and I laughed like an escaped mental patient. I yelled into the sky.

"I AM ALREADY WET YOU TWAT, SCREW YOU!"

I screamed out with laughter, and lifted two fingers into the air and waved them at the rain clouds, laughing like a hysterical maniac.

Chloe ground down her hips and gave a long wail of a moan, Baz gasped, as he felt his hips buck upwards, and his body tensed up. Chloe wailed, smiled, and then flopped forward sweating, and as she hit his shoulder, he lifted his arms around her with a smile, his words breathless.

"God, I love living with you." Chloe stiffened, lifted her head and frowned, as she tried to breathe.

"We don't live together, why would you say that?" He looked down at her lay across his chest.

"Chloe, I have not been home in weeks, and when I do, it is only for clean clothes, most of my shit is here." She sat up and looked at him.

"No, it's not... Okay, you have a few things here, but it is not like everything you own is here." He gave a laugh.

"Wow, you looked so freaked out at the moment, I mean, is it really that bad having me around?" She stared at him, a look of fear on her face.

"I love to have you here, I mean, I have not fucked someone else in.... OH FUCK!" He gave a laugh, as her eyes went huge.

"Ages?" She swallowed hard, and slid off him, looking petrified. Baz sat up as she moved to the edge of the bed.

"Wow, is it really that bad thinking you may just have slipped into something good? Jesus Chloe, we have been doing this for years." She turned and looked at him.

"I know... It is just... Well, you know... Oh fuck!" He sat smiling.

"Chloe, I frigging love you to death, you know this, out of all the places I want to be, this is the one place I am happiest, is that really so bloody horrible?" She gave a long sigh.

"Baz it is not that, you know I love having you here, it's just... Well, I just never thought I would get..." He gave a giggle.

"Attached?" She nodded and swallowed hard, and turned to look at him.

"I don't want to mislead you, have I done that?" He shook his head, and leaned forward and took her hand.

"Look, stop getting all freaked out, honestly, I am happy with this. Chloe, I mean what I say. I care about you more than anyone realises, including you, and I want this, you know, this happiness, whatever this is?" She nodded, and gave a gasp of relief.

"Yeah, I get it... I mean, it is not like you're asking for marriage, is it?" He gave a slight chuckle.

"I would if you wanted it, I mean, look at it from my point of view, I have invested well, I have shit loads of cash, I adore your free spirit and will never change that. To me you are the most beautiful woman in the world, and I am forty one years old, so I am wise enough to understand things more." Chloe felt the jolt to her system, and felt slightly panicked, she turned back to him as he smiled at her.

"Are you mental, no one is crazy enough to marry me, I am unstable and wild and way too freaking free spirited. I mean, be honest, we have both fucked other people?" He shrugged.

"I like this, I like what we have, I could do this on a more permanent basis, as I said, if you asked, I would definitely marry you, or not. I just want this to continue, it is the happiest I have ever been, I mean, I have not slept with anyone else but you in three years." Her eyes widened even more.

"Fuck off, what about all the groupies around the bands?" He shook his head, and shrugged again.

"They are just kids, I want something more me, more woman, and I am telling you Chloe, to me, there is no one more woman than you, I frigging love sex with you." She gave a nod and smiled.

"I have had a lot of practice, and I do love screwing, especially you." She stopped and stared at him, and then stood up quickly.

"Oh Fuck... Am I in an actual relationship?" He gave a roaring laugh, as he looked up at her from the bed.

"Fucked up, isn't it?" She nodded swallowing hard as her eyes grew huge.

"What the fuck are we going to do Baz?" He could not help but laugh.

"Chloe, calm the hell down, is it really that bad being close to someone not Abby?" She shook her head, but she looked terror stricken.

"Well, no, but I mean, oh fuck am I in love with you, I mean, holy fuck, is that why I love being around you so much, Jesus Baz, is this love?" She was sweating and looking intensely panicked. Baz shook his head and smiled.

"Hell girl, I know how I feel, I suppose the question is how do you feel about things? As I said, if you want more I can go there, if not, then chill out and we will stay as we are. Only you really know how you feel, I am happy going with the flow at the moment, this really does suit me, whatever it is." Chloe shook her head, and looked around the room, she looked like she was starting to unravel.

"Oh fuck, I need to talk to Weena, actually no, fuck that, I need Abby."

I staggered into the kitchen dripping and giggling to myself, outside it was pissing it down, I turned to the kettle and clicked it on. The cold water helped, but suddenly I was not enjoying being drunk. I stood dripping as I spooned in the coffee powder and extra sugar, being drunk is overrated, and horrible. The kettle clicked, and I lifted it to pour. God, I felt depressed, even being pissed was no longer fun, what the hell has happened to me?

I made my coffee, turned the heating on, and stripped, and dropped my soaking wet clothes in the laundry basket. I still felt weird as I sipped, but I felt a little more stable as I saw my phone and picked it up, and headed back towards the bedroom door shivering, bed felt like a good idea.

I made it up the stairs, well, I sloshed some coffee swaying, and walked into our room. It is so strange, most of the house has been decorated, and yet when it came to this room, we have left it exactly as it was. It was still covered in tiny flower wall paper, although, there were more photos on the wall, one was all of us stood naked at the tor, all those years ago, wow, we had all changed so much.

I pulled back the duvet and climbed in, fluffed up my pillows and grabbed Birch's, and set it behind me, then leaned back and lifted my coffee. I sat in bed holding it with both hands and sipped, my stomach was reeling, I don't think I will ever drink again. I plugged in my phone, and the screen lit up, I had five messages and... I stared at the phone.

"Thirty eight missed calls, what the hell?"

I opened them up, they were all from Birch, I gave a sigh, I was not in the mood to deal with it now. I was too tired, and still pretty drunk, I put the phone back on my unit. I sat back, lifted my cup, as I looked around the room with all the pictures of us, Roni and Will, plus mum and dad, and of course Avril. I closed my eyes, there were too many memories here, I needed to be elsewhere, but I was too drunk to drive, and I felt so unbelievably tired and weary.

I finished my coffee, it did not settle my stomach, and I really did not want to lie down, so I just sat back and closed my eyes, tried to relax, and quell the churning within me. Say hello to the night blasted into the room, I opened my eyes, and turned to the unit and looked at my phone.

"Oh God, I will have to speak to her, but why now?" I lifted it up without looking and hit answer.

Chloe came flying out of her room. "Oh Fuck... Oh Fuck... OH FUCKING HELL!" She swallowed hard, and lifted her phone to her ear as she flew down the stairs.

"Oh FUCK, FUCK, FUCK!"

"Hi."

"Abby... Oh fuck, ABBY I AM IN SO MUCH FUCKING TROUBLE!"

"WHAT?" I sat forward, as Chloe panicked in my ear.

"Chloe what the hell is wrong?" My heart had started to beat really fast, she sounded terrified.

"Chloe are you alright, you are not in danger, are you?"

"OH FUCKING YES, I AM, I AM IN DANGER OF ADMITTING I MAY OR MAY NOT BE IN LOVE. ABBY, YOU HAVE TO HELP ME, WHAT THE FUCK DO I DO?"

"Huh!" I heard her swallow hard, and then take huge deep breaths.

"Abby, don't say anything, but I think Baz wants to marry me, what the fuck do I do?" I put on my speaker phone and stared at it a minute.

"Holy shit Chloe, what are you going to do?"

"I DON'T FUCKING KNOW, WHY THE FUCK DO YOU THINK I AM RINGING?"

I sat back and gave a long sigh, I had no idea what to say, I looked at the phone, my mind reeling, and then burst out laughing. Chloe pulled the phone away from her ear.

"Don't laugh you twisted bitch; I am having a crisis... Are you pissed?" I nodded.

"Pretty much, I fell off the bridge into the stream pissed." Chloe smirked.

"Glad I am not the only one, that's a relief. Abby what the fuck am I going to do, everything has snuck up on me, and I think I am actually in a real relationship? Oh Fuck, I am screwed." I was still laughing.

"Chloe, Baz is a really cool guy, he has been with you for bloody ever, I just thought you knew." Chloe shook her head.

"Why the fuck would I? I paint and I fuck, I mean we have had a wild ride and I love him being around all the time... HOLY FUCK, WHAT HAVE I DONE?" I was still laughing.

"Chloe, Baz really does love you, I mean, my God, I see more of him in the house than I do Birch, and you said it yourself; you love having him around. I think its sweet."

"Fuck off Abby, you are too pissed to say that, it's not sweet, it's a fucking crisis."

"Why? I mean, Chloe, he makes you happy, I really do not understand what the problem is..." I froze on the bed, there were grumblings and weird things happening inside me, I snatched up my phone quickly.

"Chloe, hold up."

I jumped off the bed, and ran to the toilet, yep, there was definite movement in my stomach. I banged into the door, as I felt a surge, fell to my knees, and lifted the lid just in time...

YERK... SLOSH! Chloe pulled the phone from her ear and screwed up her face, as I gasped and retched again.

"Fuck Abby, no one wants to hear that."

YERK... SLOSH. "Oh God." YERK! Chloe held her phone at arms length and shuddered.

"Oh man that is fucked up... Are you alright, call Birch?"

YERK! Chloe gave another shudder.

"Oh, that is not good Abby, what have you eaten?" I gave a gasp and sat back.

"Nothing yet, I just sat out with a wine or eight. To be honest, I drank the bottle, which I am regretting now." Chloe frowned.

"Where is Birch, I thought she was meeting you?" I shook my head.

"Nope, Richard pissed off with her to Paris." Chloe looked puzzled.

"But you guys were supposed to be having a break, what has Birch said?" I gave a long sigh.

"Not much, she said she forgot." Chloe shook her head.

"That cannot be right, she never forgets a thing. Abby are you okay, I can come down there if you want me to?" I smiled, and looked in the toilet and shuddered.

"Oh god, that looks disgusting, Jesus what are those green lumps, I don't remember eating them?" Chloe gave a violent shudder.

"Abby, please, just flush it, I do not want description, I am a painter, my mind is already too vivid." I reached for the handle and pulled down.

"Oh shit, they float." Chloe cringed.

"For fucks sake, stop looking and close the fucking lid, oh wow, you are really fucked up, do you know that?" I shrugged.

"It is good to check, I actually feel better without the floating green bits inside me, although what the fuck are they?"

"Abby, shut the fuck up, you are freaking me out. Abby, what are you going to do, Birch should be there, you know who has done this don't you?" I gave a sigh, and lifted my phone off the floor.

"Chloe that is all over with, it is in the past."

"Bollocks! Do not tell me you are buying that, we both know it is utter shit, she has always been there stirring the pot, that bloody woman never forgives anything."

I smiled, I loved her to bits, she always has my back. I took a deep breath, and walked back into my room for my cup, and headed back down stairs.

"Oh Chloe, I am so lost I have no idea what to do, I won't deny, it has crossed my mind, we are a right pair. Honestly, I think Baz loves you pretty deeply, and I also think he understands you like I do, but you know what, I am the last person to ask. My marriage has lost its sparkle, and is heading for the sewer with those green floaty bits. It seems these days; I cannot get her in a room for more than ten minutes before she is off again. I guess it is the risk we all take, we just hope the love is forever, but that is not always the case." Chloe shook her head.

"Abby, I have no idea what is going on in your head, but I told you once before and I will say it again. No one will ever love you like she does, I told you two months ago you were both doing too much. I told her too, you guys are solid, even if both of you are being too stupid to see it. She loves you Abby, just sit and really think hard about all you two have done, and find her inside you again, I mean it Abby, do not give up on her, because if you do, you will hate yourself forever. Abby I am really worried, let me come down there."

The kettle clicked, and I poured another coffee and smiled, her belief in us two had always been total, I loved her for that. I looked at the phone.

"Chloe, I tried. I am here and she is in France, what the hell should I do?"

"Well, you get over all the bullshit negatives, and do what both of you have done for us, for starters. Abby, for fucks sake, fight for her, let her see the truth." I gave a small smile, but sighed.

"Chloe I am so tired, I am not sure I can." Chloe understood that.

"Abby, you are burned out, so is she, at some point she will drop. Look, rest up, and do what you do best, write... I mean for fucks sake, how long has it been? Abby, that cursed fucking book has your answers, I know it is on your laptop, and I am going to hate myself for saying this, but read it, read the Snow Queen and remember."

Wow she wants me to read the book, I never saw that coming, I sat in the chair next to my phone with a coffee, and lifted my legs to the seat.

"Okay, I hear you, so what are you going to do, I do think Baz is serious, and you know what, most of us treat him as part of the family already, he has been there that long?" Chloe gave a smile, as she leaned against the island.

"How do I know he will stay though, come on Abby, everyone thought the same about Terry, and he just pissed off and married that girl from the cybercafé? Honestly, I always thought we would end up together at some point, I thought he understood me." I leaned back in the chair.

"Honestly Chloe, I think Baz is different, but at the end of the day it is up to you, I think maybe you should take your own advice. Chloe sit and really think hard about everything you two have done, and decide how you feel about it all. I spent four years doing that, and when I thought I had lost her, I got pissed and almost swallowed a jar of pills, but in a way that helped, because when she came back, I told her I loved her, and you know the rest." Chloe gave a wide smile.

"You know what, you still do, and whether or not you can see it, she still loves you. There is no one else out there for either of you, so if that red haired bitch is making waves for you two, make bigger fucking ones back so that Birch sees them. I mean, come on Abby, you are smarter than all of us, show the bitch who is boss again, and show Birch who really loves her." I felt the tears fill my eyes and gave a sob.

"I do love her Chloe, I really wanted her here with me, I am missing her so much, it feels awful without her." My tears dripped on the table, and I sniffled up.

"I am sorry, I don't want to cry, but you are all I have left, and I am so lonely Chloe, I really need her here with me, and all you guys around me again, I miss it so much, don't you?"

Chloe nodded and gave a sniffle, lifted her arm and wiped her eyes.

"Yeah, I do, but we all grew up and moved on, I am so glad I have you, I mean it Abby, you are so important to me, so please do not do anything stupid, because I really need you in my life. Look, have a good cry and a good sleep, and just remember everything about her, and then do what you do best. I cannot believe I am saying this, but if you have to, write another fucking possessed book. Abby, fight for her, and all of us, because the others might not see it, but they need you, and they need Birch, so come on, get fighting." I nodded and smiled, and took a really deep breath.

"I love you too Chloe, and I need you in my life too, I just wish you were gay, because I really need a good shag about now." I giggled.

"Oh God Abby, I am so fucking straight it is unbelievable, you have no fucking idea how straight I am." She gave a chuckle.

"Abby, fight for her, she is the only woman you will ever sleep with." I nodded at the phone; I knew that.

"Thanks Chloe, I really needed to hear a friendly voice. I think I will turn off my phone, shut the world out, and take some time for me to puzzle things out."

"Okay Abby, look if you need me, just message and I will be down in a flash."

"Thanks Chloe, I love you." She smiled, and nodded.

"Yeah, I love you too, eat something... But not green." I gave a giggle.

"I will... So will you be okay now?" She smiled and nodded her head, which was stupid as she was on the phone.

"Yeah, I will be, I panicked a little but I will be fine now. I am going to think about a lot of things, and decide what to do. I will talk to you soon Abby, look after yourself, and click those keys... Night."

"Night."

Chloe gave a sigh as she ended the call, and slowly walked back up the stairs towards her room, Baz was flat out in bed and she smiled as she saw him, her voice was low and very soft.

"I reckon I could handle his dick for a little longer." She lifted the duvet and slipped in, and cuddled up close to him, and gave a happy sigh.

I slipped into bed and lay back, my head was clearing more, and my stomach had eased a great deal. I closed my eyes and thought about everything Chloe had said. She was right, maybe we had lost sight of things, and maybe Katie had noticed, I have never trusted her, the only question was, how was I going to deal with this without confronting Katie? The last thing I wanted was another huge confrontation and turmoil, I was not strong enough for that, although, I think Chloe has given me a really good idea! Thanks Chloe.

Chapter 3

Going Dark.

Richard turned in the doorway, looking irritated.

"Jemi, it is an important debate, you need to be there." She sat on the bed.

"I am tired and exhausted, and I don't want to be there. You set me up Richard, you knew she wanted me there, why the hell am I here?" He gave a very irritated sigh.

"I do what the boss says, and it is important for the Dixon Group that we honour international recognition. Jemi, we just need to get through this, and then you can go back to your little princess bride. So please, it starts in forty minutes." Birch leaned back on the bed.

"Tell me Richard, how does it feel to be Katie's number one ass kisser, knowing she will never fuck you, because you don't have boobs and a vagina? Do you enjoy being her Simp?" She smiled as his brow furrowed, and his cheeks turned red, his anger was rising.

"I mean it Jemi, I don't want to have to go down there and tell Katie you are refusing to appear, you know how pissed off she will get, and no one wants that, do we now?" Birch chuckled.

"Seriously, that is your best, look, you ridiculous little puppet, let me be quite clear, not only am I a major shareholder of the Dixon Group, I am a shareholder in K.O. Do you honestly think I fear Katie? My God, you must be a bigger bloody idiot than I pegged you for. Go tell her, and see what she does, go on. It will be nothing, because she knows as well as I do, if she tries anything, her controlling interest will mean shit. Dead's and me will vote against her, and so will my mum, because she will always support us. You have forgotten who the real boss is, and guess what you little prick, that would be me. I will appear as stated, but I am telling you now, once I set foot back on British soil, you are no longer my representation, I am done with your ass kissing bull shit."

I had not slept well, and had suffered bad dreams, so was
up early, my mind racing as I thought about a way to change
everything for the better. Talking with Chloe had helped. It had
given me many ideas, and a plan was forming of how to end all
my problems. What I needed was coffee, and a way of bringing
back that feeling of our youth. In a way, all of us had forgotten
who we were, and lost sight of everything, and it had been during
that long dark four year period of my life, I had gained the
clarity to move forward. Maybe it was time to go back there, and
recreate the past, and hopefully through that darkness, illuminate
everything.

Chloe was so right, the Snow Queen held the answer, we had
always been about the dark little beastie and her queen of the
snow, that was who we were. Those days of darkness had been
our Winter, and the glitz and glamour of public life had become a
Spring and Summer. As much as it had been our dream, I could
now see it as the thaw of Spring, and it was destroying my queen
of the snow, and I had to find a way to use the darkness to save
her.

I sat at the desk in the study that was her grandfather's, it was
her room of memories, and I had to use it to make her stop and
think. A memory of many years ago, had been stuck in my mind,
and the clarity of why, was starting to shape in my thoughts. It
was of the first time I had ever entered this room; in the summer
of the year we were married.

She looked at me and shook her head, her eyes sparkled
slightly, her voice was quiet and reflective.

"I loved him dearly Deads, this place is very special to me, I
have spent many hours in here, sat listening to him tell me of his
life. I want you to write in here, this place is special, I want you
a part of it too, so write at this desk as he did, write something
wonderful."

I understood, and I had my plan, but it was as extreme as
winter and as cold as ice, but it was my biggest chance of bringing
back the snow, and so I hammered out my thoughts. I had not
slept well, and woke up in the middle of the night, and had sat in

bed thinking of the snow queen, which was stuck in my head, and as I did, I brought together everything I had been thinking about for months. The truth was, we had drifted, and I was losing her, and Chloe was right, I needed to fight, and it started now. After an exhausting six months, I felt I knew just how to do it, and as Chloe had pointed out, it started with a story.

It would be a short but powerful story, and I already had forty thousand words down, and could feel the overwhelming power of my keys, as I hammered away adding more and more. God, it was so good just to sit in silence and write, it had been way too long, and I needed this. I really needed to get all my thoughts back in order, and writing this would do that, as my thoughts ran down my blurred fingers from the speed I was typing. Oh wow, Chloe knew me so well, and I am not sure why that surprised me so much. I sat back and lifted my cup, the word count read eighty nine thousand words, it felt like it was a word for each memory of her time with me, although, I did probably have ten thousand times that.

I looked at the document, smiled, leaned forward and clicked print. In the corner behind me the printer came alive, and the white sheet slid off the full tray, and began its chugging. I lifted my phone and tapped open my call history, there was another nine missed calls from Birch, I had put it on silent, so had not heard it ring.

I stood up, lifted my cup as I scrolled down the call list, I saw the name Andy EFG, and I tapped it, his number came up and I hit call. I walked through into the kitchen, and lifted the kettle to check if it was full enough, then clicked the switch, as I heard the phone ring, he picked it up.

"Abby, how nice, how are you, it has been a while?"

"Andrew, I need some business advice, what are you up to this evening, I am in Devon, but heading your way, and I wondered if we could meet up?"

"I have nothing planned; what kind of advice are you looking for?"

"I have some new ideas, and I may want to liquidate some of my assets. I am thinking of setting up something new business wise, but I want to talk first, and see what you think. I might book something if your free, and we will have a sit down chat with a meal, would that be okay?"

"Yeah, I would love that, I mean hell, how often does someone like me get to be seen out with a gorgeous and famous author? Call me when you hit London, and give me the details."

"Brilliant, thanks Andy, I am looking forward to it."

I ended the call as the kettle clicked. I made a coffee and walked back to the study, and watched as the pages printed off. I sat back in the old seat, and sipped my coffee, and drifted into thought, as all those memories of our time together flowed through my mind. I was glad I listened to Chloe, just remembering, brought all of it back. In many ways it was painful, how the hell could two people so in love lose their way so easily?

For years we worked side by side on the council, or side by side with D&D and it had been so much fun, and yet once we stepped down from the council, and back into public life, everything went pear shaped. The Dixon Group sucked us back in, and without realising, we gave back to them all of the control. It tore us away from each other, and if anything, just understanding that, made me realise, as long as Katie was connected to the group, we would have problems, everyone else had forgotten, but not her, she still had an axe to grind, and boy was she grinding it.

I knew the answer and prepared for combat, and as the document finished printing, I closed it down and clicked on the camera, and prepared to record something I would post to my web site in a few days. The camera app opened, and I looked at myself, I looked rough as hell, under my eyes was black from lack of sleep, but in a way that would help. I took a deep breath, smiled, and hit record.

"Hi everyone, it has been a while since I posted a video here on my site. This year has been so busy, I feel like I have been swallowed up by everything, and to be honest, I am here alone in my secret little hiding place taking a little time out. Honestly guys, I love you all, but I am exhausted, and I have had so much to deal with from the releasing of the final book of the Krisandra series, I have not even had time to write, and I need to." I lifted my coffee and took a drink.

"I am on here today, as I need to stop. I cannot do this for much longer, I am so burned out it is unbelievable, and honestly,

I am losing touch with everything around me, and that is very frightening for me. So, I wanted to tell all of you face to face as it were, that after a huge amount of thought, and I mean months of agonising, I have decided today, to take a hiatus and walk away from public life. I want to stop before it stops me, because I have lost sight of everything that has meaning in my life. As someone once told me, you cannot write if you have stopped living, and boy, have I stopped living. So, I am stopping in hope of sorting things out so I can write again." I took a deep breath, and just let it all flow out of me, and felt a few tears fill my eyes.

"I love you guys, but honestly, I have nothing new to offer you all, I have ideas, but nothing as yet to write, because I am so stressed and tired, I cannot think. You guys have been with me every step of the way, and so I felt I needed to sit and let you all know in person, before the press write some garbage about me, because they will, so you all now know the facts. I will be at Curio Live America, I would never let them down, and I have a few other things to do, but for now, the spot light on me is being switched off. I have some plans, but I have made a big decision, and I am leaving the Dixon Publishing Group, and taking some time out for me, and I hope you all understand that. Thanks for everything guys, and I will be on the Curio site and this site a lot more, so I can still, as always, talk to you all. I love you all, I will rise again from the shadows, so take care until you hear from me."

I hit stop, then save, that would do, I would post it Sunday night, and finally be free, but before that, I had to get moving to avoid the Friday rush back to London.

Katie looked really angry as Birch walked to the side of the stage, Birch smiled as she moved out of view and into the wings, Katie's face was showing her anger, she pointed back on the stage.

"What the fuck was that, you hardly said a word?" Richard cowered behind her; Katie looked irate.

"What the fuck is, I agree completely with Amanda, she raised a valid point, or Norman was absolutely right, I could not have said it better? You were fucking out there to participate, and what the fuck is texting during a bloody debate, you looked bored shitless?" Birch smiled.

"I was, I would rather be at Sunny Bank, but your little ass kissing ferret reminded me, I have a contract that says I must appear, so I did, my contract says nothing about participation." Katie blinked, and could not believe what she was hearing.

"Don't play smart arse with me Jemi, we are here for a reason, and that is as one of the leading experts in your field, these people wanted to hear what you thought." She shrugged.

"They did, I completely agree with all the others, I am glad though you said one of, because all of them out there, were just as competent as I am. I wasn't even needed, isn't that strange?" She smiled.

"Can I go now; I have a call to make?" She seethed.

"You are a fucking smarmy bitch, what is wrong with your little princess bride now?" Birch turned back, and stared at Richard.

"Wow, that sounds familiar." She turned to Katie.

"I still have a major stake in Dixon Group, so does my princess bride, so let me be quite clear." She pointed to Richard.

"When we land at Heathrow, fire him, stick him with someone else, because I will never work with that little shit again, have you got that Katie?" Katie shook her head, and gave a snort of a laugh.

"You don't have the authority to do that; Roni will never allow it." Birch smirked and walked off.

"Test me and see." She gave a little giggle.

"I am off for a bath, and I will be locking the door."

I packed what little stuff I had taken out of my bag, which was mainly my laptop, left my wet things hanging in the kitchen to dry, and loaded the car. Having booked a suite, I headed back to London once again.

I still felt really tired, but kept the windows open and played Avril really loud, it was fun, we had not done this in ages, and so alone and without Birch, I did it anyway, and silly as it sounds, it made me feel a little rebellious again.

The drive was longer than I wanted, but that gave me the space to think, and plan. I arrived by six, visited the hotel shop, bought a few things, then booked in, grabbed a shower and dressed. I phoned Andy and told him my room number, I wanted this private, so we would eat in the room. I mean, it was hardly a room, it had a bedroom, bathroom and large spacious living room, complete with dining table, it even had a small kitchen. By the time Andy arrived, I was dressed in black jeans and a long top, having just finished drying my hair. I switched my phone off, and answered the door.

"Andrew, thanks for this, come on in." He walked in with his briefcase, and looked around.

"Wow, this place is wonderful. I brought a selection of paperwork; to be honest Abby, you were a bit vague, so I have several forms depending on what your requirements are." I poured a wine, and offered him a glass.

"All I want is mainly transfers and sales, I aim to pass back some stock and sell some." He lifted his glass as he put down his case. There was a tap on the door, and I walked over to it and opened it, the staff had arrived with our meal. I sat back on the sofa, as the staff set everything up, I was aware of privacy, and so smiled at him.

"How are things going for you these days, you have come a long way since I first moved my accounts, you were a junior back then I believe?" He gave a nod.

"Things are good, and yes, I have worked my way up, but I have a good firm with good benefits, I cannot complain."

I watched the staff, as they prepared the meal, the waiter turned and beckoned us to the table. I got up, and Andy lifted his case and we walked over and were seated, I sipped whilst they served, I smiled at the waiter and handed him a twenty.

"That will be all for now, I will call down when we require it." He gave me a big smile.

"Thank you, Miss Watson." He made his way out of the room, as I lifted my knife.

"I hope you don't mind, I ordered the food, honestly, I am starving." He gave a nod and looked at me.

"So, Abby, what is all this about, it feels very cloak and dagger, is everything alright, you are not in some sort of trouble are you?" I gave a giggle, and shook my head.

"No, nothing like that. Andrew, I am really tired and burning out, so I am going dark for a little while and falling off the scene. It may surprise you, and this is in the strictest of confidence, but I want out of the Dixon Group, I want my freedom back." He frowned and looked at me with a strange stare, I shrugged at him.

"What?" He sat back, and just looked at me with a confused look on his face.

"Abby, when you say out, you mean out completely, you know, sell up and everything?" I gave a nod.

"I want to go solo; I want to move away from the corporate world, and go small and independent. I have been thinking about it for some time, and so I felt before I acted, I would talk things over with you. I am looking at setting up my own operation, I thought Sanctuary Press would be very fitting."

He sat back in his chair, he looked at the table for a moment as he chewed, he looked back up at me, and I could see his mind was trying to work things out.

"Abby, you do know the Dixon Group shares alone are worth about ten million, probably more, if I offer them up? Obviously, I know people who would snap your hand off for one." I gave a smile.

"You mean Katie? Andrew, I know she has made enquiries into trying to get more, you see the thing is, I do not want to sell them, I want to pass them to Jemi. You know, just transfer them over, you can do that I know." He looked shocked.

"You two are alright, I hope? Abby, I have to say, I am struggling with this, I can tell you now, Jemi will be really unhappy. The woman is a bloody nightmare, every time I send her a profit report, she rings me up and complains. It is strange, but she does not want any more cash, if I am honest, working for her depresses me, because every time we make her tons more, it makes her unhappy." I gave a giggle, and I sliced into the beef.

"I do love that about her, look Andrew, I have no control of my life, they arrange things and do things, and to be honest, I just want control, and I want to take a long break. I have not written in ages, and at the moment, all I want is to hide away, sit alone and write new material, it really is what makes me happy. I also want my life back, honestly, I am beginning to wonder who the hell I am, I never have time for me." He understood.

"But Abby, you can do all that without giving your shares away, just bugger off somewhere and write, they will be earning whilst you are gone." I nodded.

"But I want freedom, I want to have complete control over any new works, and to be honest Andrew, as long as Katie is involved with that company, I won't, and neither will Jemi." I lifted my fork to my mouth and chewed, oh God, this was wonderful, I was so hungry.

"Andrew, look at it this way, if I leave, Anita my publicist will be free, I can get her to take on Jemi, so she will not be stuck with Katie's puppet. Anita understands our life, she is also a very important aspect of D&D. In one swift move, I free up Jemi and me, do you see how that would work?" He raised his eyebrows.

"You do know this will make waves?" I smiled.

"Not if I sell her back her K.O shares it won't, she will be too busy gloating to notice she has been outplayed." He gave a little chuckle and shook his head.

"I cannot deny, that is actually pretty smart thinking, so I take it, I approach Katie, handle the sale and then what, because you know Roni is going to be really pissed off about all this?" I nodded.

"Yeah, I know, let me deal with that, just get those shares transferred from me to Jemi, and then approach Katie to make an offer, and I do not want them too cheap, make her really stretch for them. I want to extract every penny I can out her, I mean it Andy, really push back, she thinks she is getting her own way, and I will let her think that, but she needs to be slowed down. Pin her down on price, and do not budge." I pulled a piece of paper out of my pocket, and slid it across the table.

"Here, you will need this." He picked it up, and looked at it, he looked confused.

"What is this?"

"My new temporary number, as I said, I am going dark for a while. I bought it today, this will be the only way to reach me, my usual phone is switched off. I need to write with no interruptions." He gave a sigh.

"Abby, you are being straight with me aren't you, if there is trouble between you and Jemi, you would tell me, wouldn't you? Abby, she adores you, and somehow, I am getting the feeling she does not have this number." I gave a small smile.

"Andrew, you are right, she does not have it, only you do. Things have been strained and she is busy, and I need some time out, and my freedom. Move the shares, handle the deal, and help me set up Sanctuary Press. Jemi will see me soon enough, for now, I am going to hole up here, live on room service, and do what I do best, I am going to write."

We finished our meal, and he passed me all the relevant paperwork, which I signed, and by ten thirty I was sat back on the sofa, and my eyes flickered, I was totally exhausted. Andrew got up and lifted his case.

"Abby, you look utterly wiped out, I will go, I do think you need to get some sleep. Thanks for tonight, I know it was business, but honestly, it has been really nice to sit and chat a little. You know, I am always there if you need someone to talk to, just give me a call." I smiled as I stood up.

"Thanks, I have enjoyed it too, but yes, I am completely burned out, I think I will get in bed." He lifted the do not disturb sign off the table.

"I will make my own way out, and hang this as I go. I will transfer all the shares and let you know when it is all done. Abby, take better care of yourself, you may not see it, and maybe she has lost sight of it too, but you both really need each other. Talk soon."

I stood, as he walked to the door and waved, I smiled as he slipped the sign on the outside handle, and then pulled the door closed behind himself. I picked up my two phones and walked into the bedroom, and pulled off my top, and unbuttoned my jeans, and then slipped under the duvet, and snuggled down, I missed Birch, so hugged my pillow.

I slept for most of the next day, and woke around six in the evening, I ordered coffee, and sat on the balcony as I slowly came to life. It was Saturday evening and London was busy, and I needed to clear my head. Once I was awake, I walked back into my room, slipped on my jeans and top, and grabbed my denim. I pulled the long brown haired wig out of my bag and sat at the mirror, and smiled as I remembered Birch, and her secret operation Pop Tart.

I combed my hair up, slipped on my wig, and headed out of the door, I really needed a walk, even in the busy streets, it would be nice to simply be anonymous for a while.

The night passed, as I walked around London, lost in thought remembering the few times that we had been able to avoid the press, and walk uninhibited around the city. I smiled as I walked, remembering her soft voice, infectious giggle, and calm manner. I came back to the hotel, had something to eat, and then headed to bed, as I lay in the dark remembering all the joy we had together, I curled with my pillow, and wept, until I finally fell asleep.

Sunday arrived, and I was awake and busy, sat at a small table, having had breakfast, and was looking at my laptop. I checked out my social media, then logged into my blog and uploaded the video. Once it was up and live, I disconnected from the Wi-Fi. I was not aware that Birch had rang everyone in search of me, as she slowly unraveled in France.

Birch was pacing around the room, she was packed ready, but had the keynote address to deliver. She was panicked, and had been crying for half the night. Richard knocked on her door. He walked in.

"Jemi they are ready for you… What the hell has happened; you look like death?" Birch grabbed her notes, and pushed them into his hands.

"Here, take them, I have a flight to catch, I am going home, I need to see Deads." He gave a sigh.

"Jemi, may I remind you; we have an agreement, you have a key note, and a gala meal to attend." Birch spun around on him.

"Yeah, about that… You knew about Abby booking us time off, and yet you and that red haired slapper conspired to fuck that up for me, well guess what, you have the speech, and you have a good appetite, so Bon Appetite? Katie screwed us over once before, and there is no way on this earth she will do it again, try to stop me, and I will break your nose. I have a flight and cab waiting, go kiss your boss's ass, we are done Richard, oh and by the way, the short name for Richard is dick, and honestly, it is so fitting, so fuck you, fuck that red hair slapper and have fun, ta ta!"

She grabbed her case, and pushed past him, as he stood looking shocked, insulted, and lost for words. Birch hit the lifts and entered, and saw him as she pressed the button, he was stood staring at her, she smiled, and gave him the finger.

"Bye bye, ass kisser." The doors closed, she leaned back on the wall, and gave a sigh of relief, and closed her eyes.

"Jemi, you fucked up, now go fix this."

Chloe looked at Edwina looking startled.

"What do you mean her phone is dead?" Edwina turned the laptop around and there on the screen was Abby's blog, and the newly uploaded video.

"Watch that and catch up, something is really wrong, and Birch is going into melt down in France." Chloe nodded.

"Well yeah, she should be at Sunny Bank but that red haired bitch has screwed things up again. See, I told you she was still up to her tricks, but OH NO, you would not believe it. Well clever knickers, explain to me just why exactly her promoter has put her in France when she should be in Devon?" Edwina looked pissed off.

"Okay, now shut the fuck up and watch the video, God, you are such a fucking smart arsed bitch. I am going to the library to see if I can track her down." Chloe stared at her.

"She is at Sunny Bank, pissed, crying, alone and falling in the stream, I mean, God Weena, look where she is sat." Edwina shook her head.

"Where the hell is that, I have never seen that at Sunny Bank?" Chloe gave a smirk.

"What, you did not sneak in and have a peep, I did, it is a really cool room?"

"Chloe, that room was supposed to be private and off limits to all of us." She shrugged.

"I only peeked; I was curious."

Birch was out of the cab, at the desk, and grabbed her ticket, she spoke fluent French which helped, and she was quite famous now. She put her case on the check in and lifted her laptop bag to carry on with her, and then made her way to the seats to wait to be called. Her phone rang, it was Roni, Birch clicked the button.

"Mum!"

"Okay Jemi what the hell is going on, and where are you, and what the hell is that pinging noise in the background?" Birch gave a sigh.

"I am in Paris at the airport."

"What the hell are you doing there, you should be at the farm house?" This was something she had wanted to avoid.

"Mum, I screwed up, my schedule has been so busy, I forgot what day it was, I mean seriously, I come out of one event, and Richard just tells me where to go next, so when he said Paris, I just got on the plane. I know, I screwed up, Deads rang me and when she found out I was here, she flipped and hung up on me, and her phone has been off since. Mum, I left the conference, actually, I left Richard my speech and told him to give it, and I am trying to get back as fast as I can, I have a hire car waiting at Heathrow for as soon as I land." She heard the sigh.

"I have nothing here on the books at all about you doing the Paris convention, as far as I know, this is not us, and as soon as I saw her video, I knew something was wrong. Jemi, she needs you, and you need to get your ass over here and at her side. I warned you about this, you have been too preoccupied with your books and the bright lights, go to her, and sort this out, you know what will be happening in her head, get there as quickly as you can." Birch nodded.

"I will, and what video?" Roni gave a gasp.

"Read your notifications, she posted to her blog a video, and it does not bode well. Look, I will try and get hold of her. Jemi, hurry. Alright, I will call you if I hear anything."

The phone went dead, and she looked at the screen and opened her emails, there was the notification from Abby's website. She clicked the link and slipped her blue tooth ear phone in one ear, the video came up and started to play, and Abby looked exhausted, and very sad. Birch noticed instantly the redness around her eyes, she had been crying. Birch swallowed hard as she watched.

"Oh God Deads, please wait for me, oh God, do not do something silly, Sweetie, I am coming as fast as I can, please wait for me."

Edwina sat in the library, on the phone to Luke.

"You may as well stop Luke, she has disconnected her internet, she is not stupid, if she goes online, she will know I will find her. She said she was going to drop out of public life and she has. This has been planned if you ask me, Abby would not be so prepared if she had only just thought of it."

"What has Birch said?"

"She has got a flight and is on her way to Sunny Bank, hopefully she has been too busy to see the video, oh hell, if she sees that she will fall apart." He gave a long sigh.

"Shit, no one wants that mess, okay, I will stick on her phone, but as yet it is still switched off."

"I am going to hang here for a while, Chloe is upset, I just want to make sure she is okay."

The call ended and Edwina lifted her cup, got up, she walked through the door into the hallway, as Chloe came down the stairs with her bag on her back. Edwina frowned.

"Where the fuck are you going?" Chloe looked at her in disbelief.

"Sunny Bank, Abby is alone, and she needs me, I am going to help her." Edwina gave a long exasperated sigh.

"Chloe, Birch has left the conference and is on an early flight, she is on her way there now, we need to wait here and see what happens. Chloe, this must come from Birch, we need to leave her to sort this out, they both need each other, let them realise that alone." Chloe gave a sigh, which showed her frustration.

"Okay, I will park outside Seth's old house, that way I can be there in a few minutes." Edwina gave a chuckle.

"Chloe, this has to be Birch, I know how much you love her, but give both of them a little space, trust me, we will see them smiling soon enough."

Chapter 4

The Thaw.

Birch landed at Heathrow, and went to the car rental to pick up her car, she filled in the forms, got her keys, and two hours after leaving the French airport, she was on the road heading south.

By the time she made it through the traffic and to Sunny Bank, it was 15:09. As she pulled up, she felt her heart break, there was no car, and she had really wanted there to be. She got out of the car, grabbed her bag, and opened the door.

"Deads, are you here?" She knew it was pointless, she walked through to the kitchen, and saw the wet things hung up, and gave a sigh.

"Oh Deads, what has happened?"

Birch reached out her arm and grabbed the leg of the jeans, they were still really wet, the kitchen smelt damp, so she pulled them down and opened the back door. She needed to wash some things, so opened the washer door, and then she smelt it, the softest of scents, she lifted her top to her nose and held it there as she breathed in, and her eyes filled with tears. Birch flopped down in the chair, and just shook, as she held Deadly's top to her face, and wept.

"Don't leave me Deads, I am so stupid, and I don't want to live without you." She broke down.

Anita sat back and looked at Tabby, she looked worried, and tired, as she shook her head at her.

"It was part of the deal I made with her; she had to have breaks and be at home, hell, one of the reasons I got the job was because Katie was killing her. She did three weeks in the States with just three days off, I wanted Jemi on my books, but her events were clashing with Abby's. Roni took her off me and put Richard in place, I warned Abby he could not be trusted. Oh Christ Tabs, she told me about Katie but I thought all that was done and over with.

I should have taken more note of her words, when she said she
wanted out, I just thought of all the gigs for a while so she could
write, I didn't think she meant everything." She leaned forward
and rubbed her face.

"I hope to god Jemi gets there and sorts all this out, I am so
scared at the moment, I hope she does not do anything stupid; I
really should have seen this coming."

Andrew sent me the text message. 'It is done, all Dixon Group
shares have been transferred to Jemi, and made none returnable
to you. I have sent the requested offer for the K.O shares to Katie,
but not had a response yet, apparently, she is in France at the
moment. Tomorrow I will work on sorting out the legal papers for
Sanctuary Press, and will let you know when I need to see you for
signatures.'

I gave a sigh of relief, I was almost free, now I had one more
job to do, I rang room service and requested a maid, and then I
lifted my new phone, and typed the message. 'Anita, it's Abby, I
need you to ring my friend's phone, mine is off, as it stops Edwina
tracking me down, call me as soon as you get this."

I waited for the tap on the door, I walked over and opened it
with a smile, she came in and looked around, and then frowned
and looked at me.

"The front desk said you needed a maid." I nodded.

"Yes, I do, I am going to send a text, and over on the table is fifty
pounds. All I need

you to do is answer, and pretend you are a friend, and then say,
hold on I will get her, then hand me the phone, can you do that?"
She looked at me strangely.

"Yes, it is nothing illegal is it, Miss Watson?" I giggled.

"No, it is not, I am hiding away to write, I need a break, so I
cannot use my own phone. You must not tell anyone I am here; I
really need to be left alone to write for a while." She nodded.

"Okay Miss Watson, I understand, I have seen how the press
treat you." I smiled and pressed send, then handed her the
phone.

Anita had tears in her eyes as Tabby hugged her, her phone
pinged and she snatched it up and opened the message and
frowned, Tabby leaned in to read it.

"Jesus Nita, call her." My new phone rang and the maid swiped it up and answered.

"Hello… Who is this… Anita, good… Yes, she is here, give me a minute." She smiled as she passed the phone to me, I winked and pointed to the money, she gave a nod and walked over to pick it up, I held the phone to my ear.

"Anita, just give me a minute, will you?"

I opened the door and the maid left smiling, and waved, I closed the door quietly. I could hear her on the end of the phone, she sounded upset, and like she was crying.

"Anita, just listen, I am at a friend's house, but will be leaving soon, so just listen, and for God's sake stop crying, I am fine, as I said, I have gone dark for a while." I heard her snort and take a breath.

"Okay, I am listening, but firstly, tell me you are safe and not going to do anything stupid?" I gave a long sigh.

"Anita, I am fine, I am going to sleep and write, and I am not about to do anything to threaten my life, if that is what you mean? As for stupid, I have been doing stupid stuff for most of my life." She snorted into the phone.

"Okay I am listening." I sat down and lifted my wine glass.

"Anita, I am leaving the Dixon Group, so I want you to hear it from me first. Look, I have loved working with you, but you can freelance, so we can still work with D&D together." I heard her gasp.

"You are firing me?"

"No, I am leaving, I will no longer be published through Dixons. Anita, I really need you to help me, I want you to take over Jemi. I don't care how you do it, but you need to get her away from Richard and take care of her. Look, he is killing her, so I am asking that you do for her, what you have done for me."

"Abby if you are moving company, I will happily move with you, I love our working relationship." I knew she would say that.

"Anita no, I am going to be using a small company, and they cannot afford you, call it me helping out a small business, like I did Ella. Anita, listen to me, Jemi is in trouble, you have to get her account. Please Anita, I really need you to do this as a friend, same terms and conditions, everything, just talk to Roni, and sort this out for me, you are the only person I can trust." She gave a sigh.

"Alright, I cannot really refuse, can I? Abby, I wish you had talked to me about this, you know we are great friends, I would have helped you. I hate this by the way, and I know what you are up to, it is not exactly hard to work out, but I still think you are wrong."

"Trust me Anita, and just get her account, if I am out of the loop and she is with you, we are both home safe, and that is all I want, to protect her."

"I take it you have not spoken to Jemi; she was stuck at the airport falling apart when I spoke to her? Abby, talk to her, she is thinking the worst. Abby, no matter what you are thinking, she still loves you as she always has."

"Anita, do you honestly think I don't know that, why do you think I am doing all this? I am fighting my ass off to protect her, she has no idea and she will not admit it if she did, this way solves my problems once and for all. When I am free of the Dixon Group, things will settle down, trust me, help Birch as you have me." She sighed.

"Roni is going to be heartbroken, your books have meant the world to her, knowing you started with her and built up your career." I nodded as I sat back.

"For now, I am leaving my books at Dixon, I owe Roni that much, just help Birch, I have plans in the making, and soon she will see what I am doing, is the best for everyone. Okay, I have to go; I will call you again when all this is sorted."

"Abby, thanks for talking to me, and please watch yourself, you are burned out, you need to take better care of yourself, I know you, remember? I am sad I cannot work with you; it has been the best time of my life; I am going to really miss it." I smiled.

"We still have Curio Live America and the auditions to do, and that is all D&D work, the Dixon part of that contract is complete. For what it is worth, I have loved every minute of it also, and we are still best mates, you know where I live."

"Yeah, have no fear, we will be seeing each other plenty, good luck Abby, please take care of yourself."

"Yeah, see you soon."

I ended the call, and turned the phone off, and then lifted my glass. I looked at my laptop sat open on the table, I got up and walked over to it, and sat down, I put my glass at the side, read the last five lines, and then started to type.

With the clothes washing in the machine, Birch stepped out into the back garden and looked out at the trees, her eyes were red and puffy. She looked at the garden and spotted the bottle and the wine glass on the grass, and frowned. In the kitchen her phone bleeped, and she turned in the doorway and ran over to the table and snatched it up, it was a message from her mum. 'Video Call Now!' She gave a sigh.

"Oh God, do I have to?"

It was not unexpected, after all, she had walked out on a conference and fired Richard. She grabbed her laptop and walked around the stairs to the study door. Birch entered and walked up to the desk, the place was as it had always been, except, in the centre of the desk, was a pile of paper, she moved round to look at it.

'When the Snow Thaws. By Abigail Jennifer Watson.'

(A tale of a Snow Queen, lost in the thaw.)

Birch felt her breath catch in her throat, and sat down with a bump, she stared at the manuscript and felt afraid.

"Oh crap, if this is goodbye, I am not sure I can handle it Deads."

Birch placed her laptop down at the side of the desk, and opened it up, it started to boot as she stared at the pile of white paper. She lifted the first sheet and read it. 'For Jemima, my lost queen of the snow.' She felt her hand start to shake and her eyes filled with tears.

"Deads, please don't do this, please don't end us, if is this is you saying goodbye, I have nothing left."

The video call came up on the screen and the tune played, and she jumped out of her skin. She reached over and clicked the answer button. It took a few moments to load and her mum appeared; she did not smile.

"Jemi, we need to talk, I have heard from Richard, he told me what you did... Are you crying?" Birch gave a huge sniffle, and leaned her screen forward.

"Mum, I am at Sunny Bank and she is not here, but she left me this, and I don't know what to do. I have been so frigging stupid, and I am terrified if I read this, I will lose her forever." Roni leaned forward into the screen.

"Is that a manuscript?" She nodded.

"It is part two of the snow queen, you know, the special book she wrote me." Roni gave a sigh.

"Okay Jemi, Look, I need to know what has happened, just what exactly have you done, fill me in and then we will discuss the book." Birch took a deep breath, sniffled, and wiped her eyes.

"I fired his ass mum, because he does everything Katie tells him to. I have been working none stop with booking after booking, and they are always when Deads is at home. Mum, we hardly see each other, and when we do, I am so tired I fall asleep. Mum, yesterday he called her my little princess bride, and the minute he did I realised. Then when Katie was pissed off with me, and she called her exactly the same, everything fell into place, and I knew they were working together to keep us apart, so I fired him, I think I pointed out he was a dick as well. I packed my things and came straight here, I have only been here just over an hour, but Mum, she was not here, and I just wanted to hold her and tell her how sorry I am, and now, I have this." Tears streamed down her face, and she gave a huge sob.

Roni's phone started to ring, and she saw Anita's name light up on it, she looked at Birch and lifted her finger for her to wait.

"Jemi, it is Anita." She picked up the phone and answered.

"Anita, I am glad to hear from you… She has, Oh Christ."

Roni's face clouded over, and Birch gave another sniffle and wiped her eyes, Roni stared at Birch, as she listened, and then gave a sigh.

"Well yes, it makes sense, and actually I was going to call you, as Jemi fired Richard today, walked off the job, and flew home to Sunny Bank… No, she is not there… What friend? So, when you say she is withdrawing, does she mean all of us?" Roni gave a nod.

"Okay, yes, I get that… She is, well that is not a bad thing, well not for her, I cannot say I am happy about this, I am not, but to be honest Anita, it makes good sense. What about her other works, is she moving them, I mean, has she given you any idea at all?" She gave a sigh.

"Okay, yes, thanks Anita, I will make it official in the morning, and do the paperwork... Well yes, but do not worry, I can easily sort that out... She will, well thank God for that, she is devastated and a bit of a mess at the moment, I will let her know... Thanks Anita, yes, I will talk to you soon, goodnight."

Roni looked up as she ended the call, and looked right at Birch, who appeared to be watching with eyes filled with hope, she lowered her voice as she put her phone back on the desk.

"Jemi, Abby has officially left Dixon Publishing." Birch gave a gasp, and her eyes opened wide.

"What... Mum, stop her." Roni gave a smirk.

"How Jemi? Her contract was an open ended one, she can leave whenever she wants, and I am sorry, but she has quit the group. She is now a free agent, but she specifically requested that Anita approached me and asked me to replace Richard with her as your agent, and I have said yes. Anita is now your full time promoter, under the same terms as she was with Abby." Birch filled up with tears again.

"I have lost her haven't I, that is what this story is about, this is her saying goodbye?" Birch shook as her tears dripped onto the desk; Roni leaned forward into the screen.

"Jemi, she has not left you, don't you see, she is trying to protect you, oh Jemi, how could you think such things? Abby loves you so much, can you not see what she has done to protect you? I mean yes, I am not happy to lose her, but I cannot deny, she is brilliant." Birch gave a snort, and wiped her eyes on her sleeve.

"How is she brilliant, I am so confused, Mum, she has left the company?" Roni smiled.

"I think you need to read that story, because honestly, she is so amazing. Jemi, like you, she spotted Katie was getting back to her old games, the way she explained it to Anita was that she did not think she was trying to get you into bed, she felt Katie was keeping you apart, by only picking events that coincided with Abby being at home. It makes sense, she creates tension and division, and stands back as you drift apart. Jemi, Katie is the lead promoter, she knows all our bookings in advance, she has to, as she provides all the equipment. Abby is brilliant, wow, I wish she would work for me in the publishing arm." Birch shook her head.

"Mum, I don't understand, how does her quitting help me, I want her with us, and at my side." Roni raised her eyebrows.

"Yes, and Katie knows that, and as long as she does, simply because you both work for the same publisher, she will have advanced notice of both of your movements. Jemi, do you understand what she has done, she has left, and that frees her from any advance notice to Katie? Jemi, that also frees up Anita to take on you, and in doing so, takes Richard completely out of the loop, which means Katie just lost all of her aces. She has actually defeated her without blood, precisely to keep you together, she is not leaving you, she is defending you, so she does not lose you. Personally, I think it is brilliant, she lined up all her bishops and rooks, pinned the queen down, and moved straight into checkmate."

Birch took a deep breath and relaxed a little and wiped her eyes again.

"So, I have not lost her?" Roni smiled and shook her head.

"You have not lost her, I mean honestly, how could you even think that? Jemi, she has gone dark to write, she has not written a word in eight months, and she needs to write, and so that is what she is doing. She did tell Anita she would talk to you soon, I would say, in the meantime, get some sleep and read that manuscript, I think you may find everything there, written in a way only you will understand."

Roni talked for a little while longer, until she could see Birch was a lot calmer, and then she blew her a kiss and ended the call. Birch went into the kitchen and made a coffee, and then headed back to the study, she sat down and started to read the first page.

Back at home, Edwina sat at her computer, reading all the latest news and looked pissed off, Deb's had arrived and was sat in Abby's seat, Chloe was sat at the spare computer and Anthony was leant against the table. Anita had phoned to fill them all in, and Chloe was looking smug, Edwina looked at her over the monitor.

"Okay, so you were right, but think about it, what she has done is pretty smart. She is completely free now and can do whatever she wants, she has nailed Katie's ass to the floor without facing her or saying a word, it is a really genius move." Deb's nodded.

"I just wish I could talk to her." Chloe's eyes moved to her.

"She is writing, and let's be honest, it is ages since she did any, this is good for her, she has no distractions at all. I just wish I knew where she was, I am not sure she will eat properly." Edwina sat back in her seat and stretched.

"She will be in a hotel, room service, but no interruptions, lots of writers do it. I just wish she had come to me and talked." Chloe frowned at her.

"How? None of you are here anymore, and be honest we do not exactly get together a lot, I am the only one she has left. I am always here when she needs me, you guys are hardly ever around these days." Edwina narrowed her eyes.

"I am here three days a week, I am always around to talk to." Chloe gave a snort.

"You are here from ten till two thirty, and never have time to talk, you are too busy, hell, all I get is a quick coffee, we never see any of you at weekends." Deb's looked hurt.

"That is not fair, we have families Chloe." She gave a nod.

"Yeah, you do, but isn't Abby also family? Let's be honest, we are doing a huge Curio event, and yet only Birch and me are going with her at the moment. None of you have arranged anything with us, and it is only just over a month away. So, are you guys in or out, because she has been working her arse off till the early hours every night, getting it ready with Birch?" Deb's looked even more guilty, and Edwina gave a sigh.

"Aden has been working on it, and I am overseeing him, you know Chloe it is a lot of work?" She nodded.

"Yeah, it is, why do you think they are both so burned out? Weena, you were right by their sides for the first one, so you know how hard it is. Let's be honest, you could get through stuff a lot better than Aden, but you are too busy playing shop with Luke. Guys we are the Curio's, not Aden, or anyone else, we called it Curio Life because it was us, our life, our story, but it is not anymore is it, because all of you have got your life, the life you wanted, and all of you have forgotten what we were meant to be about." Edwina looked really pissed off.

"You know what Chloe, you are out of order, I really resent that, you know I did not want to leave, but we have a kid, and we are entitled to have a life as a family you know?" Chloe got up out of her seat.

"I never said you did not have the right, but one week Weena, that is all we have asked for, and yet no one can find the time. Let's be honest, Abby and Birch are too polite to say something, so they take it all on themselves, what the fuck happened to all girls together, do you resent that too?"

Chloe walked out of the library as Edwina fumed, Deb's put her head down and Anthony took a deep breath.

"She has a point, darlings, I still live here, but it has been forever since I sat with them and just talked, the new shop extension has stretched me too much." Deb's gave a nod.

"Yeah, I have loads of time at home, I could have made more time to help, Chloe is right. Abby would never ask us for help; she would take it all on her shoulders and struggle with it. I will talk to Jimmy tonight." Edwina flopped forward in her seat.

"Crap, schooled again by my sister, what the hell has happened to us?" Anthony shrugged.

"We let life get in the way, and lost sight of two of the most important people in our lives, and Abby has had to fall on her sword before any of us could realise we had abandoned them. I will clear my books and tell Michael to get some time off, it looks like we are going stateside again." Edwina nodded.

"It is during the school holidays, I will talk to Luke, we will work something out for Sammy to have fun in shifts." Debs gave a long sigh.

"I feel awful, I will talk with Jimmy tonight and see what we can work out, Chloe is right, we are the Curio's, and we should all be a part of this. I will swing by the nursery tomorrow and talk to Deli. You know, I must admit, it would be nice to all be together again, I am not sure about you guys, but I do miss it." Edwina smiled.

"Yeah, me too, I do not have much crazy in my life these days, I mean, to be honest, life seems a little dull at times, we need to arrange a get together before the event, and break the ice again."

The night passed slowly, page by page as Birch sat with a desk lamp on, whilst outside the rain lashed down. She had a box of tissues on the desk, and would occasionally give an excited giggle or chuckle, and wipe her eyes. On the floor was a wide circle of white used tissues, but they were not the usual circle of a blubbering wreck, they had become a circle of happiness, of relief, and joy.

Finally, she reached the last page, and held her hands to her heart, finished the story, she gave a gasp as she turned the last page over and laid it down on all the others. She sat back in the chair and took a deep breath, and then burst into tears and bawled her brains out.

"It's so beautiful... I don't deserve such love... Oh Deads, you are a nicer person than me... I am an utter shit and so stupid, but I love you too." She sat there and wailed the house down, she shook in her seat grabbing tissue after tissue, some things never change.

Birch stood up hugging her box of tissues and staggered out of the study and up the stairs, she walked into the room. The bed was not made, she stripped, still sobbing, and climbed into bed, she pulled Abby's pillow close and cuddled up to it, and breathing the soft scent of Abby, within minutes she was fast asleep.

Chapter 5

The Power of a Woman.

It was Monday morning, and I was flat out in bed, having been up most of the night writing. At E.F.G, Andrew had been having a busy morning, as Katie flew in from France, and came straight to his office. He smiled as he handed the papers over to her, she frowned as she looked at her solicitor.

"It is a bit fucking expensive, wow, the little princess bride has high expectations, does she really think I would pay that much?" Andrew sat back in his seat.

"Those are the terms and the price for your company back, it is up to you, she did tell me that she was quite happy to vote against everything you proposed, and make your life a living hell. She told me she would quite enjoy that for what you have done." He sat forward in his seat.

"Sign and pay, or leave, Abby tells me Chloe is very interested in buying them." He smiled, as she swallowed hard.

"Fucking little smart arsed princess, God, I hate her, she is too dammed clever for her own good." She leaned forward in her seat, and snatched the papers out of his hand, gave a sigh, and signed.

"God, this is the second time that little witch has screwed me." Andrew smirked at her solicitor as he watched her sign, and then looked up at Andrew.

"The cash transfer will be today." He lifted his phone and sent a text.

"It is going through now to your companies account." Andrew gave a nod, and sat back, as he lifted the papers and checked them, and gave a nod. Katie fumed.

"I hate her, I do, I wish I had never met her." Andrew gave a casual nod.

"You know Katie, you never learn, why don't you just leave them alone, you have your business and it is thriving, isn't it time you gave up?" She scowled.

"If I need advice, I will see a therapist, just take care of the money and stay out of my private life." He smiled.

"If you need a suggestion, I would strongly recommend Sweetie's Retreat, it has some highly skilled professionals." Her solicitor smirked; she stood up looking irate.

"Is that it, are we done?" Andrew calmly stood up.

"I believe we are; Abby will be delighted." Katie turned with a scowl.

"Gerald!" She stormed out of the office; Andrew smiled as he walked to the door to watch her leave.

As Katie stormed down the office, at the far end dressed in paint covered dungarees with a vest, Chloe appeared. She saw Katie storming towards her, and her eyes turned to a look of dark thunder. Katie faltered as she saw her, and gripped Gerald's arm, Chloe scowled, slipped her arm behind her back, and Chloe's voice was loud.

"WHAT THE FUCK ARE YOU DOING HERE!?" Katie slowed, as Chloe pulled a paint brush out of her back pocket, and spun it in her hand.

Katie panicked, as Chloe picked up her pace, and came marching down the long office at high speed, she screamed, and ran between the long lines of desks pointing at her, and trying to cover her boobs with her other arm.

"You stay the fuck away from me you mad bitch, I mean it, I will call the law and press charges for assault." Chloe scowled at her.

"I warned you to stay away from them."

Katie gave a terrifying squeal, and ran down behind the desks screaming, as everyone in the room watched completely at a loss as to what the hell was happening. Chloe stood smiling, as she watched Katie reach the stairs, she yanked open the door and fled screaming down them. She spun her brush in her hand, and slipped it into her back pocket, and smiled at Gerald.

"Not a fan of art that one."

He gave a mighty laugh, and watched as she sauntered past him, heading for Andrew, with a beaming smile.

Inside Andrew's office, Chloe gave a big smile as she sat down, he looked a little surprised.

"Chloe, this is very unexpected, what can I do for you?" Chloe sat back in the chair.

"This place has grown, I met your fiancé coming in, she is pretty, you done good Andrew." He gave a smile.

"Yes, she is a wonderful woman, it is not long now, we will be married in August, you did get the invites, didn't you?" Chloe nodded.

"Yeah, we will all be there." Chloe leaned forward in her seat.

"Andrew, I talked to Birch this morning, and she told me Abby has given all her Dixon shares to her." He gave a loud sigh.

"Chloe, as much as you are a client of this company, that is confidential information, I really cannot discuss that with you." She sat back and smiled.

"I know, and I am not here about that." He frowned.

"Then why are you here?" She gave him her biggest, most beautiful smile.

"You... How did Abby transfer shares when she is off the grid, and no one can contact her, which means, you know where she is?" He gave another long sigh.

"Chloe again, that is confidential, honestly, I cannot betray her trust."

She nodded, stood up, and put her hand in her pocket, and pulled out a polythene freezer bag. Andrew looked appalled as he saw her place it on his desk, with a used condom inside it, and shuddered. Chloe gave a long sigh.

"Honestly, Andrew you are forcing me into a corner, I am so sorry, I really do think you are an ace guy. Times are desperate, and that calls for desperate measures, I did not want to do this." She unclipped her dungarees, and they fell to the floor, then she pulled at her vest and slipped it over her head.

Andrew went into complete melt down, as Chloe picked up the bag and opened it. He shot out of his chair looking utterly terrified, his voice was really low, but filled with utter panic.

"Chloe, what the hell are you doing, you cannot take your clothes off in here, I will get fired?"

She gave him a big smile, and pointed to the door, then reached into the bag and pulled out the condom, both of them screwed up their faces, Chloe shuddered.

"Fuck, I hate these things." She gave another shudder.

"Ew, it is cold… So, Andrew… I am going to walk out of here naked, and tell everyone, including your fiancé, we just screwed on your desk, and you were fucking amazing." She held up the used condom.

"Wow, Baz is really healthy; I mean, that is a lot for a guy his age."

He shook his hands in the air, as he stepped back from his chair, his face was bright red, and he was sweating like crazy, his voice was low, but filled with terror.

"Are you fucking insane, why the hell would you do that?" She smirked, and was actually really enjoying herself.

"Where is she Andrew, I need to go to her, she needs me?"

It was cheque mate and he knew it, his heart was pounding in his chest, as he pulled out his handkerchief and wiped his face. He looked at her with terrified eyes, and shook his head slowly.

"Please Chloe, don't do this, please, I really love Julie and want to marry her. I know you love Abby, but I promised I would not tell a soul."

He wiped his face again, Chloe turned for the door, and was as cool as a cucumber. She stepped out of her dungarees and reached for the door handle; he went into even higher levels of panic, and raised his hands as he panted to stay breathing.

"Okay… Okay, please put your clothes on. Jesus Chloe, are you trying to kill me?"

She turned from the door, and reached for the empty plastic bag. He pulled a piece of paper out of his pocket and handed it over the desk, as he took deep breaths to try and calm down.

"It is room 142, please hurry and get dressed." He flopped down in his seat and wiped his face again, Chloe smiled.

"Andrew, you are a great friend to all of us, but as much as you think you do, you have no idea who Abby is. I won't tell the others, but I am going to her, and I am going to help her, like she always has me." He gave a nod, and was breathing better.

"I get it, I do, I know how much you guys' care, she does not look well, and I am worried about her." Chloe pulled up her dungarees and clipped them back at the top, she rolled up the bag and slipped it into her pocket.

"Caring for Abby is our job, let us do what we do best, and

thanks, and I am sorry, but you have to understand as much as she thinks she can live in the dark alone, she can't. She needs Birch, and Birch needs her, and I am going to help them sort this all out." He nodded and wiped his face again.

"Christ, you lot are a bloody nightmare, but honestly, I really admire all of you for the loyalty you hold for each other, we need more of that in the world, even if it does push me to the brink of breakdown." She gave a giggle.

"Baz says I have great tits, what do you think?" He swallowed hard.

"As much as I tried not to look, tell Baz he is bang on the money." She gave a beautiful smile and walked around the desk, and kissed the top of his head.

"You are a great friend to all of us, and we appreciate that, thanks Andrew. I will go to her now and help her."

He took a long deep breath and calmed down, Chloe waved as she left the office, and he closed his eyes for a moment. He spoke quietly to himself.

"Christ, if she did that to me just for a room number, what the hell did she do to Katie to make her run screaming out of the building?" He took another long deep intake of air.

"She looks so calm and innocent, but Jesus, she is bloody scary."

Room service woke me up, and I pulled on a long top and staggered to the door, and pulled it open, the waiter pushed in the food trolley, and Chloe followed him in eating a piece of bacon, she smiled.

"Hi Abby, look, breakfast." I stared at her, and could not believe she had found me.

"Chloe, what the hell?" She grinned and pulled me into a hug.

"I missed you, and I was worried about you. Seriously, turning off your Wi-Fi will only stop Edwina tracking you down, I have other more cunning ways. I mean, honestly Abby, I was always going to be here for you." I gave a sigh, and lifted my arms round her, and squeezed.

"Thanks Chloe, you are really quite surprising, and it is nice to see you." She squeezed me harder.

"I am really going to yell at you for this you know? Just not yet, you need to eat, I can feel your ribs."

I smiled, she never changes, even now after all these years she is simply her, and she is adorable. Somehow, age has changed all of us, but not her. I leaned back and looked at her bright shining eyes.

"I really love you, do you know that?" She smiled.

"Yeah, still not going to sleep with you, oh God Abby, I am so straight it is unbelievable." I giggled, and kissed her cheek.

"You are missing the shag of a life time, God, I am so pent up, I am probably wetter than you are." She gave a shudder and stepped back.

"Yeah, save it for Birch, you are putting me off the porridge." I chuckled, God, she was wonderful.

I tipped the waiter and he left us alone, and we sat on the sofa eating as she told me all about what was happening, and I filled her in on what I had in mind. Chloe told me about poor Andrew, and I sat laughing like I had not laughed in years, she just sat there smiling and took my hands in hers.

"I have missed this Abby, we do not do this enough, none of us do, and trust me, I have told all of them." I smiled and gave a nod.

"Yeah, you are right, shit Chloe, when did you become the wise one?" She giggled.

"Fuck knows, I am hoping it's a phase and will soon pass." I smiled.

"Poor Andrew, he is such a quiet and respectful guy." She chuckled, as she lifted a piece of bacon, and winked.

"Hey, he told me I have great boobs and Baz is right, I bet he is not that quiet in the bedroom." She winked.

"So, what are we going to be doing, the shares I get, and in a way Katie, but Abby, what about Birch, she is really hurting you know?"

I felt that pang of guilt growing inside me, and felt my own discomfort, and shuffled on the seat.

"Chloe, I had to do this, I had to disappear and arrange everything first. I know it makes little sense, but Chloe, I need to be free again, I need to cut all the shackles, because they are dragging both of us down. I know this appears hard, but honestly, this is the only way I can save us, because as uncomfortable as it is to admit, Birch and myself have been drifting and lost sight of what is important, and I really need to get her back on track with me. I told Anita I would talk to her soon." Chloe gave a nod and smiled.

"I can see that Abby, but you know, if you had come to me and talked to me, I would have helped you do all this behind the scenes."

I understood that, she had become my closest friend over the last few years, the fact she was sitting cross legged in front of me, in a place no one would find me proved it.

"Chloe, there is more to do, and actually, you can help, as I need some artwork, a logo." She frowned.

"Okay, so what do you need?" I gave her a big smile.

"I am starting my own publishing company, it will be called Sanctuary Press, and I will need something catchy and iconic for my new AJW brand." She gave me a big smile.

"Do you need investors, I have cash?" I lifted up a piece of bacon.

"I was hoping you would be the art director; you know graphic novels are all the rage now?" She looked like she was going to explode.

"Oh fuck yeah, Abby, I am so in... In a completely straight way, just so you know." I giggled, and put out my hand.

"Welcome to the company Miss Pemberton."

Chloe gave me the most beautiful smile as I shook her hand, wow, I have missed this so much, this is what Curio life should be, all of us working together side by side.

It was Monday, and after my upload to my blog yesterday, the press were having a field day, and all the papers were full. I was having a breakdown, divorce was in the air, coverage of Birch's dramatic absence from the conference was plastered everywhere. It was the break up of the century, and they were loving it. Birch had become the heroine, and I was trashed, as speculation ran rife about where I was.

Outside the house, reporters filled the path, at the surgery and all over Wotton reporters were asking questions, and for the first time in years, everyone in Wotton had gone tight lipped. Roni was under pressure as her phone rang off the hook, and so eventually as Anita arrived in Manchester, looking exhausted, Roni held a press conference in a hotel in the middle of Manchester, and the place was packed.

Anita walked in first, followed by Roni, as the cameras flashed, and every news channel had their cameras pointed at them. They both sat down, and Anita leaned into the microphone.

"Good morning, ladies and gentlemen, to begin, Doctor Veronica Dixon, is going to make a statement, after which there will be questions." Roni sat forward.

"Good Morning... I will start by officially announcing that our Author, Abigail Jennifer Watson, has made the decision sadly to part company with Dixon Publishing. For myself personally, this has been both a shock, and it has deeply saddened me, because as you all know, she is also my daughter in law. However, considering the sorts of treatments she has had from the press and their utter disregard for her welfare, combined with the very heavy load of her celebrity status and demand on her to constantly appear, I am not completely surprised. I will say that currently, all of her works to date, will be remaining with the Dixon Group, and continue to be supplied to all retail and wholesale outlets. As for her future works, Abby is now free to decide how she puts them out."

She sat back and Anita pointed, as the long list of questions was asked and replies given. At first, they were cordial, but it was not long before the tabloids joined in, and the whole tone dropped.

"John Douglas, National Mail. Doctor Dixon, is it true that there has been affair after affair, which is the real reason Abby has left your daughter?" Anita went to lift her arm to ignore the question, but Roni touched it. She looked right at the reporter.

"Mr Douglas, why am I not surprised to see you here? You are assuming that Abigail and Jemima have separated, and I read that utter piece of trash you wrote in this morning's paper. Tell me please, which skip did you root in to find that? My daughter and Abigail are as strong as they have always been, and sadly this is not about their relationship, it is about the grueling workload of two successful authors and their stage work. Honestly, you are so blinded to the truth, I was considering raising the funds to buy you and all your staff at that rag you work for guide dogs."

Anita sniggered, as some of the other reporters laughed, Anita leaned forward.

"May I remind everyone, that this is going out live to the Dixon website and on River TV, so please, if you wish to misquote Doctor Dixon, we will be posting the full press conference later." She pointed.

"Angela Tomkinson, Readers Today. Doctor Dixon, after Abigail posted her video yesterday, all of her readers are very concerned for her welfare. Please could you let all of them know she is fine, some of our readers really are quite worried about her." Roni smiled.

"Abby is going to be fine, the biggest problem for her has been the grueling workload and also that of her wife, they have barely had any time together. She has also been prevented from writing, which is also her greatest joy in life, and so very wisely, she has created a scenario that has allowed her more time with her wife, and more time to be creative and start writing again. I know of one thing she has written, but I am sure now she has time, rest, and space, she will be happier and healthier."

And so, it went on for over forty minutes of questions, and as she spoke, Chloe took some time out having been assured that Abby was fine, and after watching her eat, walked across London for extra art supplies.

The door banged, and Edwina turned in the kitchen.

"CHLOE IS THAT YOU?" She walked to the hallway opening and saw Birch as she dropped her bag looking exhausted. She had found it very hard to get her car in through the gates as reporters mobbed the car. Edwina ran down the hall and swept her into a hug.

"Oh Birch, we are so worried, I am so glad to see you. How are you?" Birch gave a weak smile; her eyes were still puffy.

"I just want to be alone Edwina."

Deb's and Deli appeared in the kitchen, looking pale and worried, Birch saw them and smiled.

"We will all be fine, I know what she is doing, and why." Deb's swallowed hard and her eyes filled with tears, Deli saw her, and her eyes filled up as she looked at Birch. Deb's gave a sniffle.

"I am so worried about her and you, please don't break up, please stay together I love you guys so much." Birch walked down the hall, and pulled her into a hug as her tears filled her own eyes.

"We won't Deb's, I will never let her go, you all know that, and believe it or not, all of this, well, this is Deads fighting for all of us. As I said, I understand what she is doing and why, trust me, we will hear from her soon."

They sat around the island and drank coffee, as Birch gave them all an idea of what she thought Abby was attempting to do, and in a way it all made sense, and all of them relaxed a little, Birch sat back and smiled.

"I have missed this guys, you know, us, all girls together, it is nice." They all smiled, it was actually, Deb's gave a nod, and blew her nose.

"We have too, you know Abby is right, we all lost sight of each other, not just you two, all of us and we have been talking about Curio Live. You know Birch, it is a lot of work, and we all want to be involved, both of you need rest, why not let us do more, after all, it is supposed to be a Curio event, so let us help." Birch smiled.

"Sweetie's, we would love that." Suddenly there it was, that side of her no one had seen for a while. Edwina's phone rang, an she lifted it up, and gave a sigh of relief.

"Finally, it's Chloe." She hit the button and lifted it to her ear.

"Chloe where the hell are you, it's chaos here, the press are climbing the gates, I have Luke putting together a security team?"

Chloe was stood in the centre of Piccadilly Circus, with a brown haired Abby, she giggled as she looked at all the traffic.

"I am with Abby, and she is fine, and don't you go tracking me either, I have your blue stick, so you won't find us. I told you Weena, she needs me, and I am with her. What are you lot doing?" Edwina smiled, and covered her phone with her hand as the others watched on, she rolled her eyes.

"She is with Abby, how the hell she found her I have no idea, but she has, and Abby is fine." There were gasps all around the room, and Birch smiled, Edwina looked back at her phone.

"We are all here in the kitchen, Birch needs to take her car back for six tonight at the airport, so I am going to go with her in Petal and then drive her back, but apart from that we were all sat here worrying about Abby."

"Hang on Weena... Wow, he is fit, that is a fine ass... Okay,

Abby says, drop the car at the airport at five, and I am already in London, so I will grab her and take her to Abby. She really wants to see her, she is missing her, but she has done shit loads of writing. Abby says, tell her to let Gloria drive, and I have no fucking idea what that means." Edwina frowned, and looked at Birch.

"Who the fuck is Gloria?" Birch sat up, and gave a beaming smile.

"Oh Sweetie, she is an ugly bitch, but she is very useful at times." Edwina looked puzzled and she looked at Birch.

"Take the car back for five, Chloe will meet you and take you to her, she is missing you." Deb's reached over the island and took her hand, and gave a huge smile, Birch suddenly looked instantly happy, and then looked around the table.

"Oh crap, I look a right sight, I have to go and get ready." She jumped off her seat and ran up the hall, and everyone gave a chuckle as they heard her thunder up the stairs to her room.

Back at the hotel, with burgers and beers, Chloe looked at her watch, and slipped her hand in her pocket.

"Okay the press conference is over, and Philip told me she would be back in the office with Anita about now." She slipped a blue USB drive out of her pocket.

"Put this in your laptop and then connect back to the internet, and do not worry, Edwina and Luke will not be able to find you."

Edwina sat back in her seat as Sammy sat eating in the kitchen with Deli and Deb's, she gave a broad smile, and she looked over her monitor at Luke.

"Got her, she is in Hampshire... No Coventry... No Newcastle." She banged her fist on the desk.

"I fucking hate Chloe, the thieving bitch, she was not lying, she has been snooping in my fucking hiding place again!"

I looked at the screen and smiled. "Hi Roni, I am so sorry, I did not want to leave but I had to." She smiled back at me, and gave a soft nod.

"I won't say I am not utterly heartbroken, you were my star author, but Abby, I really understand, and actually I think you are quite brilliant in what you have done. Abby, you did not need to hand back the shares, Jemi was devastated when she got the notification." I understood that, but Roni did not fully understand my plan.

"Roni, it has to be a complete breakaway to work. I had no other choice, because I was going to lose her, and I had to fight to stop that happening. Birch lost sight of everything, she was blinded by it all, and I had to do something so big, she would finally notice, do you understand that?" My eyes filled with tears.

"Roni, it has been so long since we had a night together, we have not made love since last year, we were becoming strangers. I had to show her, I had to make her see it was killing me, and I wanted to save us." Roni wiped her eyes.

"Oh Abby, how could you think you would lose her, why didn't you talk to her?" I shook my head.

"When Roni? That is the point, we were living separate lives, I wanted so badly to talk, but she was never there when I was, and I knew why, I had to fix it, I had to."

"Abby, why didn't you tell me, I am the boss for God's sake, you know I would have done everything in my power to help?" I nodded.

"I know, but this time, it had to come from me, but sadly this is Birch, you know how stubborn she can be? I had to do something that would really make her sit up and notice." Roni gave a nod.

"You are so smart, you always have been, and yes, trust me she has noticed. She is really hurting Abby; she was so afraid she would lose you. Have you spoken to her yet?" I shook my head.

"Not yet, I will soon, I wanted to talk to you first, and have everything else in place." Roni lifted her cup, and her green eyes twinkled, she had aged, and appeared to have whiter hair than she ever had, although these days, she had taken to tying it back a lot more. She gave a smile as she put her cup down.

"I must admit Abby, I am very curious as to your next move. Will you be taking your currently published works away from us and reissuing them?" I shook my head.

"No, I keep my word, nothing will change in respect to those books, but for my new books, I want something different. Roni, I am setting up my own imprint, not competing, this one is just for me, and some graphic novelists I know of. I will at some point be announcing Sanctuary Press, a company built around the AJW brand. With that and D&D, I have everything I need, Chloe will be a part of it as art director, and I have a few other connections for printing. I will use some of the companies D&D have, and have already bought 100 ISBN numbers ready. My new stuff to begin with will be books or short stories, but I have also been working on the full story of the Curio's, sort of an autobiography told from my point of view, it is about two thirds done, and I have a few other books that need finishing to put out if I need to. Roni, I want to just be at home, and cuddle Birch, I want what we lost back." She gave me a big smile.

"It appears this has been coming for some time, you are very well prepared. Abby, I love you, and if I can help I will, do you need an investor, because if you do, I will back you?" I gave a chuckle.

"I am fine Roni, thanks to Katie I am well funded, she paid treble the price for her shares, I felt it was somewhat ironic, yet fitting." Roni burst out laughing, and shook her head.

"Oh, wow Abby, you can be ruthless, but well done you, that was a smart play. I am glad you are fine, but if you do need funds, I am always here. Talk to her Abby, she needs you." I gave a nod and smiled.

"I am shortly; I really need to see her and hold her. Roni she now knows how serious I am, I have shown her how much I still want her. I hope I fixed that red haired witch now enough for her to back off for good, because if she pulls this shit again, all us Curio's will be in the graveyard stashing her body." Roni gave a giggle.

"I do hope you invite me, hell, I would pay to join in. Abby, good luck, and thanks, I really needed to see you were fine, we are all very worried about you."

"I need Birch, and to just be alone with her, and that is on the cards, and then all will be well again. We will both see you soon."

She gave me a wave, and ended the call, all I had to do now, was take a shower and then talk to Birch.

Chapter 6

True Love.

Birch and Deli came down the stairs, and Edwina and Luke hugged each other as they pissed themselves laughing. Deb's sniggered and held her hand to her mouth, as Birch stood with long red hair, and bright blue eye shadow, looking uncomfortable, in one of Michael's old hoodies, and baggy grey sweat pants. Deli staggered behind her in high heels and a long white wig, that Anthony had once worn to impersonate Avril for Abby.

"Birch I am not sure we can pull this off, I mean, you are tall and surprisingly slender for forty, I put on weight after having the kids." She swayed, on her high heels, she had not worn any for ages, Edwina smirked and gave a shrug.

"Breathe in that stomach, hold your breath and wave, that should do it." Birch lifted her big bag, and slipped it inside the waiting rucksack; Edwina smiled.

"Drop the car off, and Chloe will be there waiting to take you to Abby. Birch, use this time to heal you both." Birch smiled.

"I will Sweetie. I just need to see her." Edwina slid on her dark glasses, and smiled.

"God you are a hideous bitch, go on, go get her." Birch giggled.

The press stood at the gates watching, movement at the door brought a murmur of excitement, and cameras came up, a tall redhead came out, and there were groans, and then Birch stood at the door, and there was an instant explosion of flashes as the redhead got in the hire car. Deli the Birch impersonator, waved like a lunatic.

"BYE SWEETIE, AND THANK YOU, I LOVE YOU!"

The gates swung open, and the Birch lookalike stood waving at the door, as the cameras continued to take picture after picture, as the hire car shot off.

Behind the door, Edwina hung on to the waist band of Deli, as she swayed, waving like a lunatic, and Deb's sat on the stairs with Luke hysterically laughing. Little Sammy looked confused, as Deli stepped back and almost fell over. Edwina was laughing so hard, as she pulled Deli into a hug.

"Oh my God, that was so funny, you were brilliant." Deli smiled, as she pulled off her wig.

"I hope it worked, those two need a break." Sammy frowned.

"You are not Auntie Birch, where is she Aunt Deli?" Deb's sniggered.

Birch pulled into the lot, but there was no sign of Bess or Chloe, she headed inside and dealt with the paperwork, and then walked out of the door, looking for an orange camper. She stopped dead in her tracks, as she saw me leaning against my car, I smiled.

"Wow you look like a right fit bird, I love red heads, they are banging."

She smiled, and her eyes filled with tears. I held out my arms, and she walked over to me and buried her face in my neck, as I pulled her close and just felt the joy of holding her. She gave a huge sob.

"I am so sorry Deads, I was so scared I had lost you; it has been horrible without you." I pulled her tight.

"I know, I am sorry too, but I had to do this Birch."

I pulled her back and lifted her face to mine, her eyes were huge they were so close, and sparkled with her tears. I leaned in and kissed her, and her arms came around me, and oh my God, it was heaven, I had yearned for this for a long time.

Camera flashes alerted me to the presence of the press, I had been spotted, I should have worn a wig, but I did not care, I pulled back, smiled, and pulled off her wig.

"That is better, that is my snow queen." She gave a giggle and smiled.

"Come on, we have been busted, let's get out of here. Seriously, that eye shadow is not at all your colour." She gave a slight giggle, as I opened the door, she jumped in, and the reporters scrambled, we knew this game well.

I jumped in the driver seat, turned on the engine, and headed for the barrier, I drove around the roundabout, and Birch looked back.

"Deads, shouldn't we have gone that way?"

I smiled at the wheel, as I braked hard, and an orange van pulled out of a lot behind me. I came back round to the roundabout, as the press followed us, and then headed for the barrier. Chloe hung out of the window, Baz was driving, and she waved like a maniac. I got my ticket ready, and then watched as Bess swerved into the centre of the road skidding across it, and Chloe screamed with delight. My window came down as Birch watched looking shocked, the ticket went in, and the barrier went up, Bess had blocked the road completely.

I put my foot down, floored it, and we were away, as Birch flopped back into her seat, and reached across and put her hand on my leg, I turned and glanced at her.

"We are free Birch, I am free, there is nothing she can do now, both of us are free of her forever, it is time to live again."

Car horns beeped like crazy, as Chloe walked up the road with a big smile, and a handful of leaflets.

"Can I interest you in a live stream from the USA, it will feature Curio Live America?"

All of the press frowned and scowled, and swore at her, Chloe looked at them all and just laughed at them all looking pissed off, as they leaned out of their car windows angry. She looked back as Baz started the engine and Bess roared into life. She faced the press with a giggle and screamed.

"LEAVE THEM ALONE, YOU HAVE DONE ENOUGH DAMAGE AND CAUSED THEM ENOUGH PAIN. I AM HEADING HOME IF YOU WANT TO FOLLOW, THEY HAVE GONE WHERE YOU WON'T FIND THEM!"

She gave a wave, and then skipped off to Bess, and jumped in with a giggle, and the barrier went up, as Chloe and Baz drove through, there was no sign of Abby and Birch. Chloe laughed in her seat, and patted Baz on the leg.

"That was awesome, God, I fucking love you." Baz glanced at her.

"I love you too, you know that." He glanced back at her and she was sat frozen, and as white as a ghost.

"You alright, you look like you have seen a ghost?" Chloe swallowed hard.

"I just said that out loud, didn't I?"

Baz laughed as he drove watching the road, as Chloe stared at him looking absolutely petrified, He gave another little chuckle.

"Chloe, honestly, you are the love of my life, I have been with you for a decade now, and I am happy with this. I have never hidden it. As I said the other night, if you want more I can go there, because honestly, I get it, Terry pissed off and left you in the lurch. I do, but hey, I was there then, and I'm still at your side now, and I have every intention of being around for a long time. You know, I have never asked any girl, we are not that much different, but hell, I am up for asking you." She gave a shy smile.

"But why Baz, honestly, I am not that special, and I cannot say I won't cheat on you, and I don't want to hurt you." He glanced at her and gave a smile.

"Not special, you must be having a laugh. My God girl, look at you, you are stunningly beautiful, and you have a huge wonderful heart, and honestly, you are the most loving woman I have ever met. I feel so safe with you, and I fucking love you more than you will ever know, I have for years." Chloe turned pink, and put her head down.

"No one has ever said that to me before, no one has ever said such lovely things, and I don't know how to deal with that Baz." He smiled.

"Just accept it, all of it is true, and I am happy to say it more if you need to hear it, because I will tell you a million times if it helps, because it's the truth." She looked up and her eyes were filled with tears, and her cheeks were really red, and her voice was soft.

"I do really love being with you, Baz, you make me really happy." He turned, and winked at her.

"Hearing that makes me feel like the biggest man alive, and happier than I have ever been." She gave him a big smile, he pulled up at the lights and stopped on the red light, and turned in his seat.

"I am really serious Chloe, I will marry you tomorrow, if we have to set the terms and conditions in advance, then fine, and if that means we take sex out of the equation and we get to play once in a while, I am so fine with that. I have watched you do it with others at parties, and honestly, it was hot. Look, the thing is, us Chloe, me and you, it works. Trust me, I will sell my house, studio and all my shit and come live with you, because I will never take you away from Abby and Birch, I am fucking serious girl, I want you to be my wife." She swallowed hard.

"Really, I mean, honestly Baz don't fuck with me, because I will fucking stab you, if this is a piss take?"

He opened his door, got out, and walked around the front of Bess, the lights changed to green, as he came round to her door. He opened it, and offered her his hand, as cars behind them started to beep. She frowned.

"Baz, the light is green, what the fuck are you doing?" He smiled, leaned in and took her hand and pulled.

"Baz, are you mental?"

Baz pulled, and unclipped her belt, and slipped off her the seat, the cars behind were going mad beeping like crazy. He gripped her shoulders, stood her in the middle of the road, looked her in the eyes, and slipped his hand into his pocket. She gasped as he went down on one knee and looked up at her, she swallowed and felt panicked.

"Baz for fucks sake, we are in the middle of the road, and everyone is really pissed off." He shrugged.

"Fuck em, this bloody thing has been in my pocket for ages. This is my best chance, and I am frigging well taking it." He lifted up his hand, revealing the small box, opened it, and she saw the sparkle.

"Chloe Pemberton, you are the love of my life, and I so desperately want to marry you and have you to share the rest of my life, so I am asking, with terms and conditions arranged first if needs be, but will you marry me?" He winked, and then glanced to the side.

"Say yes quick, I think I am about to be arrested." The blue lights flashed on his face. She looked to the side and then back at him and then nodded.

"Yeah... Yeah, I will... Holy fuck did I just say that?" He stood up and pulled the ring out of the box.

"Too late now, you said it out loud."

He slid the ring onto her finger and tears filled her eyes, as she leapt into his arms, and he smiled.

"Have you any cash on you, I might need bail money love?"

Chloe squealed with happiness, and looked at the police officer walking down the road with his pad.

"Officer please, don't nick him, I just said yes, and we are going home to shag, then get married." Baz looked at her and smiled, and her eyes were bright happy and smiling, he was so happy.

"You won't regret this, I promise Chloe, no one will ever hurt you again..." The officer smiled and closed his pad; Baz gave her a wink.

"He put his pad back, quick, let's leg it before he changes his mind."

With loud happy squeals from Chloe, Baz ran around the front of the van as the lights went back to green, and jumped in, and set off, he looked in the mirror where the officer stood smiling.

"Fuck that was close, I thought he would nick us for sure." Chloe squealed with delight, and looked at the ring on her finger.

We had hardly made it through the door, and I was tearing her clothes off. God, I had a huge need, and as I pushed her across to the bed in the hotel room, I could feel her pulling at my clothes. I pushed hard and she fell onto the bed, and I was on her, kissing and touching, I needed her touch so badly.

Say hello to the night started to play, and I gave a sigh. "Ignore it."

She had already pulled it out of my back pocket, answered and put it on speaker phone.

"ABBY, BIRCH... OH MY GOD... OH MY GOD, I SAID IT, HOLY FUCK HE ASKED AND I SAID IT." I lifted my head out of Birch's boobs.

"NO FUCKING WAY!" Birch frowned.

"ABBY, I DID, I SAID YES, WE ARE GOING HOME TO FUCK, OH MY GOD, HE IS MENTAL, WE DID IT IN THE ROAD." Birch lifted her head up, and frowned.

"Did what in the road Sweetie, did you screw in broad daylight... in the road?"

"BIRCH I AM SO HAPPY, BAZ ASKED ME TO MARRY HIM AND I SAID YES." Birch looked at me and looked shocked, I giggled.

"Chloe, she is lost for words, but honestly, we are both really happy, you know what, he is a wonderful guy, and you know we all love him." She gave a giggle.

"He is, isn't he? I am going home to tell Edwina." Birch frowned.

"Have you not told her yet Sweetie, I thought she would have been the first?"

"No, you guys are the first, I really wanted Abby to know, guys, I want to be as happy as you are, and he makes me that." I could not help but smile, she had more right than any.

"You know what Chloe, both of us are really stoked for you, and yes, go and be gloriously happy. I am about to go down on Birch."

"Shit... Fuck... Sorry guys, I just got excited and wanted to tell you, give her a good eating or whatever it is you call it, both cum hard... Carry on, I will talk soon, yeah?" Birch gave a giggle.

"Thanks Chloe, and congratulations, go have epic sex too, bye Sweetie." The line went dead, and I looked at Birch.

"Wow, Birch, Chloe is actually getting married, I mean, holy shit, we are talking Chloe, I never thought it would happen." Birch gave a smile.

"Hatty held out until she was over forty, and look at her now, cohabitating and happy with Clive, I think it's sweet." She looked down, and frowned.

"Oh God look at my belly, I am getting fat."

I looked down at her little round belly, she had hardly got any fat on her, I slid back and looked at it and then glanced up at her.

"You could get liposuction." She frowned.

"I heard it is painful, Sweetie, I don't like pain."

"Well then, you have no other choice."

She frowned not understanding. I pushed my face down into her belly, and blew out as hard as I could, and she screamed out with laughter.

"DEADS, SWEETIE, NO... IT TICKLES, SWEETIE STOP, I CANNOT TAKE IT, HA HA HA HA!"

She thrashed on the bed kicking and screaming, and it was wonderful to hear it, as I blew harder and she screamed out, possibly disturbing everyone in the hotel.

Edwina sat in the kitchen with Anthony, Deli and Deb's. Luke sat with Jimmy at the table; Michael leaned on the fridge. All the kids were out in the garden, when the front door exploded open and crashed back, everyone jumped out of their skin with the noise from the bang. Chloe came panting into the kitchen.

"WEENA... WEENA WE DID IT!" Deb's rolled her eyes.

"That is hardly news Chloe, who haven't you done it wi..."

Chloe stood in the doorway with her hand up showing her bright sparkling engagement ring, beaming with the biggest smile ever. Anthony stood up and stared at her hand, there was utter silence, his voice was quiet, almost lost in amazement.

"Chloe darling, is that what I think it is?" She smiled at Edwina.

"Weena, he asked, and I said yes."

Deb's hand went to her mouth, and Edwina smiled as her eyes filled with tears, and she snatched her into the biggest hug ever, and just bawled like a bitch, Chloe frowned.

"Wow, drama much Weena?"

It took a few moments to sink in, and then suddenly the room erupted like a bomb going off, and Deb's, Deli and all the others dragged her into the hugest hugs. Anthony stood back and smiled as he looked into her bright dancing eyes, he had tears in his eyes.

"Honestly darling, I am so happy for you, I really am lost for words. I love you so much darling, I honestly do, and you deserve such happiness in your life. To be honest, I never thought there was a man good enough, but I am happy to be wrong, because he is a good man, he really is." He pulled her into his arms and she snuggled into him.

"I love you Anthony, you know that right? You are my brother in every way." He breathed into her shoulder.

"You have always been my precious little sister, and I cannot deny, I am so happy for you at the moment."

"DRINKS." Jimmy held up two bottles. And suddenly it was party time at number three Waterside Lane... Again.

I gave a happy sigh, as I lay on top of her sweating, red in the face and smiling like a mental patient, her arms were around me and we both panted, and I snuggled into her neck.

"I have missed this, Oh God, I really needed it." She took a deep breath and lay facing the ceiling breathing hard.

"Deads, we still need to talk, there are things to sort out between us." I gave a sigh.

"I know, just not yet. Birch, I want this, just this for the moment, just hold me, I have missed it and yearned for this for months." She gave a small smile.

"Yeah, me too, but Sweetie, as much as I do not want to move, I really need a pee, unless you want to get into April showers, I have to move."

I gave a sigh and sat up on her waist, and looked down at her, and she looked as radiant and beautiful as ever with her long white hair with faint patches, spread all over the sheets, her snow white skin, and those insanely gorgeous green eyes.

"You are so beautiful Birch, honestly, you still take my breath away."

She smiled and went a little red, I slid back and climbed off her, and she sat up, and slid off the bed, and ran to the toilet. I walked over to the phone and lifted it up as I heard her pee.

"Birch, I am ordering food, what do you want?" Wow, she can really pee.

"Anything, I am starving."

"Hello, hi, room service, this is room 142, can we order food please?"

As I have often said, news travels faster than email in Wotton, and the word was out, as the celebration raged. Edwina took Chloe by the hand and into the study, and then bawled her brains out as she watched Chloe phone her dad and tell him the good news. Baz did not have a mum and dad, they had died when he was twenty two, but he did have an aunt, and so together they both told her the great news, and Edwina wailed even more.

We sat at the table as we ate, there were interruptions as we talked, and some tears were shed by both of us. I know some of what I said hurt her, but I had promised to always be honest with her, and so I told her straight up, how it felt to be alone and lost without her. Admittedly, she had told me she felt it too, and as cold as it was, I asked how?

"Birch, be honest, you got lost in the fame and the power of it all. I am sorry, but if it had not been for Izzy, Sweetie's Retreat would be closed down. You were just too busy enjoying the spotlight, and that is why Katie pounced at the chance to lure you in. Birch, Katie played you, and you went along with it." She looked really upset as she looked at me, I lifted my glass and took a sip.

"Birch, I love you, God, have you any idea, but honestly, I was at the bottom of your priority list, you just did not have time." She nodded her head and looked down; her voice was soft.

"I know… I see that now, it was not my intent Deads, never think I don't care, I do, but why all this, why all the secret deals and behind the scenes planning, why not just come straight out with it?" I took another sip of my drink.

"Birch, I tried, but you would not listen, it is why I wanted us to go to Sunny Bank. I needed you sober, awake, and alone long enough to tell you how I was feeling, because honestly, you were starting to sound like Katie, and it scared the living shit out of me."

She took a deep breath and pushed her plate away, and sat back, and I could see her thinking about everything. Her eyes moved up to me, God, I loved her when she was like this, and it was really turning me on.

"Deads, why the shares, why transfer them to me, I really do not want or need them?"

"You will." She frowned and shook her head.

"How, mum has the majority, I really do not have a need for them, I always vote with her?" I put my glass back on the table.

"Birch, your mum is 63, and your dad 64, they are coming up to retirement age, if I am right, at some point Katie will try to buy more shares. I just fleeced the bitch selling her my stock to slow her down, but both of us have seen how the share value has tripled in the last few years. Trust me when I say, the only person who can put her back in her box is you. Birch, you need to get ready, because of this it has made your mum really think, the timing is perfect and she will now ponder when to hand over the control of the group to you. With my shares you have already become more powerful, and they will be crucial to you taking over. Birch it is going to happen, we always knew it, use this time to prepare."

Birch lifted her glass and took a drink, I could see her working things out in her mind, she knew I was right, and maybe it surprised her that I had a better handle on things than she did.

"Deads I really do not want to run the group alone, I always thought we would do it together, and when your dad sold his company and moved to Miami, I just figured it would be us two, like D&D." I gave her a smile.

"Oh, it will be... Birch we are married, I will always talk things through with you, just like the Parish Council, I don't need shares for that, and honestly, I think your mum knows that."

"But why leave, why quit, you have a great portfolio with us, honestly that is the one thing that does not make sense, Katie cannot control everything?"

It was a question that had occupied my thoughts for months, and after a great deal of thought, four weeks ago I had made up my mind, it just took the latest disaster in my life to push me enough to step up and actually do it. I looked up and could see her watching my every move.

"Why did you start the retreat without your mother's backing, I mean, why Birch, there was no need to, she was behind you all the way?" She shrugged.

"I wanted my independence; I wanted the freedom to run my own ship." I smiled.

"Understand now? Birch, since my first book, your mum, Katie, even to a degree Anita, have planned out every aspect of my writing life, but like you, I have always wanted the freedom to make those decisions myself. Birch that was why I was at Uni to begin with, I wanted to be a publisher, honestly, I wish I had done it years ago. Sanctuary Press will do that for me, it is my books, my pace, and me making all the decisions. I really want that, and yes, like I would with you, I will look to you for advice at times. Birch, I have an AJW brand, and as AJW, I want control of it, that is all." She smiled.

"I completely get that, oh you have no idea how much that makes sense, I will help you all the way, I hope you know that?"

I was so happy to hear that, because secretly, I was shitting myself and hoping I did not mess up. I stood up and walked over to the sofa. Oh God, I was bloated, I had not eaten this well in ages, I sat back and lifted my legs up, and she came up and cuddled in at the side of me. I stroked her long white hair, as I sipped my wine.

"Birch, the Curio's have lost themselves, and we need to get them back to who they were. I have talked a lot with Chloe, and I think marriage to a degree and family, has taken its toll. If we want to make Curio Live US a success, we need them back as they were, I think Chloe and me are the only two left who still look remotely the same, even your hair is so faded, you can hardly see the bark lines." She snuggled back and relaxed into me.

"Deads, family and commitment has taken a lot out of them, it is not easy raising kids, juggling a business and staying the same, it is a lot to carry Deads." I shook my head as I fingered her long hair.

"I do not agree, Birch, the house was our focal point, our centre, it is where we gelled and where we planned all our adventures and mischief. I understand they have to move out to raise kids, but they all stopped visiting, honestly, I have hardly spoken with Deb's in the last four months. I cannot remember when Deli and me last had coffee, even we stopped communicating. Okay, so we have worked on Curio Live together, but it was me, home alone and you home alone, don't you miss those talks all sat round the island tossing ideas into the pot?"

"Well yes, but Sweetie, as I said, we have all moved on, we all grew up, there was nothing we could do about it, that is life." I lay my head back; the wine was kicking in and I was so tired.

"I remember a time when you would say you don't stop playing because you grow old, you grow old because you stop playing, and everyone has stopped playing, including you. I mean Christ, you live in a suit these days, what happened to that crazy wilderness, spiritual, warrior of adventure? You know, I went to see May two weeks ago; her tree is huge now and so beautiful, and I sat and talked to her. I loved how she never quit, she just held up her middle finger, and carried on being who she wanted to be, we all could learn from her."

"I wish you had told me; I would have loved to have been there with you."

"I did, but you were too busy getting ready for your big wine party at the grand ball room. Birch. I am thirty nine, forty in just over four months, and honestly, I am not ready to grow up yet. Chloe and me have resisted it, and we have every intention of living it up right until the end like May did. The truth is, neither of us want to do it alone, we want our friends there with us, because that is kind of the point of being a Curio."

"Deads, I am sorry, I did get carried away again, and I am

regretting it so much, I am not sure how close we came, but it was really close wasn't it, we almost got swallowed in it all? I read your story, and I do understand, I am so at fault, but never think it was deliberate, I never want us to break up, and I know I came to the edge of the abyss when I read that story, which by the way is written brilliantly."

"I won't lie Birch; I downloaded the divorce papers. Birch, if this had failed to get your attention, I was ready to go to a solicitor, and start proceedings. I never want to feel that lonely again, it was just like being stuck in the guest house, waiting for you to leave Uni, I will not go back there, not ever."

She sat up and turned to face me, her eyes filled with tears, and she shook with pain, I lifted my hand to her cheek, as she tried to speak. She took a huge breath and swallowed it.

"Please don't ever do that, Deads, you can never leave me. I have loved you since the day I met you, honestly, I was as lonely sat in hotel rooms waiting for the next event, and I have had too many nights sleeping alone to last me a lifetime. It was never meant to be like this. I just lost sight of things, I would never hurt you and never leave you Deads, I love you with all my heart." I smiled.

"Do you think I don't know that? Birch, you lost you, this was my cry for help, this was me screaming my lungs out in a thick mist to find you. Birch, do you know today is the first time since last year you have called me Sweetie, that is how lost you got? Baby, I really need you in my life, oh hell, I need you at my side always, that has always been the point of us, we are light and dark, Celia and Lillian, my dark little beastie to your snow queen. Birch, the spring came and it was starting to thaw, and all I could see was the snow turning to green, and as much as I hate it, I really needed a blizzard."

She smiled as her tears dripped on my leg, and gave me a nod, and then took a huge deep breath, and wiped her eyes on her sleeve.

"I need my dark little beastie too, oh Deads, I have missed this so much, I missed you. You are right, all of us need to shake ourselves up, we have Curio Live to do, but most of them have not even said if they will be there yet, how do we get them back in the frame?" I lifted my glass, and smiled at her.

"Well firstly, we need to get Deadly and Birch back on track, and then, we have a reunion, and I mean a real Curio get together and thrash everything out, it is time I think, we brought back the house meet, pray for good weather."

I was exhausted I had hardly slept in days, and she looked beat, I finished my glass and took her hand, and led her into the bedroom, the bed was a mess and smelt of sex, but I really did not care. I slid my arms around her, and kissed her softly.

"Birch, I would really love to screw you again, but honestly, I am bloody exhausted." She gave a little giggle.

"Me too Sweetie, it has felt like the longest week of my life, and all I want is to curl up and cuddle."

I kissed her again and slid onto the bed, and she climbed in and curled around me, and I felt her hand slide up and cup my boob. It had been so long, and it just felt right. I closed my eyes with a smile, and listened to the sound of her breathing, and suddenly, I was fast asleep and happy.

Chapter 7

Family, and Us.

It was gone one when I woke up. I sat up in bed, slid out and walked into the living area, and she looked up and smiled, sat at her laptop.

"Morning Sweetie." That sounded so good, it had felt like forever since I had heard it, I walked over scratching my head and yawning and bent down to kiss her.

"What are you up to?" She looked up and smiled.

"I am talking to Edwina; we are going over some specs for the live event. River's sister company, need a few things. They are really happy that the promotion in advance is going well, they just need some info for our requirements in the arena. There is coffee and milk over there, I brought some in my bag, well actually, I always have some, just in case."

She made me laugh, that bag had been on her arm every day for as long as I could remember, and for years I had been making a mental note of its contents, from lethal weapons, to an old blue Babygrow. We had always called it her survival kit, and on many occasions, it had saved the day. I must admit, it was looking a little frayed, I had sewn some of it back together a few times.

I made a coffee as she typed in her message box, I guess the game was over and the word was out, Edwina would have done a trace on Birch's laptop, so she knew where we were now. Birch looked up.

"The press are still all over the gates, those vultures never quit." I shrugged.

"Let them wait, we do not have to go home until we are ready." I saw her eyes change, as she looked at me.

"We are okay though, aren't we, I mean, you are not going to just get up and leave me are you. Oh, God Deads, please tell me we are okay?" And there it was, her insecurity flowed up and she was childlike again, I smiled.

"Birch, listen, and listen well, we are solid, stop worrying, I am going nowhere. Hell, what do think this is all about? It is why I did this; I needed you to know how I felt and that I want us to be us again." She gave a sigh of relief.

"Phew, my heart is racing, as long as we are fine?" I smiled.

"We are, talk to Edwina, I am running a bath."

It is a strange thing getting older, I stood in the bathroom, and looked in the mirror and I could see me, and yet, the Abby I see has more lines around her eyes. Her eyes appear a little more intense, and although my skin does not flare up anywhere nearly as much as it did, and it is still pretty smooth, there is a softness to it, that I felt it did not have before.

Is it strange that I would see my mum as an older person when I came back from Uni, and now I am not that far away from being the same age. I mean, okay, she was 49 when I was at Uni, I came late to her compared to others, but I am 39 years old now, and that young wild woman, that used to look back at me in the mirror everyday has gone forever, and I miss her. Oh God, is this a midlife crisis, am I heading into menopause, which is why I suddenly have gone bonkers and changed everything about my life?

Is this it, is this the slip into decay as my young heart panics and clings on to my youth with a terrified grip as I start to decay, and turn into my grandmother, holy shit I hope not? I pushed my skin back slightly towards my ears, stretching it, and smiled, there she is, there is the Abigail I know, there is my crazy dark beastie.

"You are as beautiful as always."

"Huh?"

I turned, and she was leaning on the doorframe smiling, I gave a sigh and stepped back from the mirror, it was starting to steam up as the bath was almost full.

"I am getting old Birch and I do not really want to; I want to stay the Abby you fell in love with, not become some wrinkled old prune." She gave a chuckle and walked in, and pulled me into her arms.

"Oh Deads, I don't care, honestly, I still think you are the most beautiful woman on the planet, and honestly, I like the way you have matured." She lifted her hand to my face, and her eyes danced with delight, I felt her soft fingers stroke my cheek.

"I love these little lines at the sides of your eyes, they are the result of all the times we have laughed, and just revelled in the moment." I looked into her big green eyes; they still sparkled with such life.

"Birch, there is so much I still want to do, so many things I want to write, and at times I get scared that time is running out for us." She smiled.

"Deads, age has no bearing on living, every moment is so precious, and it should be lived. Maybe we have forgotten that, I think all of our Curio family has, and maybe things do need to change for all of us." I gave a nod.

"Birch, never scare me like you have, keep talking and keep holding me and cuddling me. I have been so afraid recently, feeling I was losing you was destroying me. I could not sleep, I could not write, it has been awful. Birch I am still Abby, I am still your Deads, I know I look more like my mum, but I am still me on the inside." She gave a big smile.

"Oh, you silly, is that what has been going on in your head, you thought you were less attractive to me? Oh God Deads, that is simply not true, it was not about you, it was just life, and probably my ego. It is silly, I fell into the same trap I have always warned others about, and I got preoccupied with the glitz, and you know what is so stupid?" I stared into her bright green eyes and shook my head.

"No... What?" She smiled.

"I have over sixty million in the bank, and I don't even want it."

"OH CRAP... The bath."

I wriggled free, grabbed the taps, and quickly turned them off, and gave a sigh of relief, and looked back at her as she lifted her top.

"It feels like forever since we last bathed together." She gave me a smile as she undid her pants.

"It is, and I am really looking forward to it."

Yeah, so was I, this was a part of my life I have always loved, I suppose now we have a long history of just relaxing and talking, and laughing together submerged in hot soapy water. I climbed in and lay back with a long happy moan, as her arms came around me as I leaned back into her soft breasts, they were like two soft pert pillows, and I have always loved relaxing into them. The steam rose up with the scent of the soap, and I felt happy, I think I have missed this the most.

"So, how is everyone?" Birch tightened her embrace, and leaned down on my shoulder.

"They all have hangovers, last night they had quite the celebration, the house was filled with kids and Curio's, as they celebrated with Chloe. To be honest, Edwina said it almost felt like old times." I frowned and turned slightly.

"Almost?" Birch gave a chuckle.

"They missed having us there, she said they have done a lot of talking, apparently Chloe gave them all quite the telling off. Edwina laughed; she told me Chloe really stuck it to her about deserting the Curio cause." I gave a small chuckle.

"She has never changed; she can be only her... You know, some days I think back, and I realise she has had my back since that day she came up to us and apologised on the green. Even this week, when I thought no one would find me, she still did, she really is the most amazing friend, we are both really lucky to have her." I felt Birch stir in the water behind me.

"You know Sweetie, about that... How the hell did she find you, I mean, Edwina was going frantic and she couldn't find you?" I started to giggle, and slipped forward in the bath, and turned around to look at her.

"Oh my God, I have not told you, have I?"

We sat in the hot steaming water, as I recounted how I had met with Andrew, and then told her of how she went to his office, terrified Katie and then stripped in front of Andrew and threatened to walk down the office naked; to tell his fiancé, they had just had epic sex on his desk. I laughed so much I had tears in my eyes, as Birch squealed with delight, and there she was, that crazy teenager with a beautiful and infectious cackle of a laugh. Honestly, I thought she had lost it, but as I sat there watching her laugh and scream with delight, I knew she hadn't.

The Curio's had lost this, and it had sent them off in every direction, she had always been the happy crazy glue that held us together, and for a while she had been missing in action. I was so relieved to see she had come back, I needed her in my life so badly, all of us did. She was the banner to which we always had gathered, and I was so happy to see her, sat there screaming with delight. I think she has come back just in the nick of time to save us all again.

Little had changed at number three Waterside Lane, the house had been decorated a few times, but apart from that, everything was relatively the same. The biggest change came out in the garden, as house mates married and moved out, children became a part of our life, and with that came the phenomenon of Auntie Birch.

At the far end of the garden, surrounded by shrubs and trees, Birch built a play area, with swings, slides, and a roundabout. A small hut was erected to become a play house, and she painted it with bright happy colours, and of course, there also came a tree house. Well, I say tree house, it was more a house on stilts next to a tree, but as with all things Birch, no expense was spared, and with solar panels and endless strings of lights, the kids had a wonderful area to play.

My arch was off limits, and a small fence was erected around it, to prevent the children from climbing on it. Deli gave swimming lessons to all the kids, and by the time they were three, she had them all swimming like pro's. Around the patio, we had two small picnic benches, and when we ate outdoors, they would sit there as all of the adults sat at the patio tables.

The children brought a sense of fun and youth to the house as we all grew up, and in those first few years, we were one huge massive creative family. It was normal to stand on the balcony and look down, and see Chloe and the kids, all naked, covered in paint as they crawled about on long rolled out pieces of paper making pictures. On the flip side, there are also those moments, when the kids can test you to your limit, especially when your dad just happens to be a famous rock star, with a good reputation for trouble.

Deb's sat at the island holding her head, and looking very pale, Edwina sniggered as she walked up with a coffee and painkillers.

"You are out of practice girl; you let yourself go."

Deli groaned, her face on the cool surface of the island, and Jimmy smiled from the doorway. It had been a loud and wild night of celebration for Chloe and Baz. Deb's swallowed her coffee, and looked like death.

"I just want peace and quiet, and no sudden movements, Deli understands, don't you?" Her eyes opened, but it was too bright, she closed them again.

"Yeah... Please stop shouting." Edwina sniggered, as she turned back to the kettle.

"Look on the bright side, Chloe and Birch are not here, I am sure you both appreciate that." Deli groaned and Deb's smiled.

"I am happy for her, I am, but yes, I am so glad she is not here, she is too loud. Actually, where is she?" Edwina leaned back on the unit and held up her cup, and smiled.

"She has gone to show dad her ring, and then Baz is taking her to meet his Aunt Flo, he has no parents, and she is all he has, so he wants Chloe to meet her. She was so happy this morning, honestly, I keep bursting into tears." Edwina's eyes filled up, and she squeaked out.

"Excuse me."

She grabbed a piece of kitchen roll, and ran to the library; they heard her sob as she ran down the hall. Deb's gave a deep happy sigh, the slap of tiny feet on the patio announced incoming, Deb's closed her eyes.

"Oh God, what now?" Jenny appeared at the door and walked up to her mum; she was loud.

"Mum, will you tell Gem, he is threatening to poo in the pool again, and Sammy is encouraging him. Mum, we don't want poo in the pool, honestly, I hate boys."

Jimmy sniggered as Deb's lifted her head, she slid back in her seat with a groan, and stood up, Jimmy yelled from the door.

"GEM... NO POOING IN THE POOL, AND SAMMY, STOP ENCOURAGING HIM!"

Deb's stared at Jimmy with a confused look, and Deli shrunk back holding her head and moaned. Jimmy stared at Deb's.

"What Doll?" Her voice was very soft.

"Why... I mean, why would you? Just go out there and talk quietly to him." He smiled.

"Yeah, headache, sorry Doll." Deb's turned to Jennifer.

"If he tries again, tell your dad."

She walked slowly back to the island, and flopped back in her seat. Jenny walked over and tugged at his hand, he looked down and smiled at her.

"Dad, I think Helen pissed in the pool, she stood sort of still and shuddered, and I knew Dad, she pissed." Deb's eyes moved towards Jimmy, as he looked down at his daughter.

"That's okay Doll, just don't tell your Uncle Anthony, it sort of freaks him out." Jenny gave him a big smile and ran outside.

"Thanks Dad." He looked up and saw Deb's watching him, he shrugged.

"What! Deb's, it's all just water."

I lay back on the bed, still wearing my damp bath robe, which was wide open as Birch crawled up me with a smile, I was red and breathless.

"Was that nice Sweetie?" I pushed my head back into the pillow.

"Oh God yes, I really need this, it's perfect, no kids, no house mates, it is almost as good as Sunny Bank." Birch sat up on my waist and her eyes dulled, I gave a sigh.

"Birch, it is over, leave it there, we are together, have talked and sorted out the things we needed to." She put her head down.

"I am sorry, I cannot help it. Deads, I feel so guilty and stupid, I am supposed to be the one with the answers, and I completely fouled things up." I sat up and pulled her into a hug.

"It is done, please, I am so happy today, I have not felt this good for a long time. This... You know, just us, this is how it is meant to be, so let's just go with it and smile." She felt so warm and soft in my arms, as I sat there, and just snuggled into her.

"You know Birch... Birch... Birch?" I gave a long sigh.

"Bloody hell not again, do you have a button you just press?" She was fast asleep... Again, I am sure I have told you... Yeah scratch that, I know you all know by now?

"Christ, I am too old for Yoga positions like this."

Having finally wrestled her softly back onto the bed, and slid her under the covers, I smiled at her, and stroked the hair from her face.

"Sleep is good, you really need it, sleep well my snow queen."

I climbed off the bed, and headed over to the table where my laptop was open, and my last document task barred down. I clicked it open, read the last few lines, and started to type. Maybe it was knowing I was free, maybe it was the excitement of saving my marriage, I am not sure, but suddenly, I felt alive, and my creativity was flowing at high speed down my arms, and into my typing hands. I was lost to the world in the red mist of focus, and the lines were pouring out, and I felt more alive than I had in years, the day moved on, as I wrote away, feeling happy again.

BANG!!!
"I'M HOME!" Deb's stood by the stove, with Deli.
"In the kitchen." Wild screams echoed outside.
"AUNT CHLOE... AUNT CHLOE... AUNT CHLOE!"
The group of wild children came racing and panting through the door, Chloe beamed with delight, and went down on her knees with a huge smile, and the kids all mobbed her.
"CAN WE PAINT, CAN WE?"
Chloe looked up at Deb's as Sammy climbed onto her shoulders, and Gem hung from her neck. Deb's gave a sigh as she looked at her excited eyes.
"Their dinner is almost ready, maybe later, if they behave." Anthony rolled his eyes.
"Good luck with that one, now she is back there is no hope of it, she is more feral than they are."
Deli sniggered. Chloe looked down at the group around her, Sammy was sat proud above her, as Helen and Jenny held her hand, and Gem clung desperately to her neck.
"Okay guys, you heard your mum, dinner first, so all of you be good, and eat your dinner nicely, and then if you do, we will all paint something."
Happy yells and screams echoed around the kitchen; Deb's giggled as she drained the potatoes. Chloe lifted Gem up on the island, and winked, Sammy was still on her shoulders.
"So, what have you been up to little man, have you had fun?" He gave a smile and nodded.
"I peed in the pool." Anthony froze in the kitchen; Gem gave a big smile.
"When mum was in the hot tub, she farted, and when I popped the bubble, it smelt horrible." Deb's turned looking horrified.
"GEM!" Chloe giggled.
"I did one once in there, and it bubbled like a gargling crocodile." All the kids laughed, as Deb's looked at her going beetroot.
"Chloe, do not encourage him, it is bad enough Jimmy is always

making wise cracks that should not be known about by children." Chloe shrugged.

"We all fart, and mine was spectacular that day, well, I was impressed, and even Birch laughed." Gem gave another giggle; Debs rolled her eyes and looked at the children.

"Okay, Kids, places." They scattered, and headed for their seats, and sat down, Deli and Deb's began to serve up the meal, as they all looked excited and happy.

I was happily typing when two long slender white arms came around me, and I felt her head on my shoulder. I leaned slightly over to her as I finished my sentence, and then lifted my arms up, and gave a happy sigh, she turned and softly kissed my neck and I shuddered, her voice was so soft.

"I am sorry, normally I would not disturb you, but I heard you typing, and came in to see you here tapping away, and I had an unbelievable desire to just hold you. I am so happy you are writing again Sweetie." I turned my head and softly kissed her.

"It feels good, I have really missed it, I have needed this for a long time. Maybe I needed to get out of the house to focus, I am not sure, I just know it feels wonderful." She slipped back a little and kissed my head.

"I will make coffee, I could eat, what about you, shall I order something?" I sat back, and watched as she filled the little room kettle.

"Do you know what I would really love?" She turned and her eyes sparkled.

"Sweetie, you are going to wear me out." I gave a giggle, as her eyes twinkled.

"That would be nice, but I think the best thing ever would be to put on the wigs, and go for a walk, and buy some fish and chips, and then just walk, talk and eat them." Her eyes sparkled, and for the first time in a very long time she bounced on her heels.

"Sweetie, I would love that, oh I want to do that." It was nice to see it, I had missed it so much, and in a silly little sort of way, it made me happy.

With giggles and chuckles, we headed into the bedroom, and I gave a sigh of relief as Birch pulled out her boot cut jeans, a top, and denim shirt. We messed about laughing and then pulled on our wigs with masses of giggles. When we were finally ready and chuckling, just for laughs we snook out of the side door, just like we had that day of the live event in London, much to Katie's annoyance.

Arm in arm we walked up the street, and I smiled as I remembered Roni and her high pitched squeaks, as she saw us and laughed, I gripped Birch's arm, and looked at her.

"Birch, did you ever find out what your mum did with that picture of us that first day we dressed as pop tarts?"

Birch glanced at me, her long red hair lifting slightly in the gentle breeze, and gave a sigh.

"Oh Deads, don't ask." I frowned.

"Why not?" Her eyes moved back to me.

"The bitch had it made into a calendar, and sent it to everyone accept us for New Year. I believe your mum hung it in her bedroom, because every time she looked at it, she had to run to the toilet, she laughed so hard. She still has it in a box under her bed." I gasped with shock.

"Jesus Birch, why didn't you tell me?" She smirked.

"I got my own back, I made a calendar of twelve naked pictures she had hidden, especially with one, where she was drunk in Italy, and had climbed up a fountain of a nude man. She held his neck and pretended she was screwing him. I sent that to all of her friends and relatives. Your mum told me she nearly fainted when she saw it, my great aunt did." She giggled. I was shocked.

"Holy shit, was she mad at you?" Birch sniggered.

"No, she has no shame, she autographed it and sent one to Izzy at the retreat, it is in her office still today, she loves it." I giggled.

"Wow she is pretty cool, God, I would die if someone did that with pictures of me." Birch stopped and stared at me, she swallowed hard, I felt the cold prickle of terror run down my back as I stared at her.

"Oh God... Birch... Please tell me you have not made one of us and sent it out?" I could feel the blood draining from my body with terror.

"Yeah... About that." I let go of her arm and stepped back, I could feel a panic attack coming on, and shook my head.

"Oh God, what did you do?" She gave a snigger, and smiled.

"Oh, you are just too easy, oh you silly." I gripped my heart, and breathed out as she gave a cackle of a laugh.

"Jesus Birch don't do that; you just scared the shit out of me." She leaned in and kissed me.

"You are just too easy, it takes all the fun out of it, sorry Sweetie." She kissed the side of my cheek and laughed out loud. I took a few deep breaths; she had scared the hell out of me. She smiled.

"Sweetie relax, I only made one out of all the filthy sketches Chloe did of the Curio's, it was very well received." I gave another loud gasp.

"WHAT! Christ Birch, does Deb's know, oh my God, she will freak if she finds out?" Birch shrugged.

"It was a great calendar; I personally loved the one with Brent blowing off Anthony as Michael ploughed him from behind. The one with you sat on the sawing horse, well, I mean, that was an amazing sketch, although thinking back, I am not sure it should have been October, what do you think?" I was stood frozen staring at her, and heading back towards cardiac arrest.

"What the fuck is wrong with you, why would you do that, Jesus Birch, what if that gets out, you know the press will lap it up?" She smiled.

"I didn't really." I gave a long gasp; I was freaking out.

"No, I only sent it to Chloe, Edwina, Deli and Deb's, oh, and your mum." And I was freaking the fuck out again.

"Birch are you insane, Christ, I don't want my mum or... Oh hell, did Patrick see me masturbating?" I was sweating, what the hell was wrong with her? I leaned forward to breathe.

"Birch, you watching me masturbate is kind of sexy and fun, but Patrick?" I stood up, and felt sick.

"Oh God, what if he wanked off to it?" I was shaking.

Birch gave a hysterical laugh and snatched me into her arms, and I could feel her tummy wobbling, my heart was pounding inside me, she giggled in my ear.

"Oh Deads Sweetie, I do love you, but honestly, you are so easy to wind up." I took a deep breath, and tried to calm down.

"Seriously, Birch, tell me the truth, is this a wind up, because I think I am having a panic attack?" She leaned back and kissed me softly.

"Deads, I am just playing with you; I would never embarrass

you like that." She looked at me with a smirk on her face, and raised her eyebrows.

"Although, is it weird that I found the thought of Patrick wanking off to your pictures strangely erotic?" I looked at her with utter disbelief.

"You know you are messed up right?" She gave a loud cackle of a laugh, and dragged me off to find a chip shop.

We had such a great evening, walking as we ate chips and fish with our fingers, and talked about everything. It has been such a long time since we had done this, and once again I saw that quiet side of her, and listened to her soft infectious chuckle. It is strange, for the last four months I had thought I was losing her and we were drifting apart, and yet walking and talking and listening to her, it felt the same as it always had, like nothing had changed since I was eighteen.

We screwed up our used papers, and she dug out the baby wipes, and we cleaned our fingers, then hand in hand we walked back to the hotel, to see the press were there. The word was out, we had been discovered, and Birch took my hand and led me down to the car park, so we could use the internal elevator to avoid them. I gave a sigh as we got back to our room, and flopped in my chair.

"I thought we would get longer, I really hoped we could avoid them for at least a week." Birch rubbed my shoulders.

"I know Sweetie, it has been nice, just us two alone with the space to talk, but you know what, maybe it is time to go home." I nodded; she was right. I lifted my hand and clicked save on my document.

"You pack, I will sort the bill out, and then let's head home." She leaned down, and kissed my head.

"YUK!!" She spat and screwed up her face.

"Fake hair, and it tastes musty." She spat again, and I giggled as I stood up, she is so bonkers, she spat again.

"Sweetie it's not funny, it tastes horrible, I don't like it."

Chapter 8

Sad Partings.

I let Birch drive. Wearing dark glasses and baseball caps, with our hair up, she sped out of the car park, and turned away from the mass of exploding camera's. They know my number plate, I lifted my phone to the dash, and it connected.

"Call Edwina." My phone bleeped, and then the phone rang, she picked up at the other end.

"Abby, are you alright?"

"Edwina, we are on our way back to the house, the press have found us, so we are coming home, get the gates open, we will not be long."

"Will do, I will get Michael and Luke to clear the road, Abby there is a lot of them, Anita is here, she just got back from Manchester, she just said she will wait for you."

"Okay, we should be about twenty minutes."

"We are on it, Abby, drive safe."

I giggled, if only she knew that my psychotic wife was finally behind the wheel, and we were heading back at speed.

Is it strange that we now have a whole range of strategies in place to deal with press? It is ridiculous really, but that is the life that Birch and myself have to live by. As we hit Waterside Lane, and our dark glasses went back on, Birch skilfully maneuvered the car through the gates, as Michael and Luke pushed reporters out of the way. The flashes exploded and shouts and screams could be heard, I just looked down, and left Birch to it, she was well practiced in this, and of course completely bonkers, so she just drove at them.

We finally made it inside, and gave a sigh of relief as Luke grabbed our bags, Anita pulled me into a hug.

"I am glad you are safe, I was so worried about you, honestly, I would have handled you both, you know that? Oh Abby, I wished you had not left, I am so disappointed to lose you." She did look so sad, but I gave her a smile.

"Anita, you have not lost me, we are friends, and we will work loads with D&D." It did not really do much to lift her spirits.

"I know Abby, but it will not be the same, I love our day to day working partnership." Birch leaned in.

"Sweetie, I will keep you busy, I will act all crazy and psychotic to keep you on your toes." Deb's grinned at me as I smirked.

"She does know she does not have to act, doesn't she?" I smiled, and pulled her into another hug.

"I have missed you Deb's, it is nice to see you back home, where are the kids?" Her eyes moved up.

"They are in bed, the new bunk beds in Izzy's old room are a big hit, Jimmy is up there reading to them."

The kids' room, was once again Birch's idea. We have two sets with pink sheets, and two sets with blue, and they are placed on opposing walls, so girls get one half, and the boys the other. With six kids in the house, it can get busy, so at night, they all share one huge room, and to date it has been a hit. Edwina and Deli have kept their rooms, and they do stay occasionally, but nowhere near as much as they used to.

Edwina handed me a coffee, and I turned, and saw Chloe sat on the floor in her studio, she was watching me. I smiled and walked down the kitchen, and she gave me the hugest of smiles.

"Chloe, I want to see that ring, just to make sure I am not dreaming." She jumped up and came quickly towards me, she looked happier than I have ever seen her, and I have no idea why, but my eyes filled with tears.

"Oh Chloe, I am so unbelievably happy for you."

I felt her arms come around me and hug me so tightly, as I threw mine around her and gave her the biggest hug ever.

"Wow, who would have thought after all our millions of conversations, you found him, and he was already at your side. God Chloe, I am so happy." She leaned back and her eyes were more alive than I have ever seen them.

"Thanks... You know, when we talked, I was terrified the other night, but when we talked again in your hotel room, you really made me see things in a way I have never looked at. Honestly Abby, without you, I would never have said yes, and I am so glad I did." I was lost for words and just cried; she smiled and lowered her voice.

"I see she is back; I am so thrilled Abby. See, I told you, you two belong together, you fought good girl, and look, you are both free of her now. Just live Abby, both of you, just be who you have always been, you know I hate to point this out, but you both forgot." I nodded and pulled her back into a hug.

"I love you Chloe, be so happy the world shines around you." She giggled.

"I could put glitter on my tits if that helps?"

I chuckled, and squeezed her harder. Birch appeared and pulled her into a hug, and I left them to talk, and came back up to the island and lifted my cup, Anita was watching me, I knew that look.

"No, you are no longer my agent." She gave a sigh.

"The press won't leave until you do Abby." I gave a sigh.

"Do I have to?" She giggled.

"Give me one more time to be your publicist, call it a parting gift." She was making this impossible for me to refuse.

"Okay, one last gig together, and no more." She chuckled.

"Good, when you rang saying you were coming back, I rang your mum to borrow the church hall keys. Tabs is there now with Morty and Creamy setting things up. We have forty minutes to get ready." I gave a sigh.

"God, I hate agents." She giggled.

Forty nine minutes later, having washed and got ready with Birch, we stood at the bottom of the steps with Tabby and my mum. She was worried about me, after all I had been out of touch, and the press had pretty much attacked me.

Anita walked up on to the stage, where a long table had been set up, with microphones. Edwina was at the lighting desk, and had a small camera set up, to stream the press conference live to my web site. Anita made her usual introduction, and I slipped on my mirrored glasses, and took a huge deep breath, Birch took my hand and squeezed it, and we walked up the steps and onto the stage, and boom, there was an explosion of flashes.

We sat down side by side, and I prepared to make my statement, and at this point I have to say, I have grown to hate the sound of camera shutters clattering. I looked up.

"Ladies and Gentlemen of the press, there has been too much speculation about recent days, so I would like to address the issues that have been presented before me. Can I firstly say, I never read the garbage you write." I looked at my sheet.

"Firstly, I am tired, and I have been so busy, I have not written a word of new material in eight months. My last book tour was a hard one, and I am run down, unwell, and simply exhausted. Yes, I have decided to part company with the Dixon Group, and it has not been the huge break up all of you have speculated about in your papers, I simply wanted a change. I have spoken to Veronica Dixon, and it was a nice happy friendly conversation, so I am sorry to disappoint you. It has been a sad occasion, as for myself, this will be the last time that Anita Dickinson represents me, and she has become more than just an agent and someone I relied on, she has become a very dear friend, and I will actually miss her a great deal." I lifted the glass of water off the table and took a sip, it was gin, I smiled.

"As for breaks ups and divorce, for God's sake, please find something original to write about, as you can see, and as you plastered all over today's papers, one does not kiss a partner you are divorcing. Sadly, for you, we are both very happy and still committed to each as we have always been, and may I add, will celebrate our tenth wedding anniversary shortly, so please just stop with the nonsense." I sat back, and the room was silent, Birch gave a quiet snigger, Anita pointed.

"Julie Kent, Daily Informer. Both of you, when pictured in today's picture kissing, it was stated that you Doctor Dixon were crying, if you are both so happy why? Is it not true that you were crying because you thought Abigail had left you?" Birch shook her head.

"Miss Kent, have you any idea what our life has been like? We have hardly been in a room together in six months, yes, I cried, I had no idea she was picking me up, and was so happy to see her, I burst into tears. That is not very uncommon you know, and I do, I am a therapist. I am sorry we were so happy; I am sure you would prefer we fight, but that is just not the case."

"But you walked out of the conference in Paris and Katie O'Reilly delivered your speech." Birch gave a smile.

"I was not meant to be there, the Dixon Group were not aware

I was, and I was fed up and pissed off about it, and just wanted to be home with Abby, so I left." She looked lost for words. Anita pointed.

"Thomas Jennings. National Daily News: Abby, you look really tired, what are your plans, because there is the TV production of seeds of summer and Curio Live USA? Are you going to be well enough to do them, because a lot of people are concerned you are not?" Birch chuckled as I leaned into the mic.

"Thomas, the Curio's is a massively important aspect of who I actually am. There is no way on this earth I would miss it, seriously, if I was ill in bed, I would make them wheel it on the stage so I could play my part."

"Oh, I would totally do that Sweetie." I giggled as did other reporters.

"Look, I am tired, and I am burned out a little, but I am now completely free of commitments, and what I intend to do, is rest and write, nothing else. When the time comes, I will walk on that stage and lead the charge of the Curio's into America, and I will love every minute of it." Anita pointed; I smiled as I saw who she was pointing to.

"Janet Banks, Lifestyle Magazine. Miss Watson, you have left the Dixon Group, where does that leave your books, and any new work you do, will that be a D&D thing now, because it does look very much like you are distancing yourself from what was in fact the family business?" I smiled.

"Miss Banks, I really love your hair, I do think auburn is your colour. Anything I have published with Dixon, is staying there, as for new works, when I actually get them written, I have an idea of how I want to present that, but it will not be with D&D, that is a promotions and event company, not a publisher. When I decide, I will ensure all of you know, for now, I am just enjoying some home life and relaxing and not in a rush to return to public life."

"No offence Miss Watson, but what about your fans, they have been very loyal to you?" I gave a nod.

"I love my fans, and yes, they are loyal, and they are actually my number one priority, as I am sure many reporters screaming my name at events have been frustrated by. As I said, I have something in mind, and they will be the first to know through my website, which is actually carrying this live as we speak.

Understand, to me, they come first, and then everything else after. I have nothing new to offer, and I want to fix that by writing for them, which I will now do. They are very precious to me, and I will never hurt them, and that is where my thoughts are." Anita pointed.

"Jessie Everet, American freelance. Doctor Dixon, can we have an update on Curio Live, as it has been a long time coming, and a lot of us over the water are very excited?"

"Oh Sweetie, we are excited to. At the moment it is going well, we have a lot of people offering their time and services. River TV as you know, have a sister company in the USA and they are handling all the promotion and set up over there, and we are talking to them every day. There will be a lot of merchandise available, most of it designed by Chloe, and I don't want to give too much away just yet, but we will have a lot of surprises, even some the Curio's do not know yet. So, all I can say is wait and see, but we can assure you, it will be worth watching." She giggled. "I am getting very excited." Anita leaned into the mic.

"Ladies and gentleman that is all for now, if you wish to know more, you have my number, and Doctor Dixon will be available for extra questions at a later date. Tonight, concludes my role as publicist for Abigail Jennifer Watson, and can I just say, it has been the biggest thrill of my life to work with her. I have learned so much from her, and she has been an inspiration and I will always be very grateful to her for that. From tonight onwards I will be the official representative for Doctor Jemima Dixon, and I am really looking forward to working alongside her. Thank you for your time, and we will see all of you at the next one."

I turned and saw tears in Anita's eyes, and it hurt to see it, I stood still for a moment, and Birch understanding stepped out of the way. I pulled her in to a hug and heard her sob.

"I am sorry Abby, I did not want to cry, but I am really going to miss you, it has been the best ten years of my life representing you. It has been such fun, and for me, a dream come true."

The camera's rattled off picture after picture, as I leaned back, and held up her face, and smiled.

"I was honoured to work with you; there is no doubt in my mind you are the best in your field. Anita, this is not goodbye, we are friends for life, and I will always be there if you need me. Thanks for everything, you literally changed my working life, and made it a happy one. Hey, look on the bright side, we still have D&D, so this is not the end." She smiled.

"I love you Abby, I have loved every second." I smiled, and she wiped her eyes.

"Me too, come on, we need a drink."

She smiled and nodded, and I took her hand and Birch's and we left the stage. Anita wiped her tears as Tabby hugged her, and smiled at me, I understood. I hated leaving her too, but I knew, I had to make a clean break, and sadly, Anita was a part of that, and the most painful part of the process.

There are two great things about knowing our Vicar Gail, the first being, the Church Hall backs on to the Vicarage, and the second being it has a gate from the back of the hall, through the vicarage garden. We snook out, we knew the press would be waiting, and secretly jumped in our car that was parked next to the gate to the show field. Gail and Floyd jumped in, with us, as the nannie was watching their little one, and soon with a lot less reporters, we rolled in through the gates to home, Anita and Tabby were right behind us.

We all arrived back home, and drinks were poured, as we stood in the kitchen and talked, Anita was back on the job sat talking with Birch, as the others larked around, but seeing Anita so upset had got to me. I hated leaving her behind, I really wanted to poach her, and had I been with any other publisher, I would have, but I simply could not do the dirty on Roni.

I slipped out of the kitchen, and walked up to the library, it was empty, and I sat in my seat and clicked on my computer, I leaned back in my chair as it booted up, and sipped my drink, as the computer linked to my laptop upstairs and started to update all the new story files. The door creaked and I looked up, Tabby smiled.

"Have you got a minute?"

I gave a nod and waved her in. Tabby slipped in and closed the door behind her, she came round and sat in Birch's chair, and she smiled as she looked at me with dark eyes.

"Abby, I wanted to thank you." I frowned.

"What for?" She gave a soft smile and leaned on the desk.

"She is hiding it well, but she is devastated, because you will never know how much her job has meant to her working for you. I have been with her a long time, and I have seen how much your influence has rubbed off on her. You know, I am not sure you are aware of this, but you have been her idol and her mentor, and she has learned so much working with you, not just as a publicist, but as a person. She has cried for the last few days, she is so broken hearted, but she does understand, she has been worrying about you for several months now behind the scenes. You probably do not know this, but she has had some very big rows with Katie behind the scenes to try and get her to ease up on Jemi." I knew nothing of it, and gave a sigh.

"Tabby, I am not sure I can take this, honestly it is killing me, leaving her behind is the hardest part of all this, but she works for the Dixon Group. At the moment, I have no definite path, she will be without work, which is why I asked Roni to let her take on Birch, it will keep her close to us." She reached over and patted my leg.

"She understands that, she does, and I know she has D&D and so this is not the end, but she loved getting up every day, knowing she was working for you, she was a fan girl long before she met you. You know she once told me, that it impressed you that she had prepared so much to meet you by reading all your blogs, Abby, she had been reading them as you posted them. She read handed death when you first published it, and bought everyone as they came out, and they are so tatty, she has read them so many times. She is a massive fan, so working for you, has been a dream come true, and it has made me so happy to watch it." I felt a lump in my throat.

"I love her Tabby, I love her like a sister, I have always thought of her as one of us, and I always rang her first when we got great news. You know Katie was making my life hell, and I was seriously thinking of just quitting writing, but then she came along, and to be honest she was gutsy. She just walked in stated her case and then gave me a list of others who she said were almost as good as her, and that was when I knew I would work with her, and I am so glad I did. My life has been so much easier with her on my side, I wish I could give her more, but I have no direction at the moment, and as yet only a few ideas of what I want to do. Tabby, I really need a break, I need to write and relax with Birch for a while." She gave a nod.

"We both know that, and she is glad you will get it. Abby, do you know the story of how we ended up together?" I shook my head.

"No, we were on holiday, and she took you to bed, is about as much as I know." Tabby giggled.

"I won't deny, I fancied her like hell, and I was not sure if she was straight or gay, so I hit on her and hoped. I invited her to my room, and on the nightstand was Sanctuary Arch, and she picked it up. Honestly, I just wanted to tear her clothes off, but she started to talk about the book, and suddenly it was two hours later, and we had been like a pair of fan girls all night. When she said she worked with writers, I had no idea it was actually you. We had sex in the early hours of the morning, simply because we ended up talking about seeds of summer and got really turned on. I knew then, I did not want to let her escape, so I asked her to meet me later, which was on the nudist beach, and bugger me, if you weren't just sprawled out in the sun. Honestly, I was blown away. Her love of your work was so deep and passionate, it really turned me on, and became the reason we got and stayed together, we have been a right pair of fan girls ever since. She has twenty eight Abigail t shirts which she wears at home when not working." Tabby gave a wicked grin.

"Don't tell her you know that; she will kill me. Her favourite hoodie is the carnival hoodie you gave her. I mean, the thing is worn out, and full of holes, but she will never throw it away. This has been her dream job, and without realising you have made her really happy, and I am really grateful to you for that, because I love my life with her, and I love seeing her smile." I gave a long sigh and leaned back.

"God Tabby, you have not made this easier on me." She shook her head.

"Do not misunderstand me Abby, we both think you need the rest, and you need to write, and no one understands that better than her. Jemi will be good for her too, and I actually think a change will do her good, but I wanted you to simply understand, how much joy you have given her, and as I said, thank you for it." I smiled.

"I get that, I do, and I am grateful, you know it was a two way street, she gave me as much joy, working without the pressure of Katie made a massive difference to my life. Even now, I still feel I owe her so much for that."

"Abby you are free, just enjoy your time, and write something epic for us to lust over and rave about." I gave a giggle.

"I will, you can be sure of it." She patted my leg.

"Awesome, I will really look forward to it, and just so you know, I still want that book you started at Sunny Bank, I have not forgot." I giggled at her excited eyes.

She leaned over and kissed my cheek, and then got up and left the room closing the door quietly behind her. I sat back lost in thought and smiled, Tabby was right, I had equally as much fun with Anita. I remembered so much of working with her for Dixon and D&D. God, we had done some laughing, and messing about, and the crazy thing was, the only reason I could break free and set up my own publishing imprint, was because I learned it all from her.

Anita, bless her, has taught me everything, and actually was the one who has given me the confidence to achieve my oldest dream. I leaned forward, and clicked the file on my computer, and it opened, I gave a little giggle as I clicked back to the first page and read the title. 'The Publicity Girl.'

I scrolled down to the dedication page, which was blank, and wrote. 'For my biggest fan girl, and her twenty eight T shirts.' I clicked the page link and went back to where I left off, which read, 'Chapter Thirty Nine.' I dropped the line and wrote in the chapter title. 'One Last Night of Press.' I smiled as I started to write, this had been a book that was ten years in the making, and it had been written on all those free moments I had over the years in hotels, or home waiting for her calls. It was in a sense our autobiography, except the writer was Jane Aston, and the publicist Beth Waters.

Even though it was a story of fiction, it was actually our story, of how I thought she was the enemy, and she became one of my most valued friends, as I worked with her on all sorts of crazy adventures in the world of writing. The crazy thing was, it was fast and funny, and really gripping, and not one word of it was fiction, but most importantly, it was my tribute to a most amazing woman.

Edwina leaned on the door and smiled as Anita and Birch came up the hall, she gave a slight giggle, and beckoned to them. Birch understood, and tip toed up, and Edwina pushed the door so it opened a crack, and Birch and Anita looked in. Edwina gave a smile and whispered.

"It is a long time since we have seen that, look how happy she looks." Anita watched with amazement.

"I have never seen her when she is actually writing, wow, look how happy she looks." Birch smiled as she watched.

"I never get tired of seeing that, oh you have no idea how turned on I get watching her like this, it is like she is on some spiritual plane, and communicating everything through her mind. Oh god, I am getting wet." Anita stepped back.

"I am taken, and we have a contract that forbids it." Edwina giggled.

"I love seeing her like that, because actually, that is the real Abigail Jennifer Watson."

I was hammering away completely unaware of everything, living the words and travelling through time, and the happiest I had been in a very long time, Birch smiled.

"She is finally free, and is living again, now she can write."

It was late when I finished, the book was finally done. I saved the file, and then plugged in my flash drive and made a copy, I pulled it out, slipped it in my pocket, flicked off the light and headed upstairs.

Birch was still up sat at her desk reading and typing, I walked in and yawned, as I looked at her.

"You are up late." She looked up.

"Not really, it is not even one yet, the others all left early, I think we are all too old to party all night." I flopped over her shoulder and kissed her neck.

"Yeah, we have become old women now." She giggled.

"Hardly, and anyhow, don't they say life begins at forty?" I smiled, considering I was a few months away, it was a nice thought.

"I am not ready to be old, not yet, I still got lots of naughty left." She gave a giggle.

"Now you are talking my language Sweetie, we had fun tonight, it was nice, the girls missed you, but they all understood. Although Deli and Anthony were not here, and you know maybe it is just me, but it does appear hard to get all of us in one room."

"Deb's said Deli was here most of the day, she left because Eric was unhappy about something, and where is Anthony?" Birch leaned back.

"He has gone to visit Michael's uncle; they will be gone over night." I nodded, and leaned back and slid my hand in my pocket, Birch spun round in her chair.

"So how is the writing going, you looked really into it when I looked in?" I pulled the flash drive out of my pocket, and handed it to her, she looked confused.

"I finished it, that is one of two I need to finish." She stared at the drive in her hand.

"You wrote a book in three days?" I gave a chuckle as I walked to the bed, and sat down and undid my jeans.

"No, hell I wish I could. I have been working on that since I finished Shoots of Summer, I finished it tonight. It will need editing, and so forth, but yep, it is a completed first draft. I have another story I started years ago, I think I will get back onto that one next, I think I only have ten or so chapters to go." Birch looked blown away.

"Sweetie, Shoots of Summer was ten years ago, how come it has taken so long?" I slid off my jeans and gave a happy groan of pleasure.

"I did not know the ending until tonight." I flopped back on the bed and relaxed.

"What is it about?" I yawned; I was exhausted.

"Read it and see, I think it will be a good start to a new imprint, and something unexpected." I sat up and pulled off my top.

"Don't stay up too late reading, it makes you grumpy." I slid up the bed and pulled the duvet up, and slid down under it, and gave a titter. I knew her so well as she spun round in her chair and plugged the drive into her desktop, she was possibly my biggest fan girl.

I lay back and heard her gasp as she read the title, I snuggled into the pillows, and watched her turn in her seat.

"Sweetie, is this about you and Anita?" I gave her a smile.

"Yeah, it is our story, written in the same style as Shoots of Summer." She gave me a huge smile.

"Oh Deads, what a lovely thing to do, you know she cried tonight, she is so upset to have lost you, honestly, I feel mean taking her on for me. Is there no way you can keep her on?" I gave my head a shake.

"Birch, I will not screw your mum over, she works for the Dixon Group, I am no longer their author, keep her with you, and with D&D. I want her close, you know, I am really going to miss her, she was my ideal publicist, I will never find another as good as her." Birch gave a sigh, she understood, her eyes twinkled.

"So, what is this about?" I frowned at her.

"Birch, it is our story, written from a fictional stance."

"Cool."

She spun in her chair, and looked at her screen, and then she started to read, I relaxed, and just enjoyed resting and closed my weary eyes. Life was good again, as I breathed out happily. 'Say hello to the night' I opened my eyes.

"I don't believe it, what now?" I grabbed my phone and clicked answer.

"Hello!"

"Abby, oh Abby, it's Louise from the Tea Rooms." I sat bolt up in bed, suddenly I was wide awake.

"Louise, what is the matter?" Birch spun around in her chair.

"Abby, we lost her, we lost Lillian."

"What?"

I felt the tears fill my eyes, as I looked up at Birch and gave a sob, Louise was on the phone breaking her heart and trying to talk. Birch was up on her feet; her voice held a sense of urgency.

"Sweetie, what is wrong?"

I felt a huge pain travel up my insides and into my throat, and I gave a massive painful sob, as I looked up at Birch, and found it hard to talk, and my voice was quiet and trembled.

"I lost Lilly." I broke down as Birch grabbed my phone.

Chapter 9

Lillian's Last Trip.

The next few days were terrible, I felt utterly lost and broken hearted, Birch was the same. We wanted to go straight to Celia, but Louise told us she had been collected at the hospital and taken to her sisters. The truth was, there really was nothing we could do, and it hurt so badly, I found it hard to not constantly burst into tears.

Lillian, had suffered a stroke, she was seventy two and still working every day, I could not believe it. Birch managed to get Celia on the phone, she was utterly devastated, which was to be expected. They had been together for almost fifty years, and had started sleeping together in a time when it was taboo to do so. It was something I had always admired about them, they were devoted to each other, and had hidden it away for a very long time, but no matter what, they had stayed true to their feelings and each other.

In many ways, they had been the example that had helped me come to terms with my feelings for Birch. After that first summer with Birch, and then coming home alone, when most people called me, and trashed me as I walked around the village, Lillian had always made a point of stopping me to ask how I was.

I remember one afternoon, after being home for just over four years, I met her outside the book shop, and she asked me if I would like to walk with her, I was so lonely at that time, and in so much pain, and she smiled and took my hand, and walked me down to the canal. We stood at the bridge and looked out over it. Lillian looked at me with a sad smile, and held my hand.

"Abigail, you are such a lovely girl, and I can see you have so much love inside you, I am worried about you, you must take better care of yourself. Abigail, I taught English for many years, I think I have a good sense of people, and I think, you will find that she will come back, she will come looking. Abigail, the feelings you have should not be hidden, and you should let go and let them out."

I shook as I stood there, and the tears rolled onto my face, as I sobbed, I really wanted to, I missed her so badly, and this was the first time anyone understood.

"Lillian, I want to, honestly, I do, but she is not into women. If I tell her, I will lose her forever, and I am so utterly scared of losing her." She gave my hand a squeeze, and pulled out a handkerchief, and handed it me.

"Abigail my dear sweet child, how can you possibly think that? Oh dear, I thought you knew Birch well. Look Abigail, I have been around a long time at the side of Celia, and we have seen it all, we know who will, and who won't. When you have lived with a hidden secret like we have, you learn very quickly, and to be honest my girl, if I honestly thought Birch did not love you, I would not be standing here talking. Abigail, the girl adores you, it shines out of her like a beacon, can you not see it?" I shook my head.

"To be honest Lillian, no, I have so many doubts about everything except her, but I am terrified she will not want me if I say something. I miss her so much Lillian, it hurts, and Madge will not leave me alone, and without Birch, I feel afraid to speak up to her." She smiled a sad smile at me.

"We know, we have seen how bad it is, but Abigail, just think of Birch and speak your mind, she is there inside you wrapped up in all those wonderful feelings you hold for her. Abigail, Celia and I talk a lot, and whether or not you believe it, one day, it will be you who stands up and heads the council, and when you do, she will be right at your side, trust me, I know people." I smiled at her and wiped my eyes.

"My dad has always said you were the best English teacher he ever had, and my mum has always spoken of you fondly. Lillian, I would love to be up there with her, I really would, but at the moment, I am struggling just to get through each day without her, it hurts more each day she is not here. I mean, I know I am being selfish, she has to finish her doctorate, but I really am missing her. I was with her every day at Uni, and now I am so lonely without her here." I started to cry again. She gave her head a nod.

"Abigail you must not lose hope, no matter how hard it gets, believe in her. Do you think after that summer and all the goings on, plus two years together side by side do not count? Abigail, dear child, they count for everything, you will see, a day will come when she will breeze into this village, and it will be like she never left, and my best advice to you, is take better care of yourself, and wait, she is coming, trust me."

I sat back on the bed, and wiped my eyes as Birch wept, Birch sat opposite her eyes filled with tears.

"She knew Birch, and she believed in us both, and she was so right, because that day came, and you came hurtling into town, and swept me into your arms, and we have been together ever since. I have no idea how she knew, but she was even right about the council. That day changed me, after that, it became my dream, my heart's desire. I knew, if you did come back, I was going to tell you, I was not going to hide anymore, I was going to listen to Lilly, and look you in the eye and tell you I was in love with you. Birch, she changed my life, it is why I wanted so badly to be your Lillian, I wanted to be just like her, with the same devotion as she had to Celia, and I have been." I wiped my eyes as Birch sat sobbing.

"Birch we will have to go soon, and honestly, I am not sure I am strong enough to say goodbye to her, I really do not want to." Birch stood up and dried her eyes.

"We must Deads, we owe her that, and so much more. Take my hand, be my Lillian and honour her words. Come on Sweetie, we have to go."

It is funny, it has been impossible to get all the Curio's in one spot for a good few years. Today, on one of our saddest days, Birch and I walked hand in hand across the green towards the Tea Rooms, and there they were, all stood together in black, awaiting us. I suppose the Tea Rooms, has played a massively important role in the lives of the Curio's, it is where we have gathered and met up, where we have laughed so hard, we spilled our drinks, or gasped for air as we choked in shock. It is also where I faced my darkest moment of life, as I held a bleeding Birch, and Lillian and Celia phoned the ambulance that saved her.

We have argued with Madge, and they were always there in the background silently supporting us, using the gossip network with pure skill, as we fought for the right to be us. They always encouraged us to simply be us, and stand up for what we believed in, and walk proud.

Birch and I have often said, the players may change, but the village will always remain the same, but today, a change so vast will happen, the village will never be the same again, at least, not for me. Lillian will no longer be in the Tea Rooms, rattling her tea cups as Birch makes sexy comments, and saying things like 'Oh My' as she shakes with the thrill, or 'Oh Dear' as she swallows hard and contemplates a sexual advance from Birch. It will never feel right without her. No, today, the village will change for me forever. I felt the sadness intensify as I approached the group with the heaviest heart I have ever felt. Everyone nodded with red eyes, but little was said.

Bev wiped her eyes as she looked at me, she was dressed in a suit of black, and honestly, I have never seen her look so good. She blew her nose and tried to smile, but her eyes were as red and puffy as all of ours. I saw her tears fill her eyes, and it was heart breaking.

"I bloody loved her to bits Deadly; I shagged her and Celia a good few times, and she was a fine old bird, I tell ya, God, she knew how to make me cum."

Deb's looked horrified and gave a shudder, Anthony looked positively appalled, and shuddered, Birch gave a little snigger. I cannot deny, it made me smile. I lifted my hand and touched her arm.

"We all loved her Bev, in different ways obviously, but she was special, there was no doubt." Birch looked solemn as she put her arm round Bev's waist.

"She was a wonderful person Bev, who did not miss a trick, I mean, let's be honest, she was one of a few who actually saw Deb's when she had hair down there." There was a loud gasp, and Deb's went purple.

"You said we would never mention that again Birch, I mean, how could you, it was embarrassing?" I tried not to, but Chloe put her head down, and I sniggered as I watched her shoulders shake.

Bev nodded.

"Aye Lilly had a good amount of hair down there; you know, it proper surprised me a woman of her age would have such a hairy minge. I bet I have swallowed a good few of them in me time, I certainly pulled a few out of me teeth."

Anthony screwed up his face, and gave another look of utter disgust, even Michael who was normally quite accepting, looked completely grossed out. Edwina smirked, and Chloe kept staring at the floor, Birch looked away, and I knew she was smiling; I dared not to look as I knew I would laugh too. A tall man in a black suit walked up to us, he looked round at all of us.

"Mrs Dixon?" Birch and myself looked at him.

"Yes." He gave a sad smile.

"Miss Ford Baxter requested that you two accompany Miss Thorpe Willingham. It was her express wish, that Birch and Abigail, joined Celia on her last journey, and that the group of Curio's followed behind, so would you please come with me?"

I looked at Birch and swallowed hard, and suddenly I was very nervous. Birch took my hand, none of us had seen Celia since it had happened, she had been staying at her sister Cissy's house. He led the way, and opened the door to the Tea Rooms, and we walked inside. I was not mentally prepared for this, and I am not sure Birch was.

Celia stood in a black suit, holding a single Lilly next to the long casket, I have no idea why, I did not really know what to do, so I walked right up to her and pulled her into my arms as tears filled my eyes.

"Celia, I am so unbelievably heartbroken and sorry."

She pulled me close and I felt her shake a little as the undertaker closed the door. Birch moved in and hugged her with me, both of us sobbed. Celia's voice quivered as she spoke to us.

"Girls, she really admired and loved you, she wanted you here, she cared deeply about both of you. She always told me she saw you as daughters, because she had no family to speak of, but all those times we had visiting you at home, she said always felt like visiting her girls."

I could not help it, but hearing that just broke my heart, and I sobbed even harder. As did Birch. Celia stroked our hair, and her voice lowered.

"Girls, I need you to be strong for me, she would want that. This is so hard, and I want to be strong for her as I always was, but I need you to help me."

I looked up and tried not to cry, her face was filled with sadness and I hated seeing it. I swallowed hard and nodded at her, and lifted my hankie to dry my eyes. Birch was finding it harder, and she gave a huge sob, and lifted her hankie under her hair as it fell around her face, she gave a sniffle and looked up. Celia smiled at us both.

"That is the spirit, she would like this." I gave a nod and sniffled.

"We will be there for her, she was for me at a difficult time, I will be for her."

Birch gave a nod, but was unable to talk. Celia nodded and turned to the counter. There was a row of shots lined up on the top, Celia looked at Deb' and the others as they all stood weeping.

"All of you, take a glass and we will toast her one last time."

I took a huge deep breath; Birch was finding her composure. We walked up to the counter and all lifted a glass; Celia led us all back to the casket as the undertaker watched on. We stood in a line all facing Lillian. Celia raised her glass.

"To Lillian, all girls together." I smiled and lifted my glass with Birch, and all of us spoke.

"Lillian. All girls together."

We downed it in one, and my throat exploded, this was high quality rum, Chloe coughed and patted her chest.

"Oh My, that was strong." Celia tittered, and I saw her smile, she nodded at Chloe.

"Oh my, indeed." The undertaker stepped forward.

"It is time Ladies."

We all placed a lily each on her casket, as the church bell gave a solemn ring out across the village. Lillian was lifted up, and Celia took hold of mine and Birch's hand, and took a deep breath.

We stood in a line, behind us Bev wept into her hankie, as Anthony and Michael stood either side of her, comforting her, which I thought was really sweet of them. Behind them, Chloe, Deb's, Deli and Edwina waited to follow. Lillian was lifted up, and Celia took a deep breath.

"One last walk together my love, one more walk around the green, this time is for Lilly."

It hurt so much to hear it, and I really tried hard to hold it all in, but it was so hard because my heart was breaking. The procession began, Louise and Stacy stood either side of the door watching with tear filled eyes, and Celia stopped.

"Come girls." She let go of my hand, and reached out to them.

"Walk either side of Birch and Abby, you belong here with her."

I had to agree. Celia took one hand, and Stacy the other, and holding hands we followed Lillian, as she was taken down Green Street, and onto the high street.

The road either side was filled with people, as the bell rang out, and the procession slowly walked around the green and up Church Rise. Bev wailed into her hankie behind us, I had never seen her so moved or upset, as everyone at the sides of the road lowered their heads in a mark of respect. I felt it was nice for her to be honoured this way, Lillian had been a central part of village life, the Tea Rooms was a pivotal part of life around Wotton, everyone at some point paid them a visit, and had a cup of something.

Marjorie stood at the church gates as we approached, I have not seen her for a while, and she looked older, sterner, and also a little frailer, she held a hankie and dabbed her eyes. Regardless of what had happened in our life, for all of the time she had lived in the village, she had always been the first customer of the day, and greeted Lillian and Celia, as they opened up shop, and I could clearly see, that like me, she too felt a deep loss. She gave a nod as she noticed me watching, and I returned it, and felt the gravel of the path crunch, as we entered the church.

Rev Milton stood at the door at the side of Gail, Lillian had requested he play a part, and Gail was happy to let him join her, so he came out of retirement for one more day. He was seventy six years old, and yet as it appeared, still going strong, although he looked very sad, and a little bit frail, as we passed the door, and with Gail, he led us into Church.

The service was sad, but lovely, Gail handled it with such gentleness, and was clearly as upset as all of us, she spoke beautiful words. Birch sat at my side and held my hand, both of us wept buckets, as in front of us, Celia broke down and was comforted by Stacy and Louise.

Gail gave the eulogy, as Celia was incapable, and then the moment came which I had been dreading, Birch had been asked to give a few words on behalf of us all. She got up, and walked to the front, it was so strange seeing her stood in a church, dressed in all black, she faced the front behind the lectern, as Lillian lay behind her.

"Celia, Ladies and gentlemen, this will be so hard for me, but Lilly asked, and how could I refuse?" Her eyes were red and blotchy, and her hair hung down her back, and she looked serene and beautiful.

"When I came to this village for the first time twenty one years ago, I was loud and brash, and I will not deny, I was seen as trouble and a problem. I was young, inexperienced and still very much involved in trying to discover what kind of a woman I was going to be. There was a very important part of me at that time, that I really was not fully aware of, and being here and not being accepted was difficult and challenging for me. Lillian and Celia embraced and accepted me, long before I even accepted myself, and at that time, it meant a great deal to me." She lifted her hankie and dabbed her eyes.

"Over the years I have realised they saw the truth of me, and they did not sit in judgement, if anything they encourage me to be myself. Standing here today, I cannot tell you how hugely important that was to me. Recently, I heard a similar story told to me by my wife, of how Lillian came to her at one of her darkest times, and gave her hope, and the strength to continue."

I felt the tears again as I watched, Lilly would never know how much that meant to me, and I sobbed into my hankie. Birch saw me and filled up, and she too wiped her eyes, her voice was a little broken, but she held it together.

"Each and every member of our Curio family has a similar story of support, encouragement, and the love shown them by Lillian. I am sure as I look around this church today, all of you could say the same." There was a lot of movement, and it was clear a great many had responded.

"That is who Lilly was, she was a teacher, an educator, and a person who had the ability to show and share a great deal of love and kindness. Many times, I have heard the saying, that in Wotton the players may change, but the village will always remain the same, and I have always agreed with that, except today." Birch turned and looked at the casket, covered in flowers, and gave a nod, and then turned back, tears rolled down her cheeks and she struggled a little.

"Today, the village has changed forever, because a very important player has been taken away from us, and it hurts to say, that her loss will be so great, that without the love and the kindness of Lillian Ford Baxter in the Tea Rooms, this village will change forever. Her loss is a mighty blow to this community, and all I can do today, is try to emulate her, and offer, my love, and my support to Celia as a poor substitute. Rest in peace my beautiful soul Lilly, may your spirit walk ever around us, in the love you gave to us all. Thank you."

She burst into tears and headed to me; I pulled her close as she sobbed bitter tears into my shoulder. Gail conducted the rest of the service with a hymn and a prayer, and Rev Wallace gave the blessing, and once again Lilly was carried out of the church, and around the back, where a freshly dug grave was ready.

Rev Wallace walked forward as we all gathered around, and he almost fell over the casket, Gail and Floyd grabbed him in just in time. All of us threw out our arms to catch him, and lent forward, Deb's gave a slight squeal. We all gasped a sigh of relief as we leaned back, with the panic averted, and somewhere behind me I heard Hatty.

"Who let that doddering old bugger out, he does know this is for Lilly doesn't he?"

Birch and I, put our heads down and sniggered, so did Celia, Chloe nudged me in the ribs and gave a small giggle.

"Pack it the fuck in Abby, I always get a rollocking for laughing at funerals." I sniggered again, and felt her shake at my side. Rev Wallace looked round confused.

"Is it this hole?"

"And now we know why he only ever had one child."

"Hatty for the love of God, this is a solemn event."

Chloe sniggered, and I snorted. Birch wobbled at the side of me, and Rev Wallace stood looking at the casket, appearing confused.

"Who is it again, did they say Celia, oh dear, lovely woman, yes, yes, quite lovely." Hatty piped up.

"For fuck's sake, give him his glasses, she is only bloody there right in front of him."

"Hatty shush; will you behave?" Birch blurted out a giggle, and my shoulders shook, Chloe kicked me. Rev Wallace noticed Celia.

"Oh, and there you are, I did wonder." He looked confused and turned to Gail.

"Who is this again?" Gail whispered.

"Oh yes, yes I remember now, small woman, liked tea."

"Praise the fucking lord."

"Hatty, this is a church, will you behave."

"Hey Flick, do not let him bury me, I will probably end up under the bloody green."

Birch lifted her hand to her mouth, and snorted a laugh, I was fighting so hard not to laugh, Chloe gave a little strange squeak, and her shoulders shook and Edwina slapped her, which made Birch laugh even more and set me off. Titters broke out all around us.

Finally, Reverend Wallace got it right, with a lot of help from Gail, who in all fairness had a fixed smirk on her face throughout, the service was completed. We all walked down to the gates, and hugged Celia as we passed through, and then waited in a group. The Tea Rooms was the chosen venue, and caterers had been hired, and today the premises were closed and roped off for the funeral party only.

I stood in the Tea Rooms with a cup of coffee, next to the counter, it felt strange not having Lillian here, as an army of hired staff waited on everyone. Madge came up to us and gave a respectful nod.

"Doctor Dixon, I liked what you said about Lillian, it was very accurate and heart felt, I found it quite moving. Thank you, I feel you showed her immense respect and honour." Birch gave a smile.

"I think Lillian touched the life of everyone one way or another Madge, it felt right to point it out, we loved her dearly as I know you did too, I feel she will not be replaced easily." Marjorie gave a grisly smile.

"I believe you are right Doctor Dixon; I considered her a cherished friend; I will miss her." I looked at Madge.

"We all will Madge." She smiled and nodded.

Isn't it strange, there has been so much that we have disagreed with about each other, and yet there are also things in which we have complete agreement, Lily being one of them. Birch was right, she really was irreplaceable, and her kindness, caring and sweet manner would be hard to replace. I have no idea how Celia will cope without Lillian, I know to be without Birch would destroy me, I had a taste of that once, and I hated it. I turned to Birch and looked at her, she gave a soft smile, as I lifted my hand to her cheek, and she leaned on to it.

She looked tired and worn out, her eyes were red and puffy and duller than normal, and her skin was as white as snow. She had no idea how much she meant, I could write volumes, and still not even remotely touch the tip of the depth of my love for her.

"I cannot imagine being without you, if I lost you, my world would be over. Birch, we have stopped living, all of us have, and we need to start living, because honestly, none of us know how long we have got, and I want to live a life worthy of you." I could see all of the group looking at me.

"A life worthy of all of us, we have become disconnected, and we need to find a way back. We are the Curio's, and that is what we are all about, crazy and chaos, and being true to ourselves living free, and I think it is time we all started acting like us again." Deb's looked at me and gave a sigh.

"That is all well and good for you, but Abby, it is not that simple." I shrugged, and turned to look at her.

"Why not? Deb's I am thirty nine, forty in a few months, but you know what, I am not ready to throw in the towel and get old just yet. I am still filled with life, and I want to live it in true Curio spirit, as me." Everyone was watching me; she shook her head.

"Abby, some of us have kids and may I add, responsibilities, it is just not that easy." I was so surprised at that, it threw me for a second, and to be honest, made me a little angry, and although I didn't mean to, I snapped back.

"What, and I don't? You know what, you all moved out and left me, Birch, Anthony, and Chloe behind. That house costs a fortune to run. Do you remember the all girls together policy, well the four of us have a huge responsibility now, because we run that house? Birch has her business, so does Anthony, and Chloe has her art. Okay, so I have stepped out of the limelight, but I still had the responsibility of someone I really care about losing her dream job, because Anita is heartbroken, and that really hurts me deeply. Do you honestly think because you Edwina and Deli have moved on I do not worry my ass off about you guys, because I do, every minute of every day?" I looked around the circle.

"I am a Curio, hell, I was the reason it all started, and I feel it deeply, and yes, I am knackered like I have never been before. You know what Deb's, if you have so much responsibility then fine, turn around and walk out of that door, walk away, but before you do, go on that site with all those kids. You bloody well tell them straight, it is over, you are quitting, because other things are too important to you. Do it and do it soon, because in just over a month I will be on that plane, and if your life is too hectic, then quit, and I will find someone who can fill your shoes. That is my responsibility Deb's, those kids who keep killing themselves because no one else wants to be responsible for them." Birch grabbed my hand.

"Deads, we get it, look, we are all upset, just leave it." Deb's had tears in her eyes, and everyone else was silent, I gave a sigh.

"I am sorry Debs, Birch is right, I am upset, I am absolutely broken hearted, because daft as it sounds, I never expected Lilian to go yet, and I am hoping none of us do soon. Just take a look around at the pain and the hurt in the eyes of everyone here, just look Deb's. We all feel like this because we knew Lillian and loved her, well ask yourself this, who feels like that for all those kids, who are so alone and so broken, they took their own lives? I feel that Deb's, I love all of you deeply. I get it, I have said enough, but you know what, someone had too, and again, that is my responsibility. I really need to be alone now."

I pushed through them, and walked out of the Tea Rooms, and into the fresh air, I felt angry and upset, and needed to calm down. I walked onto the green, and my heart felt so utterly broken as I burst into tears. Birch looked at Deb's.

"She is upset Sweetie, she really cared about Lilly, you do not know the full story, but she was very important to Deads, and she is in a lot of pain. She thought I was going to leave her alone, and she is still fighting with all that, don't hold it against her." Deb's gave a sniffle, and looked at Birch.

"I love her, she knows that, but honestly Birch, she was right,

I hated her saying it, but Abby does not lie. I have let everyone down, I have let her down, I should have been around. I would have spotted her pain long before any of you, and I should have been there for her to help. I will make it up to her." Birch smiled.

"She loves you Sweetie, she loves all of us just like Lilly, that is what makes her so special." Deb's nodded.

"I know, I love all you guys too."

I reached the bottom of the green, and Birch came running after me, she grabbed my hand and stopped me, I turned, and she pulled me into a hug. I gave a long sigh into her.

"I am sorry, I do not know what came over me." Birch gave a smile.

"From where I was stood it looked like a burst of complete honesty, you were not wrong Deads, they have forgotten what we all once stood for. You were right to point it out, I can think of better places than the middle of a funeral, but hey, that's you." I looked up into her bright green eyes.

"Birch, this has scared me, I am your Lillian, and she is gone. Celia is alone now. I know it sounds daft, but when they lowered her into that hole, that could have been any of us. It came so fast, no one expected it, and it made me realise that you or me or any of the others could be gone that quick. I am not sure I could deal with that, because we have so much life to live, but they are all starting to act like my mum when I was at Uni. They have stopped living, all of us have, well, except Chloe, the rest of us have all let ourselves be ground down and become stifled, we have got to get back, we have to live again, because those kids need us." She smiled.

"You are not wrong Sweetie, but let's take it one step at a time, they all heard you, so they know. Take a break and rest, and let's see what happens, because I somehow think the power of a Dark Little Beastie, is greater than you realise." She leaned down and kissed me softly.

"Take me home, and let's get naked, drunk, and screw like bitches."

"Birch it's not Friday. Uni rules do not apply." Her eyes grew bigger as she moved her face closer.

"Abigail Jennifer Watson, you are my most favourite author,

and do you know what I really want to do at this moment?" I giggled and shook my head, she leaned in close and whispered softly in my ear, I shuddered.

"Oh hell, screw Uni, I left years ago." She gave a squeal, grabbed my hand, and we hurried down the green in the direction of home.

Chapter 10

Deli's Dilemma.

Eric and Deli had done well, between her nursery, and his paint ball company, they had worked hard and bought a house on Garden Street, two doors up from where Deli had grown up. The Alpha team had ruled supreme, apart from one encounter, when the all girls together team had kicked their ass.

With two children, Joshua aged seven, and Elizabeth aged five, like everyone in Wotton, they appeared to be a normal, conservative happy family, but behind the scenes as I was about to find out, there was going to be a big change.

Six years ago, Eric and the Alpha's decided to invest big, and sold the paint ball company, and bought a rundown night club in Oxendale. Gavin was a DJ, and Colin and Peter ran a pub, so with some training, Eric got his liquor licence, and Club Empire was modernised repainted and opened for business, and in the early years it had been a big hit. Trends come and trends go, and Oxendale is a big place, with a lot of clubs, and Team Alpha had become stuck in a rut, as none of them could agree on anything when it came down to how to revive the club.

The problem was made worse by the fact that they spent all day and night at the club, drinking, and partying. Deli was left at home, running her nursery business, which employed six, the house, and taking care of two children, which was mainly why we had hardly seen her in months. Deli and Eric were at breaking point, as the bills piled up, and the profits were being sucked away by the excesses of the Alpha's.

It was a week after the funeral of Lilly, and I had been stuck in the house, Birch had returned to the practice, where most of her clients had been moved to two other new counsellors, June and Mary, and she only saw three clients a week. She was now the head consultant of the practice and three UK based Curio Clinics, as well as being a very successful author. Izzy managed all of the operations with her as usual, and Sweetie's Retreat was a massive and very profitable operation.

The truth was, I was bored, and Deb's was busy, we had a very tearful reunion in my bedroom, where we sat and talked for three hours as I filled her in on all my plans. It felt good to make up with her, I had felt bad for two days, and had been writing like crazy as I finished yet another book, which I handed to Chloe to get an idea for a cover. Deb's needed to get some paperwork to Nigel, and I was bored, so I offered to drop them in to him, they were important for the next big council meeting.

I got myself ready and headed for the door, I came out of my room, as Chloe came very quickly through her bedroom door, closed it hard, and stood looking at it. I stopped, not quite understanding what she was up to, she turned her bedroom door knob, pushed the door a jar and peered in, I frowned and walked up to her, and patted her shoulder.

I kid you not... The scream from Chloe as she shot up into the air, almost burst my ear drums. I will not deny, I jumped with her and also screamed, as it scared the shit out of me. She spun around looking terrified, and gasped.

"ABBY, DO NOT FUCKING DO THAT; YOU SCARED THE LIVING SHIT OUT OF ME!"

She was as white as a sheet, panting, holding her heart, I leaned in to look at her, I felt really concerned.

"Chloe are you alright, you are shaking, and are you sweating?" She swallowed hard.

"I had a fright." I nodded; I understood that.

"Yeah sorry, I thought you had heard me." Chloe shook her head rapidly, and breathed in, and gave a long breath out.

"No Abby, before that." I frowned.

"How do you mean?" Her eyes went really wide, and she swallowed hard again, and wet her lips.

"Abby, I think that fucking book is haunted."

"Huh?" She gave a slow nod, and her voice lowered.

"I am telling you, there are unnatural things in that book, which escape when you read it, things start to creak." I smirked; I mean, I tried not to.

"Chloe, it is just a manuscript." She shook her head.

"Abby, I am telling you, you have done it again, that fucking thing is possessed. I am warning you now, if that fucking thing is raising Gwenda from the dead, I am fucking moving out."

I tried not to giggle, but you know me... I gave a snigger and reached for the door handle; she grabbed my hand looking terrified.

"What the fuck are you doing?" I nodded at the door.

"I am going in to look." She shook her head.

"Abby, please, I love you, but honestly, if you go in there, I cannot guarantee you will come back out. There are unnatural things lurking in there released from the book."

I sniggered, turned the handle and walked in. Her room was the same as always, I was glad the wardrobe was shut, something far creepier than ghosts lived in there. I saw the manuscript on the bed where she had left it, and looked back.

"See, there is nothing here." Chloe peered around the door at me, and gave a long sigh, then swallowed hard.

"Chloe, it is a ghost story, that is all. It is written to give the readers the jitters; it is the same as in movies. It is not real, it is psychosomatic, you read creepy stuff and it makes you feel creepy and nervous, that is all."

Behind me was a creak, like an old mansion door opening, just like I described in the book. I will not deny, I felt a cold tingle run down my spine, and the goosebumps lifted on my arms. Chloe's eyes got bigger and bigger; I swallowed hard.

"It's the frigging wardrobe, isn't it?"

Chloe nodded looking petrified, I turned slowly, and saw the door open a crack. Okay, so my heart was pretty much pounding in my chest. I turned really slowly, and could just make out the worn yellow of Percy through the door crack. I frigging hate that teddy, it creeps the shit out of me. Chloe gave a squeak at the door.

"Abby, don't open it, there are things that should not be seen in there."

Yeah, she got that right, it was her perverted teddy for starters. I reached out, and Chloe whimpered and slid back a little, so only her eyes peeped round the door frame. I saw my hand shaking, what the hell was wrong with me, I was a fully grown up rational woman? It was probably just a faulty catch, after all, it was an old wardrobe, and knowing what was attached to the front of Percy, it was clearly just the pressure on the door, that was all.

Suddenly the doors exploded open, and Percy came out at full speed. His huge cock went straight between my legs, as he hit me full on, and knocked me flat to the floor, and I screamed. Oh hell, did I scream, never in the history of man, has such terror in a scream been heard. Chloe screamed just as loud and looked down.

"I am sorry... I didn't mean it." Yep, she pissed all over the carpet.

I lay on my back under Percy, his large moth eaten furry face pressing against mine, as my arms and legs waved in the air like an impression of a dying fly. Filled with panic and utter terror, as I tried to fight him off me, screaming at the top of my lungs.

"GET HIM THE FUCK OFF ME!"

My heart rate was headed very quickly towards cardiac arrest, and pounding in my ears, as suddenly Percy was yanked off, and I saw my chance to escape. I came flying out of the room and slammed into the opposite wall, breathing faster than an express train, and shaking like a leaf. Chloe banged the door closed and held the handle fast, she was breathing as fast as I was, she looked back as she shook.

"See... See... I fucking told you, that book is haunted."

Honestly, as mad as it sounded, I was starting to agree, never in my life have I been as terrified. I slid down the wall next to my room, and sat on the floor trying to breathe again, and could not believe I was saying it, but hell I was terrified.

"Oh God Chloe, I am so sorry, you are right, something here is as weird as hell." I was sweating like crazy, and wiped my face.

Down the hallway, Edwina's door opened and she fell out, followed by Birch who was crawling on her hands and knees, and both of them were pissing themselves laughing, Luke staggered out holding his sides, his face as red as mine, and I knew it.

"You fucking rancid bitches, that scared the living shit out of me." Chloe was dumb struck as she pointed to her door.

"WEENA, I PISSED ON THE CARPET, YOU COW!"

Luke leaned on the wall gasping for air, Edwina was lay on her back still screeching with laughter, and Birch looked up red in the face, with tears in her eyes.

"Oh Sweetie, I am sorry, it was meant for Chloe, not you, but

Sweetie, it was so funny."

She flopped on the carpet and squealed with laughter. I slid up the wall, my heart still hammering in my chest, and staggered down towards them with weak legs, Edwina looked up at me, I was really pissed off and she knew it.

"What?" I glared at her.

"What... Is that frigging all, I almost had a heart attack, Percy tried to shag me. Do you even remotely understand what that is like?" Birch looked up and sniggered, I glared at her with hate.

"Sweetie, you were the one who said we needed to act like Curio's, so we did." Edwina sat up, I was lost utterly for words, Chloe frowned.

"Yeah, be goofy and fun, not fucking haunt my bedroom, I thought Percy was possessed by Gwenda." Chloe looked at me.

"Percy is a good shag, if you want give him a go." And suddenly, I was sure, I will never ever feel sexual again. Birch stood up and pulled me into her arms, I was still shaking. I could feel her tummy wobble as she held me and tittered in my ear.

"Oh Sweetie, I am sorry, it was just a test run." I gave a long relieved sigh, and took a deep breath, and then leaned back and frowned.

"Test run... For what?" Luke smiled at me.

"Do you remember the first carnival we did, well we are thinking of making a Curio haunted house, there has not been one since the arts college did theirs, so we thought this year we will build our own." I understood that.

"Yeah, haunted Percy's jumping out of cupboards, that will bloody terrify anyone." He gave a smile.

"Well, you know, we thought something like skeletons and monsters." Birch's head snapped round.

"No skeletons, Sweetie, I don't like skeletons." I sniggered, and felt my heart rate slow down a little.

It took a while for Chloe and myself to fully calm down, which we did over a coffee at the island, as Birch and Chloe filled in Luke and Edwina on 'The Old Renshaw Mansion,' which was a gothic sort of ghost story. I had started it eight years ago, and so over the last week, having re read it, I finished it off, and now had two books to release when I was ready. Having calmed down and feeling a lot more relaxed, I had to go to Nigel's to deliver the papers for him and Molly, and Birch decided to tag along, but kept occasionally tittering. The good news was, the press were gone, and I was free to come and go without having to fight my way out of the gates.

We drove up Waterside Lane, towards Meadow Cottages, I still think the name is stupid, it's a farm house and barn, and pulled up outside Nigel's house. It still feels strange visiting Nigel, I always feel that dark presence, as if Primula is around watching, but on the up side, him and Sophia are still going strong and are actually very happy, which has been really good for Nigel. Sophia like all of us has aged, she is forty, it is hard to believe, but she has aged well, although her skin still looks a little orangey brown to me.

Birch has warned her many times of the dangers of sun beds, but her hair which is still bleached, is always immaculate, and her dress sense and style is never out of date, and Rupert has flourished under her care. Nigel smiles so much more and is calm and more relaxed, and nowhere near as nerdy as he was. He has a goatee now, which looks idiotic, but Sophia loves it, and likes to stroke it, which okay, creeps me out, but hey, each to their own.

Nigel was at work, but we were invited in for tea, so we headed inside, and sat at the kitchen table. The house is immaculate and stylish, she really does have a great eye for interior design, and even though this is a very old building, it always feels fresh and modern. Sophia poured the tea, as she talked.

"It is nice to have tea with my friends, yar." Yep, she still says 'yar,' but it does not irritate me as much as it used to. I think I have grown used to it after so many years.

"I had tea with Deli yesterday; I have missed it." I frowned.

"I thought you two, had tea all the time?" She turned, and smiled.

"We try to when Eric says it is alright, yar." Birch looked up from her biscuit.

"Does she need consent from Eric, that does not sound right?"

I glanced at her, she pounces on things quicker than a cat on a mouse, but I was right up there with her. Sophia carried the cups to the table, and put them in front of us.

"Eric is not the same, I liked him, but not now he makes Deli cry, yar." I knew nothing about it, and by the look of Birch, neither did she, her eyes moved to me and then back to Sophia as she sat down.

"Why does Eric make Deli cry?" Sophia looked up with bright blue eyes.

"He spends all her money on his club, which I must say, is so last year, yar." I was lost for words, why had Deli not said anything?

"Sophia, the nursery is safe though, Deli is doing alright, isn't she?" Sophia smiled.

"I love working there, it is a kind place for children, I will miss it when she sells it. I get sad about that, yar."

Okay, so suddenly I was heading back into panic, I had loaned her the money interest free to set it up. This was Deli's dream, and there was no way on this earth I would watch her lose it.

"Sophia, why is Deli selling the business?" She gave a sad sigh.

"She has to save the house, but I don't know why, it is still on the street, yar." She looked puzzled, I looked at Birch.

"I am going to the nursery." She gave a nod, Sophia smiled.

"I love the nursery, it is a kind place, I have lots of little friends there, yar."

Twenty minutes later, we jumped in the car, and I connected my phone, and rang Deb's, it took a moment for her to answer as I pulled onto upper Waterside Lane.

"Hi Abby, is everything alright?"

"Yeah Deb's, I just wanted to know, have you heard anything about the nursery closing?"

"Well, it is shutting at the end of June for four weeks for a refit, is that what you mean?"

"Deb's, Sophia has just told us it is up for sale."

"Really, well I have heard nothing about it. Abby, why would she sell it, she loves the place, you backed her, has she not said anything to you?"

"No Deb's, but I am going to find out."

We arrived just in the nick of time, Deli was stood with Josh and Lizzie, locking the gates, I pulled up, and rolled down my window.

"Jump in, we will give you a lift. Actually, where is your car?" She looked really nervous; Birch leaned across me.

"Sweetie, we know most of it, get in, we are having coffee, and we are going to talk." Deli looked at the kids, and then back at Birch.

"Please Birch, I know you are doing this for the best, but honestly, just leave it, do not get involved, I can handle it." I looked at her.

"Deli don't make me ask twice, get in the car, I am already involved, I talked him into dating you, and I helped you finance that place. Now do as Birch says, because you know what she is like, she will hassle the shit out of you until you do." Her eyes filled with tears, and she looked afraid.

"Eric will be really mad." Birch stared up at her.

"Nowhere near as mad as I will be if you do not get those sweet little kids and your ass in this car. I mean it Deli, my dark little beastie and me will leave you here and go straight to Oxendale. Sweetie, someone is going to start talking, and it is better if it's you." She gave a sigh, and pulled open the door.

"Come on kids, get in." I smiled, as I looked at them climbing in.

"Who wants to paint with Auntie Chloe?" They both screamed in the back seat, and Birch giggled, Deli climbed in, and we shot off back to the house.

It was an hour later, when we all sat in the living room, Chloe was keeping the children happy, and to be honest, herself, as I sat with Birch and Edwina and talked to Deli.

"If you are selling your business, it cannot be a small thing, and I want no bullshit Deli, this is us. Tell me, how bad is it?" She looked at me and her eyes filled with tears.

"It is not all him Abby, it is that Gavin and Duke. They have turned the place into a strip bar, and they have a swingers club planned for upstairs, they have topless dancers and barmaids. Oh Abby, it is an awful place, we are hundreds of thousands in debt, and he just won't stop spending. If I don't sell the business, I might lose the house, I did not know, honestly, I didn't, but he got a second mortgage to finance it all, and they are spending money so fast, he has fallen behind with the payments. I have lent him everything I have to try and clear the debt, but we are so far behind, if we do not pay up by July first, they are taking the house. I sold the car just to buy food."

I sat back and gave a sigh, and looked at Birch, she was watching Deli very closely.

"I know you do not want to hear this, but is he screwing around?" She lifted her hand to her face, and tried to wipe her eyes.

"I think so." Birch nodded.

"You think so, or know so?" She gave a huge sniffle, and took a breath.

"I do not know for sure, there are rumours, but Birch, I do not know how, I just know, I feel it." Birch leaned forward, and took her hand in hers.

"So that is a yes then. I trust your instincts." Edwina looked at us both.

"What I want to know, is how the hell does he get a second mortgage if Deli was not involved? It is a shared property; how could he get it without her having to sign?" Deli shook her head.

"It is not shared, everything is in his name, including the house. I only found out a few weeks ago, because I was cleaning the bedroom, and a shoe box fell off the closet shelf, and all the letters were in there." Edwina looked really surprised.

"Seriously? Deli, I do not know of one single married couple who do not jointly own the house between them. I have never ever heard of a couple where the man is the only name on the mortgage." She took a deep breath, and Birch gave her hands a gentle squeeze, and looked her right in the eyes.

"Okay Sweetie, firstly, you will never lose your home, because this is also home, so do not worry. Secondly, you are not selling your business, Deads helped finance that, because it was your dream, and you are not giving that up. The question I want to ask is a very important one, and you do not have to answer, but I have to ask it." Deli nodded and understood, Birch gave a sigh.

"Deli, it is up to you, and we will support you, but honestly, do you still want to stay married to Eric, or do you want out?"

Wow, she does not piss about, I mean, talk about cutting to the chase, but there again, why am I surprised, she is so like Roni at times? Deli took a deep breath, and wiped her eyes, she looked at Birch, and gave a slight nod.

"Birch, it makes no difference, I am married to him, and I only have until July first, if he goes down, they will take everything away, including my business. No matter what I do, I am going to lose everything." She burst back into tears, and Birch leaned forward and pulled her into a hug.

"Oh Sweetie, I thought you knew me better, you are my house sister, and I have sixty million in the bank gathering dust." She pulled back, and looked her in the eyes, and knowing her as well as I do, I sat back and waited for Birch's plan to take all Deli's pain away, honestly, she is amazing.

"Okay Sweetie, listen to me now. I am going to buy the nursery, that way, it will not be included in your assets. You are going to sell it me for two hundred pounds, and then he will not be able to take your money. We will take you home, pack all yours and the kids' things, and then you are moving back here, where you are safe. Now, we have done this before, so we know it works. When everything is settled, I will sell you back the business, and it will be legally safe from him forever. Is that okay, because if it is not, we will work something else out?" Deli took a deep breath, and looked down.

"I do not deserve you as friends; I have hardly helped out with anything; I should have been here supporting you." I smiled.

"Deli, you had enough on your plate, and as I have told you, we should have known about this sooner." She nodded.

"I am sorry guys, I really am; I have let all of you down." Edwina smiled, and pulled her into a hug.

"You were being you, which is kind of the point of us, and we are not friends, we are your sisters, remember, all girls together? Come home Deli, we miss you."

So, for the second time in her life, calls were made and once again, everyone teamed up to help Deli move back home, well, all accept Chloe, Birch and myself, we had other things to deal with.

In all girls together style, we showered, and Birch and I did a little quick fondling, dressed to impress, and jumped into my car, and headed off to Oxendale, for a night out at Club Empire.

At number twenty two, Garden Street, Deli sorted through her things, and told everyone what she needed. Morty, Alex, Creamy, and Bongo, followed Luke around the place with Jimmy. Deb's was at home watching all the kids.

With Petal and a much bigger van, bags and boxes were packed, and shipped out of the door, to be taken to Waterside Lane. Deli wept a lot, as she organised, her biggest mistake had been mentioning to me that Eric had hit her twice. Not hard as she put it, but when I had questioned her as to did it blacken her eye, she had tried to change the conversation, so that was a yes. Edwina set up a scanner and a laptop on Deli's kitchen table.

"Bring me the shoe box." Deli frowned at her.

"What for?" Edwina gave her a sympathetic smile.

"Deli, he is backed into a corner, he will apply pressure, we need insurance just in case he plays dirty. Look, no one wants this, but we have to protect you, and so I want copies of everything to back you up. I hope we do not have to use them, honestly, you have suffered enough. Deli, let us do what we do best, all girls together style." She gave a nod, and went to get it.

It took four long hours to sort and pack what the kids needed, Deli was not bothered about the furniture, and just took a few things she valued. Her room at home still had everything from her flat in it, so she tearfully packed her clothes, and Jimmy leaned in on the door, as she looked up and wiped her eyes.

"I never thought he would turn out like this Jimmy, he was such a nice guy for a long time, but that bloody group of his friends, they have changed him, and not for the better." Jimmy gave a sigh and walked in, he pulled her into his arms, and the tears once again flooded out of her, he held her tight.

"I know Doll, but you know what, you are safe and protected, and honestly, anything at all you need, just ask, Deb's, me, and all the others are there for you."

She wailed into his shoulder, and he felt so angry inside, Eric better stay the hell away from him, because the way he felt watching Deli cry, he knew, he would rip him apart.

The house looked a tip by the time everyone was finished, Anthony arrived, and as everyone headed out to the van and cars, he took Deli's hand, as she stood staring at her destroyed living room.

"I gave him my best years, I loved him so much, and I treated him with such care. I mean, look at his beautiful children." She was holding a silver framed picture of them. She gave a sob.

"What happened to him Anthony, why did he change so much? Honestly, there have been times recently, I hated him. I tried so hard, and he did not even notice I was alive." Anthony gave her hand a squeeze.

"I know how you feel Darling, I really loved Brent, but it was just not enough. I hung in there, but the fact is, he hung out with others who changed him, and he moved on without me, and it tore me apart. It probably means little at the moment, but Deli darling, I love you, and I will always be there for you, no matter what, and so will all the others." She turned and snuggled into him, and he put his arms around her.

"It means the world to me Anthony, and I love you too. You know, I always wanted mum and dad to have another child and give me a brother, but now I can see why they did not, because I got you." She looked up and smiled, and his eyes filled with tears.

"I am, and always will be." He rolled his eyes.

"Oh Dear, look at me, you got me all sentimental and twitching, come on, let's go home before I bawl my brains out, and dampen the carpet."

With her arm around his waist, she walked out of the house, locked the door, and walked down the path. At the gate, she turned and looked back and wiped her eyes.

"I am not going to cry anymore Anthony; I have cried too many tears alone in that house."

He smiled, and took her hand, walked to the car, opened the door for her, and she climbed in. Edwina turned around, and Deli smiled.

"Take us home."

Chapter 11

Club Capers.

We walked along the pavement towards the doors, which were lit up in blue and purple neon. Two large bouncers were stood outside with a golden rope across the entrance. Birch snuggled into my arm.

"Sweetie, I am quite excited." Chloe smirked.

"To be honest, a bunch of naked girls twirling, I get that at home all the time." Birch turned and looked at her.

"Chloe, I looked on the internet, this place has guys too."

Suddenly, Chloe was excited, I giggled, as she smiled. In a way I felt sad, I never in a million years thought Eric would turn out like this, but now that I think back to the men in my life, I should have known, I had lousy taste in men. I gave a sad sigh.

"You know, I never thought Eric would end up in a place like this." Birch looked surprised.

"You didn't, Sweetie, his sister runs a large chain of sex shops, I do not think it is a big reach to work out how he got the idea?"

"Yeah, but Birch, A swinger club?" She shrugged.

"As you know Sweetie, I have no issues with people's sex lives, and let's be honest, a swingers club sells lots of lube, sex toys and condoms. If you think about it, his sister will probably do very well out of this place."

We reached the door, it was a private members club, Birch pulled out a stack of twenties with a smile, and seductively leaned in to the bouncers.

"Oh Boys, please tell me you two will be free later?"

The rope unclipped and we were in, although, it did cost us two hundred quid... Each! We were in, and as we walked through the doors, I was actually quite surprised. I looked around the place, it was pretty up market, and not at all like I had imagined. I had somehow thought it would be dark and seedy, but it was in fact very stylish with a lot of stainless steel. Down the centre of what was a long room, was a cat walk like stage lit in neon blue and purple, and had seats along the whole length, where men in suits, and sexily dressed women, watched a girl in just her thong, with really long legs, twist and gyrate round a steel pole.

The bar ran down the whole side, which had a mirrored back, lit again in blue and purple, with a row of topless, attractive, G-string wearing young woman serving. The seats were lush and padded, we headed over to the bar, the seats swiveled so we could drink and watch, Birch was loving it. Chloe lifted her phone and took a picture of the girl, and I frowned at her, she shrugged.

"Edwina wants pictures, she might bring Luke here, and I get to paint her." It made sense to me, so I went with it, Birch excitedly grabbed my arm.

"Let's go sit next to the stage." I looked at her not quite understanding.

"Why?" She looked confused.

"To watch her dance, Sweetie." I shook my head.

"Birch, other women don't turn me on, is she turning you on?" She looked shocked.

"Hell no... I just want to imagine it is you, so I can stuff money in her knickers." Chloe rolled her eyes.

"She gets fucking weirder by the day."

I gave a giggle, and let her lead us to the long stage, cat walk like thing with poles on it. We all sat down, and Birch was really excited, she pulled out a wad of cash, I pointed to the sign.

"Birch, this is a high class place, you do not touch the girls, you use the envelops, and hand them to those girls with the boxes." She sat back and pouted.

"Well, that is no fun at all."

We both giggled, and I lifted my drink, as she pouted and put her money away. The girl who had seen the cash, and was wiggling and twisting in front of us, rolled her eyes and moved on to another guy.

To be honest, watching strippers and pole dancers is not as much fun as you would think. It really is quite boring, and I cannot help but wonder, just what is it that gets men so turned on about it, surely, it is more fun to go home and actually have sex?

We got up and moved back towards the bar, a tall young guy

turned, and looked Birch up and down with a smile, as Chloe leaned over the bar and waved, to order more drinks. He leaned into her.

"Hello, you delightfully beautiful lady." She gave a sweet smile.

"Well, hi handsome." He raised his eyebrows.

"Please tell me you dance in the back?" Chloe gave a giggle, as I watched lost for words, I mean, these people really do not piss about. Birch gave a little girlie giggle, and touched his shoulder.

"Oh Sweetie, I have danced everywhere." She leaned into him, and was close, acting more seductive than I have ever seen her.

Was it me or was this guy getting excited, I looked down and noticed...? And that was a definite yep! He thought he was going to score with her. His smile was getting bigger and bigger, actually, that was not all.

"If I may, I would love to enquirer as to if you do extras." She patted his arm playfully.

"Oh Sweetie, I am a little pushed tonight, but I suppose I could do a quick tea and biscuits." Chloe blurted out a snort and looked away, I was becoming alarmed. He frowned at her.

"Is that something new, I have not heard of that before?" She giggled like a little girl.

"Oh Sweetie, it is a northern speciality, you know. there is nothing like a good dunk, munch, and slurp." Chloe snorted again, and he looked really excited, and this was moving well beyond my comfort zone. I leaned into Birch, and whispered in her ear, feeling slightly panicked.

"Birch, this guy is asking you for sex, you know, EXTRAS?" She gave me a big smile.

"I know Sweetie." Her eyes danced with devilish delight, she turned back to him, and winked.

"So, what is it worth to you?"

I was starting to really panic, he was literally growing, and his pants were really sticking out, and oh shit, Chloe had noticed. He smirked, and looked at her semi exposed boobs.

"I have cash, a lot of cash, and a room close by." Birch smiled a sweet smile.

"I have a lot of cash, I hope you can match my stash, because I could never do extras with someone not equal or better." He gave a smirk, and a cocky smile, I was completely shocked she was going this far. He moved even closer and his thing was almost rubbing on her.

"I have twenty million reasons why you should take my room key." Birch gave a big disappointed sigh.

"Really... Oh that is a shame, you would need to at least triple that just to match me, and I was hoping for more." He looked instantly confused, and frown at her.

"You have that much, then why the hell are you lap dancing?" Birch smiled, and leaned in, and kissed him softly on the cheek.

"Sweetie, I am not a lap dancer, I am a sex therapist, and it costs a hell of a lot more to see me than those girls. When I do find someone that I like enough to have sex with, and trust me, I know a lot, do you know what I like to do to them?" His eyes opened really wide, as she leaned right in and whispered into his ear, his eyes moved to me, and that made me really uncomfortable.

He gave a shudder, and I looked down, oh yeah, that was really disturbing. Birch leaned back and lifted her drink, and then pointed down.

"That must feel very yucky, I would go clean up, you know, freshen things up a little." Chloe looked very impressed, as he looked down, and turned away to go clean up, she looked at Birch.

"Birch, you know I admire you, and so I am going to ask, and I know I will regret it, but what the hell did you say to make him cum in his pants?"

I looked at Chloe with that what the hell are you thinking look, it failed, this was sex and she needed to know. Birch leaned against the bar and chuckled.

"Oh, that is easy, I told him in a very naughty dirty voice that Deads and me would strip naked, stand over him, play with each other, and make each other squirt all over him." I gave a violent shudder, Chloe gave a satisfied smirk, she appeared impressed, I looked at them both in horror.

"Don't include me in his frigging messed up fantasies, you two are really screwed up, you know that?" Birch could see I was really uncomfortable, and she slid her arm in mine.

"Not much longer Sweetie." I was not sure what she meant, she pointed at the mirror across the bar, I looked up, and realised she could see right across the stage and past the dancers.

On the far side of the room stood Eric, with his arm around a very young blonde in a golden bikini, it was easy to tell, he was rubbing her ass, and she was really enjoying it. The lights dimmed, and a voice I recognised, came over the speakers, it was Gav.

"Ladies and Gentlemen, live on stage two, for your entertainment, Helga and Nadia, will begin a live girl on girl sex show." I gave a sigh.

"Really, is that how low he has sunk, Jesus, poor Deli." Birch gripped my arm.

"Come on we are up."

She pulled, and I grabbed my glass, Chloe followed, as Birch dragged me along, she was way too excited for my liking. We moved to the stage, but I could see Eric was also on the move with his golden bedecked female. We ended up right at the front of the stage, as Helga and Nadia started to kiss and grope each other.

I did not really notice much, my eyes were on Eric, as the lights were down, and he was moving slowly with his new woman, towards a doorway. I looked down and Birch had her head lay flat on the stage, and was staring up at the girls, as they were bending and twisting and moaning. I felt a twinge of horror. I leaned down to her, and felt a little panicked.

"Birch, what the hell, stand up for Christ's sake." She pointed at the girls.

"Sweetie look, oh that is really amazing, could you bend like that and get me just there?"

Chloe smirked, as I looked up at the two girls, unable to comprehend what the hell they were doing to each other. Birch looked up with excited eyes.

"Does my little button get that big, so you can suck it?" Oh hell, I felt my cheeks redden, Chloe leaned with a smile.

"Mine does, Baz measured it for me." I turned feeling appalled and looked at her.

"What the hell, why would you even ask, actually scratch that, what the hell made you think of it to even ask?" Birch turned and looked back at me, her eyes were huge and dancing.

"Oh Sweetie, she is good, I mean, look at the size of it. That is massive, it is huge." She held up her pinkie finger and wiggled it.

"Wow, I am really impressed." My legs felt weak, and I gave a violent shudder.

"Birch, can we go now please, Eric has gone into that room?" Her head popped up from the stage.

"Oh shit, yes, come on, we need to talk with him alone."

Crazy as it sounds, I was so glad to get away from that stage of women with oversized clitoris's, hell, my wife is messed up.

We headed across the room, much to my great relief, and up towards the door. Birch pushed, and it swung open into a corridor. At the end of which was a red door, and between us and the door, was Gavin, I gave a sigh as Chloe squeezed past and smiled.

"Gav, wow, it has been a long time." He looked at all three of us.

"What the hell are you three doing here?" Chloe winked.

"I am getting married, we came to see Eric about a private hen party, you know seeing as I have not much longer in the free lane, I want a few extra stamps on my card." He shook his head.

"He is busy at the moment, and does not want to be disturbed." Chloe moved in closer, and put her hand on his chest, her voice went low and sultry, as she gently pushed him against the wall.

"You know, I often wondered about that day in the paint ball arena. You know, when I think on, it was pretty cold in there, and you looked pretty stressed out, and it made me wonder." I watched as her hand slid south. He gave a gasp, and Chloe giggled. He swallowed hard, and shook his head.

"Look guys, you cannot disturb him, he will not like it." The sound of a zipper going down, matched the motion of Chloe as she lowered, he looked down.

"Oh Fuck." Birch looked at her watch.

"Three minutes Chloe from now." Gav squeaked; Birch smiled.

"Here is the deal Sweetie, go longer than three minutes, and we leave, if not, Eric gets visitors." He gave a slight pant, and leaned his head back onto the wall.

"Oh God." He jerked up, and closed his eyes.

"OOOOH!" Birch smiled at him.

"Was that nice Sweetie, although one minute twenty, oh dear?" Chloe jumped up and looked at him, she moved forward and kissed him, and I knew what she had in her mouth, and felt my stomach twist. I was repulsed; God she is such a slut.

"Oh Chloe, I love you, but you are so many shades of messed up, I just have no clue where to begin."

Birch led the way as we stormed past Gavin, who still had his pants around his ankles, and so was unable to stop us. We reached the door, and Birch shoved it open with a crash, and there was Eric, with the girl bent over his desk, and he was planted balls deep inside her. To be honest, I was heartbroken. He stared at us in shock, still holding her hips, Birch lifted her phone.

"Don't stop Sweetie, she was enjoying that." Click! Birch smiled at her, and bent down and waved, the girl looked confused.

"Hi, I am Birch, that is Deadly, and that is Chloe, and you are who exactly?" She lifted a hand off the desk, and gave a small wave, as she panted.

"I am Candy, that's with a K." Birch giggled.

"Oh, then you really are a Sweetie." She chuckled.

I stared at Eric with utter hate, I had trusted him, he looked embarrassed, and was going very red. I was not sure if it was anger or shame, but I was pissed off, and it showed, he just stood there holding the girls' hips, he blinked.

"Look Abby, this is..." I snapped in.

"What... Not what it looks like, is that what you were going to say, because it looks to me like you are balls deep in Candy with a K?" He gave a sigh.

"Abby, just calm down, and let's be grownups and talk." I was seething.

"I trusted you Eric, I wanted someone special for Deli. She has been hurt enough, and I bloody well trusted you to be decent, so yeah, start talking, and tell me why the hell you hit her." He shook his head, as I took a pace closer.

"It was not like that Abby." I took another step closer.

"Did your hand hit her face?" He gave a gasp.

"Look Abby, just calm down." My eyes were burning I was staring so hard.

"Just answer the question, did your hand hit her face?" He lifted his hands off Candy, and she slid out from between us, Chloe pulled her away to the side.

"Abby, I would not describe it that way." I screwed up my fist, and my arm came up, and I threw everything I had in it.

SMACK!!!

Chloe gasped as his nose exploded. Blood shot out everywhere, as he reeled backwards and hit the floor, I stared down at him.

"Was it like that, or like this?" He panicked, and lifted his blood covered hands up.

"Okay, you made your point."

My heart was pounding inside me; Birch leaned over and click! She took a picture, as I stared at him on the floor, and then the tears came.

"How could you, she is so sweet and loving, and she worshiped the floor you walked on; you utter piece of shit? I trusted you to love her and cherish her. Well trust me, you will never hurt her again, because if you do, there is no rock you can hide under that will hide you from me, AM I CLEAR?" My tears dripped onto his exposed legs.

I turned, and walked to the door, and looked at Gav, with his shirt hanging out. I sniffled as I tried to compose myself.

"You know Gav, at school when you were on the team, I really considered screwing you, but one minute twenty, wow, I am so glad I didn't." I walked back up the corridor, and headed back into the club. Chloe and Birch followed behind me, and Chloe looked at Birch.

"See what I mean, she can be really bloody scary." Birch smiled.

"She is my dark little beastie, and I am so turned on right now, I want to measure my clitoris." Chloe gave a violent shudder.

"Promise me Birch, never ever tell me if you do. Oh Birch, I am so fucking straight it is unbelievable."

Birch gave a loud cackle of a laugh, and then hurried to catch me up.

Two hours later and feeling hurt, I leaned on the door of Deli's room and looked in, she saw me and smiled, as she folded a jumper.

"It appears we have done this before." I nodded, and walked in.

"How are you doing?" She sat on the bed, and I sat at her side.

"I am relieved, hurt, a little frightened, and sad." I took her hand in mine, and gave it a squeeze.

"Things will get better you know? If you look at it, Deli, it was not all bad, you two had some great times, and look at those two adorable children you have. I just looked in on them, they are so beautiful. Look Deli, we have all been through some pretty dark times, hell, I just went through a pretty awful one. You know what, if there is one thing to learn from this place, it is firstly you will never be alone, and it will get better. Your business is safe, and this house is a stable place, I mean, the people are not quite as stable as I wish, but here you have nothing to fear."

She leaned over onto my shoulder, and I let go of her hand, and lifted my arm around her.

"I know Abby, honestly, I know." She gave a small chuckle.

"You know it is crazy, but I have always called this place home when talking to my mum, I used to call the other house Eric's house, how odd is that? It always felt like his and not ours if that makes sense? Even though it has been a sad day for me, weirdly enough, I felt relieved when I put the kids to bed here."

"So, what are you going to do now Deli?" She gave a long sigh.

"I want to create as stable an environment for the kids as possible. I also need to contact Bradley and tell him to put the renovation back on hold until I own the company again, and then I want to help get Curio Live on track. I live here, and to be honest, I have not been on the site nearly as much, I want to make up for that." I patted her leg and got up.

"Don't worry about the renovations, we talked in the car, they are going ahead under Birch's ownership, Chloe and Me will be covering that cost with Birch, call it a welcome home gift."

"Abby, it's thousands of pounds." I walked to the door, and then turned back to look at her.

"Deli, I bought a new cup last week because mine got dropped, and that is the first time in two years I have actually spent some money. Deli, all of us are doing well, we have this great house, I have the latest tech, a wardrobe stacked with clothes I hardly wear, and I have a bank account filled with more money than I will ever spend. Let me use it for something with meaning, let me use it to build your dream, because that will really mean the world to me." She looked at me, and shook her head.

"Always the bloody writer, using words in a way no one can

refuse, you know you are impossible right?" I smiled.

"It has been said. I am going for a coffee, and then to find out what weird and strange notions my wife picked up tonight, sleep well." She gave me a big smile.

"I will, night Abby, sweet dreams."

Ten minutes later I returned to our room, holding two coffees, to find Birch sat up in bed, with her knees up. The moment I walked in I was suspicious; she had that guilty as hell look. I narrowed my eyes as I looked at her, and she became uncomfortable, as she looked up.

"What you up to Doctor Dixon?" She shook her head, and then smiled.

"Nothing Sweetie." Yep, she looked guilty as hell, and the smile gave it away. I had pretty much worked out what.

"You are measuring it, aren't you?" She giggled, and her eyes danced.

"I might be... Sweetie, why the hell do rulers have that bit at the beginning before the measuring bit, mine is so small it does not reach all the little lines?"

I sat down in my desk chair and sipped my coffee, as I watched her fiddle under the sheets. I shook my head in pity.

"My God, you are messed up. Birch, why the hell does it matter, and honestly, measuring it, whichever way you look at that, it's bloody weird?" She looked, up and lifted out a plastic ruler.

"I am just curious, I wanted to know, and if you think about it, it is good research for work. So, is yours bigger than mine, do you want to find out? You know Sweetie, it could be fun." Man, she is so strange, and yet weirdly enough, this is turning me on.

The following day felt a little more normal, I came down to breakfast to see Edwina had arrived early, and was pouring coffee, as Chloe sat staring at her cup lost in thought, whilst Anthony and Michael got ready for work. Birch ran around grabbing things with a slice of toast in her mouth, and Deli was getting the children ready for the nursery, and trying to do their hair, eat, and keep the kids tidy. It felt nice, as Edwina placed a cup in front of me, and I smiled. I was not ready for words yet.

I sipped my coffee and waited for the door to bang, and as

everyone disappeared, after a quick, "Bye Sweetie and a kiss." Silence descended on the house. I sipped, and Chloe watched, I looked over my cup.

"What?" She smiled.

"It is nice having Deli back." I nodded.

"It is, although, it is a shame Eric is a shitbag, I really wanted him to be a good guy." She lifted her cup and sipped.

"I am glad you and Birch are okay; I mean, you are okay, aren't you?" I smiled as I sipped.

"Yeah, Anita has moved a lot of extra dates off her to give her more time at home, and also help with the Curio Live event, we have a lot to do Chloe." She gave me a small smile.

"We will do it Abby, stop worrying. Baz is going to help, and so is Jimmy and Debs. Honestly, we all want to be involved, we all talked, and it is not fair all of this has to be on yours and Birch's shoulders, we will do more, and it will be good for all of us."

I gave a nod, I was a little intimidated by it all, this was a huge event compared to the last one, and we really needed our A game. I sipped down more coffee and thought, then looked at Chloe.

"What?" She smiled.

"We are more like we were, last night, Birch was really weird, and Deli is back, and all of us mucked in as a team to help her. I have not felt this happy in ages, it felt like us back then, looking out for each other and going to help out. They lost sight of it Abby, you were right you know." I sipped more coffee and was starting to wake up properly.

"About what?"

"At the funeral, being a Curio is a big responsibility, but it is a responsibility we all have, not just you. I know it started because of you, but all of us made those videos, all of us helped build that website, and all of us went on it and talked. I told them all you were right, and I told them we need to back you two up more. I think they have listened, because all of them want to help in this, just like last night. You still look tired; you need to rest up and let some of us carry it for a while."

I love her, I do, she is so sweet, and so caring at times, but that is Chloe.

"I will be alright Chloe, I really needed Birch, I was missing her and yet I could not get her to see it, and it was eating me up inside. I am fine now; she understands and things are getting back on track." She gave a nod and smiled at me, and got up, and headed for the kettle.

"Good."

It is funny how life goes around in circles, we all drifted once before, and it was Birch that came back, and brought us all back together. It has happened again, only this time it is me who is fighting to pull us all back. I feel for Deli, she was evicted and ended up here, and now faced with losing everything and being threatened with eviction, she has returned. Is life just a series of crazy circles, I often wonder if it is, and if this is a whole life of just going round and round?

Katie has tried yet again, and last time Anita found herself looking at leaving the Dixon Group, and yet I made a choice and brought her in as my agent, and now I am the one that has to a degree cut her free, and I know she is now considering what her future will hold. Although, considering everything, my reputation for picking lousy men seems pretty on point, my taste in guys really sucks, is there any man I like who is not an ass hat? Maybe that is the point of being a Curio, I have often contemplated that time when we all sat together and I asked Edwina, 'why does his gayness matter?' It does make me think, especially at the moment, as we are about to embark on a whole new chapter of Curio life as we finally move abroad.

In my mind, the definition of Curio, put as simply as I can, would be Curio: A person who is curious about everything pertaining to them. A person who has rejected the socially defined labels, pertaining to their sexual orientation. A person who sees themselves as a whole, and not just defined by their bed partner. To me that makes sense, my sex life with Birch is so wonderful and fulfilling, and yet it would be wrong to say that is all she is, because it is not. She is so complex, and so deep and has so many wonderful attributes, and yes, sexually she is amazing, but that is not the reason I love her, I loved her deeply long before we slept together. I came out of my thoughts and Chloe was watching me, she smiled, lifted her cup.

"You know Abby, I can almost see you thinking, what has your brain in overdrive now?" I put my cup down.

"I was just thinking about life, and the millions of conversations Birch and I have had over the years. I suppose it is because we are going to do another Curio event where people will be asking questions." She nodded.

"Okay, so where are your thoughts today?" I sat back and gave it a moment, and then looked up at her.

"It is quite mental if you think about it, people meet and talk and feel a buzz, and then they grow together and really get into each other, and all this happens before the sex, and yet today, everything is still being defined by the sex. Look at marriage, and monogamy, the marriage is defined by being faithful, and none sexual with others. Adultery is still the biggest cause of divorce, but think about it Chloe. People come together and they save and scrimp, and build a home and have kids to create a family unit, and all those years of talking and sharing a life become worthless the moment a dick is put in another person's hole. I really love my life with Birch, but if I found out she has slept with someone and not told me, I would be upset, but the crazy thing is, I would not be upset she had sex, I would be really hurt she hid it and did not feel our marriage was strong enough to deal with it." Chloe gave a nod as she thought about it.

"Baz and me will probably cheat on each other, which is why we have talked about it, we have promised to be honest about it. I really love Baz, but I know he is no angel, but come on Abby, I am no angel either, so we have agreed to be honest about all of it."
I understood that, and in a way, I was glad to see she was being really thoughtful about the relationship, I looked at her.

"What about kids?" She gave a laugh.

"Abby, I am thirty nine, I think that ship has sailed." I shrugged.

"You never know, hell Chloe, you are really fit and in good shape, you eat really healthily, you know it is not completely out of reach." She smirked.

"A little shit Baz could be nice, but honestly, look at what we have. What with Sammy and Deb's kids, and we now have Deli's. Abby, we have loads of kids in our life, and I love them all to bits, they are as much mine as they are theirs."

I had to smile. she sounded like Hatty, and was right, we were both surrounded by lots of really wonderful children, but I cannot deny, a few years back I did wonder, what it would be like to have a baby Birch. I am sure any child she bore would be an amazing child, and my thoughts turned to Lillian, and that day when she talked to me. I could clearly see, that she had been surrounded by them all her life, they were other peoples, but she still considered them like her own. You see what I mean about circles, here we are sat together, just Chloe and me, and it is almost like we are becoming younger versions of Lillian. Life is one big crazy circle.

Chapter 12

Moving On.

Talking with Chloe, and really thinking about how at times life feels like it is repeating circle, brought to mind that day Birch returned, and her revelation about the shares she was given as gifts. She always told me, she felt no need for it, because she had not earned it herself, and I really understood that.

Roni gave me shares in the Dixon Group, and I was also given shares in K.O. I was just handed them, and over the last ten years, the income from them has been substantial. The tour of the States with Katie brought in three million dollars in revenues for me, and then of course, I have had book sales, guest speaker fees, and appearance fees. The crazy thing is, my trust fund has always provided me with a really good income, I really did not need the rest, which is why I helped Deli and Ella. The truth is, apart from the house costs, I need little to live, so my money has just sat in the background gaining interest, and now I can say with confidence, I am a millionaire on paper and in cash in the bank. I really understand Birch now, money is just a tool, not something to be worshipped. I do not need this house to be happy, I was happy in the guest house living with Birch, it is still some of the happiest moments of my life.

Is it crazy that it feels like too much to deal with, so I ignore it? Birch and I have done so much to try and help others during our life. I have bought artwork, helped other writers get their books out, and encouraged a lot of people to embrace themselves and live their life to the full. We have invested in G5, and put well over a million each into D&D to create a platform to do promotional events, and especially with Chloe, it has made such a huge difference to her life, but I always sit back and wonder if it is enough? One thing I do know is, having sold my stock in K.O, and handed back the Dixon shares to Birch, has given me a huge sense of relief.

Today was a day I was not really looking forward to, I had to meet Birch at two, so that we could go around to see Vanessa Douglas in her office on Station Road, for the reading of Lillian's will. Honestly, I was surprised when we got a call, I had not expected or actually wanted any part of her estate.

I walked up to the retreat, and stepped in, Alex looked up and smiled, Gill was on the phone, and as usual, there was a line of seats, with several people waiting. I walked through the swinging doors, and saw Izzy in the office, I gave her a wave, and moved over to her door and leaned in.

"I have missed you Izzy, you should come around one night and chill with us." She gave a chuckle.

"I hear you have been stirring up the world?" She leaned back in her chair.

"You did good kid; I warned her you know? I told her she was taking on too much and risking everything, but you know what she is like, she is her mother's double and as stubborn as they come."

"We are fine now, honestly, I actually feel so much pressure has lifted off my shoulders." She leaned back in her chair and looked at me.

"Deadly, what are you going to do though, Katie could have been fixed you know? Hell, I would love that job, was there really a need to leave. You know Roni has a massive distribution network; you would be a fool not to tap into it." I smiled.

"Izzy, Roni knows what I am doing, and we have talked, and I will be again, but I am not going back to Dixon, I have other plans." She gave a shrug.

"I admire your pluck, I really do, and if I learned anything living in that mad house, I know you, and how you operate with complete determination and drive." I gave a little giggle.

"Go on admit it, you miss it… Just a little bit, you know we all miss you, don't you?" She gave a cheeky smile.

"Honestly, I do a little, it was never dull, that is for sure. Look, I promise, I will pop by one weekend and we will have a fry up on the patio like we used to." I nodded.

"You know I will hold you to that." She smiled as Birch came running down the stairs with her coat, and gave a gasp as she came up at my side.

"I am ready Sweetie. Be back in a bit Izzy." She snuggled into my arm, and we walked outside, Stacy and Louise were stood waiting for us, they both gave a nervous smile. Stacy looked at me.

"Can we walk with you guys; we are a bit nervous?" Birch nodded.

"How are you two holding up?" Louise gave a small smile.

"I am doing alright; I am going to miss her a lot." Stacy nodded.

"Me too, she was so sweet, she was lovely to work for. It will be so strange working there if it reopens." I frowned.

"If, has Celia not decided to continue?" Stacy shook her head.

"She has been talking to my dad, he is the estate agent, you know Celia is seventy six. She acts like she is only forty, but I suppose without Lillian, she has decided to retire. Dad says her sister wants it for her daughters, but she was horrible to Lillian, you know, about her being with Celia? Cissy was set against it, and Lillian despised her for it."

It was so weird to think about, I just could not imagine the Tea Rooms being run by someone else, it felt alien, and just not at all right. I looked up the street where it stood with its powder blue paintwork, and all its little glass windows with lace curtains. I looked at the girls.

"What will you do if they sell it, will you still have jobs, because you two have been there for a long time?" Stacy smiled.

"We have, we got full time contracts as part of the TARTS program, and it was such a wonderful place to work, we never left. Celia and Lillian were good to us; I would hate to see her sister ruin it." It got me thinking.

"Yeah, me too."

We turned into Station Road, and walked down to next door to Pemberton's, it felt like Wotton was becoming a different place, even Derek was talking of selling up, it felt like there would be a lot of new faces in Wotton before long, and I was not sure how I felt about that.

Vanessa Douglas, was the leading partner of Douglas, Watkins and Preston, a large group of family solicitors. We knew of them because they counted the Parish Council vote each year, and most of the wealthy people in the village used them. There had been a Brimley in the practice, which was Patrick who was with mum, but he had sold out his share to Vanessa. I liked the inside, it was all fitted out in wood panel, and had a very Victorian feel to it all.

Vanessa sat behind her solid highly polished dark desk, as the four of us sat in front of her, I looked around at the door.

"Is Celia late?"

"Celia... Mrs Dixon, Celia will not be coming, the will has been read, this is just the legal matters pertaining to it, and their execution. So, if we are ready, I will make a start." I nodded and felt like an idiot, so sat back. She opened her papers and looked at Stacy and Louise.

"Girls, I am sure you are aware that Lillian was a very rich woman, her father was very big in the diamond business, and you two have been a huge part of her later life. She cared for you both very deeply, and so she made a provision for you both, and I have two cheques here for the sum of fifty thousand pounds each. She wrote that she wanted to make sure both of you were well cared for.

Stacy looked shocked; Louise filled up with tears. Vanessa smiled.

"She really loved you both, she spoke often to me about you in her dealings. Now for the important stuff. I am sure both of you are aware there was, well let's just say, a family problem with Cissy, Celia's younger sister. The fact is that Lillian and Celia were both equal partners in the business, and so as a result, and due mainly to her family issues with Cissy, Lillian has left both of you an equal part of her shares, so you both now between you own half of the Tea Room business and premises. Celia being the other owner of a half share."

I gasped, I mean wow, that was an amazing act of pure love and kindness. Stacy and Louise looked at each other not quite sure what to do, they were clearly lost for words. Vanessa continued.

"I have spoken with Celia this morning, and I am sure you are aware, she has decided to retire, and so her share of the business will go to sale. I will warn you, Cissy has already made a bid, but girls, you know this business is a big opportunity, and if you can raise the funds and buy Celia out, you will own a business valued at almost a million pounds. It is not just the tea room trade, it is the building, the contents, and all the stock and equipment, this is a very lucrative investment for the future. Celia has made it very clear to me, that if you can both raise the funds, she will give you the first refusal, if not it will more than likely go to her sister, who will become the third partner in the business." Stacy looked shocked; she leaned forward in her seat.

"I do not wish to sound too rude, but how much money do we have to raise, because I have forty, and with Lillian's money that makes ninety thousand?" Louise wiped her eyes, and gave a sniffle.

"I can probably raise one fifty with Lillian's money, that will give us two forty between us, is that enough?" Vanessa sat back in her chair.

"Girls, Cissy is offering much more, but to be honest, if you want my advice, it needs to be at least six to match bids. The building alone is valued at seven, and the business as you know, generates as much." Stacy flopped back in her seat, and shook her head, Vanessa smiled.

"Girls, this is a very well known and respected business, I am sure those in finance will look upon you favourably. You have fourteen days to see if you can raise the capital, Celia made it very clear you would need some time." Stacy looked at Louisa.

"You handled most of the managerial side with them, do you think we can raise it, I really trust you, Lou?" She shrugged.

"Stace, that is a lot of cash, we would be better talking to your dad, he knows about this stuff. I say we try and see; I don't want to just leave; it will be like losing her all over again." Her eyes filled with tears, and Stacy pulled her into her arms and hugged her. I looked at Vanessa.

"They are buying it, I will provide the capital, tell Celia, we bid seven hundred thousand, and if Cissy ups it, fine, so will I, but these girls are having that business, and will continue the legacy of Lillian, I will ensure it. When do you need the money?" Birch smiled, and leaned into me.

"I do love you, Sweetie; you really are my Lillian." Louise swallowed hard.

"Abby, that is a lot of money to borrow off anyone, honestly, I know the business is booming, but it scares the hell out of me to borrow that much." Stacy nodded.

"Honestly, you are as scary as your books at the moment." I giggled.

"Look girls, Cissy will ruin it, we can work out the details, be it a loan or once the deal goes through, bring me in as a silent partner or investor, either way, those Tea Rooms are staying in the hands of someone who will cherish them, and run that business properly. Look at it this way, if you do not buy it, where will you work, Millington, Oxendale, or somewhere else. Lillian and Celia gave you those jobs to keep you in Wotton, and I intend to ensure you both stay here, run it as it should be, and honour her memory." They both burst back into tears, and I looked at Vanessa.

"Sort out the paperwork, and I will bring in my people to help sign everything over, and provide the capital." Vanessa gave a nod and smiled.

"She spoke very highly of you Abigail, and she loved you very much, I can really see why." Birch gave a giggle and squeezed my arm. Vanessa looked at her papers, and then moved to her drawer and opened it.

"Jemima, Birch, Lillian requested you were given this, it is her diamond and sapphire brooch of a tree. She wrote, it reminded her often of you two, as it had the tree of the birch, and blue beauty of Abigail's eyes." She handed it over in a small box and Birch looked down at it, I saw the tears drip to her lap.

"Abigail for you, I have these ear rings, which Lillian stated had the exact colour and sparkle of Jemi's eyes, and with there being two, that is in fact, one for each eye."

I swallowed hard as I took it and looked at Birch, her eyes sparkled with her tears, and Lillian was perfectly right. Vanessa smiled.

"I also have this instruction to transfer one million pounds into the account of Curio Live USA. Lillian really wanted to do it herself, but sadly, she fell short of the mark, but Celia told me, that she thought out there was a lot of Abby's and Jemi's, and she wanted to help them through you two." Birch took the notice and looked at it, she gave a huge sniffle.

"Bless her, she was so lovely, this will help a lot of hurting young people. God, I miss her." Vanessa gave a smile.

"If you want my thoughts, I think her spirit will live on in you four, and a lot of people will be better for it. Jemima, send me the details for the Curio account, and Abby, I will be in touch soon with the paperwork. Good luck girls, go change the world for Lilly."

There were a lot of hugs and tears, as we returned home with Louise and Stacy, and I rang Andrew and talked with him, he took over and offered to contact Vanessa and act on my behalf. He offered the girls, his services to act for them, and arranged a meeting at our house in Wotton for two days later. More changes were coming to Wotton, as the players changed, and life took on a different state. Celia met with Stacy and Louise alone in the tea rooms the following day.

A few hours after their meeting, she turned up at the door, and I welcomed her in with the biggest hug ever. I called Birch, and she came flying home, and Celia wept as she saw I was wearing the ear rings, and Birch was wearing the brooch. We had coffee and talked, Lillian had left her a lot of money, and so she had decided to buy a cottage over near Hastings, which was where her and Lillian had met.

Celia told us, she felt older with her gone, and knew her time would come soon, and so she had every intention of spending her last days, walking the paths on the cliffs, as they had in those first days of their meeting, and falling in love. She sat with a smile, and looked at us both.

"You know on the day that you married, you did not whisper soft enough, all of us heard it, and it gave Lilly such a thrill, because Abby, she felt you and her had so much in common. She often told me, that Birch reminded her of me in my younger days. I will leave Wotton safe in your hands, knowing that there is a love here as deep as ours."

Oh God all of this was killing me, I had this huge ball inside me that hurt, and in the back of my mind was that same fear, that even though she tried, Lillian left, and Celia was alone, and it terrified me to think that could be Birch and I.

Within a week, Andrew sorted everything out, and the Tea Rooms, were placed into the hands of their new owners, and I was officially made a silent partner in the business. Stacy and

Louise moved out of their flats, and into the upstairs three bedroomed house, and advertised for new staff through the TARTS program.

Andrew also went through all the paperwork, and with a new logo designed by Chloe, Sanctuary Press was formed, and I was officially a publisher, even though as yet, I had not published anything. I kept it very quiet, as for now I did not want anyone to know.

Deli settled into a routine, and Eric for now, was nowhere to be seen, but the house was cleared, and placed on the market and snapped up fast, after all, this is Wotton and considered a desirable place to live. He made arrangements to see his children at his mother's house, and even though I hated him, I was glad that he wanted time with his children.

Deli was busy with the preparations for the nursery refurbishment, and Michael, who was now a building supervisor for Bradley, was put in charge of the job, which made things ten times easier on Deli. Under Birch's ownership, there was no shortage of cash for the job, and Birch mucked in, with ideas and little tweaks to perfect the design. We spoke to Margaret, even though she still scared the hell out of me, and she arranged for a legal representative to move forward with divorce proceedings for Deli. Life settled a little with two more kids in the house, we all slowly got back to normality.

Behind the scenes, after my rant at Deb's during the funeral, everyone was booked in and involved with the Curio tour, including Jimmy, who took over transport, accommodation, and everything to do with it, after all, he had toured there many times, and understood things better than we did. Gill and Aden became regular visitors, and stayed over a few times, as we all worked on the actual event, and the technical side. But the nicest thing of all, was this was a D&D event, and so Tabby and Anita arrived, and we all got down to business as usual. There were a few moments where we bumped shoulders as we worked, and she smiled, it did feel familiar, and I will not deny, I enjoyed it. I really had missed working with her more than I realised.

One new rule there was of us working, was there were more breaks, and so Birch and I got a lot of time together alone in our room, although everyone had to get used to shutting the door during sex, as Deli's kids were far more curious than Deb's, and there were one or two embarrassing moments especially involving Chloe in the studio with Baz.

We moved through June, and one morning I woke up as something heavy landed on the bed, and there were wild giggles and chuckles. Yep, the crazy lady had remembered. I opened one eye, and she sat there grinning like a maniac, and holding out a box. To be honest, looking at her crazy face, had it been a knife, I would not have been surprised.

"Sweetie, I am excited. Happy Anniversary."

Crap, this was a trap, I needed coffee, but it was our tenth wedding anniversary, and as soon as I touched that box, I knew she would explode like a nuclear glitter bomb. It had to be handled with precision and care. I slid myself slowly up the bed in a seated position as she chuckled and sparkled, wearing a big happy smile, she shook the box at me.

"Open it."

I pulled my knees up very slowly as she hummed with anticipation, then quicker than a striking cobra, I snatched the box, and launched myself off the bed, and ran for the door as fast as I could. Her head snapped around, she squealed, and then came tearing after me. Having learned my lesson, I jumped over the banister, and landed in the hall, as she thundered down the stairs squealing with joy, and I came sliding into the kitchen, slid on the floor and yanked open the cupboard under the island. Birch bolted into the kitchen, to find me holding a large box, she came to a shuddering halt laughing, as I smiled.

"Happy Anniversary Baby."

She looked at me. her eyes dancing with excitement, she was such a kid at times, but I actually loved that about her. Birch took the box and giggled as she opened it, Chloe, Anthony and Deli leaned in to see it. In the box was a folded black piece of cloth, she put the box down and reached in, and lifted it out.

"What is it, Sweetie?"

The cloth unfolded and she saw a hoodie, she lifted it up, and a small red box fell out, and back into the big box. Birch smiled as she looked at the logo of my arch, with the words in gothic lettering above the logo, reading 'Sanctuary', and below the arch was, 'Press' I leaned in to look at it.

"Today is my first official day of trading, and it felt fitting, because Baby, you are the reason I have peace and sanctuary, you saved it, and you brought it here, and this house, this home, and most importantly you Birch, you are my sanctuary." Chloe leaned around to look at it.

"Whoa is that my logo?" Birch giggled, and turned it around to show everyone, I lifted the small red box out and kissed her.

"Happy Anniversary."

She put the hoodie down and Chloe spread it out to look at it, Birch opened the box and gave a gasp. I leaned forward.

"It is an eternity ring, a symbol of commitment."

I lifted it out of the box, and it sparkled, it was after all platinum and covered with the highest quality diamonds and emeralds, I lifted her hand and slid it slowly down her finger.

"Birch, ten years ago today, I gave you a ring, and swore my love to you, and so today, as I slide this on, I will renew that vow, because I will love you until my last breath and beyond." I looked up and smiled, and her eyes filled with tears, and she exploded, and threw her arms round me.

"I ALMOST LOST YOU, AND I LOVE YOU SO MUCH. BWA HA HA HA!" Chloe rolled her eyes.

"Wow, drama much?" Birch sobbed into me.

"I love you so much Deads, I was so scared I would lose you, but I will love you forever." I held her tight.

"I know baby, I love you too." Chloe coughed.

"I hate to spoil a good moment, but do we get one of these too?" I giggled.

"Under the island, each bag has your name on it." She gave a happy chuckle and dived down under the island, and started pulling out bags.

"Deli, Anthony, Weena, Deb's, Anita, Tabs, where is mine?" I smiled.

"Right at the bottom." She pulled and lifted it up, hers was a deep blue one.

"SCORE!!"

Birch slipped back and wiped her eyes, she looked at her hand and smiled, her eyes shone so brightly, and she looked beautiful.

"I am so happy Deads, I got lost for a while, but you came looking and found me. I am sorry I hurt you; I really do love you;

you are all I have ever wanted." Her eyes twinkled.

"Open yours."

"I did." She frowned.

"When?" I gave her a smile and lifted my hand, to show the eternity ring and matching bracelet.

"On the stairs, and I love it, its black, it's gothic, but most importantly, it's beastie." She smiled a radiant smile.

"You have always been my dark little beastie." Anthony wandered over holding up his hoodie.

"I hate to ask darlings, especially while you two are putting all our love to shame, but what is Sanctuary Press exactly?" I turned and smiled.

"My new imprint, I am now officially a publisher, and I have two books ready to go, I just have to sort out the distribution, and then I am going to press, with two books at once. 'The Publicity Girl, and The Old Renshaw Mansion.' I figured if I am going to keep my fans happy, I will give them two at once." He leaned in and pulled us both into a hug, and smiled at me.

"Happy anniversary, you know, I am not sure why I am surprised, you really are an inspiration to all of us, but good luck, and congratulations."

He kissed us both on the cheek, I do love him, he is lovely. Chloe stood looking at her hoodie, as she held out her arms and twisted in it smiling.

"This is banging… By the way, you do know it's twenty past eight don't you?" Birch squealed.

"Crap, I am late."

Suddenly the house was filled with panic, and after a mad rush, and the hugging and kissing of children, the front door banged, and the house was quiet and back to normal. I giggled as I sat with Chloe, the chaos of mornings always made me laugh, I got up and filled my cup, and turned to Chloe, she smiled.

"So, what you up to today?" I gave a sigh.

"I have a lot of paperwork to do for the new company, and I need to call Roni, as she is helping me with distribution, and then, as always, it's back to Curio Live." She gave a giggle.

"Me to, I have images to approve, I tell you Abby, those Yanks are a pushy lot, they want the finest detail on everything." She gave a sigh.

"Are you working in the library?" I gave a nod.

"I can do; all my coms are linked." She lifted her cup.

"Good, we can keep each other company."

We headed off to the library, with coffees in hand, Chloe took extra biscuits, and both of us plopped down in front of our computers, and began our day. The time seemed to slip by as I filled in online registration forms, and endless requests for the items I would require, and also went over all the PDF files of the signed paperwork from Andrew. In my drawer under my desk, I had my new bank cards and cheque book, and I added the online account to my own private account, so that everything was linked together and all in one place. After several hours, I sat back and stretched my arms, to take the ache out of my back.

"I need coffee and food." Chloe leaned back with a sigh.

"Yeah, me too."

I flopped forward in my seat and spun around, and my computer burst into life, it was a video call, I frowned as I saw the name of the caller, Chloe came around and leaned over.

"Who the fuck is Janet Bannon Attorney?" I shook my head, and clicked the button.

"No idea. let's see."

The screen opened, and a woman of about mid forties sat at her desk, behind her was a huge book case filled with embossed leather bound books, she smiled.

"Good morning, Miss Watson, you are Abigail Jennifer Watson, the daughter of Edwin, brother to Phillipa, are you not?"

I was more than a little surprised, she had a strong southern American accent. I gave a nod.

"Yes, that is me, please could you tell me who you are?" She gave a big smile and sighed.

"I have to say Miss Watson, you are not an easy person to find, I finally tracked your father down in Miami to my surprise, and he gave me all your details. I called your phone a week ago and left messages, but your phone was turned off. My name is Janet Bannon; I am an Attorney in Law here in Missouri USA." Chloe turned, and headed for the door.

"Christ, more Yanks, I am done with them for today." I looked at the screen.

"Nice to meet you Miss Bannon, just what exactly is this about?" She nodded, and shuffled some papers on her desk as if she was reading something. She took a few long moments, and then looked up and smiled, and I felt a little nervous for some strange reason.

"Miss Watson, I represent the American estate of Phillipa Watson, I have managed it since her death, and have been continuing my role as family attorney to her daughter Amanda. I am aware of you from her will, and I believe, in regard to Amanda, you met her briefly ten years ago, when she was a guest at your wedding." I nodded.

"Yeah, I remember her, she stayed with my father in London, although, I must add, I did not really spend much time with her, as I was being married and left immediately on my honeymoon. Is Amanda alright, she is not in any trouble, is she?"

Janet's face clouded a little, she gave a nod, and paused a second, it looked like she had stumbled a little on her words as a strong emotion gripped her. I have no idea why, but my stomach squirmed, and I felt a little afraid. She gave a slight cough to clear her throat, and as odd as it sounds, I suddenly felt a deep sense of dread.

"Miss Watson, I am sorry to inform you, but she passed away twenty six days ago, in a severe traffic accident, which is the reason I have been trying to get a hold of you. I am sorry to be such a bearer of bad tidings, and I am sorry for your loss."

Just for a moment, I was at a loss for words, I had felt my breath catch in my throat, as I remembered her at my wedding, she was only young. I felt a huge wave of emotion pass through me, and was a little shocked. I took a moment to try and think, Janet smiled.

"Are you alright Miss Watson?" I took a deep breath, and gave a nod.

"Yes, a little shocked, she was only young." Janet gave a sympathetic smile.

"Yes indeed, she was thirty one years old." She took a breath, and seemed quite affected by it, I could see she obviously had a close bond with her. She gave me a smile.

"Miss Watson, are you aware of the history of the family, I am not sure if you are? Amanda married Peter Fairbanks, he was the son of a very wealthy local family, who had a lot of dealings with international importing?" I gave my head a shake.

"No, to be honest I know my dad flew to the wedding, and stayed in touch with Phillipa's family, he was very close to his sister, but I have heard very little about them. After he and mother divorced, he did not talk much about family." She gave a nod and understood.

"To be blunt Miss Watson, the Fairbanks family come from old money, and they have a very high opinion of themselves. They considered Amanda to be of a lower standard to them. Heavens knows why, Phillipa was a very successful woman, I believe she had quite the life in London? When she passed away, her London office got in touch because I was situated close to Amanda and had represented a few of her husband's business dealings, which is why I am currently making this call. Miss Watson, Peter was cut off from his family, but with the help of Philippa's inheritance and myself, both he and Amanda did very well, they lived a good successful life, and so, sadly when they were both killed in the accident, it left their children in a difficult position." I swallowed hard as I felt the sudden shock hit me, and I went ice cold. My voice was a little strained, as I suddenly began to understand the situation.

"They had children?" She nodded.

"Yes Ma'am, they have two, Daniella, and Jessica., they are nine and seven years old... Miss Watson, I am going to lay my cards out on the table here. The Fairbanks family have completely rejected any notion of taking care of these children, they want nothing whatsoever to do with them."

I felt a huge jolt and looked up; Chloe was stood holding two cups of coffee staring at me looking white faced and shocked. I looked back at the screen.

"But they are the children of their son." She shook her head very slowly.

"I have tried Miss Watson, I got a cease and desist order from them yesterday, they want nothing at all to do with them." I felt my heart rate increase, and actually I was in utter shock, as it all made my head spin.

"Miss Bannon, where are they?" She gave me a smile.

"For now, they are in the family home being cared for by their nanny, I have ensured they have funds and all the staff are paid, and I see them every day. Miss Watson, I will be blunt, I have failed to provide for these children through the Fairbanks channels, and now I am looking towards the Watson side of the family. No matter what people say, these children are family, but I am under a lot of pressure as the care services are pushing to place them into care, and I want to avoid that. Miss Watson, these children have a sizeable inheritance, and anyone who takes care of them, will be well rewarded." I suddenly understood what she was saying, and everything was starting to make sense, I looked up at Chloe.

"Phone Birch now, I need to have her here." I looked back at the screen.

"Okay Miss Bannon, I think we are both on the same page here, just what exactly are you proposing?" Chloe put the cups down and grabbed her phone, and dialed. Janet Bannon gave a smile.

"Miss Watson, I did some digging, so I am aware of who you are, and I am also aware you will be travelling to the US within a month, and the reason why you are travelling here. Look, I will be blunt, all I want is to sit and talk with you and your partner, which is why I am calling, I would like very much to meet and discuss their welfare. I can stall the courts for at least a month longer, but time is running out for Daniella and Jessica. Will you meet me?" There was no doubt in my mind at all.

"Yes, I want to meet and talk. Miss Bannon, I need to talk with my partner, my email is AJWdark, at AJW dot co dot uk, send me all the details, and I will be back to you in the next day." She gave a big smile and her eyes teared up slightly.

"Thank you, it has been so difficult for the girls, talk to your partner. I will send some pictures over to you. Miss Watson, thank you so very much, I will look forward to hearing from you." The call ended, and I flopped back in my seat, Chloe looked at me.

"Birch is on her way, Abby, you must bring them here, they are family, they need us."

I smiled at her; she was so wonderfully lovely, and in the back of mind, I was thinking something similar.

Chapter 13

Watson Business.

I sat at the computer with Birch, Edwina and Chloe sat around me, looking at pictures of two young children. It was clear that they had family resemblance to me, they clearly had a lot of Watson in them. Daniella had long jet black hair and bright blue eyes, and Jessica had sort of a blondie brown hair and dark brown eyes. They were cute, there was no doubt. Chloe smiled at me.

"Danny looks just like you as a kid, although Jessie is sweet looking too." I nervously looked at Birch.

"Their parents were killed, and their dad's family do not want them, Birch, I cannot come to terms with that, I mean, look at them, they are just young kids." I knew Birch was looking deep into me, and she was reading my thoughts.

I cannot deny, seeing them had stirred something deep within me, and as I sat there looking at them, something from a long time ago woke up inside me, and my thoughts moved back to the past, as I sat in Deb's room at her home and we talked. We were almost thirteen and watching The Railway Children on DVD. She lay back and put her arms behind her head.

"I want at least three kids, and defo a girl, what about you?" She turned and looked at me. I nodded.

"Not sure how many, but I would like a kid one day, you know, not straight away, I want to do stuff first, but yeah, maybe when I am about thirty. I would love someone to look up to me like I do mum and Hatty. I guess it would be nice to be that important to someone."

I came out of my thoughts looking at Daniella, wow Chloe was right, she did look so like I did back then. Well apart from the fringe, I did not have one back then, but those eyes, they really did look like mine. Birch was looking at me, and I blinked out of my thoughts. Her voice was soft, and I could see she was holding back.

"Deads, we do not even know them, they have not even met us. I know what you are saying, and it is appalling what his family has done. If you are thinking what I think you are, it will mean massive changes, and you have always said you have never wanted the responsibility of kids. Deads, this is not a game, this is forever, for life." Chloe nodded at both of us.

"Baz and me will adopt them if you want, they are beautiful, we will help them." I had to smile; Birch looked at me, she had that really Roni look to her, it was her serious face, and it really bothered me. Her eyes shone in the brightest of green, as she stared at me, which made me feel a little uncomfortable, her voice lowered more.

"Can we talk privately, upstairs?"

I felt a cold shudder run down my spine, and nodded. Birch smiled and took my hand. I got up out of my seat, and followed her onto the stairs, and she quietly led me up to our room and closed the door, this did not bode well, we never closed the door. She looked at me and came across the room, and took my hands in hers. She was stood very close, and her eyes looked huge.

I was waiting for the punch line, and I did not want to hear it, but I knew she would be right. I really did not want it, because deep down inside something was gnawing at me, telling me I had to save them, and I felt guilty and selfish, because she didn't, but I did. I was going to be forty, and I had fought so hard to get back the closeness with my mum.

I love mum so much, and we had become so close over the years and I loved it, and as crazy as it sounds, I had reached that point in my life where I wanted to have that. I want a daughter to be that close with me, I wanted to be that support and that huge figure that Hatty was to me in the life of another, a younger me. I looked at her and swallowed hard, trying to suppress the millions of feelings building inside me. She looked scared, and I understood why. Her voice was caring and soft.

"Deads, this makes me really nervous, you have always said never, so I need you to really think and think hard about this, because those kids have lost their parents, and I know how that screws kids up. The last thing they need, is an act of good will that turns sour on them, it will fuck them up forever. Sweetie, this is not a game, this is their lives." I looked into her eyes.

"Birch, I am well aware of that, look, this is not some fad you know, I am bloody serious about it. Birch, they are family, that is Watson blood in their veins, they are our family." She let go of my hands, and started to pace around, I watched her. She turned; her face looked like she wanted to cry.

"Look Birch, I am well aware that you too have said you don't want kids, which is why I got Chloe to call you."

She turned and stopped, and took a deep breath, I could see she was fighting some pretty powerful feelings, she stared at me with her intense green eyes, and slowly shook her head.

"Deads, don't give me hope, and then snatch it away, please Sweetie, do not do that to me."

I felt my insides crash; I was pushing too hard. For years we had talked, and both of us had made it clear we would never have kids, but I had this nagging memory in the back of my mind. It was back in the Summer she returned, we had gone through hell, and I had screwed up in a major way, and honestly, I had fouled things up between us forever with Kyle. We had talked a lot, and in a way, it was the very first time we had to a degree looked at life together further than just in the moment. I had told her of all my doubts and she just calmingly replied.

"I left you once, I hated it, so it is not in my plans, as for kids, if you want them, cool, we will go get some, and I don't need to fall in love, I am already in love, and no matter what happens, that will not change, and so I just go with the flow."

I had always remembered that moment, I have no idea why, but since talking to Janet, it had really come up in my thoughts and stayed there, and I suppose, I was hoping after all those conversations, it was still true. I gave a sigh, she was close to tears and I could feel it, for the last few months we had not exactly been the most stable partnership. Recently, we had come so close to breaking apart, and I could sense she was afraid that would happen, and this would split us. I looked her right in the eyes.

"I get it Birch, honestly, I do, we have both always said we did not want kids. Look, I am sorry I guess I got my hopes up, I mean, we have ten years of talking behind us, I have no idea what I was thinking, you don't want kids, it is okay." She blinked.

"I would love kids, I have an amazing relationship with my

mum, I just knew you didn't want them, and you have always given good reasons as to why." That hit me right in the face like a bat.

"Wait... What, but you said." She gave a long sigh.

"Deads, I wanted your kid, yours, but that is not really possible is it now, I mean, come on, I can be flaky but I am a realist? Sweetie, I never wanted some random blokes donated sperm, I wanted yours Deadly, can you even comprehend that? I married a woman, but I want her child."

I was lost for words. I flopped back, and sat on the bed, my head spinning, and a thought popped into my head of her with huge bunches running around behind her granddad, and I smiled.

"I would have loved a little Birch running wild like Gem does. I told you three years ago, I would love a little Birch, but we both knew it was not possible. Hell, for a moment back then, I even considered asking Anthony." I looked up at her staring at me, she had tears in her eyes, and she gave a sob. Her voice was high and squeaky.

"Deads, they have your beastie blood in them, but I am afraid you are not thinking this out properly. This is one hell of a commitment, and you have to be one million percent into this, and I am not sure you realise that. I almost lost you, I came so close, and it terrified me, what if you do this and then decide it is too much, will I lose you?" Her tears dripped off her chin, onto the carpet.

Oh crap... I felt like shit again. I got up off the bed, and walked over to her, and pulled her into my arms, I hated it when I made her cry. She snuggled into me, wow, she had not been this unstable and insecure in years.

"Birch I am not going to leave you, hell, I vowed that this morning." She pushed her head into my shoulder and wept.

"But you thought about it Deads, you downloaded the divorce papers." I gave a sigh, yep, I was an utter shitbag.

"Birch, come on, don't cry I hate it." I stroked her hair down her back. She did have a point, I had really thought about it, but we had overcome that.

"I cannot help it Deads; I am absolutely terrified at the moment." I squeezed her tightly, and let out a long flow of air, I had wanted to avoid all of this, and I had no idea how I could sort this out.

"Look, I will understand if it scares you and you do not want to do this, I really will." She looked up, and her eyes sparkled brighter than I have ever seen them.

"Deads you do not understand." I felt a lump in my throat, and shook my head.

"Birch I am trying, but you are not making sense." She gave a huge sob, and breathed in and swallowed.

"I am terrified Deads, not because I don't want them. The thing is I do, as soon as I saw her with that dark hair and bright blue eyes, all I saw was you. My God Deads, if you had a baby, that is exactly what she would look like, it is the closest I will ever get to having your child."

BOOM! My mind was blown, she gave a huge sniffle, and wiped her eyes on her sleeve, I looked at her.

"So, all this... This is because you want them, you are being straight with me, aren't you? Birch, you actually want them here with us as guardians, parents, whatever it will be?" She nodded at me.

"Yes... Deads, I can do this, I am ready, I have been for a while, the big question is are you, because I will not toy with a child's life, it has to be all or nothing?" She looked at me with those huge sparkling green eyes, and God, I loved the determination in them, I felt a huge wave rush up inside me.

"You know, I have always thought you would make an awesome mum, well you have kind of been to that lot stood listening by the door." She smiled and gave a giggle, then sniffled and looked at the floor and sniffed up.

"I know, they think we are so stupid."

I smiled at her and she looked up hopefully at me. She could be so silly, she had no idea how relieved I was, because I knew I was ready for this. My heart was beating, and I felt a twinge of excitement, as I looked into her green sparkling eyes, call me crazy, but I really wanted to do this. I just knew the time was right, and I was ready to commit everything to this. I swallowed hard, and smiled.

"Birch, Baby, will you have my baby beasties, and be a mum with me?" She gave me the most beautiful smile, and threw her arms around my neck with a squeal, and I pulled her close.

"We have a lot of talking and planning to do Birch, this will not be easy, oh God, we have even more yanks to deal with." She looked up at me and softly kissed me.

"I love you Deads, you know, this will make us a real family like Deb's, Deli, and Edwina." I smiled, and felt a huge wave of relief.

"We still have a lot of legal shit to deal with, I hope to god you have friends in the trade that understand all this, because we will need a lot of help." She gave a sniffle and wiped her nose.

"I will get right on it; we need to talk to this woman, and find out what she needs." I nodded and looked at the door.

"OKAY, YOU CAN COME IN NOW!"

The door exploded open, and Chloe and Edwina came racing in, and threw their arms around us, with loud excited squeals, Chloe bobbed up and down.

"Guys, I am so stoked; I am going to be an auntie." I looked at Birch, as Chloe hung from my neck, and frowned.

"She does know she already is right?" Birch giggled.

"Who cares, she is happy."

As I have said many times, gossip in this place is faster than email, especially if you tell Chloe. Within the hour, mum and Hatty sat in our kitchen, Hatty was over the moon she was going to be a Nana as she called it. My mum was more business like about things.

"Abigail, this is not a game, being a parent is no light matter, you can trust me on that one." I lifted my cup and took a sip.

"Mum, this is not a done deal yet, we have a hell of a lot of formalities to go through, and this may well blow up in our faces. Look, we know what we are doing, Mum, I am ready, I want this, I really want this and so does Birch. Honestly, tell me the truth, do you doubt us as parents that much?" Hatty stared at my mum, as she put down her cup.

"Abby, you misunderstand me, honestly, I think Birch and yourself will make wonderful parents, I mean, look at how well both of you have guided your own little family, Deb's, Edwina, Deli, and Anthony have all flourished under the guidance of you two." I frowned.

"You missed out Chloe, she is a wonderful and lovely person." Hatty sniggered.

"I think the jury is still out on that one, but she has my vote." I looked at my mum.

"Look, we both know this will not be easy, and we are ready for all sorts of mishaps, but look at it from our side, we have you, Hatty, Roni, and Ellen for support and advice if we need it. Deli lives here with two children, and she is qualified in this stuff. God Mum, you will not find two other people with such a huge support network around them. Hell, Birch is a bloody therapist, and Sue at the practice has years of trauma experience with kids, she has certainly helped Chloe and me out." My mum gave a big smile.

"Good, I just want to make sure you were thinking seriously about this, and it now shows that you are. If you want my opinion, I think these children will be lucky to have you as guardians." I gave a sigh of relief; I had panicked for a moment. Hatty patted my hand.

"You are doing good kid, your mum is right, they will be lucky to have you, I for one am very proud of my daughters." I smiled.

"We love you too Hatty, and we are proud to have you as a mum too." She giggled.

It felt like a long day, I got back in touch with Janet Bannon, and she video called us back, and Birch and myself sat with her and talked about every aspect of what was possible, including adoption. There was a lot of legal red tape, but our biggest asset, was that I was a blood relative.

Birch made it clear, that even though we had decided, the children had to have a say in it, after all, if they did not like us, we were screwed. Our only option was to fly out as soon as we could, so that we could meet with them, and then take it from there. Before that, we had to take care of some business, tomorrow was Friday, and a very important day for Wotton.

We got up early and headed into the village, today was the reopening of the Tea Rooms. It had been closed since Lillian's death, and after all the legal transfers were done, I talked to Louise and Stacy about a few extra added touches. Chloe painted a beautiful new sign, that read 'Celia & Lillian's Tea Rooms, somehow it felt wrong to change it, and after all, this was about honouring Lilly's wishes.

Louise and Stacy had hired two twenty year old girls through the TARTS program, both with brand new powder blue uniforms, and with Louise and Stacy, dressed in their best shirts and slacks, and wearing powder blue aprons, the Tea Rooms was cleaned, sparkling, and ready for business, with a very special guest of honour.

Celia had found a house and was ready to move, but she had waited especially for this day. Green Street was blocked off, and tables were set up, and a bright blue ribbon was stretched across the walkway between the tables.

At precisely ten o'clock, the doors to the Tea Rooms opened, and Stacy and Louise stood smiling either side, as Celia walked down the gap towards the ribbon. Birch and myself stood smiling next to Vanessa and Marjorie, Celia took a pair of scissors and waited for quiet. It felt like the whole village had turned out. Celia looked at us and smiled.

"Ladies and gentlemen, you have no idea how happy I am to see our two girls stood together as partners and new owners of the Tea Rooms. Lilly and myself loved them like they were our own, as we did many of you stood before us." Her voice trembled a little, and I held my breath.

"She would be so happy to see us all today." She bit her lip and took a pause, and I felt Birch's hand slip into mine and give it a soft squeeze.

"She would be so proud of our girls for taking this on, and keeping a tradition that goes back thirty five years, to when we first opened. I shall retire happy, knowing my beautiful Lillian's wishes have been met, thanks to the kindness of someone she was deeply fond of, Abigail." She looked at me and my eyes teared up.

"I now know, the spirit of my Lilly remains in Wotton. Ladies and gentlemen, the Tea Rooms is open for business as usual."

She cut the ribbon to tremendous applause, and the Curio's stepped back and all of us looked at Marjorie, I smiled with tears in my eyes, and held out my hand to offer her to go first.

"Marjorie, some traditions are worth keeping, I believe there is one in place that must be adhered to."

Celia smiled, as Marjorie who looked very emotional gave a nod, and walked towards the doors. Stacy and Louise stepped back and headed behind the counter, and Marjorie walked in, looked at them, and smiled.

"Good morning, ladies, and what a wonderful morning it is."

Somehow that felt very fitting, Celia winked and took Birch's and my hand, and we followed Marjorie into the Tea Rooms. We sat down at the back, a table full of Curio's, and Celia, and we had our first coffee in the newly reopened Tea Rooms.

Now it felt back to normal, I looked around and saw Hatty with mum, and even Agnes and Bethany, sat with Marion. It felt good, but as I watched the counter it was clear something was missing. I felt Celia take my hand and squeeze, I turned, and she smiled.

"She is here Abby, I feel her."

Chloe slurped her coffee, looked up, and went white, and looked nervously around the room. Birch sniggered.

The counter was busy, and the seats outside filled up, and the new waitress's Francesca and Linda whizzed around ensuring everyone was served. I noted Louise and Stacy keeping a good eye on them.

Before we left there was a short lull, and with Birch and Celia we walked up to the counter to see how things were going. Louise and Stacy were happy, and Birch being Birch, and considering this was after all the tea rooms, leaned in over the counter.

"So, girls, you are living together now?" Stacy frowned and looked at Louise, and then back at Birch.

"It's not like that; we have a room each." Celia gave a chuckle, Birch shrugged.

"You have been naked at our place, so you know how good looking you both are, you know, and you two are very close." Stacy swallowed hard, and looked at Louise.

"Oh, I am so straight, I am like spaghetti straight Birch." Celia gave another little chuckle, as I leaned over the counter and looked at Stacy right in the eyes.

"Yeah, but spaghetti is straight only until it gets HOT... and WET." I raised my eyebrows, and Stacy went bright purple, and the cup on the saucer in her hand rattled.

Birch gave a huge cackle of a laugh, and Louise sniggered. Celia stood there with the giggles, some traditions are worth keeping, she looked at both the girls with a big smile.

"Get used to it, it is those two."

I held Birch's hand, and swung it as we walked out of the Tea Rooms, Deb's winked at Stace as she followed, life in Wotton, was as always, continuing.

Summer was coming as we walked down the green, and I stopped for a moment to look around. Birch slipped her arm round my waist, and I just looked at the paths filling with people milling around the shops and looking in windows. The buildings looked pristine, with their sandblasted stone, bright paint work, and signs that were old world and traditional. It really was a beautiful and picturesque place to live. Birch leaned over at my side, and rested her head on mine.

"It really is beautiful, isn't it? You really did live up to your word, and made sure it was preserved and beautiful for another one hundred years. You know Sweetie, I just realised... When you think about it, when it comes to some of the most powerful women to run the council, you know, like when we first arrived back from Uni, and it was Madge and mum who were seen as the one's forging the way forward, in the scheme of things, you are one too." I frowned and looked at her.

"Did you just say I am a Madge?" She giggled.

"No... But think about it, some of the young kids in this village will see you in the same way I saw Madge and Flick back then, you know, powerful iconic women of the village." I turned and looked at her.

"You did, you just called me a Madge, what are you implying Doctor, are you saying I terrify small children?" She gave a giggle, and pulled me into a hug.

"No Sweetie, but you know, you are one hell of a role model for young women around here. I just like to think you are a more Sweetie kind of role model, not all brooding and scary as Madge was." I looked into her green dancing eyes.

"Did you just call me a sugar coated Madge?" She burst into laughter, and gave a huge cackle.

"Deads stop, I am being serious." She stood back and looked at me with a smile, and tilted her head to the side.

"Deads, you really are an inspiration, I mean it, the young women of this place should look up to you. Think of all you have achieved, and the fight you had to get there. You know from where I am stood, you really are so incredibly inspiring, and one hell of a good example of how to live here with respect and kindness." I gave a shrug.

"I was just trying to survive, it was not that inspiring Birch, half the time I was unsure and terrified, I still am to a degree, and what about you? Birch, you have done equally as much, if not more? You know, I hate to point it out, but you know, for a couple of transient whores, we did pretty good." She gave a smile.

"Okay, we shall call it a team effort, and we shall walk around, and look inspiring to the young." I gave a smirk.

"To look remotely inspiring today, I need more coffee, what time are you back in work?" She gave a sigh.

"I've got an hour, and then I have a group therapy session." I narrowed my eyes.

"It's not... You know... Them... Is it?" She gave a loud cackle of a laugh.

"No, Sweetie, that was yesterday, and Izzy does that one, even I find it a little intimidating." I giggled as I slipped my arm back round her.

"A little, even now, if someone hums, my leg starts tapping, Christ, they freak the hell out of me."

I gave a violent shudder, and she giggled. She took my hand, and we walked slowly in the warm sunshine back towards home.

Am I an inspirational woman? I am not sure about that at all, I mean, I understand I won a council election by the highest majority ever, but seriously was that all me? Let's be honest here, Primula wanted to drag the whole bloody village back into the dark ages, and my God, she was bloody horrible and terrifying. I am not convinced I was that inspiring; I think I was more the better option as no one wanted what little freedom they had tearing away.

The carnival that year was a massive hit, actually, so much so we have done it every year since, but on a slightly smaller scale, although there is always a circus or fair, and the laser light show. The Wotton dramatic society handle the green play to start it all, and there have been some really fantastic little productions, but did I inspire all that?

No, I didn't, it was a massive team effort, and to be honest, it was in fact, Birch's idea, not mine. She does that a lot, comes up with some form of madness, and shoves me forward as the token voice of the group. You see this is the point, it has always been a team effort, we all muck in and it does not matter at all who gets the limelight, we use our best skills to help each other, we always have.

I came back to Wotton and had to fight like hell just to be accepted, it wasn't inspirational, it was hell, and it took me a long time to get through it, even now there are days I get panicked and haunted by it all. It is like now, Birch and I have sat and done a lot of talking, well, we did last night, we were up until two discussing everything, because honestly, I am so excited that we have the slightest chance of being able to help raise two kids that are actually my family, but we have so much to do and work out before we fly to the States.

It is going to be yet another massive change that will drastically change our lives, equally as drastic as standing up to my dad, or moving out of the guest house, and telling Birch I was in love with her. All those times began another great adventure in our lives, and so far, they have been wonderful, but behind the scenes I was always terrified. Birch has always been so calm about things. I came out of my thoughts and she was looking at me smiling, we were stood in front of the front door.

"What?" She moved in close as the door swung open.

"I know what you are thinking, and Deads, we will be fine, and they will love it here." I swallowed hard.

"Birch as crazy as it sounds, I really want this, I want them here safe with us, but I am also terrified, it is a huge change. I want it, honestly, I am hiding it, but I want it so much. Please promise me, be there, be there at my side through all of it, and never give up on me or them." She pulled me into her arms, and I rested my head on her shoulder.

"Deads Sweetie, I sat at Sunny Bank reading your story and it broke me, because I saw how short sighted, I had grown. Honestly, I felt I had betrayed you in the worst of ways, and it was devastating to me, but it was also the best thing that could happen, because you opened my heart, and my true love for you poured out and engulfed me. It was like the biggest moment of clarity in my life ever. Sweetie, I will never do that to you again, not ever, and I will be right at your side through all of this, I swear it." I gave a sigh into her shoulder.

"I needed to hear that Birch... Thanks."

I slid out of her arms, and she looked down and kissed me softly, and my heart just melted. With her arm round my waist, we walked through the door and into our home.

Chloe came bolting down the stairs towards us looking irate, I looked at her.

"Chloe are you alright, what the hell has happened?" Her eyes were wide, and she was red and sweating, as she pointed behind her back up the stairs.

"Abby, I mean it... If you do not burn that fucking book, I will, and trust me, I fucking mean it. Put it in a crypt, cover it in salt, and fucking burn the thing."

She took a huge gasp of new air and stared at me.

"If you have broken Baz, I will never ever fucking forgive you." I felt a bolt of panic hit me, swallowed really hard, and looked up the stairs.

"Oh shit!"

Chapter 14

Auditions.

For two days I have been sat on the floor looking at pictures, and honestly, my head is mashed. My mind has been preoccupied with thoughts of the children, and Birch's reaction, and to make thing more complicated, I have the auditions of the TV series, of Seeds of Summer. I have rows of pictures of girls and guys, all with a large picture and a rough biography underneath. Birch walked into our room and I looked up.

"Sweetie, have you seen this one, I mean, okay she is auditioning for Willow, but actually, I really do think she would be better for Bram." She sat down, and handed it to me, and I looked at her.

"Well, she does have blue eyes and blonde hair, so that is a good start." I gave a sigh.

"I don't know, to be honest Birch, pictures say so little, I mean, what do they sound like? I want to hear them talk?" She leaned back on her arms.

"Yeah, I suppose so. Well look, we have an idea of who will be there, so when we watch, it will give us a much better idea."

The clause I had negotiated with Anita and the makers of the series of Seeds of Summer, was I got to have the overall say when it came to picking the main cast. After all, this was actually based on actual events, and honestly, I wanted it right. Anita had done a lot of negotiating on this, so I was well placed, and because it was a partnership with River TV's streaming service, I did have a pretty good working relationship with everyone.

The time arrived, and with a clip board filled with possible candidates, we jumped into Anita's car, and were whisked off to a theatre on the edge of London, where all the back seats were filled with possible hopefuls.

We were met by the director's personal assistant, given ID

badges, and walked down to meet the director David Willis, I had met him once, but only briefly at a meeting, he shook my hand and smiled a lot. At his side was a surly pale looking guy with short rough shaggy hair, he had a jumper around his neck, which I have no idea why, but it bothered me. He introduced himself.

"Hi... Brandon Cole, screen writer, can I just say, I love your work." I took his hand.

"This is Jemi, and that is Anita, they are part of D&D." He gave a smile and bobbed around a lot.

"Lovely to meet you all."

He appeared pleasant enough. We sat in the row in front, we were centre stage, and behind us right at the back was a large group of hopefuls, all sat holding scripts and doing a last minute cram of their lines, they looked really nervous and intimidated.

The stage had a few props, chairs, an old sofa and a single bed, I noticed a table with a few towels, paint brushes, scissors and a comb, so felt all was well, and I sat back with Birch and Anita, and we were handed copies of the script. Birch was really excited; it soon died as the day went on as the hundredth name was called. I was feeling frustrated, we had seen a lot of girls, but none of them really felt like they fitted the parts. We had selected twenty for a short list, and this felt like it was going to be a longer day than expected, unless I found a way to really get to see the truth of these actresses.

I heard the name, and looked at my clip board to find the girl's profile. She nervously walked on stage. She was tall with long brown hair, and walked with a very good posture. She announced herself as 'Emily Thatcher.' David leaned over the back of the seat between Birch and myself.

"We rather fancy her for Bram." I nodded, I looked at her on stage, she was watching me.

"Emily, please could you read the intro to the book, I see you have a copy in your pocket." She looked confused; Brandon leaned over.

"Abigail, just a quick word. It is better if she reads from the script, it makes it easier on us." I stood up, and turned around to face David and Brandon.

"Look guys, I am not feeling this, give me a little latitude, will you? Let me play around and really get a sense of these people, because honestly, I don't think we are getting anywhere." David Shrugged.

"If that helps Abby, I am fine with it." I nodded.

"Thanks." Brandon did not look happy, I turned and looked at Emily.

"Emily, I take it you have read the book?" She nodded.

"Yes Miss Watson." I smiled.

"Call me Abby. So, who is your favourite character, and I mean the one you love most?" She gave a smile.

"I really love Willow, but I do not have the hair, I am more Bram looking." I knew it, this was what I was missing. I looked at her.

"Emily, this lovely woman is Jemi, I want you to copy her, and I mean, just do exactly as she does, okay?" She frowned; I looked at Birch.

"Stand up and say hello." Birch stood and gave a big smile; she lifted her hand and gave a little wave.

"Hi Sweetie." Emily did the same and as soon as she said it, I smiled.

"Hi Sweetie." I turned back to David and pointed back behind me.

"That is not Bram, that is without doubt Willow." He looked surprised.

"Really... Well, I never?" I looked back at the hopefuls who had made it through into the last stage.

"Will everyone gather on stage please in a long line?"

Brandon was not happy, but David appeared to be enjoying this, he winked, and I smiled. I turned back to the stage and looked at Emily.

"Emily, start learning the lines, congratulations, you are going to be Willow." She looked stunned, and her face lit up.

"Really... Oh Miss Watson, thank you so much." Birch giggled, as Emily did a little dance on her heels, and Anita laughed.

"Oh my god, there is two of them."

The group assembled on stage, and I grabbed Birch's hand and pulled her up, and we walked out of our seats, as I whispered in her ear, she gave a giggle as we reached the aisle, and together walked down to the steps of the stage. David leaned forward in his seat as Brandon turned and complained.

"David this is not how we do things, we have a protocol, she cannot just pick a random person out and tell her she has the part, we have not talked about it." Anita turned around and looked up.

"Actually, she can, this is her work, and part of the contract you signed states clearly, she has full control of main cast selection. Brandon, let me tell you something, that up there on that stage, that is the real life Bram and Willow. Abby based her book on what we now know as the Curio's. Gemma, is really Debbie, Melanie, is really Chloe, Scarlet, is really Edwina, and Daniel, is really Anthony. So sit back and watch, and those two will give you a perfect cast, and trust me, with those two, forget protocol, I have worked with them for ten years, and they do not know the meaning of it."

He flopped back in his seat complaining under his breath, and David smiled as he watched us on the stage with all the young actresses. Birch walked over to Emily, and took her hand, and walked her to the side of the stage.

"Sweetie, you are going to be me, I am so excited." Emily looked shocked.

"It's true then, you are the real life Willow?" Birch smiled, and gave a big nod.

"Yes Sweetie, I mean, the green hair thing is a bit wild, but what else could she do, I mean honestly, if she called her Birch, well it would have blown the game." Emily gasped, not able to contain her shock.

I gave Birch a nod, as everyone lined up, as I turned my back to them all. Just for reference, the character in the book is Gwen, but as we all know in real life, it is Bev. Birch gave a giggle.

"Hi Gwen."

"Guard your vagina!" I turned around and looked at them all.

"Who said that?" Two girls looked frightened and lifted their hands, I nodded.

"Both of you step forward." One of the girls looked panicked, and looked at me.

"I am so sorry Miss Watson, it just slipped out, I am sorry." The other girl looked at me and nodded, I smiled, and looked at the one who had spoken.

"What is your name?" She looked down at the floor.

"Jean Collins." I lifted my clip board, and flicked through the sheets, she was auditioning for Scarlet, the computer geek. I opened the script and found the part I wanted; it was a rough breakdown of each episode.

"Jean read the part from page 156, Gwen has arrived and Bram walked into the bedroom to see a panicked Gemma. Just read the Gemma line, and give it some feeling like you are really panicked and afraid you will be raped." She gave a nod and flicked through the scrip, she read the line to herself, and then took a deep breath.

"It's her, isn't it? Oh no.... I am the weakest; she will force my consent first.... Please Bram I just decided, I am not gender fluid, I don't want that mouth pleasuring me down there."

She sounded great, but I frowned and lifted the script, and read the lines, I glanced at Birch who was looking confused. I turned around and looked across at David and Brandon, and lifted the script up, and felt my anger rise.

"What the hell is this shit?" Anita gave a giggle; I stared at Brandon.

"Did you write this pile of crap, because I frigging know I didn't, have you even read the book?" Birch gave a giggle, and looked at Emily.

"Oh Sweetie, watch this, God, she is so sexy when she gets pissed off." Emily gave a little, dare I say, Birch like snigger. Brandon sat forward in his seat looking offended.

"Miss Watson, you have to understand, this is TV, not books, we have a completely different way of phrasing things, and there is a certain set of all inclusive pronouns that are acceptable these days." I felt so angry as I stared at him.

"You mean virtue signaling, PC bullshit? Do you even understand the point of this book, have you even read the whole why does his gayness matter part? There is bloody reason this book is written this way, and it is the whole reason the end of the book is like it is. This is my work, my lines, my frigging book, and you have no right to use a virtue signaling hatchet, to completely destroy it. The whole book is about bullying and shaming, it is about shunning all the labels of society and redefining one that is appropriate to just them. How dare you call this utter garbage a script." Birch gave a happy chuckle, and put her arm around Emily.

"God, she is glorious, I am so wet for her at the moment." Brandon stood and looked close to tears.

"I have worked for the biggest and the best, I worked for the national theatre, my work is all over the BBC, and quite frankly Miss Watson, I find you crude and utterly unprofessional." He turned and looked at David.

"Either she goes, or I do." Anita sniggered.

"Brandon, this is her book, if she goes, there will not be a story, well not one worth watching." He gave a huff, flicked back his head, turned, and stormed down the row towards the isle flapping his hands.

"That is it, I will not stand by and be insulted, I feel victimised, utterly triggered and violated, I am leaving." Both Birch and Emily turned at the same time and waved.

"Bye Sweetie." Anita shuddered, as she watched them.

"Holy shit, that is scary." I looked over at Emily.

"Emily, can I borrow your copy of the book a moment please?"

She came over and handed it to me with a smile, I winked, and then flicked through the pages to find the piece I wanted. I walked over towards Jean and handed her the open book, then pointed.

"Read that line, and make me believe in you."

She looked at the book and then looked up as I walked back to the front of the stage.

"It's her, isn't it? Oh shit…. I am the weakest; she will rape me first…. Please Bram I just decided, I am not gay, I don't want those teeth down there." I smiled, and Birch gave a nod.

"Okay that is two, congratulations Jean, you are going to be Gemma."

She gave a huge smile, I pointed to Birch, she handed the book to the other girl, and she ran over the stage to where Emily and Birch both hugged her. I looked at the other girl who was stood forward.

"What is your name?"

"Karen Halliwell Miss Watson." I nodded and flicked through the sheets; I had noted her attitude. I looked up.

"You are auditioning for Bram?" She nodded, I noted her

stance, and looked at her, she was nervous it was clear, but also a little more confident than any of the others.

"Tell me Karen, are you gay, or straight?" She looked nervous, and looked back at the others, she turned and looked at me.

"I am straight, oh I am definitely straight."

"How straight?" She stood sort of leaning to one side.

"Oh, I am straight alright, and I mean, I am really straight." Birch giggled.

"Say... I paint and I fuck." She looked panicked.

"I paint and I fuck." I glanced at Birch.

"Do it with attitude." She stood up straight and looked really cocky.

"I paint and I fuck." Birch giggled, and I smiled.

"Very good, I like it, tell me, have you actually read Seeds of Summer?" She looked guilty.

"Not completely Miss Watson... I have read the first ten, and I am going to read the rest, and If I get a part, I promise I will do, honestly." And suddenly 'Boom!' There was Chloe, her body movements her attitude and her sincerity.

"Congratulations Karen, you will be Melanie the artist, give me your address, and I will send you a copy of the book." She gave a huge smile.

"Thank you, I won't let you down, I promise." She ran off over to Birch and the others and they all hugged. David leaned over in his seat, and spoke quietly to Anita.

"Do not worry about Brandon, I have a young script writer who begged for this script, he is quite a fan of Abigail's, we will make some changes. I must say, I am really enjoying how she is selecting the cast." Anita gave a nod.

"In real life, these characters are based on her closest friends, trust her David, because if you do, the fans will love this, and she has one hell of a lot of fans."

I walked across the stage to the first girl in the line and handed her the book, she took it, and I walked back to the front of the stage, and looked at them all.

"Start at page one line one, and when I say next, pass the book on to the next person to continue from that point, okay?" They all nodded. I closed my eyes. "Right... Begin!"

"There comes a time during those hallowed days of university, when you sit up rather abruptly, and the seriousness of the moment hits you bang in the face."

"Next."

"I talk of that moment when through the haze of the wild days of leisure time, alcoholic binges, and the endless slipping between the bed sheets."

"Next."

"With some spotty faced literature nerd, that the fog of your wonderful life clears, and you realise it's time to go home for the summer."

"Next."

"There is no doubt that this is that moment of crisis and panic, when the sudden realisation that all of this wonderful lifestyle, is about to end, as it grabs you and drags you back to the sobering cold light of day. Going home should be a happy, wonderful experience, but for myself, it felt like I had escaped from prison, only to be caught on the run, breathing the fresh taste of pure freedom, and I was about to be dragged back kicking and screaming."

"Stop." Birch smiled. I opened my eyes and looked at the girl holding the book.

"What is your name?" She swallowed, and I noticed her leg tremble a little.

"Paula Johnson, Miss Watson." I looked at Birch and she was smiling.

"What say you Birch?" She gave a little chuckle.

"Sweetie, she is perfect, I mean look at her." I smiled.

"Well Paula, you will never get a better recommendation than that, because she lives with the real Bram. Congratulations, the part is most definitely yours."

She gave me a huge smile, wow, she had the long blonde hair, the bright blue eyes, and the perfect accent and tone to her voice, it was like listening to myself. Okay, it was a little creepy, but I could not deny, she really was like a younger me."

I finally picked Penelope Walters, for Scarlet, aka Edwina, and an almost lookalike of Bev, called Jane Patterson. All that was left was the part of Anthony as the guys lined up on the stage. It was not easy, they were all tall, mainly blonde, and all of them would play the role well, Birch came up to my side as we watched, and one of them flicked his head and lifted his hand to slide back his fringe. I pointed.

"You... What is your name?"

"Kevin Leigh." I walked over to him; Birch followed.

"Are you gay or straight?" He looked surprised and frowned.

"Straight, can you not tell?" Birch giggled; I looked at him.

"What makes you think you can play this part?" He went straight into character.

"Darling please... I had a friend who killed himself because he was gay, I always told him, be proud, be you." Birch fondled my bum.

"That is Anthony, Deads." I gave him a nod.

"You know, I have a lot of fans who love this story, you might get some flack for a gay part?" He nodded.

"I know how hard it can be Miss Watson; he was a great mate, I saw what he went through." I was sold, and gave a nod.

"Yeah, my friend has been through hell too. Congratulations Kevin, do your friend proud and play him, and make the whole world sit up and take notice." He gave a big smile.

"He would like that, Miss Watson." I patted his shoulder.

"Well done, you earned this part." I turned and looked out across the seats at Anita and David.

"That is your main cast David, get the script right, and you will have a hit." He stood up and stretched.

"Have no fear Abby, we will, and you will get it before anyone to approve." He clapped his hands.

"Can anyone not selected please leave the stage and thank you for coming in, we have your details for a chance of other parts."

Birch slipped her arm around my waist as we looked at the small group all excited and happy.

"Wow Deads, is it me or is it really scary, that we are looking at young versions of ourselves?" I chuckled.

"Emily is good, to be honest all of them are, do you think people will notice, I mean, the book is about us after all?" She pulled me close as Anita walked up onto the stage with David.

"To be honest Sweetie, what does it matter, think about everything that has already been written about us, hell, what else can they write?"

It was a good point, I had been dragged by the press through the mire for years, and to be honest, they had been pretty terrible. David invited us with the new cast for a drink across the road in the local pub, and so all of us headed across the road and sat back and relaxed.

The talk was loud and happy as I got asked a million questions, Emily was stuck like glue to Birch, mimicking her and the funniest thing was, she did not even realise, she kept looking at me with bright happy eyes and pointing.

"Sweetie, she is so like Willow, she is marvellous."

She had completely forgotten that all Emily was doing, was copying her. Anita was hysterical laughing at the two of them. I was happy, I wanted this production to be a good one, and by the time we had to leave, I hugged everyone, ensuring Anita had their numbers, I told them all that they would have to visit one weekend and meet the Curio's.

We arrived back late, and Anita came in for a drink of coffee, we were all tired and it had felt like a long day. We sat in the kitchen talking, and Birch updated Anita, and as it came time for her to leave, she stood at the door and pulled me into a hug.

"It was fun today; I really enjoyed it."

"Yeah, me too."

I watched her walk down the drive and jump into her car, she was heading home to Tabby, and I smiled as we turned to head for bed as Birch locked the door. The house was quiet, the kids were asleep, and Deli had her door open, I could see her sat on her bed with her laptop on her knee, she was on the Curio site talking to the others.

Birch held my hand with a smile, she was happy and relaxed, we walked into our room and I headed for my desk. I sat down in front of the computer, I had not been on the Curio site for a couple of days, I clicked the icon and it opened. The site showed there were new uploads, so I sat back, and clicked the video section, and stared at the screen in shock. My breath caught in my chest as I saw a young girl sitting on her bed, I clicked the link, and the video began to play.

"Hi... I am Daniella, Danny, I am nine years old, not far off ten, and me and my sister just lost our parents in a traffic accident."

I felt a huge surge run through me, as I saw her stumble on her words.

"I am okay, I am sad, really sad and my little sister is having a hard time with it all, the local services want to put us into care, because my dad's family hate us. They do not want to help us, and I really do not know why, and I am really scared at the moment." Tears filled my eyes, as I watched and I gave a big sob, Birch turned to me in her seat.

"Sweetie, are you alright, what is it?"

She slid over to me and looked at the screen, and I saw her face cloud over. I wiped my eyes, and looked back at the screen, she was wiping hers and trying to talk.

"I know this is crazy, but my aunt is actually a Curio, I have never actually met her, and she is going to come over to meet us, and I could end up leaving home and moving to the UK. I came on here because I am so frightened, she won't like us, and we will end up separated, I don't want to lose my sister, she is all I have left. I guess I thought you guys on here would know what to do."

I could not talk as the video ended, I just sat staring, tears rolling down my face, I mean, how do you answer that? There was a ping, and I looked to see a comment posted. I scrolled down and Deli had commented.

'Do not be afraid, your aunt is a wonderful person, and she would never allow that to happen, trust me, I have known her a long time, and she will only ever do what is right for you.' Birch smiled, and leaned into me and pulled me close.

"God Deads, she is so like you, same tears, same fears, hell, it is like watching your video all over again. You need to sit with her face to face, and give her a reassurance that everything will be fine." I swallowed hard as I stared at the frozen picture.

"How do I do that Birch?" She turned and looked at me.

"Oh, Sweetie you silly, I have told you. Be you... Simply that, and trust me it will flow out of you and surround her in love." The screen pinged, and I saw another comment posted, it was Chloe.

'Honestly girl, listen to Deli, you really have nothing to fear, and all of us cannot wait to meet you. Although the UK is freezing in Winter, so pack lots of socks if you come.' Birch squeezed me and smiled.

"Look Deads, Chloe is on the job, she will be fine now." I leaned back and snuggled into her as she leaned over me.

"I want to talk to her so badly, but honestly what do I say, I am a weak substitute for her real mother?"

"Deads, just tell her what is in your heart." She leaned back and slid in front of her seat, and suddenly I knew what to say, I shuffled forward and clicked the comments box.

'Danny, you really do not need to be afraid, no one will do anything to make you unhappy, and making sure you and your sisters stay side by side is the most important thing for all of us. The Curio's are on your side and in your corner, and no matter what it takes, we will not let you or your sister down, and that is a promise.'

I hit enter and it posted, and I prayed she would read it soon; I looked at Birch, and she was typing, she looked so focused and I had to smile.

"Birch, I am glad we are going over sooner, and did not wait for the live show." She gave a small smile.

"Me too Sweetie, they need us, and we will be with them very soon."

Chapter 15

Cold Dealings.

Since posting her video, the response on the Curio site had been massive, and there was a really long list of really nice comments. I cannot deny, having seen them, I had a new found love of the Curio Life site, it had always meant a lot to me, but now it meant everything.

It was two days later, and we had been driven to the airport at two in the morning by Chloe, where we had hugged her goodbye, and flew direct to Chicago, where we had a one hour stay over, and then boarded a plane to Jefferson City Missouri.

When we landed, it was just gone seven in the morning US time, and my body clock was all over the place. I had slept on the plane, and so I felt wide awake and happy, I saw the customs officials and grabbed Birch's arm. Even now, I still panic when I see them, having never forgotten my moment of terror when stopped at Heathrow. In fact, such is my fear, that once Birch had packed, I snuck back into our room, and unpacked and repacked her case. You know, just to make sure.

We made it through customs with nothing to declare, although they did inspect my laptop bag, but knowing who I was, I soon sailed through, which was a huge help. We came out to the usual line of drivers and excited family waiting for people holding signs, and I almost walked past a tall American bloke holding a sign for, 'Watson.'

I guess it is silly, but I am now so used to being Mrs Dixon, it simply does not register with me. I was alerted to him, when he stepped forward and announced.

"Excuse me Ma'am, but are you Miss Abigail Watson?" I stopped and looked at him in his chauffer uniform.

"Yes, that is me." He gave me a wide smile.

"I am here to collect you Ma'am, I was sent by Mrs Bannon, I will be driving you to the hotel." Birch smiled, and leaned into my ear.

"I like you being a Sweetie Ma'am." Yep, flying makes her stranger.

He was really polite, and tall, I mean, wow, he towered above us. He was called Jedidiah or Jed for short. We needed cash, because I really needed coffee and according to Jed it was going to be a long drive. He showed us to the exchange, and Birch pulled out a huge wad of twenty pound notes to change, you have no idea how much it bothers me that she always has so much cash on her, and I have never understood why she has never bought a purse?

With two huge take out coffees for me, and one for Birch, which I had to haggle about as obviously straight coffee over here is weird. I cannot deny, I have no idea why they have to have such a huge list of coffee, most of which look more like an ice cream than an actual coffee, and why all the weird names, and why so many, asking for a coffee, is now like listing the ingredients of a cake?

We headed to the limo, and jumped in, sat back, sipped the brown nectar of life. Yeah, about that... Us Brits make better coffee; however, it accomplished the task, and I relaxed, as Birch looked out of the window pointing out things.

"Sweetie, this place is beautiful, it is like old western America meets modern America."

My mind was elsewhere, I was feeling nervous, there was a lot riding on this meeting, and to be honest, I was terrified. I know it sounds crazy, but I really wanted to be liked by them, and I knew I was building my hopes up, but for a few days I had been sat with Chloe talking, she was so excited, and having talked everything through with Birch, I was too.

Oh God, am I going overboard? I really want to do this, I want them to like me and grow close to me, oh crap, am I broody? Has that all womanly part of my hormone system kicked in, and finally my womanly urges are raging? Christ, if I look at a baby and go, 'awe, it is so cute,' I will kill myself.

The hotel was some distance away, and I spent most of the journey lost in space, thinking about what the next twenty four hours of my life would be like, and worrying myself to death. We finally arrived, the limo door was opened, and it jolted me back to reality, I slid out and Jed smiled.

"Don't worry about the bags Ma'am, I will have them brought in."

He lifted his hand and clicked, and a bus boy ran out as the boot opened. He closed the door, and we followed. The first thing I noticed was the humidity, it was swelteringly hot, I was glad to get inside which like the limo, was air conditioned, and I followed Jed to reception.

"Mrs Watson and partner, the Bannon account." The clerk nodded, and spun the book around, and we signed in. Jed gave a polite bow.

"I hope you enjoy your stay ladies, both of you have a nice day." I went to pull a twenty dollar bill out of my pocket and he smiled, and placed his hand on mine.

"Don't you worry none Ma'am; I am very well provided for." He smiled, turned, and walked out; Birch watched him leave.

"You know Deads, people here are very polite, I really like it."

The room was like many others we have stayed in, it was large and airy with a soft bed, it had a bathroom, and best of all large doors and a balcony. In UK time, it was somewhere around four in the afternoon, but I was feeling tired, I slipped off my shoes and lay back on the bed, and just relaxed. Janet had left us a letter, she had booked a table in the hotel restaurant for seven tonight, and also wanted us to meet her in the lobby at two this afternoon. I relaxed; I slept on the plane but suddenly felt exhausted.

Birch sat out on the balcony and sipped a coffee, as she set up her laptop, mine was going cold at the side of the bed, as I slipped into sleep. I was awoken by Birch; she sat at the side of me smiling.

"Deads, you need to wake up, we will have to go shortly, I made you a fresh coffee." I sat up feeling groggy, and yawned, she handed me the cup.

"Have a wash and freshen up, it is really warm here."

I sat sipping my coffee as I slowly came round, I had not slept well for the past week, and to add to that, the jet lag had completely wiped me out. I licked my lips, as I looked round to get my bearings again. With the windows opened wide, a soft warm breeze blew in, but thank God for the air conditioning, I looked up at Birch as she brushed her hair.

"Will it be this hot at Curio Live?" She smiled at me as she pulled the brush down and screwed up her face as she found a knot.

"If it is Sweetie, I am doing it naked." I giggled, well there was an idea, I mean hell, we would certainly raise the funds we needed. I slipped off the bed and walked into the bathroom, I felt hot and sticky.

"Birch, how long have we got, have I got time for a quick shower?"

"Be quick Deads, I just jumped in, had a quick wash down and jumped out." I peered around the door.

"You had a shower?" She turned and smiled.

"It was hardly a shower, I stood under it, did a fast rub down to get the sweat off and jumped out."

"Wow, you shower cheated on me." She giggled.

"You were tired, this has been emotionally draining for you, so I let you sleep a little more. There is a huge bath, how about later we slip in together?" I gave her smile, and nodded.

"Yeah, I would love that."

Having had the quickest shower ever, which I will not deny, made me feel so much better and awake, I dressed in a long skirt, and loose fitting thin top, and headed down to the lobby, Janet was waiting, and walked up as we left the lift.

"Abigail, Jemima, it is so nice to finally meet and talk in person." She shook our hands and guided us to the dining room, as we walked, she talked.

"Okay, the paperwork is going through, and as long as you are both happy and the children feel they can do this, we will proceed. Unfortunately, news travels fast, and before you meet the girls, I thought we should attend to some unsavoury business." I looked at her puzzled.

Oh god, was my past coming back to haunt me, was my wild teenage behaviour documented somewhere in the inner files of the FBI, and it was all about to be cast into the light to yet again shame and destroy me?

"How do you mean, unsavoury business, are we in trouble?" She gave a smile.

"Oh Honey, you have nothing to fear, however, there is a representative of the Fairbanks family who wishes to speak with you." I swallowed hard.

"Why do they want to see me, I thought they saw my family as trash, and wanted nothing to do with this?" She shook her head.

"They see everyone as trash, but nevertheless, they want you to meet with them, they specifically asked for this, which is the first time they have reached out to me, so I assume it is important."

We walked into the large dining room, where a table was laid out, and two men in suits sat talking. To the sides, two heavy men in all black wearing sunglasses, watched us, I assumed they were body guards. As we approached the men, both stood up, one was impeccably dressed and dripping in gold, and had a smug smirk on his face. I have met men like this before. He was about early forties, had the right perfectly tailored suit, immaculate hair, groomed to perfection, and was utterly full of himself. Colin Richmond from Curio Live came to mind, he looked like they belonged to the same set.

The other man was very well dressed, around mid fifties, and looked stern, we approached the table, and he gave me that rehearsed business like smile, and held out his hand. He oozed charm.

"Miss Watson, I am delighted to meet you, I am Matthew Fairbanks, Peter's older brother."

And yep, I hated the shit bag. I took his hand and shook it, noting the rings and manicure. I reached out my arm to Birch, he did not even acknowledge her, and cut in before I could speak.

"This is Walter Parker, our family attorney." He gave a nod. Matthew gestured to the table.

"Please, be seated, this is an informal meeting, let's relax and talk a while."

I noted his speech was not that accentuated, and he spoke very good English. I sat down, and he smiled at me as he sat, I looked at him and his attorney.

"It's Dixon." He frowned.

"What is?" I smiled.

"My name, Watson is my maiden name, but I am married, so its Mrs Dixon." He looked at Birch, and then back at me.

"Oh, do your type do that? How lovely, I wasn't aware of that." I felt Birch tense.

"We do, so why do you wish to see me, I must admit Mr Fairbanks I am a little surprised, I am assuming you are not a fan of my books?" He smirked.

"We believe that you will be taking over the welfare of the children, so father thought it best we meet and talk, and there are one or two legal matters to sort out, of which we would like you to oblige." I gave a nod.

"Oh, how rude of me, would you care for a drink, I believe you drink gin and lemon?" Birch leaned in.

"Not really, we prefer rum and cola, that is very kind of you, thanks."

The lack of a Sweetie in that sentence told me everything I needed to know. Matthew lifted his arm, clicked his fingers, and the waitress appeared.

"Bring the ladies a rum and cola, and I will have a scotch, single malt, on ice." She gave a nod and walked off, he looked at me, as he watched until waitress was out of ear shot.

"Mrs Dixon, we are led to believe you will take the children to your family home in the UK, can you elaborate on your intentions, and what your plans are?"

I sat back for a moment and considered the question, I cannot deny, I could not understand why he would ask that. He watched me with that air of smugness about him, and my instincts were already talking to me, he was one person I could never trust.

The waitressed arrived and served the drinks, I thanked her as he watched me, she smiled and left. I lifted my glass and took a sip, oh hell, I needed this, this guy was a conceited arse, and I was finding it hard to remain polite. I sat back in my chair and looked at him.

"Mr Fairbanks, in response to your question... No." Janet twitched, Birch took another quick sip of her drink. He frowned and leaned forward.

"Excuse me?" Yeah, not so cocky now, was he? I looked him in the eyes.

"Why do you care? You are their legally responsible family, and yet you have cut them out completely. You have made it more than clear your family have no interest in your brothers' children at all, so why do I, another family member, have to justify anything at all to you?" He looked at his attorney as if he had no answer for that, and then he looked back at me, I could see he was struggling with a response.

"Mrs Dixon, you must be aware of who my father is, he wants to know how these children will be raised?"

I smiled at him, my mind racing, as I sat there just thinking that this is possibly the most disgraceful human being I have met, and I knew Martin Hinkley. I took a breath, and looked him right in the eye, and tried to hide my anger.

"Mr Fairbanks, I know little of your family or father, but I am assuming he is a man who has never heard the word no in his life. To be quite frank, he has made it quite clear what his position is on the children, and so the way I see it, it is none of his business how those children will be raised. He turned his back on them, and so therefore as far as I can tell, is forfeit to any information regarding their future." Janet smirked again.

Walter leaned in and whispered in Matthew's ear, he gave a soft nod, and then looked at me, and gave a long sigh.

"Mrs Dixon, I really do not think you fully understand the situation here." I gave a nod. He had no idea how much I understood this, I grew up in a village full of people like his family.

"I understand this full well, I grew up with a father who was a brilliant accountant, I have seen every scam and protectionist trick there is, and watched my father unravel it. So why don't we both stop talking in circles, I am well aware of why you are here, so cut the crap, lay your cards out on the table, and let us all have a good look at them."

Birch gave a snort and lifted her glass, Janet put her head down and he looked positively shocked. I smiled, I knew his type so well, for years I listened to dad rant about them. He just sat staring at me, and I leaned back lifted my glass and sipped, I lifted my eyes above the glass.

"Yes, I am English, we do not dance around like this over the water, we talk straight and do not try to con people, as I am sure your international business dealings have shown you that. So, what have you got in mind?" Walter looked at me, as Matthew sat looking dumb struck.

"Mrs Dixon, I am sure you are aware there is a trust fund for the children that will need to be managed?" I nodded, and there it was, it is always money with these sort of people.

"I am, and my accountant will no doubt wish to see it, and look it over to see if it can be enhanced." He frowned.

"Enhanced, how do you mean Mrs Dixon?" I took a sip of my drink, and placed the glass down. I breathed in and looked at him.

There it was, the money grabbers just assumed I was here for the money, typical posh stuck up pricks, all they care about is the money. It made me so angry, it was all they cared about, and the lives of the children were meaningless to them.

"I want my financial team to look it over, check its performance, and then, if possible, make it work to its maximum potential. These girls have suffered enough, I would like to be able to know in later life, things will be easier for them financially." Matthew looked confused.

"If that is the case, why are you here?"

Birch leaned forward, and I knew she had gathered the intel she required. I sat back and watched her go to work, God, I love her.

"Mr Fairbanks, may I call you Matty, good?" She smiled at him.

"We are more than financially stable; I know you know that because it is clear you have looked into us. I think it is reasonable to suffice, that you are here to try and work out if we are here to steal all the children's money, after all, I am assuming Peter invested some of his money into it. Let me be quite clear here, we do not give a rat's ass about the money, if it makes you happy, I will gladly ensure Pete's contribution is handed back to you, because even then, we will still ensure it grows at a very good rate for their future. We are here for the children, and to try and do what is right for them, which is what a proper family do. I take it, you are here to make us give some form of guarantee, we are not after daddies' cash, am I right?"

She sat back in her seat and smiled at him, and raised her eye brows, he looked astounded and turned to Walter, who appeared to have been completely thrown. I am not sure they are used to such straight talk. Birch lifted her glass.

"Show us the paperwork, that is why you are here, so let us get on with it. It is blatantly clear you want to be anywhere we are not... Oh and Sweetie's trust me; the feeling is mutual."

Janet had her head down, and was biting her lip, I was busy staring at Matthew who was growing more and more uncomfortable. Walter leaned down and lifted his case onto the table, God I love Birch, she is so tuned in to people, and she just sits, watches, and learns. Walter slid out some paperwork from his case, now we were really getting down to the brass tacks of it all.

"Mrs Dixon. My employer, Mr Fairbanks senior, has had these papers drawn up. They are an agreement that asks you to state that you have no interests whatsoever in the Fairbanks estate, and agree to never approach the family, in any legal format for any monetary recompense. I have another that will request you do not disclose any information to these dealings, or connection to the Fairbanks family at all, and another to state you will take full legal responsibility for the children." Janet gave a long sigh, as she looked at the two men with utter contempt.

"My God, you are all lower than a snake's belly."

Birch leaned over and pulled the papers across to look at them. She laid them on the table in front of me and leaned in to read, honestly, I was shocked at how cold they were.

I am not sure why really, every time I had encountered the very wealthy, they had always been the same, the smell of money in their nostrils and the reek of control stamped all over them. I had worked my ass off to get where I was, and okay, I was a millionaire, but it had taken years to get here, but this lot, they were that slightly so called better class, they were billionaires, and they lived on the control of others, and they turned my stomach. Birch looked up from the paperwork.

"We would like to look these over with my legal people, before we sign. I am sure we can have them returned by tomorrow, although, this one you can take back now, we do not sign gagging orders, which this clearly is." She sat back in her seat and looked at Matthew.

"You know Matty, when we walked in you looked down on us, like we were lower than you. I am aware of your families' dealings, your investments, property management, and your two hundred million dollar estate in the Hampton's. Granted, I have a lot of money in investments and savings, and understand that even I am not in your financial league, but may I point out, wealth, is not a measure of character. Having done a little investigation, like I know you have of us, I am aware of who your family are and how many billions you have. But you know, looking at your family, I think you have a nerve to treat us as lesser. Your own personal history is not so sparkling, and your brother Scott's is downright sordid, and yet you sit and presume to tell us what to do, as if your billions give you the right to do so. Well, let me correct that little misunderstanding for the purpose of helping you gain a little wisdom. We are no angels, but we are not the demons your family has been in the past, yes, we too could pay people a lot of money like you do, to gag them, we choose not to. So, in regard to that piece of gagging legislative bull shit you have there in your hand, I will offer this old northern English saying... Simply put, Screw You."

He sat looking utterly bewildered, Walter just stared at Birch with a scowl, it was clear he was offended, and had no like of either of us at all. I stood up and lifted the papers from the table.

"You know Mr Fairbanks, I find what you have done reprehensible, vulgar and very distasteful. Your brother has two very beautiful children, and yet you chose this path and completely ignored the fact, that those children are grieving for the loss of their parents. How cold can a person be, it is utterly shameful behaviour? I can assure you, those children will have a stable loving home, and a very high quality of life, and if I am lucky, they will grow up to be nothing like your family. I am assuming we are done here." Matthew looked up at me, like nothing I said meant anything.

"One more thing, we want my grandmother's ring returning." Janet looked at me.

"Peter gave it to Amanda; it was her wedding ring." I nodded and looked at him.

"I cannot do that, Amanda and Peter's estate was bequeathed to both of the children, and so that is rightfully their property, and their decision. I will talk to the children and convey your request, and if they wish to, I will help them return it to you, would that be agreeable?" He looked so pissed off, and weirdly enough that made me happy, he snapped at me.

"FINE!" I smiled.

"Good, we are done... By the way, we shook hands, it is probably better if you wash it, I will be. Good day gentlemen." I dropped a twenty dollar bill on the table.

"That is for the drinks, I would hate for you to be out of pocket." Janet sniggered, as we turned and walked away. She gave us a big smile as she hurried up to our side.

"Well holy moly, if you two aren't just the dandiest little fire crackers I ever met, never in my life have I seen that family squirm such. Ladies, I am buying you a drink." Birch giggled, as she grabbed my arm and snuggled into it.

"Sweetie, are we a pair of dandies?" I winked.

"Yankee doodle do." We laughed, as we headed for the bar.

We sat in the bar, and Janet talked about the family, and how badly they had treated Peter and Amanda. There was no love that was for sure, she talked of how much they were resented locally, and how cold and cruel they could be. She made it clear they could be ruthless, and to be wary of them. Birch needed the documents scanning, and Janet offered us the use of her equipment at her office, so Birch got on her phone and made a call, ran up to the room, grabbed her laptop, and we jumped in Janet's car, and drove to her office.

Janet ran a much bigger operation than we realised, we sat in her office as her clerk scanned the documents, and placed them on a flash drive, and Birch booted up her laptop and connected to Roni via video call. Roni appeared smiling.

"Hi girls, how are things going?" Birch gave a wave; it always amused me how she waved to her mum.

"Mum, I need a favour." She smiled.

"Why does that not surprise me?" Birch shrugged and smiled.

"We have some documents, and we need them looking at fast, this Fairbanks family are bloody cold and ruthless, and they want us to sign a few things, and I want a Dixon Group legal opinion on them fast." She gave a nod.

"It is late here Jemi, but I will get right on it, how are the girl's, are they alright?" Birch sighed.

"Honestly mum, the further away from that family, the better I will feel. Email me as soon as you can, and let us know what you think. I have not got very long, but give our love to dad for us, we love you mum." She gave a sad smile.

"Those children deserve better from them. Alright Sweetheart, I will be all over this and get it moving for you, is there anything we can do to help?" Birch nodded.

"Yes, I need you call Edwina, I called a while back, she needs a little more info, so update her for me."

While Birch had a quick chat with her mum and filled her in on the day's events, I stood on the opposite side of the office, at the tall window with Janet. I liked her, she felt like one of the good guys, I watched as she stared out at the sky.

"You really do not like them, do you?" She gave a sigh.

"Abigail, they make my skin crawl with their fake smiles, and their false morals. They are cruel and deceitful, and those children are so lovely, and they deserve better treatment than they have been given. They are grieving the loss of their parents, and all that family care about is protecting their assets, I despise them."

I turned and leaned my back on the glass, and sipped my coffee, and watched Birch as she giggled with her mum.

"We have a lovely home, Janet. I hope you will visit; I live around some very lovely people. Chloe is an artist and she will adore them, and possibly spoil them. Edwina is bright and so clever with technology, and she holds a love and protection for her sister stronger than any I have ever known, she will love them. Anthony is the kindest and most caring person I have ever met, I love him so much, he is my brother in every sense of the word, and Deli, oh Deli will love them to bits. My best friend is Deb's, and she is the most loving person I know, she is a huge softy, and an amazing mum. Honestly, the house is filled with so much love, and as for that one there, they will love her, she is quite bonkers, but in a very lovely way. These children will learn so much from her, and their lives will be massively enhanced just knowing her, and I should know, she has made my world so beautiful and wonderful, she is the joy in my every waking minute."

I turned and she was stood smiling at me. She gave me a nod, and looked at Birch talking to her mother.

"I know she went on the site Abby, I visit it, I saw the video, and I saw how you all supported her. I talked to her and she was so relieved, you know, you are not the only one who is nervous, they are too. Abby, they need a home filled with love, they have been through a lot, and from the little I have seen, I think you are perfectly placed to give them that." I felt the lump in my throat, and my eyes filled up with tears.

"I want that for them, I really know what it is like to feel unloved and unwanted, I do not want them to suffer like that, I really don't, they have been through enough." She handed me a tissue.

"I do believe they will heal in your care. Abby, you will never know how relieved I was when I spoke to you. Oh, you have no idea, how worried I was. Yet as we spoke, and I looked at you, I knew that you and Amanda had so much in common, you know you really do look like her. It was quite shocking when I first saw you, the family resemblance is remarkable. I am very pleased to see you here, and I was proud of the way you stood up for them today, I do believe I made the right choice contacting you."

I wiped my eyes and gave a sniffle as Birch ended the call, and came over to hug me.

"I really want this Janet, I know there is a lot of legal red tape, but I really want to protect them from those vultures, and help them heal. We really need you to help us and make this all work out for their best, and I am so grateful for all you have done." She gave me a smile as Birch hugged me.

"I will make you a deal. I will work my ass off for you two, and those lovely children, and in return, I want the best seats in the house for me, my two boys, and my husband, for Curio Live." Birch gave a giggle.

"Hell Sweetie, if we can pull this off, you will have back stage passes." She smiled and raised her cup of coffee.

"Ladies, you have a deal."

Chapter 16

The Gothic Sting.

Janet drove us back to the hotel, and dropped us off to prepare for the evening meal, we both felt tired, as the jetlag was really kicking in. We slipped into a bath together, and I just relaxed in the hot water, with Birch's arms around me and it felt lovely. I leaned back and gave a long happy sigh.

"Oh God, I need this." She gave a little chuckle.

"You really impressed me today Deads, I was so proud of the way you handled everything, you really stood up for our girls." I turned and glanced at her.

"Our girls? Birch, we still have a lot of legal stuff to do first." She smiled.

"Janet wants what is best for them, trust me, she will work herself to death to get those two to us. I like her, she is our kind of people."

I hoped so, if the truth be known, the Fairbanks family scared me, they were cold and calculating, and I had a feeling we had not heard the last of them. Birch leaned back.

"You know Sweetie, you tense up when you think about them, you worry too much, they are not as powerful as they think they are. You know, I love mobile phones; I love all the apps I have, they are surprisingly versatile, especially the voice recording app." I turned feeling a shock to my system.

"You recorded them?" She smiled.

"Sweetie, you are the love of my life, you were protecting our girls, and so I was protecting you. I hate to point it out Deads, but I was not born yesterday."

She gave me a big smile and I started to laugh, God, I love her so much, even now, she never fails to surprise me.

Once we had soaked until the water went cold, we sat on the bed, dried each others hair, it was so nice to be naked in the heat. We dressed casually in skirts and loose tops, and made our way downstairs to the restaurant, to meet Janet. She smiled as I walked in and stepped to one side, and my heart lurched in my chest, Birch gave a gasp.

"Hi ED!"

"DAD!"

I ran over to him as he smiled, and I pulled him into my arms, and almost crushed him. He put his arm round me; he walked with a stick now. It felt like I had not seen him in so long. Angela smiled as she saw me. I slipped out of his hug and he smiled, he looked so old, but his eyes appeared filled with life.

"It is lovely to see you Abigail, I have missed you." I wiped my eyes.

"Oh Dad, I am so happy to see you." He had tears in his eyes, as he smiled, Birch pulled him into a huge hug.

"Ed, it is lovely you came for her, I am so thrilled, how are you?" I pulled Angela into a big hug.

"Thanks for bringing him. Oh Angela, it is so good to see you both, I am completely thrown." She gave me a big smile as I wiped my eyes.

"He has been following the progress, he is so happy you are taking Danny and Jessie, the loss of Amanda and Peter gave him quite a shock. Oh Abby, you have no idea how much this means to him, he is so happy." I nodded.

"We are family Angela." She smiled.

"They are lovely children, have you seen them yet?" I shook my head.

"Not yet, we will be meeting them tomorrow."

She took my hand and gave it a squeeze, and then we turned to the table, where Birch was helping to sit my dad down. We both sat either side of him, and he smiled and took both of our hands and held them, he looked at Birch and then me.

"What you are doing for those girls is so wonderful, I am so proud of you both."

He looks older every time I see him, his hair has really thinned, and his face has more lines than ever, but he has a great tan, and his eyes have more life in them than I have ever seen.

Janet sat down, and the story unfolded of how she had contacted my dad and spoke with him. He took over the story of how Amanda and Peter had stayed with them for four weeks two years ago, and how Peter had talked for a long time about how his family had treated him. Since that time, they had remained in touch by email, and talked a lot. Dad had helped them set up the trust funds, and had actually recommended the American branch of EFG to manage them. He held my hand throughout all of it.

We ate a meal, which was a bit of a shock, as I have never in my life seen such huge plates of food. On my last visit to the States, they were big, but these were massive. I struggled to eat it all, whilst my stick thin wife, devoured the lot. He sat at the end of the table with us sat in front, to each side of him, and as the plates were cleared, he took both our hands and gave a big smile.

"Girl's I will not deny, that as much as I love you both dearly, it has saddened me that you would never know the joy of being parents. I was not the best at it and made many mistakes, but I will not deny, having such wonderful daughters has been the joy of my life. I love you both deeply, and I am so proud and also so delighted that now, both of you will understand the joy of raising children. We are a family, Phillipa was very dear to me, I loved my little sister deeply, and her daughter was such a wonderful woman, and to be honest, she and you Abigail are very similar. Taking these children and giving them a good home, has brought me great joy, and I know Phillipa would be so happy if she was here now to see this."

I wiped my eyes for the hundredth time, as he squeezed my hand, and smiled at me, and I could see the happiness radiate from him, and it was clear how much this meant to him.

"I love you so much dad. But we do not have them yet." He smiled at me.

"You will, I have made sure of it." I frowned, and Birch leaned forward.

"Ed, you have not done anything shady have you?" He gave a little titter.

"Oh, Jemima you disappoint me, I thought you understood me?" She gave him that what are you up to sort of look, and he gave another titter. He sat back.

"I know the Fairbanks very well, actually better than you realise. When Graham almost brought our company down, it was mainly due to their dealings. You see, there was a group of five companies that conspired together, to fix certain deals. They were the ones that masterminded the deals, they made billions illegally. When it came to the courts and prosecution, somehow, they managed to riddle out of things, and all traces of their involvement disappeared, and Graham and the other three all went to prison, which was right and just." Birch gave a smile.

"I take it you can prove this, because if they had connections to remove all traces of their dealings, Ed, it will be hard to prove anything?" He smiled.

"When I realised, they were the ones that had arranged all the deals, I knew then, they would slip out of noose, and so moved quickly to protect the company I built. Angela scanned every document before we handed them over. I have everything on a hard drive nice and safe. I sent an email and message to Edwina; the moment I heard about you considering taking them. You know, I never understood how people did not realise she masterminded the hacker group. I mean, that girl is too bright for her own good. I have been regularly sending her information since."

I gave a giggle and Birch grinned at me, my dad turned and gave me a smile.

"Abigail, to protect those children you have the means, if you really have to, use it, but protect them with everything you have, they are family, our family, and it means a great deal. Those shits have had it their own way for too long, if you need to, clip their wings. Although, just the sheer mention of it, should hold them off you." He winked.

He was a sly old dog, and possibly my saviour, I leaned in and kissed his cheek, and he smiled at me.

"Thanks Dad, you know, you are wonderful?" He gave a giggle and looked at Janet.

"You heard nothing of this." She leaned in.

"Excuse me? Sorry Edwin, y'all was talking, and I really got distracted, I am afraid to say, I missed out, what was it you were talking about?" She gave a big smile, and he chuckled.

The evening wore on, and it was clear my dad was tired, and I was feeling wiped out, we were still on UK time, so for us back home it was getting late. My dad excused himself, and we had another round of hugs, he was staying for a few days, so we promised to meet him for another meal. I hugged Angela, and thanked her for bringing him, and sat with Janet, her phone was pinging like crazy, and she gave a sigh, I looked at her.

"Is everything alright?" She looked up.

"Are you girls ready for round two? They are on their way back demanding a meeting, and they have an army of attorneys." Birch looked at her.

"How long have we got?" She looked up from her phone.

"About two hours." Birch nodded.

"It is enough, our room now." Birch lifted her phone and dialed, as she walked.

Ten minutes later sat in our room, I had eaten too much and was sated and sleepy. Birch was on her phone and laptop, talking to Edwina and Roni in a group chat, with her head set on. Janet paced around in the bathroom, talking on her phone, and I sat doing nothing relaxing and wishing all this would just go away, and we could just be left to deal with this on our own. Birch nodded and smiled.

"Good, you are a wonder, yes, I am here waiting." She nodded, and then pulled off her head set.

"Okay Sweetie, we are all ready, well, we will be shortly. I am waiting for Frank." I frowned.

"Who the frig is Frank?" She gave me a beautiful smile.

"A friend of Coding Cube." I sat up on the bed, and felt a cold shiver run down my spine.

"Oh Jesus, what have you done?" She stood up, and walked towards me.

"Why does your suspicious little beastie turn me on so much? Deads, relax, we are protecting our girls, nothing more."

I felt a tinge of panic, I knew her so well, and she was way too confident for my liking. She pulled me up off the bed, and pulled me into her arms and kissed me.

"Please, Birch, do not do anything illegal that could blow up and hurt the girls, I could not handle it if they get hurt because of us." She kissed me again softly, and her eyes sparkled.

"Deads, what I have in mind is not technically illegal. I mean, it would depend on the judge if I executed it, but as long as we don't, we are safe. You know, a hint is a very powerful thing."

She smiled, and I felt terrified. Oh hell, she can be dangerous and crazy, and at the moment, I was so scared, I needed her stable. A knock on the door announced the arrival of a package for Janet, the knock that came moments later panicked me, as a large round spotty faced guy in a baseball hat, and baggy jeans, stood at the door. He waved and lifted his hand, and gave me a thumbs up.

"Oh wow, you are here, I am such a fan, I have got everything you have written." He pulled a tatty copy of Sanctuary Arch out of his pocket.

"I mean, hey, it's cheeky, but come on, how could I miss this chance?"

He held up a pen and I smiled, and took the book. It was well worn, and very tatty, but I liked that, he bobbed about in the hall looking very excited.

"Could you sign it to Frankie Fingers?"

Birch sniggered, and suddenly, I was regretting taking the book off him, and I never wanted to know why he was called that. I signed the book and handed it back.

"Thanks for reading my work, Frankie, I appreciate it." He looked blown away, and held it like it was the crown jewels.

"Oh wow, the guys will be so pissed, I actually talked, and you spoke back, this is so cool and totally rad."

He took a deep breath, and just held it in, and okay, I was really weirded out. Birch sniggered. I came back into the room, and Birch disappeared with him, which bothered me more than you would think. Janet came out of the bathroom as her call ended. She held the packet that had been delivered in her hand, she tore it open, and out slipped a ring.

"I hate doing this, but I spoke with Daniella, and she understands, and so here it is, her mother's wedding ring."

I looked down at the ring, it was gold and diamond encrusted, and it looked very old. I felt my stomach churn, I hated this. I was hating that these people just felt like they could order us around like we were some sort of disposable prop in their way. I hated their smugness and their arrogance, and everything they stood for, they made me nauseous. I looked up at Janet, and I could feel the anger rising inside me.

"I hate this, Janet; I hate what they are doing. They have lost their parents, and this is their mother's ring. You know, I can tell you every detail of my mother's ring. I have looked at it a million times growing up, it is that significant in my life. It is a symbol of who she is, and this, this ring, it has the same meaning to those children, and they want to tear it away from them for what, monetary value? Oh God, I am so angry, I really wish I could summon the vampires as my characters do, I would serve every one of them a gothic sting they would never forget."

She took my hand and closed it around the ring, and held my hand softly. Her voice was soft, southern, and filled with care.

"Abby, if this is the price of their freedom, Honey, I am sorry, but it is worth paying. Take it, use it, and then I can fast track everything, and bring them home to you in the UK safe." I held the ring tight.

"This is going to be my last weapon to shield them, if I know Birch, she has something terrifying and scary in mind. Honestly, she is a genius, a completely bonkers one, but she wants to do this as bad as I do, and I know her, she will pull out all the stops, and give it ten thousand percent for them."

I took a deep breath as she walked back in. She smiled her big glorious smile, she was wearing an ear piece, with a curly wire, that had a little button on the wire around her neck, and she looked like a secret services operative in her black suit. I gave her a wary look.

"Have you joined the FBI, what the hell Birch?" She smiled, and was way too happy.

"Are we ready?"

Yep, she was vague, which meant up to something, and I was probably better off not knowing about any of it, she had that spring in her stride that always made me very nervous. She grabbed her laptop, and headed for the door.

I was wearing my black business suit, which was a copy of the one Ella had made for Chloe's first art exhibition, I had worn the first one to death, so had two more made. I love them, they looked professional and stylish, and they were so comfortable, especially with the lace fluted sleeves of the blouse, to wear and work in. The problem was, even with air conditioning, they felt hot.

The Fairbanks had taken over one of the conference rooms, we walked in to the obligatory long table of dark wood, lined with a long line of seated officials, sat in suits and holding papers, which I knew were irrelevant to the matter. Roni did it all the time, so I was aware of how this game was played.

In the centre of their side of the table, two seats were empty, and behind them stood Matthew and an older looking distinguished looking man, I assumed he was Mr Fairbanks Senior. He turned and scowled at us as we entered, I noticed Janet had four of her staff already sitting down. We walked to the allotted seats, and old Mr Fairbanks leaned into Matthew and whispered. Yep, I knew this game too.

Birch sat down opened her laptop and started to type, I remained standing behind the chair, as I looked at the two of them behind the seats whispering to each other. The old man looked at me like I was filth, turned, and leaned on the seat, in a stance of power. Really, did he think that power play would work on me? I live with a psychologist? I leaned on the back of my seat, to mirror him, and smiled, he appeared not to approve. He looked me right in the eyes.

"Miss Watson, may I be candid?"

"It's Dixon, I do believe I informed your son of that earlier today, please keep up." He looked irked, as I smiled.

"As your son has probably informed you, we prefer candid, it cuts out all the bullshit, so please, carry on."

He gave an angry sigh, he clearly did not like me, but I had grown used to that over the years. He looked at me with a fixed stare.

"Mrs Dixon, I do not think you quite understand your place, you are out of your league, and quite frankly out of your depth. You are here in a foreign country, and you have no idea of the power I hold? Now you can either play ball with us, or you can kiss goodbye to any hope of getting your application through the legal system. Trust me, I have a long reach, and I can pull strings that will ensure those children never leave this country, and you never get control or guardianship of them. I want that ring, and I want those papers signed now, or else I will destroy you. I hope you understand me?"

I watched his temples pulsate as his face turned red, wow, he reminded me so much of Madge around Birch twenty years ago. I took a moment, and ran my tongue around the inside of my mouth, I glanced down at Birch's laptop, she needed more time as I realised what she was doing.

"Does anyone have a bottle of water, us Brits are not accustomed to this hot weather, we like the rain, it is cooling?"

He looked at me like I was insane, and it was clear, he did not like my dismissive attitude. One of his minions passed a bottle across to Janet, and she handed it me with a smirk. I took my time, fixed my eyes on him as I took a swig and swilled it around the inside of my mouth, then smacked my lips loudly, I noticed Birch jerk, and put her head down. Taking a deep breath, I put the bottle down on the table.

"Mr Fairbanks. If what I believe you said is right, then if I do not do as I am being told, by what I believe is actually the sixth most powerful man in America, then you intend to pull all your little minion strings, bribe a few judges and officials, and pretty much screw up my chances of becoming the guardian of Danny and Jessie forever. I think I am right as understanding that as you will fix it, to bugger their chances of leaving the USA, is that right?" He smirked.

"Finally, some sense, my God you Brits can be stupid. I am glad to see we understand each other." His minions gave a titter.

"Look girl, just sign the papers, hand over the ring, and trust me red tape will disappear." I frowned.

"Isn't that illegal, I am fully aware this is not my home country, and I have no wish to break the law?"

He gave a smug smile and looked at his son, he had power stamped all over him, with his neatly combed grey hair, manicured nails, and perfectly timed moustache. He was arrogant as hell, as he smirked, I watched Birch's lap top watching him enjoy his own smugness.

"Jesus, the woman has no idea, has she?" Everyone gave a giggle. He turned to me.

"Little lady, I control everything, the law is irrelevant, I am the one who makes them, and everyone including you will obey."

I pulled back the seat, and pushed it behind me, and moved in closer to the table. In all honesty, walking down here I had felt really frightened, but as I stood there looking at his smug smile, I could feel my anger boiling up inside me. I glanced at Birch and she winked, I knew she was ready and that was all I needed. I slipped my hand in my pocket, pulled it out, leaned over the table, and slapped my hand down hard onto the surface. Everyone stopped giggling, and the room went silent. I stared at him across the table.

"Wow, you really are a worthless piece of shit Mr Fairbanks." I lifted my hand revealing the ring.

"Are you seriously telling me that this old ring is more important to you than the life of your grandchildren, so much so you would actually break the law, to get it, and cast them adrift? My God, you are the most cold hearted and vilest creature I have ever encountered, and I write gothic horror for a living?"

He gave me a look of pure hate, and leaned across the table stretching out his hand for the ring.

"How dare you, who the hell do you think you are, do you know who I am?" I put my hand on the ring and pulled it back towards me, as anger burned up inside me, my voice sharpened its tone.

"I am well aware of you who are, and what you think you are, but I am not done yet, so if I was you, I would listen up, and listen good, because this is not over until I say so, not you."

Yep, my temper was flowing up and I had lost my mind, but you know what, I was Flicks' daughter, raised by her and Hatty, and it was starting to show.

"Birch!"

I stood back and folded my arms, as the ring sat on the table out of his reach, and he was possibly the most pissed off he had ever been. Birch typed quickly did a few clicks, and the large screen at the end of the room came to life as the blue tooth connected, and her laptop appeared on the screen, it was black and blank.

"Will someone close the blinds; I would hate Mr F here to miss something important?" He looked really pissed off. As one of his minions stood up and pulled them closed, and the room darkened.

"What the hell is this?" I smiled.

"An education. Oh, how I do love dark things." He frowned. Birch giggled; Matthew sat down in his seat.

"Mr Fairbanks, I am sure you remember Graham Banner, well

some friends of my adorable wife, also remember him, and twelve years ago they were quick to act. I am sure you must have heard of Coding Cube?"

He swallowed hard, oh he remembered Graham alright. I smiled.

"As I said, I write gothic horror, and this Mr Fairbanks is yours. I noticed as I leant down you saw my necklace, and also my boobs, they have grown a bit and I don't blame you looking, I am actually quite proud of them. As you can see, my nickname, as my most beautiful wife named me, is Deadly, which is what the necklace you were admiring says, and it is for good reason. You see Mr Fairbanks, it is not I, it is you who are out of your league and out of your depths. I live in the world of modern tech, and you only fear the press, and of course, you are expert at ensuring courts lose all evidence on you, so it disappears. Nothing truly disappears Mr Fairbanks, especially on the internet, which appears to be something you have little understanding of, which is why I have to sign that sheet of garbage your son offered us today. I cannot deny, as I think about it, just how minor league your family is. To prove it, let us see as an educational exercise only for now, let's see how I do not have a clue as you just stated, and let us see how you use illegal activity to increase your wealth."

The large screen flickered and a gothic face appeared, God, Chloe is an amazing artist, a deep voice spoke in a creepy gothic manner.

"Welcome to Coding Cube, and for our latest project, meet Gerrard Fairbanks, billionaire tycoon, and soon to feature on this web site."

I smiled; God Edwina and Luke were brilliant. The pictures changed to a computer desk top as web pages being formatted popped up in tiny windows, there was a stream of documents and emails, detailing all the illegal activity of the whole Fairbanks business, and not all of it was with Graham. It looked like Bongo, Morty, and Creamy had been hard at work, which considering the time scale was quite amazing. I looked at him as he stared at the screen looking really upset, and dare I say it, afraid. I smiled.

"You see Mr Fairbanks, you are not quite as smart as you think, and if there is one thing I have learned about life writing fiction, it is that no one is immune from the sting of the darkness."

Birch was watching the screen with a huge smile on her face; she gave a happy sigh.

"I love live streams; they are very educational."

On the screen, an image of this room from a small camera set behind me on the wall, showed Mr Fairbanks smirking. His voice rang out loud from the speakers.

"Little lady, I control everything, the law is irrelevant, I am the one who makes them, and everyone including you will obey." He turned white, and looked at me.

"Why you sly devious jezebel." I nodded.

"Yep, pretty much, I am a gothic novelist in defence of my family. Sit down Mr Fairbanks, and we will get down to business, and we will be polite, reasonable, and cordial."

He flopped in his seat, and the room was utterly silent, as image after image of documents appeared on the screen. I pulled forward my chair from behind me, sat down, and took another drink of water. I was calm, precise, yet sweating my chuff off, but I was also happy knowing I held the keys to Danny and Jessie's freedom. He looked at me.

"How much do you want?" My voice was soft and quiet.

"I want one memory for Danny and Jessie, nothing more. If I am honest, I never want to hear or see the name Fairbanks near those children again. You see, unlike you, we find there is more to life than money, to us, family is the most important thing of all, which is why we are here, so the price of our silence is exactly that. You stay the hell out of the legal system, and let us follow each step through, and do this legally and above board. You can keep your money, we do not need it, and to be honest, we never wanted it. All I want for your granddaughter's happiness, is the memory this ring holds, for those two girls, as they saw it on the hand of their mother every day. Mr Fairbanks, I assume you want this back for a reason, and I would hazard a guess, it is because it is a memory of a woman you deeply cared for, and so therefore you understand me perfectly, and also how important it is to Danny and Jessie?"

I noticed I had hit something deep inside him and smiled.

"I have not enjoyed this today, Mr Fairbanks, it was needless, and I am sorry for you at the moment, because it is clear by your actions you have lost your humanity. I am quite sure, that whoever owned that ring, would be a little disappointed with you today for your callous behaviour, and such ill treatment of your son's children. Honestly, it gives me hope seeing you sat there remembering her, because I hope it will gain you some humanity back. Leave us and the children alone, leave the ring for them, and considering I am the only person alive who can stop Coding Cube publishing what they have, then we have the makings for a deal. I will sign your papers, but not a gagging order, and we will literally disappear into the night. Do we have a deal?"

He sat back in his seat, and just looked at me, but he gave a slight nod.

"I have to give it to you Mrs Dixon, you have me by my balls if you pardon my French." I smiled.

"I do, but play nice, and I will be gentle." Janet and Birch both smirked, he leaned forward and reached out his hand.

"We have a deal Mrs Dixon." I leaned in took it and we shook; he held onto it.

"I admire your pluck, I seldom meet people who have the guts to stand up to me, you have my respect and my best regards."

"Thank you, and fear not, those children will be loved and very well cared for, and as long as you stay out of our way, not a word of what happened here will ever be spoken of." He nodded.

"I do not doubt that at all Mrs Dixon, I give you my word, there will be no repercussions from us, and for what it is worth, I wish you well." I smiled.

"Same here, have a good day."

Birch slid the two signed documents across the table, and Mr Fairbanks signed them and handed us a copy back. He stood up, gave a courteous nod, and with his son, he walked out of the room. All his minions shuffled their papers, popped them back in their cases and followed, and I sat back in my seat and gave a huge sigh of relief, I am so glad I got to sit down, my legs were shaking like hell.

Birch slid up to me her eyes bright green and dancing, she had a huge smile on her face.

"I am so turned on about now, you would have to sit over there to measure my clitoris." I burst out laughing, I winked at her.

"Baby, if it is that big, stay behind and I will give you a blow job." There was a cough.

"Really, wow, you two are so messed up."

I looked over her shoulder and saw a tired looking Edwina on the laptop. I leaned forward and smiled.

"Thanks guys, you just saved two lovely kids from more pain. Edwina, what you did tonight, means as much to me, as the day Chloe first walked into an empty studio with a new easel, does to you. Honestly, you paid us back in full today."

She smiled and gave a nod; she fully understood the depths of that.

"Guys, just get them and bring them home to us all." Luke, Creamy, Morty, and Bongo, leaned in and I waved.

"Guys, I owe you many fully cooked dinners for this." They all laughed and waved as Edwina closed down the screen. I lifted the ring and turned to Janet.

"This belongs to two little girls we know." She had tears in her eyes.

"Wow... Just wow... I just witnessed the highlight of my career. Holy moly ladies, that was the most thrilling experience of my life."

Birch sniggered, and smiled at me as she whispered in my ear.

"She has obviously never measured her clitoris then."

I started to giggle and she gave out a loud cackle of a laugh. Yep, she is mental, but my God, she is a genius, and adorable, and she helped save my ass again, and that is a Curio thing.

Chapter 17

Danny And Jessie.

By the time we reached the room, I was fried, I stripped and fell on the bed, and pushed my head into my pillow. Birch slipped on to the bed and snuggled up to me.

"Are you alright Sweetie?" I groaned into the pillow.

"I am so tired, but happy. I have no idea how you pulled that off, but I am happy you did." She gave a small chuckle, and softly kissed the back of my shoulders.

"Frank did it for me. He fused the lights in the other two conference rooms and slipped the tiny camera up near the ceiling, so it would be hard to spot." I groaned.

"Never ever tell me why he is called Frankie Fingers." She giggled.

"Seriously Deads, you saw him, did you think it was sexual, I mean, my God, no one wants that. No, he has his fingers in many pies." I shuddered.

"Even when you say it in a nice sweet voice, it sounds perverse and creepy as hell." I felt the bed shake as her tummy wobbled, she lay her head on my shoulder and it felt nice.

"We saved our girl's Deads, we came through for them."

I smiled into the pillow, our girls, why did that sound so wonderful? It was my last thought as I slipped into the world of dreaming.

I felt the bed move, and a weight landed on my waist.

"Sweetie wake up, I made coffee."

She says the most romantic things, and I love her, I opened my eyes, and she was sat there smiling. Crap... She was excited.

"Deads, we get to meet them today, and I am so excited." Her face suddenly changed.

"I am also terrified, oh God, what if they hate me?"

It amazes me how she can go from glitter bomb madness, into

manically depressed death zombie so fast, I am sure it's a skill. I have a theory, that there is no middle ground with Birch, she is like a metronome ticking from one side to the other, happy to sad, to happy, to sad.

"Birch, they will love you, how could they not?" Her eyes lit up and sparkled.

"Do you think so?"

You see, straight back up to cloud nine, it is fascinating. I sat up and grabbed my cup, she was going to fizzle then explode, and I needed to be more awake to contain the madness she would become. I sometimes think I am not really her wife, I am more of her handler, always yanking back on the leash, as she leaps up at everyone.

It was not easy getting up this morning, my body clock was out of whack, and my stomach was reeling. Birch ran the shower and we jumped in together, and I felt like I was on auto pilot, I looked at her as she washed me down.

"Birch, I am terrified." Her eyes moved up to me.

"Me too Sweetie, but I also have a sense that things will be fine, it will feel strange at first, but it will be fine." I felt the tears, as the huge emotion bubbled up inside me.

"Birch, I really want this, but look at my life, every time I got my hopes up, my whole world collapsed around me. Think about it, my books failed, I lost you as you stayed at Uni, we lost May, we lost Lily, Birch I want this so badly it hurts, but I am so afraid we have done all this, and it will just go tits up as usual."

She pulled me close and held me tight, her voice was really soft and caring.

"You listen to me Abigail Jennifer Watson, and listen good. Yes, the books tanked, and then they rose again, I came back and have not left your side since. May and Lily has been painful and hard, but that is life, but this, this is the best thing for our girls, and we know it and believe me they know it. So, dry your eyes, you need to look your best today, because they are depending on it."

I breathed in and gave a sniffle, and looked up at her. She smiled at me, and she had such love in her eyes, I really had no idea how I would manage without her.

"Deads, this is just nerves, it is you overthinking that is all, it is a huge step for both of us and a little scary, but we will hold hands and take it together, you will see." I nodded and swallowed back the tears.

"Yeah... I love you, Birch; you have no idea how much it means to be doing this with you." She smiled.

"Come on, I will do your hair, we have two little beasties to meet." I smiled, and she leaned her head to one side.

"Better?" I nodded.

"Yeah... Loads."

Picking out clothes was a nightmare, the business suit might look too scary, it was hot, and I thought skirt, but all mine are black, so finally I decided to go with casual, after all, I wanted them calm and relaxed. Janet picked us up, and my heart was hammering in my chest, it was not that long a drive, and soon we approached iron gates with security guards, it bothered me a little.

Janet explained they were her people, as she had been concerned about the Fairbanks, so had brought them in, it was sort of scary that they posed that high a threat. The house was not huge, a little smaller than ours, but it was old and as white as snow. We pulled up, and I stepped out onto the white gravel drive in front of the house. It was beautiful, and as I looked up, I am sure I saw a small face, as it bobbed down under the window. I smiled as we walked to the door.

We were welcomed in by Rosemary, she was the nannie, and honestly, she looked a bit scary, she was quite stern looking and very abrupt, I wondered how strict she was with the girls. We were shown into a large living room, it was nice, and modern, but very tastefully done, Birch looked around and nudged me.

"Hey look, they have the same sofa's we do." It made me smile.

Above the open fire place, above a thick lintel, there was a large picture of Amanda and Peter. It was beautiful, and I could see what they meant, Amanda looked very similar to me, although she had dark hair naturally, I didn't, I took after my mum, and was blonde and dyed it. Her eyes were bright blue, and very similar to mine, it felt strange.

I remembered meeting her at my wedding, she looked about nineteen or twenty, she gave me a huge hug and wished me the best, and we posed for pictures. It was fleeting, and yet it had stayed, I had thought then she was similar, you could certainly tell we were related. There was a cough behind me, and I turned around, and my breath caught in my throat. Both of the girls stood there on either side of the nannie looking terrified and afraid. Birch smiled, and gave a little wave.

"Hi Sweetie's." Jessie smiled. The nannie looked down at them, her voice was stern and abrupt.

"What do we do girls?" Danny came forward and held out her hand.

"It is nice to meet you, Aunt Abigail."

I was lost for words, and my eyes filled with tears as I took her hand. I have no idea why, I just acted on instinct, and snatched her in to my arms, she stiffened, and then softened.

"How are you, are you alright, I do not know about you Danny, but I am terrified?" The nannie coughed.

"It is Danielle." I looked up at her, my God, Madge would love her, and Henrietta would adore her.

"I am her aunt, I think I know how to address a member of my family, that will be all thanks, I would like some time alone with my nieces." She looked shocked.

"I am not sure..." I grew up in Wotton, and had spent my life seeing how the rich handled their staff, and as much as I had always hated it, I knew the procedure.

"I said that will be all, I am sure you have things to do, they are safe with me, I am family. You are dismissed for now."

She nodded and stepped back; Janet winked. I let go of Danny and dried my eyes. Birch was on her knees hugging Jessie. I looked down and Danny was smiling; her voice was soft and quiet.

"Thanks, she is a real pain." I gave a giggle.

"Tell me about it, I live in a village full of them."

Birch let go of Jessie and dragged Danny into a hug, and I crouched down and lifted Jessie into a hug. She smiled at me, and honestly it was such a Chloe like smile, I giggled.

"Hey there, how are you doing?" She smiled.

"You look like my mom." I glanced back at the picture.

"Yeah, I do a bit, who would of thought it?" She gave a little giggle, and looked at me.

"Do you know, you are shaking?" I smiled.

"Yeah, I do that when I am scared." She frowned.

"Are you scared of me?" Birch gave a titter.

"Probably the nannie, Sweetie, she is a little creepy." Both the girls giggled.

We settled down on the sofa, and the girls sat with us. Janet went looking for refreshments, Jessie was really curious and asked a million questions, I felt Danny was a little quiet. I looked at her sat at my side.

"Are you okay, or is all this too much too soon?" She looked at me.

"I have read everything about you. You know, you are really famous, and you do a lot of stuff, won't we just be in your way? I love the idea of London and England, I have always wanted to go there, but will you be taking Nannie to watch us, because to be honest, if that is the case we may as well stay here?"

She was so young, but she was bright for a nine year old, I sat back, and leaned on the back of the sofa, and twisted a little to face her.

"I suppose I am famous, and I have been busy this year, to be honest too busy, and I have stepped out of public life for a while. Danny, I am a writer, to be honest most of the time I live in an old t shirt, and wander round all day coming up with ideas for new books. Chloe and me are pretty scruffy and tatty and just relaxed. I have taken a break, a long break, because I want to be home more, you know being famous is over rated, at heart I am a bit of a home body." She nodded.

"So, you will be home a lot?" I nodded.

"Yeah, I hate all the glitz and glamour. As you probably know we have the Curio Event over here in July, but apart from that, I have nothing else booked. Look Danny, I am not going to lie, I really would love it if you came to live with us, but at the end of the day this is your life and your choice, I am not going to force you." I lowered my voice.

"And as for that gargoyle of a nannie, oh dear, she has got to go." She gave a giggle.

"I would love that, she is horrible." I winked.

"Tell me about it, although you know, I could write her into a horror story, I bet that would terrify my readers."

She started to laugh, and it was so nice to see, I looked back and Jessie was sat on Birch's knee talking.

"You live with a naked artist; does she not get cold?" Birch giggled.

"Oh Sweetie, we turn the heating up, she sits in her studio next to the kitchen and paints all day. It is all she does, she paints and she fu...umbles around with sketches and stuff." I looked at Birch and raised my eye brows, she giggled.

Janet arrived with coffee, snacks, and cold drinks for the girls, and they sat with us answering questions about England, Wotton, the Curio's, the house and everyone in it. I cannot deny they were thorough. They asked us if we would like to walk outside, and so after our drinks, we took a walk.

The house had big grounds, not as big as ours, but it was large enough. They had a pool, patio, and a long lush lawn with trees. Danny explained it had to be kept cut short because of snakes, which completely freaked out Birch, much to their amusement. Jessie talked none stop, telling us about everything, Danny went quiet, I looked at her and smiled.

"How are you really, I am worried you know?" She stopped as Birch and Jessie walked on. She put her head down.

"I am trying to be brave, I am, honestly, but I miss them so much." I heard the sob and it broke my heart. I walked over to her and pulled her close.

"It is alright, you do not have to be brave around me, just let it out."

She buried her face into me, and threw her arms around me and sobbed, and I felt utterly useless as I stood there, holding her close with tears in my eyes, stroking her hair.

"Danny they were your parents, and it is fine to be sad and miss them, you do not have to hold it in around us, just let it all out, you cannot live with all that pressure inside you."

I gave a sniffle and looked up, and Janet was stood smiling at me, she gave a nod, as Danny wept, and honestly, it felt heart breaking. I could not imagine what it is like to lose a parent, let alone two, losing Lillian almost destroyed me, and Danny was so young, and life felt so cruel. I looked down.

"Danny, all I can promise is I will always be there if you need me, I will keep you safe and protected always." She looked up and her tears shone in her eyes.

"What even from dad's family, because they hate us?" I gave her a smile, and sniffled.

"Don't worry about that lot, we fixed their wagon well and good, they will not be causing any trouble with us." She looked shocked.

"Really, I am so scared of what they might do?" I stroked back her fringe.

"You never need be afraid again, they are gone forever, I made sure of it. Hey, there is a reason my nick name is Deadly, ask Janet." Janet giggled, as Danny turned and looked at her, she gave a nod.

"Trust me, yesterday, old man Fairbanks was shaking in his shoes, I was there, and she was as scary as any of her characters, I saw it with my own eyes." She turned back and I smiled as she looked up at me.

"I told you; I will never let anyone harm you, and I meant it. Hey trust me, I am a Curio." She smiled.

"Will we be Curio's if we come to live with you?" I looked at Birch as she walked up. She shrugged and smiled.

"Someone has to follow on behind us, we could train them young, you know hone their skills." I gave Danny a squeeze.

"It looks like I will be talking to Edwina, we may have to expand the site for some younger users." She smiled.

I gave Danny a hankie, I had bought a few with me, and used a lot of them, and we walked slowly back towards the house, and Janet filled us in on a few ideas she had.

"Even fast tracked, the legal papers will take a while, and there will be a lot to do here, so what I think would be appropriate, is after you fly back, I bring the girls over for a visit, so they can get used to the place, and see it for themselves. I think that way, it will ease the change before any final decisions are taken." I agreed.

"Yes, I think that is best, this has to be their choice, I will not force them Janet. I will not deny, having met them, I really want them with me, I want them safe, and not in a care facility. I want them to be happy, and I do think we can help with that, but this has to come from Danny and Jessie, no one else." Birch nodded.

"Especially that gargoyle of a nannie, I do not like her, she is far too severe for my liking, children need to be handled with more care and less of the Hitler youth tactics, where the hell did you dig her up from?" Janet gave a sigh.

"Guess, they put her in place a while back to oversee the children, I think it is more their way of keeping an eye on things." Birch shuddered.

"She wants sending back to the crypt she crept out of." Danny and Jessie giggled.

We sat for a while longer, and I signed all of my books for Danny, she had a full set, well not seeds of summer I was relieved to see, she was only nine after all. Her mum had bought a copy of each one as they came out, and she had read them a good few times. It was such a lovely day, and my heart was fit to explode I felt so happy. I was so relieved we had all got on well, but the clock was ticking and I was dreading it, the time to leave was approaching. Danny looked at me.

"When do you fly back?" I gave a sigh.

"Tomorrow at noon, honestly, I don't want to go, but look, we can talk on video chat whenever you want to, and you have my private number now, so we can talk whenever you need. I will get things ready at my end for your visit, I am really excited that you will come to see the house. Looking at Birch, she is ten times more excited, she will go bonkers when we get home, so if your room looks like a huge rainbow bomb went off in it, that will be her doing, so be prepared." Danny smiled.

"She is very lovely, I can see why you married her, I really like her." I smiled as I looked at her.

"Oh Danny, she has so much love inside her, she will cover you in it. Although, between you and me, she is quite bonkers at times." She giggled.

"I can see that too." We both gave a little snigger as she looked up.

"What... Hi Sweeties?" She waved, and we both laughed.

Leaving was terrible, I felt this huge pain inside me pulling at my insides, and yes, I wept buckets as I hugged both of them. I wiped my eyes and looked at them both stood together.

"Listen to the gargoyle, just for now, and don't piss her off, and whenever she gets to you, just say, England soon in your minds.

Keep that thought strong, and I will see you both soon, and show you the Curio house and all the crazies we live with. Okay?"

They both smiled and Jessie threw her arms around me.

"I think I love you already." I hugged her hard, and pulled her close as my breath caught in my throat.

"I know I love you both already. Come and see me soon."

I stood up and bit my lip, Birch was in tears, I was in tears, we were a right pair as we waved from the car, and drove away, Birch exploded into masses of tears.

"I DON'T WANT TO LEAVE THEM WITH THAT GARGOYLE, BWA, HAH, HAH!"

I hugged her hard and wept with her, honestly, it was pretty pathetic.

We arrived back at the hotel, a little more emotionally stable, and sat in the bar with Janet, and signed all the paperwork that would be required. Having seen us with them, she was going for full legal adoption. I was not aware, but she had filmed quite a lot of us on her phone, and she told us she would start the process immediately, and get it fast tracked due to the circumstances, which was that basically they were alone, with a nannie, and waiting to move to England.

She also noted that there was a hostile element to their father's family, and she would use it, she knew a lot of the local judges did not like them, two in particular. It is funny, but we had only really known her for a few days, but it felt like we had known her forever, and I was so grateful to her for all she was doing, and I wanted those children away from the nannie as quickly as possible.

Dad arrived and we all sat together and talked of our day, and we both showed all the pictures we had taken, and gushed about how lovely they were and how nice they were with us, and how excited we were they would be coming for a visit. Honestly, we were like a couple of fan girls. Dad just smiled and held my hand.

"You have no idea how wonderful it is seeing you both like this, I am so happy for you both. I cannot express how much happiness it has given me to know you are both doing this, it really has brought the greatest of joy to my heart girls."

In a way, it made me very happy also, just seeing him smiling and that twinkle in his eyes, was so nice. For so many years of my early life, he had been surly and moody, it was nice to see him happy. I have had my ups and downs with him, but at the end of the day, I was happy for him. Angela had stuck by him for many years, and as strange as it was at times, she had been good for him, and actually given him a lot of happiness, and I was grateful to her for that. It is strange how the bumps in the road shake everything up, and when everything falls back, it is different, and yet, it works, how peculiar that it is?

We headed up to our room completely wiped out, it had been an emotional day, and as I curled around Birch. We snuggled up, and I lay on my pillow, with my mind filled with all the happy thoughts of the day, and two beautiful girls hugged me, and in a strange way, it made me feel complete, for the first time in a long time.

The morning was chaos as we prepared to leave, Birch as always, packed her case at the last minute, and the car was already here, and she was sitting on her suitcase trying to shut it.

"Sweetie, it won't fit in, why, it fitted in before?" I smirked.

"Been a while since I heard you say that." She giggled. I gave a sigh.

"Birch, you need to fold stuff, lobing it all round the room, and then just scouping it up and tossing it in will never work." I walked over and sat on it, and the case closed tight, she looked at me.

"Sweetie, did you gain weight?" I scowled at her.

"Are you calling me fat?" She smiled.

"Well, no, well not really." I gasped.

"Holy shit, you think I am fat... I can simply get off you know?"

"Oh God, please don't, I will never get the thing closed." CLICK.

"Oh thank God for that, I never thought it would shut." I stood up.

"Good job one of us has a fat arse." She bit her lip, and her eyes twinkled.

"Deads, that is not what I said." I looked at her as I grabbed my case and pulled up the handle.

"No, but you were thinking it." She smirked.

"See, oh my God, you actually think I have a fat ass, screw this, I am going."

I shouldered my bag and walked out pulling my case, she came running out of the room dragging her case, and closed the door then ran down the hallway.

"Deads, Sweetie, it was not like that, you know I love your ass." The lift doors opened and she made it just in time, I glanced at her as she smirked.

"My ass may be fatter; but my boobs are still pert." She gave a gasp.

"NO!"

She grabbed her boobs and felt them, and frowned, and then turned and felt mine, the lift doors opened and she was stood there holding my breasts. I smiled at the man stood staring at us, Birch realised, and pulled her hands off quick.

We came out of the lift giggling like girls, and a happy looking business man went up in the lift. We hugged dad and Angela, signed out, and jumped in the car, and I took a deep breath as we headed back to the airport.

"I wish we could have stayed longer, I wanted more than a day with them, it would have been nice just to see them once more, before going home." Birch leaned on my shoulder.

"I know Sweetie, but we will see them soon enough when they fly over."

We arrived at the airport, and Jed helped us get our bags inside, and then tipped his hat and left us. We walked together to the desk to hand over our tickets and get bag checked. As we stood there waiting for our boarding passes, I felt a soft tap on my shoulder. I turned to see what I assumed was a fan.

"Danny, Jessie, what are you doing here?" I looked up to see Janet, Danny smiled.

"We came to see you off, it is alright, isn't it?" I pulled them both into my arms.

"Alright, it is amazing, and I am so happy you did."

We sat together, and Janet handed us copies of the paperwork, she had been to the court clerk first thing, and had everything stamped and in the system, wow, she was unbelievable. We had coffee and chatted, laughed and giggled, it was so nice, and a wonderful little surprise. The flight was called, and we hugged and said goodbye, and yep, we balled our brains out again.

I sat at the plane window and waved with my eyes full of tears, I really wanted to take them home now, and watched them wave like mad as the plane slowly pulled away. As the plane lifted into the air, I tried to look back and keep the airport in sight for as long as possible, I hated leaving them behind, it felt gut wrenching. As we lifted into the clouds I sat back, and Birch took my hand as she wiped her eyes with the other.

"Sweetie, the process has begun, I know it is hard, but we have to be patient and let the wheels turn. We are closer now than we were, and with each passing day we move nearer, and eventually, our girls will come home."

She was right, but as you know, I hate waiting. I was exhausted and closed my eyes, we were homeward bound, and once again, everything in my life was changing, I gave a sigh.

"At least going back to Wotton, I do not need contacts anymore." Birch sniggered.

"Why, did you get them tattooed?" We started to laugh, oh God, that was a weird day.

Flying is actually pretty amazing, landing not so much, I don't think I will ever get used to it. Walking into arrivals, I smiled, there they were as always, Chloe came running towards me and looked around.

"Where are they?" I smiled.

"Chloe, there is a lot of paperwork and stuff to do before we get them, it takes time." Her face dropped.

"I wanted to see them."

I smiled as Edwina and Deli came up and hugged us, and as always there were the press. There is no dodging public life, we hurried out to Petal, and jumped in as they screamed my name, and I ignored them. Edwina drove, and we hurtled away, heading home to Wotton. It was a long evening of questions and pictures, and a few tears, before everyone was finally happy enough, and I could head upstairs to my soft bed. I slid under the duvet, and was out like a light, drifting through dreams, with a happy heart.

THUMP!

I sat bolt upright in bed. THUMP! I jerked, and gave a sigh.

"Oh God, what the hell is she up to now?" THUMP!

"Oh... argh... Will you frigging move you twat?" THUMP!

I slipped out of bed, and staggered towards the door, her old room door was open, I walked up the hall and leaned in.

"Birch, what the hell are you doing?"

The wardrobe was lay on its side with the doors tied shut, and she was puffing and heaving, she looked up.

"Hi Sweetie." I stared at her, I had not had coffee so felt incapable of speech, but forced myself.

"Birch, what the hell are you doing, and why is the wardrobe on its side?"

"It fell over Sweetie when I was leaning it."

She pushed with all her might and gave a screech; it was going nowhere. I knew I would regret asking, yet felt compelled to do so.

"Birch, why exactly were you leaning the wardrobe in the first place?" She looked up.

"I was moving it, and it fell over, and now the bastard won't budge." She strained and nope, it was going nowhere.

"You know Birch, I really hate to ask, but did you empty it first?" She looked back up at me.

"CRAP!"

I turned, I was not mentally prepared for this, I needed caffeine, and headed for the stairs.

"Sweetie, you are a genius." Yep, I was about to invite children into a lunatic asylum.

Chapter 18

Mirrored Life.

There are times where I question my sanity, for example the recent events in this house living with the white haired mad lady. We have been back for four days, and for every waking moment we have not been working on Curio Live America, she has been banging and scraping, and God knows what in her old room.

We are all banned, as she is determined she wants to do something special for the girls when they come here. We have had delivery after delivery, and I am starting to worry a little, she has even changed the combination on the lock to keep us out.

I was sat in the library going over a few things, as today I had invited the cast of the new Seeds of Summer TV show, to come and visit, and meet the inspiration behind the characters. I was a little excited about it. Anita and Tabby had arrived, as they would be filming some of it, and I had instructed Chloe, clothing had to be worn. She compromised by wearing a huge baggy Battered Taco t shirt off Baz, which in all honesty, fitted her like a dress would.

I was happily clicking away, when the mad lady appeared, looking likely to explode rainbows and sparkles all over the place. She hurried in, her eyes wide and shining, and grabbed my hand.

"Sweetie, it is finished, come and see it."

I gave a sigh, I had been dreading this moment, she had been full on Sophia for days talking interior design, honestly, I had started checking Insta on a regular basis just to be sure. She was way too excited and dragged me up the stairs, talking at high speed, honestly, I was thinking of giving her crack to slow her down. We reached the door and she stopped out of breath, and turned to me.

"Sweetie, this is so cool, honestly I was inspired." I saw the door and the two pictures, and pointed.

"Birch, what the hell? You cannot use a grave stone sign on a kids bedroom door."

She turned and looked at them, there was a grave stone with a D on it, and a fairy, holding a J. She frowned.

"Sweetie, I asked them what they wanted, and this is what they asked for." Okay I was a tad wrong footed.

"Danny asked for that?" She nodded.

"Yeah, she loves gothic stuff." And suddenly, I was panicked, and went ice cold.

"Oh God, please tell me the room does not look like a grave yard or a crypt?" She smiled.

"Deads, I did exactly what they asked for." I felt my stomach churn, and the sense of dread devoured me.

"Oh Hell... Okay, show me." She stepped back, and swung open the door, and I gasped.

The room looked like an old gothic novel. It had four poster beds, old cabinets, and it felt like stepping back into early Victorian England, and actually, I frigging loved it. I walked in and it took my breath away.

"Wow Birch, honestly Baby, it is breath taking, although it feels more like Bram Stoker and Mary Shelly are coming to visit. Honestly, is this what they asked for?"

She nodded, and lifted up her laptop, and showed me a lot of clipped pictures.

"See, this is what they sent me, and so I went online and got everything to do it. Obviously, it is very Dracula era, but it is also sort of Peter Pan, Alice in Wonderland, fairy fantasy orphanage as well, which is what they wanted. Look Sweetie, Jessie has fairy lights."

She clicked a switch and the whole bed lit up, it was so beautiful, I just stood lost for words as I looked around the whole room, and then a thought occurred to me, and I looked at her.

"Why have you not done our room like this? Honestly Birch, I could die in this room, it is everything I write about." She smiled at me and watched me, and tilted her head to one side.

"Sweetie, our room is themed on the guest house, I don't want to change it, I love our room as it is."

I smiled; she was right. I will never forget the day I moved in and how hard she tried to make me feel more at home. I had been living in the guest house for four years, and she was so worried I thought the house was too big, she modeled my room here on it. I turned and pulled her into my arms.

"You are so amazing, I am sorry I doubted you, it truly is a most amazing room, and I am sure the girls will love it." She smiled.

"The bath looks like a crypt; do you want to see it?" My heart froze.

"Oh shit, really, won't that freak Jessie out? I mean, Birch, she is only seven, and she is sensitive." She gave a big smile.

"You are just too easy, I left that as it was, although I have stocked it up with loads of bath products, all natural of course." I smiled.

"I love how you care so much about them, honestly Baby, it blows me away." She smiled and slipped her arm round my waist.

"I want them to be happy Deads. Look, they have little Victorian writing desks to do their homework on, I have bought them new laptops. Danny's is on the fritz, and Jessie has not got one, that gargoyle says she is too young. I hid them in the desks, and they have their name on them, so it will be a big surprise for them."

She is such a kid, and yet she is this big beautiful, mad as a hatter type of kid, and she has so much love to give. The girls will be so lucky to have her in their life, I really was utterly blown away by it all."

"Birch, where is the old bed, because that was once our bed too?"

"I got Morty to put it in the attic, it fitted into the spare room really well, because it is such a huge room, so it is now a four person guest room." I pulled her close and kissed her.

"Birch, we have to get ready, the cast will be here soon, so why don't we lock this room up for now, and go prepare? I love what you have done to it, I really do, and I think the girls will adore it." She smiled and her eyes sparkled.

"I hope so Deads, I want them to love it so much they never want to leave." I understood that, she was trying to hide it, but she wanted them here as badly as I did, and waiting was getting to her as much as it was me.

She went to pick up her laptop, and I leaned back and peeped in through the bathroom door, it was as it always had been. I heard her snigger.

"I knew you would check; you are just too easy; it takes all the sport out of it."

The cast arrived dead on one, and Birch and I met them at the gates, they all looked really excited. David with his assistant, and a new young guy called Mike, all climbed out of a mini bus they had hired. We met them and welcomed them, and we walked slowly up the drive, as they all marvelled at the house. I stopped by the garage.

"I suppose we really should introduce a star member of the cast." I clicked the button, and the garage door started to open, Emily gasped and pointed.

"Is that Poppy?" Birch giggled.

"That is Petal, but yes, Abby wrote her as Poppy."

They excitedly walked into the garage and admired her, she was still looking like new after all these years, Birch took excellent care of her. It took quite a while, as they climbed in and out and sat in the back with big smiles. They really were into it, and eventually we entered the house, and headed into the living room.

"This is where we all lived in Shoots of Summer."

Emily was following Birch round mimicking her, which Birch had no clue about, she just thought Emily was being her normal self and loved it. Luckily, they were all over eighteen, so I suggested a drink, and we headed to the kitchen. Karen spotted Chloe and honed in on her, she stood at the door looking awe struck.

"Miss Pemberton, may I come in please, and get a feel for your studio?" She looked up and smiled.

"Yeah sure, come on in and have a look." She studied Chloe and sat at her side, studying her posture.

"I believe you normally paint naked?" Chloe nodded.

"Yeah, but you know, guests, Abby made me wear a shirt." Karen nodded.

"What is it like, I have never been naked with other people before?" Chloe shrugged.

"I love it, it relaxes me and chills me out, I paint better. I don't really worry about it, I am okay with my body, so I never really think about it. I mean, it's not a sex thing with others, it's only sexual if you make it that way." She nodded and was taking it all in.

"Yeah, I get that."

I was talking away and turned around, and in the studio, Chloe was sat naked, with a naked Karen, talking and showing her how she held her brush. Birch leaned into me.

"You know it's a skill; she can get people naked in seconds." I looked at her and frowned.

"What, and you don't?" Emily noticed us talking and looked at the studio.

"Cool, can we be naked, Willow is always naked." She pulled up her top, and I looked at Birch.

"See what I mean?"

Suddenly the kitchen table was filling with clothes, and I just figured what the hell, and left them to it, after all, it was Seeds of Summer and there would be nudity involved. David and Mike did not appear to mind, although it was noted they stayed dressed, as did his assistant.

David introduced me to Mike Harris the new script writer, it appeared that Brandon was so insulted that he had sworn never to work with David again. I walked Mike up to the library, and I sat at my desk as he lifted up the script.

"Abby, Dave told me you are really unhappy with what we have, and want a rewrite, I was hoping we could talk?"

I noticed Paula Johnson slip in and sit quietly watching. I nodded, opened my draw, and pulled out my copy of the script.

"I am unhappy, because it is not what I wrote. I understand there may be some changes, but all this PC nonsense is firstly not how I wrote it, and secondly, it will kill the show dead, my readers will hate it."

I spun my pen in my hand, and Paula leaned forward and grabbed one off the spare desk and tried. I smiled as she frowned, and tried to move her fingers to match mine. Mike looked at the script, I pointed.

"I don't want to be gender fluid, that is bloody stupid, read the book, there is a reason it is written that way, look." I grabbed a copy off the shelf and opened it.

"All you have to do is read the book. Bram clearly states, we are all as bad as Vera, that is because we had been using the same slang terms society used. Now you tell me, do you honestly think anyone will buy into gender fluid, that can mean anything? Gemma does not want to be gay, full stop." He nodded.

"Yeah, I see your point, okay, here is what I will do, I will go through the book and use your words instead of Brandon's, will that be alright?" I dropped into my seat.

"Yeah, I would love that. Look Mike, this is my work, and honestly this story means a lot to me, I do not want it chopped up with a PC hatchet, I want it true, or at least as true as it can be." He smiled.

"David wants you happy, so I will run every change by you as we do it." I gave him a nod.

"That will be fine, I would love that."

The day progressed, Deli had been at her mum's, Edwina and Luke arrived, and finally Anthony and Deb's, and we all spilled out into the garden, with more drinks, as our little study group asked questions and talked with their counter parts. I headed into the kitchen to refill my glass and Chloe followed me in.

"Abby, I think I am freaking out." I giggled.

"Is another Chloe too much for you to handle?" She shook her head.

"No, actually, she is pretty cool, she paints and fucks, I totally get that. It's that fucking Emily; she is too good. I mean, some days I can just about handle Birch's madness, but fuck Abby, there is frigging two of them now, and it is fucking with my brain. Don't even get me going about the weird Edwina, it's fucked up."

"Hi Sweetie." Chloe turned, panicked, and legged it back outside. I smiled.

"Emily, how is it going, are you getting a feel for the real Willow?"

"Sweetie she is wonderful. I mean, she is pretty awesome and such fun." I nodded, suddenly I understood Chloe.

"Has she told you of her book?"

"Yeah, about that, why does Chloe get weird around it?" I shook my head.

"No idea, maybe it is an artisan thing."

She gave a cackle of a laugh and I shuddered. Oh hell, there was two of them! What the hell have I done; she was creepier than the gargoyle?

I wandered out and Anita stood watching the group as they followed our house mates around. Deb's was being Deb's and was deep in conversation, talking on a philosophical level about the underlying truth of the character with her counterpart. Anthony and Kevin were examining the female actress's hair, and waving their wrists around, and Edwina was on her laptop explaining the code that created the live stream and destroyed Nigel's computer files with Penelope. Anita watched and smiled.

"You know Abby, it is a little bit weird, having two of you all, they are actually really serious about portraying all of you properly. I am actually quite looking forward to seeing this. David told me he spent all day yesterday walking around the village taking pictures to give the set people ideas. I get the impression he really wants to do this production justice." I understood that.

"The problem is the script, the dialogue is the most important aspect, and Brandon hacked it to death, I am hoping this new screen writer pays a little more attention to the plot. This series will rise or fall, depending on whether or not it is true to the book."

"It will be Abby, I spent a lot of time talking with David and Mike a few days back, about the importance of keeping the language the same as the book." She turned and looked at me.

"How are you doing, you know, how are you feeling. You have not said much about your US trip, did it go alright for you?" I understood she was worried, and I smiled.

"Anita I am fine, honestly, Birch and I have done a lot of talking." My smile widened from big to huge.

"I am trying not to get my hopes up, but the paperwork is going through to adopt Danny and Jessie. Oh God Anita, I want to explode I am so excited." I lifted my phone out of my pocket and opened my picture file.

"We had such a wonderful visit; we really did get on well." I showed her the pictures.

"They are bright and witty, and God, I just really felt this was right. They are coming to visit, I hope you will come and see them, honestly, I just cannot wait." She gave a big smile, and put her arm round my shoulder, and squeezed.

"I am really happy for you Abby, we have talked a lot on the road over the years, and I was never sure you would take the step, but honestly, I am thrilled for you two, I really am. Maybe it was time for you to slow down and take a time out, maybe this is fate."

I really did not know, it had fallen at just the right time, I had not actually thought about it, but she was right, the way my schedule had been, I probably would have missed the call. Maybe it was time to think more about my life, I certainly had been in the last few months. I stared down the garden.

"I really want this Anita, I really want to be home more, and with Danny and Jessie here, I could get back to me."

"You know I have to ask, I don't want to, but I need to know. Abby, was it my fault, was I pushing you too hard?" I turned to her and frowned.

"No, not at all, Anita never think that, you paced everything perfectly, it was her pulling strings, trying to keep us apart. Birch's schedule was double mine. It was never you; I loved our routine and the way we worked. It was actually the hardest part of stopping, and probably why I hung on so long, because honestly, I did not want to stop working with you." She bit her lip and gave a nod.

"Thanks Abby, I really needed to know I was not the cause, I would never have forgiven myself if I had caused that."

Anthony walked up and looked at me, he put his hand on his chest and stared at me, then flicked his wrist and swung it round.

"This Kevin is really quite good for a straight guy, but please darling, tell me, I am nowhere near as flamboyant or dramatic as that."

I looked at Anita lost for words; she sniggered and looked down. I looked at Anthony, and tried my hardest not to smirk.

"Anthony, you know I love you, but honestly, Kevin is pretty spot on." He leaned back on his heels and just stared at me.

"Abby darling, I could go off you, you have a wicked streak in you."

With a flick of his wrist, he spun around and marched off down the garden, and we both burst out laughing. David came walking along the patio, he gave a big smile as he stood at the side of me and Anita.

"Abby, I have to ask, but is that the Sanctuary Arch?" I nodded at him.

"Yes, it is. It was on the canal; it was the place that I ran to and hid from the world. They were going to demolish it, and Birch saved it, and brought it here as my wedding gift." He gave a gasp.

"So that part of the book, the scene where Bram confronts Willow with the truth of herself, I hate to ask, but did that really happen in real life? I mean, you do not have to answer if it is a painful memory." He turned, and looked solemnly at me.

"I knew parts of the book were based on facts, but Abby, I never realised that part was true. I know it is cheeky, but could I take some shots of it for the series, I mean only if you're comfortable with it?" I gave him a smile.

"David it was twenty four years ago, and honestly, I am fine. Come on, I will open the gate and let you get a good close look at it." He looked mind blown as we walked down the lawn.

"When I wrote Sanctuary Arch, David, in a way, I took a very negative part of my life and I turned it into something positive, and in doing so, it helped me change my outlook. This old part of a Victorian pump house has become something deeply precious to me. You know, Birch did a lot of research on it, and she discovered that when they were building it, in order to save costs, they recycled a lot of stone from a church that was being demolished, and that is why it ended up with arched windows." Anita turned and looked at me.

"Really? I never knew that." I nodded at her.

"Yeah, I was so surprised, so you see the arch is a lot older than the brick, it really is gothic."

We reached the fence, and I saw Paula stood staring at it, it always surprised me how people are drawn to it. I unlocked the gate and David walked in with amazement in his eyes; I looked at Paula.

"If you are going to play Bram, then you need to be closer to feel its power, come on."

She looked stunned and walked up to the gate; she stared at the arch as she stepped in. I loved the reverence in her manner as I closed the gate, and walked with her towards it. I stood in the corner with Paula, and looked at her.

"I stood exactly here, I was sat in the corner crying when Birch found me, and she leaned over and embraced me, and as we spoke, I got freaked out and stood up, and she almost fell down the banking, which was about there. Those lines you will read are all exactly as it happened, and I was right here. I shook so hard I could feel my back hitting the wall."

There was a click, and David took a shot of us both together as I explained the scene to her, she was awestruck, and a little emotional, she looked up at me with tears in her eyes.

"Abby, you are so brave, how do you get over something like that?" I smiled at her.

"Paula, when you are on set, the answer will be simple, Willow. For me it was Birch, remember that in the moments that follow. Without her, I would never have had the guts to confront this, and I would probably have been haunted by it forever. It was Birch who saved me, her love and devotion. Show that when you play Bram." She swallowed hard and smiled, and wiped her eyes. I stood her in the corner and looked at her.

"Feel the power of love in that spot, soak it up and use it."

The poor girl, I could see the emotions bubbling inside her, but somehow, I felt it was right, she had to understand the importance and the significance of this place if she was going to be Bram.

We both posed for some pictures, and Birch and Emily joined us as David took some shots of us together at the arch. He was so blown away and so grateful to us all, the afternoon moved on, and it started to rain slightly, and so we headed inside. As I walked up the grass, I looked at David.

"You know David, before Birch could move the arch, it had to be laser scanned for structural defects, I have those scans and a perfect digital three D mock up of it. I could send you a copy if you want to recreate it for the set?" He stopped, and looked stunned.

"You would do that?" I shrugged.

"David, I want this right, I want it as close to the book as possible, this is a very important part of my writing life, but also my own private life. Promise me you will keep as close to the book as possible, and you can have a copy of the actual arch on set. Somehow, I think Paula will give the best performance of her life stood under the real arch."

He nodded, and I knew he understood me, and that was all I wanted. Seeds of Summer was a massively important thing to me, it was how Chloe and I made friends, it was where Deb's and me reconnected, and where Edwina and Anthony joined us for one glorious summer together.

It was also the moment when Petal came to us and Deb's gave Lillian the treat of a lifetime, and also the Summer that me and mum stopped fighting. Most important of all, it was the summer when I fell head over heels in love, and discovered the best part of Abigail Watson, which was the depth of love I had to give to one of the most amazing people I had ever known. It was my summer, Abigail's Summer, and it had changed my life forever.

We headed indoors, and some of them were shivering, it was still cool for June, so they added some clothing, and we all piled onto the sofa to talk. We all sat down as one, and they all watched us, and then sat on the other sofa across the room, and suddenly, we had a mirror image of ourselves. Emily snuggled into Paula exactly the same way Birch did me, and I cannot deny, it was a little unsettling.

Birch snuggled up, stopped, looked across the room, she turned to me and looked a little concerned.

"Sweetie, I am freaking out." Deb's sniggered and crossed her legs, Jean copied her, Chloe leaned over to Deb's and whispered.

"See... It's fucked up, and it creeps the shit out of me."

Anthony had the answer, and in true Anthony style, he looked right across at Kevin.

"Tell me darling, are you a top or a bottom?" He looked at Anthony, and looked a little unsettled.

"Pardon?" Birch sniggered. Anthony sat back, and leaned his arm on the back of the sofa, his wrist just high enough to swirl round as he spoke.

"Oh Darling, if you are going to play me, you simply have to decide." Kevin looked really freaked out, and Edwina sniggered.

They were good, of that there was no doubt, they had our mannerisms pretty much down, but at the end of the day they were not us, and in that I knew, one of us would always flip things over to create humour and discomfort, it was what we did best.

All in all, it was actually a fun day. They were all so happy when they left, and hugged us all so hard. It was nice to see all my housemates make them feel so at home, and welcomed. As they got into the mini bus and all talked wildly about what they had learned, David took my hand with a big smile.

"I have no idea how to thank you; I am sure they all have some amazing ideas and we will all sit and do a lot of talking about the book before they hit the set. I promise Abby, I will make sure this production makes you proud. Thanks for everything, all of you, I was blown away by your kindness."

It was nice to hear it, and we all smiled and waved as they drove off, and then walked back up the drive to the house. Birch slipped her arm round my waist.

"You know Deads, I am a little concerned about Emily, she has some very strange behaviour at times." I smirked.

"Really, why do you think that?" I noted the others were listening. Birch pulled a strange sort of face.

"Sweetie, didn't you find her a little odd, and to be honest, just a tad unhinged?" Edwina sniggered behind me.

"No, Birch, I thought she was delightful."

"Really?" She stopped and looked at me.

"Sweetie, be honest, she was a little bizarre, I mean, for a moment I thought about suggesting she call in the retreat to talk to someone, you know get her checked out?" I smiled at her.

"I am not sure she is that strange, I mean, come on Birch, they would not let anyone out on the street that bonkers." She scoffed.

"Well to be honest, if she plays Willow like that, she will make her look like an utter basket case, and come on, let's be real here, she is the sanest one in the book." There were sniggers all around, and yet, that is why I love her so much.

We headed for the door and Edwina gave a smirk and looked at the others.

"Now do you see my point, you fill their head with all that psychobabble, and let them play with the mad people, and they just end up joining them. That is why I stick to code, it's rational." Chloe rolled her eyes.

"Says the woman with a fetish over her flash drive." Edwina spun around and glared at her.

"It is not a fetish, I just don't want ten thousand fucking dick pics on it, you know for an artist you are pretty fucking colour blind, yours is the green one, mine is the red one."

We all laughed as we walked through the door for coffee, and in her oblivion, Birch happily went on with her madness. The house was back to normal, and somehow, it felt really great.

Like all things in my life at the moment, I was back in the library working on Curio Live America. It was Saturday evening and we had a lot to do. Birch and Edwina were on their computers, and Anita sat opposite me working on the spare. Tabby sat at the table going over formats with Chloe, and Deb's was wandering around providing back up ideas and coffees. I sat back, and stretched.

"Okay, we have pretty much set the guest list, wow, this is going to be a pretty busy event."

I lifted the steaming coffee Deb's had just put down for me, and brought my legs up onto my seat as I took a sip. My computer started to play the video call tune and Birch looked up, I smiled.

"It's mine." She chuckled as she typed. I clicked the icon and felt a jolt of excitement.

"It's Danny." Everyone stopped and looked up, I clicked the answer call, and her face came up and she was smiling.

"Hi... I got great news." I slid down on my seat with a huge smile.

"Cool, what is it?" She looked at someone off camera, smiled, and looked back at me.

"Janet is here, and if it is alright with you, we can fly out Tuesday for a week?" My heart almost exploded.

"Really.... Oh God yes... Yeah, please come over as fast as you can, I really want to see you."

Birch was all smiles and everyone seemed to lift their spirits as I grinned from ear to ear. She looked so happy, and I was too. Oh God, I was so happy inside I wanted to scream.

"Yeah, it is going to be awesome, Janet told me to tell you, she has booked a car from the airport, you know, less press and all that, but I am so excited. I really want to see you guys and the house and everything." I nodded at her just smiling, and I felt the tears in my eyes again, Birch slid her chair round next to mine and leaned in.

"Hi Sweetie... I am so excited." Danny smiled, she looked so amazingly happy, and it was good to see it, I took a deep breath and wiped my eyes.

"Danny where is Jessie?" She leaned in and lowered her voice.

"Homework, you know, the gargoyle?" I giggled as Birch frowned.

"Well, that is not fun, it's Saturday." Danny nodded.

"I know right, but that's the gargoyle for you." I giggled.

"Danny we are thrilled and I am really excited, oh God, I cannot wait, we have a big surprise for you, and I know you will love it." Janet leaned in and waved.

"Hey ladies. I have booked a room at the Hunter's Arms for me; I thought it will give y'all some space and quality time. We should be in London about just gone noon, and then we will head right over to you." I nodded; my face was stuck in a fixed smile.

"Janet, thanks for this, honestly, it has made my year, I hated leaving them, Oh God I am so emotional, and I want to scream at the top of my lungs. We will be here waiting, oh God, I am going to be watching the clock for two days counting the seconds. Is there anything we need to do?" She shook her head.

"Be you, be happy, that is the only requirement of the job." I was smiling like a mental patient. Birch pulled me close and hugged me as I wiped my eyes.

"Oh Sweetie, we can so be that, I am so excited, I just cannot wait." Janet looked really pleased.

"Okay we will have to go, I have more paperwork and a few things for your attention, but things are progressing nicely, so I will see you both Tuesday." Danny waved, and we both waved back, and the call ended, and Birch threw her arms around me, everyone in the room was smiling.

"Sweetie, our girls are coming home." I took a huge breath.

"Birch it is just for a visit, we are not there yet." She pulled back, and she looked at me, her eyes were huge, insane and very happy.

"Deads, we are closer, oh God Sweetie, we are so much closer." I pulled her close and more tears rolled down my cheeks.

"I know baby, I know."

Chapter 19

Pre Arrival Nerves.

For the next two days, Birch was running around the house like a rooster on crack. Her excitement was bubbling over, and she was permanently in a state of utter insanity. I was in a constant state of buzzing excitement, but also semi panic attack, and sporadic explosions into tears.

I really did not want to get my hopes up too much, but how could I not? I don't think I had ever wanted anything so badly in my life. There had been utter chaos in the house Saturday night, as the excitement levels blew the roof off.

Once we settled down a little bit, which took several hours, it was decided that we would keep this a house only topic, and keep their arrival quiet. Chloe gave her most solemn promise ever, she would not say a word, so as Wotton continued as normal, all of us had to hide our joy, as much as is possible, and carry on as normal.

I hardly slept Monday night and sat up in bed, my mind reeling with endless thoughts. Birch was out cold; I really have no idea how she does it, I felt like it was the calm before the storm, except this was one storm I welcomed.

It is funny really, I have spent a lot of time looking back this year, and I wondered if it is something to do with me approaching forty. Is this yet another part of the process of aging, was I settling as I approached this landmark in my life and taking stock? I was not sure, maybe it was reaching that point of crisis and making such massive decisions that would change my life, which I did when I considered leaving the Dixon Group and cutting all ties to my public life.

Being involved with the Seeds of Summer production, had made me revisit those times and those memories, and in doing so it had brought a lot back. Losing Lillian certainly has, and being able to see the changes in my friends really got to me as they slipped into the routines of normal life. It had shaken me so much to lose touch with them, that I made a stand, and as a result, recently, I have seen signs that all those crazy and wild young house mates I began this journey with, have come back to life a little.

Having Deli back home, and having Deb's and Jimmy visit more with Edwina and Luke, has made such a difference, and on Saturday night I noticed something else, something that got me quite by surprise. It is the love and support of all of us pulling together to bring Danny and Jessie into our lives, that has really reunited us all. In a strange way, they are the reason the Curio's are pulling together harder than ever to make our next huge production of Curio Live a success.

The Curio family is growing, and as Birch and myself head towards that milestone of parenthood, the Curio's are right behind us, and honestly, it has brought joy to my heart. As I sit here in bed and think about my life, I remember thinking that I was looking forward to being thirty. Back then, I did not feel the angst that others appeared to feel, I was actually looking forward to it. Here I sit in bed, months away from being forty, knowing that my life was about to change again, and it would be a huge change for Birch and myself, and yet, I was not worried, and was really looking forward to it.

I have come to learn that life has a funny way of taking you through phases, and they are not at all on a rigid schedule, they come when they are ready. In their mid twenties, and early thirties, Deli, Deb's and Edwina, knew they wanted children, but I didn't, and I felt odd at the time. I had even made it a point of avoiding babies, out of fear of triggering my hormones and becoming broody, and now, I can see I am ready. It has finally happened, and here I sit knowing as of tomorrow... Actually, scratch that, it is three in the morning, so today, I will get the chance to take my first steps into parenthood, and I really want it so badly. My phase has started ten years later than everyone else, but I am fine with that.

I guess the sail is down, and Birch and I are just bobbing along and going with the flow, although, I do think we are going to need a bigger boat.

"SWEETIE, SWEETIE WAKE UP!"

"Huh?"

"Sweetie, it is today, and I am so excited."

"Huh?"

I felt myself shake violently, with the sound of a half crazed psychopath drifting into my ears.

"Sweetie, you have to wake up, they are coming and I need you wide awake and normal."

My eyes snapped open, I felt groggy, and I looked up at the half crazed lunatic with long white hair and the biggest green eyes ever.

"Normal... No offence, but what the hell do you know about normal, it's a street you have never walked down?"

"Huh?" She smiled and leaned back.

"Sweetie, our girls are in the air and heading here, oh God, I am so excited." I think the violent and hysterical screeching and shaking, had already informed me of that.

"Okay... Okay, Birch, I am awake." She smiled a sweet smile.

"I made coffee."

You know, she always says that like it is a newly found skill, the fact that five billion people a day can do it escapes her mind. Just to add to that, I admit, there are at least two billion people on this planet that are completely devoid of all sanity, and yep, they are the tea drinkers. Case in point, Madge, Henrietta and Agnes, Marion gets a reprieve, she drinks coffee occasionally.

I slid out of bed, holding my cup, I had no intention with sitting until the glitter fairy exploded, which I felt was imminent as the pressure was building, and I was not sure she could contain it, as she was zooming around at high speed checking everything off the list.

Why the hell did Izzy give her the morning off? Actually, scratch that, I know why, the bitch knew she would be like this, and decided to keep her well away from all the other crazy people. It was a good move, after all, no one wants a head cheerleader for the loonies hanging out at the retreat. Sadly, that placed the maddest one of all in my lap, yep, I am so going to get my own back on Izzy.

I sat down in the kitchen, and looked at Chloe sat there with a fixed smile on her face. Oh crap, Birch has triggered Chloe as well, I am surrounded.

"What?"

"Abby it is today, your babies are coming home." Oh yep, she is sliding down the weird street as well.

"They are hardly babies Chloe; they are almost ten and seven." Deb's walked in and glanced at me, as she headed for the kettle.

"Yeah, I might have known you and that mental patient you married, would find a loop hole. Yours will arrive house trained, that cuts out all the screaming, shitting, and tantrums. Hell, when you told me Birch would just nip out and get one, I figured Oxendale, possibly London, I never saw shopping in America coming though." I frowned.

"Deb's, it was not shopping, their parents died, how could we say no?"

She lifted her coffee and came around me and kissed my head, and sat down beside me.

"I think what you are both doing is wonderful, honestly, my best friend a mummy, it is lovely. Those kids are lucky to have both of you, even the loony, no doubt she will find their inner crazy, and the place will be back to normal, looking like an institution again soon." I looked at her.

"I will not really be a mummy Deb's, they have a mum, but they lost her, we will be more like guardians." I suddenly realised and stared at her.

"Why are you here?" She smiled.

"Abby, today you get to see the kids you hope to adopt, honestly, where else would I be? Oh god Abby, I think I will bawl my eyes out, I have dreamed of this."

"You have?" She nodded, and tears flooded out of her eyes.

"Oh Abby, you will make such a wonderful parent, you have no idea how much it will mean to me to see it." I felt the lump in my throat, and the tears filled my eyes.

"Do you think so?" She wiped her eyes.

"How can you not Abby?" Chloe gave a sniffle.

"Guys don't, you are setting me off."

I turned to look at her as the tears welled up in her eyes. Oh God, this was killing me. Birch walked in, took one look at us, and burst into tears, and that was the set.

"I AM SO HAPPY; I LOVE ALL OF YOU, AND I AM GOING TO SEE MY BABIES SOON!"

She threw her arms round me, and I was instantly covered in hair, as we all broke down, my God, it was pathetic.

After a long round of hugs, coffee, and passing around the tissues, with red blotchy eyes, we all calmed down, and I was hoping, I had finally shed enough tears to remain dry eyed for the rest of the day. I wandered up to my room, as I needed to do something, as I noticed I was checking the clock every nine minutes, and it was driving me insane.

I sat at my desk and opened my website; it always made me smile reading the comments of my readers. Ten minutes later Birch walked in and I was breaking my heart, as I wept like a checkout girl in an onion shop. Birch fell to her knees and looked at me.

"Oh Sweetie, are you alright?" I looked up with eyes like pickles on forks, and gave a huge sniffle.

"My readers are so lovely, and they are going to miss me."

I leaned on her shoulder and bawled my brains out. She pulled me into a hug, and held me. I took a while, and I sat back wiping my eyes as I breathed.

"Birch I cannot take this, my hormones are raging and I cannot control it, if I cry anymore, I think I will dehydrate, and just blow away as dust." She smirked. I took another deep breath and looked at her.

"Is there nothing you can prescribe to kill my hormones dead in their tracks; I cannot cope with this?" She frowned and went serious.

"Deads, why would you do that?"

"Huh?" She looked at me.

"Sweetie, if I gave you those kinds of pills, you would never want sex again." I blinked.

"Oh Crap, it's a catch twenty two, I am caught between being Primula, or an emotionally retarded sexual weeping basket case." She shuddered and looked panicked.

"Please Sweetie, don't talk about it, it's freaking me out." I smiled. Finally, something to sedate her, now all I needed was something to sedate me. I took a deep breath.

"I need to think of something that will sedate me in a way I will stop crying, something that will occupy my thoughts. Yeah, that is good, you have always said it is mind over matter." She nodded at me; I stood up and walked around thinking out loud.

"It has to be something fun and exciting, and maybe a little weird, yeah, that should do it." Birch jumped up with a wild excited smile, and clapped her hands together.

"Sweetie, I know, I know, I could measure your clitoris."

"Huh?" I looked down at my jeans.

"Would that work?" She looked way too excited for my liking.

"Screw it, I am desperate, and totally messed up." She went as giddy as hell, as I undid my jeans.

"I will grab my ruler."

Ten minutes later I came sliding into the kitchen at high speed, as Chloe and Deb's looked up.

"Quick hide me, the crazy is trying to compare our dick sizes." Deb's coughed, choked, and sprayed coffee all over Chloe, who was frozen staring at me.

"Huh?" I moved over to Deb's who was turning blue, and gave her a good hard slap on the back.

"Sweetie, Sweetie, wait mine got bigger."

"Oh Crap!"

I turned and legged it for the garage. Deb's carried on coughing, and tried to wipe up her mess. I ran into the garage in a panic, and looked left, then right, and saw Petal. I climbed into Petal and threw the blanket over me; in hope she would not notice. Birch looked around with wild eyes.

"Where did she go?" Chloe frowned at her.

"She said you were measuring dicks, is there something I should know Birch?" She smiled.

"I got mine to six millimeters, it could be seven like Deads, I am not sure. Do you want me to measure yours?"

She was waving her ruler and Deb's was looking lost, confused, disturbed. Chloe shot out of her seat, and stepped back.

"Whoa, you are fucked up, keep that thing away from me. Oh God Birch, I am so fucking straight it's unbelievable." She smiled, and waved her ruler.

"Sweetie, we all have a little wiener, you know, even you straight girls." Chloe shook her head.

"Not me, I am all woman, and you are so waving at fucked up in the rear view mirror, having kids has made you really fucking weird... I am going to my room and watching porn, it is so straight it's fucking unbelievable." She spun on her heels and legged it, leaving Deb's all alone, looking over her cup. Birch smiled.

"Hi Sweetie."

I heard the scream of terror, and then suddenly the garage door burst open, and Deb's shot in gasping for air. I peered out from under the blanket, she saw me, yanked open Petal's door and climbed in. Deb's lifted the blanket and shot under it shaking at my side.

"You need to get her fixed Abby; she is way weirder than normal... Are you really seven millimeters?"

"Huh?"

We stayed inside Petal for another thirty minutes, until the house appeared to be really quiet, and then we tip toed out, and peeped around the kitchen door. All was clear and the house was silent, so we walked into the kitchen. I cannot deny, it worked, I felt much more relaxed and stable as I walked onto the stairs, and nowhere near feeling any more tears.

It was extreme, of that there was no doubt in my mind, but I was happy it had worked. I walked along the hall towards our room, and heard the distinct sound of buzzing, I closed my eyes. Oh God what was she up to now?

I walked into the room and saw Birch bright red in the face, lay back her legs akimbo with a vibrator in one hand, and a ruler in the other. She saw me and gave a massive gasp.

"I made it past seven."

I spun around and walked right out of the bedroom; I was so not mentally prepared for that. As I walked back towards the stairs Birch wailed.

"OOOOH GOD.... EIGHT!"

Yep, Deb's was right, she has deteriorated into full blown insanity. I moved onto the stairs and the doorbell rang; Deb's was walking up the hall.

"I WILL GET IT!" She pulled on the door and I gasped, as two bright happy faces looked up at me.

"DANNY, JESSIE!" I ran down the stairs. Janet smiled.

"We got in early, and the traffic was actually quite good."

Tears exploded out of me as I dragged them into my arms. Behind me the stairs thumped, as Birch appeared fastening her pants, then thundered down towards us.

It was a moment of mass excitement, as we all talked at high speed, and I hugged them several times. Oh God, it felt so wonderful to have them here, as Birch squealed and laughed and wiped her eyes.

Calmness finally descended as we stood in the hall side by side looking at them, and smiling. I took a deep breath.

"Welcome to our home guys." Deb's was blubbering and wiping her eyes, as I looked at her.

"Guys this is my oldest and best friend Deb's." She pulled them both into a hug. Danny looked around the hall looking impressed.

"Wow, you live in an amazing house." I smiled.

"With hope, you will too if you want to...?" She smiled at me, and it just warmed my heart. Birch was on fizzle and growing more excited by the second.

"Sweetie's, do you want to see your room?" They looked at each other and then nodded, and Birch grabbed their hands and almost dragged them up the stairs.

"It is so wonderful and I am so excited, I think I am going to explode." I smiled as we walked up the stairs with Janet, Deb's was wiping her eyes.

"Abby that is the happiest and most excited I have ever seen you, and it was so beautiful, I will never forget that moment, not ever, I am so happy for you right now." I took her hand and smiled.

"Thanks Deb's but we are not there yet. We have a ways to go, and they have to want to come, but honestly, I am so happy right now, I don't think I have ever felt such joy in my life."

Yep, Birch was making the girls dizzy as she flew around the room showing them everything. They just watched and smiled. I walked in and stood near the door, bless her she was completely mental, but she was so happy, and I knew how desperately she wanted them to feel at home.

The revelation of a new laptop each, brought screams of happiness, and a few tears, I walked up to Danny and pulled her close.

"It is a lot to take in, and she is sort of crazy with happiness today. Settle in, have a good look round, and we will all be in the kitchen when you are ready, okay?" She looked up and nodded. I smiled, and grabbed Birch by the arm.

"Give them some space Birch, they need to get used to the place." She stopped, and took a breath, and then came down to earth with a bump.

"Yeah, sorry, I got carried away, you are right, let them settle."

I took her hand, and we all headed downstairs and left them to it. We sat in the kitchen as Deb's made coffee, and Janet filled us in.

"It has been a long flight, and they were so excited, I would imagine at some point they will just pass out. I will be right at the hotel if you get problems or have any questions." Birch understood

"You know, we have a spare bed, you could have stayed here, we would love to have you with us." She understood that.

"Look, they need to see what life here is like, they need to find out how they fit in, that will not happen with me buzzing around, and to be honest, you two need to establish a bond, although I must say, with your meeting and all the video calls, both of you have made a magnificent start. The Adoption so far is flowing through, and I do have more papers for you to sign, but we will do that tomorrow. To be honest ladies, I am really tired, and need a good sleep." I gave a nod as I lifted my cup, and looked over it.

"I just want them to be themselves and go at their own pace, I want no pressure on them, and I hope through that, they will choose to stay, because honestly, I have this huge feeling inside me and I want to let it out, but until they choose, I cannot." Janet completely understood that.

"Your father told me, you would grow to love them very quickly, he said it was the finest quality of both of you, your ability to show great love to people." I felt the tears again.

"He said that?" Birch took my hand in hers, and Janet smiled at me.

"He certainly did, and to be honest, I have seen it." I wiped my eyes, and smiled.

"I cannot help it, I have really started to care about them, they are such beautiful and amazing children." She smiled.

"And that is the loss of the Fairbanks, they were too short sighted to see it, but not you two."

Chloe leaned on the door as the girls talked, and tapped softly, they both looked up and she gave a small wave and smiled.

"Hey, I am Chloe, I live across the hall, welcome to the neighbourhood." They both chuckled, Jessie smiled at her.

"Aren't you the naked painter?" Chloe nodded.

"That's me. I figured I would wear clothes today, you know, not freak you out first day. How are you guys doing, it is a bit mad here today?" Danny gave a smile.

"Our whole life is mad at the moment." Chloe walked in and sat crossed legged on the floor.

"Yeah, I get that, I really do. Look guys, just be you, that is all we do, and in no time, you will just slip into it all. This is a great place to live and there is always someone around. My studio is right next to the kitchen, and I am pretty much there all the time as I paint all day, so if you need a chat or company, just drop in, okay?" Danny gave a nod, Jessie looked at her.

"Can we see it now?" Chloe smiled and stood up.

"Yeah, as I said, it's always open. Come on, I will show you."

We were all talking when Chloe, Danny and Jessie, walked through the kitchen towards the studio. I turned on my seat and watched, as she took them inside and talked about her art and how she painted, and they fired about a hundred questions at her. I sat smiling, she was so lovely with them, and somehow, I felt, if they did decide to live here, Chloe would play an important role in their life. Deb's smiled and winked at me, I frowned at her.

"What?" She gave a giggle.

"I have seen those eyes before, they are your mums, she looked just the same watching you in the garden, the eyes of an ever watchful parent." I gave a giggle.

"You're just soppy, you always have been." She giggled, but raised her eyebrows at me.

The girls hung out with Chloe for a bit and then came back into the kitchen, and I went through everything with them. Birch being Birch, had stocked up on crisps, biscuits and canned fruit juice, so I showed them were everything was stored.

They got a tour of the cellar, and the attic, and then we went down to the library, which Danny loved. Deb's gave her the low down on all the books and which ones she loved most, and after the living room, we went out into the garden to see the pool, and of course, my arch.

Danny got so excited when she realised this was the same arch as was on the cover of her book, and I walked down the garden with her. I told her the story of how this had been my place of safety as a child, and how when they were going to demolish it Birch saved it, and we moved it here. I unclipped the gate and let her inside, and she beamed with delight as she stepped onto the stone floor, and gasped in awe.

I stood back watching her, she really did look like a miniature me, it was quite uncanny. Danny stood in the corner like Willis had, and smiled.

"I get it, I really do, wow, this makes the book ten times more exciting. Oh wow, you know Willis was lucky to have this, so were you." She put her head down.

"I don't really have anywhere like this."

I felt the pang run through me, and I walked up to her and pulled her close.

"Danny, while you are here, this can be your place too, if you need it, come to it, I do and it helps me a lot. I have had some dark moments in my life, and sitting here alone, to shed tears or puzzle things out really helped me get through it all. So, if while you are here you need it, then please just walk down here and take your time, but also remember, I am here to, and you can always come to me and talk, okay?"

She nodded and swallowed hard; I sensed the surge within her passing. I took her hand.

"Come on, let's join the others."

When we got back to the house, Janet was getting ready to go, she was tired, and needed to rest. Jessie wanted to know where she was staying, so we decided to walk into Wotton, and walk her back, that way both of them knew where she was.

We set off down Waterside Lane, turned onto Manor Road, and then at the bottom, turned onto the high street. Jessie was very chatty and asked Birch billions of questions as she held her hand, and Birch was happy and cheerful answering away like it was the best day of her life. Jessie had really taken to Birch, she was pretty extroverted, and so they naturally paired up. Danny was a lot like I was at her age, quiet, her mind always thinking as she took it all in, and I felt a really big connection with her.

We walked up to the Hunters, and Janet turned and hugged the girls. She looked at them both and gave a big smile.

"Alright girls, you have my number, and I will be staying here, so I am not far away if you need me, alright? Settle in and have fun, and I will see you tomorrow."

She gave them both huge hugs, and it was clear how fond she had grown of them. We waved goodbye, and there was something I really wanted to do. I took the girls hands, and we walked up Church Rise, and I peered in through the gallery door. Mum was in the back cleaning up; she looked up as I walked in.

"Abby, what a lovely surprise, I was just tidying up a bit before closing."

I gave her a big smile, and she looked at me in a curious way, I was so excited.

"Mum, I have got a huge surprise for you." She looked puzzled. I turned and looked into the shop.

"Guys... This is my mum."

Danny and Jessie walked in with Birch, and my mum looked speechless, as her eyes filled with tears, I smiled at her.

"This is Danny, and that is Jessie... They are just here for a week, but fingers crossed, yeah?"

She pulled them both into a massive hug, and exploded with tears.

Chapter 20

First Day Parents.

I lay back on the bed, and I was exhausted, it had been one hell of a day. Mum gushed with excitement of tears, and then gave the girls fifty pounds each, and a guided tour of the gallery.

She walked back home with us and hugged the girls, and crossed the road home to tell Patrick all about it, she was so excited and that was lovely. When we got back in, Deli was home with Josh and Liz, so Danny and Jessie had company around their own age, and Edwina turned up shortly afterwards with Luke and Sammy, and he ran down the garden with Chloe.

Edwina had arrived with burgers and fired up the barbeque, and we all sat out on the patio and ate our meal, and so far, the girls were enjoying themselves. Anthony arrived late with Michael, and he too gave them spending money, which they loved, as it looked nothing like American dollars.

They were both pretty tired, and it was not long before Jessie curled up on Birch's lap and her eyes flickered, and it was decided bed would benefit them more. I sat on the bed as Danny and Jessie snuggled down, they loved their room, and even though tired, they had both had a lovely day. I leaned over and kissed them both on the head like my mum had always done with me, and wished them goodnight. I pointed out we would be right next door if they needed us, and headed to my room.

I lay back on the bed my body aching, it had been an emotionally draining day, as Birch slid off my jeans, I looked down, she looked at me strangely.

"Everything alright Sweetie?"

"Just checking you don't have a ruler." She giggled, as she crawled up the bed.

"Oh Sweetie, I would love to play measurements, but honestly, I am wiped out."

We slid under the duvet, and she snuggled into me, considering she was exhausted she was still very excitable. Her arm came round and cupped my boob.

"Today was the best day ever Deads." I smiled as I snuggled back into her.

"It was, wasn't it. Oh Birch, I hope they say yes, they want to live here; I think I am falling in love with them, and I am trying not to, but I cannot help it, I really want them to live with us all the time." I felt her move.

"I know, oh God Deads, when Jessie looks at me, I melt, I just want to grab her and squeeze her to death, she is so adorable, and Danny is so like you, oh you have no idea. I watched her today, and that awkwardness and her vigilant eyes, all I could think of was you when you first came to Uni."

I closed my eyes, and drifted, I adored Jessie there was no doubt, and I completely understand Birch, I had spent half the day resisting the urge to cuddle her. Danny was more grown up, in fact she surprised me a lot considering she was only nine, well almost ten. The memory of watching her walk around the arch played back in my mind, Birch was right, I think she has many of the qualities attributed to me. It made me wonder, is that why I felt I had such a strong connection with her? I drifted into sleep as I heard Birch's soft breathing in my ear, and my dreams were filled with images of the girls from the day, it was such a happy day.

I felt the bed moving, and I heard Jessie speak. "I got frightened."

"Oh Sweetie, see come here, climb in." The bed moved again, and I felt Birch snuggle down.

"You are safe here Sweetie, you have nothing to be afraid of."

The duvet in front of me lifted up, and I felt the small figure slide in, I gave a smile and moved back, as Danny wriggled back to me. I pulled her close.

"Are you okay?"

"Yeah, I had a bad dream."

"Okay, settle down, and sleep dream free, here you are safe." I cuddled around, and heard her give a happy sigh, and then I drifted back to sleep.

Edwina smiled, as Chloe stood at her shoulder with two cups of coffee.

"Wow look at that, who would have thought it?" Chloe chuckled.

"I think it is sweet."

The four of us were out cold, all cuddled together, and toasty hot, Chloe placed down the cups, and Edwina softly shook Birch and whispered.

"Birch, you will have to get up, or you will be late for work."

Birch took a deep breath and opened her eyes, and realised who was asleep in front of her, she smiled, and Edwina chuckled.

"You all look so adorable; I really did not want to wake you."

Birch carefully wriggled free, and slowly sat up, Chloe handed her the coffee, she blinked, and took a sip, she was still groggy, but whispered.

"Jessie got frightened, and when I got like that, mum let me sleep in her bed." Edwina gave a nod.

"Abby looks so happy; I think Danny has really taken to her." Birch looked round.

"I hope so, I think they both need each other. I think Abby gets her in ways none of us ever will."

It took a lot of wriggling for Birch to weave her way out of bed, Jessie stirred and opened her eyes, and saw Birch tip toeing to the bathroom with her coffee. She sat up and looked at me and Danny, still sleeping. She yawned and then slid over and put her chin on my shoulder, and her little arm came over as she shook Danny. Danny gave a jolt and opened her eyes.

"Danny, I am hungry."

I felt the bed move as Birch popped her head round the bathroom door with a toothbrush in her mouth, and waved.

"Hi Sweetie." Jessie slid off the bed and walked to the bathroom, where she stood and watched Birch clean her teeth.

"Does everyone here sleep naked?" Birch stopped brushing and looked at her, still holding the brush in her mouth.

"I am not sure, I know Chloe does, you know, I am not sure about Deli or Anthony, we should ask them." Jessie gave a nod; it made sense to her.

I sat up in bed, saw the coffee and reached for it. Danny sat up at my side, and looked around.

"I love your room, and I really love Avril, I have all her albums." I sipped.

"Of course you have, you're a Watson and have a taste for the finer things." I handed her the cup.

"Want some?" She took it and looked at me.

"Nannie says coffee is bad for children." I shuddered.

"Nannie needs staking out in a ring of salt and burning." Danny giggled, and took a sip.

"My mom used to sneak me coffee in a morning, when Nannie was not looking." I turned to her.

"So, she has been with you a while?" She nodded and handed the cup back.

"She came when Jessie was born, my grandfather sent her, mom said it was always to spy on us, she did not like Nannie, but dad kept her on to keep the peace."

"Yeah, if you want something to keep the undead away, she is your man, God she is ugly." Danny giggled at my side and I looked at her.

"You have seen her, Jesus Danny, she is one ugly woman." She gave a laugh, and we sat there laughing. Birch popped her head round the door, and smiled a frothy smile.

"Morn..." She lifted a finger and disappeared, we heard her spit, she reappeared. "Morning Sweeties." Jessie popped her head round the door.

"I just peed." I giggled; she was so like Birch, it was scary.

I slid out of bed, and pulled on my kimono, Danny was stood looking up at the paintings on the wall. I walked over and stood at her side.

"That was painted when I was nineteen, Chloe did it from memory, as she was living in Oxendale whilst I was at Uni."

"It caught my breath; it looks just like my mom." I put my arm around her shoulder.

"It appears like the Watson gene is strong in all three of us." She turned and looked at me.

"Three?" I nodded.

"I am a natural blonde, but honestly, your face, your figure, that was me at ten. When Janet first sent me your pictures, it was like looking at a younger me." She smiled.

"I like the idea of looking like you and mom." I patted her cheek, and smiled.

"You do... let's go eat."

"YEAHHHHHHH!"

Jessie and Birch came running out of the bathroom, heading for the kitchen, I smiled, wow they were so alike.

As we walked downstairs, I briefed Danny about the chaos of the morning routine just to prepare her, and pointed out I rarely speak, until I have had at least three coffees. We walked in, and sat at the island. Luke and Edwina had stayed over, so Sammy was sat at the table with Liz and Josh. Jessie had joined them, and was looking round.

It was at this point we encountered our first Anglo American obstacle, namely cereal, Jessie had never heard of any of them. Chloe pointed to her bowl with her spoon.

"I love the cinnamon squares, they are banging." Sammy sneered.

"Sugar Flakes." Josh shook his head.

"Choc poppers." Jessie looked confused as she looked at the boxes, Chloe stood and took her bowl over to her.

"Here try one first."

It started a chain reaction as Jessie got to try each one, and then with a big smile she pointed to the Choc Poppers. Josh gave a big smile, and nodded, it made Birch giggle.

Edwina placed a cup and a plate of two slices of toast in front of me, and smiled, Danny looked at me.

"Can I have the same as you, will that be alright?" Edwina gave a smile.

"One coffee and toast coming right up young lady, wow, I think we have another writer in the house." I giggled, and she smiled.

"I love writing, I am not great, but I just love doing it." I shrugged.

"There are days I still doubt my work, to be honest, I think Handed Death, could be much better." She looked amazed.

"It is brilliant, how could you doubt it?"

Deli and Anthony got organised, and Birch flew around grabbing papers with a piece of toast in her mouth, and Jessie looked up at Anthony.

"Anthony, do you sleep naked?"

The whole room stopped and looked at him, he looked totally out of his depth, then flicked his wrist and looked at Jessie.

"Jessie darling, you will learn in this life, that some things should remain unknown and mysterious, and that my little sweetness, is one of them." Chloe looked at me and smiled.

"That was a pretty good recovery." I nodded, Danny smiled at us and lifted her cup. The clock ticked, and with a quick.

"Bye Sweetie, bye Sweetie, bye Sweetie." She flew for the door to catch up Anthony, Deli, Josh, and Liz, the door banged and silence descended, and we gave a sigh of relief. Edwina grabbed Sammy; he went to school in Millington.

"Come on little man." She grabbed her keys.

"I will be back in a bit, Sam will be here shortly, don't forget Abby, Anita is coming so hide that package that just got delivered." I looked round.

"What package?" She smiled.

"I have no idea, but it was for a certain new publishing company, and it felt heavy."

"No way, already? Wow they printed that fast."

I jumped up, and ran down the hallway to the library table, where there it was, a large brown oblong package. I picked it up and hurried back to the kitchen with a huge smile. Danny looked confused.

"Is it important?" I looked up.

"This is top secret, hush, hush, especially from Anita." I opened the package, and lifted it out, wow, it was awesome, Danny leaned over.

"Is that a new book?" I handed it to her.

"It is a test print, I have to go over it and make sure there are no mistakes, but yes, that is one of two I will be putting out under my own company. Danny this is a massive secret, no one outside of this house knows, okay?" She looked up at me with a big smile.

"The Publicity Girl, it sounds great, what is it about?" I sat down at her side.

"It is based on my working life with Anita, sort of like Seeds of Summer but not as naughty. We had a lot of fun together at our events, so I turned it into a story of friendship. She has no idea, so I want to surprise her." Danny looked at it and her eyes sparkled.

"I have to go through it, but when I am done, if you want, you can have it." Her eyes almost exploded.

"Honestly?" I nodded.

"Yeah, I get a free author copy of the final print, so once I have inspected it, you take it, I will sign it for you." Her face was such a picture, Chloe smiled at me, and winked.

Jessie wanted to paint naked with Chloe, which made me laugh. I had work to do, so I turned to Danny.

"The house can be a little quiet during the day, so what do you want to do?"

"Deb's recommended me a book, and I want to read it, I am still a bit tired, so want to relax if that is alright?"

"I will be working in my room, so if you want, I am not writing, it is Curio Live stuff, you can crash on my bed and read. Janet is coming at one with some paperwork, okay?"

I headed upstairs, and sat at my desk, I had a long list of tasks to sort through set by Edwina and Birch, so I got stuck in. Danny appeared and sat back on the bed with her book. I find there is something wonderful, about the sound of the soft turning of a page, and it was nice to sit working, and hear them turn.

I had been at it a while, and I sat back with a sigh, my back ached, and I stretched, Danny looked up.

"What is it like, you know, being a famous writer?" I spun around in my chair.

"To be honest Danny, it is hard to say, I was talking with Jo, not long ago, and both of us just felt like we were ordinary writers." Danny frowned.

"Jo, who is Jo?" I chuckled.

"Yeah, sorry, Johanna Friel." Her eyes nearly exploded as she sat up on the bed.

"You know Johanna Friel, and you call her Jo... I love her books; the Forest of Dreams series is the best?" I shrugged.

"She is a part of the Dixon Group, we did loads of events together, she lives just over the hill, we meet for coffee all the time, would you like to meet her?"

She swallowed hard, and I thought her eyes were going to explode, her voice was almost hoarse.

"I would panic and hide; she is amazing at fantasy realms." I gave a chuckle.

"Danny they are all just normal people, I mean, look at me,

this sat before you wearing nothing but a kimono, this is the real Abigail Jennifer Watson. It is not the parasol toting, black eyes, and long gothic dresses, stood in front of the press. Although, I love the dresses and the parasols, I have loads, but Danny, that is the show biz side of it and honestly, I hate it. I love the fans, it is wonderful to meet them and talk to them, but I detest the press, you will see that when you read the publicity girl."

"Yeah, but, Joanna Friel, she is a legend." I giggled.

"Wow, fan girl much Danny?" She laughed. I got up and lifted my mug, I needed coffee.

"Can I ask you something personal?" I turned and looked at her, she slid to the end of the bed, I nodded.

"Danny, I would hope you feel safe enough to ask me anything, I would like you to." She nodded and looked me right in the eye.

"You are adopting us, aren't you?" I walked over and sat at her side.

"Janet thinks that is the fastest route, and it will get you away from that nannie quicker, but Danny, it will only go through if you and Jessie agree to it. It has to be your choice and your decision, we both made that very clear to Janet." She nodded.

"I understand, I do." I looked at her.

"But?" She smiled.

"I can tell you are a writer." She took a deep breath.

"If you adopt us, we will become your daughters, yes?" I nodded.

"Legally, yes you will." It did not take a lot to see where this was going. She looked at me, I could see she was puzzling something out in her mind.

"Danny, it is okay to say it, I have a pretty good idea where this is going." She gave a sigh.

"Okay, so if I am to become your daughter, that means you will be my mum. That is the right English word, isn't it?" I took her hand and gave it a soft squeeze.

"Danny, I have no intention of replacing her, and neither has Birch, that is not what we are about. Your mum will always be your mum, no one can ever change that." She nodded, and looked at me.

"Yeah, I understand that, but won't everyone expect us to call you mum?" I gave a sigh, not unlike my mother, which was weird.

"Look, I want you to feel at ease, and you can call me whatever you want. Danny, there is no pressure here, I am not your fascist nannie. You go with whatever you feel comfortable with, alright?" She nodded.

"Yeah, thanks, I was worrying about it, and did not know what to do." I leaned forward and kissed her head.

"We are all just going with the flow here Danny, we have worries as well you know? I don't want you sat worrying, you can come to me or Birch anytime and talk about everything, and anything. Don't bottle it up, take a hint from your sister, and just let it all out." She giggled.

"She does not have a filter on her mouth; everything explodes out of her." I chuckled.

"Now that I understand, I have a wife who is just the same." She gave a big laugh, as I stood up.

"Somehow, I think this week both of us are going to have to cope with a lot of wild loud noisy shenanigans." I turned with my cup.

"I need coffee, let's see how messy your sister is." She got off the bed, and followed and put her arm around my waist.

"Thanks, I am glad we talked." I gave her a squeeze.

"Anytime kid." And suddenly, I was Hatty, oh my life was getting really strange.

"What are Shenanigans?" And that, was a very good question.

We both looked at Jessie.

"Jesus Chloe, what did you do, use her as a brush, and just roll her on the canvass?" Chloe's eyes sparkled as she looked at Jessie.

"That is the coolest idea ever, come here." She grabbed a new canvass and lay it flat on the floor.

"Here, roll on it." Jessie gave a happy squeal and lay on the canvass and rolled around, and the paint smeared all over it, I shook my head and looked at Danny.

"Which one is the seven year old?" She laughed. Chloe lifted up the canvass and inspected it, she turned it round a few times and then nodded, and turned it to show Jessie.

"This is pretty brilliant, with a few added touches, it will be an inspired work of art." I frowned.

"It looks like a kid went mental on it." Chloe gave me that look of an artisan.

"You write with words, we write with colour, stick to books, this is art."

She placed it on her easel, and gave a satisfied nod. I grabbed Jessie by the hand; she looked like she had exploded a rainbow.

"Come on, you are going in the bath." She gave me a big grin with red, yellow and purple cheeks. I shook my head and took her upstairs.

When Birch told me she had restocked the bathroom, she was not wrong, we had ducks, octopus, sharks, shells and little crocodiles. There was a water wheel and a bubble blower, and enough boats to take the whole population of London on a sailing trip. I filled the bath and wondered just where Jessie was going to fit.

I rolled up my sleeves, grabbed a sponge, and a huge bar of soap, and started to scrub, to attempt to at least find the little girl under the colour. It took a while, and I lifted her out of the tub wrapped in a towel, and carried her into the bedroom. She stood in front of me as I rubbed her down and dried her off, with a happy smile.

"You are nicer than the nannie." I looked up at her.

"Really?" She nodded.

"She rubs me and it hurts, and I cry." I stopped rubbing and felt a huge surge rise up inside me.

"You cry?" She nodded.

"I don't like her; I want to stay here." I sat up, and my eyes filled with tears.

"I want that too Munchkin." She put her arms round my neck, and hugged me hard.

"Don't cry. Tears are not for bath time anymore." I wiped my eyes and looked at her as she stepped back, and smiled.

"Yep, you are right, no tears at bath time, baths should be fun." She nodded.

"I think so too." I wiped my eyes and smiled, and held out my hand.

"It's a deal, no tears at bath time." She took my hand and shook it.

"Deal."

Oh God, my heart is melting, I really am starting to love them, and want them to stay forever. There was a cough, and I turned to see Janet stood in the doorway, she was smiling with Danny at her side. Janet stepped in and smiled at Jessie.

"Hi, I heard you got covered in paint?" I gave a snigger. Jessie looked up proud.

"I made Art; Chloe showed me." I gave a giggle.

"I could not tell which was child and which was rainbow, but she is all clean now."

Danny offered to help finish her off, and her clean clothes were already laid out on the bed. Birch had an hour free, so rushed home, and we sat with Janet and went through the paperwork. Suddenly, I noticed something and looked at Janet as I lifted the paperwork.

"Their names are Fairbanks Watson?" She nodded.

"It appears Peter was so angry at his family, when he married, he took her family name above his own, which in his father's circles was unheard of. I heard it created quite a storm at the time."

We signed each of the papers, as Janet explained them, Birch appeared to really understand all of this. Some of it was above my head, but she had been studying the American adoption system. We provided all the financial details, family history and endless other facts that left me confused and bewildered, and by the time we finished, I felt brain dead. Chloe in clothes provided us with coffee, and as we talked the girls joined us, Danny had dried Jessie's hair for her.

Jessie climbed onto my lap, and faced me with a smile, she leaned forward and snuggled into me, and I pulled her close.

"You okay Munchkin?"

"I like bath time now."

I chuckled as Danny sat down, and listened to Janet explaining what the court procedure would be from now on. Birch slid her arm round her, and pulled her close as Janet spoke.

"I am pushing this as hard as I can, but realistically, with no hold ups, it can take a month or more." I looked at Birch.

"A month?" She reached out her hand and took mine in hers.

"Sweetie we are closer, it will be hard, but we are almost there."

I gave a sigh.

"The sooner that nannie gets the boot, the happier I will be, I don't like her idea of care, it is too hard on them."

While we were talking, Anita arrived with a car full of boxes. Chloe helped, and they quietly stacked them in the corner of the room. She smiled and waved to the kids, they did not know who she was, but waved back. Janet finished her conversation with Birch and sat back in her seat; she looked at me across the room.

"She used to sit for hours on Amanda like that, I have not seen her do that in a while." I gave a snort.

"I am not surprised, that nannie is as cold as a freezer, where the hell did they dig her up from?" Janet gave a smirk.

"She has been with the Fairbanks family for a very long time. From what I can gather, she was in service to Mr Fairbanks senior, and took care of all his children in the Hamptons."

It did not surprise me in the least, just thinking back to him stood in that conference room, he was as cold as they come, no wonder he hired the ice maiden to watch his kids, and grandchildren.

Janet finished her coffee, and took the children up to their room to check in with them, we headed into the library, where Anita opened a large packet with passes in it.

"These arrived just as I was about to leave."

I looked at the printed passes, they looked awesome, with a half a union jack flag, cut diagonally across them, with a stars and stripes across the bottom half, and the big Curio Live logo stamped across them. All the passes for us had our names printed on them with a QR code, and the rest were visitors passes.

I sorted them out into piles, for Deb's, Edwina, Anthony, and Chloe, and then I held a pass up and looked at it, it read Daniella Watson, Birch giggled as she looked at it.

"She will be thrilled Sweetie, when do we tell her?"

"Not yet." I turned to Birch.

"I know it sounds crazy, but I do not want them to think we are trying to buy their love." She smiled and nodded.

"I get it, I do, but Deads, we will be in America, they can come visit us, that is the point." I gave a sigh.

"Birch, I know that... Oh God, Birch, I don't want them to leave,

I want them to stay. I am sorry, how can I not care about them? Birch, I do, it has only been a day, but it has been so wonderful. Danny talks to me, and she trusts me, and Jessie is so adorable, and I loved bathing her; it was like my mum and me all over again. Oh God, I am going to have a breakdown next Tuesday, I know it."

She smiled and pulled me into her arms, and held me tight. I snuggled into her, I know me, I know what I am like, and I knew, I just knew when they left it would tear me apart.

"Deads, we are so close, just hang in there. Look, if we need to, we will travel to Curio Live ahead of the others, and go via Jefferson. Look, between now and then, we can do more days, they won't be completely alone, we can be there for them. We may have to attend the hearing, so we will stay for a few days and do that. The thing is Deads, as long as they are happy, sooner rather than later, they will be here for good."

Chapter 21

Our Girls.

We were all sat in the living room talking Curio Live, when Janet appeared smiling with the girls, she appeared pleased everything was progressing at a good rate which relieved me. Danny sat at my side and I pulled my arm around her, as Luke explained the technical requirements of the event.

The event was pretty big, and situated right in the heart of Las Vegas, Birch had it up on her computer, and Danny was watching the images. For the first Curio Live, we had done everything in London, in one big conference centre, but for this we were taking a different route, not only would we be live from the newly refitted Spire Mobile Centre, at the same time, events would be going on in two of the nearby hotels, so rooms and events were pretty much close together, and this was Vegas, so there would be no shortage of things to do. Danny looked at me.

"That place is huge, are you not going to be scared?" I smiled.

"Honestly, it terrifies me, but the house lights are down, so even though I know there will be twenty thousand people there, I will not be able to see them, which really helps."

"We have lots of buckets Sweetie." Danny frowned.

"Buckets?" The all sniggered, I looked at her.

"It is shameful, I get so nervous I usually yerk, as soon as I come off stage."

"Yerk, what is that?" Chloe giggled.

"She pukes like crazy, you know, vomits?" Danny shuddered, and they all laughed.

The door banged and Deb's and Jimmy arrived, Danny stared at him like he was some sort of holy figure, she patted my leg.

"Is that Jimmy Blazer?" Birch smiled.

"Yes Sweetie, Deb's is married to him, didn't you know?" She shook her head, and swallowed hard.

"No, I know she married someone famous, I just didn't know it was him, the kids at school rave about the Taco's." He walked in, saw us and walked up to Danny and held out his hand, and she went really shy, it was kind of cute.

"Hey Doll, how are you doing, I hope my mates here is taking good care of you?" She swallowed again, Birch sniggered, and Danny lifted a shaking hand.

"Hi... Jimmy... Dan... I mean Danny... It's nice to meet you, I mean it is insane to meet you, my friends adore you." He smiled and winked.

"What's not to love Doll?" I giggled; she had gone snow white. Jessica sat up on Birch's knee.

"Danny and Marci have pictures of you on their bedroom wall." Danny turned instantly beetroot; I patted her leg.

"Give me a lift with the drinks Danny." I got up and took her hand, as her face burned red. I walked into the kitchen and undid the cellar door.

"Cool off down here, and help me with the beers." She nodded, and followed me down the steps, I turned at the bottom.

"So, you are a Taco's fan?" She leaned on the table.

"I was so shocked, did I look like an idiot, oh God, please tell me I didn't?" I shook my head.

"No, you looked like every fan I have ever seen meet him, he is a great guitarist, and his lyrics are getting better with each album."

"But they broke up." I nodded.

"I know, I have heard some of the demo's of the album he is working on with Floyd, who by the way, is married to our local vicar, you will meet him at some point." Her eyes opened wide.

"Floyd lives here as well?" I nodded, as I lifted a case of beer.

"If you want, I will ask Deb's to show you the studio, it will look great on Insta, your friends will be blown away."

"I don't have one, I am not old enough yet." I suddenly realised.

"Okay, how many of them know of and follow me?" She shrugged.

"A lot of them." I winked.

"Well then, as long as you are okay with it, we will snap a few pics and put them up, once the paperwork comes through." She frowned at me.

"Why then, and not now?" I smiled at her.

"I am just being careful Danny, honestly, I do not trust the

Fairbanks. When everything is legal, and you are safe, then, but we can still take loads ready." She smiled.

"Yeah, that would be cool." I winked.

"To your mates back home, it will be beyond cool."

I walked up the steps with the beer, and into the kitchen. I popped the box down, and opened the fridge door, and pointed to the large almost empty shelf.

"Pull the cold ones to the front, and line the back with new ones, I will grab the rest."

I left her restocking whilst I went and got more, and as I came back up, I heard Jimmy talking, I stopped and watched, she was on her knees in front of the fridge, she was a little star struck, but not as red.

"Well, you see that is it Danny girl, we wanted a more softer touch, but them two wanted to keep crashing and banging, and if I am honest, home life with kids and stuff, is pretty great, so I needed to slow down a bit. Will we do something again, honestly Doll, I cannot say, but what I can say is, I never rule stuff out." She nodded and smiled; he opened the can she had handed him.

"So, how is life here for you, it's a bit different from the states ain't it? Mind you, no girl could ask for better than Abby and Jemi, two of the top they are, proper clever an all. I tell you what, them two, best and kindest alive they are, I would have had me whole wedding to Deb's completely screwed if it had not been for them two, best gig ever they are."

I had to smile, he was a lovely guy and he meant well, and Danny was just soaking it up, I clumped on the steps and came up and he winked.

"She is a lovely kid Abby, reminds me of you she does." He winked, and walked off to the living room. I put the box down and looked in the fridge.

"Yeah, I think we will get a few more in, Jimmy and Luke like a can or two when they unwind. See, he is just a nice guy, talented, but an ordinary nice guy." She smiled.

"He loves you and Birch." I nodded.

"We are a group of really close friends Danny, we look out for each other, and take care of each other." She gave a nod and lifted a can to put in the fridge.

"I can really see that, I think it is nice, that everyone I have met really likes you both." Anita popped her head round the door.

"Guys, I am going to sort the boxes, are you coming?" I gave a nod.

"There in a moment."

We stocked up, and then headed back to the living room, all the boxes had been stacked on the table and everyone sat round, as Anita stood next to the large low coffee table.

"Right guys, you all have a sample of each, they are ready to start rolling and printing, but we need one main one that will go super mass production. So, take a look, and we need to decide tonight, because I have to confirm by email straight away so they have enough stock."

Anita lifted the boxes, and handed them round, everyone had their name on a box, Birch got excited and giddy with Jessie.

"I love presents; I am excited." I looked at her.

"They are not presents; they are samples."

Anita handed me mine and put Aden and Gill's on one side with Morty's. Everyone was opening them up and pulling out the T shirts, hoodies and base ball caps, as Danny and Jessie watched smiling. Anita turned and put a box on Danny's knee, then handed one to Jessie.

"I had to guess your size, so they may be a little baggy." I smiled as I looked at Danny.

"Everything alright?" She nodded and smiled.

"I did not expect one, I am a little surprised." Behind me Jessie held up her Curio Live shirt with a squeal, I patted Danny's hand.

"Look, you know we want you here, and we are not putting pressure on you, but while you are here, you are one of us. Sammy, Josh, and Liz have one, and you both should too." She smiled, and her eyes sparkled with tears.

"You are so like her; you have no idea how like her you are."

I pulled her close, and she gave a little sob, Deb's smiled across the room, as her eyes filled up, she gave me a nod as I held Danny tight, and I leaned my face down onto her head.

"It is alright, I understand, as I said, no matter what, she will always be your mum, and Danny, she will live on in your heart for the rest of your life... I tell you what, bring your box and come with me."

She wiped her eyes on her sleeve, and I took her hand, and I walked slowly up the stairs. She sniffled and wiped her eyes, as I led her into my room, and crouched down under my desk, and pulled out a leather bound album. I sat Danny on the bed, and sat at her side, and I opened the book.

"This is my wedding album." She leaned in and gasped.

"That's your wedding?" I smiled with fondness.

"Yes, it was such an amazing moment in my life, I have a video of it, which Bongo filmed for us."

I flicked through the pages and stopped at a picture of her mum and dad stood either side of me by the arch in the garden, she gasped. I pointed at it and smiled.

"Danny, do you know, what is the most amazing thing about that picture?" She frowned.

"It is my mum and dad with you at your wedding, and you look so beautiful." I smiled and shook my head.

"No, the most amazing thing is you are in it too." She looked puzzled.

"How?" I gave a small giggle.

"Not long after that was taken, I left for my honeymoon, and when I got back, my dad was so happy, because your mum had emailed him, and told him she was five months pregnant, and not even realised. It was quite a surprise, but she had not suffered any of the normal symptoms like morning sickness, so she just did not know. Danny the most amazing thing is you are there at my wedding, growing inside her, how cool is that?" She smiled a wonderful and radiant smile.

"Really?" I nodded.

"You were at my wedding, pretty awesome if you ask me." I slipped it out of the album, and handed it to her.

"Here, take it, I can get another printed. I will get you a frame, and you can put it in your room, and that way, she will always be close to you." She took hold of it and looked down with a smile.

"Thanks... This means a lot to me, Jimmy was right." I patted her leg.

I got up and reached up on top of the wardrobe where I had a box of assorted frames. We got a lot as wedding gifts, and we had not used all of them. I found a nice sterling silver one, and handed it to her. She got up and hugged me, and then walked to her room to frame it and placed it by her bed. I left her for a while as I looked at my wedding pictures, it was such an amazing day, and one of many happy times in my life with Birch.

When I walked into her room, she was lay on the bed fast asleep, I gave a smile, slipped off her shoes, and pulled the duvet over her. She was hugging the frame close to her heart, and even though I felt a lump in my throat, I felt good, she was happy, and that really was all that mattered to me.

Birch walked in with Jessie wearing a large Curio Live t shirt sleeping in her arms, she smiled as she walked over to the bed, and I pulled back the duvet, and she gently lowered her in, and pulled the cover over her. We quietly walked to the door, and I turned, and felt Birch's arm slip round my waist, she whispered quietly.

"Is she alright?" I nodded as I watched her sleep.

"Yes, she is missing her mum, but I had that covered, she will be fine now." I felt her pull me close and lean on my shoulder.

"Deads, I love this, I really do, I want this forever." I nodded, and slid my hand on to hers.

"Me too, look at them, they are so adorable, you know, I cannot for the life of me understand how that awful family could turn them away. I want them forever."

We pulled the door to, and headed back downstairs, to debate Curio Live logos.

The following morning it all started again, kids and cereal, coffee, running around madness, and then boom, silence, and the sipping of coffee. Bliss, and Jessie who was not quiet at all. I chewed my toast and sipped my coffee, as Chloe who had been out, piled the table up with pads and crayons, and Jessie got stuck in colouring. I glanced at Danny.

"What would you like to do today?" She looked at me.

"Are there any more shops locally, I would like some sneakers, I forgot to pack mine?" The golden words were spoken by Chloe.

"If you are going shopping in Oxendale, I am in." I smiled.

"Cool, let's shop."

My car was good, but this was shopping, so we needed volume, which could only mean one thing... Petal!

We got ready, it was sunny so I handed out sunglasses, I as always, wore round mirrors, and we headed out playing Battered Taco and headed for Oxendale. We both briefed the kids on the route, Chloe sat in the back strapped in with Jessie, and I let Danny sit up front.

"Shopping is not a sport, the queen of shopping is without doubt Birch, but she has to work, so it is up to us, but girls, listen up, it is an art form, that requires precision and care."

We hit the shopping centre and did what we did best, we pissed about, much to the amusement of the kids. We laughed and screamed with delight, ate ice cream, ran like maniacs and generally had a great time. We entered the shoe shop, and Danny ogled all the shoes, I walked at her side as she looked around, and an assistant appeared.

"Miss Watson... We are delighted to see you, please won't you sit down, we will be happy to show you anything at all you desire." I lifted my sun glasses and winked at Danny, she giggled.

"Get her anything she wants to see; I want her in good shoes." We sat down.

"Yes Miss Watson, would you like coffee or another refreshment?" I looked at Danny, she was loving this, and nodded. I smiled at the assistant.

"Two coffees would be lovely, thank you." We both giggled, when she nipped off.

Strangely enough, this is the first time this has ever happened to me, but hell, it was fun. Danny pointed out shoes, and the assistants brought them to her to try on. Chloe was getting similar treatment opposite us, and Jessie was loving it. After an hour, and posing for pictures, we headed out, and they both had two new pairs of shoes. Next was clothes and my favourite shop.

To be honest we went a bit mad, I bought Birch three pairs of pants and two tops, and the two girls staggered out with loads of clothes, it was mental, but so much fun. We piled Petal high, and headed home to try them all on. The four of us gathered in my room, tossed clothes everywhere and looked at ourselves in the full length mirror. It was so much fun, as we finally gathered everything, and I laid out Birch's new clothes on the bed.

Danny and Jessie headed to their room talking excitedly, and Chloe sat in my chair smiling.

"You know what Abby; you are a great mum." I smiled and sat back on the bed.

"I am really loving this Chloe, but it is going to kill me sending them home." She gave a smile, and sat up in the seat.

"Abby it will not be for long, you know, I was talking with Baz last night, and he said considering it is Curio Live in a couple of weeks, why not just rent a place in the run up, so you can be near them?" It was a nice thought.

"There is too much to do here, I would love to, but Chloe, we still have a hell of a lot of organising before we fly out."

The simple fact was, we were now right in the midst of the biggest Curio event we had done, and we were at a crucial stage as all the planning came together. It was a big event right in the heart of Vegas, and we had planned it to be big and bold. We would be live in the arena, and it would be streamed worldwide live and unedited, with a five minute delay.

We had lived for weeks in video calls talking and organising, simply to guide all of those taking part in the event. There were seminars, workshops, talks from professionals in the field, as well as a host of celebrity guests, making presentations videos, and entertaining, at one point we had thirty video crews filming all over the globe. It was going to be a massive four days of fund raising, and we needed at least two hundred million dollars to pull it off. We had planned to stop at each of the three sites to film, in Pennsylvania, Missouri which we picked because of Danny and Jessie, and California, before heading to Vegas on what would be a four day break, come working trip.

It was going to be exhausting, but fun, there was no Katie, no walking around in pairs, free run of the hotel floor, and even though they did not know yet, Danny and Jessie were coming with us. Birch arrived home and came up to change, we were still excited about shopping and she pouted.

"I love shopping Sweetie." I pulled her close.

"I know baby, but look, we bought gifts." She saw the clothing and her eyes sparkled.

"I love gifts."

I smiled as she slid out of my arms, grabbed a new pair of bootcut jeans and slid them on, they had little rainbows around the bottom of the legs and on the pockets, she loved them. She pulled on the long green flowing silk top, and smiled, I gave her a wink.

"The girls picked that out for you; I am glad you like it." She looked at herself in the mirror.

"I love it, I will go and thank them."

She ran round to the other room as I picked up her clothes and noticed Danny's new shoes, she had been in such a rush to try on her new things and then put them away, she had forgotten them. I picked up the bag and walked round to their room, and heard the din before I got there.

I walked in and Danny was looking panicked, Birch was sat on the floor bawling her brains out, Jessie pointed at Danny.

"She broke her!" Danny looked terrified, and shook her head rapidly.

"I didn't do anything, honest."

She was becoming really panicked and upset, as Birch wailed the room down, sat on the floor bawling her brains out. I gave a sigh, and put my arm round Danny's shoulder; she was trembling.

"Danny it is fine, she is emotionally unstable at the best of times, calm down, it is fine." She clung to me, as Chloe leaned in and smirked at Birch.

"But I didn't do anything, all I did was ask her if I could leave some things in the wardrobe until we live here."

I felt my breath catch in my throat, and looked down at her as my emotions swirled around inside. Birch looked at me and wailed even louder, as Danny looked at me for reassurance.

"You want to live here?" She nodded as she looked up at me.

"Yes, didn't Janet tell you?" I shook my head, and tears filled my eyes, and my voice went all squeaky.

"No... She didn't." She looked at me, and smiled.

"Both of us told her, this is what we want, we want to be here. you know, with you guys?" I smiled as my tears dropped off my nose. Birch bawled her brains out even more. I had to swallow to speak.

"Oh Danny, Jessie, we want that more than anything else in the world, we hoped, but we did not know, but we really want you too. We want this to be a happy fun home for you, and a new start." I wiped my eyes, and she turned and pulled me into a hug, and looked up at me.

"I really want to live here, and so does Jessie. I love this house, and all the amazing people, and honestly, you two are the kindest people we know. We told that to Janet, and she said she would help us do it." I gave a huge sniffle, and nodded, it was hard to talk, and I had to breathe, but I smiled.

"I really want that too, I really do." Jessie hugged my leg, looked up and pointed at Birch.

"Can you fix her; she is really loud?" Chloe sniggered.

"Fuck no, we have been trying to do that for years."

I knelt down in front of Birch, and I smiled. She was weeping and wailing and saying I have no idea what, because she had so much snot up her nose and tears streaming down her face, I could barely understand her. Chloe handed me a huge pile of tissue, and I gave it her.

"Birch, Baby, you are scaring the girls, you need to calm down."

She nodded and pushed the tissue into her face and blew. It made a loud rasping sound and the girls giggled. I gave a sigh, and Chloe handed me more tissue, and I wiped her eyes.

"Look at you, the girls picked out that top for you, and you are covering it in tears. Go to our bathroom, wash your face and breathe, and we will talk about it in a bit."

Birch nodded, and blew her nose again, I helped her up, and handed her more tissue, she walked towards the door, and looked at Danny.

"I am sorry I frightened you, but you made me so happy I could not hold it in." She started to blubber, and walked out quickly. Chloe shook her head.

"Hell Abby, she is the biggest kid in here." Jessie gave a giggle.

I sat the kids down on the bed, Danny was calming down. I looked at them both and smiled.

"Okay, you both have to understand that Birch is absolutely brimming with love, and honestly, at times it just explodes out of her. But do not be frightened, because it is because she feels so deeply, and because of that she has started to love you both very much. She is the most amazing person I know, she is so clever, and so brilliant at planning things, but I will warn you, she is bonkers a lot of the time, but you know what?" They shook their heads, and I smiled.

"She will love you and protect you and fight to the death for you. Birch is the most loyal person I have ever met, she is honest, and never lies, but sometimes she explodes and cries, but what you see is the love she feels. Do you both understand that?" They nodded at me and smiled; Jessie took my hand.

"Will she be alright now?" I smiled.

"Yes, she will calm down, and just think of the joy you two just gave to her, and it will make her very happy." Jessie nodded at me.

"Can I go see her?" I gave her a smile and patted her leg.

"Yes, go see her, it will make her very happy." Jessie jumped off the bed, and ran off to see Birch, and I looked at Danny.

"Will you be alright now?" She gave a long sigh.

"Now I understand, yeah, I will be fine."

"Come on, I need a coffee after all that wailing, my God she is loud." Chloe walked down behind us.

"Tell me about it. God, drama much." Danny giggled, and slipped her hand into mine.

Chapter 22

Family Feeling.

Birch calmed down and was really happy, and deep inside I wanted to explode, I was so overjoyed, but unlike my insane wife, I was trying to hide it. We spent the evening sat in the garden, and once again, Birch had outdone herself, and bought masses of inflatable swans and ducks, and a huge floating hand. So, we did what we always do, we stripped and dived in.

The kids followed and I ended sat on the huge hand having water pistol fights with everyone. Danny and Jessie laughed and screamed with Jenny and Sammy, as Debs tried to climb on a huge duck, and kept falling off back into the water. It was pretty hilarious, but exhausted and happy, the day ended with us tucking the kids up in bed, and kissing them goodnight.

Friday started much the same, except Birch had the morning off, and summer was coming, and the day was warming up. We packed up a huge bag, and headed off in Petal to Dursley Woodland for a massive picnic. We spread out the huge tartan rug, and set up our spot, Janet joined us as we threw frisbee's, spun in hula hoops, and batted badminton shuttle cocks all over the place.

We spotted butterflies, saw a few dragonflies, took millions of pictures, and stuffed ourselves with sandwiches and cake to the point of exploding. Danny read her book for a while, and I sat lost in thought as I looked at the old travelling rug blanket. It had seen some memorable times. We used it at the Oxendale festival, when we went camping, took it to Glastonbury, and also, Birch made love to me on it under my arch on the side of the canal, and she knelt on it when she proposed. It had seen so much over the years, the blanket alone, could tell the story of my life with Birch.

We had parked next to the retreat, so as the morning ended, we packed up lighter bags, loaded ourselves with the hula hoops, and we walked slowly back down the passage at the side of the hardware shop, and crossed the road onto the green. I slid my arm round Danny's back.

"Have you had a good day?" She looked up and smiled.

"Yeah, I love the life you live here, you go places and do loads of great stuff, we cannot leave the grounds at home, except for school, but we get driven and picked up by Nannie, so I love it here." I smiled.

"Most people think this place is boring, but I never really have, I always found something to do when I was a kid." We crossed the road, and turned towards the retreat.

"Hey you!" I stopped and smiled.

"Hatty, where have you been?" She gave me a big smile.

"Giving you some time, and looking at you two, I think it has paid off." I looked down at Danny.

"Danny, this is my second mum, this is Hatty."

She lifted her hand, and Hatty brushed it aside, and pulled her into a huge hug, just like she always had with me.

"I don't shake hands with precious people, I hug them."

She gave her a huge hug, then grabbed Jessie and gave her a huge squeeze, and Jessie giggled. Hatty looked at me and her eyes just sparkled with life.

"I just watched you walking over the green talking with Danny, and fuck me Abby...Oops, pardon me, God Abby, you reminded me of Flick, just like she was back then. Oh girl, it has made me so happy." I smiled at her and could see she was close to tears, and I was really hoping she did not cry, because I was fighting it back with a smile.

"I am happy Hatty; I don't think I have ever been so happy." She smiled and winked.

"It shows Abby, oh God it shows." She looked at Danny and Jessie.

"So, I now have two adopted granddaughters, I hope you will both be outrageous and wild, and not at all as boring and stuffy as Edwin?" Danny smiled.

"We will try." Hatty sniggered.

"That is all I ask, here a little spending money." I smiled.

"Hatty, you know you don't have to?" She winked at the girls.

"Bugger off Abby, these are my family too, and I can spoil them whenever I want, it is what a good nana does."

The girls both giggled, and I nodded, I really understood that, she had been there for me always, and I owed her so much. She handed both the girls a twenty pound note each. She gave me another hug, and squeezed me so hard.

"I am off for a coffee with your mum, go enjoy your family. God, I am so proud of you Abby." Oh God, I was going to cry again. She said goodbye with more hugs, and headed off up the street, and Jessie waved.

"Bye Nana Hatty." Birch looked at me and her eyes filled up, oh shit, she was going to explode again. We loaded Petal, and Birch had to go, but Jessie was craning her neck looking.

"Is that where you work?" Birch smiled.

"Yes Sweetie, would you like to have a look?" I was grateful it was Friday, and not Thursday, thank God we went shopping yesterday.

We all entered, and the girls behind the counter all got excited and wanted to meet Danny and Jessie. Meg and Alex raved with Gill, and it took forever to get through into the back rooms, as Izzy came out of the office to meet us.

Izzy looked at us, and her smile said it all, I stood there with my arm around Danny and holding Jessie by the hand, as Birch beamed with delight.

"Girl's this old broad, is probably the coolest person I know, this is Izzy."

She smiled at us and I could see the huge emotions swirling inside her, she looked at me and winked.

"Wow kids, you just look perfect together." She knelt down, and looked at Jessie.

"Oh my, what a cute little button you are, I bet you are as noisy as Jemi is?" Jessie frowned.

"No one is as loud as her, she screamed the house down crying, and it was really loud." Izzy gave a titter and nodded.

"Yeah, I have seen that mess." Jessie nodded.

"I know right." I giggled; oh god Chloe was rubbing off on her. She looked up at Danny.

"Wow, you look like your mum, and Abby, I bet you are the quiet one, who loves to read all day?" Danny nodded, and smiled, Izzy winked.

"Yep, another one who hangs out in the library all day. So how are things going?" Danny was a little shy, and I smiled, she looked at Izzy.

"We really love the village, it is a nice place to live, I love the house, I cannot wait till we live here." Izzy gave a smile.

"You will have such fun girls, I know those two mental patients and what they are capable of, oh God, I am so happy for all of you, honestly, I could just explode." Jessie shook her head.

"No don't, we have seen that mess already." Birch sniggered, and I could not help but snort a laugh. Izzy smiled and looked up.

"I shall try to contain myself." She giggled as she stood up.

"Come on, I will give you the tour."

And with that, Izzy took their hands and showed them every room, and told them what it was used for. Danny loved the room upstairs where Aden worked, she took pictures of it on her phone. He had three large screens with Curio Life on two of them, and on a third he was working on something new. He turned around in his seat, and smiled.

"This will not be live until the event, and as you can see, we are taking the site to a younger audience, although we will need a face for it." Danny looked at me and I smiled at her.

"Mine is too old, we need a Curio who is just the perfect age." She looked astounded.

"Me?" I shrugged.

"It could be, why are you interested?" She gave me a big smile.

"I would love to help people the way you have, and I would defo do it." I nodded. Oh god, she is sounding like Deb's now, what the hell have I done?

"Okay then, it is a deal, I will talk to Edwina and see what needs to be done." She gave me a huge hug.

Birch had a group therapy session, so had to leave us, and go back to work, she kissed the kids and left us, and after what had been a long time, we jumped into petal and headed for home. We unloaded Petal into the kitchen, sorted everything out, and then Janet and I sat for coffee whilst the kids went up to their room to put their money in their piggy banks, yep, they both had one each, Birch had thought of everything. Janet smiled at me.

"You know, they are really happy here, I hate taking them back."

I took a deep breath; I was trying not to think about it.

"It won't be for too long, and they still have some school to finish, and we will be back for Curio Live. We have not told them yet, we thought we would wait until the last minute, you know, just in case." She reached across the island and took my hand.

"Y'all will get them, the Fairbanks so far have been true to their word, Abby, it will go through, have some faith honey."

I nodded, I could not deny, I was feeling scared and unsettled, we were so close, and these last few days had felt like a dream come true. The social worker was due at four, and I was nervous, Janet could see it.

"Y'all have a lovely clean home, and there is such love here, you will fly through the inspection with flying colours, now don't you worry none, you got this." I nodded.

"Still nervous, we want this so badly, and I think they do to. It is frustrating, I am their family, they should not have to be parted from me." She smiled.

"Sadly, them are the rules. Look, you have all passed all of your background checks, your financial profile is more than stable, all your assessments have been one hundred percent. Honestly, they cannot fault you on anything, this will pass right through the court with no problems. Trust me, I have dealt with people who have a hell of a lot less than you two, and they breezed through."

I knew it was just my own insecurity, but hell, the press have been attacking me for years and writing some pretty bad things about me, and there in the back of my mind was Roni, and that first week at her house, and her voice felt like it was on a constant stream through my mind.

"It is not easy growing up with two professionals like us as parents, my work especially attracts a lot of attention, especially the books I publish. Jemi was raised in the shadow of them, and she took quite a lot of ridicule for it, I almost considered giving up my practice and becoming a teacher because of it."

It was my biggest fear, once Roni had seen her daughter suffer so much because of her public image, she had almost quit. I did not want that for Danny and Jessie, it terrified me that they would be hurt because of it, and I knew Oxendale High well, and the cruelty of children. Deb's, Nigel, Me, and especially Anthony, had been through it. It was hard and painful, and I was so afraid that my children would suffer more than we had because of my books, or Birch's practice. No matter what anyone had said to date, I knew the press, and I knew how cruel they could be, especially where it concerned me.

The girls came down, and Janet sat with them in the living room and explained what would happen with the social worker who was going to visit, and then she left. I had work to do and was sat in my room on my computer, when Danny came in with her book and sat on the bed. She was reading 'The Publicity Girl' and I heard her giggle and spun around in my chair, she looked up and smiled.

"This is such a good book, and it's funny. I love how you and Anita went skinny dipping in the Loch in Scotland, and the wind blew your clothes away. Did that really happen?" I gave a giggle and smiled as I remembered it, I got up and walked over to the bed and sat down.

"It was funny, I mean at first, we were terrified, it was getting dark and we looked everywhere, but we could not find them. Anita had her arm up covering her boobs and her other hand between her legs as she ran back to the hotel. Oh Danny, it was hilarious. We made it back to the hotel, but obviously we did not want to just walk in, so we snuck around the side, thank God we were on the ground floor and I had left our window open a nick. I was pretty skinny, and I went first, and slid in through the window, the problem was it had a locking bar, so would not open more. Anita was a little broader behind than I am, and as she slid through her ass got stuck, so she was there with her bum, showing her... Well, you know, lady parts to the grounds, and this Scottish guy walks up."

I started to laugh, I could not help it, the giggles bubbled up inside me as I remembered it. Danny started giggling with me, I took a deep breath, and tried to stop laughing.

"He looked at her ass hanging out of the window, and he says. 'Are ye advertising, or are ye in need of a push, because lassie, that is a very tempting sight?'

I was yanking on her like crazy, but she would not come through, and panicking like mad he would, well you know, do something he shouldn't. Anita just looked back and said to him.

'For god's sake man, stop thinking with your willy and give me a push, I got goosebumps on my ass." Danny looked at me shocked.

"What did he do?" I wiped my eyes; I was laughing so much.

"He walked up to her and I was freaking completely out, and he just put both his hands on her ass, and smiled, and said, 'Tis a fine ass lassie, but aye you're right, I can feel the pimples growing.' Then he pushed, and she came flying through the window."

Danny started to laugh, and it was so lovely and infectious, and I laughed with her, it took me a good few minutes to calm down, she smiled at me, and nodded at the book.

"I love this, you know, you and me, and this book is insane, it's brilliant and a really good read." It was nice to hear her say that, and I gave a nod.

"I love this too, Danny I will not deny, I am so very happy at the moment, and we are both loving having you guys here." She smiled.

"Yeah, we are too, it is nice here."

Birch was back just in time, and at four, as Belinda Ford Davis arrived to do the assessment, I put my arm round Danny, as we walked down the stairs to meet her. She began her inspection, and looked at the girl's room, our room, and the living room, kitchen and library. We then walked out into the garden as she looked at the patio, the hot tub, pool and play area, which thankfully, Birch had been smart enough to have surrounded with safety matting.

We talked, and she asked what provisions we had in place, and what our future plans were for the children. Back inside, she sat in the living room and talked to the children. I was nervous and it showed, so much was riding on this, but Birch was a seasoned professional in this field and took charge from the moment she arrived, and she was very business like. It took almost two hours, when she stood at the door and gave a nod.

"Thank you, both of you." My heart was beating in my chest; she looked at Birch and smiled.

"Jemi, don't look so worried, you know, you two have a beautiful home, and a lovely life and I have clearly seen how much the children care about you. To be honest, just for the big wigs, put a fence around the pool, I won't mention it, but if others check, you will need one." Birch smiled.

"It will be done straight away." She looked at me and smiled.

"You and Danny look good together; I can see you have bonded well." I took a deep breath and smiled.

"I have grown to care for them a great deal." She smiled, Jessie ran down the hall and looked up at her.

"Are you the scary lady Chloe said was coming?" She gave a giggle.

"I can be, but not here." Jessie gave a nod.

"That is good then." Birch giggled as Jessie hugged her leg.

Belinda said goodbye with a smile, and we all gave a huge sigh of relief. I grabbed a coffee and returned to work in my room, and before long Danny sat on my bed reading, and Jessie lay on the floor colouring. Birch came up and sat in her chair and logged in to her com, and as a family we all chilled out together.

We sat working as Danny read, and it was nice peaceful and relaxed, when suddenly there came the most terrifying scream from the stairs, and my heart froze, we all looked at each other.

"JESSIE!"

I came hurtling out of the bedroom followed by Birch and Danny, and ran to the top of the stairs, my heart was in my mouth, and fear was coursing through me, as I skidded onto the top step, and saw Jessie stood on the bottom of the stairs screaming her head off. I saw Bev, she looked up and smiled.

"Hey Deadly, hey Jemi." She pointed.

"Banging lungs on this one, I take it, this is one of em?"

I gave a massive sigh of relief, as Birch smiled, and walked onto the stairs, and down to Jessie.

"Bev Sweetie, what a nice surprise." Jessie turned, and ran to Birch; she buried her face in her leg.

"She has holes in her face." Bev bobbed at the bottom of the stairs, and lifted a hand to her cheeks.

"Oh, aye, I reckon I am getting too old for em, so I pulled em all out."

I hadn't realised, Chloe had come out of her room and was stood with us.

"Well at least we have a Bev alarm now. See, I told you she was as loud as Birch." Danny was gripping my hand tight; I turned to her and smiled.

"That is Bev, Birch's oldest friend, she looks as scary as hell, but honestly, she is one of the sweetest people I know. Come on and meet her."

Bev had a bag on her shoulder, she opened it and looked inside as Birch walked down with a really nervous Jessie, Bev smiled, and pulled a small teddy with a little tutu on, she smiled.

"I am on me bike, so not got room for bigger ones. I know it is not a fairy like, but I thought you could make wings with Deadly, she is good with stuff like that."

She held it out to Jessie. Birch smiled, as Jessie reached out and gave a smile and took it.

"You need to fill your holes up; they make you scary." Chloe sniggered.

"I am pretty sure she has, many times, and honestly she still scares the shit out of me." Danny sniggered and I looked at her.

"Did you get that?" She nodded at me.

"Yeah, I have read seeds of summer." I felt shocked.

"How, I thought you were not allowed?" She gave me a wicked smile.

"Petra Wallenson had a copy, so I hid it in my locker and read it at breaks, it was brilliant by the way."

I still felt shocked, oh my God, was I becoming my mother? We reached the bottom of the stairs, and Bev held up a little vampire teddy.

"You look like Deadly, so figured you would like this." Danny gave a big smile and took it.

"Thanks Bev, it is cute, I love it." Bev bobbed on the spot.

"Banging."

We grabbed drinks and headed into the living room, and Bev talked of the centre and how well it was going, she had six staff working with her, all employed from the Curio site, and she was loving it. It is strange, we took a risk on Bev giving her the job, but honestly, she has really stepped up to the plate, and she runs the grounds really efficiently, and they look pristine and beautiful.

I sat in my usual corner, and Danny snuggled up against me with her teddy, and as Birch, who had Jessie on her knee talked, joined by Baz and Chloe, Danny looked up and quietly talked to me.

"You have two mums; how does that work?" I smiled.

"Hatty is very special; she is my mum's best friend and they grew up together. To be honest, things were not always easy between me and mum, there was a time when how it looked was more important to her than anything, including me. I was told how to be, how to act, and what I should look like, it was not a good time for me." She nodded.

"I get that, I do, Nannie is like that and I hate it." I slid my arm round her.

"It made me so unhappy, I went to Manchester way up north and she freaked out, but that is where I met Birch, she was my roommate at Uni, and that was where I fell hopelessly in love with her. That was when I got the hair, the dark clothes and I became who I was going to be." She smiled.

"A brilliant writer of gothic stories." I nodded.

"I suppose so. Birch nick named me Deadly because of my dark hair, she called me her dark little beastie, and yes, that was where I decided for sure I wanted to write, and I wanted to write the sort of stories I wanted to read."

"So how did that all make Hatty your second mum?" I gave a chuckle.

"My parents were so busy living the right and decent kind of life, they could not see I was so unhappy, Hatty did, and I would go to her and talk. She was a teacher at the time, so I felt understood me, and in a way she became my lifeline, but apart from that, she has always been there. Hatty changed me as a baby, pushed me in my pram, saw my first steps, heard my first words, she was always there, and so we grew close. I love her just like I do my mum, she has been there for me all my life, and always there when I needed her."

Danny thought about it for a minute, and then snuggled into me. It was strange really looking back, before Birch she was the only one I could depend on at one point in my life. I have often wondered what would have happened if she had not been there, and where I would be now in life. I am not sure it would be with Birch. Bless her, she has always had my corner. She gave a sigh, and I looked down.

"I can see how that works, but you and your mum are okay now aren't you?" I nodded as she looked at me.

"Yes, now we are fine, I think Birch had an effect on her, and through that she started to see the real me. We have talked a lot over the years and we have grown very close since I came home from Uni." She smiled and snuggled into me more.

"That is good, I like the idea of you having someone you can talk to like I can with you."

"You will always be able to talk to me about anything, I never want anyone to feel the way I did, it feels terrible and really hurts."

I sat back and relaxed, my mind drifting in the many thoughts going around in my head. Danny had made me remember so much of what I call the old me, the girl before the hair, the girl who was hurt to see her father kissing another woman. The girl terrified of the choir master, and heart broken because I let a guy I thought I loved take my virginity. The girl who felt invisible at home with her parents, living in a room, where no one spoke to her for days, and cried into her pillow at night, and it hit me head on. My eyes moved to Birch who was watching me. She smiled; her eyes twinkled.

"Birch, Curo Life Junior, is massively important, in fact, it is more important than any of us think, I just realised, there are people out there, like I was before Uni, and we need to help them." She smiled at me, and gave a nod.

"I know Sweetie, Izzy and I have had some long talks with Edwina, and we are working on it, I wondered when you would realise." I looked down at Danny as she watched me.

"Have you ever written a blog?" She shook her head.

"No not really, I did an online diary for a couple of years. I have thought about it, but never really known what to write about, why?"

"Curio Life Junior will need a blogger, someone in that age range who understands things for that age group, such as bullying, peer pressure, and deep sadness, the job is available, and I will help with the editing, so what do you say, do you want the job?" She sat up with a huge smile on her face.

"Honestly, you trust me to write for Curio Life, I would love that?" I smiled as I nodded at her.

"We will need to work together, and plan it all out, it will need an introduction, and then specific topics, but that should not be a problem, those who post will give you those. It is what I do, I read the posts, and then research the facts and then blog about it, I think we will make a great team, what do you think?" I thought her head was going to explode, and possibly her face split her smile was so wide.

"I would love that, it would be so amazing, and I could ask Izzy as well for input, because let's be honest, she has seen it all." Birch chuckled.

"Oh boy has she, you will never know the depths she has gone to, but to be honest Danny, I have a clinic full of really experienced counsellors, so you can get great advice from all of them, I am sure they would love to muck in."

She sat there looking happy and proud, but smiling at me, and she had a little sparkle in her eyes, it made me so happy to see it.

"I want to be a Curio, but I want to earn my spot, and not be there just because I am your daughter, well about to be, I really want to make a mark on the site. Although, I am secretly terrified, you must not let me make a fool of myself, you will tell me won't you if I need to up my level for the site?" I gave a chuckle.

"We will go over every article you write and look at it in depth before it is posted, and trust me, we will help make you look good." She looked around at Birch and Bev; Jessie was asleep on Birch's lap.

"Oh my God, I am going to be a real Curio."

Chapter 23

Mum's Together.

It was Saturday, and in three days, the girls would be going back to the USA, and I was feeling it. It was a busy day, most of the Curio's were here and busy, Anita was on the spare computer, Birch was at hers, and Edwina was coding. Deb's was sat at the table writing content for our intro's, and I had just finished two blog posts, and in the living room, Baz, Aden and Jimmy sat together with laptops working on the final stages of travel accommodation and stage presentations.

Morty and Alex were editing video at the kitchen table, Tabs sat with Chloe in the studio looking at artwork for the event slides, and kids were running all over the house. Yep, it was a mad house, made madder by the fact that we had an endless stream of couriers delivering packages. I had made the brews whilst taking a pause, and had carried them all up on a tray, and was heading back to the kitchen for the second tray. I came out of the library door and turned, as above me I heard the shout.

"Jessie, please, this is important. Why are you not outside with the other kids?" I looked up, Danny was stood at the top of the stairs looking stressed. Jessie looked upset.

"But I want to watch cartoons on my laptop, and Helen said she would come watch them with me."

Danny turned and saw me, I could see her stress levels peaking, I knew that look, I had been there a few times when I was writing. Danny looked right at me, and gave a long sigh.

"Mum, will you tell her, I need to do this?"

My heart missed several beats, and it almost failed. I took a deep breath, and tried to calm down, as a huge wave of emotions crashed over me.

"Danny, relax. Go work in my room, it is quiet in there, just close the door and focus, okay?" She nodded.

"Thanks Mum." I felt it again, and bit my lip, I looked at Jessie.

"Munchkin, watch your cartoons, but not too loud, we are all very busy, and leave Danny to work, if you need something, come get me, alright?" She gave a nod.

"Alright Mum."

I gasped, and turned, and Birch was looking at me with her hands to her mouth and tears in her eyes. The emotion inside me was huge, and I was struggling to contain it, I looked at her and felt my hands shake with the tray. My voice was soft, almost a whisper.

"Birch... They called me Mum."

She nodded as tears streamed down her face, I felt my tears come, and they rolled down my cheeks. I was really struggling to keep it all inside me, she just walked out to me and put her arms round me, and squeezed. I pushed my head into her shoulder and shook, as my joy came out as tears. Deb's was in the library bawling her brains out, she had seen and heard it all, and was staring at me as she wept, with a huge smile on her face.

"Abby that was so beautiful, I am sorry, I don't want to cry, but it was epically beautiful, I love you guys so much." Birch squeezed me hard.

"She is right Sweetie; I am going to go down in the cellar now and bawl my brains out so I don't frighten the kids." I gave a sniffle and looked at her, and took a huge deep breath.

"I didn't want to cry, but Birch, I am so happy right now, I cannot explain how that feels, I just can't, it just made me so happy."

Birch let me go, and ran down to the kitchen, I heard her as she ran down the steps to the cellar, and she bawled her brains out. Chloe walked up the hallway looking puzzled, she pointed behind her.

"What is with Birch?" I took another deep breath and wiped my eyes.

"The kids just called me mum." She shrugged.

"Well yeah, you are, or you will be soon, what about it?" I looked at her.

"Chloe, do you remember that day when little Jenny ran up this very hallway, and shouted Auntie Chloe for the first time?"

I saw her face twitch, and then her eyes filled with tears, and her voice went really high and squeaky, as tears rolled onto her cheeks.

"Why would you say that, you know it makes me emotional?" I smirked.

"Times that by a hundred, and that is how Birch and I just felt to be called Mum." She wiped her eyes on her hand and nodded at me with a sniffle.

"Okay, I get you, yeah, I totally get that."

I needed a moment to calm down, I didn't want the girls to see me upset, so I grabbed my coffee and walked down to the kitchen, and just sat at the island, I could hear Birch in the cellar blowing her nose. I lifted my cup to sip, and Danny came around the corner.

"I have a problem... Have you been crying, is everything alright?" I heard Birch coming back up the cellar steps. I nodded.

"Yeah, I am fine, honestly it's silly." She nodded.

"Okay, so tell me." Oh god I felt so emotional it was stupid.

"You caught me off guard, and you called me Mum." I burst into tears, she smiled, and came and sat at my side, and pulled me into a hug.

"Sorry, I have been so busy, I was going to talk to you. I listened to you last night when you talked about Hatty, and you called her your second mum, and I lay in bed last night thinking about it. You know, you have three mums, Hatty, Flick, and Birch's mum. I talked this morning with Jessie, and we agreed, it was okay for us to have three as well, we have my real mom, you, and Birch, so we decided that it is okay, because when you think about it, you are legally adopting us, we will be your daughters."

I heard Birch run down the steps again, and muffled wails came through the door from the cellar. I smiled and wiped my eyes, and took a deep breath.

"It felt so wonderful, I got emotional, but honestly, it was happiness tears." She nodded and kissed my cheek; she looked at the cellar door.

"I take it mum two heard?" I nodded.

"She did, and it made her happier, but a lot louder, hence the cellar." She smiled.

"She does know we can hear her?" I giggled.

"Hell Danny, Satan probably can, she is bawling that hard, the vibrations probably caused an earthquake in China." She gave a giggle, and then turned to the door.

"I need help with the blog, but I think I will talk to mum two first." I nodded.

"Yeah, she will like that, wear ear muffs." She laughed as she opened the door, and suddenly Birch was really loud.

"See what I mean?" I handed her a roll of tissue.

"Trust me, you will need this."

It took a while, but Birch reappeared with red blotchy eyes and big smiles. I walked up with Danny to my room, and sat in my desk chair, and she pulled Birch's over and sat at my side, and together we worked on her introduction blog. I pulled my first ever Curio blog post up and went over it with her, to show her how I constructed it, and Danny nodded as she read it, and understood better what she needed to do.

She made changes, and I noticed how fast she typed in new paragraphs, is it crazy that this was the best thing ever? She asked questions, and I answered pointing things out, and we were both so lost to the world, that we did not hear Roni and Will arrive. They had driven down especially to meet the girls.

She stood outside the door with Will watching us side by side talking and laughing as we edited the document. Will gave a big smile and whispered.

"Wow, she is almost Abby's double." Roni gave a soft nod.

"She is more than that, she is an apprentice writer, and she has a very skilled teacher, look at them Will, there is the future of Sanctuary Press."

Roni tapped softly on the door, and popped her head in, I looked up and smiled.

"I can see you are working, if we are disturbing you, it can wait?" I shook my head.

"No, come in Roni and meet Danny." Danny gave a nod as she understood, and stood up, Roni came in followed by Will, and Danny gave her a big hug.

"So you are Grandma Roni, and I bet you are Grandad Will?" Both of them took a deep breath, and Roni smiled a lovely smile.

"I am, lovely to meet you at last, Jemi has been driving me mad giving me updates, I hope you don't mind, but we really wanted to meet you both, where is your sister?" Danny nodded.

"In our room watching cartoons. Come on, I will take you to meet her." She took Roni's hand and led her out, Will looked around the room.

"You know all these years, and I have never been in here; it reminds me of the old guest house."

He looked down and gave me a big smile, I pushed the free seat and he sat down, as I exploded with happiness. Will took my hands in his, as he looked at me smiling.

"Jemi told me she called you Mum." I nodded and smiled.

"I know it is mental, but honestly, it was the best feeling ever. Dad, they want to stay, they want this, us, all the family thing and I am so happy, I really am. Oh Dad, I really want this so badly." He gave a chuckle, and just looked at me smiling.

"I saw you working with her, I hope you don't mind, but it was so lovely to see, and my word Abby, she is almost your double." He sat back in the seat.

"Jemi is so happy, but not just because of the kids, we talked for an age last night, and she told me how happy she is to see you with them, she thinks you will be an amazing parent."

The door burst open and Jessie came tearing in, she stopped dead, and looked at Will, he turned and looked at her and smiled.

"Are you going to be my granddad?" He gave a chuckle.

"Well, if there is a vacancy, I would love to apply." She gave a huge smile, and climbed on to his lap.

"Awesome, the job is yours."

He pulled her into a hug and laughed, and suddenly I saw it, I saw what Jemi had all those years ago. With his whiter hair and happy face, he was just like Birch's grandfather at Sunny Bank.

I was happy to see Roni and Will, it had been a few months. Jessie wanted to collect leaves to paint, Chloe had been telling her about how she did it as a child. Deb's seeing all of us together told us to scoot, she could handle things, and so with collecting bags, we made our way out on to Waterside Lane, and headed for the canal.

Danny was unsure as to what a canal was, and I walked at her side explaining how in the pre Victorian era, many Irish navvies had worked to hand dig them, to create a waterway on which goods could be transported. I walked with my arm round her talking and pointing things out. We stopped where my arch had once stood, and I explained its location and why it had felt so safe. I did add there were a lot more trees, but some had been removed in order to lift sections of my arch out.

Seeing where it was made even more sense to her, and I really enjoyed sharing those moments of my life with her. Jessie held Will's hand and tugged him constantly towards the trees as he picked off good leaves, and told her what they were, and all about how they grew.

Birch linked her mum's arm, and was really happy. For her, this felt perfect, and reminded her of a dream she had when she was a child, of how she would walk out in the country with her own kids and her parents. Roni as always was very watchful, as she watched Danny and I walking and talking.

"Those two have grown close very quickly Jemi, it is nice to see it, I feel they are very alike." Birch giggled as Will lifted Jessie on to his shoulders, and she sat behind his head picking leaves.

"Not just Abby and Danny, I think Dad has found a friend for life." Roni smiled.

"He reminds me of Jeff and you." She smiled.

"I hope so, if she has half the memories of him, I do of granddad, she will have a rich life." She looked at her mum.

"I am really happy mum, look at Deads, look how happy she is, you are right, those two were destined to meet. Oh, mum, they are so alike at times, I look at them, and honestly, it is like her natural daughter." Roni could see that.

"They have been through a lot Jemi, it will surface, you know that." She nodded.

"I know, little bits have come out, but Abby has handled it superbly. I listened to her the other night talking to Danny, and she was so gentle and loving with her, honestly, I could not have handled it better. I think at those times Abby actually is the best to talk with her, she understands her in ways we never will. Moon always said it was her darkness that gave her the insight she has, and the light within her that healed, and you know what, I think she was right, I am seeing it."

"I am really happy for you Jemi, I think this time, Abby was ready. I always wondered if a time like this would come, but I was never sure." Birch smiled.

"I knew it would, it just took her some time." Roni gave a sigh.

"I am happy she got there; you needed her to." Birch squeezed her arm, and held it tight.

"You worry too much mum; you always have when it comes to me." Roni shrugged.

"I had reason to, didn't I? Jemi, you made a big sacrifice for her, come on, we have talked enough about it, she wasn't ready and you were? What if you had been wrong, what if she had never got to this place, Jemi you have always yearned for kids of your own, it was one hell of a big gamble?" She nodded.

"I know Mum, but look, I was right all along, I told you, she had to overcome the damage her parents did, and just look at her now. She is so happy, and honestly, she may never have seen it, but I did, she is going to be an amazing parent, hell she already is. Mum, we are weeks away from it all being legal, and be honest, how many times did I tell you, I did not want another guy's kid I wanted hers. I mean okay, it was a little weird, but look at her mum, Danny is almost her double, I get it is not her DNA, but hell, it is as close as I will get." Roni nodded.

"You made your point Jemi, and yes, I am delighted for you both. Just watching her with Danny, showing her how to write and build a story, honestly, I wanted to cry it was so beautiful. So what is next, do they need anything more from you two, or is it all ready and rolling?" Birch giggled at her dad walking up to trees, so Jessie could pick leaves, and her bag constantly slapped him in the face.

"The paperwork is done, all the assessments are in, social services are sending their evaluation over with Janet, and now we wait to see when we can get a court date. Janet is playing they are alone with a nannie and need a proper family, and Deads is an actual relative card to push things up the pipe, all we can do now is hope it is soon. I cannot fault Janet; she has given it her all. We are over in the states soon, I am hoping it all arrives at the same time, and we deal with it quickly." Roni understood.

"What if it clashes with your stage appearances, you have a lot invested in this, and let's be honest, you are both the main players, this is a D&D event?" Birch smiled, and looked at her.

"I love you mum; do you know that?" Roni laughed and shook her head.

"Why didn't I see that coming?" Birch smiled.

"Come on, you have done bigger. Look it is twenty hours by car, faster by plane, and Jimmy actually thinks he can get us there and back in no time if we need to. Mum, I need to be there, I need to do this at her side, those kids need us there and I will be, come hell or high water."

"God, you are so like my mother, she would not let anything bring her down, she just ploughed on through and got the job done." Birch gave her a shrewd look.

"What, and you're not? Admit it, you are so like her, hell, where the hell do you think I get it from? You are so like her at times, and I love that. Mum, we need the whole family backing those kids, because honestly, that nannie is bloody awful, and they are really unhappy there, we need them here as quickly as possible."

"Alright Jemi, if you have to run off, I will cover for you. I take it Edwina has a backup plan?" Birch nodded.

"Edwina always has a backup plan, actually she has three, and Anita has two." Roni started to laugh.

"Bloody Curio's, Katie was right, you are all a bloody nightmare." Jessie ran up and held up a big clear bag of green leaves with pride.

"Look Mum, I have one of you." She rooted around inside the bag and pulled out a bright green Birch leaf and held it up.

"See it's a birch, like you." Birch smiled.

"Oh, wow Sweetie, you found my natural side, you are a genius." She shook her head.

"Not really, Granddad Will showed me, but I did get lots myself." Birch smiled.

"You are so amazing Sweetie, and your granddad is pretty cool for finding it for you." She nodded and looked back.

"I am getting more."

She ran off back to Will, and Birch smiled and turned, Roni stood with her hand on her mouth, and tears in her eyes. She shook her head.

"I am sorry, I promised your dad I would not cry, oh Jemi, you are a mum." Birch smiled, and pulled her into her arms.

"Pack it in, or we will both end up bawling and make the canal overflow." Roni shook her head, and took a deep breath.

"I love you so much sweetheart, and honestly, that is the

happiest moment of my life, just seeing you with her like that."

"Stop it mum, you are getting me going, so pack it in."

We walked up to the locks, and as we waited for the others to catch up, I explained the principle of a lock, and Danny loved it. She smiled at me.

"I love how your mind works, and how you explain things, I have read a lot about how a writer needs to experience things in order to write about them. Looking up the bank, and knowing the arch was there, I could see it in what you wrote in Sanctuary Arch, about the knotted undergrowth, and tall thin closely packed trees. I find it all so amazing."

I sat on the low wall watching her, so young, so full of life, and wonderful dreams.

"I took a plain ordinary canal, and an old smashed derelict building, and added the darkness, and wrote what I saw in my mind. Add a swirling mist and vampire in pain, lost and alone, missing the love of his life, or death as is the case, and I had a story. Danny that is all I do. I take a little part of life and then dream about its endless possibilities, and add made up characters, and that is how I create a story. Anyone can do it if they want to, and I mean, really want to."

She nodded as the others came up the steps up to the lock, and smiled, Jessie was waving her bag of leaves.

"I got loads, and some of them are birch leaves." I smiled.

"I would hope so, the picture is never complete until you add the birch."

Birch smiled and her eyes twinkled at me, she did not need to say it, she knew, and so did I. We walked up the pathway back to upper Waterside Lane, and headed down the lane home. Birch linked my arm, and Jessie held her hand, and I pulled Danny in, and slipped my arm round her shoulder, and we walked in a line, as Jessie talked our socks off. Behind us Roni held Will's hand, and he glanced at her smiling face.

"See, I told you they would get there, and look, how perfect is that?" Roni just smiled a huge smile, for her it was a dream come true.

When we got home, it was still all hands on deck. As Edwina

filled in Birch, I walked down to the kitchen with two back stage passes. Roni was stood on the patio, holding a gin, I stepped out and came up at her side.

"You will need these, how are you doing, it is a lot to take in isn't it?" She stared down the garden.

"I have seen a lot of dreams come true today, Abby, I have never known Jemi be so happy, she wanted this so badly, and I have had a lot of pleasure seeing it. How are you two, is everything sorted between you now?" She never missed a chance.

"Roni, I was never going to leave her, I was fighting my hardest to save us, honestly, I won't survive alone without her. I know what I did was harsh, and I regret having to do it, but she had stopped seeing me. I was invisible and I had to make her see we could be so much more, and look at us, look what we have." She nodded.

"I understood Abby, but you have to see it from my point of view, she is my child, and she was in pain. That kind of thing is something only a parent feels, you will see it soon enough. Honestly Abby, I am very happy, oh you have no idea how happy I am today seeing you both like that with children. I will not deny, I am very impressed, both of you have taken the responsibility very seriously, and I am pleased, because it will pay off dividends in the future. Parenthood is a wonderful thing; I am glad both of you will experience it." I gave a chuckle.

"I thought I had missed it, I was so unsure of myself, and I did not want to repeat the mistakes of my parents, and I probably did wait too long. Roni I do know how Jemi felt, I know her, she did not have to say it. Yes, we had conversations, and yes, I knew she was dodging the bullet, but that made me even more uncertain. When Janet rang, I knew this was my time, and both of us talked long and hard, and we did not walk into this blindfolded, we know what the risks are, and we have faced them. These last few days have been a blur, and maybe it has gone a little faster than we thought, but I am no fool, I know we still have a few hurdles to climb, but you know what, for those two kids, we will do it."

She turned and faced me, and smiled. She took a breath and nodded.

"Abby, keep your feet firmly on the ground, Jemi can easily

forget, especially where children are involved. She needs you Abby to remain grounded, you understand that don't you? You still have a court appearance to make, and it is not in this country, to them, you are the outsiders. Keep her level, and get those kids, she really needs all three of you."

"I will, and I am, it may not look like it, but behind the scenes, my brain is ticking on overtime. I am preparing, and if I need to, I will buy a bloody house there and become a local." She gave a giggle.

"I am surprised Jemi has not thought about buying their house." I looked at her and she gasped.

"Seriously, she was going to buy it?" I laughed.

"It came up, I talked her out of it, we own enough property, but she would have done if the case stalled." Roni turned and linked my arm.

"So, tell me about Sanctuary Press, how are things going, do you need anything, you do know Danny will run it one day don't you? It is already there in her, so train her well. I have had some ideas, and I think we should talk after Curio Live."

She never stopped, but I liked that, she was always planning and always looking ahead, she never ceases to amaze me.

The evening meal was a loud and busy one, as everyone working stopped and joined us all out in the garden. It was getting warmer and the sun was shining, so I joined in with Birch and Edwina, and we started to prepare. The girls joined in with us, and we created a huge amount of salad, threw out some blankets, and sat on the grass having a massive picnic.

Once we had finished, as the others mucked in to clean up, Danny and myself snuck off to finish her opening blog for the new section of the Curio site, which would be uploaded once the announcement had been made. We worked until quite late, and once we were finished and slid back in our seats, we turned, and Birch was sat on the bed with a gin, smiling. Neither of us even saw her walk in, but she had been sat there for a long time.

Danny was tired, and kissed Birch goodnight, and I walked with her to her room, where Jessie was flat out fast asleep, I stood at her door and smiled, as she turned.

"I have really loved today, Danny, it is wonderful to walk and talk, and work together, it felt special." She smiled as she pulled me into a hug.

"Yeah, I learned a lot, and it was nice, thanks."

I kissed her goodnight, and she turned into her room and headed for bed. I headed downstairs. The house was quiet and still, all the kids had stayed over and were in bed, Roni and Will had gone to the hotel, and Bev was up in her attic room.

I made a coffee, and sat at the island lost in thought, as the moon shone down onto the garden, illuminating the patio. This house had been such a focal point for all of us, and it was filled with happy memories, and in the back of my thoughts I could hear Birch's voice.

"Sweetie it is just money, we can spend that anywhere, being happy is far more important than cash, if this place is too much, we will just pack up our girls, and all piss off to somewhere nicer. Deads, a house is a brick box, it is good for storing memories, but life is about making them, if you really cannot take any more of around here, then we can move." I noticed movement, and looked up, and saw Deb's making a drink, she turned and smiled.

"Sorry, I did not want to disturb you. Gem had a belly ache, which does not surprise me, but after I had sorted him, I wasn't tired, so thought I would come down for a coffee."

She sat down in front of me and smiled, I looked at her, and I knew her so well, I could see it in her eyes.

"What?" She gave a little giggle.

"Abby, we have known each other a long time, you are my best friend, you know that?" I nodded, she reached out and took my hand.

"I am so happy Abby, just watching you these last few days, honestly, I have never seen Birch and you this happy, and I mean you guys are kind of the lead cheerleaders for us lot. It is so nice to see you with the girls, you are going to be the most amazing mum, and if I may say so, you have had a lot of your mum about you of late." I gave a sigh.

"Is that a good thing though, if you think about it, there was a time when me and her did not exactly get on?" She shook her head.

"No Abby, you could never be that part of her, I mean, the mum she became after you came back. You know, I always thought it was you who changed her, like you changed me, and Anthony and

Edwina, and dare I say it, Chloe. Abby we were always your girls, you were the one that inspired us, and you were the standard we looked to. I have a great husband, and three very noisy but adorable kids, and if it had not been for you, I probably wouldn't have." I shook my head.

"Deb's you were always going to grow up to be a mum with loads of kids, it has been in your DNA since we were kids, that was nothing to do with me." She smiled, but shook her head.

"No Abby, honestly, I faked all my bravery, I lived in terror it would all go wrong, and you always had that way of just seeing it, and reaching into me and calming me. I have seen you do it these last few days with little Jessie, and I may add with Danny."

"They are great girls Deb's, they have suffered more than they should have done, and living with that nannie after all they have been through, they deserved better." She gave a little giggle.

"See... It just flows out of you, those kids needed love, they were hurting so badly Abby when they arrived, I could see it in the eyes of Danny. She was awkward and shy, just like you used to be, and she was hiding her pain well, but not from you. Honestly, I have no idea what it is, but you do have something special, and it reaches in and touches people, and I have seen you do that with Danny." I gave a soft nod.

"She is very like me I think, I don't know what it is, but I feel this strong sense of connection with her." She smiled at me, and I giggled.

"You are way too happy for this time of night." She nodded.

"I am, I am happy to see that my best friend in all the world, has two amazingly wonderful daughters. Oh Abby, when she called you mum, honestly your face, oh God, I think I am going to bawl my brains out again." She took a deep breath, and calmed herself a moment.

"Abby, I cannot tell you of the sheer joy I felt just seeing that. Honestly, it felt like a dream come true for me." I gave a slight smirk.

"You're just a soppy bitch." She giggled and nodded.

"I am, and I love you so much, and I am so happy you have two incredible daughters, and we can be mums together."

I gave her a big smile, mum's together, it sounded nice, actually, scratch that, it sounded wonderful.

Chapter 24

Curio One.

Many years ago, I drove away from a farm house on the edge of Devon, I thought that just a week, could give me enough happiness to last a life time, and I was right. Birch and I had suffered such a cruel event, that left us both reeling, insecure and afraid. We were sent to Sunny Bank, and over the days that followed, we found something so very important, which we had before that, failed to see.

Sat in the sun, cut off from the world, just us, with no interference, we found a love that was deeper than anything we had thought we had, and it is that love that has glued us together ever since. I had never realised until recently that others had it, I saw it in Lillian and Celia, and as I have seen in these last few days, we have found it with the two girls, who hopefully soon will be our adopted daughters.

Like all things, it slipped past too quickly, and suddenly, our time of picnics, walks, messing around in the garden, all blurred into one, as all four of us grew closer and strengthened the bond between us. There were some tears and moments of remembrance, as both Danny and Jessie, released a lot of their pain to us privately. Birch and I spent most nights curled together, and shared our thoughts and our happiness, and again, it bonded us a lot closer and increased our love for each other.

It was Tuesday, and they had to leave, the house had been madness as they packed, and both of them were quiet and not at all themselves. Janet had thought it was better to say goodbye at the house, mainly because of the press, but we felt different, and so, much to the amusement of the girls, Gloria and her ugly friend came down stairs to take them to the airport.

We went stealth in Edwina's car, which was a people carrier, and as much as I was dreading it, I swallowed hard and looked at the girl's as they teared up.

"No tears, this is not goodbye, and if you cry, Birch will bawl the place down and cause chaos." Danny nodded and breathed in, and Jessie put her head down, and Birch pulled her close.

"Sweetie, we will be there in just over a week. This is just one more week with that gargoyle, and you will be busy Sweetie, you have to pack all your things and get ready, because we are coming, and we will be bringing you back home." Jessie gave a sniffle.

"I wish you could come with us; I am going to miss you." I took a huge intake of air, and tried to swallow the lump in my throat, and crouched down in front of her.

"We will be there soon Munchkin. Be big and brave for us, and we will talk every day, I promise." She gave a nod, and wiped her eyes. I looked at Danny and it hurt so much inside.

"Keep saying it, write your honest journal, and cross those days off, and we will be there. I love you guys so much and this week has been a dream come true for us, so hang in there, you will be home as quickly as we can get it through the courts."

I pulled her close and tried to hold back the tears, but it was tearing me apart. I felt her arms come round me and squeeze, and the dam broke, and tears flooded into my eyes.

"I love you, and I will be there soon." She squeezed harder.

"I love you too, both of you."

Janet took them by the hand, and with their boarding passes, they walked to the gate. I stood watching with tears streaming down my face, they both turned and waved with tears in their eyes. I gave a gasp of a huge sob, as I lifted my arm and waved back. I turned, as they disappeared, and pushed my face into Birch, and just broke, the pain was as intense as leaving Birch at Uni, and it just gushed up out of me.

Birch pulled me close, and pushed her head into the side of mine, and we stood sobbing into each other, as we held each other. I took a huge breath.

"Birch, we have to wave."

Hand in hand, we walked to the window, my eyes scanned along the side of the plane, and I spotted them, as I wiped my eyes and waved. The last thing I saw, was the face of Danny at the small window, and I watched as the plane pulled away, and taxied onto the runway. I stood sobbing with Birch as we watched the plane shoot down the runway, and lift into the air, they were gone, and I had no idea how to deal with that.

We arrived home to Deb's sad face, she said nothing just hugged me, and I tried to smile, but failed. I went upstairs, and into their room, and sat on Danny's bed, the house suddenly felt so empty, and so silent, and I hated it. I felt I was surrounded by an overwhelming oppressive sadness, and just sat, quietly looking at the made beds, and praying that the court system would hurry.

The days that followed were busy, but their absence was felt by everyone. Birch was much quieter than normal, but who was I to say anything, I felt listless and empty, and just focused on the work, knowing I had to get back to America. My only joy was the late night calls. Every night at eleven, Birch and myself would sit in our room, and when the girls came home from school, and had done everything the nannie wanted, they would sit together and talk with us. It became the highlight of our day.

We would talk for two hours, and Danny told me of how her friends at school were stoked, yep, Chloe has had a big influence, about how they had lived with us, and she knew all the Curio's, and that got me thinking, and talking to Janet.

It felt agonising, but finally the work was done, and we all took a coach at one in the morning, with our bags to the airport. Jimmy was in buoyant mood, as the coach avoided the terminal, and headed through large iron gates towards a huge hanger, where outside was a massive plane. The coach stopped, and I looked out of the window, he turned with a smile.

"Now that is a fucking plane, what do you think?"

We all stared out of the window at the floodlit aircraft, the plane was painted with a massive Curio Live logo, and had the tail painted with the two flags, and another Curio logo, I looked at him shocked.

"Jimmy, we are supposed to be raising cash, not spending it." He winked.

"It has been donated." Birch turned looking puzzled.

"Who the hell donates a plane?" He gave a cocky smile, as Deb's giggled.

"The Taco."

"Huh?" He smiled, and walked down the coach.

"Well, you see, we have this fund, we called it the sit snug fund, and with every hit, some of that went into the pot. This thing has been moth balled for a while, we hired it out to a few other bands, but apart from that, we hardly use it." He gave a little giggle.

"You know we liked to travel in style, we were fucking rock stars, and a bit big headed. Anyways, the fund has lay dormant getting interest, and so I phoned up the lads and had a little chat see, and they were like, mate, fucking do it. So, as you can see, we have spruced it up, and have first class travel, and the fucking States will know when we arrive, I can assure you."

I had to laugh, bless them all, the boys had really helped out over the years. We had a long wait, as all our luggage was loaded. Finally, were waved off the bus and an airport official checked all our passports, and allowed us to walk up the steps on onto the plane to meet the crew. It had taken three hours, and I was really tired as I looked around the plane, and I was blown away by how amazing it was, Birch was as giddy as hell.

The plane was big, and inside it looked more like a huge living room than a plane, all of us were really excited, Jimmy smiled as he held out his arms.

"Welcome aboard Curio One. We have a bathroom with shower, toilets, and at the back there is four bedrooms if you need one, I know I will."

He winked at Deb's and she blushed, trying to restrain her kids who were going mental. Birch gave me that smile, and her eyes sparkled, she jumped on the spot.

"Sweetie, we are going to join the mile high club."

I had to admit, I was sold, God, I am so weak really. We had to sit down, and buckle in for take off, and the captain came on over the speaker.

"Welcome to Curio One, we have a few more checks, and then we will make our way onto the taxi way, and will be awaiting permission to take off. Please sit back and relax, and as soon as we can, we will head for take off. Watch for when the light goes green, as we will be airborne, and you will be able to move around. Good luck with the event, we will all be supporting you." Jimmy winked.

"Only first class for my mates."

I could not deny, he really had blown me away, and the plane was so amazing I was lost for words. I hate waiting, and it felt like it had taken forever before we finally made our way towards the runway. Outside the plane revved up, and Birch took my hand, as it began its long run up the runway to take off. Birch leaned on my shoulder.

"Deads, we are getting closer to them, and we will see them soon, I am so excited, I want to hold them so badly." I squeezed her hand.

"I know, oh Birch, I cannot wait, I really need to see them. It has felt like hell, just like sitting in the guest house hoping you would walk through the door, we cannot get to them quick enough."

The light pinged and turned green, Birch grabbed at her belt and undid it, I undid mine and relaxed, I hated take offs and landings. Birch pulled my hand.

"Quick Sweetie, hurry." She yanked me up, and almost dragged me down the plane, Chloe looked at Baz.

"You know what they want, don't you?" He winked.

"Oh, hell yeah, let's join them."

Birch dragged me into the little room, with a wicked glint in her eye. She smiled, turned me round, and pushed, and I went sprawling back onto the bed.

"Oh Sweetie, I have always wanted to do this."

She bent over and undid my pants, and I giggled, her eyes were bright, excited and wild. I felt them slide down my legs, she looked down and smiled, and I snapped my legs open fast and she blinked.

"Oh yeah, my dark little beastie, we are really going to fly wild tonight." She pulled at her top and I grabbed mine and yanked it up, her pants hit the floor, and with a squeal, she launched herself on to me.

Gem looked at Deli. "Where has everyone gone?" Deli smiled.

"Mummy and Daddy need a nap sweetheart." He looked at the back of the plane.

"Great, I will join them." Deli panicked, and grabbed his hand.

"Why don't we all play a game, and let them sleep a bit first?" He nodded.

"Okay." Deli looked at Suki, and gave a sigh of relief. Somewhere in the back of the plane Deb's wailed.

"OOOOH JIMMY!" Jenny rolled her eyes.

"God, not again!" Edwina giggled.

This was a big event, and everything had been factored in, including child care. Deli took the lead and brought in two people she had worked with. Suki and Rachel were qualified nannies, and so they had the mammoth task of caring for the kids with us all. This was a big event, but having kids along, meant it was also a holiday for them, and so some trips in between things had been arranged.

We had some filming for the event to do which was a week away, and Morty, Bongo, Creamy, Alex, Aden and Gill, had taken a week earlier flight to go straight to the venue and start the big preparations. They had the mammoth task of overseeing all of the setup, both in the main venue hall, and the exhibition halls. We would be jumping from place to place on route to Vegas, there was a lot of publicity and press to do, which yes, I was not keen on, but this was D&D, and Anita was on the job. We would fly to New York, do the press and publicity, and then head to Pennsylvania, which was the next state, and the first new Curio location.

I was tired, hot, and smiling as Birch looked down at me.

"Was that nice Sweetie?"

I lifted a limp arm and pulled her close, and kissed her, and just felt so relaxed and calm. Her eyes sparkled.

"We screwed on cloud nine." I giggled, and gave a breathless pant.

"Baby, you took me higher than that, I am exhausted." She smiled at me; her face so filled with love.

"I love you, Birch; you have no idea how much." Her smile was soft as she kissed my nose.

"I have always known how deep it is, why do you think I am here going for our kids? Deads, I could never raise kids with anyone else; I know things got strained, but I have never stopped loving you, and I never will... But Sweetie... I am so shagged out now."

She flopped onto me, and I giggled as I held her tight and just relaxed feeling her close. Her breathing changed to that soft low rhythm, and I closed my eyes feeling happy, and slid into dreams of two young girls running towards me as I threw my arms around them, as we shot through the sky heading towards them. My sleep was long and deep.

I gave a stir, and felt the little body close, and snuggled up, Deb's soft voice filtered into my brain.

"Guys we are almost there." I opened my eyes, and Deb's grinned at me.

"Did you hug Danny that tightly?" I frowned, not quite awake, and looked down and saw Jenny snuggled up close, I smiled. Deb's watched me with twinkling eyes.

"She snuck in with Helen, but they looked so cute with you two, we left them." I yawned.

"It's okay, I was dreaming of Jessie and Danny, I thought it was them, it felt nice." She gave a little chuckle.

"Good, there is coffee and food, and I think some bacon left." The bed jerked.

"I love bacon." Deb's giggled as Birch looked around, and opened her eyes.

"Hi Sweetie." She leaned over and saw Jenny, then looked at her side and saw Helen, and she gave a soft smile.

"I wondered why I was dreaming of Jessie."

I managed to wriggle free without waking Jenny, and slid on my pants and top, and yawning, made my way up to the front. Anita was flat out on a sofa, and Tabs sat eating bacon, she picked up a plate and handed it to Birch.

"Here, I saved you some."

Birch gave an excited giggle and sat down at her side, I yawned as a stewardess handed me a coffee, I nodded a thanks and she smiled. I sat on the seat next to Birch as she chewed, slowly coming to life. Out through the window, it was mile upon mile of soft white clouds, it looked so idyllic, almost as if we could run around on them. Above them was a deep pure blue, and it was just so beautiful to look out on.

I turned back to the plane, Edwina was asleep with her head on Luke's lap, Anthony and Michael were curled up together on one of the sofa's, and Gem had climbed on with them. Anita snored and Birch and Tabs giggled, Deli was in the spare room with Josh, Liz and Sammy.

Jimmy carried the still sleeping Jenny in, and placed her gently in her seat, and Deb's followed with Helen. They rested them down and strapped them in, and then wandered off, and returned with Sammy, and Josh, and strapped them in as they slept. Jimmy always surprises me, and I have no idea why, his days with the band were wild for certain, and he is without doubt a rogue, but watching him with his kids, I see a different side, almost a different guy.

He is so gentle and caring, especially with Deb's, he really is a guy of many skills, and loving his family is the biggest. He really is a great guy, and Deb's is still so madly in love with him after all this time, and I love that, I really do. Deli appeared carrying Liz, and smiled as she sat down next to me, Liz was groggy, and not quite awake, she gave a huge yawn, and I smiled. Deli slid her down between us and buckled her in, and then sat back, and fastened her own belt, I looked down and grabbed mine, and locked it in place then nudged Birch, she was sat chewing and smiling.

"Lock it up Baby." She giggled and chewed more.

"Oh Sweetie, I will never lock you out of it." Deli sniggered, she smiled a wide smile and handed her plate to me, I looked at it.

"Christ Birch, how much have you had?" She clicked her belt in, and took the plate off me, and took a new piece and bit into it.

"Apparently, not enough, and I am not talking bacon here." I smiled.

"Oh, I am so going to overdose you later." She giggled, and leaned on my shoulder.

"Sweetie, do you think a strap on will show on the Xray at the bag check?" I felt a cold shudder run down my spine.

"Oh God, you didn't?" She smiled and swallowed her bacon.

"You are just too easy; it takes all the sport out of it." Deli gave a giggle. Deb's looked at me across the plane, looking panicked.

"They don't though, do they?" Birch sniggered.

"Oh Sweetie, just cover the kids' eyes." She turned purple, as Jimmy sniggered. Chloe appeared wearing a Curio Live t shirt, she looked around and yawned.

"Anyone seen my pants?" Edwina sat up and looked at her.

"They were hanging where you started, in the bathroom. My God, you are a slut." Chloe smiled.

"Yeah, I am, but I am Baz's slut, and he loves it." Birch gave a snort, as Chloe turned, and headed for the bathroom, showing her bum.

Landing was as always for me traumatic, I hate it, and was glad when we hit the floor, and rolled down the runway. Birch squeezed my hand, almost as if she had read my mind, we were here, in the states and moving closer. We taxied onto a side run, and the plane came to a stop. Once again, we would have to wait, and I was feeling more and more impatient, all I wanted was to get to them, and hold them.

The bags had to be unloaded, customs need to visit the plane, and it felt like forever, but it allowed us time to freshen up, and get our makeup done. Birch handed me coffee, as I sighed and watched through the window, it was early morning here, and outside a long line of black cars pulled up, and our luggage was checked, and then loaded into the cars, and as always, the TV cameras were waiting for us.

Danny bounced up and down as she looked at the TV, the nannie scowled, Danny looked back, pointed, and Jessie sat up.

"Look... Jessie look, they have landed, they are here, mum and mum are here."

"She is not your mother; they are your aunt's." Jessie looked up and frowned.

"No, they are not, we have three mums." She scowled at the TV.

"You are both ridiculous, no one can have three mothers." Danny looked back, as the plane on the TV wheeled towards a line of black cars and a press stand.

"Abby and Birch have three mums. Hatty, Flick, and Roni, and so we can too. I have my real mom, and also Mum Abby, and Mum Birch." The nannie scoffed and turned in the doorway.

"You are just foolish children, nothing more, what a stupid notion." Danny winked at Jessie, and then as Jessie slid up beside her, she put her arm around her and looked back at the TV.

"They are here Jessie, they will come soon, I just know it."

The door was opened once the steps were in place, and all we could hear were wild screams, I really was not prepared for this, as I looked out of the window. The balconies of the terminal were filled with people, waving flags and screaming out. Below us on the tarmac, was a barrier, behind which were loads of press, Anita moved in to my side.

"They are unloading the luggage, there is no rush, you and Jemi go first, and lead everyone down to the press, smile Abby, I know you hate them, but this is not the UK and we need this to start well. Keep them happy until you get my signal, we need to get the kids off and into the cars with the nannies."

I gave a sigh, she knew how much I hated this, but this was a D&D event, and it had to be a success, we had a lot riding on it. Birch put her arm around me, she was loving this. The crowds were huge, River had been streaming everything it could on the Curio's, and they had really built up a huge fan base in the states for us.

"Look Sweetie, they all came out to see us, and they have flags." I had to smile, even now she was such a kid at times, I looked around at Chloe and the others, as Tabs, and Baz helped round up the kids.

"Are we ready for this?" Everyone smiled.

"Okay Curio's, let's go and sell our sweet asses, and give all the kids over here some hope."

Danny bounced up and down with a huge smile on her face, she was sat right in front of the TV, with tears in her eyes.

"Jessie look, there they are." She wiped her eyes, as she screamed a yell of delight. Danny smiled a huge smile.

"I am here mum, and I am watching, we are both here."

The camera zoomed in, and there I was with a big smile, dark eyes and dressed as always in black. Danny gave a gasp, and just sat back, and smiled as she sniffled.

"She is here."

The noise was insane, as the breeze carried the screams and yells of the supporters, and Birch took my hand and we walked onto the steps, and began our walk down. Anthony and Edwina followed, and then Chloe Deli and Deb's, and the yells and screams just intensified. Birch gave a chuckle, and waved at them.

"Get ready America, the Curio's have arrived." I gave a laugh, as we walked towards the press, and into a blizzard of flashes, and a million cameras.

Behind us Tabs with Baz and Luke helped the nannies get the children down, off the plane, and stewarded them towards the cars.

Danny and Jessie were all smiles as I walked up to the camera of RTSS, the American wing of River TV, and John Dalton, the lead reporter. I had met John a few times in London as we did some pre-recorded messages for the event, so we had got to know him quite well. He gave me a big smile.

"Abby, Birch, welcome to America." I smiled into the camera.

"It is good to finally be here, I have been very excited as the days got closer, and I am here now." Danny took a huge breath, and smiled, Birch leaned in and waved.

"Hi Sweeties." They both knew it was more for them, than anyone else.

"Guys you have so much planned, this is going to be a big event, and in between you have some break time, tell me what do you have planned?" Birch gave a giggle.

"We have a lot of surprises, and there are a few people we really want to see, and we will soon." I gave a smile, and nodded.

"We have some people over here, and as soon as we are free, we will be going straight over to see them, so this for us is going to be a working, come happy family holiday."

Danny smiled, and pulled her hands to her mouth, she felt the excitement inside her bubbling, Jessie looked at her.

"Does she mean us?" Danny smiled and nodded, never taking her eyes of the TV.

"Yes Jessie, they do, it is their way of letting us know they are coming." John Dalton pushed his mic closer.

"Abby, there is a lot of speculation in the UK about the fact you have been seen with a young girl, who looks very like you. Can you shed some light on it for us, is it true you had a daughter in secret?" Danny gasped and her hands fell to her lap; I gave a chuckle.

"There is always speculation about me, do not believe everything you hear. I am here for Curio Live America, there are many incredible children out there, who are in pain, and in need of some love. My priority here in the states is to do everything to give them the love and support they need, this is not about me, this is about them." He gave a nod.

"The UK press today is filled with pictures of you and young dark haired girl, and there are a lot of different rumours and speculation. Are you sure you cannot shed just a little light on it for us, we would love to know who this mystery child is?" Birch squeezed me tight, and I just smiled at the camera.

"America has some very precious and special children in it, and that is my aim, to be there for them, it is why all the Curio's are here, and we aim to change their lives. We want everyone watching to stand by us and support us."

He gave a big chuckle and shook his head; the press knew me better, and knew I would not deviate from my stance. Danny sat smiling, she understood, and she could feel the huge burst of happiness growing inside her. John Dalton gave a smile and looked to the side.

"Abby, I can see the cars waiting, both of you, good luck, and we are all looking forward to the event. I will see you there in Vegas, and we will talk more."

"Thanks John, I am looking forward to it." I looked right into the camera.

"See you soon." Danny smiled, and nodded.

"I cannot wait."

We walked along the line, answering questions and giving out details of the event, and talking it up with the press There was a lot of speculation, the British Press were apparently writing up a storm about our mystery child, which was a source of amusement for Birch and I. It felt like it took forever, and we finally made it to the end of the row and I saw Anita, and she gave me a nod. I walked with a smile to the cars, Birch held my hand as we waved at all the fans, she was happy and giggling.

"Sweetie, do you think they saw us?" I smiled even more.

"Oh yes... She was watching, and she heard me, I know it Birch, I really do know it."

We jumped in the car and I pulled out my phone, and there was the message. 'I watched, and we are so excited, come soon.' Oh God I felt so amazing, Birch leaned in as I typed.

'We are here, not long now, we are heading to you soon."

I sat back in the seat, and closed my eyes, and I could see them in my thoughts. Anita climbed in, with Tabs.

"Okay stage two, it will be about forty minutes driving." I opened my eyes, and frowned.

"I thought we are in New York?" She smiled.

"We are, but you know Jimmy, he wants this all to be very special, he is road manager for this trip, so just sit back and relax. I know what a pair of control freaks you two can be with your planning." Birch turned and looked at me.

"Sweetie, I am not a control freak; do I control you at all?" I smiled.

"Baby, you know that look, that sultry sexy look you have, well, I cannot deny, when you do that, you have total control." She gave a giggle, and turned away, then turned back and I had butterflies in my stomach.

"You mean this one, you sexy little minx?" I took a deep breath, and swallowed hard.

"Oh hell, yeah!" Anita and Tabs burst out laughing.

Chapter 25

Road Life.

I looked through the back window, and turned to look at Anita, sat holding Tabs hand.

"You know, I hate to point out the obvious, but New York is back there." She smiled.

"I know, Abby, relax, not long now and you will see."

I slid down back into my seat, this felt all wrong, Birch appeared not to care, she was too busy looking out of the window taking it all in. The cars turned, and I looked out of the window, and frowned, Anita smirked.

"We are here; you will like this."

I was not convinced; we were in a large yard filled with big buildings with roller shutter doors. The car stopped and the driver got out, walked around, and opened the door. I peered out seeing nothing that remotely looked like a hotel.

"Where the hell are we?"

Anita giggled and slid out. Birch climbed out and looked around as I got out at her side, well at least there were no press. I looked all around, we were in a massive yard, surrounded by large steel fronted doors, it made no sense, and the others were looking equally as confused as I was. Edwina shrugged looking puzzled as our luggage was lifted out of the backs of the cars and placed to our side. I looked at Birch.

"Have your Wiccan witchy senses picked up on anything, because I have not got a clue what is happening?" She gave me a smile and her eyes twinkled, and then she jigged on the spot.

"I hope it is a surprise; I love surprises." Yep, she was still bonkers.

The cars drove off, and I cannot deny, I panicked, I was in a strange country with no transport, in the middle of God knows where. I looked at Jimmy as he walked out in front of us, all the others were looking round looking as worried as I was. He gave a big smile.

"Are we having fun yet?" Chloe frowned.

"What the fuck Jimmy?" That pretty much summed up my feelings. He smirked.

"My fellow Curio's, may I present to you, the Curio's American Tour." Birch jumped up and down and clapped excitedly, and I stared at her.

"Why are you so frigging happy?" She looked like she was going to explode, then thought about it.

"Sweetie, I don't know, but I am excited."

"Birch we are in the middle of nowhere, we could be raped." She smirked.

"Oh Sweetie, he better be really frigging good, it's years since I had a dick inside me."

Behind me there was a loud clattering sound, and then the sound of engines, as something burst into life, I turned to see a large hanger filled with white coaches, Birch danced.

"Sweetie we are taking the bus; it's been years since I have been inside one of them too." I was momentarily lost for words.

Four white double decked coaches moved slowly forward, and then broke apart, and drove up the side of us and around in front. They were huge, white, and had Curio Live written in large letters up the side. Jimmy stood in front of them beaming with delight.

"Your tour buses await. Bus one, Abby, Birch, Anita, Tabs and Rachel, that bus is also the centre of the Curio tour, for interviews and working." He looked so happy.

"Bus two, me, Debs, Jenny, Helen, Gem, Edwina, Luke and Sammy." Chloe smiled,

"I hope the third is the fuck bus, if it's not, I am jumping on Abby's." Jimmy smiled.

"Bus three, Anthony, Michael, Chloe, Baz, Deli, Josh, Liz, and Suki... Okay everyone put your bags next to the door and load up, we head off in fifteen."

Okay, I will not deny they looked great, but a bus? I wanted a hotel, hell, at this point even a shitty motel would do me. Birch was over the moon and jumping and clapping, and very excited, yeah, she is a loony. I walked towards bus one, as Jimmy talked to the driver, and he gave me a big smile.

"Cool hey, Doll?" I frowned.

"It's a coach Jimmy, how is that cool, and why four when we all fit on three?" He winked.

"Abby, these are not just coaches, these are luxury tour buses, these things are the dogs' bollocks of road trips, I know, I have lived on loads."

Birch was elated, and did not waste a second and jumped happily on board, with a squeal of joy, I looked at the white bus. He put his arm around me, and walked me to the door.

"Look Doll, you and Birch need rest, and we have a lot of miles to cover, so this is a hotel on wheels. The last bus has crew on board and a kitchen with two chefs, we have an event to talk up, the kids will be safe, and when we grab Danny and Jessie, you and Birch will have loads of alone time with them. Honestly Doll, I want you all to have that." I gave a sigh, and smiled.

"You are as barmy as the white haired crazy lady, but thanks Jimmy, I get it." He smiled.

"Go on, get on board, these things are plush."

He was right, there were large sofa's, tables, loads of spare comfy seats, a kettle, a TV, satellite internet, a video intercom, and a small kitchen. It had a small set of steps at the back, which went up to another floor, where there was a corridor with cabin beds, a shower, toilet, and much to my delight, two rooms with a double bed, one of which had our name on the door. It even had wardrobes. I was impressed, and Birch was delighted as she opened little cupboards to look, and see what was inside, and sprawled on the seats.

The thing was massive, and spacious, which felt weird, and really beautifully decked out in highly polished wood, and soft padded seats. To be honest, it was bigger than the guest house. The windows had blinds, we could roll down made from thin wooden strips, and air conditioning, I was lost for words as Edwina climbed on and sat down and smiled.

"Honestly guys, I was worried, I have been on coach trips, and they make me puke, but you should see ours, it is pretty bloody posh, too posh for an Oxendale council estate girl like me." Birch leaned back in her reclining seat.

"Must admit, I love it, I could live in one of these." Edwina pointed to a folder on the table.

"There is an itinerary in there with all the stops on, some work, and some fun for the kids. Our first big stop is Pennsylvania, of which we are not far away, and then a day's ride to Missouri. Not long guys and we will grab them, and take them on tour with us." I nodded.

"When you see Jimmy, thank him Edwina, I actually really love this." Anita came out of the back with Tabs and Rachel, and lifted the file, she flipped it open, and sat back, Edwina got up.

"I am still tired, and you look exhausted Abby, get your head down, we have a good drive ahead of us."

I nodded. She got up and left the bus, and then the doors closed, and the driver, who was called Mike, gave us the heads up, and the bus rolled out of the compound and onto the road. I walked to the back, Edwina was right, I pulled off my top, slipped off my pants, and slid into bed, I was so tired, I had hardly slept since the girls left.

River TV or RTSS as they were known over here, had two guys, who would help with filming and documenting the tour. We wanted to make a video at each of the places we wanted to renovate, to show the places in advance, as well as show life on the road. There were press invited to join us on the buses at certain points, and so there would be a lot of interviews. I loved the fact, that if I wanted to be alone, I could just go to our room. It was pretty amazing; Jimmy had factored in everything. It was not long before I was fast asleep, and downstairs, Birch, Anita, and Tabby, sat with Rachel sipping gin and relaxing.

Behind us on the other buses, all the kids were finally in bed, as the sun slipped down, our buses drove on through the night, and soon pulled up at a truck stop for an overnight rest, we were in Pennsylvania, and just miles away from our first potential Curio site.

I was awakened by Chloe, as she sat on the bed with a large tray.

"Come on you two, only this once, here is breakfast in bed."

I smelt the coffee before my eyes opened, and was not even aware Birch was in bed with me, Chloe smiled and pointed to the tray.

"Two coffees and toast for you, and for the lunatic, a full English, which is fucked up because there is no tomatoes or fried bread, but sadly there are beans, so your bus will stink with her in it." She smiled.

"How are you?" I sat up and yawned, and reached for a coffee.

"I am fine, please don't all keep going on about it. I get it, I have not slept much, but I had a really good sleep and I feel better, and we are heading for them, and I will be okay after that." She gave a nod and smiled.

"Cool, I get it, just doing my job and keeping my eye on you two." I nodded.

"I know, thanks."

Breakfast in bed whilst on the move is a strange experience, we were heading to the first site. Down below us, Edwina and Anita sat talking with Julian Erikson, the camera man, they were also filming the whole road trip for a special River feature. Birch sat in bed with her eyes closed eating; I looked at her as I chewed my toast.

"How come you never miss?" I watched her stab a mushroom and lift it up and put it in her mouth.

"It is easy Sweetie, I peek, memorise the plate and then eat." I stopped mid lift with my coffee.

"Wow, the force really is strong with you." She giggled.

The site for the first Curio Centre, was a rundown mansion, with eighty bedrooms. For a while in the 1920's it had been a glamorous hotel, and then it had become a rest home, and finally a care facility for the mentally disturbed, complete with bars on the windows. Chloe looked at it and shuddered.

"You will feel right at home here Birch, fuck, it looks creepy."

I sniggered as we walked in through the doors, it was rundown and smelt musty, there was a lot of damp. Birch spun around in the huge hall, and looked at Chloe.

"Those paranormal investigator guys did a show here, seriously, all sorts of weird has happened in here, last thing at night, the walls moan." Chloe shuddered and looked round.

"What like Gwenda?" Birch nodded.

"But way worse than that." I smiled as the colour drained from Chloe's face; she turned to me.

"We are filming outside, right?" I nodded. Deb's turned and winked.

"What was that?" Chloe went into meltdown, as Birch turned her back and shook, Chloe looked around.

"Shut the fuck up with those bat ears Deb's, I mean it, I am already freaking out." Birch held her hand up.

"Shush, did you hear that?" Chloe dithered on the spot.

"Yeah, fuck this, I am waiting outside." She turned, and legged it through the door, Birch gave a huge cackle of a laugh.

It took a while to set up, so we all stood back and waited under a really old tree, the grounds were unkempt and the place had been vandalised badly. It was getting really warm, Birch was happily looking round at the place, no doubt, she had a vision of what it would be like. She looked at me, as Ethan was checking the sound.

"Psst... Deads, I wonder how many people have been buried here." Chloe slapped her arm hard.

"Will you shut the fuck up, I am shitting myself already. Abby, please hurry so we can just go." Birch giggled, and Deb's smirked, Edwina rolled her eyes and then suddenly jumped and spun around.

"Who touched me?" Chloe's eyes went huge.

"Yeah, fuck that, I am going hiding under my bed on the bus."

Edwina fell about laughing, as Chloe ran for all she was worth to the bus, Birch was leaning against the tree laughing so hard I thought she would pee, I shook my head.

"You are so cruel, poor Chloe."

Deb's was red in the face and wiping her eyes chuckling. I was called over and finally got to film my slot. I stood on the doorstep, as Julian with some sort of harness and floating camera, got ready. Ethan counted me in on his fingers, and I smiled and waved.

"Greetings America, from the great state of Pennsylvania, I am Abby, and I am a Curio." I started to walk slowly, and smiled at the camera.

"I am here, at what we hope will become one of our Curio Centres. As you can see, it is a little run down, but we don't mind, because we have big plans for this place, and when we are finished, it should look like this."

I paused, as I knew there would be a artists impression slotted into the film. Ethan patted Julian on the shoulder, and counted me in on his fingers, and I began to walk again.

"We are hoping to raise a whopping one hundred and fifty million dollars over the whole Curio Live event, so we can take places like this one, and bring them back to life. This hopefully, will become a modern well equipped mental health facility, for the thousands of people who visit the Curio Life site daily. People dealing with issues of homelessness, abuse and victimisation. Every day, young people are finding themselves in situations they cannot cope with, and as a result, feel so desperate they take their own lives. It is so sad, that in this bright world of modern technology, there is nowhere where they can get the help and advice they so desperately need." Ethan held up his hand, and I paused.

We walked down the path a little so they could line up the shot, and then we continued. I stood in one spot with the building behind me.

"We need your help and support, which is why we have travelled over from the UK, to ask you in person, to please help us, by making a small donation, and encourage your friends to do so. With your help, we can not only save lives, we can improve them, and over this four day event, we will show you all of the ways in which we can do that. So please America, we are here, and we are asking, help us. Help us to rebuild this, and two other centres, America, we need you, your youth need you."

"And... CUT!" He looked up from behind Julian.

"Brilliant Abby, that was a superb take, we will not need more, that is brilliant. Okay, you guys are done, we will just shoot some more footage to edit in of the place." I smiled, and Birch jumped up and down and clapped.

"Sweetie it was wonderful."

I was glad, I just did not want to waste time, all I wanted was to get back on the bus for what would be a long twenty six to seven hour drive, and to finally grab the girls.

Julian and Ethan filmed the footage, and then headed to the crew bus, as the first reporters climbed on board, and we were joined by Anthony, Edwina and Chloe, as we all sat and answered questions as the bus roared down the highway heading for Missouri. We talked as a group, individually, and once again the question of the mysterious child came up. Apparently in England the papers were full of it, as one picture was circulated of me walking across the green with Danny. One of the reporters showed it to me, it was a good picture, it did amuse me, because there was no doubt, Danny did look like she was my natural daughter.

The headlines were asking, had I given birth in secret, and kept the child hidden from view to protect her, and who was her father? The story was running wild, and every time it came up, I looked at them and blankly told them, I was only here to talk about Curio Live, and I could see how frustrating it was for them, which made me a little bit happy.

Birch completely embarrassed a female American reporter, when she asked Birch, and she quipped with the response of.

"Oh Sweetie, she is small petite and very tight down there, trust me, I think I would have noticed a baby's head on my tongue, if she had given birth."

Edwina and Anita fell about laughing, as the reporter shuddered, and looked appalled. It was a noisy affair, we laughed and joked with each other and actually, the press really got into the joke with us. At the truck stop they jumped out to move to the next bus, and interviewed Chloe and Baz, as well as Deb's and Jimmy. Chloe and Baz had created a stir with the announcement of their engagement, and the American public had really latched on to it, as they saw news reports from the bus, of them sat together holding hands.

I saw a few, and Chloe was a little shy and awkward, and the public lapped it up. So much so, as we travelled through towns, we began to see people standing at the sides of the road with signs wishing us well, I really loved it, and it filled my heart with joy.

The kids were having a wild time, Jimmy had all sorts of crazy games and silly things to do, we even stopped in a layby for a couple of hours to fly kites, and walk in the long grass, I loved it. America is huge, and some parts of it are so beautiful, I stood in a field of long grass, and Birch held me close as I smiled.

"You okay Deads?" I nodded, all around there were screams of joy.

"I want to see them, I was texting her earlier, we are closer baby. I just want to hold them again, it is crazy, but I have missed them so much." She smiled and pulled me close.

"I know, I want to hold them too, I wish America was different, we could have had them with us all the time in the UK, but we have to play by the rules. Deads, we are closer, we will see them tomorrow."

I nodded and pushed my head on her shoulder, yeah, the press missed nothing, and suddenly the image of us completely in love was beamed all over the world. Although, it was not such a bad thing, they had written enough stuff about our break up, in a way I was glad America was setting the record straight.

Fun over, and it was back on the bus with a meal, and the press moved to bus four to relax. We finished the meal and sat back, Rachel was on duty and Suki was sat relaxing with us. Deli joined us with Chloe and Deb's, as we all just crashed and laughed, it was becoming a fun trip, and it was clear, it was doing all of us good to be back together again. I had a full stomach, felt chilled out, and was a little tipsy for the first time in a very long time. My phone rang, and I saw Janet's name, I snatched it up.

"Hi Abby, where are you... Exactly?" I frowned, and looked out of the window.

"Hang on, I will find out?" I walked down the bus to the front, where Flynn was driving.

"Flynn, just how far are we from our destination?" He was watching the road as we thundered along.

"Well, we are right on schedule, we plan to be there by one tomorrow afternoon, why?" I put the phone to my ear.

"Janet, we will be in town about one tomorrow afternoon why?"

"Abby, I got us in court tomorrow at eleven in the morning, can you not get here quicker, I could use you in court?" I looked at Flynn.

"I need to be there by eleven am, can it be done, it is really important?" He thought for a second.

"The way I see it Miss Abby, give me two spare drivers. We have a layover of four hours over night. If I have an extra driver, we can go on and the others can catch up later, but if we do that, you can be there on time. It will be a push, but we will do it." I gave a sigh of relief.

"Birch and I are fighting to adopt two girls in the court, and we need to be there." He smiled.

"Then don't you be worrying, I will get you there, I promise." The relief I felt as I lifted the phone was unbelievable, I took a deep breath.

"Janet we will be there, I will call you as we get closer."

"Oh, Abby that is wonderful, I will text you the full address, and be waiting and have everything ready for you."

"Janet, thanks for this, I really miss them."

"They are packed up and ready to leave, and they are really missing you too. Abby, get some sleep, you will need it, I will talk tomorrow."

"I will, thanks Janet." I looked up the bus, and could see Birch watching me with hopeful eyes, I smiled and her eyes twinkled.

"Flynn, get us there, and I will owe you big time." He smiled.

"Just get those kids, that will be fine by me." He lifted his radio and called Mike.

Birch slipped into my arms, and I leaned into her shoulder, and gave a long sigh.

"We are in court tomorrow at eleven, Flynn will leave the group, and we will drive all night, but we should be there just in the nick of time." She pulled her arms around me and hugged me hard.

"We will be Sweetie." I closed my eyes, and just enjoyed being held in her arms, I could feel the insecurity bubbling away inside me, and I was starting to get scared.

Danny nodded on the phone, as Janet explained everything to her, while Jessie sat watching cartoons on the TV.

"Danny, they are driving overnight, to get here on time, and Abby promised me, she would be there. You must be in school, so let us do what we need to do, and as soon as we know something I will call you." She swallowed hard.

"They will definitely get here?"

"Oh sweetheart, if there is one thing I know about those two, it is they will be there honey. Danny, they want you with them so badly, trust them, they will not let you down." She took a deep breath and gave a nod to the phone.

"We want to be with them, you must let me know straight away. Janet, I am scared they will try to stop us. You know what they are like, and I have had enough of her being here, she is nasty and frightens Jessie."

"Danny, listen to me carefully. Tell no one, do you hear me? Say nothing at all, especially to your nannie, just act normal and go to school, and we will call you as soon as we can. We are all working really hard, so try and sleep, I told Abby to get some, we all need to be on our best game tomorrow, alright?" Danny nodded.

"Okay, what about my sister?"

"No one Danny, not even her, just act normal. Alright, I have to go, I have a long night of preparation to go through, to be ready for tomorrow."

"Alright Janet, I will try, and I will not say a word. Will I see you soon?"

"You will see me tomorrow. Try and sleep, goodnight honey."

"Night Janet, and thanks."

I sat in bed, and I was not sleepy, my mind was alive and I was lost in thought, as I considered everything. It was dark outside and the bus was motoring on. We stopped at the truck stop, had a few rapid conversations, and then refueled, and we were back on the road leaving the others behind.

Once we had spoken in private to Mike, he was on board, and pulled the spare driver off bus four. Edwina went on the press bus and informed the press that we would be travelling on ahead, as Birch and I wanted some time alone in private with a friend. So, after a few questions, which Edwina pointed out was a private friendship thing, and none of their business, the reporters backed off, and carried on talking to the rest of them.

I spent a long time sat in my bed talking to Edwina on the phone, and she told me she wished me luck, and they were all with us in spirit. I had a quick chat with Anthony who was worried about me, and he was so lovely, he told me yet again to take better care of myself, it was sweet and nice. I finally put my phone on charge after texting Danny to tell her I was coming and not to worry, and I sat back and drifted into my thoughts.

The truth was, in a way I felt like I had come round in a huge circle. My childhood had been a happy one, for a lot of it, my mum had been wonderful and fun. I had such happy memories of her, and the things we did, but then she went on the council, and after that she changed, as did my father. I had always thought it was village life that got inside them and changed them, I don't really know, all I know is, from that time onwards I felt like I was slowly being caged and moulded to be something I was not.

As I hit my mid teens, I felt more and more isolated, and became quieter and more introverted, and then gran who lived in the guest house died, and my mum changed overnight. My rebellion to go to Uni in Manchester caused utter chaos, and mum screamed at me and flatly refused, so much so, I felt more and more caged and more and more depressed, to the point where I took an overdose in the bath.

I remember waking in a cold bath, a week before Uni, I had lied to my parents and told them I was going to Exeter with Deb's, I even lied about the dates. One morning, when dad had gone to work, I called a cab, loaded my trunk, and snuck out of the house to catch the train, leaving my mum a note in my room. Oh boy did that cause problems. Meeting Birch was the best thing that had happened to me, she was everything the village were not, and I really settled into the life of a quiet student, although my parents went mental, and I had a lot of really horrible calls. That first term was hard, as the fury of my parents took a long time to calm down, and when I refused to come home for the holiday and stayed alone in my dorm, they backed off.

I always thought Hatty had something to do with that, and it was then, I really felt alive and started to live. Over my two years, I grew to love Birch more and more, which was challenging for me, as I did not see myself as gay, to be honest, I still don't.

Losing her was hard and painful, not unsimilar to how I feel now, and living alone and writing was really difficult, as I missed her so much. When she came back it changed my world, we fought side by side against the village, and finally we won over and joined the council, but I always knew it would not be forever, I would never let them change me like they did my mum. Recently, I felt Birch was changing and drifting away, she lost sight of herself, and I fought hard to get her to see that, even though I knew I hurt her, but the truth was, I was starting to feel, like we were both being caged, and all those feelings came back, and they were just as dark.

I am almost forty, and yearn to move forward, to be honest,

I still feel like Abby the rebel with red and black hair. Inside nothing at all has changed, the outside has a little, but not the real me. I am still inside working things out and fighting to get through, but at least I have seen Birch return back to herself. I won my fight, and cleared the decks with nothing particular in mind, I just wanted Birch. Then Janet rang, and I felt a massive urge awaken inside me, and here I am sat in bed heading towards a court house, ready for another fight with Birch at my side.

Tomorrow, my life could change forever, I could actually, if lucky, become a parent, and I know after a week of being with our girls, I am ready, and I really want this so badly, but I also know, that the odds are against me. Don't ask me why, but tonight I have a gut feeling telling me I have not heard the last of the Fairbanks family, and if I am honest, I am very frightened tonight, because I have no idea what dawn will bring.

"Sweetie, Deads, wake up." I opened my eyes and she smiled at me, oh God she is so beautiful, does she know how much I truly love her?

"Deads, we are almost there, come on, you need to be wide awake when we get there, we have about an hour to go if the traffic is clear." I sat up and rubbed my eyes.

"What time is it?"

"Nine thirty." Suddenly, I was awake.

"Birch, we have to be there at eleven, what if there is traffic?" She smiled.

"Deads, calm down, we will make it. You need a shower, and put your black suit on, and I will do your hair, now come on, get going and let Flynn and Mike get us there." She handed me a coffee. I looked into her bright green beautiful eyes of hope, and yet I felt my hands trembling.

"Birch, I am really terrified."

Chapter 26

Court.

I dropped the towel, and reached for my pants, Birch sprayed me with masses of deodorant, I coughed it was so strong.

"Birch, will you pack it in, I don't want it down there, I just shaved." She smiled.

"Sweetie, I know you, we will arrive, you will panic, and that makes you sweat. No one wants stinky next the them in court." I frowned as I looked down at her.

"I have never smelt of sweat." She looked at me and raised her eyebrows. I was shocked.

"When?"

"The health spar, after jogging, you were stinky, stinky, stinky, and no one wants stinky." I giggled.

"Well, no, that builds bad bacteria, and we must kill, kill, kill, it with piss." She gave a snort of a laugh.

"Oh Deads, that was fun." I sniggered.

"Which part, me pissing in the water, or you standing up, pulling up your hooch and washing her hair?" She gave a loud cackle of a laugh, and stood up.

"I wasn't washing her hair; I was jet washing her eyebrows off." I started to giggle.

"You are a wicked woman, poor Brandy, she probably had therapy for years."

Once dressed, I came downstairs, Anita was watching her phone, it had sat nav, and she was tracking our progress. I felt my stomach twist, as I leaned over her shoulder, whilst Birch yanked the knots out of my hair. She looked up and smiled.

"Almost there, not much longer, we should make it just in the nick of time." I nodded, and felt my stomach lurch, Birch pulled back my hair, snapped a hair band in it and then turned me round to look at me, she gave me that happy smile.

"Stunning." I felt panicked.

"I look alright, like a good parent, you know, oh Birch, you would tell me, wouldn't you?" She giggled and gave me a soft peck on the lips.

"You can be my mum any day, honestly, you look smart, professional, and tasty. Oh God, I am going to be horny all day now." I swallowed hard.

"I don't want to look tasty; I want to look respectable; I want those girls." She smiled, and gave me a hug.

"Sweetie, just so you know, if the judge finds you tasty, and wants you, go into his office lie back, close your eyes, open your legs and let him have at you. If it gets us the girls go for it." I looked at her with horror.

"Why do I have to screw the judge, what is wrong with your vag?" She smiled and winked.

"Oh Sweetie, your clitoris is bigger, men like that in a woman." Tabs started laughing, I looked at Birch.

"You are frigging messed up, and weird as hell today." She smiled.

"I am nervous, but not sweating."

I hate waiting, my eyes were fixed on the clock, and it had already ticked past ten thirty, and I was starting to really panic. We pulled into the courthouse parking lot, which was not that big, at ten fifty, we had ten minutes to spare, and hardly any time to prepare. Janet was waiting at the door and looked relieved, not as relieved as I was.

We hurried inside, it felt just like the courthouse in Oxendale all over again, and honestly, for the first time in my life, I wished the Shredder was with us, Janet spoke fast.

"Okay, not the judge of my dreams, we got Judge Phineas Reinhold, he is a stickler for detail, so be precise, and answer clearly, and refer to him as Your Honour. When he speaks to you, look him in the eyes, with this one, eye contact is very important. I am not sure where he lies on the Fairbanks front, but he has a good reputation for being fair."

I was becoming more and more terrified, the closer we got. We stood outside waiting to be called, and I adjusted my clothing, and felt my hands tremble, Birch took my hand and smiled, Janet turned to me.

"Remember, you are a blood relative Abby, around here, blood counts for everything."

I nodded, and took a deep breath, the doors opened and we were called in. We walked into the courtroom; it was actually more modern than I expected. I suppose I had seen 'To kill a mocking bird' too many times, I had just assumed it would look like that.

At the front were two long tables, Janet showed us in behind one, and we took our places as she opened her files, her assistant smiled and leaned in.

"Stand when he enters and follow the lead of the bailiff, and only speak if asked a question, and if asked, for this judge, you stand up to answer." Both of us gave a nod, I was trembling like mad.

The bailiff called out. "ALL RISE!" I stood up at the side of Birch, and swallowed hard, I was sure I was going to pull a Rosie, and I really wished, I had not eaten any toast.

He walked in like a man with purpose, actually he was quite old, but hell, he was fast, and he was tall. The guy was a giant, with masses of white hair, he looked stern, actually as he sat down, and the bailiff called us to sit, he looked at me, and he had a mean stare, yep, I was utterly intimidated. He looked through his papers as the bailiff read out the case and case number, he looked up.

"Mrs Dixon." We both stood up, and he gave a sigh.

"Mrs Abigail Dixon." Birch sat down, and I was scared shitless, but I locked eyes on him, for fear of him not taking me seriously.

"I am Abigail Dixon, Your Honour." He nodded.

"I believe you are a relative?" I stood frozen, and trembling.

"I am Your Honour, Daniella and Jessica's mother Amanda, was my first cousin, I am the children's legal aunt." He nodded.

"Please be seated, I understand you are English, and not accustomed to our legal system, but I can see Mrs Bannon has educated you well in our procedure, I commend you."

I breathed out a long sigh of relief. I was utterly terrified, and in the back of my mind I was just praying he liked me enough to see how badly I wanted this. For the next two hours, a long list was called by Janet, they were specialists and experts who all testified to our competence financially, and domestically. I sat rigid for the whole time, in a world of fear, my whole body was in panic and dread, terrified to move in case anything I did would work against me.

Janet got up and gave an overview of all our credentials and suitability, and constantly pushed the blood relative narrative. He hardly spoke to us, apart from ask to repeat our qualifications. Birch was polite, eloquent and very respectful, and it took her a while to list them all, he appeared impressed.

Once everything had been given, he sat back in his seat for a moment, and then leaned forward.

"Mrs and Mrs Dixon, I have to confess I am not clued up as to the competence of this Social Services of your country, and that bothers me. I would have preferred a reputable assessment done by our own health care system; I have great respect and admiration for their work with the care of our young children. Can you enlighten me to their competence?" Birch stood up.

"Your Honour, as you are aware, it has been stated that I am a highly qualified clinical psychologist, who runs my own practice, and three mental health centres in the UK. I work with all ages of people, as do my staff, and we get referrals on a daily basis from the British Social Services, whom we work very closely with. As a clinician, and author of three books, and the author on over twenty published papers in my field, I can assure you, they are a world class service, that has my complete and utter confidence. If they were not, I would not use them." He nodded.

"Thank you, Mrs Dixon, or should I say Doctor Dixon, for I believe that is your correct title?"

"It is Your Honour, although today, I stand before you as a simple member of the family." He nodded.

"You may be seated; it is duly noted." She sat down and I tried to smile, Janet looked tense, and I will not deny, I was worrying like crazy. A loud voice echoed from the back of the courtroom.

"Your Honour, may I approach the bench?"

I knew that voice, and felt my heart jump into my mouth, I turned to see Mr Fairbanks senior stood at the back of the court, and I felt a huge surge of cold rise up inside me, as I fought back the tears, as in my head I whispered.

"Please no, do not do this, don't take my children away."

Judge Reinhold looked with some distaste at Fairbanks, and I felt Birch's hand slip into mine. The judge stared at Mr Fairbanks.

"What purpose would approaching serve?"

"I believe I have important missing information very relevant to this case, Your Honour."

I was fighting my hardest, but I could feel the tears rising, I knew it, I had felt it last night, that sense of dread and foreboding. I knew it, I had thought it, but hoped it was not true. Had they stayed clear of us just for this purpose, why had I not just given them the bloody ring? The judge nodded.

"You may approach." Mr Fairbanks nodded.

"Thank you, Your Honour."

Janet got up and walked to the bench as Mr Fairbanks approached the judge, they all leaned in and Mr Fairbanks spoke. The judge nodded, and then asked a question. It was far too quiet for me to hear anything, I sat trembling, watching with tears in my eyes, as Birch held my hand. Mr Fairbanks said something, and Janet was asked to step back. I could feel my heart pounding in my chest as the judge looked at me, and then back to Mr Fairbanks. Tears rolled down my cheeks.

The judge nodded, looked at me again, and then Mr Fairbanks walked back to his seat at the back, he did not even look at me. Judge Reinhold sat for a moment, and it felt like forever as he viewed the courtroom, it was clear something was on his mind. Never in my life have I felt so much fear, my stomach was churning and I wanted to vomit. I closed my eyes for a moment and tried to focus, as I felt the long silence, and my hope died in my chest, leaving a terrible pain. Birch moved slightly, and I opened my eyes and tried to breath. I saw the judge, he was watching me, and then he looked around at us all, with his hard looking face, and I felt utter dread as hopelessness washed over me. I could feel the pain rising from my chest, and I looked down and gave a sob, he banged his gavel hard, and I flinched, it felt like a death sentence, he spoke in a loud voice, as looked down heartbroken, at my shaking knees.

"Motion granted." He banged the gavel again.

I jumped and looked up, and I had no idea what was going on, what was granted, had Mr Fairbanks got some sort of motion we did not know about? The judge leaned forward.

"Mrs Dixon." He looked right at me, and I stood up shaking like a leaf, my voice almost died in my throat.

"Yes, Your Honour."

"Dry your eyes, the motion has been granted. Thank you for a very respectful appearance, and good luck with your charitable cause, I wish both of you well." I smiled.

"Thank you, Your Honour, thank you very much." He smiled a grim sort of smile.

"COURT RISE!"

Everyone stood up and he stood, nodded to me again, turned and walked out. I was shell shocked, and still completely unsure of what had happened, and I think Birch was the same, I turned to Janet and she smiled.

"What is happening?" She smiled, and lifted a hand to my face.

"Oh Abby, look at you, your legs are shakin like a grass hopper, bless your sweet soul. Abby, you and Jemi have done it, you are officially Danny and Jessie's moms." I swallowed hard.

"We are?" She nodded.

"Yes honey, you did it."

I smiled as tears streamed down my face, I felt Birch push her head into my shoulder and she just wept. I turned around and slipped my arms around her, although it still felt so unreal, I was not sure I believed it.

"Baby, we did it."

I pushed my face into her and broke down, and we both just stood holding each other and wept. Anita was jumping, she dragged Tabs into her arms and gave her a huge kiss, and then they turned and hugged Rachel, and then all of them turned to us, Anita leaned over and pulled us close, as I gave a huge sniffle.

"Guys I am so happy for you." I looked up and she was smiling, and crying, and I think I was in some sort of shell shock. Janet tapped my shoulder.

"I have some paperwork to be stamped and taken care of, go sit outside the door, calm down, and wait for me." I nodded and wiped my eyes; Birch took a deep breath and smiled such a beautiful smile.

"Sweetie, I want to see our girls." I smiled.

"Yeah, me too... Birch, they really are our girls." Her red puffy eyes opened wide.

"I have to text mum."

I stood outside wiping my eyes, I looked a right sight. Up the corridor Chloe Deb's and Edwina came hurtling towards us, saw us and stopped dead in their tracks, Chloe stared at me, with my red blotchy eyes wiping them as Birch wept on Anita's shoulder. She swallowed hard, and looked really frightened.

"Well?" Edwina and Deb's looked panicked as hell. I smiled.

"We did it, they are our girls."

I think that has to be the most amazing smile I have ever seen on Chloe's face, and then she just exploded, and all of them dragged me and Birch into their arms, and it was loud, crazy and Curio... And probably the noisiest this court house has ever been.

At Amelia Watkins School, there was to be a special assembly, and everyone in the school was instructed over the speakers to go to the school hall. It was noisy and not something normally done, so it was somewhat exciting to get out of class and have an assembly.

Once, all were inside and the doors closed, we got the text. I had the papers, and had washed and cooled off my eyes, and Birch had redone my makeup. As we all parked at the side of the road out of sight. Inside the hall, there was a lot of talking as the children looked at each other, not understanding what was going on. When the signal came, three of the four large white Curio Live busses drove into the school, and parked in a long line.

I was in my full gothic attire, of long top, long heavy black skirt, and a long duster. We were met by the principal, who knew Janet well, and the six of us with Jimmy, were escorted to the side door, and led to the side of a large stage. The principal walked up the steps and crossed the stage to the microphone. There was an instant silence.

"Good afternoon, everybody. I would like to say I am very proud of this school today; I realise this is somewhat different from the normal school routine, but as you are all aware, we have been raising funds for the Curio Live event, which was organised by Miss Daniella Watson. Well, I am happy to say, your efforts as a school have been noticed, as this school has raised fourteen thousand dollars." Marci elbowed Danny, in the side.

"You will get an award for this, just watch." Near the front Jessie smiled.

"That's my big sister." She looked very smug and happy. The principal smiled.

"To be noticed is a good thing, but to be noticed by our guests, is remarkable, so may I introduce to you all. The Curio's."

There were gasps as we all walked up the steps, and on to stage, and everyone suddenly went wild. Wow, it was loud, I could see where Jessie got it from. We stood in a line looking out on hundreds of cheering applauding happy faces.

The principal stepped back, and I smiled as Birch and myself walked up to the microphone. It took a while to quieten enough to speak.

"Hi, I am Abby... And I am Birch, we are Curio's."

There was another explosion of cheers, and we all laughed, and smiled, and I saw her, and looked right into her tear filled eyes. The school quietened, and I leaned into the mic.

"Danny, Jessie, would you like to come up, you have helped raise a fantastic amount of money, and it should be applauded."

Danny was shoved by Marci, and walked slowly down the centre, Jessie just legged it, and came hurtling onto the stage, and Birch pulled her into her arms.

"Hi Sweetie." Jessie leaned into the mic.

"See Peter!"

She pulled out her tongue, and Birch gave a chuckle. Danny walked up the steps, and came towards us. I pulled her into my arms, and almost crushed her, and very quietly spoke.

"Don't say anything, but we won." She gasped and looked up, as I smiled.

"We did. You are coming home, starting today." Tears filled her eyes and I smiled. I stood back up, and looked out at all the students, as I held her hand.

"Guys, what you did as a school is truly wonderful. Every penny we raise counts, and to have all of you put in so much effort, and raise so much means the world to us. It is the last week of your term I believe, and so what we are going to do, is take Danny and Jessie on tour with us, and they will both have full access to all of Curio Live. We have spoken to your principal, and Danny is going to do special updates for your school website every day throughout the whole event."

The whole school cheered, and I pulled her to my side and put my arm round her waist. It was a wonderful moment, and I was feeling levels of happiness I never thought possible. We stood for a few minutes, and then I guided her back, and Edwina, Deb's, Anthony and Chloe stepped forward, and Birch and our girls came off the stage. I turned and grabbed Danny and just hugged the hell out of her.

"Go to your classroom, and grab your stuff, your bags are already packed and on the bus. You are coming with us now, and when we are done, you are coming to England forever." Jessie screamed and punched the air, God she was loud.

"NO MORE GARGOYLE!" Birch giggled.

"Nope, but we have Bev with holes in her face Sweetie." Jessie frowned.

"You should make her fill them in; they are scary." I smiled as I released Danny and looked down at her.

"No more tears, that time is done." She smiled, and I wiped her cheek.

"There is a row of really huge buses out there, yours is number one, get your stuff, and get on it." She gave me a huge smile, turned and ran as fast as she could holding Jessie's hand.

It was two hours later, when we all finally boarded the bus, having met Danny's class, posed for pictures, and watched Marci go ten shades of red when she met Jimmy. Janet hugged the girls, and the Curio's were in party spirit. The press arrived, but were held back until Danny and Jessie were on the tour bus, and then they took pictures of us at the school. But they were not allowed on coach number one, and for now, every Curio was silent.

We waved out of the windows, at all the students, as the busses pulled slowly away, and Danny, and Jessie snuggled up to us, and I finally had a chance to breathe and relax, which involved a gin. Jessie looked at Birch.

"We are going to live on a coach?" Birch, smiled and nodded.

"Yes Sweetie." She looked at us and frowned.

"But where do we sleep?" Birch giggled.

"In our bedrooms." Jessie looked around, and narrowed her eyes.

"I don't see a bedroom." I gave a nod at Jessie.

"Munchkin, we have eight, which one do you want?" She looked at me and then Birch, she obviously did not trust her. Birch giggled and took her hand.

"See Sweetie, they are upstairs." She walked her to back, and Jessie ran up the stairs and looked down the corridor, she saw the bunks and ran to them. She pointed at the bottom one.

"I want that one."

I giggled as Birch peeled a sticker, and stuck it on the end, and Jessie gave a reassured nod, she had staked her claim, and climbed into the bunk. I handed Danny a sticker.

"Pick one."

She gave me a big smile and climbed up to the one above Jessie, peeled off the sticker and slapped it on the side. Birch smiled and leaned in to her.

"Happy now?" Danny smiled and nodded her head.

"Yeah, I am really happy, thanks mum, and mum." Birch leaned in and kissed her cheek.

Like all things with the Curio's, we were off to location two to film, and as we began to drive towards our location, which was an old local hospital, I sat back at the table looking at the lines I had written for Anthony and Deb's, who were going to film a joint presentation. My mind was drifting as I thought back to the courthouse, as we stood waiting for Janet and Mr Fairbanks walked up to me and offered his hand.

"I believe I may have overstepped just a little, but I can assure you Mrs Dixon, it was for your benefit."

I took his hand and shook it, as he lifted a hand to ask me to step aside from the others. We walked away from the celebrating group over to a large window, and he stopped and turned, and looked at me.

"Phineas is a very honest and fair man, I have known him a very long time, and I can assure you Mrs Dixon, he cannot be bought, I cannot as you stated, fix him. The problem is he is very set in his ways, Mrs Bannon is a very capable attorney, but I am afraid Phineas has no understanding of things, well, let me say, in distant lands, and he does not trust what he does not know, especially your British health care services."

I understood that, but still could not quite understand why he stepped in on our behalf.

"I am not certain what you said or why you said it. If I am honest, I thought you wanted nothing to do with Danny and Jessie. So, I cannot deny, I am a little confused." He smiled.

"I understand that, our last meeting was not a pleasant one. Mrs Dixon, my son Matthew is a very capable business man, if I am honest, it is all he knows. He is not a warm man; I would say you were quite correct when you told him he was cold. His sister Freda is very much the same, and as I think you are aware, their brother Scott, has a reputation for living a wild lifestyle, and although he is very likeable, he is seldom sober. If you want my honest opinion none of them are suitable parents, and I see that in the children they have raised." I looked him in the eyes, and could clearly see he was watching my every move.

"So, are you telling me Mr Fairbanks that you did this for the good of Danny and Jessie, because I am sure Peter and Amanda would not see it that way?" He smirked.

"Whether you believe it or not Mrs Dixon, I admired Peter, he broke away and that took guts, but I will add, this family has a certain reputation, and in that, Peter threatened the unity of it. As was the case, we had no other option than to close ranks. You know, Peter wanted to separate, and what I did to a degree protected him, I gave him what he wanted, and as I expected of him, he rose to the occasion and prospered. It is a cause of great pride and also great sadness to me."

I could tell by his tone, that he meant it, and I could see the sadness in his eyes.

"Mrs Dixon, I want his children cared for, I want what is best for them. I may not have appeared to have shown that, but the answer to their happiness does not lie within my family. I hoped that your side of the Watson family, would ensure that, and as I have seen, in recent days, I was correct. Daniella and Jessica have been quite a handful for their nannie, and her reports very clearly showed the impact you and your partner had on them. From my point of view, I could see it was a very positive one. I came here today to ensure the case went through, nothing more,

I had no intentions of interfering, but knowing Phineas as well as I do, when he floundered, I decided to intervein." I gave a nod of understanding.

"He would have ruled that your services made the assessment, which would have taken much longer?" He gave a smile, as he nodded.

"Nannie made it clear; her position was becoming untenable, I made sure the adoption went through today, whilst you are in this country. There was no fixing, I simply stated that my family had also made a revue of your status, considering these were Peter's children, and we found you both to be more than satisfactory. As I said, I have known him a long time, and I knew my word would carry a lot of weight with him." I smiled; I actually smiled.

"They will have a good home, and they will be well cared for, and they are loved dearly already." He smiled.

"I believe that showed in the court room. I am well aware of your circumstances Mrs Dixon, and have complete faith in your abilities to raise and defend them. I must admit, you remind me greatly of their mother, she was quite the little power house at times. It is a shame, those two would have been a wonderful pair at the top of the family business. I believe that concludes all matters, and so I feel it is only right to wish you well, and offer my congratulations, live well with your children, and good luck." He smiled.

"Thank you, I can assure you, they will have a happy life." He nodded.

"Good day to you, and good luck with your fund raising event."

He turned, and walked up the long corridor, and I was left feeling torn, and not quite sure where I stood with him. Was he a hero or a villain, I really did not know? Birch came over and slipped her arms around me.

"What did he say, because honestly Deads, I was terrified we would not win, until he stepped in?" I gave a sigh and looked at her bright excited eyes.

"He convinced the judge that the social services were indeed worthy of making a full assessment, and then told him, that the Fairbanks family felt we were more than capable. He helped us Birch, he stepped in when he knew the case would fail on a technicality, and ensured it didn't. Birch, I am not sure why, I just felt, he thought we would be better for the children than his own family." Birch looked back; he was just leaving the end of the corridor.

"Well yeah, I mean, look at the bloody nannie, Christ, no one wants that gargoyle raising their children."

I printed out the sheets, although Anthony and Deb's pretty much knew the script off by heart, and I stayed on the bus with Danny and Jessie whilst Birch oversaw the filming. Jenny, Helen and Sammy came on board and hung out with the kids, and brought with them a stack of board games. I left them to play, with Suki watching over them and headed upstairs to my room, and slid out the paperwork Janet had given me.

It felt almost surreal, I had pushed myself to breakdown worrying, and now I had finally done it, and it felt so good, but I was utterly wiped out by it all. Now would come a time of huge change in our life. Before heading to the school, we had visited the house, and had packed what we could of Danny's and Jessie, and loaded it into the hold of the coach. It made me smile to see their rooms all boxed up, they had been so sure we would win, and in a way, I loved that. Danny had such belief we would get her, and in a way, maybe that is why we fought with all we had. The door opened and I looked up, Danny smiled.

"I have laughed and cried so much today, Mum, I am feeling tired and want to be quiet." I patted the bed.

"Me too, I feel exhausted, I found the court case very hard and emotional, but hey, look, we are all together, and that really is all that matters." She crawled onto the bed and snuggled up to me and looked at the papers.

"Is that it, just a few sheets of paper?" I nodded as I stroked her hair, and looked down at her.

"It does not look much, but for Birch and me, this is the most precious paper on the planet, because it makes us a family." She smiled, and closed her eyes.

"I like that, I really like that a lot." I lay back and closed my eyes.

"Yeah, I do too.

Chapter 27

The Curio's.

With the filming done, we settled down to a relatively normal life, I mean, we were living on a bus, with Birch, actually, and Jessie. We headed to California, and on the road, there was a lot to do, and Danny wearing her pass, sat at my side as we talked over the event, or checked plans and schedules. She became sort of an assistant, and to be honest, I really liked it.

We filmed the location in California, which had once been a hotel, but had been boarded up for twenty years. Chloe and Edwina filmed that one, and then Jimmy declared, it was day at the beach time, which presented a problem, we had no swim suits, and naked bathing was not allowed on the beach. Birch squealed with delight 'Shopping' and so with that, we all went on a big shopping trip, and I actually bought a bikini, yeah, I know, weird right?

Jimmy was on the ball, and we were taken from the busses by black SUVs into the shopping district with a platoon of security, and it felt really odd having big guys in all black escort us everywhere. We headed to a reasonably isolated beach, although there were still a lot of people, and we organised our day, watched over by our minders.

We messed around and had fun, although our little press core found us, and soon picked up on the fact that the girl in the British papers, was actually on the bus with us. It made things difficult, but I stuck to the line that I had stepped out of public life, and was only here to promote the Curio event, and the security helped keep them as far from us as possible. It was a fun day, although it should be noted, Birch refused to eat on the beach, and kept watching the sky. The seagulls here were big, and she was taking no chances.

After an exhausting day, we headed back to the bus, through an army of fans, it appeared the word had gone out, as to where we were. We signed and talked and smiled, and soon I was crashed out and fast asleep, as we headed to Vegas. It was almost dawn when we hit the outskirts and pulled in to wait. The sun was not quite up and I had been sleeping a lot, but was awake. The bus pulled up, and I got off to stretch my legs, and walked off the roadway onto the sand.

It is strange, because this is quite a barren place, just miles and miles of sand and red stone, covered in small spikey shrubs of grey and green. They stretched right out to the rough shaped mountains in the background, and in the light of the sun as it started to rise. I found it breath taking, and utterly beautiful, as I stood alone drinking my coffee.

The sky was getting brighter, and I waited for that first full beam of the sunlight, and smiled to myself, as a very precious memory slipped into my mind. I was stood there lost staring at the mountains, when I felt a small arm around my back, and looked down. Danny stood at my side, and I slipped my arm round her shoulder. She smiled at me.

"I woke up and went into your room, and you were not there, what are you doing?"

"I am stood here remembering, and enjoying this beautiful place."

"What are you remembering?" I smiled more to myself than anything.

"Yule, twelve years ago. Birch got me up at five in the morning, it had been snowing for days, and it was freezing cold. She took me up to the top of the hill above Wotton, and as the sun rose, she smiled with tears in her eyes, happy to see my face lit by the first light of Yule. It was such a beautiful moment in my life, because then, she did the most unexpected thing ever, she went down on one knee, and asked me to marry her." Danny's voice was soft.

"Wow, that must have been mind blowing?" I nodded.

"It was, it threw me completely. Oh Danny, I loved her so much, and it all came gushing up inside me, and I froze, hardly able to talk. It was such a huge moment in my life, so precious, so special. I told her yes, and I have been happier than I ever thought possible. Many people do not see it, or understand it, I mean, she is completely mental, but oh God Danny, I hope one day you find a love as pure and as deep. You know, I stood in that court terrified, no one will know how so utterly scared I felt, but I glanced to my side and she was there, watching everything, taking it all in, and just knowing that, a part of me felt great hope, and it was right, because look, here you are." She squeezed my waist, and looked up at me and smiled. CLICK!

"Got it, that is the picture I am going to paint." We turned, and Chloe smiled.

"That is an amazing shot, oh God, as soon as we get back, that is going on canvass. Chloe walked up and showed us the picture, and it was lovely, I was looking down, Danny was looking up, as we stood facing the sunrise with our arms round each other. It was beautiful.

"ARE WE HAVING BREAKFAST YET, I AM HUNGRY?" I looked at the bus, where a little naked Jessie stood on the step watching, Chloe giggled.

"God, Birch is a bad influence on that one, look at her, twice as loud as anyone else and stark bollock naked, Christ what have we done?"

It was still some time before everyone was up, so we raided Birch's grain bars, and sat outside as the sun warmed the morning, drinking coffee and crunching seeds as Jessie called them. Actually, I have never eaten one, and they were rather good. It was hot here; the temperature was rising rapidly.

It took a while for everyone to rise, and breakfast was served, and we headed off with a grumpy Birch, who had a hangover, towards Vegas. Birch sat looking rough and I smiled at her.

"Birch Baby, Vegas, hotels, and huge big baths." I winked, and she smiled.

"I love baths." She frowned and put her hand on her head, and groaned.

"DO YOU HAVE A HEADACHE, MUM?"

I could not help but laugh, as Birch shuddered at the table. Danny giggled, as Jessie looked round at everyone.

"WHAT?" Birch jumped, and I bit my lip.

As we hurtled through the desert, and Vegas loomed up in the distance, we all sat as Edwina connected her blue tooth to the TV screen, and we watched the time lapse footage of the stage being erected in the arena, it was pretty cool. Morty had done a brilliant job, but I must admit, my stomach churned a little and Birch giggled, yep, we would be needing buckets.

The drive into Vegas was amazing, to be honest the place is massive, far bigger than I expected. The coaches pulled around the back of the hotel, and went down an underpass to an underground parking area. Gill and Creamy stood waiting, as an army of staff came out to take our things. Each was instructed with the right room numbers, and with our luggage, we were taken to our rooms, which were on the thirty fifth floor. Yeah, I stayed well away from the windows, which were huge and looked out and down on the Vegas strip, it made me giddy just being near them.

Danny and Jessie were in our suite, as it had two rooms, and they both ran around like maniacs looking at everything. This place was plush, it was a high class suite fit for a queen, and as soon as I saw the bath, I knew what I would be doing for the next hour.

We had pretty much got most of the floor to the Curio's and crew, which was wonderful, Jimmy and Deb's had done a brilliant job of arranging everything. Chloe and Baz were on one side of us, and Deb's and Jimmy the other. Anthony and Michael were across the hall, with Edwina and Luke to their left, and Anita and Tabs to their right. We had our own conference room for meetings, which we made our headquarters, and operations room in the hotel, and a very long corridor, which revived a lot of memories for Chloe and myself.

The bath was huge, it could easily fit five, and was set on a dais, so we stepped down into it. It was all marble and felt a lot like a Roman bath. I filled it with hot water and bubbles, and holding Birch by the hand we stepped down, and felt the utter joy, of submerging in the water. We had wine and glasses, and as I leaned back against her, she handed me a glass, oh this was luxury indeed. I closed my eyes and breathed out with joy.

"Oh baby, I have wanted this for days." She gave a long relaxed gasp.

"Oh Sweetie, this is bliss."

"I AM HAVING ONE TOO!"

Yep, she was way too excited. Jessie came running in stark

naked, and SPLOSH! Foam and water went everywhere. There were bubbles, and then she appeared through the foam with a huge mound of bubbles on her head. I took my hand off my glass, and giggled. Jessie had huge wild eyes.

"OOOh.... OOOH IT'S HOT!" Birch giggled. Danny walked in giggling in a robe; I pointed.

"Jump in, the more the merrier."

She gave a big smile and slipped off her robe, and came down the steps slowly, and lowered herself into the water, and gave a sigh as she leaned back and relaxed. I snuggled back into Birch.

"This is the life." She leaned on my shoulder and kissed it.

"YUK... Soapy!" Danny and Jessie giggled.

Bubble bath is creative stuff, as we messed about making hats and beards, and decorating each other. It was fun, and we spent most of our time pissing about and just laughing, it was so much fun. Washed clean, and with blown dry hair, and fresh clothes, we headed down to the restaurant VIP area for a meal, which was loud and fun. Danny was taking snaps, she had exclusive access to us, and she was writing her blog for school.

The meal over, we returned to our room, got ready, grabbed our passes, and then headed out across the way, to the huge round arena. Tickets for the event were one day tickets, or a full four day pass, all the side events were done in two of the hotels at the sides of the Arena, and they were all free.

I took Danny by the hand, and we walked out onto the stage, which was massive, and we stood at the front and looked out. Around us the crew were still working, checking sound and lights, and the whole place was a mass of activity. Danny shuddered.

"Oh wow, this is big, are you terrified?" I smiled as I looked out.

"I am always terrified Danny, even in a small theatre. I think it is the fear that drives me to succeed, although my stomach will churn on the night."

"I think you are really brave, all of you are." I looked down at her.

"I believe deeply in Curio Life, I absolutely think it is a place for good, and I have seen first hand the good it has done. Danny, so many lives have been improved or saved because of it, and when I go on that site, and I see the eyes of those hopeless young people,

I know deep in my heart, I want to do the best I can to help them. It matters so deeply to me that I do." She gave me a nod; I could see she understood.

"I am a Curio; I will do more to help." I patted her shoulder.

"That would be a nice thing kid."

Birch and Jessie appeared on the stage, and decided to see if they could shout so loud, Edwina and Aden would hear them in the booth at the back of the Arena, and they were really, really loud. We left them to it, and headed out of the arena, and into the hotel next door, and walked round visiting all the stands and exhibitors from charities all over America.

Danny was introduced as a new Curio, and we shook hands and talked to all of them, and thanked them for joining us and being a part of it. Jessie arrived and loved it, she got bag loads of goodies, as did Danny. At the end of the hall was a small stage, with the huge RTSS logo above it, this was where most of the guests would be interviewed by River Television Streaming Service, who were the cable company, carrying the whole event live. Deb's and Chloe stood arm in arm as they talked, and I walked up the steps with Danny, and slid my arm round Deb's and smiled. John Dalton spoke into his mic.

"Wow, what a huge surprise, we have Abigail Jennifer Watson, here live at the booth in what everyone is calling Curio City today. Abby, what a thrill, we are all ready, tomorrow this all begins, you must be excited?" I smiled at the camera.

"We are, and nervous, this one has been four years in the making, it is a big event, and we are hoping America jumps on board, and shares in the madness with us for a very worthy cause." Deb's giggled.

"It is going to be a real spectacle, that is for sure." John smiled at me.

"Abby, there is a lot of speculation about your own health, how are you, will you be fine up there?" I nodded and looked at Danny and winked, and then back at the camera.

"Honestly, I am fit and healthy, I have been resting up a lot and getting sleep, I was just so exhausted from the endless publicity events. It wore me out, but I am back and I am here, and we are ready to roll." He nodded as the camera panned out, and he looked at Danny.

"Now, I have to say, there has been even more speculation about this young lady, who has been seen at your side a lot lately, and I have to ask, are the rumours true, did you and your wife have a secret child?" Chloe burst out laughing, and Deb's started to giggle, I chuckled, and looked at Danny.

"Birch and I are both one hundred percent female I can assure you. Everyone, this is Daniella, and she is our latest addition to the Curio's. She is a very special lady, and we have something very special in mind, which we are not going to reveal until the event. If you really want to know, tune in to find out more, and everyone out there, send in a dollar, we will do so much good with it." He lowered the mic to Danny.

"So, you are a new Curio, tell us what is that like for someone so young?" She looked a little nervous.

"It is exciting, and crazy, and a little bit terrifying, but I am having loads of fun." He smiled.

"So, you cannot give us a hint?" She shook her head.

"No, but you will see if you tune in, and donate, this is a very worthy cause." I smiled, as John looked at me and smiled.

"I take it you have been teaching her Abby, that was a response not unsimilar to your usual responses." Danny giggled; I gave a nod.

"She has been my unofficial assistant for this trip, and she is really bright and learning a lot from all of us." He smiled at us all.

"Abby, Chloe, Debbie, and Daniella, thank you so much for stopping by, I am sure our audience will really appreciate it." We all nodded, as he turned to the camera and began talking.

"Up next, Brad Regan is in the south hotel, and he is talking to Edwina, and the technical team for Curio Live, so over to you Brad."

We walked down the steps and made our way back through the stands, nodding and stopping to do a few selfies, and signing pictures, and then headed outside and walked slowly in the really warm night, to the hotel. Birch and Jessie had disappeared; Chloe breathed out.

"This is fucking massive guys, I am not sure about you, but I am shitting myself." Danny smirked.

"Don't worry Chloe, we have loads of buckets." Deb's burst out laughing, as Chloe looked back at her, and then me.

"Fuck, these two are just mini versions of you two." I giggled, and gave Danny a squeeze.

We got back to the hotel to find Birch with Luke and Jimmy and skate boards. Birch and Jessie sat on the boards, and then Jimmy and Luke ran like hell down the long corridor pushing and let go. Birch and Jessie screamed like banshee's as they came hurtling towards us, I looked at Chloe and our eyes sparkled.
"Oh yeah, I am doing that."
We both laughed as Birch landed in a heap, and we grabbed the boards and ran up the hall. Danny was laughing like mad as she saw us sit down, and Luke and Jimmy prepared. Wow they can run, holy shit it was fast, and I screamed my lungs out.
Danny was stood next to the wall with Jessie, as we flew past at high speed screaming. Chloe was loving it, and Danny and Jessie came running down behind us. We were out of control, travelling at speed heading towards the end of the corridor, when there was a ping, I looked at Chloe.
"Holy shit... Holy shit... OOOOOOOH SHIIIIIIIITTT!"
We shot through the elevator doors as they opened and...
SMASHHHH!
We hit the back wall of the lift laughing like mental patients, Danny leaned around the door laughing like crazy, as we lay tangled in a pile, and laughing our asses off, Jessie looked round the door.
"Oh wow, that dent is awesome." I was giggling, as I looked up and saw Roni and Will. Roni gave a sigh, and looked at Will.
"Just who exactly are the children?"
"GRANDDAD WILL!"

We staggered out of the lift giggling like naughty school girls, as Roni looked at us and shook her head. Birch pointed at us down the corridor with bright sparkling eyes.
"Ha ha, you got busted!" Chloe and me sniggered with our heads down, Roni looked at Danny.
"They are supposed to be responsible parents." She smiled.
"I love them just the way they are." Roni smiled and winked.
"Yeah, me too." Will walked up the corridor with Jessie on his shoulders, to Birch, he smiled at her.

"I am so proud of you two, oh Jemi, so proud." Jessie nodded.

"Yeah, they are bad ass."

Birch giggled. Will leaned in and kissed Birch on the cheek. Sammy and Jenny came running down the corridor and snatched the skateboards off us, Roni smiled at me.

"You look really happy Abby." I smiled, as I stood with my arm round Danny.

"I am, we got our girls, they are with us forever." Roni grinned, and took a breath, and then hugged us both.

"Oh Abby, Danny, you have no idea how happy I was to get that text. I phoned Flick and her and Hatty were in tears they were so happy." I nodded, my mum had sounded crazy happy, but blubbered a lot.

She stood back and wiped her eyes, but she was smiling so much. I took her hand and we walked back to our room, as Jenny and Sammy shot past us, we all stood together and Will looked at us, all four of us.

"I want a picture." He lifted his phone, and the joy in his eyes was so lovely.

"The two best looking daughters, and the two cutest granddaughters in the world, oh wow, I am a very rich man." Click. Jessie frowned.

"You are not selling us." Birch and I snorted a laugh. Will smiled and crouched down.

"You four are so precious, there is no one who could afford you." Roni smiled; Jessie nodded.

"My mums can, they are loaded."

Bless her, she is so cute and beautiful, but Danny is right, just like Birch, she lacks a filter on her mouth.

Tomorrow was a big day, and we were as prepared as we could be, at seven in the evening, we all gathered on stage with all the crew, there was a hell of a lot of us. Birch climbed up onto the staging for the drum kits of the bands that were booked in, and she looked down at all of us as we all stood with our arms round each other. She smiled and her eyes danced.

"We have all come a long way, since the night the six of us built that site and filmed our videos. We have grown in number as one large family, Jimmy, Michael, Luke, and your guys."

Edwina passed out glasses of wine to us, and juice to the kids. Birch smiled at me.

"Deli, you came next, and Baz, Anita and Tabs, and all the children, and this week, Deads and me were blessed with Danny and Jessie. We are all bound by love, we lost our way for a while, but these last few days being together, travelling and sharing our days beside each other, has been such a wonderful experience. I love you all so deeply, you have no idea how deep it goes, you are my brothers and sisters, daughters and sons. Guys, let's do this in style... The CURIO'S."

We all lifted our glasses. "CURIO'S." Jessie looked up.

"AND ME." I nodded, and raised my glass.

"AND YOU." She smiled, God, I love her so much, Birch giggled as she watched us all.

Tomorrow was going to be a long day and as much as we loved to party, we all needed rest, so we all walked out into the night air, and walked towards the hotel. I must admit, it is one of the things I love about the strip in Vegas, well, apart from the lights, but we are pretty well known, some would even say celebrities, and yet we really do not get that hassled.

People spot us and take pictures, the press certainly do, but because this is a place where you run into stars all the time, people are sort of use to it, and so they allow you some space, and I like that. Birch had Jessie on her shoulders, and was holding Danny's hand, and she was happy and giddy, and I just loved seeing her that way. These girls had no idea how much love had entered their lives, but I did, and as I saw Birch look down and talk to Danny, as Jessie laughed, I just felt unbelievably lucky.

Luke's large arm came around my shoulders, and he pulled me close.

"Wow, you look like a very happy person. I have seen that look in Weena's eyes when she watches Chloe with Baz." I smiled.

"I am Luke, I was just thinking how lucky I am." He squeezed.

"She is an extraordinary woman, and honestly, you have two really wonderful children, Weena and me are so happy for you both. We were talking last night, and making Danny a Curio, was a smart move, we need people to continue after us. I hope Jenny and Sammy at some point step up, I think what all you have built is so amazing, I think it should go on." I nodded.

"I would like it to, we have all done so much good with this Luke, but we need to do more, young blood will do that." He smiled.

"You know, when I came that first night, you know, to do some coding?" I sniggered.

"You mean reboot Banger Bobbles?" He sniggered.

"You know what I mean? I met you all, I knew Chloe, but I met Deb's, Anthony, Birch and you, and even then, I could see what an amazing group you all were. You know you were pretty quiet and shy; you sat in your corner watching and saying little, and yet I could see you had a quality I had never encountered." I looked at him, and laughed.

"Yeah, I was the first woman you met who did not want to bang you." He gave a roaring laugh, I giggled with him, and nodded at him as he smiled.

"Abby, I am being serious, God you have changed, you are not bloody quiet anymore... No, what I am trying to say, is I see it in Danny too. She has it, and I have seen how she leans to you, and I love how you have embraced it, and taken her under your wing. She is a bright girl, with a bright future. Abby, you have done something wonderful for her, and I think it is lovely."

"Yeah, still don't want to bang you." He shook his head and gave a huge laugh, I smiled.

"I get it, I do, and actually, I feel very close to her too, and thanks Luke, thank you for making the wishes of one of my best friends come true. Edwina means so much to me, and you have made her really happy." He smiled.

"We all done good, but you know what, I got the best advice ever during the carnival, and I listened and took it." I turned and looked at him and frowned.

"You did, what?" He smiled.

"It was from you; you patted my shoulder and told me. Don't fuck it up." I started to laugh, and we walked in through the hotel door.

The night was moving on, the kids were in bed, we had bathed again, and I lay in a cool soft bed as Birch curled around me and gave a soft happy sigh. I felt her hand slide up and cup my boob, she kissed my shoulder.

"Deads Sweetie, we are naked, alone, and in a hotel, we have never stayed in before." I giggled and wriggled back into her.

"Really, and what do you have in mind Doctor?" She giggled.

"I was thinking rude, hot, and very, very naughty." I gave another giggle.

"Oh God, you really know how to make a girl happy." The door opened and Jessie walked in looking sad.

"What is up Munchkin?" She climbed on the bed and crawled up to us.

"My bed is too big. When I lie across it, I don't reach the other end." Birch gave a giggle.

"Sweetie that is good, it gives you lots of space to move around." She frowned.

"Why do you hold mums' boobs?" I looked down, the duvet had slipped, and Birch was still cupping me.

"It makes me feel safe and secure Munchkin." She looked at me, and nodded.

"Are you scared of falling out of bed too?" She crawled over to Birch's side of the bed.

"You can hold my boobs as well mum, because I don't want to fall out of bed either." I stifled my giggles as Birch looked really down hearted. I looked at her.

"What... Hey, we signed up for this together?"

She gave a sigh and rolled over, and I laughed. Danny stood in the doorway watching us, I gave a smirk, and lifted the duvet up.

"Come on, there is room for one more." She smiled, ran over, and climbed in.

To be honest, it is nice, I love having a proper family, it feels right, and makes me so happy.

Chapter 28

Curio Live America.

The house lights went down, and Edwina sat at her console at the back of the arena wearing her head set, at the side of her, sat Morty and Aden. She watched the dark stage.

"And stage lights five, go..."

There was a buzz all around the arena as soft lighting lit the stage, and either side of the stage, two huge screens came to life and flickered. The large screen at the back came to life and flickered in a soft red, and then a large Union Jack flag appeared, and the buzz of the crowd intensified, as it tore from the top left corner, right down to the bottom right, and as the torn flag fell away, it revealed the stars and stripes of an American flag. The speakers buzzed.

"Ladies and gentlemen.... Welcome to a Dixon and Dixon Events, partnered with River Television Streaming Services event. This is Curio Live America."

A Curio logo appeared above the flags and the crowd went wild, and it was deafening. The thump of a drum beat began, Thump... Thump... Thump, and as the music kicked in, the crowd started to clap.

The back screen changed and as the music played, pictures appeared of us getting off the plane and a montage of our whole bus journey began to play, showing all the Curio's working having fun, and generally laughing and smiling. The clap from the audience was deafening, as the pictures changed to the time lapse of the stage being built and assembled, and as it reached the part of the built stage the back screen lit up with the Curio Logo, and the music stopped.

"Ladies and gentlemen... Miss Abigail Jennifer Watson."

The crowd roared, and Birch kissed me, as I took a breath, adjusted my face mic, turned, and walked past a smiling Danny, out onto the stage as huge roar lifted in to the air, it was mind blowing, as all the spot lights hit me. Edwina smiled as I walked down the centre of the stage.

"God, she has such presence, look at her, she is a fucking rock star."

My heart was pounding as I reached the centre of the stage and smiled, it was deafening, and I gave a small laugh. The two enormous side screens showed me up close.

"Hello America."

The roar was so unbelievable, I was blown away. It was so loud I could hardly hear my laughs as I waved. Birch jumped up and down, as she watched the monitor, she looked at the crew.

"That's my super Sweetie." Danny laughed at her side. I had to take several breaths, as finally the crowd began to settle and I nodded my thanks.

"What a welcome, wow, thanks guys." I looked back at the screen; it was once again the Curio logo.

"Ladies and gentlemen, fellow Curio's, hi, I am Abby, and I am a Curio." There was another massive roar, and I laughed, this really was remarkable. Again, I had to wait, for it to quieten.

"The Curio's are a group, of some of the kindest, most caring, and loving people I have ever met. We started out as a group of friends sharing a house, who were targeted, victimised, and shamed. We were labelled whore, transients, trash, slut, puff, and referred to, as like that. It was a difficult time for us, because as young twenty four year olds, we had no way of showing others what was happening in our home village, and it hurt, and was painful, and the cause of many tears. One night, we decided to create a web site, on to which, we all uploaded a video telling our story. A blog was added which I wrote, to chronicle the life we had, the bullying and suffering we encountered."

Behind me pictures of that first site came up on the screen, showing all our video clips ready to play.

"We made the choice, to reject the labels people were giving us, and pick one of our own, because most of the bad things being said about us were all targeted at our sexualities, hair styles, dress sense, and our sex lives, and we were so much more than that. A label that notes only your sexuality, is a label for just one part of your whole, so we picked a label that took into account, our whole being. It covered our hopes and dreams, our loves and passions, our interests and our hobbies, and most importantly, who we were as people. We chose a label, that was based on our curious natures, as young people learning about who we were, and who we wanted to be, and as you know, we shortened it down to Curio." I smiled as the crowd roared.

"Ten years ago, we did Curio Live London, and from that we have bought, renovated and refitted out three mental health facilities, because through our website, we have now been contacted by over thirty three million young people, who reached out to us for help, guidance, and advice, and in some cases, support and shelter. A great many of these people, were in this country, and it has taken some time, and four years of planning, but tonight we are all delighted to be here with the hope of doing the same over here in the USA." Another roar erupted.

"We have three sites lined up, one in Pennsylvania, one in Missouri, and one in California, where we hope to build mental health facilities that will be the very best in their field. They will be bright, new and modern, with the latest equipment, and the highest quality trained staff in the field, and trust me, my wife is a trained Clinical Psychologist, and she sets a very high bar to jump at." I looked to my side and she waved, with a huge smile.

"This will take a lot of money, and we need to raise at least one hundred and fifty million dollars to do all three, but to begin with, we will start in Missouri, with a run down hospital, and then we will do the others. Every penny that can be raised, will bring hope, care, support, and a chance to rebuild the lives of the young. Too many of our young people take their own lives each year, because they feel lost, alone and unloved, and have no other way out of the misery they live in. America, we need you, we need you to help us, so what do you say. ARE YOU WITH US?" The roar of the crowd was deafening, and I could not believe the power of their response.

Alison Williams walked on from the side of the stage, wearing a huge smile, I lifted my arm.

"Ladies and Gentlemen, one of your hosts for the next four days, Miss Alison Williams."

She leaned in and hugged me, and I waved and walked from the stage. Birch was bouncing around laughing and clapping like a maniac, as I came off into the wings at the back, she took one look at me.

"Oh shit." Grabbed the bright yellow bucket, and handed it to me, and YERK! Birch shuddered.

"Oh Sweetie, you really need to stop doing that, it really is very unattractive." Danny looked really worried.

"Are you alright?" I looked up and nodded... YERK! Chloe peered over the bucket.

"What is it with you and green bits, you only ate toast?" Birch shuddered.

"Chloe Sweetie, please stop." She gave another violent shudder, even Danny took a step back.

On stage, Alison Williams talked of what was happening, how to donate, and where to go in order to purchase the massive range of merchandise, in person, or online. She detailed a whole list of events planned over the next four days, and just like last time, the long row of boxes appeared to show the rising total, and thanks to the Curio's, the band, and G5, it was already above three million.

I gave one final yerk, into the bucket. I really have no idea why, but I just cannot seem to get over it. I have done thousands of stage appearances, and pretty much most of the time, I yerk. Chloe once pointed out, that by now, I have probably thrown up three times my own weight, which appalled Birch.

I made my way to the dressing room, and rinsed out my mouth. I had done the opening, and was back on stage later, Deb's was fitted with a mic, she was going to go and talk with three famous actors, and get them to tell their stories, before we did the presentations of the Pennsylvania property, which Birch would handle, and then we had our first live act, which was a band. So far all was going to plan.

I sat back and relaxed a little, I had to appear at one of the stands for the events in one hour, which would be live streamed to the main stage, Danny was coming with me, Jessie had gone shopping with Will and Roni. Edwina would hand over to Aden and Luke, and she would be joining us with Anthony. We were live, streaming, and for the next four days, it would be manic.

With security, we headed over to hall one, in the hotel on the right of the large Spire Mobile Centre, and we arrived at a stand for suicide prevention. A guy called Dirk, had a mic, and for the next hour and a half, we talked, signed pamphlets and gave out information to help young people, all whilst doing a live interview, which was streamed to the stage. It still surprises me the number of adults who approach us with fears for someone they know, even here in this huge country that has some of the world's leading health care, it astounds me how many are suffering alone. I have heard too many sad stories to last me a life time.

Although it was funny when I handed Danny a pen to sign with, and a lot of young people asked her. I stood for a moment with a smile, as she nodded and asked questions, and gave out some great advice from the pamphlets, she looked like she was really enjoying herself. We stood side by side as we talked and signed, and I swung my hips and bumped her, she giggled and looked up, her bright blue eyes filled with fun and excitement, I winked, and got handed another book to sign.

Anthony stood at her side, as always keeping a watchful eye, and giggling with her as he made funny comments. Hearing her chuckle and laugh with him was so wonderful, he is such a great guy, and I love him so much.

We had a quick lunch, and headed back to the arena as we had stage side seats for the band, and Danny just exploded with joy, as she stood bobbing about watching the band. It was wild and she was loving every minute taking hundreds of pictures. I stood back with Birch, watching her, her face was so happy, I suppose for her, someone who had rarely been out unless accompanied, this was the most amazing thing that could happen. It reminded me very much of that night at the Railway Inn, on my first ever trip to Birch's home.

Edwina appeared in her head set, she smiled as she saw Danny bobbing and dancing, she pointed her finger across the stage.

"Jenny and Sammy are over there going mental; they love this band."

Edwina fitted my head mic, Birch still had hers on, she smiled as she lined it up against my cheek, and then pointed.

"There is a red bucket there, you know, just in case, I believe you appalled the crew earlier, no one wanted to rinse the yellow one, so they threw it in the skip out back." She chuckled.

"Okay you are wired and ready, Luke will be counting you in."

She kissed my cheek.

The band were bowing as the crowd roared, and Danny was just star struck, and giddy, she was having so much fun. Birch took my hand, and gave it a squeeze.

"Are you ready for this?"

I nodded, and took a deep breath, as the band ran past me and the black curtain came down to hide the instruments, as roadies crawled like mice all over them taking it all apart, to leave the stage ready for the next band. I heard Luke in my ear.

"Abby, Birch, you go on three... Two... One... and go, we have projection."

Holding hands, we walked onto the stage to a rousing applause, and together we stood side by side, and smiled at the audience, Birch was giddy.

"Sweeties, wasn't that wonderful, wow, what a great band." Above on the large screen, a picture came up of an old run down hospital in Missouri. I took a deep breath.

"Ladies and gentlemen, earlier my wife Birch talked you through the specifics of what will be our first centre, so you all have a pretty good idea of what will happen there. Tonight, we want to talk about a very special person, who touched our lives and made a huge difference, we want to talk about this very special lady." I looked up and felt the tug inside me. Birch squeezed my hand, and looked out at the audience.

"Ladies and gentlemen, this beautiful lady, is Lillian Ford Baxter, she is one of a partnership that ran the local Tea Rooms in our own village at home. Lilly was an ex teacher, and for almost fifty years of her life, she had to hide who she was, because she was in a same sex relationship, at a time when it was shunned and shamed by society." I took a deep breath.

"Lilly was someone who over her long career, took care of many young people, and she helped them, supported them, and advised them. She had the biggest heart I have ever known, and she showed such love. She came to me at a time in my life, when it was very dark, and I was really struggling to cope, she was gentle and caring, and showed me a level of support, that helped me to make it through the darkness. I did not ask her to, and wasn't looking to, I was lost and alone, and scared, because I was so isolated and so lonely." I gave a sniffle and wiped my eyes, as the huge wave of emotion washed over me, as I remembered that day, Birch took over.

"That is who Lilly was, she had to hide her own lifestyle, but she still reached out to others, she referred to us as her girls. All of us in the village felt we were safe under her watchful gaze, she encouraged us to be us, and not hide, and we loved her very deeply for it. It is impossible for a same sex couple to have children, but that did not stop Lilly, she loved us all, and she treated us like we were her own. She really was a most remarkable woman, and sadly earlier this year we lost her, as age overcame her." Birch breathed in, and I squeezed her hand, and took over.

"In her will, Lillian left the sum of one million dollars to Curio Live America, and her instruction was to keep helping others like we were. All of the Curio's knew her and loved her deeply, and would like you to know, that the hospital we have already bought in Missouri, will be named The Lillian Ford Baxter centre for health and well being. It will be a lasting tribute to her, and will continue to help young people for a long time to come." I wiped my eyes, and smiled, Birch looked back at the screen where it showed a large picture of her.

The audience rose from their seats and gave a huge applause, and I knew at home in Hastings, Celia would be watching, and like me crying, but she would be happy, knowing her spirit would continue. Birch smiled at the screen.

"Here is to you Lily, we love you."

We walked off stage, and I took several deep breaths, Danny stood holding a bucket, Birch giggled.

For today we were done, a band was set up in Germany, and it came on the live screen to be streamed to the event. After that, for four years documentaries had been filmed, with celebrity guests, and they would be screened all night, with highlights of the day's events. Chloe and Deb's were handling press with Anita, and we had some time off, and made our way back to the hotel. We walked into the lobby, and Janet ran to us and dragged us into her arms, she was gushing with happiness, as a guy with two boys stood behind her smiling.

Janet introduced us to her husband Ralph, and her sons,

Douglas, aged 13, and Toby, age 10, who Danny and Jessie knew as they went to their school. We were heading for food and to meet Roni, so invited them to join us, Janet was overjoyed to meet Roni and Will. We sat down with meals and talked, Jessie was bouncing all over the place talking about her shopping trip, Roni assured Danny, there were bags on her bed for her too. Yep, they are spoiling them as bad as Hatty and Mum. Roni smiled, and her eyes twinkled.

"Abby, don't be a party pooper, I am having such fun, and it is so nice to have grandchildren to spoil." I smiled.

"Okay, you are off the hook." She smiled at me.

"I am loving this Abby, and if you want my honest opinion, I think it is doing you a world of good, it is like tonic, although you do know, you have three children really, because she will never grow up?"

I looked at her across the table talking to Douglas and Toby, and gave a soft smile.

"I don't want her to Roni; I want her to stay just as she is." Jessie nodded.

"Yeah, we don't want another gargoyle." I gave a chuckle, and leaned in to her.

"No, we don't." Roni smiled at me; I could see the joy in her eyes.

We were all really tired by eight, it had been a really long day, but there were three more to go, so we headed back to our room. Jessie hung limp from my arms, she was wiped out, so we put her in bed and tip toed out. Danny had a shower and I dried her hair.

"I read the blog, it is good, your school should be loving it. I mean they have some pretty exclusive pictures of us all chilling out, I love the one you got of Birch staring into space, maybe we should get you a better camera."

"Really, I would love that."

"We have press, and then we are free for three hours, I think we should go and buy one." She turned and looked so excited, and I smiled.

"If you are going to do the work, you will need the tools."

She skipped off to bed happy and I slid in next to Birch, she giggled as she pulled me close.

"You call my mum; you are spoiling them just as much as she

is?" She kissed my shoulder and I quivered, as she moved slowly down to my neck.

"Oh God Birch, oh yes Baby, oh hell I need this." She pulled up the duvet.

"Quick Sweetie, just in case she wakes up." I giggled and slid down.

"Oh Doctor, you can be so naughty." She gave a quiet squeal of happiness, and I started to tingle.

Day two started with breakfast in the conference room, as Edwina covered all the nights activities and film that had been shot by the hundreds of people who had got involved. She gave us the details of the day's events; this would be an easier day for us, and had been planned that way, as set up had been tiring. But before all of that, we had the one part I hated the most, we had press and Anita smiled at me, she knew for me this would be torture.

The good thing about this one, was we would all be together, unlike my last experience of Curio Live with Katie at the helm. We assembled in the back room, Danny was nervous, and I held her hand.

"Remember, keep it short factual and only Curio Live, you can ignore any questions about your personal life. You know Danny, you do not have to do this." She shook her head.

"I want to, I am just nervous, that is all." Chloe winked.

"Don't worry Abby, I have got her back." I smiled at her; she looked around.

"Where is Jessie?"

"She is with Suki, they have gone to a kids game place with Jimmy, and the rest of the kids." She nodded.

"Good." I frowned.

"Why?" She smiled.

"Jesus Abby, if we put her out there none of us will have any secrets left." Birch giggled.

"She has a point Sweetie, out there we need to filter things."

I was stunned, how could she of all people even say that, this was Jessie's role model talking? Deli looked nervous; it had been some time since she had done this. I patted her shoulder.

"You will be fine, it all comes back, and honestly, you will wish it didn't." She nodded, and we all took a deep breath, as Creamy opened the door, and Anita guided us in. The long table, the mic's, the flashes, I did not miss this.

We sat down, and Danny was between Birch and myself, Anita looked around, and made all the usual Curio questions only statements, and then it began, and the questions flowed, and most of them were pretty nice and respectful, but there is always one.

"Paul Williamson. Chicago Today, Miss Watson, you are a pretty huge celebrity name now, some would even say an A list celebrity, are you not just leveraging your fame to make money for this event?" I was about to answer when Danny spoke.

"I don't think she is any bigger than a famous and in demand Doctor of three massive titles, or a rock star's wife. I realise I have not been here long, but from what I have seen behind the scenes everyone here is treated equally. The stage time over the weekend is pretty equal, and I should know, I have the schedule."

Birch smiled, she was defending me, and she noted it. Anthony picked up the thread.

"You know darling, there are some who have said I have the stage presence of a goddess, I mean, these girls are good, but who does their hair. Let's be honest, I helped make all of us look wonderful."

Birch and Chloe sniggered, and the reporter looked lost for words. I smiled.

"Mr Williamson, I opened up the event, mainly because I have a long list of events to attend, and so I did the opening, and then I headed off to spend a day at many of the booths in the event, Anthony was on the booths before we even went live, as was Deli, and as you saw, I was followed shortly after on stage by Deb's and then Birch. We have a massive list of very famous stars and musicians appearing, who actually asked us if they could participate. This has nothing to do with fame; this is about making sure those centres get built." Anita pointed.

"Paula Swinton. UK National Daily, Daniella, there has been a lot of speculation about your sudden appearance with Abby, and the papers in the UK are asking where you came from, could you shed any light on that for them?" I looked at her, she knew she did not have to answer.

"Miss Swinton, wasn't it? There is a really good reason why I am a Curio and why I am here, and that will be revealed over this weekend, for now I cannot say. I have spent time with Abby, as she has given me help with blog posts, she is a writer, which other Curio would I ask?" Chloe looked round.

"Not me that is for sure, my spelling is terrible, actually, Abby will you give me lessons too?" We all giggled, and I smiled and winked at Danny, wow, she was really holding her own. Anita pointed

"Jessie Everet, Freelance. Guys you finally made it, and we are so thrilled to see you all here, and even with a new little Curio. Danny, I have read your school blogs, wow you have done some amazing stuff, I bet your school mates are thrilled, and you have got some great inside pictures. How does it feel to have such unlimited access?" Birch leaned into the mic.

"Jessie we are only here because you have been banging on about this at us for years, will we be getting a break, or will you be crusading for Curio Live two next?" Everybody laughed, especially Jessie.

"Guys I love you. Danny?" Danny nodded and smiled.

"I have some great pictures, and Abby has done a lot to help, but the blog is great fun, and I am really enjoying doing it. I have not had time to talk to my friends; you have no idea how busy it has been. I know there are loads of messages on the site and I will answer all of them soon." Jessie smiled.

More questions came, and finally after an hour Deli, Edwina, Chloe, Debs and Anthony were as exhausted as I normally am, they had answered so many. Anita finally called it a day, and we all thanked everyone and walked out to a barrage of flashes, and as soon as we were inside, we all mobbed Danny, she was amazing, and we congratulated her with hugs and praise. I was blown away by her performance.

She was happy and smiling and her eyes danced, Birch slipped her arm round my waist, and leaned on my shoulder.

"Sweetie, I think you made another writer." I glanced at her.

"At least mine is quiet, what the hell have you created?" She giggled

"She is loud, but oh God Deads, I adore her, she is so cute. We did good, we got two amazing kids, I am so proud of Danny today." I smiled as I watched her with Chloe, laughing and talking.

"We have; they really are amazing."

We had a break, and a drink, and then headed out to a camera shop, Creamy came with us, just in case. Let's be honest, the guy is a giant, no one is going to mess with him, well, I mean, Deb's did.

Okay, so I have a great camera, my dad bought it me for Christmas three years ago, so I am quite skilled. Camera people, they talk about stuff I have never heard of and they go on and on and on. My head was spinning as the two shop assistants raved, Birch did not help, she jumped up and down and clapped excitedly saying Oh really every minute, I looked at her, as the guys nipped off to get more.

"Do you understand all this?" She gave me a blank look.

"Not a word of it, but they get so excited I cannot help myself." And that was me done. Danny was laughing as I looked at her.

"I have no idea at all about this stuff, I say, point and pick one, and pray it has an instruction book Edwina can understand." She nodded.

"Good plan."

We looked at them all, and she randomly pointed, and I looked at the camera, it looked like a camera so I was in. The assistant returned, and we showed him our choice, he looked at it and smiled.

"Oh yes, a really good model, yes, that is a wise choice." Birch looked at it and got cocky.

"Well obviously Sweetie." I glanced at Danny and she sniggered; I looked at the assistant.

"Do you have anything that is just a point and shoot, it is for a seven year old?"

He looked offended, and pointed to what I presumed he saw as mass market garbage. I picked one up in a box, and smiled as I placed it on the counter.

"This one as well please."

We came out of the shop, and headed back to the hotel, I had phone duty, so Birch took Danny off to meet with Chloe, and I headed for the call room. I was surprised to find Roni, Will and

Janet on the lines, they had volunteered. I sat down and plugged in, Deli sat at my side, and between us we both got on with taking calls. I actually secretly love doing this, it is such fun when I answer and say 'hi this is Abigail Jennifer Watson.' The phone goes quiet for a second and they usually respond with 'Really?' I love it, and let's be honest, if they were going to donate ten, by the time I am done, its twenty.

It was yet another long day, and I flopped on the sofa in my suite, as Birch handed me a gin, and Jessie ran round taking pictures, and Danny sat on her bed with Chloe, who knew everything about cameras, she had slept with a few photographers, why does that not surprise me? She has actually learned a lot, and so it was nice, as Birch sat at my side and leaned on me with a huge smile.

"I am so happy Sweetie."

I really understood that, I had felt it since they boarded the bus, and just felt this huge ball of joy constantly growing inside me. We had done good, and I was so happy, I just wanted to dance and yell and scream about it, I just needed a rest.

Chapter 29

Curio Family.

Sunday was a mega busy day, and flew past in a blur of stage appearances with famous stars, phone calls, and booth visits, as well as masses of press. There was a grand ball, with tickets at two thousand dollars each, which honestly, I was not thrilled about, it was the promoters call, and they had sponsors for everything. My mind, was a whirl of gin and questions, when I fell into bed and was asleep in seconds.

Monday was the final day, and all of us were tired, as we had our usual morning meeting and quaffed lots of coffee. Today was the big day, as we would launch the new junior platform, and Danny wanted to announce it. Edwina had the site upload with Danny's new video, and her new first Curio blog post, which we wrote weeks ago, but with her new camera, she had taken better pictures, and they were added, ready to publish.

We had the stage set, and everything was ready, my head mic was fitted, as I stood at the side of Danny, who had one on to, and I looked down at her, as Roni came to the end of her filmed feature.

"Will you be alright; do you want a bucket?" She did look pale; she shook her head.

"No, I am determined to do this, I really want to." Wow, she could be so like me at times. Edwina patted my shoulder as Roni walked smiling towards me.

"Abby your mic is live, get ready, we have just uploaded the new pages, and you are free to go."

I winked at Danny, took a deep breath, and walked onto the stage, to a thunderous applause. I stood in the centre of the stage, and smiled out at the audience and waited for the place to quieten down.

"Ladies and gentlemen, today we are going to broaden out the Curio Life web site, and add a new special feature. Before we do that, I want to talk about our new Curio Daniella, or Danny as we all know her. If you have been on the site in the last few months, you would have seen her video, and understood her concerns and worries. But there is so much more to her story, which is why, she was brought into the Curio fold." I glanced to the side and saw her smiling.

"In recent weeks there has been a lot of speculation about who she is, and why she has been seen at my side in the UK and America. So, having spoken to Danny, I wish to clear that up." I took a deep breath, and the silence surrounded me as all eyes were on me.

"Danny's parents were taken from her and her sister in a tragic accident not that long ago. Yes, she looks like me, she has the dark hair and the fringe, and beautiful bright blue eyes, but please ignore the press, she is not my love child, or secret baby. Her and her sister, are the daughters of my recently deceased cousin." I paused for a second, as there were murmurs.

"When my wife and I heard of this, and discovered that her and her sister were alone, we did what any family member would do, we went to her aid, and as a result, my wife and I have adopted her and her sister... Yes, you heard that right, we adopted them, and so they are now members of the Curio family household."

The place was so silent you could hear a pin drop. I smiled as I looked out, and noted a few members of the press.

"Danny's video, made all the Curio's think, and we realised there was a place where we could help more, and so with that in mind, we worked with Danny, and have created a new part to our platform, and so to tell you all about that, please welcome new Curio, Daniella Watson, or simply Danny."

The arena exploded with noise as she walked on smiling and waved, wow, she had guts that was for sure. In the wings Birch and Roni, watched with tears in their eyes, as she reached me and took my hand, and faced the audience. It was not so bad; the lights were so bright she could not see much. I squeezed her hand, and she took a deep breath, it took quite some time, before it was quiet enough for her to speak.

"Hi... I am Danny, and I am a Curio."

The room exploded again, and she gave a laugh. She stood smiling, and I looked down and watched her carefully, she was trembling a little, but she really impressed me. At just nine almost ten years old, I thought she was the bravest kid alive. The noise died down, and she smiled.

"Ladies and Gentlemen, I am lucky, I have two amazing women in my life today, who love me, cherish me and support me, but how many young people under eighteen are out there who do not? Not that long ago, I lived in fear, that my sister and I would be separated and put into care, and for me, that was terrifying. Actually, it was a lot scarier than this." She giggled.

"Today, a new feature has been added to the website of Curio Life, it was literally published, and went live, as I walked on. The new feature, is Curio Life Junior, and it is a place to talk and get advice from trained professionals, and other people who have been through the darkness and come out the other side, and it is aimed at under seventeen year olds only. It is a secure site, with a lot of administrators, who will work out of a specially created centre in Oxendale in the UK. We understand all kids have parents, and at times, they do not like what their parents say, and this is not a site that will overrule your parents, but it will give you a place to just talk things through, and that as I know, really does help."

She turned and looked up at the screen, and the site came up, with her first blog post on it. She smiled when she saw it.

"Kids want to talk, and sometimes just be heard, I did, but I had no one, until my new mums came to help, so it is live, it is up, and I will be on there talking. Curio Life Junior awaits you."

There was a massive round of applause and cheers, and I stood looking out feeling overwhelmingly proud of her. I glanced to my left, and saw Deb's as she walked on from the side of the stage and she handed a note to Danny, I frowned, Danny opened it and read it and then gasped, she looked at Deb's.

"Really?" Deb's pointed out into the audience. Danny looked up and gave a huge smile.

"Oh my God, I am so excited. Ladies and gentlemen, for one night only, please would you welcome to support Curio Live America, the reunited Battered Taco." My jaw dropped as I heard Floyd's guitar wail, and that usual, yet cleaned up announcement, as the curtain behind us rose quickly.

"ROCK IT OUT THERE, CURIO'S, FOR BATTERED TACO!"

The stage exploded with flash bombs, fire, and masses of smoke, as the crowd went wild. We hurried off, and Danny bounced in the wings clapping and screaming. It is probably a good thing we turned her mic off. Roni looked at me and smiled.

"Oh hell, she is as loud as the other one, when you press the right buttons."

Suddenly, as I watched Danny jump, dance and scream, I could see myself, age nineteen, stood in a field with Deb's, Chloe, and Edwina, as we screamed and bounced to Battered Taco at the Oxendale Festival on that long glorious, wonderful Summer, of so long ago, and I just stood and smiled.

The guys roared through their set, Jimmy was wild and loving it, so was Floyd, and I saw Gail who had flown in with them, across the stage with Dylan, Jenny, Helen and Gem, as they watched their dad as he played live, wow, that must have been so magical for them.

Isn't it funny, how things go around in a circle and remind you of yesteryear? I could see Jenny, with that look of complete devotion and adoration for Jimmy in her eyes, and wow, with her long brown bushy hair, she looked so like her mother, it was uncanny.

Oh God, I just realised Birch and I have a mini Deadly and Birch, Deb's has a mini Deb's, Edwina has a mini male Weena, and holy shit, what will we do if Chloe produces, a tiny sexually deviant copy of herself, will it all start all over again? Holy shit we are in trouble. Thank God for Anthony, because I think I am looking at the next really serious wave of crazies for Wotton.

The set was incredible, and I had to wonder why they split up, because they were brilliant, although, it felt right to have Jimmy play, just like he had at our first Live event. Danny was exhausted and almost hoarse she had screamed so much. She was so happy, for her it was a dream come true, and she did actually take loads of pictures for her blogs, she hung from my neck smiling up at me as the boys left the stage.

"That was epic." I smiled at her; I love seeing her happy.

The final films began to roll, the event was nearing its end, as the clips we shot at the three locations played as we all had made special videos for the event. As they played, a huge semi circle of seats was moved into place on the stage, and Alison Williams stood by ready, as all the Curio's were miked up with face mics. As the video's ended, Alison walked on and gave a big smile, as the crowds roared.

"What an amazing four days, and to be honest it would not be Curio Live without a last chance to chat. So, to start with, because this family has grown in size, please welcome Mrs and Mrs Dixon, and their two newly adopted daughters, Danny and Jessie."

We walked on holding hands and headed over towards the seats, as Alison sat down in an arm chair in the centre, the crowd roared out, as we sat down, and got settled, and waited for all the applause to end, Jessie sat on Birch's knee, and looked round at us.

"That was loud."

We both giggled as Alison smiled, and behind us on the screen the Curio Live logo came up with a row of empty boxes, ready for the total. Alison smiled as the crowd settled.

"Wow guys, you are a family now, last time we did this, you were about to get married. How are you both feeling?" Birch breathed out.

"Nervous... This has been a huge event, and right in the middle of setting up, we found out about Danny and Jessie, and so it has been pretty crazy." She smiled; Jessie leaned out.

"They are loud." I giggled; Alison nodded.

"They are indeed, I take it you are Jessie, I have heard a lot about you?" She nodded.

"I am a handful, Granny Roni told me that." Birch giggled, and I laughed. Alison looked at me, smirking, and trying to hold her laughter in.

"Abby, you are looking good, family life is good for you." I looked at Danny and smiled.

"I am loving it, we have two amazing girls, even if they are a handful at times." Jessie leaned over, from Birch's lap.

"She means me." Alison laughed with the audience.

"I know she does." She looked at Danny as she smirked.

"New home, new Curio Danny, it must be huge for your life, how are things going?" She gave a smile and went a bit shy, and nodded a lot.

"I am really loving it; I cannot wait to get back to the UK and home." She smiled, I pulled her close, and gave her a squeeze. Jessie leaned forward and looked at her.

"We live in a big house and a village of grumpy people; Chloe told me to ignore them stuffy old buzzards." I sniggered, as Alison fought back her laughter.

"Did she now? That is probably good advice." Jessie nodded.

"I know right?"

I was hard not to laugh, Birch had her head down, and was shaking, I turned back to Alison, as she giggled, and looked at the audience, trying to focus.

"The Curio family has really grown, last time we were here it was at Curio Live London, and we had one member who was due to give birth. So, to see how things went, let's bring on Debbie and Jimmy Battersby, and their three children, Jennifer, Helen and Gem."

The crowd roared as they walked on and took their seats. They sat smiling and waving, it was amazing, they were like a huge celebrity couple. It took a while for the crowd to settle, Alison turned and looked at them.

"Wow Jenny has grown, and you both have two more, the Curio family has really expanded, how are things guys?" Deb's smiled and looked so happy, as she held Jimmy's hand.

"We are great, living a quieter life but busy." Alison nodded, and looked at Jimmy.

"Jimmy, the Taco were amazing, is that really just a one night deal?" He smiled.

"Yeah, it was awesome, but you know, we have all moved on, we are not as young as we once was, and we have other tunes to do. Floyd is working on his stuff and Dougie, is working on some really amazing sound tracks for movies, it was banging fun, but honestly, I am knackered now." The audience giggled.

"Debbie, massive event, and all you guys have been all over the place, you handled the booths, that must have been chaotic?" She giggled and rolled her eyes.

"It was madness, but it has been great fun, and we have all loved working side by side, we are a good team, and we are not short of people these days." Alison smiled. Jessie leaned forward.

"I didn't help; I went shopping with Granddad Will." The audience roared with laughter, Birch and me both giggled, Alison smiled.

"You did, wow what did you buy?" She looked worried, and leaned forward and whispered.

"Granddad Will told me to say nothing because my mums would tell him he was spoiling me too much."

The audience roared with laughter, and I could see Roni in the wings pissing her sides laughing. Alison was fighting to keep her face straight; she looked at Jessie.

"But that's what granddads do." Jessie nodded.

"I know right."

Birch had her head down laughing, I could not help it. Deb's was holding her mouth and her eyes were sparkling as she tried not to laugh. Alison tried to regain her composure, and was smirking.

"Okay, to try and get some order, this show was a technological nightmare, which was masterminded by husband and wife duo, Edwina and Luke Jefferson, and here they are with their son Sammy."

Danny slipped her arm around me as they walked on, and sat with Deb's and Jimmy. Alison gave a big smile.

"Wow guys, I spent a little time with you and Aden up in the control box, and it was a huge amount of work, it was amazing to see you Edwina directing everything." She gave a nod.

"Yes, we have come a long way in twelve years, I must admit, there was quite a few moments of panic, but in true Curio style we got through." Alison nodded.

"The Curio family is growing, and I believe your little sister has just got engaged?" Edwina laughed.

"Yeah, it was about time." From the wings over the speakers came Chloe's voice.

"Oh yeah Weena, I was just making sure I picked the best one that's all, it took time."

Edwina sniggered as Alison and the audience laughed, and Chloe walked on in her dungarees dragging Baz behind her. Alison lifted her hand as the audience went wild.

"Chloe Pemberton, and Basil Radley." I looked at Deb's and she smirked.

"B Radley, she is marrying B Radley, please tell me it's not really Boo?"

Deb's squealed with laughter, and Birch gave a cackle of a laugh as Chloe sat down. We were all pissing our sides laughing. This interview was slowly slipping into chaos, and we all had the giggles, which the audience was loving. Chloe sat down and waved. Alison wiped her eyes.

"Oh dear, you guys have not changed." She took a deep breath, and regained her composure.

"Chloe, engaged, and now a really well known and respected artist, you have come a long way since that wonderful talk you did back in London." She smiled.

"Yeah, it's pretty much all I do, I paint and I..." Jessie leaned forward.

"You fumble, Mum Birch told me that."

Birch snorted really loudly, and we all burst out laughing, Birch leaned back covering her mouth as her eyes filled with tears, as she laughed, me and Deb's were howling with laughter. Alison was wiping her eyes, and the audience was roaring with laughter, Jessie was stealing the show. Chloe looked at us.

"See what I mean, she is never doing a press conference with us?" Alison wiped her eyes, and tried really hard to focus.

"Oh dear, she is so lovely, but hell, we will be here all night at this rate." She looked up with red eyes, and chuckled.

"You know what, let's just get the rest out. Ladies and gentlemen, Anthony Parker with his partner Michael, and Fidelity Hannigan, with her two children Josh and Liz."

They all walked on to a roaring applause, and finally, we were all out, and sat down, and Alison took a huge breath, and looked round at us all.

"This is so lovely, what an amazing family you all are. Deli, I have to ask, the documentary you made on all the British sites, that was made three years ago, and I have to say, it was a really amazing thing to watch, and also, I have to ask, was there any booth you did not visit, because you have not stopped since you got here?"

She gave a big smile as her two children hugged her and looked a little shy.

"It has been busy, that is for sure, but look, we have all flown over here for one reason, there are kids out there suffering. They need our help, and they need the American public to back them, so we can build the sorts of centres featured in the documentary. Abby and Birch have been working on this for four years solid, in between all the other things they have done, and we have been behind them, mucking in and giving them the support they need." Anthony nodded.

"You know, this all began, with Abby and Birch, it literally grew out of one conversation, and we have not stopped since, but to be honest darlings, these two loonies, have put their heart and soul into it." Alison smiled at me.

"I have heard that a lot over the years, what do you think Abby?" I smiled and looked at them all.

"Come on guys, it has always been a team effort, and yeah, Birch and I have done our fair share of late nights, but look at all this. We might have planned it, but you guys executed it, and what an amazing event it has been." Birch nodded.

"There is actually one more person who deserves the credit as well. D&D is actually a three man team, and this is a D&D event, and so everyone of you should give high praise to an equally hard working member of the team Anita Dickinson." Alison lifted her hand.

"Come on out Anita, let's have a look at you."

I giggled as I saw Tabs push Anita, and she came out shaking her head and looking terrified, we slid up and made her space at the end, she looked embarrassed and we sniggered at her. She sat down next to Alison, who smiled.

"Anita, the face behind all the publicity, you have done a marvellous job, you are around this lot a great deal, what is it like to work with the Curio's?" She looked at me and Birch and we smiled.

"They are all mentally unstable, but it has been a joy and privilege, it really has, and to help create something that has done so much good, it has been a dream job, I could not ask to work with a better group than this lot." Alison smiled and nodded.

"Yes, I must admit, we have had a lot of fun back stage this long weekend. So how did we do, that is the golden question, and the boxes are blank? We need at least one hundred and fifty million, shall we find out how much has been made?"

We all nodded, but we were nervous, and we all turned to the back screen and watched There was drum roll, the boxes flashed and then lit up one by one, and our breath caught in our throats as 379,876,361 came up, and the audience went mental. I was stunned, it was completely unexpected, Chloe and Baz were up dancing, Birch just looked stunned. Jimmy was hugging everyone, it was utter insanity, I looked at Danny and she smiled.

"We did it mum."

I nodded and smiled, and pulled her into a hug, as Jessie screamed out in joy, although I am convinced, she did not know why, for her it was a way of burning off energy, I think?

I leaned over and slid my arms round Birch, as she smiled with tears in her eyes and I hugged her, wow, she was so amazing. Alison stood up with a huge smile.

"Guys, what would you like to say to America?" We all looked at Birch as she wiped her eyes, she shook her head.

"This was more you than me Deads, this time, was you." I pulled her up and slid my arm round her, and all the Curio's stood together and I took a huge breath.

"Wow, thank you America... Your kindness and your generosity, shines out loud and proud, and we are unbelievably humbled by this. We can do so much more than we planned, thank you, all of you, from the bottom of our hearts." Alison walked to the front of the stage, and held out her arm.

"Ladies and gentlemen, the Curio's... Thank You America, this was Curio Live, Goodnight."

We stood there waving and wiping our eyes. Jessie looked up between us as we held her hand.

"We did it... Great... What did we do?" God, I love her, she is so like Birch.

It took forever to get off stage, the shock was wearing off, and it had lit Birch's crazy fuse, and she was happy and giddy and smiling like a psychopath. We had our mics removed by a smiling team of stage hands, and the atmosphere was electric, as we walked out of the side entrance with Roni and Will, it was not over yet, the crew was already at work taking everything apart, they work all night, and within two days, it would all be gone.

Roni slipped her arm around my waist; I don't think I have ever seen her as happy. She took a deep breath of the fresh air.

"I have to say, I am very proud of you all, that is one hell of an achievement Abby, just do me one favour?" I looked at her.

"Yeah anything." She nodded.

"Abby, go home, rest properly, recover, and enjoy your family. I worry about you more than you think, and you look ill. Please, for me, rest."

"Roni I am fine." She smiled.

"Abby, I am a therapist, Fine to me, means Fucked, Insecure about it, No Energy left. Go home, be a mum, and recover, please do that for me." I smirked.

"Okay, I hear you." She kissed my cheek.

"Good, because Jemi is also very worried, take the pressure off her."

We made it into the lobby, and suddenly Danny was jumped, as Marci wrapped her arms round her.

"That was amazing, and you were so cool, I mean God, I would have died up there on that stage." She stood back, and smiled at Danny.

"I am really going to miss you; you are definitely moving to the UK, aren't you?" Danny looked a little sad, and nodded at her.

"I am going to live with my mums in the village, but we can still talk on video." I smiled.

"Or you can come visit us, we have room." Marci stared at me, and then looked at Danny.

"Your new mum... She is Abigail Jennifer Watson, have you any idea how cool and awesome that is?" Birch leaned in.

"Oh Sweetie, in real life, she is a scruffy bitch, who writes naked, stinks and never brushes her hair, but yeah, apart from all that, she is pretty cool." Danny laughed, and Marci stood with her jaw open; she looked at Danny.

"Your other mum, she is the coolest Curio ever." I looked at Birch, then Marci.

"Yeah, but she farts in bed and stinks the place out, doesn't she Danny?" Danny gave a huge giggle and nodded.

"Yeah, she does." I laughed as I looked at Birch.

"So, who is the stinky now?"

We hung out in the bar, and had drinks, Danny sat with Marci chatting about the event and blogging, and showing her all the pictures on her phone, it was nice to see. Jessie flaked out, and so we picked her up, Danny said goodnight to Marci, and we headed up to our room, ordered room service and just collapsed and ate finger food. It was over, well almost. But before all that, we needed sleep.

With well over double the money raised, we were all happy when we sat in the conference room, and Edwina gave a report on the event. It appeared the Fairbanks Foundation donated one hundred million dollars, tell me that was not guilt? To be honest it did not matter, Birch was happier than ever, we had our girls, and the Curio's had bonded again, and we felt as close now as we always had. Jessie was a huge hit with the media, her lovely open and frank manner on stage had won over the hearts of a nation. Danny was a huge hit, apparently, the UK press were writing up a storm about her, and the media gushed with pictures of Birch and Jessie, and Danny and me, and for once, it was nice to see articles that covered us in a positive and wonderful manner. The British Press saturated cover of a happy loving family. Maybe we did need to all take time out and reevaluate our lives, and make a few changes.

We all did another press conference where we were happy, and misbehaving, as the jokes and sarcastic comments bounced around between us and it felt nice. It was just gone noon when we packed our bags, and like a military operation, we all moved our things down to the buses.

I think I shook a million hands saying goodbye, as the buses moved to outside the arena, and we took one last look. The stage was almost gone, as teams of men moved black boxes into trucks. Aden, Gill, Morty, Alex and Creamy were staying on for three more days to oversee everything.

We headed to the bus to finish everything off, and Anita and Birch sat at the table with laptops and paid everyone, and as they did, I printed off the invoices, to add to my file, and we had yet another D&D success. It was busy and lively, fans came to the buses as we parked in a long row, and took on supplies for the journey back, and the guys talked and signed autographs, even Danny went out to meet fans, and stood with Marci, as she smiled for pictures and signed autographs. Birch and I sat at the window and watched her with big smiles.

Birch snuggled up next to me, as I watched out of the window, and she kissed my cheek with a giggle, and I turned to her. Those huge green eyes danced and sparkled in front of me, she had not changed much, she was older, and the signs of aging were there, but she was still so beautiful. I smiled as I stroked back her hair.

"I am alright Birch, I really am. I was tired, I thought I was losing you, and it took its toll, that's all. The fight for the girls and all the waiting got to me, nothing more. I promise, I am going to be fine, I need to get home and relax, and stay out of public life. Some time at home with you and the girls is all I need, it has been all I have ever needed, just you, and now our girls, I am so fine with that."

Birch smiled that amazing smile, the one she had that very first day, when I arrived at Uni in Manchester lost, and disorientated and knocked on her door, and she had opened it with that wonderful smile and said. "Hi Sweetie"

"Deads, I love you, I always have, but honestly, at times I get frightened, because you push too hard. You are my Lillian, but I am not ready to let you go yet, I got shit loads of crazy for us and the girls left to do." I smiled.

"I hope so, because the kids are busy, the bus is empty, and we are alone." Her eyes widened, and she bit her lip.

"Oh God Deads, will we ever have sex again now we have kids, because I really need to get laid?" I smiled.

"Quick, while it's quiet."

With squeals and giggles, she dragged me out of my seat and we ran to the end of the bus, and up the stairs laughing like little girls. Outside as the Curio's all gathered around the bus talking and smiling, and signing autographs, there was a sudden high pitched squeal.

"OH GOD DEADS, YESSSSSSSS!" Jenny looked at Jessie and rolled her eyes as everyone stopped and looked at the bus.

"Oh God, not them too?"

I lay back, happy and sweating, panting for air, and rolled over and looked up at her as she gasped, she lifted her head slightly and her eyes moved down to me, as she smiled.

"Oh Sweetie, that was heaven, I was honestly starting to think it would never happen again." I swallowed hard and crawled up her and flopped on her breasts, and her arms came around me. It was so nice, and I really needed that.

The door burst open and I looked up, Chloe stood panting and looking wild.

"Guys, I am getting fucking married." Birch lifted her head.

"Sweetie, we are screwing, we know, you are engaged for God's sake, can this not wait?" She shook her head.

"Not really, it is in four hours, and I need a dress." I lifted my head up, and frowned.

"Huh?"

Chapter 30

Weird Wedding.

Chloe nodded as we sat at the table, looking panicked.

"I was out with Baz, and we saw it, and we just thought all you guys are here, and it looked so perfect a place, so why not?" Edwina turned.

"Chloe, what about mum and dad, and Aunty Doris, you know dad has always wanted one of us to marry in church?" She nodded.

"I rang him, I told him the whole thing would cost him less than five hundred quid, and you being the genius you are, would live stream it. He was over the fucking moon and wired me the money." I could not help giggle as Edwina looked stunned.

"You have got to be fucking joking... After all the months of hell I went through, with him banging on about how it looks, and it is important to do it right, and you just fucking ring him up, and tell him he will save loads, and that is fucking it?" Chloe nodded with a huge smile.

"Pretty much... Yeah." Birch sniggered, we thought Edwina's head was going to explode, Edwina stared at her.

"You fucking rancid bitch, how the fuck do you get it so easy?" She smiled.

"Told you I was his favourite." Birch chuckled as she stood up, Deb's was watching all this fascinated. Edwina was on a role, and very red in the face. Deb's looked at me.

"It's fascinating isn't it, you know, the dynamics parents have with their children? It is very romantic don't you think?" Edwina turned and scowled at Deb's.

"If she marries him today, Deb's, I am tying you to the back of the bus, and dragging your ass up the road, with all the tins, and the just married sign. So shut the fuck up, you are a soppy bitch."

I put my head down and laughed, as Deb's looked scandalised. Birch turned and looked at Chloe, she gave a sweet smile.

"Chloe Sweetie, I hate to ask, but I am kind of curious, who are you having for bridesmaids, you know, there are a lot of kids?" She gave a huge smile.

"All of em."

"Huh?" She looked at Edwina.

"I want you to be my maid of honour." Edwina stared at her; her voice was suddenly really soft and quiet.

"Honestly, Chloe, I would love that." She exploded into tears, and hugged her. Chloe looked at me.

"I want you too, and Debs, Birch and Deli, and I want Anthony to give me away. Guys, it has to be all girls together." Edwina wailed into Chloe.

"I love you so much Sis." It was funny, although I did spot a bit of a problem.

"Chloe, that is most of the guest list, Luke and Michael will be the only ones in the congregation." She shrugged.

"Fuck it, it is my wedding." I nodded, yep, I could live with that.

"So, what are you wearing?" Chloe suddenly remembered, and looked panicked.

"OH FUCK!"

Deb's and me sniggered. Birch gave a squeal, and her eyes exploded with green delight, she threw up her arms with joy, and Danny jumped.

"SHOPPING!" Yep, those are the magic words of chaos. Birch went into full scale battle mode; she stood up and looked very serious.

"Okay guys, write this down. Deb's, we need a cake, Deli, talk to the chef about food, Luke, you need to sort a live stream, Anthony, you need a suit, Sweetie, you are always impeccable, but buy something new, you are going to be father of the bride. Michael, we need a big site, actually find some nice romantic desert. Anita, find that photographer that's been following us around, Jimmy, I want a car, a stylish one, with an open top, and ribbons. Tabs, we need music and booze. Deads, all the kids need measuring, and my Sweeties, grab your bags, we are going shopping... Well don't just stand there, we have just over three hours and the wedding of the century to pull off, we have a full tilt Curio wedding to organise, now get snappy." She clapped her hands, and then took a deep breath. Danny leaned into me.

"Mum, is all that even possible, I mean, it's a wedding, in almost three hours?" I turned and gave her a smile.

"Danny, if you think Curio Live was good, sit back and watch, the true power of the Curio's has just been unleashed by the crazy shopping fairy."

We exploded out of the bus, on an impossible task, in soaring heat, but this was Birch in her full glory. She was going at warp speed with one sole aim, this was for one of the girls, and that was all that mattered. Baz stood looking at me, and I looked up.

"Abby, what the fuck do I do?"

"Do you have a suit?" He shook his head looking panicked. I pointed.

"Catch up with Anthony, he is heading that way." Baz turned, looked, gave a nod, and then ran out of the bus. I smiled and grabbed Danny and Jessie's hand.

"Come on, we need to handle the shopping fairy, prepare to be educated."

We entered the wedding shop, like a twister blowing through Oklahoma, and the shop owner looked at us, sweating and panting, looking somewhat put off by what looked to her like middle aged degenerates and their brood. She looked down her nose at us, as we all packed in behind Birch.

"Can I help you?" Birch smiled.

"We need a wedding dress Sweetie, for her." She pointed to Chloe.

I am not sure she was that impressed, we were after all, dressed in torn jeans, and mainly old rock t shirts. She gave a sigh and turned to the rail, she looked Chloe up and down, and pulled one out, Birch's eyes were scanning the rails. You see, this is that moment of sheer wonder, that has indeed over the years, stamped her as the queen of the golden card. I slid back to Danny and leaned in, and quietly whispered.

"Wait for the click, and marvel."

This was a huge store, it was filled with lines of dresses for every occasion, it would take weeks to look at all of them, but Birch would scan it like an android from the future, and within her first few minutes, all of that data would be inside her brain. The assistant pulled a wedding dress off the rail and held it up. Birch looked at it, I could see her fingers coming together. She stared at it.

"Oh, Sweetie no, she is a Curio, not a hooker." I looked at Deb's. She shrugged.

"I am on the fence to be honest Abby, I mean, no money was involved, but hell, in all other departments Chloe has them beat."

Danny sniggered. Birch looked around the store, her fingers rubbed, and then SNAP! She was off.

"No, that will just not do, we need style and creativity, elegance and a little slutty. No, I want this to be perfectly her, and that can only mean.... THIS!" She pulled the dress from the rail, and we all gasped. I looked at Danny.

"Oh God, I am so wet for her right now." I realised, as I saw her cringe.

"Oh yeah, about that, probably not what a mum should say to her daughter... Sorry." I smiled, as she shuddered, Deli sniggered.

Chloe grabbed the dress, and headed for the changing room with Edwina, and Birch went into action, as she walked down the rails. She knew the colour of the dress and the design, and she swept along pulling things out and handing them back.

"Deads, Deb's, Deli, Danny, Liz, Jessie, Jenny, Helen. Hmm let me see, oh yes, Sammy, Gem, and me." She spun on her heels.

"And now for Edwina... Oh yes, this." She looked at the assistant.

"I take it, you take gold cards?" I stood back in awe; Danny looked mind blown.

"Mum what if they don't fit?" I smirked.

"They will... Perfectly, trust me, this is the magic shopping fairy, she is a goddess of the clothing rails... Oh God I am.... Yeah, not going to say that!"

Chloe stepped out in a white dress, it had tiny yellow and very pale blue, almost white flowers embroidered around it. It cut to show her breasts off nice, but tastefully. It was on the shoulder, but they could be slipped off slightly, and split right down the back, to the nape of her bum, so it came off easily, which let's be honest, it's Chloe, it will have to come off fast. Edwina exploded into tears.

I will not deny as she looked at me and smiled, I felt a lump in my throat, Deb's was in tears, I smiled as my eyes filled up.

"Oh Chloe, you look beautiful." She blushed a little.

"Baz will like it then; I want to look pretty for him?" I wiped my eyes and sniffled.

"Honestly, you look stunning."

She smiled; Danny wiped her eyes. Yeah, about that, what is it with women and wedding dresses, that just causes us all to explode into weeping piles of mush?

With Chloe looking like a princess, which actually looking back at all our other weddings, she has complained about. Well, actually not mine, she like the footman's attire, why so suddenly does she want to look all girlie? Hmm, I think Baz has found her more feminine side? We all trooped into the changing rooms, which with kids is not that easy. Jessie struggled, and I crouched down, and smiled.

"Just stand still, and I will slip it up." Birch sniggered.

"Been there, bought that T shirt."

"MUM!" Danny looked horrified.

"Oops, sorry Sweetie." Jessie looked at me as I pulled the dress up, and she turned so I could fasten it.

"Mum, do I speak English now?" I frowned as she turned round.

"Munchkin, you speak lovely English, you always have." She looked confused.

"Those yanks say Mommy, and I say Mummy, so does that make me English?" I giggled, oh hell, I need to keep her away from Chloe.

"Munchkin, I really love the way you say mum, when I hear it, I get very happy." She nodded.

"Good, I am staying English then." Oh God, she is melting my heart.

We all came out, and stood together, all the children had pale lemon dresses with very pale blue flowers, and all us grownups had very light blue with pale yellow flowers. Chloe smiled as we stood around her.

"God guys, you look beautiful, I want to cry." Edwina frowned, and looked at her.

"Who the hell are you, and what have you done with Chloe?" We all laughed, we did look good, I glanced at Danny.

"See, told you, goddess of the clothing rails." She smiled.

Jessie was dancing around and swinging her hips, not unlike Birch at our wedding.

"I look like a fairy." She did, Oh God, she looked so beautiful, she frowned.

"I don't have a wand." Birch smiled at me.

"I am just going into the changing room; I won't be a minute." I frowned at her, and looked at Jessie.

"I will get you one Munchkin."

We all looked at ourselves in the large mirror, and I cannot deny, we really looked good. Edwina came out from behind the curtain; she pointed behind her.

"We have leakage, there is even a tissue circle." Chloe snapped her head around.

"That fucking book is not coming to my wedding." I shrugged.

"Chloe, we left it at home."

"Huh?" I shook my head as Danny looked at me.

"What book?"

"DON'T READ IT!"

Birch sat in the changing room sobbing her heart out, she looked up with red blotchy eyes, blew her nose, and tossed the tissue on the floor. I gave a sigh.

"Birch, what on earth is wrong?"

"SHE LOOKS LIKE A FAIRY, AND SHE IS SO BEAUTIFUL, BWA HAH HAH!"

Suddenly the horror of my life to come was painting itself in my mind. Parties, birthdays, school plays, the list went on, honestly, I felt I should invest in a tissue company. I knelt down.

"Birch you are scaring the girls." Yep, those were my new magic words.

"You need to calm down, she does look beautiful though, doesn't she?"

Edwina sighed as she looked at Danny, both of us sat on the floor hugging each other bawling our eyes out.

"Kid, you have a lot to deal with, are you sure you don't want Luke and me to adopt you?" Danny gave a sigh, as she looked at the sobbing mess, her parents had become.

"Mum's, you are scaring the grown ups, this has to stop." We sniffled.

"Okay Sweetie... Alright love."

Changed back, eyes dried, bill paid and everything bagged, we called Flynn for the bus. Deb's shot off for a cake with Deli, they were also to meet up with Tab's and doing a booze run, I turned and looked at Birch.

"Florist." She smiled.

"Done Sweetie, I did it online." Wow she was amazing.

Bus one was wedding HQ, so we hung up all the dress bags, and waited for our raiders to return, and slowly the plan was coming together. As each one reported in, we ticked the boxes and added to our plan, we were building up a picture of the event, it was running like a military operation, and was precise, detailed, and we were ready to move out, until...

"Who has the rings?"

"HUH?"

"OH FUCK!"

Birch, Edwina and myself, came tearing out of the soaring heat, sweating, into the shop in our wedding gowns. We slid to a halt at the glass fronted till, and gasped for air. I held my chest, as I looked at the guy behind the counter, bright red in the face, and gasped out my words.

"We need wedding rings, two, gold, plain, you know, the usual?" He smiled politely.

"Of course, Madam, what sizes?"

"Huh?" I looked at Edwina and Birch, she shrugged.

"I have no idea Sweetie, I mean he has fat fingers, which let's be honest, probably explains why Chloe is always happy." I shook my head, yeah, that was disturbing.

"Birch why didn't you measure fingers?" She shrugged.

"Didn't think I had too, I mean, you have never complained, they are slender, but they touch your spot, I mean, I totally get measuring a clitoris."

"Not frigging yours, theirs?" Yep, I was panicked, sweating, and back on the road to cardiac arrest city. She understood.

"Yeah... About that!"

She turned and legged it out of the door. I stood staring and panting; Edwina was bent over gasping for air. The door burst open and Birch came belting back in, she reached across the counter puffing like a freight train.

"Sweetie, can I just borrow this?"

She snatched the ring gauge up, turned, hoisted up her dress, and legged it back out. I gave a gasp and tried to relax. I smiled at the assistant.

"We won't be a minute... We are English."

He stepped back, honestly, I did not blame him, for all he knew, we could have just escaped from a mental hospital. To be honest, after all these years, I am not completely convinced Birch was not once roommates with Rodney.

Ten minutes later, Birch staggered in through the door, she was red in the face, sweating, and her breathing was making a really weird wheezy noise. She staggered up to the counter, and slapped a piece of paper on the glass with the ring gauge, and looked at me.

"Heee... Heee... Heee... Heee.... Heee!" She put her head on my shoulder, and tried to keep breathing. "Heee... Heee. Heee!"

The man behind the counter picked it up, read it and smirked. He turned, and lifted up a tray filled with rings. I looked at the two plainest and pointed, as Birch gasped in more air.

"Those two please." He nodded.

"Yes Madam." He picked them up and grabbed two boxes.

"Will that be cash or card?"

Birch's head popped up from my shoulder, she looked at me, and there was real fear in her huge green eyes, as she gave a little terrified whimper. Yep, designer jeans, back pocket as always, and the problem with that was... I looked down at her dress. Birch looked utterly terrified, as she clawed at my shoulders panting for air.

"Heee!" I did try, honestly, but it came out as a snort!

Edwina gave a long sigh, reached into her dress top, and pulled out her card, Birch gave a huge gasp of relief, whimpered, and pushed her head back into my shoulder. I looked at Edwina's decent sized boobs.

"What else have you got in there?" She smirked, and lifted her eye brows.

"Only girls in knickers know the answer to that." I frowned at her.

"But I don't wear knickers." She smirked.

"And that... Is why you don't know?" She smiled a smug smile as her card was handed back to her.

We walked out of the ring shop, well, actually, we sort of half walked, half carried Birch, as she wheezed her way back to the coaches with us. The walk was a lot longer than I realised. By the time we got back, we were getting close to departure, everyone was dressed, Jessie had her wand, and at the side of the buses were two beautiful white, long open topped, American cars. No idea what make, they just looked really stunning. Jimmy had put ribbons on them, and draped white silk across the seat. Okay, it was nylon, but it looked like silk. Come on we are on a short time frame here?

We gathered outside, as we organised. Baz took a cab with Luke, who was to be his best man. Anthony stood proud looking radiant, as he pushed his white carnation into his button hole. Jessie looked at him.

"If you are now Aunty Chloe's dad, does that mean you dadopted her like mum did me?" He frowned, and gave his hair a side flick.

"Good God no, why do you think her father is on the other side of the world, even he is trying to hide the fact she is his daughter?" Jessie frowned.

"You should dadopt her, she looks like a princess." Anthony smiled.

"She does sweetness, and maybe I will." She gave an assured nod.

"You should."

Birch had finally recovered the use of her lungs, as Anthony lifted his arm and escorted Chloe to the car with a smile. Edwina, Birch, Debs, Deli and myself got in the car behind, and the kids were put on the bus. Yeah, this was becoming the strangest wedding I had ever been to.

We set off, and all that mattered was that Chloe was happy, Jimmy and Michael drove the cars, and four buses followed us. Yeah, see what I mean, weird wedding of the year? We arrived, and I will not deny, I looked at the venue and even being a writer,

I found the place hard to describe. Deb's looked at me with a confused look.

"Why is it pink, covered in glitter and tin foil stars, and is that bell tower cardboard?" Birch sniggered.

"No Sweetie, it is plywood."

I smirked, as I saw The Temple of Glistening Love, set back, and sandwiched between a pawn broker, and a bail bonds office. Jessie jumped off the bus and stared at it with awe.

"DO FAIRY'S LIVE HERE?"

Looking at the vicar stood waiting, I was convinced they did. Deb's leaned over looking concerned.

"Abby, I am not sure that woman is a woman."

Birch sniggered. I had so many questions, and there were way too many answers, as my mind boggled. The vicar waved and gave a huge bright red lipstick smile; she put her hand on her heart.

"Oh darlings, you look so beautiful and scrumptious, come my petals, come and be joined." Deb's looked at me, looking confused, and a little worried.

"Abby, why is her voice so deep?" Birch sniggered as she undid the door, Deb's looked really nervous.

We all climbed out, and helped Chloe straighten her dress, all the crew walked in ready, as the vicar took each of their hands and smiled, as she batted her very long glitter filled eyelashes. I looked up and the bell tower was swaying, I nudged Birch, she had her head down trying not to look, her hand came up to her mouth, and there was a squeak, as her shoulders shook. Danny took hold of my hand.

"Mum, this place is freaking me out." Birch squeaked; I tried so hard not to smile.

"It is okay sweetheart, as a writer you need to experience everything, and oh boy we will today." Birch squeaked again. Deli looked at Danny.

"Stick with me kid, I am frigging terrified." You know, suddenly Moon appears quite normal in my mind now, how weird is that?

The Temple of Glistening Love, was without doubt, the least likely place on a list I would compile to get married in. It was basically a bungalow, with a crooked handmade, wooden bell tower on it. The whole place was pink, and covered in glitter and shining tinfoil stars, even the path, mesh fence, and steps. The only alternative colour was brown, and that was the lawn, as it had not rained in weeks here. The kids lined up in pairs with little baskets of flowers, led by Sammy and Josh. Liz and Gem came next, then Helen and Jessie, then Danny and Jenny.

There was a space, as Edwina walked in front, followed by Deb's and Deli, then Birch and myself, followed by Anthony, who proudly held Chloe, as she beamed with happiness.

The vicar stood waiting, and smiling, as the light from the mirror ball, bounced off her glittering eyelashes, black sparkling dress, diamante choker dog collar, and heavily glittered long black hair. I am quite sure if you shone a laser on her, you will see her from space.

The altar was a pink coffee table, with a huge cardboard love heart on it, and two candles, which to be honest, looked like they belonged in Roni's kitchen cupboard. I leaned in to Birch.

"Love the altar, we must get one like that at home for your prayers."

Birch still had her head down and was vibrating like a tuning fork. It was not a big place; to be honest, it was a living room. There was forty of us including the crew and guests, of which Janet and family were some. They very kindly pressed themselves into the wall, to make room, which I thought was decent of them.

We were packed in like sardines, and we were shoulder to shoulder, pulling the kids back into us, and it was so hot. I felt the high humidity was probably just us all breathing out. I could feel the sweat running down my back, as I gasped for cool air.

Baz proudly took Chloe's hand. I mean let's face it, he was the only twat with enough space to move. Anthony would have stepped back once he had given her away, but apart from sitting on Michael's shoulders, there was nowhere to go. Reverend Diamonique of Divine.

Yep, we snorted... Loudly! Began, as her eye lashes flapped like birds' wings strobing the mirror ball, and if I am honest, she was more flamboyant, than Kevin's portrayal of Anthony, which even Anthony thought was too much. I did smile though, Chloe looked so happy, as Baz made his vows, and I teared up. I loved her so much, and to see her this happy, touched me very deeply.

Jimmy was stood behind, and watching between mine and

Deb's shoulders, he whispered very quietly.

"Hey Doll, is it me, or does that vicar have a bigger love lump down there than Baz?"

And Birch sagged as her earthly vibrations took over, and her head shook faster than a nodding dog. I leaned over, an inch, to be honest that was the only space I had, and whispered to her.

"You looked, didn't you?" Birch shook violently.

"Sweetie, I am going to pee." I smirked.

"Well, we are setting a lot of wedding firsts here, so go for it, and just piss on the carpet."

Chloe looked up into Basil's eyes, and smiled, as she gave her vow.

"Baz, Oh God, Baz, I love you, I really do. I know it was not always easy with me, but you have made me so happy, you have no idea of how happy I am with you. I promise, I will love you forever." She gave a radiant smile, as she slipped on the ring.

It started like a Mexican wave with Edwina, then Deli, Anthony, and Debs, and my eyes also filled with tears, as the Reverend Diamonique of Divine, pronounced them man and wife, and they kissed. And I mean all of them!

Diamonique in her divineness, grabbed Baz and snogged the living shit out if him, and then she did Chloe, I am sure there were tongues. I covered Danny's eyes, some things should not be seen, and I knew Danny would thank me for it later. Deb's shuddered like hell.

"I am getting the fuck out, and on the bus before she gets near me, Christ she is scary."

It took a few minutes to make enough space for Chloe to actually walk down the aisle. The sound and lighting crew were really decent, three of them climbed out of the window to free the pack. It was somewhat like those kids tile games, where you have nine squares and eight tiles, and you have to move them around to make a picture. After some wiggling and shoving, and grunts and pushes. We had a space wide enough for Chloe and Baz to walk out, Birch looked around panicked.

"Deads, I am dripping." I smirked.

"Don't tell the vicar that, you may get a surprise." She sniggered.

"Oh God Sweetie, save me." I pointed with half an arm.
"Ladies room."
She disappeared, at speed. Debs was staring at the door looking panicked, as the Reverend Diamonique of Divine, snogged the living shit, out of everyone leaving. Yep, even I was disturbed, I had to use the only weapon I had, I looked down at Jessie, and pointed to the vicar.
"She knows where all the fairies and sprites live."
I grabbed Danny and Debs, and followed behind Jessie, as she marched down to the vicar, and looked up in wonder.
"Do you really know where all the fairies live?"
We slipped past fast, and followed the pink brick, glitter filled path to safety. Birch came out of the lady's room, as the vicar grabbed Edwina, and snogged the shit out of her, I think she liked Edwina. Birch panicked and ran.
"Oh, fuck no, that is one communion I am defo avoiding."
She flew past the busy vicar. Weirdly enough, Luke, who was watching on, had a bigger lump than the vicar.
Pictures were posed for, the live stream was disconnected, yeah, Morty regretted that, as we left him all alone inside to pack up the tech, poor sod looked dishevelled and exhausted when he staggered out. We all stood as a group of Curio's in front of the world's weirdest wedding venue, and had our usual group picture taken.
One car was returned, and Chloe and Baz jumped in the other one, which had a lot of beer cans tied to it. To be honest, we could not find the skip at the arena, so opted to drag them out of town. We all jumped on the buses, and followed Chloe and Baz, to a flat large area of concrete, that was in the middle of nowhere, but surrounded by desert, and we set up to party Curio Style.

Chapter 31

Back to Normal-ish.

To most people, a lump of concrete is nothing, a waste, a sign of what was, to the Curio's, it is the basis to build something.

Four buses in a line, three folding tables, two pop up gazebos, and a nylon cloth, and we had a food service area, complete with wedding cake. Add to that, a laptop wired to a speaker, and tons of fairy lights, with a bus full of booze, with a back drop of mountains set in a desert, and we had a wedding reception. Linda and the kids drove out in their car, and joined us.

The music thumped, food was served, and the alcohol flowed, as we all danced and laughed, and had the time of our lives. I walked over to the bus to refill my drink, I was pretty sober which was unusual for me, and I turned and smiled as I saw everyone relaxed and enjoying themselves. Chloe danced up to me holding a bottle, with a huge smile, I pulled her into my arms, and she wrapped herself round me.

"Wow, I am so happy for you Chloe." She leaned back, with a huge smile, her eyes filled with happiness.

"Abby, I never thought I could be like this, but I remember you know, all those years ago, when you told me, I will know when the time is right."

I smiled, and was so happy to see her like this. It felt good to know that from now on, she would not be alone, because there have been times, when I know she lay in bed at night, feeling it.

"The time is right Chloe, and he is perfect for you, he is your Birch." She nodded and smiled.

"I know, we will still be having breakfast chats, it won't change Abby, I will always be there for you." I leaned in and softly kissed her lips, I knew that, she had always had my back.

"There, I kissed the bride, and Chloe, it was such a gay kiss." She giggled

"Thanks Abby, for always being there and talking, I love you so much, in a completely straight way of course." I hugged her hard.

"Chloe, you deserve this, and I will always be there for you, as I am the others."

We partied hard, Anita and Tabs were drunk and making out, Edwina was slow dancing with Luke, the crew were dancing with each other, and we had a back drop of mountains, it was perfect. I let Chloe go feeling happy. I walked back to the table for a bottle of beer; Deli was watching with a smile.

"Hey miss lonesome, all these men, and you are not dancing." She gave a weak smile.

"I have kids to watch." I frowned.

"Not really, all the kids are on our bus tonight, bus three is the shag bus, so we moved them all out. Suki and Rachel are watching the kids, go have fun, and you know, a free night, horny crew, you might get lucky." She gave a sigh.

"God, I could use it, but you know Abby I am still married." I shook my head.

"You are bonkers, Christ Deli, he was banging the shit out of Candy with a K when I last saw him. Deli we are two thousand miles from home, and as they say, what happens in Vegas, stays in Vegas. Deli, you will have to move on eventually, and a little shameless body rubbing is a pretty good start." She gave a laugh.

"I love you Abby, I have missed you so much, it has been nice us all being together again." I patted her shoulder.

"Go on, we got the kids covered, go sate that libido."

Danny walked up and smiled, I pulled her into a hug, and looked down as she looked up at me.

"You know Mum, you lot are insane, how did we even do all that?" I shrugged.

"It is what we do, we pull together, solve the problems and do it, although, I take no responsibility for the church, that was all Chloe." She giggled, and hugged me hard.

"I am tired, I might go chill in bed for a bit." I kissed her head.

"Okay, I will be up in a bit. Where is your sister?" She pointed.

"Over there with mum making sand castles."

I looked over, and saw Birch having the time of her life, explaining the correct way to build a sand fortress. Danny slid off to bed, I lifted my bottle and leaned back watching them play together. Jessie was loving it, she plopped out her bucket, well it was an ice bucket really, and smiled, Birch was delighted, she had wet the sand to help it stick. Jessie stood up with great pride as she held out her arm, and my blood ran cold.

"Wow Mum, look at the size of this worm, it is a monster." It rattled.

I kid you not... The scream from Birch possibly broke the sound barrier, and was heard on Mars. She fled at high speed into the desert, with tears in her eyes and shaking her wrists screaming like a deranged psychopath. I froze with terror as Jimmy smiled, and walked slowly towards Jessie.

"Oh Fuck, I hate snakes... Jessie, my precious, just hold it there, that is a good girl, don't let go sweetheart, and stand still." She smiled.

"He is big Uncle Jimmy; I have never seen a worm this big." Jimmy swallowed hard.

I dropped my bottle, and moved slowly, and watched filled with terror, as Jessie clung to the rattle snake, its tail flicking around and rattling like castanets. My heart was in my mouth and I was shaking, as I moved slowly closer, slowly falling apart, I could feel the tears burning my eyes. Birch was screaming at the top of her lungs.

"Help her, help her."

The chef walked past us really quickly holding a knife, he walked right up to Jessie, grabbed her wrist, and then with one swift movement, he cut the wriggling body off, and carefully took the head out of her hand, he looked stern.

"We do not play with snakes!"

Jessie burst into tears. I ran and snatched her up, and looked at the chef with tears in my eyes, my lip was trembling, and I was shaking violently.

"Thank you, Thank you so much." He smiled.

"My pleasure, she is cute, but out here is dangerous."

I nodded, and squeezed her hard as she cried into me. I looked at Birch, she had fallen completely apart, and was on her knees weeping. I was pissed off, and it showed.

"Birch, there are even more snakes out there, get your arse back here, you daft bitch."

I turned, and walked back to the bus, clinging to Jessie, shaking and weeping, as I held her as close as I could. Deb's and the nannies were gathering the other children, and shepherding them back to the bus. I took Jessie up to my room, and sat on the bed as I cradled her in my arms.

"Jessie that was not a worm, it was a snake, and it could have hurt you. You must be more careful; this country has nasty things living out there which will hurt you. I could not handle that, not ever. I will be glad when we are back home, the worms there are safe." She snuggled into me.

"I am sorry mummy; I did not know." I put my head down on hers, and rocked her.

"It is all right Munchkin, just stay out of the sand."

I put her to bed with a kiss, Suki was getting the others ready, and then went downstairs. Birch was shaking violently as she stared at me, her eyes filled with tears, she looked the most scared I have ever seen her.

"Is she alright?" I gave a sigh and walked over to her, and pulled her into my arms and she burst into tears.

"I am so sorry, I froze and panicked, I was so terrified." She shook as she wept, and I pulled her close.

"She is fine Birch, the chef saved her, so did Jimmy. Birch that can never happen again, no matter what the danger, we go in and we deal with it and protect our kids." She sobbed and shook.

"I am so sorry Deads, I was so frightened she would get hurt, I almost died."

I could not be angry, how could I, my whole body froze up in fear? The truth was, I could not have helped her, I did not know what to do, and even I wanted to be as far away from the snake as possible, they terrify me. It was a lesson to be learned for both of us, and our first big step into parenting.

The following morning, we packed up, but no kids were allowed off the bus until Jimmy and Luke had assured me that everywhere was safe. We all moved back to our own buses and began the long drive back. It took us four days stopping off, to let the kids have fun, before we arrived at the airport, and loaded Curio One to fly home.

Jimmy arranged a van at Heathrow for when we landed, we had a lot of boxes stored in the buses from Danny and Jessie's home to get through customs. Janet took care of the rest, her team packed what was coming back here, the rest was to be sold at auction.

Coming home was nice, I had missed it, and it was snake free. Jessie had settled down and was her usual normal self, and everyone slipped back into their own routines, although most weekends, we were all together now, and the bond of closeness we shared, felt closer than ever.

Deli appeared brighter and happier, she had hooked up with a lighting guy called Tom, and had most definitely sated her desires. Danny and Jessie unpacked their boxes, and their room filled with more of their own stuff. I helped Danny sort out her wardrobe, she had some nice stuff, it was a shame it did not fit me. It was nice to see pictures of her parents on the wall, and she framed some of Birch and Me and hung them alongside.

Deb's and Anthony were busy as the summer events kicked in, which actually became great fun, because we had kids to take, and Jessie had a wild time. The village appeared to approve of us as parents, and we got some very lovely comments. It is funny really how things change, and how opinions move with the times.

I spoke to Marci's parents, and they arranged for her to come visit on the last week of August, so Danny was really excited, and for a little added extra fun, we decided we wanted to take the kids camping, but after the snake incident, I was not sure. Birch solved the problem by buying three tents, and Deb's and Edwina with the kids joined us at Sunny Bank on the second week of August. Chloe and Baz came down and stayed in the VW, which over the years Baz has almost rebuilt, and Mum and Patrick came down with us, although they stayed in the house.

Showing the kids Sunny Bank was a huge thrill, I took my car with Danny, I wanted Deli to come, but she had booked a hotel in Brighton. Once we arrived at Sunny Bank, the kids went wild, they loved it, and within an hour in the house, seeing all of the pictures on the wall, Jessie wanted bunches, and so suddenly, there was a little blonde/brown haired version of baby Birch, tearing around the place.

We pitched the tents in the back garden, next to the swing, which Luke and Jimmy helped repair with new chain, and we slept under the stars as the temperature soared. We made a fire pit, toasted marshmallows, and Jimmy brought along his guitar. I sat in the darkness, lit by firelight, holding Birch's hand, and we sang our hearts out.

It was so much fun and I loved it, and Birch appeared happier than I have ever seen her. I think in a way, this was her way of showing her grandfather her children, and it was important to her that she did. I spent a lot of time sat with a camera taking pictures of her with either Jessie or Danny, she was such a good mum, and so caring, and I could see her love flowing out of her into them, it was so lovely to see. I knew how that felt, and how incredibly special it was.

We did a few days in Bude with sandcastles and seagulls, but no chips on the beach, and we swam in the river, Jessie had big arm bands even though she could swim, Birch was taking no chances.

We came home exhausted, happy, and closer than ever. I flopped on my bed with a happy sigh, and just relaxed. Birch came in smiling, and lay at my side.

"Sweetie, the kids are swimming with Deli." I looked at her.

"Really?" She nodded, and I sat up and pulled off my top.

"Quick hurry." She gave an excited giggle, and undid her pants.

"Oh, God's Deads I need this, I love them I do, oh God, I love them so much, camping is great, but sharing a tent all the time, is not easy being hands off. I need so desperately to climax." I jumped on her.

"Stop frigging talking and kiss me." I pushed her back into the bed.

"MUM, MY TOWEL FELL INTO THE POOL!" I gave a sigh, and rolled off her.

"OH fuck!" I grabbed my pants.

"Okay Munchkin, I am coming." Birch gave a long sigh.

"I wish I frigging was." I patted her leg.

"Birch we will get there, it just takes time to balance things out." She smirked.

"Get there? We have not been frigging there for weeks." I sniggered, as I pulled on my top and looked at her, she opened her legs wide.

"It's wet, and waiting." I bit my lip.

"I know, oh Birch please, don't tease me, I want it so badly, I really do." I jigged on the spot.

"MUM!" I closed my eyes.

"I am coming." I turned, and ran out of the room, and Birch gave a sigh.

That night, I sat at my desk, once again answering messages, when Birch snuck quietly in, she gave me a big smile.

"Sweetie, they are asleep."

I jumped out of my seat mid response, and yanked off my vest, and starting undoing my pants.

"Thank God for that, finally."

I jumped on the bed, and dragged off the duvet, Birch jumped on me and we locked lips and started kissing, I was so hot and so wet, as she pulled the duvet over us.

"Oh yes baby." A little voice spoke, and I closed my eyes.

"I fell out of bed and bumped my head." Birch groaned into my shoulder. Then rolled off me.

"Oh Sweetie, come here, and let me look at it."

"Can I sleep with you mum; you can hold my boobs to stop me falling?" I rolled over, and pushed my face onto the pillow. Honestly, I wanted to cry.

The following morning, I woke to find Danny curled in front of me. I lay there feeling her warmth, she was fast asleep and looked like a sleeping angel. I looked back, there was no Birch or Jessie. I needed a pee, so very slowly slid out of bed and headed to the toilet. I walked back into the room, and Danny was sat up rubbing her eyes. She blinked and looked at me.

"What's that smell?" The wave of coldness suddenly ran over me.

"Oh shit... It has started, she has gone full on Felicity, and now has an accomplice."

Danny frowned as I turned for the door, in the hall it was stronger, I walked slowly sniffing towards the stairs, Danny followed me still rubbing her eyes. I reached the top of the stairs, and Deli's door opened, she leaned her head out.

"Oh God, she has started, hasn't she?" That was all the conformation I needed.

We made our way down to the kitchen, and yep, the mad lady was stood naked in a red apron, stirring a huge pan, Jessie was sat on a towel leaning over the cooker watching, she noticed me.

"We are making Jam." She frowned.

"What is Jam?" I walked in.

"They call it jelly in the states."

I walked over with Danny, who appeared quite interested. We peered over the edge of the pan, Danny pulled back fast, looking like she was going to Yerk.

"What is that awful smell?" She looked as green as whatever the hell Birch was cooking, Birch smiled with pride.

"It's sprouts Sweetie." I stepped back, as the horror engulfed me.

"Birch, you cannot make jam out of sprouts, it will taste like fart sandwiches."

Chloe sniggered, and I turned around, and she was sat at the far end of the long table with a coffee.

"Why are you sat over there?" She smiled.

"Because your lunatic wife is over there, cooking farts in a pan."

Is it weird that made complete sense to me? I grabbed two coffees, and joined her with Danny, and the three of us sat watching, sipping our drinks. Birch was happily stirring when Deli appeared and did not notice us.

"What the hell is that?" Birch smiled with Jessie, and they both said.

"We are making jam!" Chloe shuddered.

"God, it is scary when they sync." Deli noticed us, and looked at all three of us.

"What the hell is she cooking?"

"Sprouts!" She furrowed her brow.

"But it's jam, well it is supposed to be?" Birch looked up, and gave a big smile.

"Sweetie, we can put it on the leftover turkey and have Christmas dinner sandwiches." Chloe turned to me with a strange look.

"Is it me, or for the first time in years, did she make some sort of fucked up sense over jam?"

I was not sure, just the concept of Brussel sprout jam evaded any reasoning I had. I looked at Danny, and she shook her head looking terrified.

"I am not eating them." I grinned at her.

"It's okay sweetheart, we already have a test subject... Her apprentice." We all sniggered, as Jessie happily watched, Deli joined us at the table with a coffee.

"Is it me, or since you got the kids, has she got weirder and weirder?" I shook my head.

"No, she has always been weird, I think she is like a magnet, you know, weird sticks to her and just builds up. Let's be honest, we have just got back from the states, and that place is a continent filled with weird, she is probably at triple strength now. Never forget who she works with, they sort of top her up, but America, oh Christ, we have some strange times coming."

The thing about having children in our life, was that in a way, old familiar patterns appeared, like, school uniform shopping. As is the case in Britain, all schools now have mandatory uniforms with embroidered logo badges on them, and so once we had done all the paperwork with the local education authorities, we got a letter to tell us that our children had been accepted into Oxendale Academy.

When I was there it was a junior and high school, now apparently it is an academy? The two schools had been combined together on the same site, and some of the railings that had separated them in my time, had been removed. The school now had one head teacher to rule over the whole school complex, which felt sort of weird, and to be honest, a little disappointing. The uniform was completely different, the green of my day, was now dark blue, although the badge was still a little similar.

We were given a sheet of all the required uniform, and one afternoon we headed out to the shopping centre in Oxendale, and the school uniform shop. Danny actually sulked.

"I don't get it, I just don't, in the states we could wear what we like, I have a whole closet filled with cool clothes." She pouted as she looked at the deep blue uniform. I gave a sigh.

"Danny, this is how it is here, they think that making you all dress the same, it reduces poverty discrimination, and helps everyone fit in. Trust me, no one likes it, it is the one thing every kid has in common."

Birch lifted up a pleated skirt, and gave a big smile, and her eyes danced.

"Sweetie, I really like these, they are very feminine, and cute." I sneered.

"She is wearing pants." Danny nodded; Birch frowned.

"But Sweetie, she will look adorable in this." I looked at her.

"It's pants, I wore pants, Deb's wore pants, Edwina wore pants, and Birch, Chloe wore skirts." Her eyes widened, and she dropped the skirt.

"Oh Christ, she is definitely wearing pants then." I winked at Danny, and she smiled.

Why the hell does everything have to have an embroidered logo on everything? Even the pants had a blue stripe on the pockets? I checked the list just to make sure there was no mandatory logo required on the underwear. When I was at school, I had a school tie, and a badge on my blazer, that was it, but these days, every single item of uniform had one on, and costs five times more than the plain stuff, it was ridiculous.

The list is mental, as we walked around the store ticking things off with Jessie and Danny, who was slowly coming round to the idea. There were other girls her age in the store getting the same uniform as us, and I think it helped her see that everyone else was okay with it. Jessie was not thrilled about it either, especially the blazers. She stood looking in the mirror.

"This looks stupid, fairies don't wear uniforms." I sighed, as I sat on the floor looking up at her, as I checked it over.

"If you think about it Munchkin, a tutu, shiny top and wings is a uniform, I mean, every fairy wears those." She puzzled it out in her brain.

"Can I go to fairy school then?" I sighed, and Birch leaned over her straightening her blazer.

"Not until you are eleven Sweetie, those are the rules, just like Harry and Wizard School."

Yep, she was sold, she would go to school, and qualify for fairy school when she was old enough. Loaded up with uniforms, files and stationery, and five hundred quid less in the bank, we loaded Petal and then went shopping again, it is not easy to stop Birch on a roll. We had a fun day eating ice cream, looking in windows, and generally pissing about as normal, and arrived home, having dropped off Birch at the retreat, loaded with bags.

I spent two hours sat on my bed sewing in name tags, and then hanging all the new uniform on hangers. I was just finishing up when Chloe came in looking white faced, and freaked out.

"Abby, something really fucked up is happening, and honestly, I am panicked." I gave her a frown.

"What is it?" She swallowed hard.

"You have to see it to believe it." I frowned; she looked really terrified.

Okay, so I was worried, I slipped off the bed and followed Chloe, she walked to the kid's bedroom door and pointed.

"They are immune."

"Huh?"

I leaned around the door, and Danny was sat crossed legged on the bed, and was reading the Snow Queen to Jessie. I smiled; they looked so cute. I walked in and gave a smile as I sat down on the end of the bed, Danny looked up with a huge beaming smile.

"I really love this, it is an amazing story, oh Mum, Jessie loves it, and so do I." Jessie nodded.

"The Snow Queen is trapped and Nightshade is going to help her, it's banging." Yeah, I really need to keep her away from Chloe. I smiled as I looked at Danny.

"This is a very special story; I wrote it for Birch a long time ago." She gave a big smile.

"It is beautiful, you should publish it." Chloe leaned in the doorway.

"No one wants that, there are not enough trees to make the tissues, and that thing is cursed, it should be sealed in a crypt and hidden away forever." Danny did not understand.

"But why, this is the most beautiful story I have ever read, Aunt Chloe, you should read it, it is captivating, and it just fills me with warmth." Chloe frowned.

"You are fucked up, holy crap, you are going to be a writer, and then there will be two of you." I giggled.

"Danny, whenever Birch reads this, she cries the house down, because as she says, it is so beautiful, and it touches her deeply. It freaks everyone else out." She smiled a lovely smile.

"I get that, I do, you wrote this to her, I would imagine if anyone ever wrote something this beautiful for me, I would be the same. Mum, your love of her really shows, and I think that is so special. This is a brilliant book."

My eyes filled with tears as I saw the sincerity within her, and I smiled. Just knowing someone else understood that, touched me deeply. Chloe ran down the stairs panicked.

"Holy fuck, Danny broke Abby, if she ever writes anything, we are all fucked, I am going buying salt and matches."

I stood at the side of the doorframe next to their room, and listened, as Danny read the book to Jessie, and tears streamed down my face. It sounded so beautiful to hear it read out loud, and everything I had ever thought or felt about Birch came flowing back through me. They loved it, my kids loved it, and that meant more to me than anything else that had ever happened to me.

Birch arrived home from work, and was confronted with a panicked and terrified Chloe, who stood on the stairs and waved a shaking finger up towards the kid's room.

"Birch, you need to get up there, they broke Abby with that fucking cursed book. That thing is evil, and you need to destroy it, they broke the fucking author, those kids are fucking demons."

Birch nodded, dropped her bag, and ran up the stairs, to our room in utter panic. She arrived in our room, and I was sat on the bed surrounded by tissues, bawling my brains out. I looked at her, and cried more.

"THEY LOVE MY BOOK, AND UNDERSTAND IT'S BEAUTY, AND I HEARD DANNY READ IT OUT LOUD, AND IT WAS SO BEAUTIFUL!" Birch sat at my side, and took my hand.

"Oh Sweetie, I get that I do, but what we need to do, because it is so beautiful, is get naked while they are reading, and give each other lots of oral pleasure, until we all feel better." I nodded and sobbed.

"Okay baby." Birch gave a gasp of hope, and started undoing her blouse.

"Frigging finally!" She pulled at her blouse, and Danny walked in hugging the book.

"Mum, are you alright, we heard you crying?" Birch flopped back on the bed, with a groan.

"I was so frigging close. Chloe is almost right, it is me who is frigging cursed, and it is going to be at least ten years before they move the fuck out, oh God, I am going to wither and die, devoid of the remembrance of pleasure, it's been so long."

Chapter 32

Parenting.

The friendship between Danny and Jenny grew over the summer, and I was pleased to see it, in a way, it reminded me of me and Deb's when we were younger. Jenny would come over most days, and she would bring Helen with her, and she would play with Jessie. I felt it would help Danny overcome some of her homesickness, as she missed her school friends in the states.

She spoke to Marci a lot, and they wrote to each other long emails about what was going on in their life. I loved that Danny printed them out, and kept them in a file, and on those days, she felt the pangs of home, she would read them. As parents, I suppose we really want to do right by our kids, but I was always aware that by adopting them, we uprooted them, from their natural surroundings, and that meant they were torn from their friends.

One afternoon a package arrived for Danny, and we had no idea where it had come from, but it was clearly addressed to her with a letter, which revealed it was from Old Mr Fairbanks. The package contained her parents' ashes, and it brought back a lot of pain for her. She spent the rest of the day sat on her balcony, and did not even want to see Jenny. I talked to Birch on the phone, and she told me, just be gentle and not push anything.

I walked into her room, and out through the patio doors, and sat on the floor, mainly because I could not sit on the rails, it made me dizzy. I crossed my legs and looked at her, she had been crying.

"How are you?" She wiped her eyes on her sleeve.

"It hurts today, I really do not know what to do." She looked at me, her eyes were red.

"What would you do, I am American, as was my dad, I do not understand things in this country?" I gave a nod, it made sense.

"If this was a story, like the Snow Queen, what do you think the queen and Nightshade would want?" She swallowed hard, and looked over the balcony.

"They would want to stay together." I smiled.

"Okay, so whatever you do, keep them side by side." She sniffled, and nodded her head.

"They would want to be closer like you and mum; they did love each other like you two do." I really understood that, we had always said to each other in life and death we would not be separated.

"So, Danny, the way I see it, you need to find a special place, which is a single place, where they can be together forever." She nodded.

"They would like that, but where?" I gave it a moment.

"Okay. Listen, when my dad, Edwin was a kid, he lived on Manor Road, just four doors up from Hatty, that is where he grew up. He was seven when his baby sister was born, and she was called Phillipa. She married, but at that time, could not afford a house around here. My granddad died young, so when Phillipa was born, she grew up there, and her mum, my gran, let her and her husband live there with her. Your mum was also born in that house, and I mean in the living room one cold winters night, just like her own mother. My dad often told me the story of getting out of bed, and coming down to find out he had a sister. He loved his little sister a lot, and he also told me of the day she rang him to tell him your mother had been born at his old house."

She nodded, and wiped her eyes, and breathed in, I could see the blue of her eyes under her fringe.

"I knew she was born in England; I never knew it was in Wotton. I suppose in a way; Wotton is our family home?" I nodded.

"It is, we have a long line of Watson's going back to the early Victorian age, I will ask mum, I know she has a family tree somewhere. So, you see, this village is a place she belongs to, she was born here. I think to place her here is a good thing, and if your dad wants to be close to her, considering his views on his family, I think he would like to be here too, the only question is where?" She looked at me.

"I remember mum telling me, before I was born, they came here to a wedding, which I think was yours here. She never said

Wotton, she just said her home village. She told me her and dad walked on the hill and in the woods, and it was so special to show him the places she and her mum played growing up with her brother." I smiled.

"Well then, we can get those answers, let's go and talk to her mums' brother." I stood up and offered her my hand, she looked confused.

"How?"

"Danny, he is my dad, I talk to him all the time."

I took Danny into my room, and checked my watch, taking into account the time difference, I worked out he would be up, so I sat at my desk, and sent a text, then opened my program, and watched for the green dot. When it came on, I clicked it, the tune played and there he was smiling.

"Hi Dad, we have a riddle, and only you can solve it." He waved to Danny, and she smiled.

"Abigail, anything, what can I do for you?"

"Dad, we got Amanda and Peter's ashes today, and Danny is upset. She told me her mum took Peter walking around here when she came to my wedding, and spent some time showing him all her favourite spots. I don't suppose you know the places they went?" He sat back in his chair.

"Let me think now. As I recall she was pregnant at the time and did not know it, but she told me she would walk each day to exercise, it was something she did a lot of at home." Danny looked at me and nodded, she knew that.

"I know they walked along the canal a little, and they went for a picnic in Dursley Woods. If I am right, the day before your wedding, I went up to see Bradley to sort the final arrangements, and she asked for a lift, she really wanted to show Peter her favourite spot on top of the heath. Yes, I remember her telling him, as a child she sat up there a lot, she felt free and at peace there." I smiled.

"Thanks Dad, you have been a huge help." Danny smiled. We talked to my dad for quite some time, and finally said goodbye, and I sat back in my chair.

"The top of the heath is where the day we first got Petal, we drove up to, so we could get away from the village, it is also where Birch asked me to marry her, for me, it is also a very special place, would you like to see it?" She nodded.

"Yes please, I want to see mums special place." I gave her a smile, and leaned over and hugged her.

"Right, I tell you what we will do. It is a nice day, so let's make a surprise picnic, and when Birch gets here, we will all go up to the top of the heath, and make it a special place for you too." She looked a lot happier as she nodded.

When Birch got home, Petal was already on the drive, and packed. She changed her clothes and jumped in, Chloe and Baz joined us with Deli and her kids. We made our way to the small track at the top, and parked up, and then walked onto the heath. It was roasting hot, we sat a little way off May's tree, but Birch and myself went over to check it, and I laid some wild flowers the girls had picked at its base.

I told Danny the story of May, as we all sat and ate, and how we got permission off Farmer Sutton, who owned the land, and had planted the tree in memory of her, and she loved it.

"Do you think he would let me plant a tree here too, this was her favourite place?" Birch shrugged.

"It will not hurt to ask; I will ring him later to find out."

After we ate, I took Danny by the hand and led her to a small flat place, that jutted out from the hill, I grabbed her shoulders and moved her round, and then looked at her and smiled.

"It was probably about two feet higher, because it had snowed a lot, but there Danny, right where you are standing. That is the place Birch went down on one knee, and asked me to marry her, and I was right here where I am stood now." She smiled and looked around, and then realised.

"Oh lord, this is where Nightshade told the Snow Queen he loved her." I smiled, she was such a clever girl, Birch stood watching with tears in her eyes. I pointed.

"It is so strange, because I wrote that before Birch did it, and in this particular case, instead of me taking life and writing it into a story, the story became real life. The sun came up right there, and it just made everything sparkle and twinkle, exactly the way I wrote it, like a sea of shimmering diamonds. I stood here Danny lost for words, and that was all I could think, my dream came true." Danny gasped in amazement.

"Oh Mum, that is the most amazing thing I know of." Birch

wiped her eyes as she looked at me.

"Oh Deads, I love you more than I did then, and I love how the story has woven into real life. I never realised until now, but yes, I see it, I completely see it."

"The crazy thing was, I had bought a ring, and hoped she would mistake it, because I never thought for a second Birch would actually do the same. I had sat for hours over the months wondering what it would be like to be asked by Birch, so much so, I added it to my story. Little did I know, that days after I sent it to be published, she would predict what I had written, even now it gives me the chills to see fiction and real life collide." Jessie looked up at Birch.

"Are you going to kiss her now, because you should, you know?" Birch looked down at her stood in the long grass.

"Yes Sweetie, I am." Jessie nodded.

"That is a good thing."

She scampered off to Chloe and Baz, who were walking hand in hand. Birch came over and wiped her eyes, Danny walked over to May's tree, which was really big now, and Birch slipped in close.

"I meant it with all my heart then, and I still mean it with all my heart now Deads. I will love you forever, and beyond, you are my Lillian."

"And you are my Celia, and you always will be, I could never love another like I love you." She kissed me softly and my knees trembled, she broke apart, and my heart fluttered.

"Oh God Birch, I need us to find a frigging way to screw, and soon." She smiled.

"We will, I am already planning, and have something in mind." I smiled.

"Good, because I just soaked my jeans with just a kiss, that is how pent up I am getting." She raised her eyebrows.

"Wow my kisses are that good?"

"Yes, and I am also that desperate."

She chuckled, and pulled me into a hug. With our arms round each other, we walked slowly over to Danny, she had walked about forty paces from May's tree, and she stood looking out over Wotton. Just below her, Deli was throwing a frisbee with the kids. Danny turned and looked at me.

"I just worked out, because I can see our house from here, so if

I can plant a tree here, I will be able to see it every day from my room.”

Her eyes were sparkling, as she looked down at our house in the distance. We stood behind her, and I placed a hand on her shoulder.

“Feel better now that you know what you want to do?” She lifted her hand and touched mine.

“Yes, I do, thanks mum, I needed you today.” Oh God, she melts my heart.

“HEY, I FOUND A WORM, LOOK.” She pointed, everyone turned and looked.

“DON’T PICK IT UP!”

Chloe and Baz came up the hill smiling, I threw Chloe the keys.

“The picnic hamper is packed, take Petal back, we are going to walk. Go have some noisy time.” Chloe smiled and looked at Baz.

“See, that is why I love her so much.” Birch turned to me and pouted.

“Oh God Deads, I wish I had thought of that, I want noisy time too.”

“What, are my kisses not as good?” She gave me a big smile, and her eyes twinkled.

“Oh, they are really good, I just want more in other places.” I laughed as we started to walk towards Manor Road.

When we reached the main road, I took Jessie’s hand, and we walked slowly down until we came to the bottom, and stopped outside number seven. I looked at Danny and she looked at the old house.

“That is it, that is the house your mum was born in, literally on the other side of that window, is where she entered the world.” Jessie pointed.

“My mom was born there?” I nodded; she looked up at the house.

“My mom did good marrying my dad, his house was a lot bigger than this.”

When we got back, Birch phoned old Mr Sutton, and after explaining the story, he realised who Amanda was, and was sorry to hear of her passing, but praised us for taking her children in. He had no problems with us planting a tree, as he made it clear,

no one would ever touch that land with a brick. With his seal
of approval, plans were made, and two days later, which was
Saturday, we all trooped back up the heath, with a spade, a large
Beech tree from Norman, and some compost, and dug a hole
ready.

Deb's and Edwina joined us with Deli, and Anthony took an
hour off, and Luke, Jimmy and Baz helped dig a really big hole.
Chloe was not sure, as she looked at the size of it.

"Guys, it is ashes isn't it, and I mean, we are not like putting a
whole body in here, are we?" Birch rolled her eyes.

"Sweetie, trees like big holes." Edwina smirked.

"It will frigging love Chloe then."

We all laughed as Birch unwrapped the large root bag on the
roots, and placed the tree in, and held it, while we followed her
instructions and added a little soil. Danny opened the package,
and scattered the ashes of her dad in first, and with Jessie's help,
she spread them around. Then she poured in her mum, and
spread them evenly over her dad. Jessie picked up a big bit.

"What do you think that is, an eye or a finger?" Chloe gave a
violent shudder.

"Wow kid, you are really messed up, and creepy as hell. Don't
play with the dead, it's messed up."

She dropped it back in the hole, and we carefully filled in the
hole, with the rest of the soil and the compost, and patted it down
to compact it. When it was done, I looked round.

"Does anyone want to say anything. I think words should be
spoken." I looked at Birch. She gave a nod.

"Everyone, join hands around the tree."

I took Danny's hand, and held Jessie's with the other, and Birch
took Jessie's other hand, as we formed a circle around the tree.
Birch put her head down. We all took a moment.

"Death is but the passing from one form to another, and as we
gather, and we place these earthly remains of Amanda and Peter
back into the earth from whence they came. Know, that their
spirit will linger within the love that we hold for them, and keep
them ever close to us. The circle of life is complete, so may their
spirits be blessed, and may they shine upon their two children,
and keep them safe always. Rest safe in peace with our ancestors.
Blessed be."

Danny shook, and I pulled her close, as she buried her face in me, I looked at Birch who had tears in her eyes.

"Thanks, that was really beautiful."

I held Danny close as she sobbed into my chest, and everyone put their heads down, and gave her a moment of privacy. I looked down at her as she really sobbed, and it broke my heart to see it, but I knew it was doing her good to let it all out, somehow, I think, she had been bottling it up for a while.

The others separated, and left us alone, Birch walked Jessie off, and we were left alone, and I held her close.

"It is good to cry Danny, it is good to show your grief, and also all the love in your heart for them. But also remember, you must never forget the joy, and all the happiness you had with them, for both of them are very important as you move forward in this life. They will always be with you in your heart, never forget that, for they loved you deeply."

In a way, it is cruel how life treats us, today Danny's pain reminds me of the price her and her sister have paid for the joy in my own heart. Both of them came into our lives and have changed them, and I feel such love and such happiness having them with us, and yet there in the back of my mind, is always the reminder, that Amanda and Peter paid a high price for the joy I feel.

It took Danny a long while to quieten, and I know it did her good to do it, but standing there, above her parents, and holding her close, it tore at my soul to see this young girl, who I had grown to love so deeply, suffer such pain. She quietened down and wiped her eyes, and looked up at me.

"I am glad we did this; I needed to." I nodded and wiped my eyes.

"It is no problem, as I said, I will always be there to help you, and Birch will always be at my side." She nodded.

"Can I go home now?" I leaned down, and kissed her head.

"Yes, if that is what you want Danny."

I took her hand and we walked back to the car; she was with me as Petal was pretty full of tree on the way up. We drove back alone, and left the others to wander for a while. Birch texted me. 'Just be there for her, call me if you need me, back soon.' I let Danny in, and she went up to her room, and I walked to the kitchen and made a coffee, and then headed to my room. I looked in on the way past her door, and she was sat on her balcony looking at her parent's tree, so I left her with her own thoughts.

Things in this house, always slide slowly back to normal, and Danny spent a couple of days sat in her room, or under my arch with her laptop. She appeared to be writing, and so I left her, but kept a watchful eye on her, as did Birch.

It was the week of the fete, and everything in Wotton was preparing, our house was once again filled with papers and files, and Anthony was busy, as was Deb's. Marci was planned to arrive on Wednesday afternoon for a week to stay, her parents were using the time to spend some time in London and travelling out to a few places. We arrived at the airport, and collected them in Petal, and I drove them to their hotel.

On the way to Wotton, Danny and Marci talked frantically as they updated each other on everything that had happened. Once home and settled, as we had bought a camp bed, which Jessie claimed for a week as it reminded her of camping, I got stuck in with getting Sanctuary Press ready.

I worked long days and collapsed into bed, something of which we did not get a reprieve, as Danny was busy with Marci and Jenny, and the three of them had become quite the group, so most nights Jessie jumped in bed with us. I know, honestly, Birch and I were both gagging for it.

We made jam, which Danny entered, using fruit, and we all made a sponge cake, and on Friday we prepared our flowers and displayed them. Saturday, was steward duty, but not for as long, although we did have the D&D tent and Bess. With so many volunteers, the legacy of mine and Birch's, we only did two hours, and for the rest of the time we enjoyed the fete with the kids, which was awesome.

They had never experienced anything like this, for them it was mind blowing, but they loved all the rides and it was fun seeing them happy, and Marci was just overwhelmed with it all. I cannot deny, it was disturbing to see Birch on the carousel, grinding her pelvis on the unicorn's mane, as she rode around, I suppose we were lucky she did not sit on its face.

The good news, was that having Marci over gave Danny a

companion, and so whilst we manned the D&D stand, they could go off around the fete and have fun together, although, they were under strict instruction not to leave the show field. I signed books, and Chloe signed art prints, and we even had a few Curio fans stop by, which thrilled Danny when a few of them asked her to sign autographs. Marci was really impressed and raved about it as she took pictures, which was nice to see as Danny felt so special, and I think it did her good.

Jessie was having the time of her life, as Anthony and Michael took her walks, followed by Deli with her kids, and Edwina, and Deb's, and she was spoilt rotten with sweets and treats, and the really good news was... Yes, we got some alone time.

We snuck into the rest tent, and it was empty, so giggling like naughty girls we made our way to the lovingly known area of 'The Shag Spot.' Just to make sure we did not get discovered, we slipped around the bales into that open area that only few knew of, where we had once had sex before. I was so excited as I pulled her round, and started to kiss, I was so pent up, but finally we had a child free area, and some really desperately needed time alone.

I was hot and horny and gagging for it big time, as was Birch as I fumbled with anticipation while passionately kissing her, at her denim shorts buttons, they came open and oh my God, I was so turned on, then I heard it, and my heart froze.

"I am not sure we should be doing this Sophia, what if someone comes in?"

We froze mid kiss, and I could see Birch's eyes open really wide, as we looked at each other, and broke our kiss in shock.

"Nigel, you said you wanted hot and spicy with a little danger, well live a little, yar. Look, everyone does it here at some point, and look, I am wearing a short skirt, and I have no panties on."

I closed my eyes, please God of all the faiths, not that, not him. Birch broke away and stared at me in abject horror. We heard the sound of a zipper being pulled down and I felt the ice cold shivers flow through my entire being. Birch snapped her hands to her ears and cringed.

"Oh Sophia, this is so scary... Oh... Oh..."

We both shuddered in unison, and I felt the chill of the coldness run from her into me, as I heard the sound of sucking. Birch eyes opened wider than I have ever seen them.

"Mmm! You like that don't you, yar?"

I jerked back and dithered, and closed my eyes, as goosebumps covered my whole body. There was a long slurping noise, and Birch pushed her hands even harder onto her ears and shook violently. I rammed my fingers in my ears and wanted to YERK.

"Oh Sophia... OOOOOH."

"Ooh Nigel, yar, put it into me."

My whole body was ice cold, and I could feel all my hairs standing on end, Birch dithered looking the most freaked out I have ever seen her.

There were suddenly slapping noises, and gasping, and I retched. Nigel was actually having sex, and I could hear it all, and wanted to vomit everywhere, it was so not fucking fair. My will to live died in less than a second, with my violent shudder.

Oh God, what has my life come to, when Nigel gets laid and I don't? Birch crouched down with her hands on her ears and started to quietly weep. What had happened to us, we were once the horniest women in the village, and now we were both on track to becoming withered and dried up old ladies, as Nigel shagged more than we did? I think I want to kill myself, my life is devoid of all meaning, bereft of joy, and utterly over.

As the slapping and Sophia's moans came through the hay bales at us, and I cringed and shuddered and retched, Birch's shoulders shook, as she silently wept. This had to be the lowest point in our sexual existence, as I fastened my jeans, and pulled down my top covering my boobs, feeling utterly broken and depressed.

I, Abigail Jennifer Watson, author of Seeds of Summer, slandered and shamed for being lewd, crude, and rude, for writing a sex positive book detailing the joys and freedom of women to enjoy sex, had become a female eunuch due to parenting. I hung my head in shame, and heartbreak, and joined Birch, silently weeping.

The sound of Sophia's orgasm sealed my fate, my vagina was to remain a dry and withered husk for eternity, left to decay, as dry as a bowl of sand. I sat on the floor brought up my knees, and pushed my face into them, as I covered my ears, and wept bitter painful silent tears.

We sat apart, staring at the floor long after Sophia and Nigel left, I finally stood up, traumatised, feeling utterly devoid of any sexual feelings, repulsed and wretched. I tapped Birch's still weeping shoulders and moved to leave. We came out of the tent lost and afraid, we had entered in to that zombie stage of our lives, we were officially sexually dead, and we were on the road to becoming Marjorie's.

With our heads down, we walked slower than a funeral procession back to the D&D tent, completely broken humans, only to be greeted by Jessie who looked up at me smiling, waving her candy floss at me, in some form of ritual happiness taunt.

"I HAVE HAD A GREAT TIME, IT WAS BANGING!" I looked at my beautiful and cute little daughter, and all I saw, was a spawn of Satan, hell bent on killing my sex life.

We drove home in silence, sat side by side, as the kids in the back laughed and giggled, and I realised, we had adopted dementors, and they had sucked all the sexual joy from our life. At home, I went to the kitchen and started to make our evening meal, it was going to be salad. As I held up the cucumber and stared at it, I felt it was taunting me, and I resented it, so I took out my anger, chopping the fat fucker to shreds with the smile of a psychopath.

I had finally become my mother, and I watched my will to live, wash down the sink, as it ran off the lettuce as I cleaned it. I gave a long and desperate sigh, and looked at the water swirling around the plug, dragging my sexual liberation with it, and sighed again. Deli looked at me a little concerned.

"Abby, are you guys alright, you know you have been really quiet all afternoon?" I gave another long sigh, and looked into her happy sexually sated eyes.

"Deli, where is the most likeliest place to get raped?" She frowned.

"Why the hell would you want to know that?" I turned and looked at her.

"Wherever it is, I am going there." She smirked.

"Yeah, kids, been there, done that."

I felt the slightest glimmer of hope as I stared into her angelic eyes, oh God, was I that desperate, I was looking to Deli for advice? My God, I have sunken low on the food chain. I clung to hope, as an aura of womanly wisdom surrounded her.

"You have... Oh God, how did you deal with it?" She smiled, as Birch looked up from the island with hope in her eyes. Deli's eyes twinkled.

"School... Oh God Abby, it is the saviour of all marriages, and mid morning sex is just the best."

I wanted to kiss her, as the clouds of doom over my life parted, and I heard angels sing, as a single ray of hopeful light shone down on me. I turned to Birch, and could see the ray of hope in her eyes, she smiled for the first time in five hours.

"Baby, our kids are going to school, even if they catch the plague."

She nodded with hope, and the light returned to her eyes. We were saved, we were about to be served a seven hour window, five days a week, to screw, and my God, term could not come quick enough, actually, neither could I.

Chapter 33

School.

Like every Summer of my life, it ended with me exhausted and tired, sat at the back of the hall, awaiting the drone of the guest speaker to finish, before the awards ceremony. I was only here because my daughter had won a third prize for her Cherry Jam, the recipe of which Deli had given her.

Birch's Jam for savouries, had caused quite a stir, I would imagine in the area of the bowels, and although it had been debated heavily, there were not enough judges with strong enough stomachs to award her a prize. I was dreading my future, because I knew I was weak, and at some point, she would offer me some, and being the slave to my vagina I was, I knew I would eat it just to get laid. Hell, at the moment, if she promised to nail the bedroom door tight, I would eat every frigging pot with a spoon, just to have an orgasm.

When we finally got to the prizes, and Danny walked up with pride for her green ribbon, I stood below the stage with Birch, Jessie and Marci, and we screamed like lunatics, as she lifted her tiny little cup. She looked so happy and proud, as her eyes danced with life, oh my God, I loved being a parent. Well, it had its faults, namely lack of sex, but apart from that, I was good.

The following Wednesday we met up with Marci's parents, and they looked really happy. Twats, they had probably been shagging all week. They were nice people, who held hands, I could see Birch looking at them with a simmering hate. Yep, she was aware that they dumped their kid on us, to go off and shag for a week too. We spent the day in London, and then drove them to the airport, and waved them off as Danny wept, it was a sad end to what for her had been a wonderful week. Life returned to normal, and we had just four more days to go before school started.

That first day was awful, it started with them both standing in the hall in their uniforms, and suddenly they looked so grown up, and we bawled our brains out, to which Danny and Jessie just rolled their eyes.

Jenny and Danny were in the same year, which was comforting to us, they had grown into really close friends over the summer, so at least she was not alone. She met us at the door as Birch hugged and kissed the girls, she had an early appointment, so I drove them both to school, and walked them to the deputy head teacher's office. I introduced myself, and my children, and they were taken to class, and suddenly I hated it, and did not want to let them go.

Watching Danny turn back and smile, and Jessie walking away with a teacher was terrible, and I felt the pangs of separation in my heart, as the deputy head teacher reassured me, they would be fine. They better had be, I was a writer and had researched thoroughly how to dispose of a body, and if any kid hurt my children, there would be a death in the village. I sat in my car outside the school, and bawled my brains out for the second time today, and it was not even ten o'clock.

The house was quiet when I got home, Chloe was painting, Deli was back in her newly remodelled nursery, Edwina was with Sam in her office, and Anthony and Birch were both at work. I made a coffee, and headed to the library and sat down, and my working day began. At ten to twelve, I took a break and gave a long sigh, and lifted my cup. As I walked into the hall, the door burst open and I jumped, as Birch flew in, she was out of breath, she looked at me and I felt a twinge of panic.

"Birch, what is wrong?" She took a deep breath.

"Deads, I have forty eight minutes."

She yanked on my hand, and dragged me onto the stairs, as I squealed in shock. She was moving at speed, and almost dragging me as my feet slipped on the carpet. We burst in through the bedroom door, she turned and just tore open her blouse, as all the buttons fired at me like a machine gun burst. I did not piss about and yanked at my vest, she looked at me with the those smouldering green eyes, and oh hell, I was so up for it,

"Deads I have a need, oh God, do I have need, and honestly, I am up for anything, even anal, just make me cum the hell all over the place."

She said no more, as she went flying back onto the bed as I attacked her like a rabid animal, and she squealed with joy, as I tore her pants, ripping them down her legs, and plunged in between them.

Edwina walked into the kitchen and looked at the ceiling, where wild screams and acts of lust drifted down to her, she smiled and looked at Sam.

"I see term time has started."

"OH GOD BIRCH YES!!!! YES BABY!!!!!"

Chloe walked in and put her cup on the island.

"It's about time, Abby was gagging for it so much I started locking my door, you know, all they had to do was ask. I would have taken the kids out for a day, I love those kids, they are banging fun."

It is probably a good thing I did not hear her, because if I had, I would have punched her again.

I lay back, red in the face, sweating and panting having had two glorious orgasms, with a fixed smile, as Birch walked in from the shower wrapped in a towel. She dropped it and started to dress, she had a great body, and I know, I just explored every inch of it. I gasped at her.

"You are a goddess." She smiled, and sat on the bed, and leaned in to kiss me.

"And you are a very dark, and very naughty little beastie. Oh God Deads, I was starting to think we will never have sex again." I was still smiling.

"How long have you got?" She looked at her watch.

"Eight minutes." I pouted.

"I could go again." She giggled.

"Sweetie, I am finding it hard to walk I am so sensitive, I have to get dressed, my blouse is buggered and my pants are torn, wow, you really were a beastie. I feel ravished." Say hello to the night. I groaned as my phone lit up.

"Oh God what now?" I lifted it up, and looked at Birch.

"It's school."

There is a sense of foreboding, which I have come to realise every parent experience's the minute the word school lights up on their phone, and I was currently experiencing this for the first time. I hit the button and answered. The soft sickly voice of a woman on the other end creeped into my ear.

"Hello, Mrs Dixon, I am sorry to call, but we have had a slight incident with Jessica." I sat bolt upright feeling panicked.

"Is she alright?"

"Oh yes Mrs Dixon, she is quite fine, the problem is, she has assaulted a young boy."

"What!?"

"She is in isolation at the minute, and I would deeply appreciate it if you came and saw me after school today. My name is Laura Cole Denison." Just the mention of the name made me feel cold, oh God, was she related to Henrietta?

"I will be there at three thirty."

"Lovely, I will see you then." The call ended and I looked at Birch.

"Jessie has assaulted a boy." She smirked.

"Awesome, what did he do?" I stared at her.

"Birch, we cannot let her go around hitting kids, I cannot have my daughter being a bully." She shrugged.

"I know her and trust her, if she did that to a boy, the little shit deserved it." I fell back on the bed with a gasp, she smiled.

"Deads, don't worry so much, Jessie is a well rounded and tough little monkey, she is going to be fine. I am actually quite proud of her; she stood her ground like my kid should. Okay, as much as I really want to stay and watch you quiver, as I do slow and sensual, dirty, dirty things with you." I shuddered and felt my vagina throb.

"I have a session, Sweetie. Pick me up at three, we will go together."

She leaned over and licked right up the inside of my thigh, and for just a second, I lost all control, and quivered. She giggled.

"See you soon, you hot naughty little beastie." I quivered again, and smiled.

"I love you, you dirty slutty naughty doctor."

She grabbed her jacket, waved with a chuckle at the door, and honestly, I wanted to walk her out, but I had temporarily lost the use of my legs, I leaned back into the bed and smiled.

At three fifteen, we stood at reception with Danny, who had smirked when I told her, and waited as Miss Laura Cole Denison, grandniece of Henrietta, walked up with Jessica, who looked upset. I crouched down and looked at her as her lip quivered.

"Are you alright Munchkin?" She shook her head, and looked really sad.

"They put me in prison, and it's not fair."

I pulled her into a hug as Laura asked us to come to her office. Is it weird that I am thirty nine, almost forty, and yet I am still intimidated by teachers? I am a grown woman for Christ's sake, and yet here I am feeling all that pressure of school again, as I followed this fascist who imprisoned my kid. Yep, I hated the bitch, anyone who makes Jessie look that sad, belongs in hell, and I was plotting to send her there.

The rancid smug bitch sat in her chair, behind her cheap tacky desk, and talked like her aunt. Jessie curled on my lap upset and in tears, I wanted to bind the bitch to the chair, using her tape dispenser, set her on fire, with her cheap wooden name plate, and toss her out of the window, sending her to hell where she belonged. She talked to me like I was ten, the patronising bitch, I wanted to shave her long bleached blonde hair off, and knit it into a scarf to keep Jessie warm in winter.

"Mrs and Mrs Dixon, we cannot allow violence in school, I am sure you more than most know that Abigail, as it has always been a school policy."

Birch nodded, and I stared at the smug bitch, wow, she was lecturing me, after the years of abuse I have suffered from her self righteous aunt? Birch leaned forward in her seat.

"Laura, can I call you Laura, good? I know my child and she is not violent; Jessie would not do this without provocation." She shook her head.

"That is beside the point, she hit Thomas Watkins in the nose, and gave him a very bad nose bleed." I looked at her.

"If Jessie did that, then what was he doing to her, have you asked?" I looked down at her.

"Jessie, why did you hit Tommy?" She looked at me.

"Mum he was calling me smelly Yank, I told him to stop loads of times, but he kept doing it. I told the teacher, and she did nothing. So, I told him, if he did it again, I would knock him the

.... Out." Oh God, I really need to keep Chloe away from my kids. Birch looked at Laura, and I could feel her anger boiling within her.

"So, this Tommy was bullying our child, and the teacher did nothing, so Jessie tried to stop him, and as a result, she has been put in this isolation for what, being victimised?" Laura gave a sigh.

"Mrs Dixon, we cannot allow violence." Birch nodded, and I could see her face as it darkened. Yep, she had taken everything into account, primed herself, and was going into defence of her child mode.

"But victimisation and bullying is fine, is it? Laura, have you any idea of the impact that bullying does psychologically to children, because I do? I spend every day of my life working with people who even now as adults, have not recovered from their bullies in school. So do not sit in that chair, in front of me, someone who is a far more superior educated woman than you will ever be, and talk to me with that pompous smug attitude. I feel insulted that you treat me like I am some uneducated heathen, and lecture me on why my kid should not defend herself. Instead, get out there, and start telling those kids the real effects of bullying, like nightmares, insecurity, bed wetting, dark thoughts, body dysmorphia, and suicide. If you cannot be bothered to get your fat ass out of that seat and do it, fine, I have a team trained for just the job, and will send them in here free of charge. I think we are done here."

She sat back and looked shocked, as Birch got up and lifted Jessie into her arms, she looked at me and her eyes were blazing.

"Deads, we are going."

Danny smirked, and took my hand as we walked out. I looked at Birch, as she put Jessie down and took her hand.

"Are you alright?"

"No, I am really pissed off, it is always the same shit with these twats, they wriggle off the hook of responsibility every time. They say they have no tolerance of bullying, that just means they do not want to know about it. I have talked to so many parents who are frustrated, because they cannot get schools to take them seriously, well, it is not happening to my kids." I smiled, and Danny smirked.

I love her so much, and she has no idea how powerful she is in defence of her children, and actually, how much like Roni she can be. We walked up the school corridor, and Mrs Taylor came out of her room and saw me.

"Abby, how lovely to see you, how are you?" I gave a big smile, I loved Mrs Taylor, she taught me English for five years, I turned to Birch.

"This is Mrs Taylor, my old English teacher." Birch gave a smile.

"Really nice to meet you, Abby has talked of you often, she loved English, it was her favourite class." As we talked, Jessie pulled at Birch's hand and pointed.

"Look Mum, that is him." Birch looked down the corridor where Tommy stood with a red swollen nose, Birch looked at Danny.

"Watch your sister." Danny looked at her, and felt frightened.

"Mum, leave it, we have enough trouble." Birch walked off, and Danny panicked, as she saw Birch approach the boy and crouch down. She smiled.

"Hi Sweetie, I am a doctor. Oh, that looks really sore." He nodded, and she smiled.

"Sweetie did you know doctors can cut things off people?" She nodded, and he stepped back, she gave her sweetest smile.

"You or your friends call my Jessie, or hurt her in anyway at all, and I will cut out your spleen and make you eat it, and they taste very horrible. Do you get me?" He looked terrified and nodded. She smiled and stood up.

"Get your mum, to put an ice pack on that and the swelling will go down, okay Sweetie?" His mum walked up looking worried, Birch turned.

"Mrs Watkins, hi, I am Doctor Dixon, Jessie's mum. I was just telling your son to get you to put an ice pack on that, it will help with the swelling. I am sorry my daughter did that to him, she will be reprimanded for it." Mrs Watkins shook her head.

"He probably deserved it, he has a horrible mouth at the moment, his big brother is not a good influence. You know I am glad I met you, Taylor went through hell here, and you really helped her, I am so grateful." Birch smiled.

"Taylor Watkins, I should have known, she was a lovely girl, and yes, she made great progress, how is she?" Mrs Watkins smiled.

"She is doing really well, she works at the organic nursery, she has thrived there with Norman and Daisy, doing her diploma she is, they are such lovely people, and they have helped her a lot." Birch smiled.

"I am really happy to hear that." I walked up with Danny and Jessie, and Mrs Watkins smiled.

"Abby, it has been a long time." I smiled.

"Hi Wendy, it has, hasn't it? This place has not changed much." She shook her head, and looked at Danny.

"Wow, is this your daughter, she is your double, well, you were blonde back then, but those are your blue eyes. She looks just like you did at school?" Danny smiled, as I put my arm across her shoulder.

"She has many of my traits, and is a good kid." She nodded.

"I have followed your career, my Taylor has all your books, you did really good Abby, but we all knew you would, always the brightest in the class. I am really happy for you, especially after all that awful business, with Hinkley. I am really delighted to have seen you, but I have to go, George will be home soon, and I have kids to feed. Take care of your kids, and don't mind this bugger, he will be punished, I won't have my son hurting old friends' kids."

"Thanks Wendy, I am sorry my daughter hurt him." She rolled her eyes.

"Little bugger probably deserved it." Jessie looked at Tommy with hate.

"He did." Wendy chuckled, and waved as she left.

We walked out of school, and over to the car park, and I told Birch about Wendy at school.

"She got a lot of stick for being poor, but she was so good at English, she would have made a great journalist or writer. Another one of James's bed post ticks sadly, and after that she got with his mate George, she was pregnant at seventeen. I last saw her at a school reunion two years after school and she was pregnant again. Sad to see her today, she had such a good future ahead of her." I gave a sigh and Birch squeezed my hand.

"It happens Deads, life has that way of twisting in ways we never expect." We got in the car, and Danny leaned over between the seats.

"So, are you going to do it? Mum, you have to, I really want you to, and she said we could." I gave a sigh, and Birch looked at me.

"What?" I looked at her.

"Mrs Taylor wants to run a writer's group, and she wants me to help run it, which means basically she will sit back and let me do it all." Danny looked excited.

"Mum tell her to do it, tell her mum, she has to do it, I texted Jenny and she is in." Birch smiled and winked at me.

"Sweetie, I have told you a thousand times, you would make a brilliant counsellor or teacher, you should do it." I gave a sigh.

"Oh, Danny do you know what you have started, she won't leave me alone now?" Danny giggled.

"I know, that is why I told her, do it Mum." I put the keys in and started the car.

"Let's grab take out, I am exhausted, and I will think about it, okay?"

She sat back in her seat with a big smile, and Jessie giggled as Danny slid her belt on. I looked in the mirror and saw her smiling, oh God, I am so weak when it comes to Birch and my kids. Birch gave a small chuckle.

"So, what are we ordering?" I reversed out of the parking spot.

"Anything that does not require savoury jam." Danny giggled as I winked.

When we got home, I unpacked Chinese, while Danny told me about her day. It was very different to American school, but she actually enjoyed it. She was in the same class as Jenny, and her friend Trish, so they had helped her settle and get into the routine. She sat in front of me with a spring roll picking at it.

"I did that maths a year ago, so I am okay with it, Science was good, but honestly, Mrs Taylor is brilliant, I loved her class, Jenny does too, she is great."

I smiled, somehow, I was really thrilled that she was still teaching, and Danny had her. I sat down with my coffee, and lifted it with both hands.

"I have such happy memories of her classes, she really inspired me to become a writer, she is the reason I took English at college and then Uni. Listen to her Danny, she is the best." She smiled.

"I could see that in your face tonight, you really love her, don't you?" I gave a nod.

"Yeah, there are few like her in education today." She broke her spring roll and looked over it, her blue eyes danced.

"So, are you going to do the class?" I gave a sigh.

"Will you leave me alone if I say yes?" She smiled a beautiful smile. and I rolled my eyes.

"Okay, I will do it, do I have a choice you told Birch, and she will never leave me alone until I do?" She jumped up from the table.

"Awesome, I am going to text Jenny and Trish, they will be blown away."

She ran off to her room to talk alone, and I sipped my coffee, God, I am so weak. Green eyes, or blue eyes, or that cheeky smile, and I am putty in their hands.

I finished sorting out the food, shouted everyone down, and returned to the kitchen. Birch came in with Jessie, I looked at her, and she looked down, I looked up at Birch.

"No matter what, we cannot allow violence in school."

Danny and Chloe looked up, Baz nodded, but kept on chewing. Birch understood, regardless of the cause, violence should not be encouraged. Jessie looked down at the floor, as I looked at her.

"Jessie, you cannot go around hitting people, and so I think as a punishment, there will be no drinking coffee." She looked up and frowned.

"But I don't drink coffee." Birch nodded sternly.

"Too right, with that kind of behaviour, I am not surprised." I looked at Jessie.

"We will go easy this time, but if there is a next time, you will not like it, okay?" She nodded and gave a small cheeky smile.

"Thanks mum." Oh God, I love her so much, she is adorable.

With tea over, Jessie had to wash the pots as an extra punishment, which actually she loved doing, so with some two step ladders, she stood by the sink and played with the bubbles and washed up. Birch helped, and also helped play with the bubbles, and I went up to my room to finish off answering comments.

An hour had passed when Danny came in, and sat in Birch's chair, she watched me for a few minutes and I could feel her eyes on me, I smiled as I typed.

"You may as well ask, the death stare does not work on me, I live with Birch." She giggled.

"I suppose I am curious, I just wondered, what you were going to do in the extra class?" It was understandable, so I stopped writing and spun in the chair and looked at her.

"You want to be a writer, and I presume the others who attend do, so what would you want to know?" She sat back, lifted her legs and crossed them as she thought, and then looked up, and her blue eyes flashed under her fringe.

"I would want to know everything about a writer's life, not just how to write better, but also what day to day life is like. What it is like to have a following, the places you go and the things you see, and how you take a precious moment, and turn it into a wonderful passage like you do in the Snow Queen. You know, I really love that story." I smiled; she had read it twice now.

"Okay, so answer me this, why do you love it, what does it do to you when you read it?" She leaned back on the chair, and I could almost see her thoughts.

"What I really love is how I feel when I read it, I see the pictures in my mind, and as I read, I watch them, and that stirs me deeply. My feelings get sucked into it all, like I am feeling the power of those emotions, oh Mum, it is such a good story."

Wow, she just blew my mind. I had always thought that Birch would be the only one to see and feel all that, and yet here was Danny, almost ten, and she got it completely, it was a massive revelation.

"Danny, I just write the truth, I mean, I don't write Birch did this and I did that, but I give that moment to Nightshade and let her use it, and I watch Birch's reaction, and write that for the Snow Queen. For the declaration of love from Nightshade, I wrote what I had wanted to say for a long time, but had not had the chance to, that is all." She smiled.

"I love the way you love mum, I really do, since I first met you, I have seen how much you both love each other. I was worried when I found out you were married to a woman. I have never encountered that before, but when I walked in, and you looked so nervous, and I saw her take your hand, I really understood that, because I saw my dad do that a lot with mum. It may sound silly, but it gave me confidence, because I was scared." I gave a slight nod.

"We were both scared Danny, we wanted to take care of you so much, but all you had to do was say no, and in a way, we would have lost what became for us a very important dream. Oh Danny, you have no idea how much it meant to us, and how happy it has made us, we love all us being together." She laughed.

"Even when you are bawling your brains out in a changing room?" I giggled.

"You both looked so lovely, it caught our breath, maybe we could have handled it better, but that is us, we do not hide it." I think she understood that.

"I like that the most mum, neither of you hide your feelings, it helps me with what I feel, because I can talk to both of you about them, and that has made a big difference to me, and I think Jessie." I frowned.

"Danny, Jessie has no issues expressing herself, as we have all seen." She smiled.

"Not now, but for a long time, she was really quiet, there was a time when she would only talk to me, with you two, she has really found her voice again, and that makes me very happy."

There was a sniffle, and we both turned, and Birch was sat on the bed holding a tissue to her mouth, as tears streamed down her face. I gave a sigh, and she dropped the tissue into the circle, I was not even aware she was there. She looked at me with red puffy eyes.

"YOU TWO ARE SO BEAUTIFUL, IT BREAKS MY HEART, I LOVE YOU BOTH SO MUCH." I gave a sigh, and Danny giggled.

"See what I mean?"

Birch sobbed and pulled another tissue out of the box, and blew her nose, it sounded like a broken trumpet, and Danny giggled.

Chapter 34

Life Goes On.

Seeds of Summer the series was premiered, and with a baby sitter, Birch and I drove to London, to see the first episode screened. Ella was called, and as we walked up the red carpet to amazing screams, I felt happy, but hoped they had not buggered it up. We sat and watched, and laughed, it was wonderful, and I was thrilled, which meant David was massively relieved. It was perfect, and although some scenes were cut, just implying them, painted a good enough picture to get the full flavour of the books.

I gave the cast such hugs afterwards, all of them had done an amazing job, and Anita was so delighted at our response, Tabby was bouncing all over the place with happiness. It would be a month before it was screened on the channel, but I did not care, they had done a superb job, and that was enough for me.

Is it weird we did not stay in London but drove back, because we had Deli as a baby sitter, and we missed the kids and wanted to be home with them? We spent an hour at the after show party, and then made our excuses. After doing several interviews, we jumped in my car sober, having drunk only coffee... I know right, us two, just coffee, how crazy life is as it turns. We are mum's now, and actually, we love it, Chloe, Deb's, and Anthony stayed on, and stayed in a hotel.

The thing is, I was actually loving being a stay at home mum, and silly things like washing kids' clothes and helping them with their homework, gave me the greatest joy. I am probably the only person alive who really loves the school run, as I sit and listen to Jenny, Danny and Jessie laugh and talk in the back seat. I love writing, I really do, and it has always driven me and given me a purpose in life, but honestly, having two kids has given me a greater one, and I love it, actually, scratch that, I ruddy well adore it.

It was Thursday, September 18th, and at 2:30 in the afternoon, I was escorted into an empty classroom at Oxendale to set up for what would be the first after hours class at Oxendale Academy. It was dedicated to those who had the dream of becoming a writer. I set up my laptop and my projector, and got ready to try and teach about what it was actually like, and how a writer works, and honestly, I was as nervous as hell.

Danny was in the group, and Birch was tied up at work, so just before the end of day bell, I walked up to get Jessie, and then walked back to the classroom, where Mrs Taylor stood waiting with a smile.

"I have wanted to do this for a long time Abby, and I am so thrilled you are doing this, look."

I looked through the door, and there were about fourteen children from right across the whole school years, all sat with note books and pens waiting. To be honest I was surprised, I expected maybe four or five. She gave me a big smile, as I took a deep breath.

"Just be yourself, relax, and just tell it as it is Abby, let them really understand the lifestyle, the work life, and how your mind works. Trust me, they will learn so much, because you have no idea how much you have to offer these children, but I do, and it will enhance their life."

I nodded, my stomach churning, she walked in with Jessie, settled her at a desk with crayons, and then she looked at the assembled group. She smiled at them, as I stood waiting outside the open door.

"Class, I am delighted that I am finally able to do this for all of you. For this class, I will be using someone who knows the lifestyle of a writer better than anyone, so please welcome an ex-pupil of my English class, and a professional writer. Abigail Jennifer Watson."

It felt so strange to walk into a class room and be at the front, and not head to my seat, and also to have fourteen young smiling faces look up in awe. I walked to the front of the desk and looked at Mrs Taylor as she sat down to my side, and then looked at the room full of waiting students, of which at the back with a huge smile was my daughter, sat next to Jennifer. I smiled at the room.

"Hi, I am Abby, and hopefully, through this class, you will all get an insight into what it is like to be a writer, a real writer. A person who sits at a desk, or curls up on a sofa with a pad, and uses what they have in their brain to create, people, places, and worlds that appear out of the unknown. I was once told, by someone I looked up to, open your mind, let it all flow, and then when you have dreamed long enough, pick up your pad, and just empty it all onto the page. That is still the best description of writing I have ever had."

Mrs Taylor gave a huge smile and nodded, as she remembered well the moment. I looked around and saw several of them writing it down, and smiled to myself, because I was looking at me twenty odd years ago. I stood there in jeans, and a long top, just plain and ordinary, just being me, and looked to all those young hopefuls, and a thought occurred to me.

"Why do we write, why do we want to be writers, because that is the most important question you will ever ask yourself?" A young girl near the front put her hand up, I looked at her.

"To be like you." I smiled.

"Okay, yes, I always fancied myself as a young Shelly or Wells." I leaned off the desk, and walked around to my laptop, and looked up.

"But who am I, who is the real Abigail, do you think this is me?"

I tapped the laptop, and the screen on the wall came alive. There was a picture of me at a gala, and I was in a glamourous gothic gown with my parasol.

"Or this one?" The picture showed me on a stage sat with a row of other writers.

"What about this one?" I was stood holding my first of three Jonathon Grahams prizes.

I could almost see the glitter in their eyes. Danny sat smiling her eyes fixed on me, she knew where I was going with this, I looked around the room and shook my head.

"None of those are me, not the real me, not the real writer Abigail, those if you make it, come much later. Before that you have to do the work, you have to really knuckle down and get on with it. Too many people think putting a book out will make you famous, too many think writing a book is easy, it's not, it is sheer bloody hard work. If you are not obsessed with your story, to the point of break down, you will never write a book worth reading.

This is not a fast track to stardom, I started writing when I was your age, and it is only in the last ten years, I have felt like I made it.”

They all stared at me, and swallowed, I gave a slight smile, and nodded at them.

“Guys you have to love it so much, that just the joy of creation will drive you forward, and for most of the time you will look like this.”

They gave a gasp as they saw the picture of me sat at my desk, pounding the keys with tears rolling down my face. I clicked another one, where I was sat at my arch with my laptop on my lap, lost in thought and miles away as I wrote.

“And some days, you will look like this.” Up came the picture of the selfie of me from the guest house, with no makeup, drunk, broken, and lost to life. They all gasped as I turned and looked at it.

“Yikes, what a mess I was. That was after my first two books failed and tanked, all I wanted was to be a writer, and I had felt like I had failed, and look at me. That is the real Abigail, that is me, broken, destroyed, and lost, as I struggled. Writers look like this.”

I gave a chuckle, as I put up a picture of Danny, sat with a pad with her back against a tree in the garden, lost to the world and making notes. I looked at it and smiled, she looked horrified and looked down.

“All of you, go through your parents’ pictures, and I am sure you will find one of yourself that looks like that one.” Mrs Taylor smiled.

“If you are writing for fame, or for money, then give up. If you are really lucky like I have been, it happens, but that is an after thought, a consequence of what you do. Most writers do not even make minimum wage, most writers have a job and write in their spare time, because the only thing that is important, is the story itself.” I changed the picture, and a picture of my books came up.

“I want this group to be informal, I want over the weeks for all of you to get past my reputation, and just treat me like I am one of you, because at the end of the day, I am. I am a writer, a plain boring, cries at my desk when the story will not come out properly writer, so hands up, who is like me, who here is a real writer?" Hands shot in the air, and a girl at the back said.

"I cry my ass off when I get it wrong." The room giggled, and I smiled.

"Great, right, what do you do?" The boy looked up looking panicked.

"I yell at my brother." I smiled.

"Yep, I get moody with my house mates. You?"

"I have cried loads." The room laughed; I pointed at Danny.

"You?" She gave a giggle.

"Mum, I come to you." The whole room laughed, and I shrugged.

"Okay, but that is my point, and it is a really important one, because here in this room, is your salvation." They all looked confused, and Mrs Taylor gave a nod and smiled.

"Guys, you are writers, you have each other. Share ideas, talk out theories, express your frustrations to each other, I don't work alone, I have a mate who I bitch like crazy too. She has banged on the table once or twice, with her own frustrations, I call her Jo, we have coffee and moan about our books. You all will probably know her as Johanna Friel." The whole room gasped, and I nodded.

"You see, that is the point, as of today you all have a bond, and it is an important one, because whether you know it or not, one of the most important things you can build as a writer is a support network. You need people who get you, understand you, and what you do, and most importantly, people you can talk out your frustrations with. That starts now, here in this classroom, that is the most important tool you have."

Jenny looked at Danny and smiled, and I could already see that they were all starting to think, and starting to see each other in a different light.

As we moved through the hour, I explained more about what I wanted to do over the year, and started to talk about their first assignment, and they all looked worried, I had to smile, talk about a room of insecure nerds, I knew that look of fear. I could see the clock at the back of the room, time had gone so fast, and I was loving it, and could not help but think, why had I not done this sooner?

"Okay guys, for next week I have two assignments, the first

being, I want you all to write something, and what I want, is I want you to take an inanimate random object, and make it something else. Be creative, make it live, just let your imagination go, and write it down. I do not need a manuscript, but give me enough to show me where your writing is at. And secondly, think as you write about all those moments of frustration where you have struggled to write something, or felt it was not yet good enough, because I have done all the talking today, and next week, all of you are going to join in, and we are going to look at discussing theories of how all of us can write better."

I sat back on the edge of the desk, and they all put their things away, and yep, out came copies of the books for me to sign, Danny had not spared me. It is strange how life goes around in circles, here I was back in school, and the last time I was here, I was being inspired to write, and now here I was back again, inspiring others to write. I have to wonder, which one of these kids was going to be the next big thing?

Maybe that is how we have evolved, as I look back at my life, I watched my mum and I learned a lot from her, watching my dad certainly helped when I ran the Parish Councils Summer Fete. Even Marjorie in a way taught me a lot about who she was and who I am, I certainly gained a lot of knowledge of how to, and how not to run a council. Is that what we do, lead by example, and in doing so teach others? I think maybe it is.

Birch has always told me, there is great wisdom to be gained from the darker moments of my life, and I have seen that is true. I have certainly had my moments in hell, but I have learned a lot from my mistakes, and it will, I hope, help me guide Danny and Jessie better through their lives. Although, they too will make mistakes, and at that point I will sit with them, and look at what can be learned from it. The class slowly emptied, and Danny slipped her arms round me with a huge smile.

"You were brilliant, we loved it." Jenny nodded and I smiled, and pulled Jenny into a hug with my free arm.

"I am glad you enjoyed it; I was winging it you know?" Danny snuggled into me.

"I really loved it; I feel inspired." Jessie looked up at me.

"You talk a lot, and you call me?" I giggled as I looked down at her.

"Maybe Munchkin, but I am a lot quieter." Danny and Jenny chuckled. Mrs Taylor was all smiles.

"You missed your way in life, you are a natural teacher, oh Abby, honestly, that for me was a huge privilege." I smiled at her, and could see her happiness.

"You taught me so much, I loved your classes, and I listened to every word you spoke. I have done well in life through writing, but honestly, I owe that to you. I enjoyed today, I felt I was just passing on the knowledge, like you did for me, and it was good to give back." She smiled; I knew she understood that.

Driving home, it was lovely, as Jenny and Danny sat in the back swapping ideas and talking at a wild pace about what they could write or discuss for next week's lesson, and I just sat back as I drove and listened. They reminded me so much of me and Deb's at that age, and oddly enough, that gave me great hope.

We arrived home to food, Birch was home cooking with Chloe, Jessie ran in, and Birch scooped her up in her arms and hugged her.

"How are you, Sweetie?" She hugged Birch hard.

"Tommy was nice to me, so I did not have to batter him, and mum can talk for hours, she stood there and banged on all day, and she calls me?"

Birch giggled as I walked into the room and her eyes sparkled, as she leaned her head to one side and looked at me.

"You look happy." I smiled.

"Yeah, I am, it felt good, and I really enjoyed it." Chloe handed me a glass of wine.

"Dinner will not be long. It is good isn't it, I love doing the art group, I love how creative the kids are." Yeah, she understood. I sat at the table and relaxed.

The meal was served, and Danny and Jenny sat either side of Birch, and talked and talked about how great the class was. Birch just smiled and watched me, as her eyes danced and twinkled, she looked so happy. Jessie was listening at my side and rolled her eyes.

"They bang on too." I looked down at her and giggled, she looked up at me.

"I thought you were cool, but I want to be a brain doctor like mum, I am going to open up people's heads too, and see what they have in there. I bet Tommy does not have much, he is stupid." I gave a big chuckle and cupped her cheek.

"I think you will make a wonderful brain doctor, just stay out of Chloe's head, there is stuff in there no one wants to see." Baz sniggered. and dropped his mash; Chloe smiled and raised her eye brows.

"I know all the naughty stuff." She nudged Baz and he giggled.

After tea, we washed up, and then I headed to my room and lay back on my bed and relaxed, and Birch came in and sat on my waist and looked down at me. I was feeling at ease and nostalgic, as I looked up at her, with that long white patched hair and those intense eyes filled with mischief, I smiled at her.

"I love my life with you, I love having kids Birch, I never thought I would, but I do. I am so proud of both of them, and you are such a great mother." She smiled.

"You know Sweetie, you are too, I watch you with them, and you are so natural in the way you talk and they just open up and share their thoughts, it is a gift. Moon always told me that one day you would be a mother of great love, and she was right."

She leaned over and she kissed me so softly, it was tender and caring, and so filled with love, and I just basked in it. She had no idea how much she had inspired my life, my writing, and my creativity; she was wild chaos on legs, but she was loving, thoughtful, and the greatest companion I had ever known. My love for her was so deep it was vast, and just swept me up, and made me a complete person, from all those shattered fragments of who I was when I first met her.

You know, it is strange how life works, I remember Moon telling me at the wedding, a child would come from it and bless my life. It still freaks me out how she knows things, and yet on that very day, Amanda was already pregnant and carrying Danny, even though she was unaware of it. As a result, through her loss, I have gained two wonderful and beautiful children. Life is so strange as the circles go round and repeat on themselves.

I opened my eyes and she was sat back staring at me with a smile, God, she was beautiful. BARRRP! I choked.

"GOD BIRCH, DO YOU HAVE TO?"

"Sweetie I am sorry, it just came out, I was trying to hold it in."
I staggered out of the bedroom, my stomach churning, gasping
for air.

"That is frigging awful, what the hell have you been eating,
sewage?" Danny and Jessie popped their heads around their
bedroom door. I looked at them gasping for air and coughing.

"Stay out of our room, she has done it again." I staggered down
the stairs, as Birch stood at the top.

"Sweetie, I have a healthy diet; I did say sorry." I looked up the
stairs still wanting to yerk.

"Can you not push something up there to freshen it on its way
out?" She giggled.

"Oh Sweetie, that would be weird, but it could be fun." I
smirked. Jessie came running out of her room and onto the
stairs, holding her nose. Danny followed looking green, as Jessie
squealed.

"MUM, IT GOT THROUGH THE WALL; I DON'T LIKE IT.
MAKE IT GO AWAY!"

I sniggered, oh God, she was starting to sound like Birch, what
had I done?

Sunday was Danny's birthday, she was ten, and yeah, it was
our first time ever celebrating our child's birthday, so we went a
little overboard, and the living room was stacked with gifts from
everyone.

Birch was mental and insane as she loved presents, and yep,
I held her waistband to keep her out of arms reach as Danny
tore off the gift wrap, to reveal clothes, books, tech, and the one
thing she had always wanted, a bicycle. It was a proper lady's
bike imported from Holland, complete with basket and all the
accessories, she could finally join us on bike rides.

Everyone turned up, and Hatty and Clive added more gifts to
the pile, as did my Mum and Patrick, she looked so happy and
thrilled and made a point of thanking everyone repeatedly. All the
Curios and family arrived, and we also let her invite some friends
from school. Edwina arranged music, and we spilled out into the
garden and got the outdoor kitchen going in full swing, whilst
Birch and I cooked burgers.

It was nice to see her friends with her, I had worried a lot about her losing all her friends from home, but she was surrounded by a small group, some of whom I noted were from the writer's group, and they all sat on the grass eating burgers, crisps, endless cakes, and drinking cans of soda, it felt good to see it.

Half way through Roni and Will arrived, much to the joy of Birch, and Jessie who saw Granddad Will and made a dash for him, Roni walked over with a smile.

"She looks really happy Abby." I smiled, as I watched her sat with her friends laughing and joking.

"I am really happy for her; she has settled in well at school. She deserves this, she has had enough sadness in her life." Roni smiled.

"You two have done a wonderful thing with them, and it is clear how much it has meant to them. I have to say Abby, I have never seen you so happy." I smiled.

"I am, I always thought kids were not the answer, but honestly, those two, have shown me joys I never thought possible. To be honest, I wasn't ready for a long time, it would have been a cruel act to take kids on five years ago, and I wouldn't do that to Birch. I knew how she felt Roni, she is not good at faking, but the time was not right, now is." Roni smiled.

"You always have been the brightest, I am actually pleased to hear that Abby, if I am honest, I thought it was fear. I will not deny, I was surprised when Jemi rang me and told me about them and their parents, I did not think you would go through with it."

"As I said, the time had to be right, and it is, and yes, I really am very happy with how it has all turned out." She smiled.

"Good for you, I am loving being Grandma Roni, and honestly Abby, this has been a tonic for Will." I giggled.

"I see a lot of Jeff in him. She is a handful, but she is so lovely and wonderful." Roni giggled.

"It amazes me how like Jemi she is, I think he sees that, and it gives him back something he thought he had lost when she grew up."

I have no idea how many burgers we cooked, we were running out of salad fast, and I gave Norman a ring. Daisy turned up shortly after with more, and she brought with her a gift for Danny, which I thought was really sweet of her. It was a long day that ran until ten, Danny was happy as I sat on her bed, her room was filled with her cards, she did not want them downstairs, she wanted them in her room, so she could see them.

I sat on her bed and looked at her bright happy blue eyes, she looked so happy, I smiled.

"Did you have a good day?" She nodded.

"The best, I woke up and sat out on the balcony, and told mum and dad I was okay, and then I came down and had such a surprise. Mum, I really loved today, thanks."

It warmed my heart to hear it, she sat up and pulled me into a hug, and I felt close to tears. It is strange how quickly I have come to feel such love for these children, because I have, they feel like they are my own, and I know I would not love them more if I had given birth to them, such was the power of what I felt. I kissed her goodnight and pulled the door too, and headed for my room, Birch was drunk, and giddy, which meant she was horny, I chuckled as I undressed, and her eyes twinkled.

"Hi Sexy Sweetie." I laughed as I slipped in under the duvet and she pulled me close; her eyes filled with naughtiness."

"Yummy, I have a hot little author in my bed, and I am feeling very wicked."

THUMP... THUMP... THUMP. I giggled as the door bust open, and Jessie came racing in and landed on the bed.

"MUMS, I AM EXCITED, AND CANNOT SLEEP!"

Wow that's sounds familiar, I rolled over and looked at her.

"Why are you excited Munchkin?" She looked at me with bright happy eyes.

"What will I get for my birthday?" I chuckled.

"Munchkin, it is not until March, we have not decided yet." She nodded.

"Good I am writing a list." Birch chuckled.

"Sweetie, how long is the list?" She put her finger on her mouth as she thought for a moment, then looked at us.

"It's long, Danny told me I should wrap it on a loo roll, I am not sure I know what that is." Birch chuckled.

"Sweetie, that is the card tube inside the toilet tissue." She raised her eyebrows.

"That makes so much sense, when Jenny said she was going to the loo, I thought she was going out of the village, but she came back really fast, and I thought, that was a short trip." Yeah, she still struggles converting American to English.

Jessie slid into bed and Birch snuggled round her, I had to smile, the days used to be boring, but now they are so much more fun, especially since Birch appears to want all her work breaks in our bed.

Life moved on, I continued, teaching writing at school, I started writing more stories, and worked quietly on my next big project with Chloe, as we headed towards my fortieth birthday.

It was so magical, as the kids with Chloe piled into our room and jumped on the bed, and suddenly I had cards that had 'Mum' printed on them, and it was so special. Okay, so I cried for an hour, but honestly, it was the most precious moment of my year.

All around me the house became a hive of activity, as the Halloween Carnival was planned, which I was really excited about, as it would be our first with our own kids. Edwina was working on a new light show, which had become a massive attraction, although we did alternate the circus and fair, and only had one at a time, swapping each year from one to the other, it was after all, a lot of work for the council.

The big night came, and we all played our part, and Danny and Jessie loved it. Jessie was so excited and possibly louder than anyone else in the village as she stuffed sweets down her neck, and ended up in the toilet being sick. Yeah, we made a note for next year.

Standing on the side of the road though, watching her sat at my feet on the curb, and with one arm round Danny, and one round the crazy light fairy, was such a thrill for me. I got to see the other side, and remembered all those years ago, how Birch and I ran up the street in Curio hoodies, handing out lights and glow sticks to kids as their parents smiled with gratitude and thanks. Now that was me, standing here, grateful to those who treated my kids to sweets and gifts, oh how the world and life has come round full circle.

It snowed again at Christmas, and we took Jessie to see Santa. Yeah, I made sure there was no bulge before sitting her on his lap. She got Luke, who over the years had really honed his skills at playing the role, poor sod, she talked his socks off, with an exhaustive list. As Curio's, we selected a tree together, and yep, she cried her eyes out... Again!

This year for a treat, I bought two secret forever trees, one for the kids, and one for the biggest kid in the house. I lit them both up and waited for a response, and I was not disappointed. Birch's first forever tree is now planted in the garden, and the thing is massive, we planted it at the bottom of the garden a good few years ago, behind my arch. The thing I love the most about it, is if you look about half way up it, you will see an old weathered bauble, that once had a skeleton on it. She refused to remove it, she still has all the Pagan symbol decorations in a box at the top of our wardrobe, I bought new ones for this year.

At Yule, we walked up to the top of the heath, and stood next to Amanda and Peter's tree, there were a few tears, as the sun came up, but it was nice to do it, and make the moment special for Danny, I think she needed it.

Christmas day was mental, everyone stayed overnight, and so first thing in the morning with the table filled with kids, was insane, and so loud, I wore Birch's ear protectors wrapped in tinsel, yeah, I am not stupid.

Watching Birch sat with the kids ripping the shit out of their gift wrap was so wonderful, and so precious, I filmed it and watch it often. We all had the most amazing day, and the turkey was huge, we barely fitted it in the oven, but we had an army to feed. For a New Year's treat, we flew to Miami, and spent New Year with my dad, it really was very special, he seems so old and frail now, and has a full time nurse to help care for him.

I was so glad we went, and yet as I sat with him, and he smiled, he still had that twinkle in his eyes, the one he found with Angela. I have to say, she has been wonderful with him, and she has never faltered. I spent a lot of time talking with her out on the deck under a large umbrella, and it was nice to talk about life and all we had seen and done. I told her many times how grateful I was for all she had done in helping him accept Birch and I, because it really mattered to me more than you would think.

We flew back via Missouri, and spent a long weekend in a hotel, where we met up with Janet and her family, and Danny got to hang out with Marci, which for the kids was so special, and gave them a chance to reconnect with their earlier life.

Birch's birthday was insane, she too cried for hours, she hid in the cellar, but as we know, there are air vents down there which travel up through the walls. Although, it was hilarious watching Chloe completely freak out, as the walls of her studio started to wail, and she thought Gwenda was back. I just sat back, said nothing and waited, okay, so I may have expected this, and opened the vents the night before?

The sad news came at the end of February, and I flew back over to Miami, and sat at his side in the hospital, holding my dads' hand, as he fought to tell me how much he loved me and how proud he was, before finally passing. It hit me so hard, and was devastating. I had spent so much of the early part of my life seeking his approval, and never really getting it, and had suffered so much under his regime and coldness. As he gasped his last breath and told me, it broke my heart to finally have it, and I think just finally knowing he was proud and loved me for who I was, hit me so hard, because it felt like too much to bear.

We stayed over until after the funeral and helped Angela sort everything out, she was just crushed by it all. Shortly after we returned for Jessie's eighth birthday, which was madness, Angela sold everything, and came back to Oxendale to live with her sister. Dad's ashes came back with her, and his ashes were buried in the church, which I was actually happy about, it felt right he came home. Angela visited his marker often, as we got to see her a lot. We would drive over and pick her up, and she got to spend time with the kids, which she loved. I am glad she came back, and felt a part of us, after all, she did so much for dad, and actually, she made him very happy, and it was nice to see it.

I took my time returning to the spot light of the public eye, Sanctuary Press was a slow process, as I did not rush, I was happy just enjoying my family life. Like all things in my life, it came round full circle, and it was time to step up, and reveal what I had been up to. Edwina volunteered to help for a day as a publicist, and with her and Chloe at my side, we prepared.

Chapter 35

The Writer Returns.

I sat at my archway as it grew darker, with the red spotlight on me. It was still pretty chilly, so I wrapped in a shawl, dressed in all black, with my dark eyes, and holding my parasol, Edwina smiled as she focused the camera.

"Okay we are set, and it looks brilliant and a little creepy, it's perfect." Danny stood at her side, and gave the thumbs up, and I smiled into the camera.

"Hello my readers... Last year, I promised you all something would come when I walked away from public life, and became a little reclusive, having quit Dixon Publishing. There were a lot of rumours and health concerns at that time, but here on my website, I told you all, I just needed some well earned time off, and admittedly, I have taken longer than even I expected. In my time out of the spotlight, I have been working on quite a few projects, but I have also experienced the great joy of becoming a parent, to the two children of my cousin, who was tragically killed in a road accident." I smiled at Danny.

"It has been the happiest time of my life, and I am rested and healthy, and ready to step back into a limited spotlight, as I still have the duty of a parent, and so wish to devote much of my time to my beautiful daughters and wife. However, I have arranged a press conference for Saturday, at the large Cogs and Wheelers book store in London, where I will reveal, what comes next for the AJW brand. I think all of you will be very excited, as I will be streaming it live to this site, at eleven on Saturday morning, if you cannot be there, be here to see it. Thank you."

Edwina panned out to get the whole arch into the shot, and then lifted her hand.

"CUT!" Danny's eyes sparkled, as she felt the excitement.

"Oh God Mum, I cannot wait." I gave a chuckle.

"Danny, you have read them, you have the test prints." She

shook her head.

"No, I mean seeing them unveiled, Jenny has been keeping me up to date with what her mum is doing, and I am so excited, can I dress up, mum said I could?" I frowned at her as Edwina giggled.

"How do you mean; mum says you can?" She shrugged.

"Me and mum had an idea, and we thought it would be fun."

Oh dear, she had Birch in on the plan, this could not be good. Edwina looked at me and winked, I scowled at her.

"What do you know?" She gave me a giggle.

"Abby, my lips are sealed." Okay that did not bode well, I gave Danny a shrewd look.

"I don't trust her, what has your mum done?" Danny just chuckled.

"You will see, and it will be awesome."

You see, this is my problem, Birch is not to be trusted, and when she ropes the kids in, she is definitely not to be trusted, and now I was starting to worry. Giving me 'you will see' as an answer, really makes me panic, as every time she says that, something weird and crazy happens. I was nervous all night, and all the following day, and no matter what I tried, everyone was tight lipped, even Jessie who I can usually crack as she has a big mouth, but not this time.

Edwina uploaded the video and it went live to the web site, and she shared it out all over social media telling everyone to be there. I sat in the library talking to Deb's, as there was a lot to organise. Her store in London was huge, and it had two floors, of which the second floor was usually for promotions, special offers, and had lots of seats. What we had arranged, was a very special deal, and currently at the shop, there was a massive display hidden behind a large black curtain. I would do the press conference stood in front of the curtain, and then the curtain would draw back, revealing the display of books, at the back, there would be a table, from which I would do signings. I had done everything I could, but was nervous, I climbed in bed and Birch cuddled into me with a giggle, I did not trust her, I looked back.

"What are you and the kids up to Doctor?"

She snuggled into me and kissed my neck, and I felt the goosebumps run down my back, I quivered then realised what she was up to, I slapped her leg and she squealed.

"Sweetie, that hurt." I grinned, and pointed at her.

"Don't try distracting me with sex, what are you up to?" She giggled, and straddled over me.

"You saw through that then? Crap, I paid the kids to stay out of here for nothing." I frowned.

"You paid them... To not sleep in here?" She nodded.

"Yes Sweetie, I am really turned on, and I have a very long list of very dirty and naughty things I wanted to do to you... You know, on this, our only night alone in bed this year... Without kids... Naked and horny... But it is okay, we can talk too." I swallowed hard, and felt my leg tremble.

"What sort of list?" She raised her eye brows.

"It is naughty, and smutty, with oils and toys and things of a very deviant nature." My leg trembled more.

"Oh my!" She gave me a very sexy wink.

"It is okay Sweetie, I am happy to chat, so what do you want to know?" She smirked.

I slid my hands slowly up her front, and ran my fingertips round her boobs, and she gave a big shudder, I knew how much she liked that. She smiled and leaned back.

"Oh Sweetie, don't do that, you know it drives me wild." I giggled.

"So... About this list?" She gave a squeal, and dived on me. Oh, crap she did it to me again, I am so weak when I am around her!

I woke to the alarm going off, which was odd, as it was Saturday, and there was no sign of Birch, or the small crazy child demanding breakfast. I hit the button and slid out of bed, my legs felt weak, but considering my night of passion, why was I surprised? Birch was rampant last night as was evident from my still shaky legs. I grabbed my kimono and wandered downstairs, and walked into the kitchen for my coffee and stopped.

"What the F...!"

Danny, Birch, and Jessie all stood with black wigs with red tips, wearing black clothes, and had on dark eye makeup. Actually, Danny had my red eye makeup. It was kind of creepy and I shuddered; Danny giggled at me.

"Hi Mum, it's dress like Abby day." I frowned, she actually

looked really good, Birch giggled.

"That is what it says on your website Sweetie."

She turned her laptop around to show me, and I saw it on my site. I gritted my teeth and sighed; the cow had hacked my site.

"I will kill Edwina." Jessie looked up at me, yeah, that was unsettling, she whispered.

"I am being quiet like you today."

Okay, maybe not that unsettling, there was one positive at least. Birch came around the island, and to be honest I was a little turned on. Up close she looked really hot with black hair; she smiled at me as she slipped her arms round me. Oh hell, I was turning myself on, is that weird? She giggled.

"You know Deads, I could wear this in the bedroom." My leg trembled, and I nodded with a big smile.

"Yes please." She giggled.

"Deads is it messed up that I want to screw you, as you, and I am weirdly aroused dressed like this?"

"No idea, but I am really wet."

"MUMS!" I looked at Danny.

"We are here, right here Mum, and we can hear you." Jessie frowned.

"Why are you wet, it's not raining?" Birch turned to her; I panicked.

"Birch... Please don't, I have a press conference, and if she escapes near them, everyone will know what you are about to say." She turned back to me, and our eyes met, yep, my legs trembled again.

"Good point Sweetie, I will save it for later." I nodded.

"Trust me, that is better for everyone."

After coffee, a lot of coffee, I took a quick shower, and got ready, I was having the red eyes done today, and so took my red parasol, Danny borrowed my purple one, and Birch my black. Jessie got a child's umbrella, which Chloe had painted with black dye, and decorated with black lace. As we were getting ready, Jenny arrived and she too looked like me, she spun in the hall.

"What do you think?"

She had the wig, which I had found out Anthony acquired, they were all black, and he had dyed the tips himself. She wore a long black top and long black skirt, and had a shawl around her shoulders, and with the black eyes, she did look good. Jimmy came in and tapped his watch, and I fell about laughing. He smiled, in his wig with black eyes, and with his mustache, he looked hilarious, he winked at me.

"It's dress like Abby day Doll; I always play my part."

I couldn't look at him, Birch and Danny were in fits in the kitchen, he walked up to Birch and he winked, she had tears in her eyes.

"So, Doll, do I have a shot now?" She sniggered, and pulled him into a hug, as she cackled.

"Oh Sweetie, I think a shave first." I was wiping my eyes, he looked such a sight, I looked at Birch.

"If he had longer eyelashes, I would say he looks divine like Diamonique." Birch broke down laughing, and he looked at me and smirked.

"That was even too weird for me Doll, how the hell did those two drive past that place, and think, that is the place for us, I still cannot work it out?" I am not sure we would ever find out.

We jumped in my car, Jimmy followed, and we headed into London, and came in around the back. The shop was not open yet, and already there was a long line of my lookalikes waiting, God it is weird. We parked up in the delivery yard, but it was too late, the press had spotted my car reg plate and knew I had arrived. We walked up the back stairs, to cameras flashing and shouts from them, into the shop, and up to the top floor. Jenny was really excited as she pulled open the curtain a little bit, and Danny peeped in.

"Oh Mum, it's amazing."

At the back where I would sit signing, was a slightly scaled down replica of my arch. The boys on the shoots of summer set had made it for Debs, the full size one would not fit in the shop, so they reduced the scale. Deb's had set it up with a table in front, and two large Sanctuary Press banners hung down either side. It did look brilliant. Both sides of the shop floor running up the length of the shop, were units filled with books for sale. One side had the Publicity Girl, and the other the Old Renshaw Mansion, above which there were giant posters of the covers, Danny could not believe it, I think she was more excited than I was.

At nine the store opened, and people flooded in with the press. On the rail of the upper floor a huge screen hung down, showing my website, and the live stream was counting down. Red ropes were across both of the stairs, as fans arrived in droves and started to queue ready. I moved behind the curtain, as the press came up, I was waiting for one more thing before we began, and she arrived exactly at nine thirty as planned with Tabby, and came up the back stairs.

Anita walked in, and I was stood smiling holding a book, she saw the posters, the huge stacks of books and stopped, as her breath caught in her throat, and her eyes filled with tears. I walked over to her and handed her the book.

"I made a journal of our whole time together, and then made it into a story." She gave a sob, as she looked at me.

"This is your copy, and my heartfelt thanks."

She stood there holding it, and just shook, the picture on the front of the book was her, drawn by Chloe, holding her papers as she hurried into the house. I had seen her arrive that way for years, she gave a huge sniffle, as Birch handed her a tissue.

"I don't know what to say, it was the happiest time of my life working with you." I smiled.

"Well, now not only do you have the memories; you actually have the story." She smiled.

"I love you for this, it means the world to me Abby." I pulled her into a hug.

"It meant the world to me too, I have had such a happy time at your side, thanks."

Deb's slipped in through the curtain, she too looked like me, this was getting really weird, even for me, and I lived with Birch and Jessie. She smiled.

"I told Jimmy to leave that on in bed, a girl has to have her fantasies." She winked and I shuddered. Chloe sniggered as she stood by the door looking around. I looked at Deb's, she was way too happy for my comfort.

"Stop it, you are creeping me out." She giggled, as Birch sniggered and walked up behind her.

"Oh Debbie, you know, I am getting really wet." Danny cringed.

"Please stop, you are staining my innocence." Birch gave a

cackle of a laugh, Jenny looked really uncomfortable.

"I know you all shared the guest house, but I never ever want to know what went on, not ever." Birch turned and looked at her.

"Oh Sweetie, you are missing a treat, did I ever tell you about when Bev caught all three of us naked in bed?" Danny went white.

"Please stop?" Jenny shuddered; I chuckled as Deb's got us prepared.

The press were allowed upstairs, and set up their equipment along the front of the balcony. Edwina counted us down, and as the clock hit eleven, the live stream went active, with the pictures of the podium in front of the black curtain. It came on the large screen; the shop below went instantly silent. I took a deep breath, and with Chloe at my side, and Edwina acting as my publicity girl for the day, we stepped through the curtain and a barrage of flashes went off. Edwina lifted a hand mic, stood a little off from my side.

"Ladies and gentlemen of the press, Miss Watson will make a short statement in regard to two announcements, please wait until she has finished, and then I will direct the questions." She stepped back, as I came forward, I looked right into the live stream camera.

"My readers, I promised all of you I would be back, and here I am. I have not forgotten you, and I have a wonderful surprise for you, but first let me clarify something important." I smiled at the camera, as more flashes went off.

"Leaving the Dixon Group, was not easy for me, they supported my start, and helped me gain the attention I needed, but behind the scenes, I had always harboured a goal, a dream if you like. It was something personal, something that was mine, and of my creation, and ultimately, as I explained to the CEO of the Dixon Group, it was something I was always going to do. Today, I take a leap of faith, as I take that all important new step for me, and I am announcing a new aspect of the AJW brand, as I bring everything together under one banner, with the launch of Sanctuary Press, a new name in publishing." There was a really loud cheer below in the shop, and I giggled, and waited for it to quieten.

"This is my publishing imprint, run exclusively by myself, and my co director, Chloe Pemberton Radley. Together in unison with D&D, I will put out all new works via Sanctuary, and so with that in mind, today I am announcing the publication of two books, to make up for the gap, of which both will be available to buy in all outlets in ten days' time. Just to provide an early treat, today, here in Cog's and Wheelers London, there are ten thousand copies of each book, available only from here, and while stocks last. You will not find them anywhere else for another ten days."

The curtain slid back and below in the store there were gasps, as the full stock came into view behind me.

"The Publicity Girl, is a special story for me, based on my life with Anita Dickinson, the best in her business, and it is not unsimilar to Seeds of Summer in style, just not as graphic. I hope you find it amusing, because we had so much fun working together. The Old Renshaw Mansion, is a return to Gothic Horror, and I have been told by the few who have read it, that it is a good, creepy and at times scary story, ultimately, it is up to you. Thank you." I stepped back, and Edwina moved back to my side.

"Miss Watson will be available to sign books today, once you have paid at the till and have a receipt, you can join the line for signing, marked by the purple ropes at the bottom of the shop. Questions... Okay, you know the ropes, name and title, then question. You."

"Ben Shepperton Daily News Today. Abby, you are a family woman now, how will this impact on business and life for you?"

"Hi Ben, been a while. It won't, I am running this from home, where I am available for my children. As for other events, there will not be as many, as I do want to raise my family. I suppose my priorities have changed with children, but I am actually enjoying my life a lot more, and so will continue with that in mind."

"Peter Matterson, Book Digest. Miss Watson, it is unusual to publish two at a time, will this be a regular event, do you really have that much written already?" I gave a smile.

"Peter, this is a one time thing. The Publicity Girl I have been writing secretly for a long time, and the same goes of the Old Renshaw Mansion, but I do have several stories on the go, and have no shortage of tales to tell, so we shall see." He gave a nod, as Edwina pointed.

"John Dalton, Courier Today. Miss Pemberton, how do you figure in all this, you are an artist not a writer." Chloe stepped forward.

"Mr Dalton, oddly enough, I can read." The press laughed.

"I am creative director and an investor in this company, and I also will be involved in some of the work around the stories that are yet to be put out. Sanctuary will be working with others, as I will be looking to expand the more artistic aspects, such as graphic novels, which is something even I have played around with, so I can assure you, there is plenty for me to do. There is a big market for graphic novels, and Sanctuary aim to become a part of that, and I am actually really enjoying it all, as it is a very exciting market for young readers."

It went on for another ten minutes, before Edwina called it to a halt, and I stepped back, and headed to my table, where Danny sat waiting, she was going to be my assistant for the day. The press cleared their things, although a few grabbed Anita for her thoughts on the book. Deb's opened the ropes and the fans came flocking up, all dressed like me, it was so weird and very surreal.

The word was out, and people were piling in, people were emailing asking if Deb's had an online store with the books available, but I had been quite specific, it had to be an instore purchase. People arrived, and Danny sat at my side passing books over to me as I signed. Jessie appeared for a while, she was bored, and Deb's, had given her a stamp, so she stamped every book as I signed, and the fans loved it. Well, until she got hungry, and then Birch took her off for food.

It was a long day, but it was fun, Chloe sat in so Danny could have a break, and it felt like old times, as we joked around with the fans, and the line never ended. There were groans outside as the shop closed late, and the security let the last few in the shop get their books signed, and then it was time to rest.

We headed home and had takeout, and all sat around the table eating Indian, yeah, we would all regret that in the morning. I made a point of leaving air freshener on my desk before getting into bed. Deb's, Jimmy and the kids stayed over, it bothered me Jimmy looked like me at bedtime. I cringed as I lay in bed, knowing Deb's was having weird sex with a me with a moustache.

Birch thought it was really funny, I looked at her.

"Oh really?"

I jumped out of bed, and then looked in the wardrobe and pulled out the patched wig, pulled back my hair and slipped it on, and then looked at Birch and batted my eyes.

"Hi Sweetie." She shuddered, as I came seductively towards her.

"Oh hell, that is unsettling." I gave her a big smile.

"Oh Sweetie, don't you love me anymore?" She looked really freaked out. I crawled onto the bed, and opened her legs, and her eyes opened wide. I lowered down slowly.

"Oh Sweetie, I need this." She screamed at the top of her lungs.

"OH MY GOD, I AM A CANNIBAL!"

I fell off the bed laughing, as Chloe ran in with her hammer, she stopped dead, and stared at me, and shook her head.

"Oh fuck... You two are weirder than ever." Jessie ran in and skidded to a halt. She looked at me and then Birch, and then looked up at Chloe.

"You are right, they are so messed up, it's unbelievable." Chloe nodded.

"Told you."

The books sold out in less than three days, which I was thrilled about, and once they were released, they raced up the best sellers list. I have never read reviews, but Danny does, and she would run into my room excitedly, and read out the latest great revues. The Publicity Girl was a massive hit with the critics, it appeared, finally, I had written something they could get behind. The Old Renshaw Mansion also was received kindly, and Danny would read out lines like 'Really creepy,' and 'Superbly filled with suspense' and 'Gripping and Addictive.' I loved that she followed them so closely, but reminded her of how not to be fooled, they could also be mean, and hurtful, and she was best off just listening to the fans.

It was May Bank Holiday, and I was sat at my desk. It was really hot, and so wore no clothes, and had the windows open. I could hear the kids playing outside, Sammy was loud as he splashed in the pool with Deli and Baz. I had a few things to finish, and then I was heading to the pool, when there was a tap on the door, I looked around and saw Deb's.

"Hi, not disturbing you, am I?" I shook my head.

"No, God, Deb's you almost live here, you don't have to knock with me."

She smiled, and came in and sat down on the sofa. It is funny, because she never sits on the bed like the rest do. It is like some sort of guest house tradition; she has probably sat on it more over the years than anyone else. I looked at her.

"What's on your mind?" She smiled.

"Abby, I need some advice." I nodded.

"Okay, what about?" She looked at me, and I could see something was eating at her.

"Abby, do you regret quitting the big scene and just being at home all the time?" I shook my head; it was an odd question.

"Well, if you mean the Dixon Group, I felt I had no choice, if I didn't, I think I would have lost Birch. That vulture was certainly trying, and then I heard about Danny and Jessie, so no, not at all. I actually love being a parent, and honestly Deb's, the school group, I really love it, those kids have so much talent. Deb's, I know it sounds crazy, but I really love being a mum." She smiled and nodded her head.

"You are a great mum, Abby; I always knew you would be. Abby, I have had a really good offer for the shops, the Henley's chain want to buy me out, and to be honest, it is more money than the shops are worth. Not the village shop, I told them that one is off the table, but the other eight, and the distribution centre, they want to buy them." I shrugged.

"So, what do you need the advice on, do you want to sell?" She gave a sigh.

"Don't get me wrong, I love it, I love the book business, but it has got so big I am never home, and when I am there Jimmy is not. Abby, do you think Jimmy is unhappy, do you think he misses music?" She had me there, I had not talked to him about it.

"Have you asked him, I mean, he has enjoyed working with Floyd, his latest album will be out soon?" She shook her head.

"I am afraid to ask, if he says yes, I will be devastated, because I really do want to be a good wife." It made sense; she had always put too much pressure on herself.

"Deb's, the way I see it, the shop in the village made you happy, so it is not like you won't have that. I get it, I do, Jimmy at heart is a musician, and be honest, some of your happiest times were with him in the studio. If you are asking me, will you be happy with that, only you can answer that? If not, replace Jimmy with someone you trust and free him up to do music. Deb's, you own the company, be honest, since your dad sold his company in April, he is home more, and you are never going to need the money. It is up to you." She smiled, and nodded her head.

"I knew talking to you would help. Abby, I want to sell, Gem is young, and I want to enjoy it more like you do. I always wanted to be a mum more, and I feel I am missing some important moments." I understood that, I loved being at home with the kids.

"Then do that, be you, come hang out with me and the kids more, I would love that. Let Jimmy go back in the studio, it has been a while since he recorded anything, let him play for a while." She gave me a big smile.

"Yeah, I think I am going to do that, thanks Abby, you know I miss this, I miss us, the talking and all the fun." I smiled.

"I have always been here, with Chloe, Deli and Anthony. Edwina visits a lot more, and in the last few weeks, her and Luke have hardly gone home. Deb's, you have a room still, and there is plenty of space for the kids. Two weeks ago, when Jenny stayed over Jessie slept in the kids' room, and Jenny took her bed, her and Danny are so like us. Although while you are here, do you know who Brett Palmer is?" She frowned.

"Isn't he that rough kid from the back of Garden Street, his dad won some cash, he is about seventeen, his mum is nice, she comes in the shop, why?"

"Jenny quietly told me, he has been hassling Danny, she has been quieter than usual, Birch has been looking for intel on him."

Birch had found it, and was hot on the trail, and she knew just where to find him. He was dealing drugs at the back of the railway station near the kids play ground. She tied back her hair, put on a woollen hat, pulled up her hoodie, and approached him, with her hand in her bag.

"What you got?" He looked her up and down, in her torn jeans and old shoes.

"What you need?" She pulled a huge knife out of her bag, and gripped him by the scruff of his neck.

"Your balls on a plate for starters. I heard you have been hassling young girls for sex acts and pictures, and trying to get them into the shit you sell?" She held the knife at his throat, and her eyes burned with rage. He looked at her.

"I am not afraid of you, old hag." She smiled.

"And Sweetie, that is your first mistake. You should be polite, especially when the goods downstairs are at risk." He smirked.

"I got friends." She smiled.

"I know, I got pictures of you all dealing, and emailed them to the law today. I am not sure your friends will be around for a while, you see, they all went for a drive with the blue lights people, so it seems to me, you are alone now." He suddenly looked afraid, but tried to act tough.

"You are a fucking mental bitch; it is you who wants locking up." She smiled.

"Keep it up Sweetie, now tell me, which do you like best, the canal, the woods, or the heath, because honestly, I do want to bury your chopped up body parts in a spot you like?" He started to swallowed hard, as she pushed the knife harder against his skin, and his face paled.

"I don't want to be buried in any, I don't want to be buried." She smiled.

"Good, stay away from the girl's, especially Danny Watson, I like her, she is sweet, too sweet for your tooth. Do you understand me, and if I see or hear of you selling this fucked up shit to kids again, I am picking the spot, are we clear?" He nodded his head rapidly. She smiled.

"Good, because I am watching, and I will know."

She pushed him hard, and he fell over in the grass. Birch turned, and walked back to the bridge over the railway, Chloe nodded at her, with her big hood up over most of her face.

"Are we good?" Birch gave a nod; Chloe gave a sigh of relief.

"Fuck, you can be scary, come on, Edwina and Luke are up here."

For the rest of the year, Danny was no longer harassed, and started to smile again. At the start of the summer holiday, we booked a hotel in Hastings, and met up with Celia. She was so delighted to meet Danny and Jessie, and it was lovely seeing her again. Birch made a huge fuss of her, and we spent three of the days of our holiday walking with her on the clifftops, as she talked of how her and Lillian had walked here fifty years ago as they fell in love.

It felt so special as I took in the beauty of the place, walking with Celia on one arm, and Birch on the other, as the kids explored in front of us. Danny took many pictures, and when we returned to Wotton, we showed them Louise and Stacy, and there were many tears. I am so glad we went, and I will never forget it, in a way, I thought, just for a short while, linking my arm on those clifftops, she had a paler version of Lillian to walk with one more time.

Three months later, we got a phone call from Vanessa Douglas to inform us Celia had passed away, it was a heart breaking moment for all of us, and once again, it felt like the end of an era. Birch and I sat up that night and talked, and she told me how she was in a strange way happy, for in her beliefs, Celia and Lillian, were once again united. I will never forget watching her and seeing the absolute belief in her knowing their spirits would be joined forever, and it gave me great comfort, and in an odd sort of way, it felt like Birch was telling me, that no matter what happened, we would be joined together forever and beyond.

Celia's remains were returned to Wotton, and she was placed beside Lillian, in a very moving service, Birch was right, they were together again, and it felt right. That was the last time I saw Marjorie, four months later she too passed away, and it really felt like the end of an era, as the faces from those days when I returned home from Uni, faded away to be replaced by others, and life as it always had in Wotton, changed the players, and continued.

The following winter, we lost Delphine, and Anthony broke. It was a really difficult time, seeing him so hurt and in pain was agonising for both Birch and myself. In her will, she left everything to Anthony, and wrote him a letter, that told him, she had always seen him as the son she never had. It was such a beautiful letter, as she spoke of how proud she was of him, and the man he had become, I cried reading it, because she was so right.

Anthony put her house up for sale, and Anita and Tabs bought it, and moved into Wotton, which was great, because I got to see more of her. I had really missed working with her, and so we had coffee on a regular basis in the tea rooms, and talked of our adventures together, it always ended up the same, with both of us hugging each other in tears, I really was tempted to steal her back off Roni.

Chapter 36

Life Goes Ever On.

Life moves ever on, Deb's sold her business, and returned to the shop and village life, I continued to make limited appearances, and to write. I finally polished up the Old Wiccan Cottage, and put it out, much to the delight of Tabby, who had waited years, to finally read the novel I started that day at Sunny Bank. Birch worked on a new book, but would not tell me what it was about, and a few years passed by, and Danny was fifteen, and Jessie hit an even noisier twelve.

Danny was growing into a beautiful young woman, and she was so clever, and had set her sights on university, and studying English, Business, and Public Relations, that sounded so familiar. It was spring, and I was sat in my room editing my latest manuscript, which I had titled 'The Heart of the Rainbow,' Which was a comedy story, set on the life of a sexually deviant perverted artist. I was reading the text and was chuckling, as I sipped a fresh coffee, when my phone went off, it was Roni, I picked it up.

"Hi Mum, nice to hear from you, what's up?"

"Abby, I am in the tea rooms, fancy a coffee, I need to talk?"

"Yeah, why not here?"

"Abby, just meet me."

I grabbed my coat, and walked into the village, I love the tea rooms, Stacy and Louise had knocked the back room out to make it three times the size. They had discovered plans drawn up by Lillian and Celia, and the moment they saw them, they knew they would finish off their dream for a perfect Tea Room. Their business boomed, and yet it still remained the image of the same quaint village tea room it always had done.

It was certainly appreciated in bad weather, as it could fit three times the people into it. What I loved the most, was that on the far back wall, they had hung a large painting done by Chloe, of Lillian and Celia. It had been taken at my wedding, and in tribute to them, Chloe painted it, and gave it Louise and Stacy. I always sat with it in view, as it made the place feel like they were still here, watching over us as always.

I arrived and ordered coffee, and saw Roni wave. I wandered over and waited for Fran to bring it over. I sat down and smiled at Roni, she was aging, and her hair was whiter than ever.

"Okay, so why all the cloak and dagger, that is my genre?" She gave a giggle.

"Abby, I wanted to see you alone. I have a proposal, and if I go anywhere near your house, Jemi will know, I am sure she has bat senses." I giggled.

"She is batty enough so why not, so what is it your mind is scheming now?"

Roni sat back in her seat. She lifted her coffee and sipped, as her green eyes watched over the top of the cup.

"Abby, how would you like Anita back, I know that idiot Jeffery cannot get you out there, he has tried, and yet you resist good events?" I smirked; she had a finger in every pie.

"I would love nothing more than to work with Anita, but Roni, she is Dixon Publishing." She gave a smile as she put her cup down.

"Well yeah, unless of course Sanctuary Press bought me out." I gave a giggle.

"Why would I do that?" Her green eyes twinkled, with the same mischief as Birch's.

"Because I want you too."

Fran delivered my cup as I sat momentarily dumb struck, I nodded my thanks at her. I looked at Roni.

"Are you serious, why would you want to sell?" She gave a little chuckle.

"Abby, you know Martin Williams recently passed away?"

I nodded, I had heard and was saddened to hear it, he was good with me in the early days of my books. Roni watched me closely; she was so like Birch at times.

"Well, he owned forty five percent of the shares in DPG, Katie is trying to raise the money, but I have first option to buy, they are under market value as his son wants a quick sale. Abby, this is a very good deal, the moment you purchase, the stock will be worth double what you paid. He has agreed to sell them to you, Andrew has done the paperwork, I have it here, and I know you have the cash; the stock returns alone will pay you back in a year."

From a business point of view, it was a brilliant deal, and I could not deny, it was tempting.

"That is not a controlling share, you have fifty one percent, it will be your ship not mine." She smiled.

"Oh, did I forget to mention, I am giving Danny, a twenty percent holding as an early birthday present, and I do believe she holds twenty percent of Sanctuary, does she not?" I started to laugh.

"Wow you are so sneaky, but why mum, why sell at all?" She leaned over the table, and took my hand.

"Abby, you know how much I love you, having you as a daughter has been a joy for me. Look Abby, I am sixty six, a publishing company needs younger blood, and honestly, I will be handing everything over to Jemi shortly. You know I always wanted you two side by side running things when I went, call it a crazy old lady's dream. Abby, when Jemi met you, I knew then you would be her future, it is why I brought you in to publish you. I built DPG for you, I knew you had no interest in therapies, your future always lay in writing. Look, you run the publishing wing, she runs the therapy side of things, I get the best there is to guide my legacy. The board meeting is next week, and I know you still will not take any shares of the Group, so buy these shares and mine, let Sanctuary swallow DPG and get complete control of all your work back, and with it comes Anita. Don't tell me you do not miss her, I have read the book three times, hell, just the mention of your name has her in tears. Abby, do this, do it for me."

I gave a sigh and sat back in my chair, she looked so serious, and I knew I was wasting my time; she was actually the only thing worse than her daughter, she would hound me till the grave if I did not do this.

"You always put me in an impossible position, if I say no, I will come across looking like an utter shit. Do you and Will sit in bed at night, plotting up ways to trap me?" She gave a happy chuckle.

"Well, it's not that dramatic, but we talk."

She pulled the papers out of her bag, and I looked at them, I knew Andrew's signature well, so I signed them, she smiled, and held out her hand.

"Congratulations DPG is now yours, the meeting of the Dixon Group board is next Monday, we will announce everything then. I take it you are all still coming at weekend?" I gave a laugh.

"I am not capable of keeping Jessie away from Granddad Will." She smiled, and handed me a letter.

"Give that Danny, it is conformation of her shares, I transferred them this morning, she will need to be at the meeting too, after all, she is a shareholder." I shook my head; she was a slippery old eel. She stood up.

"Finish your coffee, I am going to pop in to see Jemi, and then meeting Andrew for lunch, Abby, for now, say nothing to Jemi, let me tell her. See you at weekend, drive safely." I smiled, she was cunning, and tricky, but I loved her deeply.

I really admired Roni, I had since the day I met her, she never ceased to amaze me at how sharp and how fast her mind worked. I sat back in my seat as I sipped my coffee, and I was actually glad. I had all my books back again, the hands of death and cursed books series were mine again, as was seeds and shoots of summer. Somehow, I felt new cover designs were required.

The weekend arrived, and Friday night after school, we packed up the kids and headed off to Uppermill. Like Wotton, it changes little and I like that, although I am glad I have a car now. I have never forgotten walking up the hills dragging my heavy case, the locals around here have good legs.

The girls got the twin room, and Birch and I got her old room, little had changed, the bed was the same one she bought during her summer living with me, which she had her dad fit, so when we came home for the last week before Uni, we could still sleep together. It still had all her bookcases minus the books, but I loved that Roni and Will had left it untouched. It brought back a lot of happy memories, even my moment of panic as Bev clumped down the hallway, and I thought I was going to be raped. I smiled as I looked at the door and Birch giggled.

"It was a fun time, wasn't it?" I frowned.

"What, panicking because I thought I was going to be raped?" She gave a smile.

"Yeah, about that, lie back and take your pants off." I lay back and giggled.

"Honestly, when that door opened and I saw her, I was scared shitless." She giggled as she sat at my side, and looked down on me as she stroked the hair from my face.

"It is silly Deads, as I look back, but even then, I was in love with you, just afraid to admit it."

"I am glad you did; Birch I have had a wonderful life with you, and the kids have just made it even better. I know we had a bit of a road block a few years back, but look at us, look what we have. I love my life, Birch." She smiled.

"So sincere and so full of love, you have not changed at all over the years Deads, and I love that." I smiled.

"Hate to point out the obvious, but you are a hundred times more bonkers than you were back then." She smiled, her green eyes twinkling and so filled with love.

"MUM, TELL DANNY IT IS NOT TRUE, TELL HER PEOPLE DON'T SINK IN THE MIRE, AND THE MOORS IS NOT FILLED WITH UPRIGHT SKELETONS!"

Birch started to laugh; she sat up and turned to see Jessie stood in the doorway.

"Sweetie, tell Danny not to be stupid, they are not stood up, they all lay down." Jessie nodded, and turned to Danny.

"See... Wait... THEY ARE LAY DOWN, THAT IS WORSE!" Danny appeared with a smirk.

"I am not sure about that sis, what would you rather do, walk on their heads, or their rotted naughty bits?" She shook her head.

"I am not walking on any."

We settled in, and relaxed with a meal, and over Saturday and Sunday, we explored Uppermill and walked on the moors with Jessie, who tip toed, and kept saying sorry to lumps, much to Birch and Danny's amusement.

Monday morning arrived and dressed in suits, we took the train to Manchester, which the girls loved. Will was taking Jessie shopping, which meant she was getting spoiled... Again. We headed into the hotel where the conference suite was booked for us. Roni's assistant had taken care of everything. We walked in to see a table surrounded by nine other people, one of whom was Katie, wow, she had not aged well, and my God she was fat. It was clear, living the high life, and first class all the way, was not good for her waistline.

She had really ballooned out, and her face had really aged, is it wrong that it cheered me up to see it? She saw me and took her chance, considering it had been four years since she had seen me to have a pop.

"What the hell is the dark princess doing here, I thought this was a shareholders meeting?" I smirked.

"If you stop talking and listen saggy tits, you will find out."

Birch giggled, and a few of the others put their heads down, Katie frowned and looked down at her breasts, as we sat down. Danny sat next to me, and leaned in.

"Is that her, the one who caused trouble before your wedding?" I smiled.

"Yep, that is the fat red headed slapper in the flesh; avoid her she is trouble." Danny nodded as she looked at her.

Roni opened her agenda, and flicked through the papers, and scanned them. She looked up at the other members.

"This will not be a long meeting, well not for me anyhow." She took a deep breath.

"You have all served me well in this company, but I am aging, and feel it is time to hand over the baton." Birch looked at her and frowned.

"What's going on?" Roni smiled and looked at her.

"Jemi, it is time, I am going to hand over to you." Birch tensed, and looked panicked.

"Whoa, hold up a minute, we have not even discussed this, Mum, I am not ready, not yet." Roni gave a sigh.

"When then, will you ever be ready? Jemi, I know you, and I love you dearly, but you cannot keep holding off to keep me propped in a seat I no longer want." Birch looked at me, and then back at her mum.

"Look Mum, not here, just give me a minute, somewhere private." Roni gave a sigh.

"Alright Jemi." She looked at the others.

"You and Abby come with me."

She stood up, and I had no choice but to leave Danny sat in her seat, as Roni walked through the door, and down a hallway to another smaller conference room. I was feeling panicked. Birch was looking angry and upset, she walked in and went straight into attack mode.

"How could you do that Mum? You do not just walk into a room and then casually say, oh by the way, here you go, it's all yours I am off. Bloody hell Mum, I have been here all weekend, and we should have talked about this." Roni gave a snort as she looked at Birch.

"Jemi, I am getting old, you knew this day would come, look, I have divided up the company, you may as well know because, I am going to announce it. Jemi, DPG has gone." Her eyes almost exploded.

"WHAT! Mum, you know I wanted to give that to Deads, and you sold it, how could you?" Roni gave her a hard stare.

"Jemi, you could not give it away, the board would oust you the moment you did. If you keep your temper down, as I was just going to say before you very rudely flew off the handle, I sold it to Abby. Well, Sanctuary Press, Abby owns the controlling interest with your daughter Danny, who has twenty percent, which is why she is here." Birch turned and looked at me.

"You bought it and did not tell me, wow, is that your knife in my back?" I went to talk but Roni cut in.

"Jemi, I was the one who asked her not to say anything, I wanted to talk with you in the break. Do not blame Abby, this is on me, and if you don't want control, I am sure Katie will have her name on the door in weeks. Jemi, when Martin Williams died of heart failure, Katie went after his shares, but I had first refusal, they were offered me by his son for a third of the price. I approached Abby, it was too good a deal to miss, and it gave her control of all her written works. Katie does not know they have been sold yet, Jemi, I was protecting you and Abby, if she had got control, we would be back where we were four years ago, I do not want that."

Birch calmed down, and sat down in a seat, she gave a long sigh, and then looked up at her mum.

"I do not feel ready to run everything yet." Roni looked at her.

"You have too." Birch shook her head.

"No, I don't, I don't have to do anything." Roni looked really angry.

"Jemi, you don't understand you have to do this, now stop acting stupid, and just take bloody command will you?" Birch shook her head, and her voice rose.

"I am not being stupid; I am not ready." Roni walked closer to her, and stared at her; her green eyes burned.

"Then get bloody ready, because you are taking over today, Jemi, please, do it." Birch stood up, and stared her right in the eyes.

"Give me one good reason why I need to, just one mum, because honestly, you are doing a great job, and you have a good few years left in this seat."

Roni looked at me, and you know that sinking feeling you suddenly get? Well, I suddenly got it and went cold. Roni's eyes filled with tears, as she turned back to Birch.

"Jemi, I have cancer!"

And there it was, my world stopped for a moment. Birch faltered, she swallowed, her voice died in her throat. I felt my insides somersault, and a huge lump grow up in my throat, as Birch stumbled on her words.

"Wait... What?" Tears filled her eyes.

"Mum... No... I mean... No." Roni nodded, and her voice lowered.

"Jemi, Abby, I start treatment next week, I am going to be ill for a while." I shook my head, and tears filled my eyes. She looked at us, as I took Birch's hand.

"Girl's, I need you. I need you to be strong for me, there is a good chance I will get through this and I am taking it for Will. Jemi, it is time, and Abby, it is time for you too. Please girls, do this for me?" I felt shocked, hurt, terrified, and a huge pain flowed up inside me.

I think we both felt the same natural instinct, as at the same time both of us snatched at her, and pulled her into a hug. I did not know what to say, it hurt so badly hearing it, I could not imagine her suffering, or even leaving us. I didn't want that, I know Birch didn't, I just held her and wept with Birch. She squeezed us hard.

"Girls, I love you both so much, but this is life, and it must be faced. We have to do this, and we have to do it now. Look, I have been streamlining and downsizing for years, and by splitting it between you both, then you have a sizable chunk each to manage.

Girls, I don't want Katie at the helm, I want you two, I built this for both of you. Jemi, Abby, you are my daughters, this is my gift to you both, use it to do good and live well, and pass it on to your daughters to secure their future, I am so proud of my girls, let me show it."

She let us go and stood back and looked at us, she smiled. I was so lost and feeling so much emotion, I wanted to speak, but I couldn't. I just stood there with tears streaming down my face, I loved her so much, and I could not bear the thought of actually losing her. Roni nodded.

"You two are Dixon women, so dry those eyes, put on your armour, and let's go and do this, and we will talk later, okay?" Birch gave a long sigh, sniffled, and wiped her eyes.

"You ask a lot of us mum, you hit us with that, and then just brush it off for a bloody meeting. I am not you mum?" She smiled.

"No Jemi, you are stronger, you have just never allowed yourself to see it, you are right, you are not me, you are my mother's double... Right, let's go back in there and dish out some long overdue karma." Wow, even now, she is still the strongest woman I know.

Fifteen minutes later, having washed our faces and grabbed a coffee, and took a lot of deep breaths, we walked back into the room. Danny was talking with Joan Harrington, the senior publishing editor of Dixon Publishing about my books, with Craig Smithers adding input occasionally, she smiled when she saw us. Katie was talking quietly in a corner with two of the other board members, her eyes followed me as we walked along the table, back to our seats. It was pretty clear to me, nothing had changed and she was up to her tricks, sneaking around to do deals that benefitted only her.

We all sat back down, and Roni continued as if nothing had happened.

"Right where were we? Oh yes, as of today, my daughter Jemima will assume head of the company, her shares will be increased, and she will have majority control." Katie leaned forward, and looked up the table.

"What if some of the board members are not happy with that?"

Roni looked at Birch. Birch looked right at her.

"Then leave, I will buy your shares now, and you can take your fat ass out of this board room, I will not deny, I won't miss you." The two guys leaning forward with her, sat back, Katie stared up the table.

"There is still the matter of the open shares of the publishing aspect of the business to discuss." Roni leaned back in her seat.

"Dixon Group no longer has a publishing company, it has been taken over by another rival, which was to be my second order of business. As of now, we are just a therapeutic practice company, which is why I have every confidence in my daughter to manage it. All of you will get a substantial payment in the next shares pay out." Katie furrowed her brow.

"Hang on a minute, what about Martin Williams, he was a major shareholder?" I leaned onto the table and smiled.

"And now you know why this dark little princess is here. Sorry Katie, you were not fast enough. I own the forty five percent Martin owned, and my daughter Danny, owns twenty percent of Dixon Publishing, leaving Roni only thirty one percent. Just to be clear here, it is Sanctuary Press, not Dixon." I smiled, as I sat back, and Danny looked at me and giggled, I looked down the table.

"Joan, Craig, this is my daughter, isn't she beautiful, we will all be working together from now on." Katie looked livid.

"You do know K.O has longstanding contracts with Dixon?" I nodded.

"I know, but there is no Dixon anymore, I just told you, it's Sanctuary Press, we took you over." Birch bit her lip. Katie stood up and glared at me.

"You fucking set me up you bitch; I should have known four years ago when you sold me your shares, it was the start of a stitch up." I relaxed in the chair.

"May I remind you Katie, because you appear to have forgotten, it was you who named me the Dark Princess, so what, are you pissed off because I am acting like one?" Birch and Roni sniggered; I waved at the empty door.

"Hi Chloe."

Katie gave a squeal, and turned around fast, and Birch, Roni and Danny burst out laughing. Katie looked back, she was livid, turned, and stormed out in a temper. I sat back and winked at Danny.

"That is how a Watson deals with problems, we wait, and when least expected, we strike. I like to call it the gothic sting."

She giggled and gave me a huge smile. The meeting continued and we all stood around as coffee was served and talked. Danny stayed by my side as she listened to me talk with Joan and Craig, and started to see how the company would be restructured around Sanctuary.

A press conference had been arranged, after the meeting, so with Roni, Birch and Danny, I walked down to the room, where Anita waited, she was surprised to see Danny and me, and looked at me with a confused look.

"Why are you here Abby, I was told this was Dixon Group Business?" I nodded.

"It is, I am here with Roni, I have advised her, and Danny is here to just get the experience." Anita looked at me.

"Are you being straight Abby?" I winked.

"Anita, I married a woman, I have never been completely straight." She giggled.

"It is nice to see you; I have missed your wit."

"Yeah, me too."

Roni signalled. Anita walked us all in and we sat down, I sat next to Anita, as the journalists looked a little surprised to see me, cameras clattered and flashes went off. Roni took the lead.

"Good afternoon, everyone. Today we see another change to the Dixon Group, as it evolves into the new era, and I feel it is time to take a back seat and bring in someone with more skill to take the therapeutic practice forward. This morning, I have handed Dixon Therapeutic to my daughter and successor, Doctor Jemima Dixon, and in order to streamline the group more, I have sold Dixon Publishing, in a merger deal with Sanctuary Press." I looked at Anita, and whispered as Roni spoke.

"Want a new job, with just two authors, because Jemi and me want a good publicist?" She looked stunned.

"Are you frigging serious?" I winked.

"Welcome home kid, I am your new boss, oh, and the little me here, she owns a chunk of the company too." Danny smiled. Anita sat back in her chair with a big smile. She pointed.

"Amy Walker, River Cable TV News. Miss Watson, Abby, did we just hear that right, Sanctuary Press has bought all of Dixon Publishing?" I smiled.

"Amy, how wonderful to see you back with a camera, I told you that the studio would bore you." She giggled,

"Yes, you heard right, Danny, and I now own the controlling interest, and as you know, Chloe and myself own Sanctuary. To be honest, I left all my books with Dixon, but I wanted them back, so I bought the company, and I have control again." She gave a big smile.

"Abby, you own D&D, so where will that leave K.O?" I sat back in my seat.

"I will definitely be keeping Joan and Craig, they have been a remarkable team for Dixon, so I am happy to have them still on board, I spoke to them a little while ago. Miss O'Reilly appears unhappy with the merger, but I am open to bids for contracts. D&D has a lot of contacts and contractors, and there is room for K.O, although we do have different working arrangements than those at Dixon, but my door is open should she wish to use it. I will say, I am delighted to regain the services of my publicist, I have missed her, so from now on, all contact for me, will be through her."

By the time we were done, it felt like a good day's work, and we headed back on the train to Uppermill. Birch was really upset and wanted to talk, so whilst the kids were kept busy, we sat in our room with Roni, and she detailed us in on her illness and how it would be treated. It had to be done soon to give her a chance, and she was starting immediately.

Neither of us wanted to leave, but she had hired a private nurse to help her, and she did not want the children to see her during treatments, as she told us it would not be pretty. Under protest, and having spoken to Will, we said our goodbyes, and loaded the car, Jessie had extra bags and a big smile.

It was hard to focus on the road home, Birch was very quiet, but I understood that. It took a few months for her to really open up about it all, as she made many trips home alone, and she saw her mother go through hell and start to recover. It frightened her, and Birch was afraid to admit that to me, a person who had always looked to her. She can be so silly at times, I knew that, we were both frightened, Roni was a massively important figure in her life.

Three years later, having spent a week alone with Roni and Will, Birch divided the therapeutic practice from the media company, which D&D bought. She sold Dixon Therapeutic to all of the counsellors that worked there. She helped them put a bid together, and as a collective the practice was sold. The only condition was, it remained named the Veronica Dixon Mental Well Being Centre, and she returned to Sweetie's Retreat, and dissolved the Dixon Group board, paying them off with the money from the sale.

The first book I published of hers as the larger Sanctuary Press, was the 'Dynamics of a Daughter, Wife and Mother, by Doctor Jemima Dixon,' and I was so proud to stand beside her and Anita, as the announcement was made. It was such a great book, and the dedication simply read. 'My love always to Veronica, Abigail, Daniella and Jessica' It was a huge hit for her, and we were all so proud of her, Roni cried when she read it, but was so incredibly proud of her daughter.

Life went on, and we helped Gavin buy out Mum and Ellen as he took over Waterside Galleries with his new model, and artist wife Sarah. Danny grew up, sailed through college and went on to Uni, and qualified with distinctions, and Jessie aced her GCSE's, headed to college, and looked for a university to study medicine.

Patrick died two years later, followed a year later by Hatty, and mum and all of us took that really hard. It crushed me to lose Hatty, and even now, I still miss her. I began to realise that the hardest thing about aging, is you lose those you love the most. She would have been pleased to know; she did not get buried on the green. At her funeral, we all opened a beer, toasted her, and then poured some on her casket as it was lowered, somehow, it felt like she would love the irreverence, and laugh at us for it.

When Farmer Sutton died, Birch bought all the heathland from his wife, and created a trust to manage it, to ensure that like Old Mr Sutton had promised, it would remain the focal point of beauty it always had been. She named the trust. 'The Memorial Heath Trust,' and gave the ownership to Danny and Jessie, to guarantee their parents ashes were never disturbed, and a plaque of remembrance was placed in front of the tree, as was, one for May.

Wotton changed little, the players changed, but the village remained the same, a small pristine village in the heart of England, representing an image, of how England once was. There were still secrets happening behind closed doors, and those who wanted control, but that is village life. It changes little, gossip is still faster than messaging, and secrets always come out in the ways people never thought they could, and adults still bullied too. We tried, and we fought, and we remained ourselves, living our life, at number three Waterside Lane, Wotton Dursley.

I often sit in a chair under my arch and reflect on my life, about all I have done, and all I have seen, and it has been a curious sort of life. I wrote an autobiography, about my curious life, and gave it the title, 'It's A Curious Thing.' I felt it best I got it down before I went bonkers, Danny will publish it after I am gone.

Curio Life continued to grow, and we turned it into a foundation. We hit Canada and did another Curio Live in Toronto, again over four days, and raised the amount to open four more centres. It is strange, back when we set up the site, all those young faces, with help and support, grew up and had families of their own, and they all became patrons of the site. The same applied to all the young, Danny, Jenny, Sammy, and Jessie as new Curio's brought up their generation, and continued to work for the benefit of all.

We suffered in our first few years together in Wotton, and in a bid to get our story heard, we gave a voice to millions, and we ended up helping a lot of people, which is something I am so proud of, and I was thrilled to see Danny and Jessie follow in our footsteps.

I am so proud of my girls, Danny; she has grown into a remarkable woman. When I first held a writing class at Oxendale High, many years ago, I set the group the task of writing about an object, and I told them to let their imagination run wild. She wrote a wonderful little story about the heath, and the love of her parents, I found it beautiful, and touching, and I wrote on the bottom, exactly what Birch once told me at Uni, 'you should expand this.' Two days before she left for university, at just age eighteen, she walked into my bedroom, and handed me a manuscript.

"I want you to read this while I am away Mum." I looked at it, and frowned.

"What is it?" She smiled looking awkward.

"Do you remember that story I wrote about the heath for my first essay for the writers group age nine?" I nodded at her and smiled, as I remembered.

"Yeah, it was a good piece, I told you to expand it." She handed over the large stack of papers.

"Well, I did it, I mean, it has taken years, and a lot of looking into the past, but it's finished. Mum don't be too hard on me; I have worked hard on this." I gave a chuckle, that insecurity I knew well.

"What is it called?" She looked more than a little awkward.

"The Children of Summer Heath, it is about my parents, and what I could put together from their letters and emails. It is a fantasy story, but I built it around their summer here together attending your wedding." I smiled.

"I cannot wait to read it." She looked terrified.

"Promise Mum, go easy on me, this is my first manuscript." I started to laugh.

"Danny, you have a huge talent, stop worrying. Look, if it needs anything, I will be gentle."

It needed nothing, it was brilliant, imaginative and wonderful, I loved it. It made me cry at times, but I think a good book should. It still is my favourite book of hers. She followed in my footsteps, and became a great writer, and when I stood down, from the school writing class, she stepped up and took it over. I sat in for a few and watched how she managed, and she reminded me so much of myself, when I first began with Mrs Taylor.

Jenny published several wonderful books with Sanctuary Press, and she took over her mother's book shop. She was so like Deb's, and it gave me great joy to see the close friendship her and Danny shared, they were so like Deb's and me at times, and at times, I saw a little of mum and Hatty in them, which gave me great hope.

Helen and Gem followed their dad into music, Helen was an

amazing guitarist, and Gem a really good drummer, but there again, he was taught by Zac. Zac was ugly, but he was a hell of a great drummer. Jimmy was so proud of them as they formed a band named Waterside Wild, and he sat in the studio, and produced their first demo tapes with Baz.

Danny grew up as a part of Sanctuary Press, we ran it together with Chloe. Between Chloe and her, we became well known for graphic novels, and built a huge following, of which I was delighted to see, Chloe produced a whole series of the Hands of Death. As I aged, I stepped back more, and let Danny take the lead. She had a great head for business, and she has done a wonderful job, and all whilst writing in her spare time, I am so proud of her. It is funny, I was convinced as a young woman I did not want kids, and yet Danny and Jessie, became so important to me in my life, they were mine and Birch' s greatest joy.

Roni died seven years later, and two years after that we lost Will, I still think to this day, her loss was too much for him to live with. I understood that, and he knew that, as he saw it in our many conversations. Will was a loving father to me at a time when my dad wasn't, and losing him broke my heart, he was such a wonderful caring man. It hit Birch and Jessie really hard.

We travelled to Sunny Bank, with their ashes, and Birch revealed one more secret, and walked me to the clearing we had sunbathed in, on that difficult week of recovery before our wedding. She showed me a large tree of white, stood alone on the edge of the clearing. Here lay the ashes of her grandparents, and I began to understand it was why she loved to sit here in silence so often when we were here, for her, it allowed her to stay close to her grandfather.

With heavy hearts, we planted another tree twenty feet away, and below with great tears and heavy hearts, we placed Roni and Will back together and laid them to rest in the place they loved the most. It was the saddest time I ever had at Sunny Bank, we stayed just a few days, and returned home.

Life felt different after that. Things continued as always, but the world felt different, not quite the same if you can understand that. Roni had a profound effect on me, I respected and admired her more than any other, she taught me so much about life, myself, and business, and I was grateful to her. I grew to love her so very deeply, and the pain of losing her still lingers within me. I often see the blue icon on my task bar, and pictures of her smiling face appear in my thoughts, and her happy voice echoes in my mind. 'Abby, what a lovely surprise.' I miss her so much, she was my go-to, when I could not muddle things out. Roni always knew what was on my mind, and was there to comfort me when I was at my worst, there is such a huge void in my life today, left by her absence.

A long time ago at Sunny Bank, I decided to compile a photo archive of our life together, and over the years it grew vast, as I recorded every aspect of all we did. It started as just Birch and I, but soon expanded to include every picture I had ever taken, with dates and places, as I recorded everything about the Curio's and the families we raised. It got so big, I moved it all onto a five trilobite hard drive, and during the many summers I had at Sunny Bank, I added all of Jeff's pictures of Birch's life.

Like Morty had once done, I labelled the hard drive, and named it, 'The Curio Chronicles,' which felt fitting. It really felt like it was the complete photo history of all of us, and every year I have added to it for well over thirty years. I often sit and put the pictures on slide show, and spend my day watching and smiling, especially now as I have aged. I do think it was the best decision I have ever made.

I got old, I look in the mirror and just see my mother, that just does not feel like me at all. I am still me on the inside, probably a more frustrated me, because I am still pretty wild and lively, but my body does not always let me do the things I want to, and it pisses me off. That is this curious life we live, I suppose?

Chapter 37

A Curious Life.

Birch came out of the retreat and took my hand with a smile, and we crossed the road and walked across the green. I stopped and looked around, Wotton was busy, and looked exactly as it always had, it felt strange, everything has aged, except this place, I gave a happy sigh.

"Nothing changes, only the people." Birch gave a chuckle.

"The faces are different, but the behaviour is still pretty much the same. I suppose Sweetie, the only real difference is we are not seen as whores and transients anymore, I guess even we are considered too old for that now." I frowned.

"Christ Birch, we are not that old, and after last night, you clearly have not aged, I would say you are naughtier now than you have ever been." She giggled.

"You are still a little beastie, it is probably a good job most of this lot do not see inside our bedroom at night, although it would be fun, I sort of miss not having the Shrew Crew slag me off." I chuckled as I squeezed her hand, and turned to the road.

It is odd how life just sneaks up on you. I have reached the grand old age of fifty nine, and yet, I do not really feel any different from that young woman of nineteen. I still think Birch is the most beautiful woman I have ever met, even if she does have pure white hair and a few wrinkles. We certainly still have a yen for sex, and our sex life is as wild now as it has always been, our bodies have changed, but we are both still in good shape, and take good care of ourselves.

Okay, so I gained a little weight, but I am not a million miles off from my youth, I do yoga and walk a lot. With Birch in charge with Chloe, we all eat much healthier these days and take our supplements, and I think all of us still look pretty good. Birch has an amazing body for a sixty year old, and she still has the energy of her twenties, which okay, at times leaves me a little breathless, but even so, there are thirty year olds in the village who look in much worse condition than us lot.

Birch really looks like her mum, her hair is shorter these days, and sadly the patches are gone, although I cannot say much, my hair is a silvery grey these days, I guess even I reached that point where dying it just felt pointless. It was cool for a long time, as I just let it grow, so I was silver which faded into black with red tips, I really liked how it looked. Anthony finds it hard these days, he has had problems with his hands, and so as he struggled, I decided to simply stop, and give him and my roots a break.

These days he is more a supervisor in his shop; he walks around his salon giving hints and tips and talking to his customers. He has trained quite a lot of girls, and a couple of guys in his time. His shop is still bright and modern, and does all the latest trends, although he is sole proprietor these days since Delphine passed away.

Things change, and yet they don't, and the circle of life in Wotton continues. We crossed the road, and walked down the passage into the woodland, I breathed in and smiled.

"I love this place." Birch chuckled.

"I love that we saved it, it is looking so much better these days, I think Colin Banks was a good choice for manager. He really has the team working well, the new benches are a good addition, as well as the stone bridge and the stream widening program, it has really given the place more character."

"I think we did good; it feels like forever ago, Danny was pestering me yesterday to go back and run for chair, but I think we did enough." Birch was looking up at the canopy of the trees, as the sun broke through in patches.

"We played our part, I never wanted to hang on like Marjorie did, seven years was enough, and be honest Deads, what else was there to do? The village looked a thousand times better when we were done, all that is left is the mundane stuff, no, I am happy having played my part, it was enough."

We crossed the bridge and headed up onto the path towards Manor Road summit. It was so much easier walking here these days, we had added a lot of new paths when we took on the Dursley Woodlands project, and there was a labyrinth of good quality sandy pathways to follow these days, all sign posted clearly. I looked at Birch as she smiled to herself, I felt she was remembering those wild times hacking back the overgrown shrubs.

"You have never regretted it, have you?" She turned, and her bright green eyes danced.

"How do you mean, regretted what?" I shrugged.

"You know, coming here, and leaving your Manchester life behind?" She stopped and turned to me.

"Deads, I told you." She lifted her hand to my chest.

"Manchester was just a place I once lived, this, this here, this has always been my home, the place I belong." I smiled at her.

"I know, but when you consider it, you did give up a lot for me." She shrugged.

"I left a lot behind me yes, but look at what I have gained, as crazy as things have been, my life has been enriched by coming here."

"Like what?" She slid her arms around me, her eyes came really close and they looked huge, I felt a little flutter in my tummy.

"Deads, I shared a life with the only person I could ever truly love. I raised two amazing kids, have been surrounded by the most amazing loving friends, and woke up to you every day for thirty six years. We also have pretty much fucked everywhere, and given each other a trillion orgasms, I think we have lived a wonderful life." I leaned in and gave her a soft kiss.

"I have loved my life with you Birch, I don't think I would have made it without you." She smiled.

"You would Sweetie, it would just have been much duller." I chuckled.

She had a point; I cannot say I have not often sat, and wondered what would have happened without her. Would I have married some dull boring man like my father and repeated my mother's life, I was not really sure?

"It has certainly not been boring Birch." She giggled as we turned and walked on along the path.

"We have done a lot, I mean let's face it, we have had some shameful sex with others, and lived a naked crazy life, and we have laughed more than I think most others have." I had to agree.

"We certainly had some bumps in the road, what with a

psychopath climbing in the window at Christmas, lousy press, Madge and her crew, and not forgetting Prim, she made life hard for a while, it has not been boring. What happened to her, I have not heard anything about her for years?" Birch chuckled.

"After she married that bent MP's son she moved to Hastings, and from what I heard she got battered on a regular basis by him. She is divorced, I think. I did hear from a therapist over there she took him to the cleaners and ended up with the house and everything he had living alone. I have wondered if she regrets treating Nigel the way she did, after all, he would never have hit her?" I nodded.

"He is better off with Sophia, she has been good for him, I think he finally found the girl of his dreams to love him deeply, that was all he ever wanted, I am happy he did." Birch smiled as we reached the road.

"Yeah, odd as they are as a couple, they both made it through, and went the distance. I was never sure they would, but Sophia has really stood by him, I think that is sweet."

We stood at the side of the road holding hands, as two large trucks trundled past heading for the village, the wind brushed past us and lifted Birch's hair off her shoulders, and she gave a giggle. It does amaze me how she still has that childlike quality; she noticed me looking and glanced at me, I smiled at her, she had no idea how much she meant to me.

We crossed the road, and walked over to the style, and clambered over it. Yeah, I am not quite as elegant at this stuff as I used to be. Taking my hand, we walked along the path that led across the top of the heath towards the two huge trees we planted. My mind drifted as I thought back through the years, Birch smiled at me, and I blinked and came out of my thoughts.

"What?" She gave a slight chuckle.

"I love the look on your face when you drift into thought, go on, tell me what that curious little writer mind was thinking." She knew me so well.

"I was just thinking back and remembering Lillian and Celia, I suppose the young today see us as we saw them back then." Birch gave a giggle.

"What, do you think they see us as a pair of naughty perverted old ladies, because Sweetie, I would be so okay with that?" I had to laugh.

"I just thought in a way we had to a degree emulated them." Birch squeezed my hand.

"The two old lesbians of Waterside Lane, and the shame of Wotton." I shook my head.

"No, Birch I was eighteen when I met you, that was forty one years ago, it is a long time." We reached the large beech tree, and she turned and slipped her arms around me.

"It may feel like a long time, but we have eternity ahead of us, it is but a blink of an eye in the span of time, and I aim to spend a huge chunk of time with you." I smiled.

"Forever and beyond?" She gave a giggle.

"Oh yes Sweetie, whatever there is after this, I am taking you there, and then on and on and never stopping."

She was so lovely, I looked at her, with her little lines below her eyes and the crease lines from her endless smiles. Those eyes were as bright as they had always been, they had danced in her face for as long as I had known her. I turned and looked down at the base of the tree, and saw the small bunch of flowers.

"Looks like Danny has been here." Birch nodded.

"Yeah, she never misses, although she did not say anything yesterday when she called in for that paperwork. I thought something was on her mind, she looked a little upset, that is probably why, she had probably been here first."

"She has been a little quiet lately, I have wondered about her. You don't think anything is wrong for her at home, do you?" Birch thought about it.

"She has been a little withdrawn, but this time of year she always goes a little quiet. I can talk to her if you like?" I nodded.

"Yeah, see if your spider senses pick up on anything, call it a gut feeling, but she does not feel like herself at the moment." She nodded.

"I will."

I took her hand, and we walked along the top of the heath looking down on the village and our home. May's cherry tree had grown huge, the flowers had fallen and faded, although it had been a real show this year, possibly the best ever. We reached our spot, and I looked down, Birch slid her arm round me, she knew where my mind was.

"It was almost thirty four years ago, oh God Birch, where has it gone, I don't want this to ever end?" She squeezed my waist hard.

"It won't Sweetie." I turned into her, and pushed my face onto her shoulder.

"Birch, we have been married for almost thirty two years, it has gone too fast, it frightens me at times that a day will come where we will not be together. I never want to be without you." She chuckled.

"Oh, you silly, love is eternal, I will always be right here at your side."

Ever since Lillian's death, it had been a fear of mine, I really could not bear the thought of her alone, or me alone without her. She felt me tremble slightly, and pulled me close.

"Deads, I can never leave you; I thought you knew that?" I breathed into her shoulder.

"No matter how you look at it, Birch, one of us will go first, and we are growing old, this life cannot last forever, it scares me to think about it."

Birch slid back slightly and lifted my face, her eyes were so green and bright, her face so pale, and her hair bright white as it was lit by the sun. God, she was so beautiful, and had such a loving face, her voice was soft and caring.

"Deads, stop over thinking it. Look, we made a vow, and we both meant it, and Sweetie, you have to believe it. I believe with all my heart, we will walk together long after this life, I will never leave you, not in this world or others." I took a huge breath and swallowed hard; I felt the tears in my eyes.

"I love you so much, and I have been so happy with you, my life has been perfect, but I do get scared. Birch, we have lost so many we love, and I cannot help it, we are all getting old. Hell, Danny is thirty this year, and married with a daughter of her own. Birch, I have not changed inside, I am the same as I have always been and I want to live for years, but I look in the mirror, and I look like my mum. I am aging Birch, and no matter what I wish for, that time will come. I want to be your Lillian forever; not leave you like she did Celia." She gave a sigh, and smiled at me.

"Sweetie, all that matters at the moment is now, this moment, this time, that is all that matters. Deads, you cannot live if you are filled with what if's, no one knows what the future holds, and you should never worry about it. From the moment we met, we have embraced the moment and lived it like it was our last, and we have made the most of every second of our life, and honestly, Sweetie that is all that counts. If you are filled with all this dread of what tomorrow will bring, you are not living, I have told you, let go of it all, and just embrace now. Come on, let's head home and make something nice for our meal tonight, and then we can cuddle up and just enjoy us for a while." I gave a huge sigh and nodded.

"I am sorry, I cannot help it, I have been feeling like this all week, and remembering a lot of our life together. I get scared, because at times it feels like we are two thirds of the way through it and heading for the final line." Birch shrugged and took my hand.

"So, we still have a third left to piss about in then." Her eyes sparkled with mischief, and I gave a small chuckle, there was always mischief where she was concerned, we started to walk.

"Deads, stop thinking of what is to come, I am not in a rush to leave here, and I have so much mischief still left in me, you know Sweetie, when you stop playing, you grow old, and I intend to keep playing."

I have never understood how she does it, and yet even now her mind is still as wild and crazy, she really is the most natural free spirit I have ever met. We reached the road and turned down Waterside Lane, heading towards home, she held my hand and swung it.

"You know Deads, you get lost in all the bad at times, you forget the good. Just think about it, we high fived shagging in the tent at the festival, we had great sex under your arch on the canal, and had a wild threesome with that guy in the yurt, it was crazy and new and amazing at the time. Although if I am honest, I was shitting myself, I will never forget looking at you riding him with such confidence, and thinking wow, she is frigging amazing." I gasped and looked at her.

"You are kidding right, why have you never told me this before? Jesus Birch, I was sat on him watching you thinking oh my God, I never thought I could ever do this. It was like the sluttiest thing I had ever done, and I was actually shocked with myself, and terrified. You looked so calm, actually, it really turned me on that you were so in control." She shook her head.

"Nope, I was crapping myself, but I got so turned on watching you, I just exploded with a massive climax." She giggled.

"It has been fun, that guest house was insane, I mean hell Deads, we shaved Deb's vagina, and you walked in on Chloe with a huge dildo in the kitchen, I mean, holy shit we were all wild."

"You went down on me for the first time there, that blew my mind at the time, I will never forget it, lying there, watching you and it was so wild, so new to me. I was a little scared, but I was so turned on because I had dreamed about it and never thought it would happen, wow Birch, I still get turned on when I think of it. I was so in love with you, and trying to hide it, but when you did that, it was like the happiest moment of my life." Birch smiled at me, and her eyes danced.

"See, we have done so much together since that moment, neither of us knew what was to come and we did not care, we just loved it and lived in the moment. Deads, we do not know what is to come now, but what we do know is, no matter what, we will love and live every second of it. Sweetie, we are not done yet, we still have years of fun in front of us."

I pressed the button and the gates opened, and hand in hand we walked in and headed for the door, she was right, I was getting carried away as usual. We walked into the hall, I love that little changes in our house, although the plants these days were huge and we had cut them back a good few times. I slipped off my jacket and hung it on the rack, and dropped my keys in the bowl, and looked up the large staircase, and a memory came to mind, I smiled to myself, I saw the pictures in my thoughts.

"Jessie please this is important. Why are you not outside with the other kids?" I looked up, and Danny was stood at the top of the stairs looking stressed. Jessie looked upset.

"But I want to watch cartoons on my laptop, and Helen said she would come watch them with me."

Danny turned and saw me, I could see her stress levels peaking, I knew that look, I had been there a few times when I was writing. Danny looked right at me, and gave a long sigh.

"Mum, will you tell her, I need to do this?"

My heart missed several beats and it almost failed, I took a deep breath, and tried to calm down.

"Danny, relax. Go work in my room, it is quiet in there, just close the door and focus, okay?" She nodded.

"Thanks Mum." I felt it again, and bit my lip, I looked at Jessie.

"Munchkin, watch your cartoons, but not too loud, we are all very busy, and leave Danny to work, if you need something, come get me, alright." She gave a nod.

"Alright Mum."

It was probably one of the most precious moments of my life, I walked onto the stairs and wiped my eyes, even now it made me emotional. It is funny really, I was so adamant in my twenties I would never have kids, and yet, when Danny and Jessie came into my life, it changed it forever. I found I had so much love buried deep down inside me, it was one of the best decisions I ever made.

I walked into my room and it was the same as always, just a small reminder of the guest house, covered in clothes and filled with love. Hell, I was fifty nine and still had Avril posters on the wall. I have never wanted to change this room, it is almost exactly the same as the day I moved in at the age of twenty four, the only real change has been a bigger wardrobe and Birch's desk, everything else was brought over from the guest house.

I walked to the patio doors and looked out on the garden, Chloe was sprawled out naked on the grass with Baz, Birch had stripped and was sat with them, as they talked and Chloe sketched. She has short hair now, it is strange in a way, as I looked at her with a side flick and hair trimmed right back. I always loved her waves of long colour that ran down to the nape of her back, but she had gone a sort of pepper grey now, and in a way, I think she had a look of Hatty about her.

Deli was in the pool swimming as normal, she had not changed much, she plaited her hair more these days, and lived a quieter life, she had dated a lot, but never remarried. I think Eric had put her off for life, he died early in life, he went at forty three from a heart attack induced by coke. He never learned, so many had told him that his mates were bad for him, and he just never listened. Deli did not appear to be too shocked at the time, I think she had cried enough because of him, and so had no more tears left. It is funny how the circle of life turns, maybe there is something to be said for Karma, maybe it does come around and balance the scales?

I lifted my eyes and there it was, stood tall and proud at the bottom of the garden, my Sanctuary Arch, I am still impressed Birch managed to move it here. She is so amazing, she gets an idea and I have no idea how, but she thinks it all through and makes it happen, I do not think there is anyone, anywhere like her.

So many feelings and memories are attached to that arch, and the crazy thing is, it is not really an arch, it is an old church arched window. It has seen all of the darkest hours of my life and all of the joy. I think all of us at some point, have had sex under that window at sunset, I know Birch and I have, God, we have pleasured each other thousands of times below it. We once caught Jessie screwing down there when she was nineteen. Oh dear, that was a funny moment, Birch looked at the face of the terrified boy and told him, 'Don't stop, the girl bloody needs that.' Poor Jessie she was beetroot, and I had to laugh.

It is a precious place with precious memories, I stood there and told Birch my vows as I looked in her tear filled eyes as I married her there, and I stood alone just a few hours later lost in thought there as I cooled down from the hot marquee, that was such a wonderful moment. I stared at it as the moment played in my mind.

I walked into my corner, and turned around and was faced with Hatty with her camera, it clicked.

"Got ya... I have waited all day for that, because that is the one I will paint." She looked at me and smiled.

"You did it kid, you broke her curse, and you followed your heart, I am so proud of you." I looked down at the floor.

"Did I really? I swore I would never marry, but I could not help myself, I want Birch more than anything else in my life." Hatty walked onto the stone, and leaned on the wall at my side, and pulled out a cigarette and lit it.

"That is why you broke the curse, Abby. She wanted something far more than Edwin, but she stepped back at the last second, and married him instead. You married your hearts desire, she didn't, because she was not strong enough, you did, and that is so very important. Abby, you did what you wanted, and you did it your way, she backed out with cold feet." I looked up at her.

"You are pretty happy now with Clive yes, you must have finally got over her?" Hatty blew out a smoke ring.

"Clive is a wonderful man, but he will always be second to her. Abby, I will never get over her, you almost made the same mistake, and I am so fucking glad you did not."

I understood that, twice I have almost lost her, and I never want to even come close to that again.

"I really want this marriage to work; I never want to lose her Hatty." She smiled.

"You won't Abby, there is absolutely no chance of that."

"How can you be so sure Hatty, people change?" She turned on the wall, and looked at me, her eyes were bright and full of life.

"Abby, I never had kids, I didn't need to, she had you. You are as much a daughter to me as you could get. I changed your bum as a baby, pushed your pram, saw your first steps, heard your first words. You are my daughter, and I love you so very much, now ask yourself this, when you came within an inch of losing her, who was it that pulled you back together?" I felt so close to her, I always have, and I felt this huge wave of emotion boil up inside me.

"You were always there, when they weren't you were, I love you too Hatty, you have always been my second mum, you know that?" She smiled.

"I won't let you fail kid, not ever, I will never let my daughter fail." I gave a huge sob and she pulled me into her arms, and hugged me closely.

"Abby, go and live, be you with Birch, and be happy."

She was right, she has always been there like a shadow watching over me. She stood by me with Martin, kept her word when I told her about my dad's affair, defended me in the village, and was there to help when I screwed up with Kyle, without her I would never have made it through. When my parents shunned me, she loved me even more, I could never thank her enough. She let me go, and I stepped back and smiled, she handed me a tissue.

"You will have to leave soon Mrs Dixon."

"Oh Hatty, you are the very first person to call me that." I wiped my eyes, and she smiled.

"I know, it was deliberate. Go on, go and get ready, you have a whole new life of adventure waiting with that insanely beautiful woman." I nodded and smiled.

"I love you Hatty, thanks for everything." I gave her another huge hug, and then she pushed me back with a smile.

"Go live."

I blinked and breathed in, God, I miss her, she was more than just another mum to me, she was my rock for years until she made way for Birch. Hatty got me in ways only Birch does, she was such an incredible person, and I loved her so deeply, she really did change my life as she fought for me with my parents. I think without her in my life, I never would have found Birch.

Her later years became so happy for her, and I was overjoyed to have her share so much of her life with us and the girls. Once she retired, I saw much more of her, and she was a regular visitor, and loved Danny and Jessie so much. I have so many memories of watching her with the girls, happily smiling and taking so much joy from it all. In a way I was happy to know my family made her happier, and she got to see the daughter she cared for so much, raise children and share that joy with her.

She painted the picture, and gave it me for Christmas a few years later, I hung it in the living room so I could remember her every day of my life, it really is beautiful. I often find Chloe sat crossed legged in front of it just staring at it, lost in thought as she tries to work out all of Hatty's painting secrets. She is such a fan girl of Hatty's, it really is quite silly, because Chloe is an amazing artist, and so talented.

Maybe Birch is right, life is a curious thing, and it goes on for as long as it can, and maybe I do need to relax and keep on going with the flow, after all, isn't that what I have been doing since I was eighteen? I turned to my desk and slipped into my seat, I had words on my mind and a new tale to tell, and maybe it was just the days of reflection I had been going through, I was not sure, but somehow, I felt that everything I had seen and done, was forming into a story.

I sat in my seat, wiggled my mouse and the screen came to life, there was a new document open and it read. "For fuck's sake, don't just sit there, write something Deads.' I giggled and clicked it down to the task bar, I loved her, she knew me so well, and it had been a while since I had done any writing. I opened a new document and wrote the line; a story had been forming in my head for a while.

The Dark Winters Series. Book One, The light from the Snow.

I was off, as I began the first chapter, and I entered into that zone where time stopped and new characters came to life as I hammered on the keys. My new inspiration was my own life, my own joy, and my journey through the darkness of my youth and into maturity beside my crazy wonderful wife. It would be a fantasy, set in a fantasy world, and it would be fast, funny at times and filled with joy, as my group of new characters fought through the darkness of their lives, and moved towards the light of love and joy.

Across the village on Rose Street, Jessie stood in the kitchen of Danny's home, and put an ice pack on her sister's face.

"Danny, you have to talk to mum, you know she will find out, she has detection skills, superior to the C.I.A, you will not hide this from them." Danny gave a wince.

"Jessie, it was an accident, I pushed him too far." Jessie stared at her.

"Really... Danny, why are you defending him, look at you? Danny if this was just a back hand it would not leave a mark like this, be honest, it was a fist. Danny, I know you try to hide it, but this is me you are talking to, this is not the first time, is it?" Danny's eyes filled with tears.

"Jessie, I have a child who is almost two, I cannot leave him, what if he tries to take her off me?" Jessie gave a sigh.

"Jesus Danny, look who our parents are, do you honestly think they will let him do that? God Danny, I thought you were smart? He will have the Shredder up his ass if he even tries, and she has not mellowed with age." She lifted the bag, and looked at the side of Danny's face.

"I hate to tell you this, but this is not going away any time soon, and you have to show up for work tomorrow, because if you don't, both of them will be round here in a shot. You know what they are like?"

"Jessie, they are not young, and he is a big guy, I cannot risk them having a go at them, what if he tries hitting them, he is too big for them." Jessie smirked.

"Seriously, that is what you are worried about, Christ Danny, mum has a bloody huge knife in her bag, do you honestly think he will push it with her? Be honest, if Chloe's story's are right, old or not, mum has a punch that impacts, she will knock him the fuck out." Danny shook her head.

"I don't want that, I don't want them hurt, please Jessie, just pretend nothing has happened." Jessie looked at her and bit her lip like Birch does as she thought. She took a moment and looked at Danny, and shook her head.

"No... I am sorry Danny, but I will not let you be one of his victims, you need to come with me now, and talk to mum. Danny, go home, you will be safe there and he will not be able to hurt you. Take some time out at home, and let him stew for a while. It might do him good, but there is no way I am leaving you here to be his punch bag. Honestly, talk to Aunt Deli, she will tell you the same." Danny gave a sigh.

"I knew telling you was a mistake, you are just bloody like mum, oh Christ, they will hit the roof." Jessie nodded.

"Probably, but you know what, both of them will also hold you and love you and take really good care of you, but most importantly, they will protect you. Danny you cannot live like this, trust me, go and talk to them, because if they find out from anyone but you, they will bloody park Petal on him. You know I am right?" Danny sighed.

"God, I hate it when you are smug and a smart ass with me, I am your older sister you know?" Jessie giggled.

"I love you sis, now come on, pack a couple of bags and I will cuddle my lovely niece, and then I will take you home. You know them, this is best done now, if you leave it, they will fry you alive for not being honest with them." Danny nodded, and let out a long slow sigh.

"I know you are right, I am just dreading it, the moment I look at mum, those big blue eyes will fill with tears and it will kill me Jessie, I hate seeing her like that." She smirked.

"God, you have no idea how like her you are, tell me, if this was me, wouldn't you be just the same?" Danny nodded and got up holding the ice pack to her face, and gave a sigh.

"Alright, I know when I am beat, come on then, let's do this while he is at the pub."

Chapter 38

Remembrance.

It is funny as I sit here at my desk, looking at my room, it has not changed since the day I moved in, but the house is quieter these days. I can still remember it clear as day, she was so vulnerable, as she showed me this room, and I was feeling the house was just too big. She had run around pointing things out in hope she could convince me; she always did try too hard. I closed my eyes and could hear and see us.

"You are impossible to say no to; you know that right?" She burst into tears, and threw her arms round me.

"Oh, Deads, you have no idea what that means to me, I was so afraid you would hate it. I missed you so much, I miss living with you, I miss sleeping with you, my life has been horrible. All the time I was doing this, I was thinking of you, it will be such fun, I promise. You will never need to look over that abyss again, I promise, I could not live if anything happened to you."

She was true to her word, she never let me down, was always there at my side standing her ground to back me up, and this house has become such a house of love. She has such vision, the memory of her sat in the library that first night I saw the house came to mind, and I could see her kneeling in front of me as I wept with joy, her words resounded through my mind.

"This is a new start, no isolation, no loneliness, and a life worth living. We came back to this village side by side, and they hated us, some of them hate us more. This is where you and I will live, and we show them, we will show all of them, that having us here is the best thing this village has ever known. All that starts, with having a house which is the envy of them all. It is also a house filled with love and friendship, I hope that now, you can see why I have done all this. Deads, just by living a good happy life, we will prove all of them wrong."

She was so right; she has always amazed me with her mind

and ability to plan it all out in advance. I have never regretted a moment of it, even if it did get weird and crazy at times. It really is much quieter now, is it mad, that for a reclusive writer, I miss all the background noise?

I miss the chats and giggles, with Deli, as she leaned in through the door of my room, and the arguments between Edwina and Chloe, as they argued about flash drives. Anthony, and his fast cutting wit, I loved him so deeply, he was such a wonderful caring man. Izzy sat pouring whiskey into her coffee, or Debbie and her shock as she turned beetroot, or Jimmy and his wild wise cracks, and crazy full of life attitude.

I loved them all so deeply, and I still do, we filled the back wall of the living room with pictures in frames, like Jeff did at Sunny Bank. I often stand, shedding a tear as I see us all, stood with Petal, or outside the yurt, Deb' s and Edwina's weddings, our first Christmas at home, my wedding, and without doubt the weirdest wedding picture ever of all of us smirking at Chloe's wedding.

Losing Anthony, and then Edwina, was hard, then Deli, and when Deb's passed away, it almost destroyed me, that was such a dark and terrible time for me, and yet I had Chloe still. She really did help me, as with Birch, we grieved together. The three of us made sure she had a good send off, and her funeral was so beautiful, and the church was packed, she would have loved to have seen all the love she gave in life returned the way it was.

It is strange, sometimes, I sit in the kitchen, and just for a second, I am sure I see Chloe out of the corner of my eye, sat there naked and painting, through the door of her empty studio. I think I miss her the most, she became such a close friend as we shared coffee each morning together. Just thinking back, it is crazy to think we ever hated each other. Chloe became a rock, in the foundation of my day to day life, and she was such a beautiful free spirit, and filled with more love than people realised.

I never really got over losing her, we shared so much together, and she always was there behind me watching my back. She never changed, her and Baz lived so happily here, right up until she was seventy one, and they were still screwing, bless her. We moved in here on the same day, and spent forty seven years, sipping coffee and talking every day I was home and not doing events.

She lost Baz, and it changed her, she missed him so much. It is funny really, she avoided a relationship for most of her life, and yet with Baz, she had a love as strong as ours. She lost Baz, and she lost her smile and stopped painting, and three months later, she slipped away quietly in her sleep cuddling Percy. Birch, and I really missed her, but as Birch explained, they were not meant to be apart, and so she left to re-join him. It made sense, as he loved her so much, and was true to his word, he stood beside her from that moment he first told her how much he loved her.

We paid the guy at the crematorium to put Percy in with her, it felt fitting they went together, he was after all her longest serving lover, and also her safe space, when she was alone and afraid.

She left Danny and Jessie her shares in Sanctuary, to her, all our children were also hers, and honestly, she was exactly like Lillian and Hatty in her care and concern for them. All her money, which was a substantial amount, was bequeathed to Curio Life, as well as her art, which totalled a staggering three thousand high quality paintings and sketches, and it felt right. She did so much good with her comments and never missed a day answering and writing to every new person that posted. She was without a doubt, the most loved Curio on the site, with the biggest heart, and I really understand that.

I suppose that is life, as the circle turns, as Birch always said, we are born, and we die, and everything in between is up to us. I remember her telling me, that the greatest quality of humans, was their vast ability to love, and this house has been a huge part of that. Birch was not wrong, it was far more than just money, it has certainly been filled with life, love, and has been lived in to the fullest by all of us, and especially all of our children.

Danny is divorced, yeah, the controlling shit hit her, and then ran into Birch and me big time, he did not last two seconds against us two. True to our word, no matter what the danger, because we were older and he was big and strong, we faced the danger, and defended our child. She is a very successful author, and now heads Sanctuary Press, she is so like me with a hint of Birch. She lives here with her daughter Verity still, and runs everything from the library, and Edwina's old office next to the garage. Verity is her double and like a mini me, I love that she took the first three letters of Veronica, and the last three of Felicity to name her daughter.

Jessie has changed little; she is so like Birch and a joy to me. She is a doctor and consultant at Oxendale General Hospital, but her main office of her practice is based at Sweeties Retreat, which she still runs with Gill's daughter, who is a qualified psychologist, and Birch still heads the board, and is a guiding hand to them. Izzy was lost to us two years ago, but like Birch, she too was always on hand to help at Sweetie's Retreat. She worked there as manager until she was seventy three, and has trained a long line of great counsellors to work at the retreat.

Jessie is happily married with two children, who she named Amanda and Peter after her natural parents, and they all live in my mum's old house, her husband Shaun, is also a doctor, and a really caring man, with an amazing sense of humour, I like him a lot, and Birch adores him.

We lost mum twelve years ago; I really do miss her. We became so close, who would have thought it when I was nineteen? After dad, she really did live her life to its fullest, and she had had such love with Patrick, and I have always been so grateful to him for that, because she was an amazing woman who deserved so much more than my father gave her. The guest house still has her art things in it, Jessie felt they served as a tribute to her, and at times I go there and sit in it and talk to her. Her last canvass was a picture of me, painted looking through the guest house window, as I sat inside at my desk typing Seeds of Summer all those years ago. She took a picture, and as Birch once told her, she finally painted it.

It is not quite finished, but it is beautiful, and it makes me remember so much. It is odd really, I still go there, and I can still see them now, all there. Birch at the table lit by the window, Anthony in the comfy chair, Deb's with her back against the bathroom wall, and Chloe and Edwina sprawled on cushions on the floor. I have such wonderful memories of that time, and such joy in my heart.

In many ways, living with Birch, I have come to understand her fascination with the mind and behaviour of people, I have sat back often these days and simply closed my eyes, and there they all are. Like a book, I can recall it all, even after all these years, the pictures just flow into my thoughts, like a recorded video, and I smile as I see them. It is a strange gift, and so many people take it for granted, and they do not realise what they are losing. Maybe because of Birch, I understand that every moment of my life has been precious and a thing of great wonder, so maybe, that is why I have never taken any of it for granted, and taken note of all we have done. It is probably because of that, I can sit here and look back, and reflect happily on those precious moments from so long ago, and relive that moment, and feel those feelings deep inside me. In many ways, even though the house has grown quiet, I know they are all still here, inside my heart, and inside my memories, and in a way, they have never left me. I will never be truly alone as I was, I can see them and feel them. I closed my eyes, and smiled.

I sat on the bed feeling utterly lost.

"It's weird, isn't it?" I nodded, as she sat at my side and took my hand.

"You know, Abby, I did not think I would ever be able to say this, but I am so thrilled to be here at your side, the night before your wedding. I never thought you would ever marry, which just shows how very special Birch is."

"Deb's, I am terrified, and I have no idea why, because I really want this, but I am shitting myself." She giggled.

"Come over to my place and chill with Jimmy and the band, they are mucking about, but it will help calm you."

I smiled, her hazel eyes filled with love, her long bushy ponytail, so filled with hope and optimism, she truly was such a good friend.

I sat for twenty minutes, as Deb's fed me coffee through a straw, Anthony smiled, and gave little squeaks of happiness, and as he finished, he reached into a small black box, and kept his hand there, and he looked at me, and twitched, I frowned, he had not twitched around me in years.

"Abby... You have been so much to me in my life, my protector at school, a sister in the village, at times you have been like a wife or a mother. Oh, dear, I feel all emotional." He wafted his free hand in front of him, and twitched again.

"Abby, I love you so much, and I am so happy for you today, so

I want to give you something, something special, and just for you. It is my heartfelt thanks for everything you have done for me."

I loved Anthony so deeply, so few saw the depth of him, to me he was mighty man, a giant of the village. His inner strength was so much greater than most people realised, and his heart was filled with so much love. He did become a brother to me, a guardian, and a huge support through my life, it is so sad he had to suffer such ridicule and bullying in his early life because of his sexuality, so few understood his value, but I did. Hell, we all did, it is funny really, because we were devoted to him, he often talked to me quietly in the garden about not understanding why he grew up as he did, he never understood how it was men that attracted him, and I always felt he missed the point. He was deeply loved by a whole group of women, because truth be known, his personality was what all of us looked for in other men, it always felt ironic to me. He was lovely, they all were, I have had them behind me since before we moved in here.

She typed in the line, and then stopped and looked at me, and smiled.

"You want the honours? Abby, you more than any have the right to activate it, just press that button and everything he has on you will go forever, and we are done."

I looked down at the keyboard, and the enter button, she smiled.

"You have more right than any of us, he has years' worth of pictures of you, so press it."

I reached over, and my finger hovered for a moment, was this right or wrong, I was so unsure, I closed my eyes, and hit the button. I gave a small gasp, and opened them, and saw the screen.

The black box disappeared and a few others popped up, and then disappeared, his computer made a grumbling sort of noise as somewhere in the background, a hidden process was activated, Edwina clicked off the monitor.

"Okay we are done here." She got up, and patted my back, and looked at Birch.

"You were right about the password, I got in first time, no need to hack it. Okay let's go before we are noticed." I looked at Birch. She smiled.

"A-b-i-g-a-i-l, he really is fucked up."

I shuddered, and felt a cold tingle run down my spine. Edwina slipped her arm around me.

"I have added a little insurance, I will be watching him, and if he tries to upload anything else, I will see it and I will stop him, you have no need to worry Abby, we have your back." I nodded.

"Thanks."

I cannot count the amount of times Edwina had my best interests at heart, there are so many times when she was almost like a mum, I really saw her like a big sister. There were so many occasions when she came through for me, and all of us really, not just the code that exposed Nigel, she created the Coding Cube site, and protected me, helped save the girls from the cold cruelty of the Fairbanks family, opened my mind to who I was when she showed me parts of myself, like she did with my dad, when she pointed out how I learned by watching him do accounts, and she would always stop me, and tell me to eat more, or get more rest.

Her organisational skills were matched only by her party spirit, and her infectious laughter, and the love and protection she gave to her little sister, which she expanded to include all of us. All of us always felt loved and safe in her presence, she really was a pillar that held us all up. In many ways, I can see why Chloe adored her so much, she was a wonderful influence on all of us.

She was a good example for Chloe, who let's be honest, needed a little at times, and yet somehow, even after we clashed at school, she became my closest friend in life.

"Fuck off Watson, this is nothing to do with you." I stepped in between her and Deb's, and faced her out, although to be honest, my head was screaming at me. 'What the hell are you doing, have you completely lost your mind?' I swallowed hard, and leaned in to Chloe.

"Leave her alone, she is my friend, so it is my business." Deb's pulled on my jumper from behind me.

"Abby leave it, I do not want you getting hurt, I am alright." I stared into Chloe's dark eyes; Chloe gritted her teeth.

"You should listen to her, because if you don't back the fuck up bitch, I will knock you the fuck out." I leaned in closer.

"Go for it!"

Her breathing increased, I was clearly pissing her off, I noted her arm twitch, and then stepped back into Deb's. I was pissed off and angry, this had gone on long enough, and yep, I was probably going to get battered, but I was not backing down. Chloe breathed in, her eyes blinked, and as her arm came up, I lifted my arm and put everything I had into it, it was my only hope of surviving the day.

I was faster, and felt my fist crunch as it hit her face, I was ready for hers but it never came. Such was the power of my anger; she went flying backwards and crashed onto the floor. I was so surprised, as I looked down at her watching her sprawled out, Stephanie Slater looked shocked and stepped back, I stared at Chloe as she held her face, and blood gushed over her hand.

"You ever touch her again, or call her mum names, and I will be back, do you hear me bitch? Stay the fuck away from her." I breathed a sigh of relief, turned, grabbed Deb's and almost dragged her looking shocked, out of the school yard.

"Come on, we better leg it before her friends turn up."

Isn't it silly how little we understand life when we are teenagers? Chloe always told me of how brave she thought I was, and yet she never understood her own bravery, if truth be known, I would never have swallowed my pride back then and faced her to apologise. I had to give her some credit, she came alone, and was summoning the courage to talk.

"Look Abby, I don't want us to be enemies, to tell you the truth, the other night I was jealous. I do not have the courage you have; I would love to have hair like yours, and I want you to know, I actually really admire you for it. I mean, look at me, I have the right top, the right skirt, and the right shoes, so as not to offend the old ones. I have a wardrobe at home full of great clothes, but I cannot wear them here, I have to sneak into Oxendale on my night off to wear them. So, what I am saying is, can we be friends, I have been a total bitch in the past, especially to you Debbie, and I want you to know I do regret it, and I am really sorry to all of you." I felt Birch soften a little.

"Chloe, friendship is earned, and I cannot deny, I am not in a rush to add you on Insta, some friend's requests are surveillance, how do we know you are not setting Abby up?" She shook her head.

"I would not do that." Deb's stepped forward.

"You already did though, didn't you?" She looked down.

"I took it down after talking to Birch in the toilet, I really am sorry, I honestly took it because you all looked so cool. I did not think others would see it, I don't have a huge list of friends on there, if I had known, I would never have posted it." She looked me right in the eyes.

"I loved your top and pants, honestly? Edwina really roasted me that night, she is a better person than I am, and then Harriet gave me a talking to the other night, and it really made me think. I want to make it up to you, but I really don't know how to."

I am not sure Chloe really understood how much she made it up to me. She stood up to me when I wrong about Birch, covered for my mum after Ozzy, scared the living hell out of Katie. She filled my every morning with a happy smile, and she was so there for me when I married Birch. She was wild and free, and swore like a sailor right up until her last breath, but she was such a loyal friend, who also played a huge role in my children's life. She was very like a younger Hatty, and maybe that was what I saw in her, and why I grew as close to her as I had Hatty, losing her was one of the hardest things I have faced.

I will never forget that morning when I walked into her room, and she was there, fast asleep, hugging Percy, with the duvet pulled up. Her eyes were closed and she looked so peaceful, with a slight smile on her face. She had aged and her hair although shorter was such a beautiful mixture of whites and greys, it was almost as if it had been painted by her. On the chair next to her bed was her picture of me lay out in the garden at my mum's house with Birch. I had always loved it, and once told her it lived and was her greatest piece of art, she would never sell it even though I had asked her a thousand times. It sat there at her bedside, and she had stuck a post-it note on it, and it simply read. 'Abby, I love you, it is yours now XX.'

I never needed to check her, I simply knew, and I felt a huge surge of emotion rip out of my heart. Her hand was on Percy's shoulder, with the only rings she ever owned on them, her engagement and wedding rings, and I lifted my hand and took it in mine. It was cold, and a huge sob erupted out of me, and I broke down. I knew from that moment my life would never be the same again, her noise, her giggles, her crazy theories of the supernatural, and her beautiful smile had painted such colour through my life, how could I let her go, how could I live here without her?

I had lost Lillian and Celia, Roni and Will, Mum and Patrick, my dad and Angela, Edwina, Deli, Jimmy, Luke, Anthony and Michael, Debs, and Hatty, and yet losing Chloe felt harder than losing all of them, and it tore at my heart in a way I never thought possible. I sat and held her hand for over an hour, as I told her how much I loved her, and how important she had become to me in my life, and I cried and sobbed as the pain was too much to bear. She was so filled with life, and lived every second of it with joy, and in many ways, she was the most Curio of all the Curio's in that sense. Even though she was as wild as she could get away with, she was without doubt, one of the most amazing human beings I had ever known. We had such fun, and laughed as we lived. I feel blessed to have known her, sat there holding her hand as I calmed down and thought of all we done, in the end, I had no choice but to smile.

"Abby... Birch?" She sounded very forthright, and business like, she had a fixed stare.

"Guys I have been thinking... I think I need to show some gesture of my appreciation, but I have hardly any cash and nothing of value, to be honest my greatest asset is sex, it's sad, but that is a fact."

We all nodded, we knew this to be true, we had witnessed her in action. She took another deep breath.

"Guys.... I am so fucking straight; I mean, you have no fucking idea how so fucking straight I am.... But..." She stumbled a little and took a massive deep breath.

"As a token of my gratitude, I am prepared.... Prepared.... Prepared to screw you both... Not at once, that is just too fucked up for me, but I will do it... As a token of thanks."

She was utterly unique, and I am sure, when she left the world, there will never again be anyone quite like her to replace her, and the world will be duller because of it. I came out of my thoughts, I had done it again and slipped off in my day dreams of remembrance, I looked at my desk top, and the picture of all of us stood next to Petal outside Anthony's salon, and gave a sigh.

"I miss you guys; I miss you so much."

The Curio's had made a name for themselves, each of us had focused on our passions, and worked hard to achieve success, all of us had gelled as a group, and faced some pretty harsh realities, no more so than gaining the acceptance of the residents of the small village of Wotton Dursley.

Like pieces of a jigsaw, we had been drawn together, and created a patchwork of personalities and creative abilities, and as odd as we all were, it worked. Raven Moon had always called us a tribe, and in many ways, I feel that is right. All of us brought something different to the mix, none of us were really that similar, and maybe that is why it all worked. I have never been too sure, I often wonder if we were all just slightly insane and had a huge capacity to love, because if there is any one ingredient of us all as a collective, that would be the one quality that was the strongest.

I sit and watch the world, yeah, it is a writer's thing, but I see how broken and isolated people have become, it is not just Wotton, it is everywhere. In many ways, Wotton is like a predictor of what the world will become to me. I have seen the two faced attitude of people, the greed and lust as they claw for more. The attention seeking and fake fronts of those who hide behind the lies they use to protect their own indiscretions. The world is hurting, people are lost and alone, as isolated as I was in the guest house, as the media and social media sites indoctrinate them with falsehoods, that leave themselves hating their bodies, their minds, and those around them.

Everything today has become a competition of fakery, as people have a adopted a ruthless persona to outdo their neighbours and relatives to feel superior and moral. I sometimes feel it all started here in Wotton, it certainly felt like it when I was nineteen. Wotton looks unchanged, but I hear all sorts of rumours about the life people live behind closed doors, and maybe that is why the Curio's were so special, we never really hid it, and we were always honest about it. We learned that from Birch, who has been my greatest inspiration, she did not shy away from controversy, she faced it, and talked honestly about her life, her thoughts and desires. Never once have seen her deny an aspect of who she is or how she lived, and I have always admired her for that, because it was that alone that gave me a voice, and the ability to write openly and honestly in my stories.

How strange my life has been, Birch has without doubt encouraged me to live in the moment and enjoy every last second, and as I sit recounting my life around my dearest of friends, I can see that I have. Many years ago, I walked out of a bathroom with my hair dyed black with red tips, and I looked into a mirror and smiled. Behind me Birch stood up with a smile and those amazing green eyes, and gave me a nod, and I knew for the first time in my life who I was, and since that day, I have been true to that person, and the wonderful thing is, all Birch said to me that night was.

"This is you, this who you were meant to be, and not who they told you to be. I love it Sweetie."

She had no idea in that moment, how so very important those words were to me, and they have stayed in the back of my thoughts for all of my life, and here I am at the grand old age of seventy seven, and I still think of that moment and cherish those words. I think it was because she was right, and maybe the world has lost sight of that, and maybe the Curio's always knew in their hearts to never forget that. I feel that is what set us apart, we refused to adhere to the so called rules of society, we cast off the names of shame, and created our own label, and without really understanding what we had done, we created something so powerful, it changed us, and changed the world of all who surrounded us.

Why does his gayness matter?

I really do not think I even understood myself when I said that, I really did not understand the implications it would have on our life, and yet within seconds, Birch was alive and leapt on it. She understood full well its implications, and it started a journey that has lasted for fifty eight years of my life. I will never forget that moment as I tried to make them realise, and when Birch said those fateful words, it rings through my mind often.

Birch sat listening to me and gently smiling to herself, as I spoke.

"Does it matter if it is a pressure group in society, or one person here, those are still her standards, not mine, or any of yours, and it is the same all over the world. Small groups of individuals, use pressure groups to get things the way they want, and that is why we have all these pigeon hole titles we have to fit into, but surely one box cannot fit all? We are examined and defined by their idea of what we should be, not who we actually are as people, that is social conditioning. The naked body is shameful, this skin colour is not acceptable, yet that one is, who you sleep with picks your box. You heard Marjorie, with her Whore, Slut, Transient, Miscreant, titles for us, she is picking the pigeon holes for everyone around here. All I am saying is why can we not take that power back off her, when it comes to us? Why can we not do the same, and reject those labels completely, and all just be sexual humans, or even better, just humans?"

"I am just curious." Everyone looked at Birch, she shrugged.

"I am.... I am curious about life, curious about people, curious about other cultures, curious about attitudes, and behaviour, which is why I want to be involved with my mums' work. I had a chance to sleep with a woman once, she really wanted me to, but I just didn't want to. I have considered it with another woman since, and if I am honest, I really wanted to, but I was afraid, so am I Bi or straight? I say neither? I say I am just really curious, because I like learning from everything I do. Every adventure in life is a lesson, and that is all I care about, learning about me and how I react to things. Personally, I agree completely with Deads. Guys there are seven billion people on the planet, and every one of us, is completely unique, so should there not be seven billion pigeon holes? I can only be me, and only I can define who that is, no one else can or should. I too hate all the labels in the world today, so I suppose if you want to give me a label, I will pick one myself, based on what I know about me, and it is neither straight or bi, it would be Curio."

Chloe sat up, and gave a huge smile as she looked at Birch.

"Oh my God, I love that. CURIO! It sounds awesome." The others all nodded, and I smiled.

"It is a great term, Birch. Curio, meaning curious about everything, curious about life in general, yeah, by that definition, I am a Curio too." Deb's nodded.

"Yeah, me too... I am a Curio, it really fits me, because I love science, and fashion, books and great sex, why should I be anything people in the village would call me? I am staying a Curio."

That single moment of inspiration changed us all, and really changed the way I thought about everything, and for me, it opened the world and allowed me to actually watch with unblinkered eyes. Birch was right, I am curious about so many things, and always have been, which is probably why I have spent my working life as a writer. Birch has no idea how the moment changed everything for all of us, and maybe that is why we have all lived so happily and close to each other, we were after all a curious family of misfits.

I came out of my thoughts as I heard the thump of the stairs, and smiled, I had no idea what she had been up to, she has done so much since her retirement I have no idea how she does it all. The bedroom door creaked open, she was in her overalls which only meant one thing, she had been in the garage.

"Deads, I did it, it works, she is running again, come on." I gave a chuckle, and looked at her smiling face.

"Oh wow, that is remarkable, after all this time?"

Her green eyes twinkled as she leaned on the door, she never fails to surprise me. The patches are gone, and her hair is as white as snow, and not as long, although she wears it in a long plait these days. She wears dungarees a lot, and refuses to wear what she calls 'Prim Clothes.' She still has that cheeky smile, although she has wrinkles like me now, but even though we have aged, she is still so beautiful to me. We have done alright, we took care of each other, we still swim most days and walk a lot, we gained weight, my boobs got bigger, but not much, and she still holds one every night as we curl up together, I think I would really miss that if she stopped.

I got out of the chair and walked slowly out of the room, and down to the garage. Petal had changed little, the girls make sure she is polished, but she is showing her age. Birch looked at me.

"There were no plugs, strange though, because I really don't remember taking them out."

She shrugged, and opened the door for me with that beautiful radiant smile, and her eyes sparkled. I was feeling very excited, we had talked about doing this for a long time. Petal has not changed, she still has her bright flowery dashboard, although it is a little sun faded in parts. The blue rosette is a little tatty but still up there swinging away from the mirror. The seat covers have done well, the driver's seat is a little worn, but it is bright and colourful with its rainbow stripes.

Getting in was not as easy as I remember, but just sitting there, wow, this brought back such wonderful memories, as I looked past the blue rosette swinging from the mirror. We had certainly done some driving in her, and we had so much laughter in her as we roared along laughing and joking a group. I would never have thought she would become so important in our life when I saw her as the rust heap she was when Birch bought her. I smiled as Birch climbed in, I almost felt nineteen again, although, I was aware of what Jessie and Danny thought about us using Petal.

"Birch, the girl's will be mad if they find out." She gave that little giggle; I love so much.

"Probably, but you know what Sweetie? This is us; it is who we are, and it is who we have always been. This, you my dark little beastie, and me, just like always, together forever and beyond. All girls together." I chuckled.

"Let's do this, you crazy Snow Queen, one more ride around the village for the Curio's, all girls together."

I laughed as we drove out of the garage slowly, and the gates opened, it is a shame Marjorie is no longer here, it would be such fun to see her scowl as Petal drove along the green once again.

"Deads?"

"What?"

"Let's go see what grew in our sunlight." I smiled, now that does take me back.

"Go for it Baby." She gave a happy giggle, and we accelerated down Waterside Lane.

Chapter 39

Deadly and Birch.

The doors to the hospital burst open, and Danny came hurrying through looking panicked, she saw Jessie in her white coat waiting, her voice was desperate.

"Where are they, are they alright?" Jessie turned, looking tired and upset.

"We do not know everything yet, they are comfortable, and for now stable. Where is Verity?" Danny was trembling, and was a white as sheet.

"She is with Jenny, she will be fine, Jess, I am more worried about them." She nodded, she understood, both of them meant everything to them, and she was trying to hide it, but she was also afraid, but did not want Danny to know.

"I have them in a private room, this way." She started to walk, and took her sister's hand.

"Danny, it is not good, we have done all we can, we need to wait and see." Danny glanced at her sister; she was close to tears, as they hurried up the corridor of Oxendale General Hospital.

"What the hell were they doing driving that fucking thing? I told them both, it was too old, hell, they are too old. Honestly Jessie, if they don't make it, I am not sure what I will do, who the fucking hell races an old piece of junk like that in their late seventies? I thought we had hidden the spark plugs?"

She was panicked and scared, and so like her mother, her tears welled up in her eyes, as they hurried down the corridor. Jessie gripped her wrist, and turned to her.

"Come on Danny, it is those two, seriously, they have never behaved, hell, they were never meant to. Those two have challenged every concept of society since the day they met. Seventy seven, and seventy eight years old, driving a bloody ancient Land Rover at fifty miles an hour, playing Battered bloody Taco, full blast. Danny, that is who those two are, and not me or you were ever going to stop them." Danny gave a sigh, and looked down as she wiped her eyes.

"Jessie, I am afraid, I don't want to lose them." Jessie stopped, and pulled her close and hugged her.

"I know, but Danny, one day we will have to let them go, those two will need to start chaos in the afterlife, God help whatever dimension they end up in... Come on, Mum Abby is sedated, but the crazy one is lucid, they are in here."

Abby lay on a bed, her face was black with bruising, she had a drip, and a heart monitor that bleeped, and she was not fully conscious. Jemi was on the other side of the room, she too was black and blue, she was heavily medicated but awake, barely. Danny sat on the bed and took her hand.

"I am here Mum." She had tears in her eyes as she looked at her.

"Oh Mum, what the hell were you thinking, look at you, Mum, you have scared me to death?" She gave a small smile.

"How is Deads Sweetie, is she alright?" Danny sobbed, and wiped her eyes, on her sleeve.

"She is over there; she is not conscious yet. Mum, you killed Petal, and honestly, I am glad, I have told you a thousand times, she was a death trap." Jemi giggled.

"Sweetie, she was fine, the brakes locked up I think, they have not been used for a while. Sweetie we just wanted one more trip in her, that's all, she was precious to us. You will never understand the joy Deads and me had with her; she was a part of us Sweetie." She gave a cough and winced.

"Danny, I need to see her, she will be frightened if I am not there." Danny sat back.

"Mum, you are only five feet away from her, she is right there." Jemi wheezed.

"It's not the same Sweetie; I need to see her. Danny, help me, I just need to see her." Danny nodded.

"Okay, I will go get Jessie, and we shall see if we can get your beds closer."

She got up, and headed for the door to find her sister. Birch turned on the bed, and slid her heavily bruised legs out. She was in pain, it hurt a lot. She slowly lifted her bum off the bed, and put her weight onto her feet, she winced with the pain. She pulled the drip out of her arm, and then saw her, she needed to get there, and leaned on the wall.

It was not far, but it was agonising, every step shot pain through her body, and her eyes watered as she gritted her teeth. Slowly, she made her way towards the bed, and gasped in pain with each step, and finally she made it. She pulled up the sheet, and slid her bum on the mattress, and then with one massive painful push, she slid onto the bed.

Birch slid up close, and faced me, and gently lifted her hand to my cheek. I opened my eyes as I felt her warmth, she smiled, those beautiful green eyes looked huge they were so close. She stroked my cheek, it was soft, and felt nice, my eyes were blurry, and she drifted in and out of my focus.

"Hi Sweetie." It felt hard to talk, my throat was so dry.

"Hey… Birch, I missed you." She smiled.

"I know, I am here Deads."

I had no idea why, but that same old dread filled my heart again, and I could sense something all around me. I looked at her, so close as always, she had no idea how much she meant to me, and how wonderful my life had been with her. I smiled at her, she was my Celia, but I felt strange, and I didn't want to leave her, I wanted to be her Lillian, but not that way. I swallowed hard.

"Birch, I am not sure I am going to make it. I'm sorry, I don't want to leave you, but I feel strange." I felt the tears well in my eyes, and started to cry.

"Deads, it's fine, honestly. Oh Sweetie, we have had such a time, you have made me so happy, I love you so much." Her eyes filled with tears; I hated seeing her cry.

"Don't cry Birch, I love you too, you are the love of my life, you always were, I have loved my life with you." I breathed in, and it felt painful.

"Birch, I am really scared." The tears flowed out of my eyes, and ran down my cheek.

"Shush Sweetie, oh you silly, so little has changed in all these years. I am here Deads, we will stay together, remember, together forever, and beyond, My Lillian?"

I smiled and my eyes cleared, and there she was, so young, so pretty, her skin as white as snow, with all that beautiful white hair with the black patches, and those deep intense green eyes.

She was so beautiful; I smiled at her.

"My Celia, my Birch, my Snow Queen." She smiled, and her eyes danced and twinkled. Her voice was soft, and filled with love and care, just like it always had been around me.

"My dark little beastie, I will never leave you, not ever, I promised, and I am here Sweetie." She leaned in, and gave me the softest kiss, and it felt so nice, so loving. I smiled.

I felt her drift, what was happening, what was this strange light feeling, my pain was going away?

"Birch, I am scared, what is going on?"

"Sweetie, I am here, see."

I turned, and looked back, and there she was, I looked around, everything was so bright.

"Birch, where are we?" She shrugged as she came up at my side, and took my hand, she gave a giggle.

"Fuck knows, I think we changed boats. Come on, let's go and find the others."

Danny stood frozen, watching, her heart breaking, but she smiled, as she saw the love and care between us.

"I love you mum's; I love you both so much."

The long beep from the machine filled the room, and Birch smiled and closed her eyes, and let her last breath flow. Danny turned to her sister, her eyes streaming with tears.

"They are gone... They went together."

Danny and Jessie stood hugging each other, as the machine continued a long bleep, and it was clear, they had both gone together. Danny pushed her face into Jessie and wailed, as there behind them on the bed, Birch held Abby in her arms. It was the act of a great love, and true to their word, they would never be separated, not even in death.

When the sad news hit the papers, they ran days of articles that praised us for our charity work, and every paper carried wonderful tributes to both of us. What twats, they trashed me for most of my life, and yet now they were cashing in on me big time, bloody hypocrites. River TV did a massive tribute, where they edited together all my interviews, and replayed much of the Curio Live events. They made a documentary about us that told our story, well most of it, and added it in five parts in between all the other stuff, it ran for a whole weekend, and was beautifully done.

Anita who had retired and wrote occasionally for a national paper, wrote a long article talking of the joy it had been to work with both of us. River TV did a two hour special with her as she talked of the joys of those early days with D&D and the insane work pace and our belief in Curio Life, as we planned the US and Canadian events. It became one of their highest rated documentaries ever to be shown.

In my home village, the place I returned to from Uni to get so much abuse, and had fought all my life to finally gain acceptance, flowers started to appear on the village green, and within days it was completely covered, all with cards expressing their sadness. It was hard for Danny and Jessie to see, because Jessie lived in my mum's house with her two kids, and Danny in ours with her daughter. I suppose it was nice for the village to see, some of the locals certainly appreciated it, especially Stacie, and Danny found it touching as she saw the frail old balding figure of Nigel, who stood at the base of the green, leaning on his walking stick, quietly breaking his heart and sobbing, next to Rupert with his wife and children. I guess we really did make a difference after all.

As we lost each Curio house mate, we left their rooms as they were, I guess it is sentimental, but Birch and I did not have the heart to change things. The kids room remained as it was, so did Chloe, Anthony, and Deli's room, I had found comfort after they had gone, just sitting there alone seeing their things and remembering them with love. Danny decided, the room of Birch and myself would remain the same, and not be touched, I think she understood me better than I realised.

A week later Danny walked around the room, that had been both of her mother's room for years, and looked at the pictures hung over the bed. A young nineteen year old Abby with red tipped hair. Deadly, Birch and Goggles stood at the notice board, the day Chloe made up with them, and they bought Petal, and the last painting of Deads and Birch, kissing at Deb's wedding, the day they made their vow to each other.

It felt painful, and her tears were hanging behind her eyes, but she was fighting to hold them back. They were the last of the Curio's, Chloe, Deb's, Edwina, Deli and Anthony had already passed, but those two hung on, loving each other the same way Celia and Lillian had, but now that era had gone forever.

Lost, alone, and in pain, Danny sat in her mother's chair, and flicked the mouse on her computer which was in sleep mode. The monitor came on and the computer came back to life, and she typed in Deadly37, and the computer opened up, and her mother's desk top came into view. It was the picture of all of them that summer, stood at the side of Petal, on that last day of that glorious summer, outside Anthony's Salon. There on the back of Petal was the artwork, which had above it. 'All Girls Together.' The original door plate, was framed and hung above Birch's desk at the side of mine

She sat back in her seat, and gave a sigh, as she looked at them all, with their bright happy hopeful faces, she had seen it for all of her life, it somehow felt fitting, Petal was in a way, also a Curio. It all started the day we found Petal, and curiously enough, it ended the day we lost Petal.

"I miss you guys; hell, the world misses you guys." She wiped her eyes.

There was a document left open on the task bar, it seemed odd, she clicked, and it came up, and she smiled, it was something her mother Birch, had done years ago, and she could not believe she still had it, it read. 'For fuck's sake, don't just sit there, write something Deads.'

Danny had spent a week crying, reading the journals of Abigail, as Abby documented her life, her feelings, and her thoughts, and Danny had worked her way through most of them, and as she sat there looking at her mother's words, 'Write Something,' inspiration struck, and she leaned forward, opened a new document, and on Abby's computer, she began to write.

The Greatest Hearts (The story of Deadly and Birch.)

There comes a time during those hallowed days of university, when you sit up rather abruptly, and the seriousness of the moment hits you bang in the face. I talk of that moment when through the haze of the wild days of leisure time, alcoholic binges, and the endless slipping between the bed sheets, with some spotty faced literature nerd, that the fog of your wonderful life clears, and you realise it's time to go home for the summer.

My mother, Abigail Jennifer Watson wrote that, as the opening lines to Seeds of Summer, and what followed was a semi fictional story based on parts of her life, as she came home from university with her best friend in the world Jemima Dixon.

Actually, what she missed out, and failed to write, was what had happened almost a year earlier, because that is where the real story began. That was the story, where a shy quiet girl called Abigail knocked on a door, and a completely naked girl, with skin as white as snow, long hair of bright white with patches of black resembling birch bark, and the most amazing green eyes answered. She took one look at the prim and proper Abigail, and smiled, said Hi Sweetie, and opened the door wider.

In that one single moment, a match made in heaven began, and over the year, Jemima, who most people called Birch, opened up Abigail's world and made her see her true potential, and in doing so, she changed, and earned the nick name of Deadly.

This is that story, based on the true life journals of Abigail Jennifer Watson, and written by me, her adopted daughter, Daniella Watson. This is the true story of Deadly and Birch, the greatest hearts that ever lived, and the kindness that flowed out of them.

Danny was off telling our story, in what at that moment, would become her biggest selling hit book. It is funny how things go round in circles, I got my first hit writing a fiction of the very same story in Seeds of Summer, isn't that a curious thing?

Did we matter? It is strange I suppose, but I have talked to and read a lot about people who were afraid to be forgotten, and yet I have never worried about it. They say, that a person can only ever be forgotten, when their name is spoken for the very last time, and I do not worry about that. I suppose I do not need to, for even though I am no longer there, I know that at number three, Waterside Lane there is a wall filled with pictures of me and the Curio's. My web site will stay online forever, filled with all the video's I filmed of me talking to my readers, and telling them how much I loved and appreciated them.

Twenty four year old me, is there in the housemate's section of Curio Life, as I introduced myself to the world, with another video I filmed for Curio Live USA, so there is no shortage of memories for people to see. There is also, an incredible statue of us on the mantle, depicting us as we were, sculpted by Clive, and it is there on view for all time. Us, the Curio's, a perfect replica of a time long past. I am sure, all of us will be mentioned often.

Most importantly, I will live on in the hearts and memories of Danny and Jessie, and also their children, and as long as there are books and digital readers, my words will live on forever, and really, I will never really die or disappear, there will always be some element of me left for the world to share. It does not really matter now to me, for I have made my mark, and I am happy that I did it with a group of the most amazing and creative people.

At the end of the day, we had a good life, actually scratch that, we had an amazing life. Was it conventional? Well, it was and it wasn't, I did things in my life I had never thought I would, especially sexually, but I also did some amazing and wonderful things, like give a home of love to Danny and Jessie, and helped provide a safe haven to my Curio family. We helped make life better for all those young adults on Curio Life, and with Birch at my side, we added to the beauty of the village.

We lived, laughed, and loved, but more than that, we gave back, and those around us felt it, and through that we did make the life of others better. I am proud of that, it was not bad for a couple of transient whores, who walked home to Wotton from the train station. It was after all, a curious time, and a curious life. My life, Abigail Jennifer Watson's life, it was my Curio life, and I loved every second of it.

More Author's
From
Violet Circle Publishing

Mike Beale. (Children's Book)

Crumble's Adventures.
ISBN: 978-1-910299-06-7
Digital ISBN: 978-1-910299-08-1

Colin Smith (Play)

Heaven knows I'm Miserable Now
ISBN: 978-1-910299-16-6
Digital ISBN: 978-1-910299-23-4

Ted Morgan. (Poetry and verse)

Wordsmith's Wanderings.
ISBN: 978-1-910299-04-3
Digital ISBN: 978-1-910299-09-8
Peregrinations of the Wordsmith
ISBN: 978-1-910299-18-0
Digital ISBN: 978-1-910299-21-0
Silhouette Soldiers
ISBN: 978-1-910299-19-7
Digital ISBN: 978-1-910299-22-7
A Menu of Memories
Digital ISBN: 978-1-910299-32-6
Digital ISBN: 978-1-910299-33-3

Robin John Morgan. (Fiction/Fantasy/Slice of Life)

Heirs to the Kingdom.

Book One, The Bowman of Loxley.
ISBN: 978-1-910299-00-5
Digital ISBN: 978-1-910299-10-4
Book Two, The Lost Sword of Carnac.
ISBN: 978-1-910299-01-2
Digital ISBN: 978-1-910299-11-1
Book Three, The Darkness of Dunnottar.
ISBN: 978-1-910299-02-9
Digital ISBN: 978-1-910299-12-8
Book Four, Queen of the Violet Isle.
ISBN: 978-1-910299-03-6
Digital ISBN: 978-1-910299-13-5
Book Five, Crystals of the Mirrored Waters.
ISBN: 978-1-910299-05-0
Digital ISBN: 978-1-910299-14-2
Book Six, Last Arrow of the Woodland Realm.
ISBN: 978-1-910299-07-4
Digital ISBN: 978-1-910299-15-9
Book Seven, Bridge Of Sequana.
ISBN: 978-1-910299-17-3
Digital ISBN: 978-1-910299-20-3
Book Eight, The Circle of Darkness.
ISBN: 978-1-910299-26-5
Digital ISBN: 978-1-910299-29-6

The Curio Chronicles.

Part One, Abigail's Summer.
ISBN: 978-1-910299-27-2
Digital ISBN: 978-1-910299-28-9
Part Two, Curio's Summer.
ISBN: 978-1-910299-34-0
Digital ISBN: 978-1-910299-35-7
Part Three, Curio's Christmas.
ISBN: 978-1-910299-38-8
Digital ISBN: 978-1-910299-39-5

Part Four, Abigail's Wedding
ISBN: 978-1-910299-42-5
Digital ISBN: 978-1-910299-43-2
Part Five, Curio's Carnival
ISBN: 978-1-910299-46-3
Digital ISBN: 978-1-910299-47-0
Part Six, Abigail's Curio Life
ISBN: 978-1-910299-50-0
Digital ISBN: 978-1-910299-51-7

Of The Ravens of Berengar Trilogy.

Rise Of The Raven
ISBN: 978-1-910299-30-2
Digital ISBN: 978-1-910299-31-9
The Countess Of Darkness
ISBN: 978-1-910299-40-1
Digital ISBN: 978-1-910299-41-8
Violet Stone
ISBN: 978-1-910299-44-9
Digital ISBN: 978-1-910299-45-6

Sword For The Sky.

Oaken of The Winds
ISBN: 978-1-910299-48-7
Digital ISBN: 978-1-910299-49-4

Other Works.

Han's Cottage.
ISBN: 978-1-910299-36-4
Digital ISBN: 978-1-910299-37-1

Find out more about our authors and their books at
www.violetcirclepublishing.co.uk